THE LAST PLANTATION

Books by Don Wright

The Woodsman
The Captives
The Last Plantation

The Last Plantation

by Don Wright

Gray Stone Press
Nashville

This is a work of fiction. All the characters and events
portrayed in this book are fictitious, and any resemblance
to real people or events is purely coincidental.

THE LAST PLANTATION

Copyright © 1990 by Don Wright

Published by Gray Stone Press
205 Louise Avenue
Nashville, Tennessee 37203

Cover painting by David Wright

ISBN: 0-9627870-0-0

Library of Congress Catalog Card Number: 90-084383

First printing: October 1990

First Edition

Printed in the United States of America

Dedicated to "Miss Ellen Wemyss,"
"MISTRESS OF FAIRVIEW"

Clayton Harris was mistaken when he said, "We who came before eighteen sixty-five have seen the last plantation."

Through you, Mrs. Wemyss, a select few of us who have been fortunate enough to know you (we who came after 1865) have been given a renewed opportunity to see "The Last Plantation," for you, and Fairview are true, genteel Southerners of the old style.

We of Sumner County love you.

—Don Wright

A map of Gallatin, Tennessee and surrounding countryside showing the approximate locations of places, home-sites, and battles that are depicted in THE LAST PLANTATION.

Map not to scale.

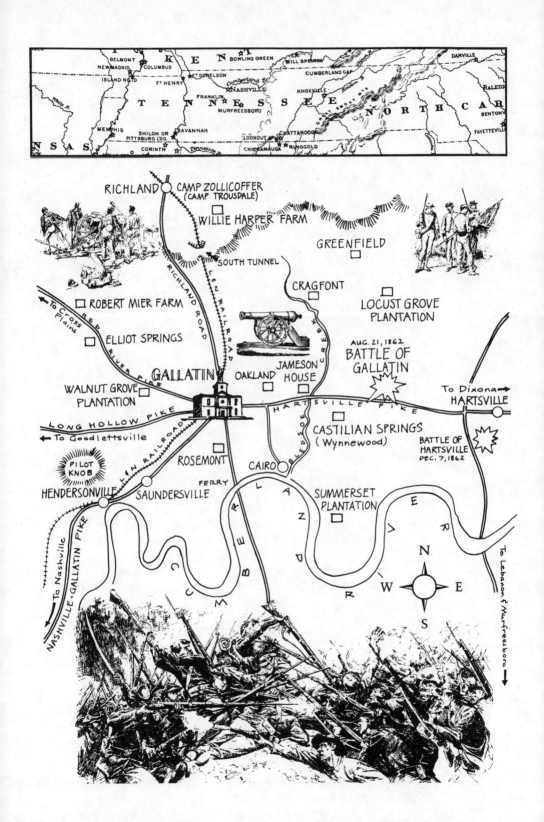

BOOK I
The Golden Days

CHAPTER 1

Young Clayton Harris leaned on the fantail railing of the *Princess* and watched the huge paddle wheel churn the muddy Ohio into a foaming froth as the boat backed into the main channel.

"I reckon eighteen fifty-nine will go down as the droughtiest year in history," commented an elderly man standing beside him.

"And the month of June will be remembered as thirty days of purgatory," Clayton returned, pushing a lock of damp, unruly black hair off his perspiring forehead.

The man smiled. "Do I detect a bit of schoolin' in your speech, son?"

Clayton nodded. "The University of Ohio."

"Well now, that's impressive."

Clayton eyed the man surreptitiously, noting that he had the look and carriage of a great gray heron stepping gingerly along a creek bank. "What is it about schooling that impresses you, mister . . . ?"

The man removed his white panama hat and bowed. "Jonathan Corrigan Summers, at your service, sir."

"I'm Clayton Harris," the young man said, offering his hand.

Mr. Summers' handshake was surprisingly strong. "I'm not usually so meddlesome in other folks' business," he said, "but I'm curious as to where a young, educated feller such as yourself might be a-goin'."

"I'm taking Mr. Greeley's advice. I'm going West."

Mr. Summers took a silver cigar box from his inside coat pocket, extracted a cheroot, struck a Lucifer, and watched his exhaled smoke trail lazily toward the churning paddle wheel. "It weren't that anti-slavery, anti-liquor, pantywaist Horace Greeley who coined that phrase, son. It was a hard-drinkin', fistfightin' newspaperman from Indiana, named John Soule."

Clayton's gray eyes showed surprise. "Most people believe Horace Greeley authored that remark, sir."

"All Greeley done was shout it the loudest and the longest."

Clayton chuckled and studied Mr. Summers more closely. "Obviously I'm not the only person who's been to college."

The old man shook his head. "I can barely read an' write."

Then, with the cheroot clamped between his teeth, he nodded at Clayton and threaded his way across the main deck, through the maze of machinery, merchandise, men, women, and children, to the stairwell leading to the upper deck, where the well-to-do passengers congregated.

Raising his gaze to the upper level, Clayton was impressed by the sheer grandeur of the scene. Tall-hatted men stood smoking cigars, while elegantly dressed women sat at small, round tables sipping cold lemonade. Frock-coated gamblers lounged in the shadows of staterooms and watched the crowd through slitted eyes, and ladies of questionable reputation watched the same crowd with eyes wide open.

For a split second, Clayton questioned his recent decision to quit college and strike out on his own with little more in his pocket than the price of a boat ticket. Although he had not yet notified his father of his decision, he was aware that had he but swallowed his pride and asked his father's assistance, he too could have been a part of that sophisticated, arrogant society above. He also was aware that even though his father was a self-made, wealthy man, he would vehemently disapprove of his son following his example by setting out in search of himself.

Clayton turned his back on the upper deck and studied the river, marveling at the scenery that swept past the rail with each revolution of the paddle wheel.

Mansions on breeze-swept heights appeared to raise their noses to the skies in an effort to avoid the stench of the river. And unnamed shantytowns, their ramshackle buildings constructed close to the water's edge, were wafting the scent of offal over the flatboats, houseboats, canoes, and rowboats that were moored to their very doorsteps. But the most wondrous sight on the river was the grand promenade of the "Brides of Babylon," as the river folk fondly called the gaudy steamboats that flaunted themselves like cheap prostitutes up and down the waterways.

Several times as the day wore on, he glimpsed Mr. Summers lounging on the upper deck, his broad-brimmed planter's hat pulled low in an attempt to shade his face from the glaring reflection of the afternoon sun as it burst in a thousand directions from the surface of the shimmering river. And even though Clayton couldn't see the old man's eyes, he felt that Mr. Summers was watching him. So at sundown, when he again found Mr. Summers beside him, he was not surprised.

"You been holdin' down this fantail all day," the old man said, resting his elbows on the railing.

Clayton shrugged. "Nowhere else to go."

"Ain't it the truth. This boat's so crowded, a body has to suck in his stomach to make room for his chest when he breathes. These riverboat captains ain't got a grain of sense when it comes to overburdenin' the boilers. Can't blame 'em much though. It's the captain who gets to the landing first and loads the most that makes any profit for the stockholders."

Clayton studied the men, women, and children clustered about him. Was the prospect of monetary gain worth jeopardizing the lives of these folks? He thought not. Then he sobered. His father would consider such squeamishness unbusinesslike, for he would not only approve, but would openly advocate such a risk.

The muscles in Clayton's jaws corded into knots; his father had always accused him of being too soft.

"The reason I came down here," Mr. Summers continued, "was to invite you to sup with me."

Clayton glanced at the upper deck. The first-class passengers were strolling en masse toward the main cabin, where the evening meal would be served. Clayton shook his head. "Thank you for the invitation, Mr. Summers, but—"

"Son," broke in the old man, "there's two things a gentleman don't do. One is, he never refuses a drink or an invitation to dinner with another gentleman. And two, he never offers to pay for it—unless, of course, the inviter is a scalawag. Then, sir, you shoot him dead for insultin' you with his offer in the first place. I can tell by the cut of your clothes that you're a true gentleman. An' I sure as shootin' ain't a scalawag."

With that, he guided Clayton toward the stairs that led to the upper deck.

Although large oil paintings and gilt mirrors adorned the walls of the long main room, it was the great amounts of food—heaped on silver trays carried by ebony-skinned servants in short white jackets and dark trousers—that caught Clayton's eye. Not even the best hotels in Columbus could boast such cuisine.

Across the table, Mr. Summers smiled at Clayton.

"If this is your first steamboat ride, eat slow and easy, son. I've been runnin' up an' down this river for nigh on forty years and I've never got used to such rich vittles. Made myself sick a time or two."

"I didn't know there was this much food in the world," Clayton said, eyeing the heaping plates set before them.

The old man cut a portion of beefsteak with his fork and plopped it into his mouth. "Each stop we make to take on wood," he said, chewing vigorously, "the stewards buy up every chicken, goose, hog, an' side of beef they can find. Fact is, they'll purchase darn near anything that's edible. A passel of folks makes their entire livin' by supplyin' the steamboat traffic with foodstuffs."

"What happens to the leftovers?" Clayton asked, making a show of cutting his steak with his knife. "There's no way the people in this room can eat all of this food."

Mr. Summers, his faded eyes twinkling with amusement at the lad's display of manners, watched Clayton lay the knife aside and delicately spear a bite of steak with his fork. "When the first-class passengers are through eatin'," he said, "the steward's helpers pile the leftovers in a cauldron and take it to the lower deck. They holler, 'Grub stock,' then get out of the way." Mr. Summers' steady gaze caused Clayton to blush, and he barely heard the old man say, ". . . 'cause those folks below are starvin' by then."

The old man pushed his empty plate aside and took a tentative sip of scalding coffee. "So you're goin' West to make a fortune."

"Yes, sir. I thought perhaps I would try Texas."

"Humph! Texas ain't nothin' but plumb full of misplaced Tennesseans. So why go to Texas? Tennessee is a dern sight closer."

"I take it you're from Tennessee?" Clayton asked.

"Yes, sir! Gallatin, near the Cumberland, in Sumner County. Why, God reached right down and touched Tennessee with his own hand. He said, 'If'n I was goin' to live on earth, this is where I'd choose.' Purty place, Sumner County, purty place indeed."

"Mr. Summers," Clayton said, laying aside his fork, "I'm wondering what all this has to do with me. I mean . . ."

The old man smiled and leaned back in his chair. "You come right to the point, don't you?"

Clayton nodded soberly, fixed his elbows on the table, and waited.

"What I need is a schoolmaster," Mr. Summers said. "Somebody with an education. Somebody with backbone. And it's got to be somebody from the North."

"I'm sorry, Mr. Summers," Clayton returned, "but I don't see—"

"You're a Northerner, an' you're educated. What I'm saying is, I'd like to engage your services, Mr. Harris."

"As a schoolteacher?"

"Exactly. And here, sir"—Mr. Summers handed Clayton a twenty-dollar gold piece—"is an advance on your wages, which we will discuss over a cheroot."

Fishing the silver cigar box from his inside coat pocket, he extended it to Clayton. "You can consider that twenty dollars the beginnin' of your fortune, Mr. Harris."

Amused and intrigued by the old man's proposal, Clayton opened the container and placed a thin black cigar between his teeth. As if by magic, a steward's helper appeared beside him and with the deft flick of a thumbnail, a Lucifer burst into flame.

Clayton sucked the cigar into life.

"Thank you," he said to the Negro, blowing a puff of smoke toward the ceiling.

The man extended the match to Mr. Summers, who took a long draw, inhaling deeply. Clayton followed suit, then burst into a loud spasm of coughing that turned every head in the room.

Mr. Summers leaned across the table. "How long you been smokin', son?"

"Not long. My father forbade it."

Mr. Summers frowned. "How old are you, Mr. Harris?"

"Seventeen, sir."

"Seventeen." The old man settled back into his chair. "You look older."

Clayton wiped tears from his eyes. "Everyone says that."

"It's good that you do. It'll come in right handy, bein' the schoolmaster an' all."

"Mr. Summers"—Clayton laid the cigar on the edge of his plate—"I know absolutely nothing about teaching school."

"Makes no nevermind. You know readin', writin', and figurin', and that, Mr. Harris, is aplenty."

Clayton shook his head. "I'm no schoolteacher, Mr. Summers. I wouldn't even know where to begin."

The steward's helpers finished clearing the tables. Most of the women and children vanished. Young mulatto women flitted about the room spreading felt cloths over the large dining tables.

Almost magically, a sign appeared above the bar: "Gentlemen Who Play Cards for Money, Play at Their Own Risk."

Mr. Summers took a speculative draw on his cigar. "Do you gamble, Mr. Harris?"

"No, sir. Unless something is a sure thing, I leave it alone."

The old man nodded. "Occasionally that's good, occasionally it ain't. But I reckon that in the long run a man'd be better off to stick to the sure things. However, life wouldn't be worth livin'."

Clayton pursed his lips, not knowing whether to be offended or amused. Stealing a glance at the old man's gnarled, work-hardened hands, he asked, "Do you play cards, sir?"

"Never. I gamble on people, places, things—and the elements—but not on the pasteboards."

Clayton was perplexed but decided to let the statement pass.

Mr. Summers crossed his spindly legs. "You there!" He beckoned to a mulatto girl standing beside the bar. "Bring my friend an' me a toddy. We'd be much obliged."

An instant later she was placing tall cups before them.

"Thank you very much, ma'am," Clayton said when she turned to leave.

The girl frowned, then moved quickly away.

Clayton looked at Mr. Summers. "Did I say something wrong to her?"

Mr. Summers sipped his toddy without answering.

Clayton persisted. "She looked as though I had offended her, Mr. Summers."

"She's a darky, Mr. Harris, and you called her 'ma'am.' There ain't a gentleman in the South what would call a black wench 'ma'am' or a buck 'sir.' Why, I reckon a Southerner would die before he'd do that."

Shocked, Clayton glanced away. His gaze locked with that of a beautiful woman sitting at the next table. Her thick, sooty-black hair cascaded over her exposed shoulders, giving her a sensual appeal that was further heightened by a pale-lavender, low-cut gown. It was the most revealing garment that Clayton had ever seen.

But it was the amused glint in her midnight-blue eyes that caused Clayton to blush, for there was no mistaking the fact that she had overheard the exchange. Then the glint was gone, screened by her long lashes as she scanned the three men sitting at her table. "M'sieurs," she said, her voice soft but businesslike, "I will open with ten dollars."

"If what you say is true," Clayton said, swinging his

attention back to Mr. Summers, "then why is that lady sitting at a table with those white men? Isn't she part Negro?"

Mr. Summers took a long pull on his toddy. "That's Claudette LaBranche. An' the truth is, she's probably more educated and sophisticated than the so-called society women who wouldn't be caught dead in her presence. Still, even though she's a bit more pampered than most, she's nothin' but a high-yellow whore, and all the education and beauty in the world can't change that a'tall."

With a nod of his head, Mr. Summers indicated the cardplayers at Claudette LaBranche's table. "Those gentlemen will gamble with her—even pay to sleep with her—but they won't call her 'ma'am.' You'd best remember that, Mr. Harris. Folks in the South'll not take kindly to a white man who treats black women the same as he does white ladies. You could see for yourself how it embarrassed that table wench. Why, son, she isn't used to that kind of talk."

Clayton couldn't have cared less what "folks in the South" thought of him, but he kept that knowledge to himself. Glancing again at Claudette LaBranche, he wondered if she were really a prostitute . . . or was Mr. Summers merely stereotyping all black women?

As Claudette LaBranche shuffled her cards, she threw Clayton a seductive smile that gave Mr. Summers' words all the credibility necessary.

In minutes, nearly every table in the room was occupied by gamblers. Waiters and serving girls stood to the beck and call of the patrons, who could signal for a cigar, a drink, or a new deck of cards without so much as raising their eyes from the playing field. It was a placid atmosphere, yet tension rippled through the room like waves in a millpond; one could hear it in the tinkling of glass, the quiet laughter, the clinking of coins, and the shuffling of currency. And as if that weren't enough, one could taste it in the layers of dense smoke, the whiskey fumes, and the lingering perfume. It was real. It was exciting. And it was dangerous.

Clayton sipped his drink and, as Mr. Summers was doing, concentrated on the four players at the next table. Two of the men appeared to be either wealthy businessmen or planters; the other—who wore a dark-gray frock coat, tight-fitting, light-gray breeches, and knee-high English riding boots that shone like patent leather—seemed more distinctive.

It took Clayton a full minute to realize that the man's expression showed not the least trace of emotion.

Following Clayton's gaze, Mr. Summers said, "George DeVol is probably the most famous gambler on the Ohio —or the Mississippi. He plays honest. He plays good. And he never takes a man's last dollar. That feller sittin' beside him, and the one directly across the table . . . they must be new to the river."

"How can you tell?" Clayton could see nothing extraordinary about the two men.

"They're crappers, workin' together. Losing to one another in an attempt to bait the suckers into bettin' more. Guess they don't know they're playin' again' DeVol."

Clayton watched the men and found that Mr. Summers was correct. The man sitting directly across from DeVol deliberately threw in a winning hand, then made an elaborate performance of losing to his partner.

When the deal was passed to DeVol, he fanned the cards, then called for a new deck. His unblinking gaze penetrated the man directly across the table, causing the crapper to shift uncomfortably.

"Son," Mr. Summers said, inching his chair away from the table, "we'd best be gettin' some fresh air. If'n I don't miss my bet, it's gonna get a mite smoky in here." The old man's eyes twinkled.

Clayton remained seated. If something exciting was about to happen, he didn't want to miss it. Sighing, Mr. Summers leaned back in his chair. He had ridden the river too many times to be excited by one more shoot-out.

DeVol's hand moved leisurely to his inside coat pocket and emerged with a round-barreled, underhammer pistol with six ugly holes in the muzzle.

"Gentlemen," he said with the slightest Cajun accent, "every barrel of this pepperbox is loaded and capped."

The two crappers jumped to their feet and eased aside their frock coats, exposing the grips of pistols shoved into their waistbands.

Clayton was afraid to breathe lest the merest movement trigger a spontaneous reaction in one or all three of the men who faced each other with such incredible confidence.

Even Claudette LaBranche seemed to be carved in wax.
Only the slight rise and fall of her full breasts gave evidence
that she was alive.

DeVol was speaking so softly that Clayton was forced to
lean closer to hear his words: "You have been cheating since
the game began . . ."

"Who says?" demanded the man standing next to him.
His friend across the table inched his hand toward his
pistol.

"This does," DeVol raised the pepperbox and aimed it at
the stickpin in the man's cravat. The click of the hammer of
his pepperbox was loud in the hushed room.

"And so does this," came Mr. Summers' slow drawl.

Clayton's head snapped toward the old man. He had not
seen Mr. Summers move, yet there he stood with a single-
shot carriage pistol in his hand, his faded blue eyes as fierce
as a hawk's. Then Clayton's eyes swiveled to a movement at
the bar. Ever so slowly, the bartender had reached up and
was pulling an overhead cord. Within moments the door at
the far end of the room burst open.

"What in hell is going on here?" The captain's eyes roved
the length of the room and came to rest on DeVol. "What's
the trouble, Mr. DeVol?"

"DeVol!" cried one of the crappers. Then, glaring at his
companion, he said, "You fool. You set us in a game with
George DeVol." Turning to the captain, the man grinned
sheepishly. "Nothing is wrong, Captain. My friend and I
will be leaving your boat at the next landing."

"No," the captain said, his face darkening like a thunder-
cloud, "you'll be leavin' my boat at the next sandbar." The
two men set up a howl of protest, but they followed the
captain from the room.

Clayton felt a twinge of sympathy for them. He even
hoped that the captain would reconsider his threat, for a
sandbar in the middle of the Ohio River was no place to be
stranded at night.

He appraised DeVol with new interest.

"Mr. Summers," he said when the old man sat down
again and put his pistol away, "I want people to react to my
name the way those two men did to Mr. DeVol's."

The old man drained his toddy, then set the empty glass
on the table. "George DeVol would shoot a crook quicker'n

he would a cottonmouth. Folks know what DeVol stands for, and they respect him for it."

"It wasn't respect that prompted the change in those two gamblers," Clayton said. "It was fear." Then he frowned. "Those crappers feared DeVol because he's dangerous. Other people, such as yourself, call the same feeling respect."

"Well, I don't much agree with that," Mr. Summers said. "A man has to work long an' hard to gain folks' respect. Fear comes a mite easier."

A few minutes later when the captain brought the *Princess* to a gentle stop, the passengers left their cards facedown on the tables and raced to the deck.

By the time Clayton and Mr. Summers pushed their way to the rail, the two gamblers had been put ashore on a small sandbar. They looked frightened and lonely in the flickering light cast by the running lanterns of the *Princess.* No sooner had the boat swung toward midstream than the male passengers drew their pistols and began taking potshots at the stranded crappers, who made long, running dives into the murky river and splashed into the safety of darkness beyond the sandbar.

"No one would care if those men drowned," Clayton said, shocked as the laughing crowd strolled toward the game room.

"Why, son," the old man said, taking Clayton by his arm and following the crowd, "the river's so shallow, them boys can dern near wade to shore."

Stopping at a stateroom, Mr. Summers withdrew a key and inserted it in the lock. "My cabin has two berths," he said, pushing the door open. "If you're so minded, you're welcome to the upper."

Clayton held back, hesitant of accepting any more favors from the old man. But when he looked over the railing to the deck below, where his fellow second-class passengers were packed so tight they could hardly lie down, he reluctantly assented.

Even though the cabin was scarcely larger than a closet, it boasted stacked bunks, a washbasin, a porcelain pitcher and bowl, and an ornate gold-leafed mirror that reflected the oil lantern attached to the wall. But the room was so narrow that Clayton had to wait until Mr. Summers was stretched out in his bunk before he could climb into the upper berth.

Clayton was not aware that he had drifted off to sleep until he was thrown from his berth to crash heavily onto the washbasin. The pitcher and bowl were shattered with such force that the water from the pitcher drenched Mr. Summers, who bolted upright, slamming his head against the bottom boards of the top bunk.

"Dern it to hell!" the old man cried. "Every time I ride one of these floatin' sawmills, this happens."

"What's happened? What is it? Did the boiler blow up?" Clayton scrambled to his feet and steadied his back to the wall as the boat groaned and shuddered. "Will we sink?"

"We done already sunk. We're sittin' smack dab on the bottom of the Ohio right now. We done run aground, son."

"Run aground, sir?"

The old man groaned and lay back in the bunk. "The pilot done missed the channel in the dark and left us high an' dry on a bar."

Even as the old man spoke, Clayton heard the captain bellow for engine reverse, full steam. The boat shuddered but did not move.

"Stuck tighter'n a wedge," Mr. Summers said.

"What will the captain do about it?"

"He's got several choices. He can wait for the river to rise, which will probably be sometime in September or October, or maybe next spring. Or he can ask another riverboat to give him a tug, which no self-respectin' captain would do if his life depended on it. Or, if we've run aground on the Kentucky side, chances are he can talk some of the planters into sendin' ten or fifteen teams of horses an' some slaves down here to try an' pull us back into deep water."

Clayton groped his way to the door and threw it open. Torches, lanterns, and candles lit the boat as though it were daylight, making it all but impossible to see into the darkness beyond.

"I can't tell which side of the river we're on," he said, reentering the cabin, "but I don't understand what difference it could make."

"If we're on the Ohio side, we're in a passel of trouble,"

came the old man's sleepy reply. Then, sighing with the surety that he would not get any rest until he had stilled the lad's curiosity, he swung his legs to the floor and reached for his coat. Fumbling in the inner pocket, he withdrew the silver case and fired another cheroot.

"It's like this," he said, taking a long draw. "The Ohio River is the modern-day holy stream. Some call it the 'true waters of baptism.' They say it's more powerful than the River Jordan, 'cause all the Jordan does is wash away a man's sins. The Ohio, on the other hand, not only cleanses a man's soul, but also changes the color of his skin."

Clayton's eyes narrowed. He knew what Mr. Summers was leading up to.

"Yes, sir," continued the old man, "there ain't no other river in the world where a blue-gum slave can jump into its waters on the South side an' come out a gentleman on the North side, cleansed of black hide and ready for the promised land—which some Yankee idiot told him was on the North side of the Ohio."

A slow anger began building in Clayton. His father and uncle were outspoken pro-abolitionists and were involved with the underground railroad. And while he differed with his father on many issues, he knew that the man was definitely no "Yankee idiot."

"But what does that have to do with getting this boat off the sandbar?" he asked, his tone sharper than he intended.

Mr. Summers appraised Clayton through the heavy cigar smoke. "Because once a slave reaches the North side and is free, all of a sudden it's beneath his dignity to work."

"What about the Ohio farmers? Why wouldn't the captain hire them to pull us off the bar?"

"A captain did that once. When he asked the farmer how much he owed him, the man told him a hundred dollars."

Clayton sucked in his breath. A hundred dollars! It was robbery.

The old man chuckled. "The captain didn't pay it. He threw the farmer overboard and ran full steam for St. Louis."

"What do the Kentucky farmers charge?"

"They make a holiday out of it, a game." Mr. Summers went on to explain that plantation owners from miles around would send mule skinners to compete in what would become a pulling contest. "Yep," he said, "a kind of holiday."

The old man crushed out the cigar, then swung his legs into the bunk. "Meantime," he said, stretching out with his hands behind his head, "I aim to get me some sleep."

Clayton was too troubled to sleep. Mr. Summers' attitude toward black people bothered him deeply. Perhaps he should return the twenty dollars and push on to Texas as he had originally intended.

Leaving the cabin, Clayton walked to the bow of the boat and studied the sandbar on which they were stranded. Crewmen had disembarked and were walking slowly along the length of the exposed bow, inspecting the hull for damage.

"We will be stranded for hours, perhaps for days, m'sieur." The voice that came from the darkness beneath the stairway was soft and pleasant.

Clayton peered hard, but could see no one. Deciding that the lady must have been addressing someone else, he turned again to the rail.

"Oui, m'sieur, I was speaking to you." Claudette LaBranche stepped into the glow of the lantern light. Instinctively, Clayton bowed.

She laughed softly. "You are a true gentleman, m'sieur." Joining him at the rail, she added, "I am afraid, however, that the trait will not serve you well in the South."

Clayton stared at the woman. He had no idea of what was customary when one was approached by a "lady of the evening." Forcing a nod, he mumbled, "Thank you."

Again she laughed, and Clayton groaned inwardly, cursing himself for being too inexperienced to react to her as would an adult.

"No," she said, laying her fingertips playfully against his cheek, "it is I who should be thanking you, m'sieur."

"I'm sorry, ma'am," he said, trying to collect his wits, "but I can't recall doing anything that warrants your thanks."

"Ah, but you have, m'sieur. In the dining hall earlier, you called that servant girl 'ma'am' and meant it. You honored her."

Clayton was taken aback, and it showed in his face.

"You are surprised?"

"Yes, very much. I was under the impression that I had offended her."

"No, m'sieur. I assure you, you did not offend her." Claudette leaned on the rail and watched the lights of the boat crew bob and dip over the sandbar. "You startled her perhaps, but you did not offend her."

She smiled at him, her white teeth glistening between her rouged lips.

"You will be very handsome when you mature, m'sieur," she said, studying his face. "Women will find you most desirable."

Clayton remained silent for fear that he might make a denial that would sound childish and silly; he was already aware that girls found him appealing, for too many had told him so. But they were mere children when compared to the woman standing beside him.

"I appreciate the compliment, ma'am," he said, pleased with his reply.

Claudette eyed him with bold interest. "You have a way of making a woman feel respected, m'sieur. It is a nice trait . . . but alas, it is one that seems to disappear with age. Grown men take so much for granted. Such a shame."

"Well, ma'am," he said, "my father taught me to respect my elders."

Claudette burst out laughing.

"You are a most confusing person, m'sieur," she said. "You give with the one hand, then take away with the other. Ah, but you are very refreshing."

With a sway of natural grace, she turned and walked across the deck, disappearing into the dining hall.

Clayton scratched his head, his brow creasing thoughtfully. He was not so naive as to be unaware of the implications of Claudette LaBranche's profession, yet he could not envision the woman as anything but a lovely lady traveling south on a riverboat.

CHAPTER 2

Sunup found the Kentucky shore alive with men, dray horses, mules, oxen, block and tackle, and spectators by the score. Indeed, the carnival atmosphere quickly caught up the passengers of the *Princess,* who cheered wildly as the teamsters skillfully maneuvered their animals in an attempt to achieve the most effective leverage while winching the boat into deep water. Slaves bounded up and down the riverbank, lashing pulleys to trees and stringing out load lines, while still others took the free ends of the heavy manila ropes into small boats and rowed furiously toward the stranded paddle-wheeler.

Streams of black soot rose into the cloudless sky from the tall smokestacks as the boilers were stoked to maximum pressure so they could assist in backing the paddle-wheeler into the channel.

"Good thing we're within twenty rod of the bank," Mr. Summers said to Clayton, "else them teamsters never would get enough tension in them lines to move this tub. Might not nohow."

Clayton smiled at the old man's pessimism. But as he considered the three hundred and twenty feet of water that separated the sandbar from the Kentucky shore, his smile faded.

By the stern of the steamer, a deeply tanned, sandy-haired youth perched precariously in the bow of a bobbing johnboat. The boy was expertly rigging a hawser to the stern.

He saw Clayton watching and grinned widely, disclosing a mouthful of widely spaced teeth. Curious, Clayton strode toward the stern, but the boy had already made the line secure and was paddling madly toward the shore.

"What's that fellow's hurry?" he asked, rejoining Mr. Summers.

"Which one?"

"The one in the rowboat, there."

Mr. Summers squinted in the direction Clayton pointed.

"The captain pays a bonus to the first teamster who gets a tight line," he said. "That's the reason those mule skinners on the shore are 'hoora'n' them hawser monkeys to hurry and tie off. They want to get the first pull, an' it looks like that towhead in the johnboat—that's not a rowboat, son—just might win."

To Clayton's surprise, he found himself caught up in the excitement of the contest, and he cheered just as loudly for the blond-haired boy as did the other passengers who had chosen champions.

"It's quite thrilling," he admitted to Mr. Summers.

"Yep, it is," the old man agreed, smiling at Clayton's enthusiasm. "But regardless of who gets the first pull, it's goin' to take all them teams of beasts workin' together to snatch this rig into deep water."

The sandy-haired boy reached the bank and jumped ashore. Catching up the lead lines, he cried out to his pair of matched bay mules and they sprang into action. Like fine-tuned machines, the animals leaned heavily into their collars, the oiled-leather breeching of their harness slapping loudly against their strained muscles, while the seasoned-hickory doubletrees and trace chains groaned and popped as the pulleys the boy had attached to the trees hummed and quivered under the stress. Both mules squatted against the awesome load, the corded muscles of their rear legs trembling like jelly, their hooves digging into the ground.

The young driver urged them on, calling for them to try

harder, to show the world what a fine team of mules they
were.

All along the bank, load lines snapped tight, singing in the
wind as team after team took up their slack.

"That youngun is good," Mr. Summers commented.
"Yep, he's real good."

"Did he get the first pull?"

"Looked to me like he did. But it was mighty close."

The *Princess'* boiler stacks belched thick, oily smoke as
the paddle wheel churned mud, silt, and slime off the
bottom of the Ohio. Still, the boat refused to move. The
teamsters ashore whipped their animals to even greater
exertion.

Then a tremor ran the length of the vessel, and with an
ease that was anticlimactic, the steamboat slid off the bar
and into deep water.

"Easy as fallin' off a log," Mr. Summers said and grinned.

A great cheer erupted from the spectators on the bank,
joined by a burst of whistling and shouting from those on
board. The boats again put out from shore and sped toward
the *Princess*.

Clayton excused himself from Mr. Summers and ran
down the steps leading to the main deck, where he fought
his way to the stern. The sandy-haired youth was wrestling
with the wet, heavy rope.

Grinning up at Clayton, he said, "Wet rope is always a
bitch after it's been stretched to the breakin' point."

Clayton nodded and leaned over the railing to assist.
"Yes, it's harder to untie than dry rope."

The boy stared at Clayton. "No shit," he said.

After a long minute of silence as both boys worked at the
knot, Clayton said, "That was a stupid comment I made."

The boy continued picking at the knot. "Pretty dumb."

Clayton tried another tack. "You did a fine job handling
that team."

"We won."

"Well, you should have. It sure looked as though you
knew what you were doing."

The boy squinted at Clayton. "I been skinnin' mules all
my life. Hell, fella. Ever' boy up an' down this river who's
over five years old knows how to handle a team. I'm just a
whole lot better than most."

"Your humility is very touching," Clayton said.

"You shore do talk fine," returned the boy, unabashed. "An' if'n I knew what that big word meant, I'd probably be pissed." He dug harder at the knot. "Course, big, fancy words wouldn't have got this boat off that sandbar."

Clayton blushed. Then he laughed delightedly. "Touché."

The boy's eyes narrowed. "I don't like folks to poke fun at me, sonny."

Clayton sobered. "Touché is a French word used in fencing. It means you touched me . . . you got me back. We are even."

"Well," the youth said, studying the knot from several different angles, "I've built a lot of fences but I ain't never heard that word a'fore. But if you say so, I reckon it's true."

Pushing Clayton's hand aside, he dug into his overall pocket and came out with a large clasp knife that he opened with his teeth. Clayton ran his tongue over his own fine, even teeth as though he might have nicked one solely by the power of imagination.

Grinning widely at Clayton's discomfiture, the boy attacked the heavy rope as though his life depended on cutting through it in one clean sweep. But try as he might, it took several hard slashes before the strands parted and the hawser splashed into the river.

Clayton expected the boy to row for shore and was starting to wish him Godspeed when the young man scrambled up the side of the *Princess* and nimbly flipped himself over the rail and onto the main deck.

"My name is Cotton Ferris," he said, sticking out his hand. "What's your'n?"

Clayton eyed the boy's fair hair.

"Naw," Cotton grinned. "I wasn't named Cotton 'cause I was towheaded. It's 'cause my ma claimed she found me under a cotton bale. My brothers an' sisters was born under a cabbage leaf . . . but not me. I was different."

Clayton shook Cotton's hand and introduced himself. He had never met such an outlandish person. Friends are made that easily.

The *Princess* lurched into motion. Leaning over the rail, Clayton pointed to Cotton's unmoored boat, which was bobbing like a piece of driftwood in the wake of the churning paddle. "We're pulling away from your skiff!"

Cotton shrugged. "Don't make no nevermind. I ain't goin' ashore. I'm goin' downriver."

"Won't they miss you? Your folks? Won't they be worried?"

"They will come mornin', when my steppappy has to chop the firewood an' do the milkin' his own self."

My father will miss me too, thought Clayton, when he finds that I have quit school to chase rainbows.

Cotton's gaze darted over Clayton's shoulder. "It's the bull!" he whispered. "He'll dump me for sure." Then he was gone, darting in and out between crates of machinery and equipment until he had lost himself in the crowds milling on the deck.

The burly boat detective stormed up to Clayton. Small beads of sweat standing like blisters on his upper lip broke and trickled into his mouth as he shoved his face close to Clayton's.

"I saw you help that stowaway come over the rail," the man yelled, spraying Clayton with perspiration. "For two bits I'd throw the both of you overboard."

Clayton wiped his face with the back of his hand. "I don't believe you want to try that, mister."

The detective frowned, then reevaluated the tall, well-built youth. A damned Yankee city slicker, he decided. "If I take a notion to throw you overboard, boy," he said, "I'll do it."

Clayton eased his left leg forward and rested his weight on the ball of his foot. "I have paid for my passage, sir, and not you or anyone like you is going to throw me anywhere."

The man recognized the subtle shift of position and took a quick step backward. From the corner of his eye he saw that a crowd had circled them, expectant and eager for a show. He didn't like that. If the boy proved hard to handle, it could very well ruin his reputation as a river tough, and possibly cost him his job.

"It ain't you I'm after," he said. "But when I find that other fellow, you'd best not interfere."

"Then you might as well stop looking for him," Clayton said, making an on-the-spot decision that took him by surprise. "I paid his fare an hour ago."

The bull's eyes narrowed. "You'd best be tellin' me the truth, boy."

Clayton shrugged. "Check with the purser."

"I'll do that." The man made a show of brushing Clayton aside, then stomped off in the direction that Cotton had taken.

"You made an enemy, son."

Clayton turned to find Mr. Summers leaning leisurely against a crate. The old man pushed himself erect and strode over to Clayton. "Do you carry a pistol?" Clayton shook his head. "Well, you'd better start packin' one or you're goin' to find yourself in a heap of trouble someday."

"I can handle myself, Mr. Summers. I was boxing champion of Ohio University."

The old man shook his head. "Son, that's fine and dandy in one of them matches where everybody knows the rules, but it ain't worth a hill of beans if a man comes at you with brass knuckles, or an ax handle. No, you'd better get yourself a pistol."

Clayton saw the bull climb the steps to the upper deck and walk slowly along the rail, searching the lower deck for Cotton.

"Excuse me, Mr. Summers," Clayton said. "I've got to purchase another ticket."

"You'd better go purchase yourself a pistol!" called the old man to Clayton's retreating back.

The detective was furious when Cotton presented him with a ticket.

"First time I ever did see somebody outsmart a bull," Cotton told Clayton. "And it's the first time in my whole life anybody ever did spend six dollars on me." He frowned. "You know I ain't gonna be able to pay you back for a spell, don't you?"

"It was worth it, just to see that fellow's face," Clayton said. "Anyway, you can pay me back once we get to Tennessee."

"Is that where you're goin'? An' you want me to tag along?"

"Yes. I'll have to talk to Mr. Summers first, but I'm pretty sure he'll approve. He certainly was impressed with the way you handled that team of draft horses this morning. And he knows that you got the first pull on the dragline."

"Them weren't horses, Clayton. Them was mules. Don't you know nothin'?"

Clayton winced at the boy's terrible English. If he did indeed accept the teaching position Mr. Summers had offered, Cotton would be his first scholar.

That night Mr. Summers had two guests for supper. He was both amazed and disturbed by the amount of food Cotton consumed.

"Son," he said when Cotton filled his plate for the third time with a heavily sauced Creole concoction, "if you're not used to this type of food, you might ought to ease off a bit."

"Eat it all the time," Cotton said, spooning a helping into his mouth.

Mr. Summers kept silent. Clayton, however, was not tactful. "Cotton," he said, "you've never eaten food like this in your life. And you're going to be sick if you don't stop."

"No I ain't." Cotton tilted his chair back and belched loudly. "Damn good vittles. Wish them darkies hadn't cleared the table so quick."

Mr. Summers shook his head. "If you work like you eat, Cotton, there's a place for you on my plantation."

"I'm a good hand, Mr. Summers. Jist you wait and see."

As the patrons called for decks of cards, whiskey, and cheroots, Clayton's gaze drifted from table to table. To his disappointment, Claudette LaBranche was not present.

Cotton nudged Clayton with his foot. "Loan me five dollars."

"For what?"

"I want to play."

"What do you know about cards?"

"I been watchin' poker games since I was knee-high. My pap had a game at our cabin just about ever' week . . . 'til he got caught cheatin' and somebody shot him dead."

Clayton was doubtful, and it showed in his face.

"You'd never make a good gambler, Clay," Cotton grinned. "A man can read your face as easy as pie. But they'll have a hell of a time readin' mine."

Reluctantly Clayton handed Cotton the money and watched as the boy strode to a nearby table and pulled out a chair.

A man sitting at the table said, "That chair is reserved for a player."

"I am a player," Cotton said, sliding onto the seat and

scooting it closer to the table.

"You're not paying attention, boy," returned the man. "That chair is for a poker player."

Cotton glanced around the table. The other players were watching with amused indifference.

The man caught Cotton's wrist and drew him close. "Get back to your own table, son. I'm not goin' to tell you again."

Clayton pushed his chair back and rose quickly to his feet. After appraising Cotton and the man thoughtfully, however, he slowly settled himself back into his chair. Mr. Summers released a pent-up sigh.

"You had me bothered for a minute there," the old man said, offering Clayton a cheroot, which was declined. "I thought sure you were goin' to embarrass the lad by interferin' in his business."

Color rose in Clayton's face. "I believe in assisting a friend if he's in trouble."

"That's fine an' dandy. But I haven't seen nothin' to indicate that Cotton's in trouble, yet."

"That man's still holding his wrist."

"Yep, but he's not hurtin' the boy none. Now, if he was killin' Cotton, that'd be a mite different. Let's see if the boy's made out of green hickory like I figure he is."

Cotton had leaned toward the man until their faces were inches apart.

"Mister," he said, his grin widening, "I was playing five-card stud when you was still suckin' your mama's titty . . . an' if'n you don't let go of my arm, I'm gonna cut your hand off an' stick it up your ass."

The men at the table burst out laughing. "Better let the fella join us, Charles," suggested one. "You'll have a hard time dealing one-handed."

Charles released Cotton's wrist. "He's no kid," he said. "He's a damned dwarf in kid's overalls. Welcome to the game, mister."

Mr. Summers eased his hand off the butt of his pistol. He alone had seen Cotton slip his hand into his pocket and open his clasp knife with his thumbnail, and he was more than relieved now to see the boy close it just as quickly.

"That boy's got spunk," he said to Clayton. "Maybe too much." Clayton wondered if that meant Cotton was made out of green hickory.

Surprisingly, as the game progressed, Cotton held his own or, if anything, won a little.

"That boy was born under a lucky star," Mr. Summers said.

Clayton agreed. Then, excusing himself, saying he needed a breath of fresh air, he walked to the bow of the boat and gazed up the river. Millions of tiny lights sparkled on the black, sluggish water and he found himself wondering which one was the reflection of his lucky star.

From the shadows, Claudette LaBranche said, "Star light, star bright, first star I've seen tonight, I wish I may, I wish I might, I wish this dream would come true tonight."

"How did you know what I was thinking?" Clayton asked without turning.

"Because I have gazed at those reflections and searched for my own lucky star hundreds of times."

Moving into the glow of the lantern, she asked, "Why do you always come to the bow of the boat instead of going to the fantail, where most of the patrons go?"

"I want to see where I'm going, not where I've been." Then he countered, "Why do you hide in the shadows tonight? The deck is nearly empty."

"I can never be by myself for more than a minute . . . unless I hide."

She joined him and rested her elbows on the railing. Tossing her head back and closing her eyes, she said, "I dislike what I am, M'sieur Harris." A faint breeze ruffled the soft ringlets that framed her face. "I am even afraid of steamboats. Do you realize, m'sieur, that nearly four thousand people have died in steamboat mishaps? Paddle-wheelers are floating death traps." She stared upstream into the darkness beyond the running lights. "I dream about being burned to death in a boiler explosion. It would be a fitting way to die, would it not, M'sieur Harris?" She laughed shakily. "Do you not see the irony of it, should I burn to death aboard a steamboat?"

Uncertain of how to respond, Clayton shook his head.

"Would not Satan be furious if God sent me to purgatory as used baggage?" she murmured as though to herself. She laughed again, but it was the nervous laugh of a woman terrified by her own thoughts. Then she whispered, "Already burned. . . ."

Clayton shifted uneasily and stared at the sky above the river channel. "Why don't you quit? Just walk away? You're pretty. You're intelligent. You could get a job or something."

Claudette smiled at his naiveté. "I am a free woman of color, m'sieur. But that does not mean I am free." Then, before he could protest, she slipped her arm through his. "Come, let's walk for a while."

As they moved off toward the fantail, she asked, "Are you going far? Perhaps to Baton Rouge, or to New Orleans?"

"No." Glancing up and down the deck nervously, Clayton withdrew his arm. "I'm sorry, Miss Claudette, but . . . I'm not sure I should be talking to you like this . . ."

Claudette's face fell. "You are right, m'sieur. A courtesan, even when she is out of bed, is still a courtesan. However, if you will try to forget it, so will—"

"I lost my ass!" Cotton was striding toward them, his face cracking into its perpetual grin. Then, taking a full turn around Claudette, he whistled softly through the gap in his front teeth. "You are one hell of a fine-lookin' woman."

"And you," she laughed, "are a naughty puppy." Turning her smoky eyes to Clayton but still addressing Cotton, she said, "I only wish your friend would take lessons from you, m'sieur. He is so very serious all the time."

Cotton dismissed Clayton with a wave of his hand. "Don't mind him. He's educated. An' you know how them book-learned Yankees is—kinda pinch-mouthed an' high-falutin', an' dumb as a rock 'bout important things."

Claudette's hand covered her mouth, but it did little to stifle the laughter that bubbled forth.

Clayton dropped his head and clenched his teeth.

"Well," Cotton said, winking at Claudette, "I gotta go. Mr. Summers an' me are aimin' to play a hand of Ol' Maids or somethin'. I just didn't want Clayton worryin' about his money, which he won't now that he knows I lost it. See y'all later."

Clayton watched Cotton saunter back into the saloon.

"I'm sorry, ma'am. I hope Cotton didn't offend you."

Claudette shook her head and laughed delightedly. "On the contrary, m'sieur, he was very amusing. In New Orleans, among the Creole aristocracy, he would be quite a curiosity."

Clayton didn't doubt that.

"Well," Claudette sighed, with regret in her voice, "I must go. But I thank you for a most entertaining few minutes. The encounter has certainly been . . . different."

After she left, Clayton pondered her words. Was he too serious all the time? He didn't think so. Should he try to be more like Cotton? The thought made him shudder. Was he pinch-mouthed? Surely not.

Hearing footsteps, he turned to find Cotton coming toward him. The boy was staring at him with something akin to awe.

"She's the prettiest woman I ever saw," Cotton said, "an' I got to talk to her in person." Clutching his heart, he staggered against the railing. "I'm in love." Then he sank slowly to the deck. "I'm in love!"

"Stop that," Clayton said, "and get up from there. People are watching."

Cotton bounded to his feet, oblivious to the stares of the late-night strollers. "Hell, Clay, they ain't a man on this tub what wouldn't sell his soul for a chance to cut Claudette LaBranche. Loan me twenty dollars."

"Cut her? What do you mean?" Clayton ignored the request.

"You are dumb as a rock! Ain't you never learned nothin'? It means to . . . why, to breed with her . . . you know? Hell, it's what men an' women do to one another for twenty dollars."

Cotton took a step backward, staring hard at Clayton. "You ain't one of them girl-boys I've heard about, are you?"

"No, of course I'm not! I just don't believe in fornication, that's all. And I've only got about six dollars left anyway."

Cotton frowned at him. "I ain't followin' you about this fornication stuff. Talk plain English."

"I don't believe that a man should join with a woman until they are married."

Cotton burst out laughing. "Ain't no wonder you Yankees are pinch-mouthed."

Although Clayton watched the shadowed places, Claudette LaBranche did not appear the next night. He would have been hard pressed to say truthfully whether he was relieved or disappointed. But she did appear on the following evening, stepping out of the shadows to take her place beside him at the railing.

"I have heard that you are leaving the boat tomorrow," she said.

"Yes. We're changing steamers at the mouth of the Cumberland."

Claudette LaBranche smiled sadly. "May I speak freely, m'sieur?"

"Please do."

"Thank you," she said, and then hesitated as though she did not know how to begin. Finally she said, "You are a fine young man, m'sieur, and if you would not be angered by a word of sincere advice from a . . . a worldly person . . ."

"I would take it as a favor, ma'am."

"Fight hard to remain as you are, M'sieur Harris," she said. "Allow no woman, and especially not the gorgeous seductress, the South, to change who you are and what you believe in. For beneath the beautiful and elegant ball gown that the South wears, you will find nothing but a tattered chemise. No, m'sieur, do not succumb to the South's charms . . . ever."

CHAPTER 3

Clayton, Cotton, and Mr. Summers stood on the upper deck of *The Whirlwind* and watched the lights of Nashville on the bluff slip past. The night was sticky, and the insects were driving the passengers to near insanity with their stinging, biting, and buzzing.

"These river mosquitoes can fly faster than this tub can run," Mr. Summers complained, fanning his face with his wide-brimmed hat.

"You ain't wrong, Mr. Summers," Cotton agreed. "This ol' boat ain't doin' but four goddamned miles an hour an' the bugs is flyin' eight."

"Boy," the old man said, pointing his hat at Cotton, "when we get to Summerset, you'd better watch your swearin'. Mrs. Summers don't take kindly to cussin', 'specially from a youngun."

"I only cuss around menfolks," Cotton said, grinning widely.

"An' that's another thing," Mr. Summers said. "That infernal grinnin' of yours is enough to drive a body to drink."

"My ma used to say the good Lord set my ears too high.

An' when he 'tached my mouth and tried to make it match, he was obliged to draw it up on the corners." The boy laughed loudly and slapped his knee, causing dust to jump from his threadbare overalls.

Mr. Summers appraised Cotton, then Clayton. The two were such opposites that he wondered at their ability to be friends. Cotton had nothing in his favor, not even such a small blessing as a handsome face, yet he loved life and lived it to its fullest. Clayton, on the other hand, had obviously been handed many advantages, yet he approached life soberly and with caution.

The old man fished out a cigar and raked a wooden match across the deck railing. Both young men, he mused, would make a mark upon the world. The question was, what kind of mark would it be?

Mr. Summers took a deep, contemplative draw. As he exhaled, a moth fluttered into his slack-lipped mouth.

"Damn!" he shouted, raking his gums with the back of his hand. "For two bits I'd disembark us right here at Nashville an' hire a wagon to carry us the rest of the way to Cairo." He pronounced it "Kay-ro."

"How far is Cairo, Mr. Summers?" Clayton asked.

The old man spat again, then grimaced. Moth dust still clung to the roof of his mouth. "It ain't far. Maybe thirty mile, as the crow flies."

"Thirty miles? Is Cairo near any real towns? Or is Nashville the closest?"

"Cairo is a real town." The old man drew on his cigar, then grimaced again as the smoke mingled with the moth dust. "But if Cairo ain't big enough to suit you, Clayton, there's Gallatin, the county seat, which is about three or four miles down the road. They's probably two, three thousand folks live there."

At the Cairo wharf, waiting for the paddle-wheeler to dock, was a barefooted Negro boy wearing a faded calico shirt and homespun trousers.

"Massa' Summers!" he shouted, clambering down over the front wheel of an antiquated, open-topped phaeton and running to the walk plank. He looked to be about twelve years old. "Massa' Summers! It's sho' good fo' you to be back, suh."

Mr. Summers nodded his greetings. "Everything go well durin' my absence, Rufus?"

"Yes, suh, everythin's been just fine." The boy fell in beside Mr. Summers, taking overstrides in an effort to match the old man's long, gangling steps. "Ole Mista Jameson's house nigger, Henry James, he done run away, tho'."

"Again?"

"Yes, suh. He purt' near got plumb away this time."

"How so?"

"Henry James done built hisself a raff in old Bledsoe Creek and near t'floated hisself clear to Gallatin a'fore the sheriff catch't him."

Mr. Summers turned to his two companions. Laying his hand on the young Negro's shoulder, he said, "Boys, this is Rufus. I'm trainin' him to be a house servant." Rufus grinned and nodded. Clayton reached out and shook Rufus' hand, drawing frowns from Mr. Summers and Cotton.

"Anyway," said the old man, "Rufus says that one of my neighbor's slaves has run off. This is the second time this year that's happened, an' sentiments are runnin' high. The slaves are gettin' more and more belligerent and dissatisfied. They're behavin' like they've seen somethin' us white folks have overlooked."

"It's like that ever'where," broke in Cotton. "Ever' owner in Kentucky is experiencin' the same thing. They say the grapevine's been a'smokin'. Yes, sir, somethin' has sure got all the slaves upset."

"Well," Mr. Summers said, "whatever it is, the darkies hereabouts ain't talkin' about it. But I feel it in my bones—trouble's comin'."

Mr. Summers turned toward a two-story brick building sporting a weathered sign that read "Higher's Grocery Store."

"Rufus," he said, draping his arm over the boy's shoulders, "you was about to let me forget the most important thing of all."

"Yes, suh, I sho' nuff was!" cried the boy happily. Then he clapped his hands while his bare feet drummed out a rhythmic tattoo that brought dust boiling up around his bony ankles.

The four entered the building through open double doors

and marched to the glass-cased candy counter.

Clayton did a full turn. The general store consisted of one long aisle, with each side packed from floor to ceiling with dry goods, farm equipment, foodstuffs, and just about every sundry one might imagine. The place had a pungent aroma all its own, not at all unpleasant.

Turning back to the candy counter, Clayton marveled at the selection: A rainbow of colors gleamed from wide-mouthed glass jars, painted boxes, and ornately decorated tins. He knew a moment of embarrassed discomfort. He had slighted the town of Cairo without ever having seen it, and he wondered if perhaps he might have also made the same miscalculation about many things concerning the South and its way of life.

"About two pounds of horehound, Mr. Higher," Mr. Summers said.

The middle-aged, stoop-shouldered proprietor scooped up the stick candy and laid it on the scales. Frowning through the bottom half of his small, gold-rimmed spectacles, he added several more pieces. "Two pounds, right on the money. Have you heard about Jameson's nigger?"

Mr. Summers nodded, passing the man a gold dollar. "Rufus told me."

"They brought him back and broke his ankles," said the grocer, wrapping the candy in brown paper. "He won't be runnin' anymore."

Mr. Summers' craggy brows drew together and his mouth turned down at the corners. "Pretty harsh punishment, weren't it? Henry James won't be doin' no work, neither. I wonder if they thought of that."

Clayton's face drained. He had heard such stories from his father's abolitionist friends; until now, they had seemed unreal. But this was real. A plantation owner had actually broken a slave's ankles because the man had tried to escape to freedom!

Anger welled up within Clayton, and he was about to voice his condemnation of such barbaric behavior when Rufus looked up at him and said, "Massa Summers, he don't never treat his folk that-a-way."

Cotton laughed and ruffled Rufus' kinky hair. "When slaves are good," he said, "owners ain't got no call to punish 'em."

Rufus nodded.

"Jameson said he was makin' an example of Henry James," Mr. Higher said, handing Mr. Summers the candy and his change. "I expect he did the right thing."

"Maybe so," murmured Mr. Summers, dropping the money into a black-leather coin purse. "Maybe so."

On the drive from Cairo to Summerset Plantation, Rufus handled the matched team of grays expertly. The old phaeton shone like new money, and considering that the narrow dirt road was deep-rutted from years of abuse by iron-rimmed wagon wheels, the rubber-tired carriage wheels rolled smooth and quiet on the well-greased axles.

The countryside was gently rolling, and even to Clayton's untrained eye, it looked to be extremely fertile. Every field they passed was alive with Negroes tending long even rows of waist-high plants.

"What is the crop?" Clayton asked. "I don't recognize it."

"Tobacco, son," Mr. Summers answered.

"Looks as if the farmers are going to have a good year," Clayton said.

"Too dry." Mr. Summers also watched the field hands. "An' we don't call ourselves farmers, Mr. Harris. We are planters."

Cotton nodded. "'Less'n we get some rain, corn won't make twenty bushel to the acre."

Clayton settled back against the warm leather upholstery. The fields looked plentiful indeed, and he found it difficult to believe that they would bring but a mediocre yield.

"Don't feel bad, 'cause you're not familiar with plantations an' such, Clayton," Mr. Summers said. "You're an educated young feller who can teach folks things I can't even say right. Why, I reckon you and me an' Cotton will learn a heap from one another."

"Now, Mr. Summers," Cotton said, leaning around Clayton so he could see the old man's face, "you ain't figgerin' on me learnin' no readin' or writin', are you?"

"You think you're pretty smart, do you?" queried the old man.

"Well, shore I am," Cotton said. "I'm a horse-and-mule man, an' I don't rightly see how readin', writin', an' all that malarkey is goin' to do me no good a' tall."

The old man's face grew thoughtful. "Well, supposin' I sent you to town to sell one of my mules. How would you know if the man paid you all the money he was supposed to?"

Cotton considered that. "I reckon I'd tell him if'n the money weren't right, I would hunt him down an' blow his thievin' head off. I ain't got no time for crooks, Mr. Summers."

Mr. Summers nodded. Clayton, who possessed an uncompromising belief in the due process of the law, was appalled. But as he opened his mouth to protest, Mr. Summers was already speaking: "Still in all, it would be a mite simpler just to avoid all that trouble by learnin' to read, write, and do figures. Don't you think so?"

Cotton glowered, then grinned. "I might go to school for a short spell, jist 'til I can count good 'nough to trade mules."

"Well, I's a-wantin' to go to school," declared Rufus, grinning nearly as widely as Cotton. "I's a-goin' to learn all's I can and be a real educated nigger."

"What you goin' to do then?" Cotton scoffed.

"Well, I don't rightly know, Mista Cotton." Turning to Mr. Summers, Rufus asked, "What is I a-goin' to be, Massa?"

"You're goin' to be one sorry pickaninny if you don't watch where we're a'goin'," the old man cried as the carriage dropped into a hub-deep rut that nearly overturned the vehicle.

"Damn it, Rufus," complained Cotton as the phaeton righted itself and threw the travelers back into their respective positions, "you nearly caused Clayton to mash the piss outta' me."

"I's sorry, Mista Cotton," Rufus said. "I reckon I jist got carried 'way thinkin' about schoolin' an' all."

"Ain't no school for slaves nohow," said Cotton. "The law don't allow it. So where in hell are you gettin' all these highfalutin' notions?"

"He's just a-dreamin'," Mr. Summers said, throwing Rufus a threatening glare.

Clayton's eyes slid questioningly to the old man. What was it Mr. Summers had said the day Clayton met him? "What I need is a schoolmaster. Somebody with backbone

. . . and it's got to be somebody from the North."

When Clayton spoke, his voice had an edge to it. "Mr. Summers, I believe we had better talk about that job you offered."

The old man stood up in the phaeton and leaned on the dashboard. Rufus swung the carriage into a lane where overhanging oak limbs intertwined to create a leafy tunnel. "We're home," Mr. Summers said. Then, settling back into the upholstery, he added, "I always did like comin' home."

Clayton took an angry breath and exhaled it; he had his answer.

As they neared the end of the lane, Rufus flicked the grays with the rein tips, urging them into a high-stepping trot that had the wheels fairly humming as the buggy sped beneath the arched, wrought-iron entry whose freshly painted sign welcomed all to "Summerset."

In the distance, sitting on a knoll, was a large, two-story, white frame house with four imposing columns supporting a Georgian-style portico.

Behind the main structure stood a log smokehouse, and off to one side was the kitchen. A respectable distance beyond, there were two whitewashed cabins that Clayton later found to be the homes of the house servants. On a hill to the right of a huge stock barn stood a row of weathered, unpainted board-and-batten cabins that housed the field slaves.

By the time the phaeton came to a rocking halt in front of the main house, a score of Negro children were bounding across the yard squealing out greetings to Mr. Summers. Then the house servants appeared, and behind them a wisp of a woman who could be none other than the mistress of the plantation.

The children surrounded the phaeton, their faces eager with expectation.

"What you-all want?" demanded Mr. Summers, stepping down among them.

A hush fell over the youngsters. They dropped their heads, then slowly raised their large black eyes and grinned with shy eagerness.

"You younguns been mindin' your mamas?"

"Yes, Massa Summers," they chorused. Clayton smiled, understanding that he was witnessing a game that had been played many times before.

"Are you certain?" bellowed the old man.

"Yas, suh," the children cried.

With that, Mr. Summers withdrew the sack of hard candy and held it aloft.

The children clapped their hands, their faces alight with grins.

Mr. Summers handed the candy to a portly Negro woman wearing a cook's apron. "See that everyone gets a piece, Trillie. The field workers too."

The woman nodded. "Yes, suh, you can 'pend on it, Masta Summers."

The old man strode briskly up the herringbone-brick walkway to the porch where his wife waited.

"I found us a schoolmaster," he whispered as he bent to kiss her cheek.

"I surely hope we are doing the right thing, Mr. Summers," she returned. An uncertain smile graced her aged but still-pretty face.

Mr. Summers squeezed her hand reassuringly. "Don't go havin' doubts now. After all, this was your idea."

"I know it was. Still, I can't help but be a little hesitant. It is against the law . . ."

"It ain't again the laws of God," he declared. "An' like you've said a hundred times before, them's the ones that count."

Drawing her down the wide stone steps to the walkway, he slipped his arm through hers and escorted her to the carriage.

"My dear," he said proudly, "I present to you Mr. Clayton Harris and Mr. Cotton Ferris. Clayton's considerin' teachin' school, and I figure on apprenticing Cotton to our overseer. Boys, meet Mrs. Summers."

Clayton bowed and kissed her hand. "It's a pleasure, Mrs. Summers."

When she extended her hand to Cotton, he shook it heartily. "Please to make your 'quaintance, ma'am."

Mrs. Summers' face lit up with amusement. "So you want to be a planter, do you?"

"Well, actually, ma'am," Cotton said, "I'm a mule skinner. Mr. Summers says I might be useful with the stock. But I know how to handle slaves, ma'am, 'cause they ain't no different than any other prime animals."

Mrs. Summers smiled uncertainly.

Mr. Summers cleared his throat loudly. "Cotton, you can either bunk at my overseer's house"—the old man pointed at a small frame dwelling that sat at the foot of the hill below the slave quarters—"or you can fix you a place in the barn."

Cotton appraised the overseer's house and then regarded the large stock barn. "No offence to your overseer, Mr. Summers, but I think I'll take the barn. I like bein' around stock."

The old man nodded. "Well, go on down there an' get settled in." Taking Clayton by the arm, he guided him toward the house.

A house servant retrieved Clayton's valise from the carriage and followed the trio up the steps and into the great hall. On one side of the corridor, doors opened into a parlor and a sitting room, and on the other side, into a library and a downstairs bedroom. The stairway leading to the upper story was a wide, graceless affair with a landing at the turn instead of the winding sweep of the more stately homes.

"You'll have to make do with the downstairs bedchamber, Mr. Harris," the old man said as he ushered Clayton into the high-ceilinged, stuffy room.

Clayton gazed happily at the four-poster bed with its lace canopy and feather-tick mattress. It was an especially inviting sight after nights spent in a cramped steamboat cabin.

There was a cherry highboy in one corner and an ornately carved armoire in another. Beside the fireplace sat a small writing desk and a Windsor chair, and next to the bed was a commode with a porcelain pitcher and matching bowl. The highly waxed, wide-board poplar floor was bare.

Clayton found the room's simplicity a noteworthy change from the bedchambers of the Columbus elite, with their imported French wallpaper, heavy draperies, and dark-mahogany furniture. He deposited his carpetbag in the armoire and joined Mr. Summers in the doorway.

Meanwhile, an elderly black butler escorted Cotton around the house and down the back walkway.

"The barn is that-a-way," he said, pointing stiffly. "They's a room in the loff, wif a bed and such. Masta say that's where you 'posed to lib."

"Much obliged," Cotton said, clapping the man on the back. "Sure will beat the three-room shack I shared with thirteen brothers and sisters. Never had no time alone. None a'tall. Yep, it'll be a pleasure havin' my own room." Cotton struck out in long strides toward the barn.

The old slave's eyes followed Cotton to the barn until the boy disappeared into the shadowed entrance. "Sho' don't understan' what ol' Masta thinkin' 'bout when he brung white trash like that home wif 'im," he said, shaking his head.

CHAPTER 4

Upon leaving the bedchamber, Clayton followed Mr. Summers to the library, which also served as the plantation office. Trillie, the housekeeper, had placed a silver tray with a pitcher of tea and three glasses on a large mahogany desk. From a corner cabinet Mr. Summers selected a bottle of whiskey and splashed generous amounts of the clear liquid into two of the glasses. The third he filled with tea from the pitcher and handed to Mrs. Summers. Then the old man passed Clayton a glass, took his own, and nodded to the young man. "To the South," he said.

Clayton returned the gesture and sipped his drink. It was cool and smelled of mint more than tasted of it, for the corn liquor was by far the most prevalent ingredient.

Studying the old man over the rim of the glass, Clayton wondered when Mr. Summers would get to the point of the offer he had made aboard the *Princess*. Even though he was certain that he knew what Mr. Summers was leading up to, he felt that it would be in his best interest not to pressure his benefactor.

But as the afternoon shadows lengthened and Mr. Summers persisted in rambling on about plantation life and the surrounding countryside, Clayton, a bit light-headed from the whiskey, gave in.

"Mr. Summers," he said, setting his glass on a table, "let's talk about the teaching job you offered me."

The old man eyed Clayton belligerently. "Son, ain't you been listenin' to nuthin' I been sayin'? I been familiarizin' you with the folks and the country hereabouts."

"Yes, sir. I'm aware of that. But what does it have to do with the job you mentioned?"

"Everything! How in the world do you expect to teach folks anythin' when you ain't got no notion as to what or who they are? A man's got to understand a body before he can teach him somethin'."

Clayton gritted his teeth; he had been too hasty. "Well, would you enlighten me as to what you have in mind, sir?"

Mr. Summers pinned the boy with a hard stare. "I want you to take the time to visit the folks who live in these parts: the Winchesters of Cragfont, the Wynnes of Wynnewood, the Jamesons on the pike, the Boddies of Walnut Grove, Dr. Daniel Mentlo at Oakland, Colonel George Elliott at Elliott Spring, Joe Guild at Rosemont, the Chenaults at Greenfield. Hell, son, those are just a few of the people I want you to meet an' get acquainted with. I aim for you to see firsthand what life in the South is all about."

Clayton nodded. "I agree that a schoolmaster should know and understand his scholars, sir, but what does culture have to do with reading, penmanship, and mathematics?"

"What I've been talkin' about ain't got a dern thing to do with the scholars! It's you who's got to be educated before you can start educatin'."

Clayton, startled by the old man's admonition, jumped to his feet. "I've got a fine education, Mr. Summers, and I doubt you'll find that I am lacking."

The old man stood up too and took a turn around the room, his tall frame bent in concentration.

"Clayton," he said, stopping to lean on the back of a wing chair, "you've got a headful of book learnin', but you ain't educated." He pointed a finger at the boy. "I want you to fully understand our way of life here, an' 'specially our slaves' ways . . . 'cause it's them you're goin' to be a-teachin'."

Clayton shook his head. "Mr. Summers, in all due respect, sir, I'll have to return your money. It's against the law to teach slaves to read and write."

The old man took a deep breath. "Son, if things keep a-buildin' like they are, there's goin' to be bad trouble 'tween the North and the South. It's brewin' like a swarm of angry bees when somebody's tryin' to steal their honey. An' any fool with half an eye ought to be able to see it comin'."

In spite of himself, Clayton smiled. "I've never cared for honey, Mr. Summers, so maybe that's why I disagree with you. I know the North and South have differences that need to be worked out, but I don't believe that the United States will go to war with itself. Why, it's been only a little over forty years since we truly gained our independence from England and became one nation."

"See!" cried the old man. "You said yourself the North an' South have differences, but you ain't even willin' to see what the South is really like! How you goin' to fix somethin' if you don't take the time to figure out why it broke?"

Clayton flushed at the old man's challenge. "Mr. Summers, I have been taught to respect my elders, but I am going to speak my mind, sir. You said a while back that the slaves are getting more belligerent and dissatisfied every day. That, sir, is because everyone in the world, including the Negro, is fed up with the institution of slavery. Yet you Southerners refuse to acknowledge that truth. I do, however, agree with one thing you have stated: Something must be done . . . and it will be. But it will be accomplished by our elected leaders, in a civil manner. Not, sir, by war. It would be beneath the Union's dignity to raise its hand in combat against a bunch of julep-drinking, soft-spoken, conceited weaklings."

The old man slammed his fist against the desk top. "Well, let me tell you somethin', you long-winded jacksnipe. I was with Ol' Hickory at the Battle of New Orleans in eighteen fourteen when we won that independence you rave about. An' it weren't no Northerners what whipped the British. Hell, the Northerners weren't even there. No, sir, it was the Southerners, with their squirrel rifles and huntin' knives and sharp eyes. So don't ever think the South won't fight for what it believes in. Furthermore, if the truth was known, it was the backwoodsmen at Kings Mountain what turned the tide of the Revolution in seventy-eight. Dern it, boy, a Southerner ain't never walked away from a fight in his life, and he won't now . . . not if the whole wide world rares up in arms again him. An' that's what the North don't understand."

Clayton bit back a defensive reply and said instead, "I don't see the connection between educating the slaves and the prevention of war, Mr. Summers."

The old man picked up his glass and took a long swallow. "There ain't no connection, son," he said, wiping his mouth with the back of his hand. "But the way I figure it, a small investment now in educatin' the slaves might return dividends tenfold should they . . . have to depend on themselves sometime in the future."

Clayton smiled again, he felt victorious. "You just finished informing me, sir, that the South won the War for Independence all by itself. Yet now, almost in the same breath, you imply that it can't beat the North."

"No, Clayton, I'm not sayin' that a'tall. What I'm sayin' is that with or without a civil war, it's only a matter of time 'til the South frees its slaves. An' when that happens, I want my darkies to have the best chance possible at a new life."

It was Clayton's turn to pace the room. "Mr. Summers," he said, pausing by the fireplace and staring at his reflection in the mirror above the mantle, "I don't believe in breaking people's feet, or in whipping them . . . or in any form of cruelty. I want you to know that."

"You've made that plain. In fact, I was dependin' on it."

Clayton studied Mr. Summers' reflection in the mirror; he could learn much from such a man, for he knew without a doubt that he had just been manipulated and outmaneuvered by a slow-talking, self-proclaimed illiterate who was blessed with an overabundance of common sense, which Clayton knew to be a ridiculous phrase, for true common sense was as uncommon as was genius.

"I'll visit the plantations," he murmured, "and I'll do it with an open mind. But I'm not promising anything. Is that agreeable, sir?"

"That's fair enough."

CHAPTER 5

Breakfast was hardly over when Mr. Summers took Clayton and Cotton on a horseback tour of Summerset, making sure that Clayton paid close attention to the slaves working the fields.

Men, women, and children were sweltering under the scorching morning sun. Yet even then they looked happy enough, moving quietly among the pale-green tobacco plants. The young Northerner had envisioned slaves chained together like prisoners, an overseer standing over them wielding an eight-foot blacksnake whip. If an overseer were present, Clayton could not locate him.

When he asked about the absent overseer, Mr. Summers told him that the man, whose name was Butler, had gone to Gallatin to purchase a new haymowing machine and would not return until late afternoon.

"Who guards your slaves?" Clayton asked.

"Nobody guards my slaves. They ain't criminals; they live here."

Cotton, sitting his horse with such ease that it was almost as though he had grown there, unwittingly came to Clayton's defense. "Well, they's one thing for sure—the plantation owners up in Kentucky wouldn't leave their slaves untended. Hell, they'd be off an' runnin' for the river a'fore you could skin a cat."

"I don't doubt that," Mr. Summers agreed. "And if I lived near the Ohio, I wouldn't be so trustin' either."

"It's them Yankee bastards from Ohio, Indiana, an' Illinois," Cotton continued. "They sneak over the river at night and stir up more shit than you can shake a stick at. Caught one of 'em, we did, and hanged his ass to a white oak tree."

"You did that?" Clayton twisted in the saddle so he could look Cotton in the eyes.

Cotton grinned sheepishly. "Well, all I did was stay in the bushes an' watch. But I seen 'em do it."

"We'd best be movin' on," Mr. Summers said, adjusting his hat so that the shade cast by its wide brim hid his face.

"Well, I did see 'em," Cotton insisted, reining his horse down a row of tobacco that extended almost as far as the eye could see.

It was mid-afternoon before the three had inspected all of Summerset Plantation. Clayton was impressed with what he had seen and heard. It was a beautiful, well-organized piece of property, and its slaves appeared to be content.

The old man thumbed his hat to the back of his head and ran a sleeved forearm across his perspiring brow.

"Yes, sir," he said, "Summerset's a prosperous plantation, Clayton. Do you have any idea of why my crops are tolerable? Why my livestock is fat an' healthy? Why my darkies are strong an' sassy?"

"I would assume that it's because of good management, sir," Clayton said.

The old man nodded. "It's because I, Jonathan Summers, rotate the crops in my fields. An' I, Jonathan Summers, am careful about inbreedin' my livestock. An' I, Jonathan Summers, pay close attention to the health an' well-bein' of my slaves. The point I'm makin' is that nothin' on this plantation is capable of improvin' itself without close supervision . . . not even my slaves."

"Darkies!" Cotton said. "Why, if'n you turned them out to fend for their own self, they'd be as lost as newborns. They ain't got sense enough to get in out of the rain."

Mr. Summers smiled to himself; Cotton had stated the case quite well.

Upon reaching the stable, Cotton reined in and asked Anderson, the blacksmith, to tighten a loose shoe on his horse. Mr. Summers and Clayton rode on to the slave cabins. Although most of the able-bodied men, women, and children were in the fields, there were a few slaves in the quarters, engaged in the numerous menial and domestic tasks that were an integral part of everyday plantation life. All of them spoke to Mr. Summers as he passed, and to Clayton's surprise, the old man answered, calling each by his or her given name.

Clayton could see that care and forethought had gone into furnishing the cabins. Each was equipped with a fireplace and serving crane, a black-iron cook pot, a table and bench, a lantern, and a rope bed. Also, each had a small sleeping loft, presumably for the children. The inside walls were of roughsawed poplar boards and had been whitewashed. The roofs were of split red-oak shingles, laid in orderly rows. As neat as the cabins were, however, due to the lack of washing facilities, the odor of the inhabitants was overwhelming. Clayton preferred to stand and observe as much as possible from the open doorway.

Mr. Summers seemed impervious to the stench, marching into the cabins and inspecting them at length. Perhaps a person gets used to it, Clayton decided. But somehow he doubted it.

When they reached the last cabin, Mr. Summers instructed Clayton to wait outside, which suited the boy fine. The old man went in, closing the door behind him. Clayton heard the murmur of voices through the rough-hewn door, but it wasn't until he heard a cry of pain that his curiosity got the better of him and he eased the door open to look inside.

A slave girl lay on a cot, and it was obvious, even to one as naive as Clayton, that she was well into her labor. He was surprised to see Mrs. Summers sitting on the edge of the bed gently wiping perspiration from the girl's brow.

Mr. Summers and Trillie stood near the foot of the bed. "Well, Pauline," Mr. Summers said, "are you goin' to fetch me a fine, healthy buck?"

The girl's glassy eyes turned toward the old man, and for a moment she tried bravely to smile. Then her face contorted with pain. "I dunno, Massa. I's a-feared I's gonna die."

"You ain't goin' to die," he assured her. "As soon as Butler gets back from Gallatin, I'm sendin' him for old Mizz Winchester's midwife, Chatty. Ain't another darky in the country can bring younguns into the world as easy as she can."

The girl tried to take a deep breath, but she couldn't. Breathing hard, she whispered, "I's gonna try real hard to bring you a fine buck, Massa."

Mrs. Summers patted Pauline's hand. "You'll be just fine, Pauline, just fine."

Lifting the worn sheet that covered the girl's body, the old lady inspected her pelvic area. "I'm surprised, Jonathan," she said, making no attempt to curb the displeasure in her voice, "that you were unaware that Pauline's time was near. I think you have become much too lax in the running of this plantation. I think you've grown too dependent on Mr. Butler."

The old man turned abruptly to a slave woman standing at the head of the bed. "Sal, you're suppose to be tendin' this girl. Why didn't you send word that Pauline's time had come?"

The woman wrung her hands, her eyes frightened. "We done ast Mista Butler to fetch you, Massa, but he say Pauline won't have no trouble wid her birthin' 'cause . . ."

"'Cause why?" Mr. Summers demanded.

"'Cause, he say de baby be only half human . . . and he say dat make it come easier." The woman cringed under Mr. Summers' angry glare.

"Goddamn Butler!" cried Mr. Summers, avoiding the I-told-you-so look on his wife's face.

Clayton was forced to jump aside as Mr. Summers stormed out the door and marched toward the main house. Catching up the bridle reins of both horses, Clayton fell in beside him. "Will that girl be all right, Mr. Summers?"

"She dern well better be! If she ain't, I'm goin' to take the price of a fine slave out of Butler's hide . . . an' slaves don't come cheap."

Clayton was not only disappointed by Mr. Summers' statement, he was stunned. Then he was enraged. "Is that all you're worried about, the price of a slave?" he yelled. "What about the fact that he got her pregnant? Doesn't that bother you?"

The old man stopped and stared at Clayton.

"Why, no," he said finally. "That don't bother me a'tall. An' don't never holler at me nary another time, son." The old man took a step, then stopped again. "Fact is," he said, "a mulatto is worth more'n a pureblood, 'cause folks want 'em for house servants. So if Butler knocked Pauline up, I'm obliged. Heck, Clayton, ain't hardly a plantation in the South what hasn't got one or two of the master's yard children runnin' about."

"Have *you* got yard children here at Summerset?" Clayton blurted.

"I ain't never held with the idea of beddin' my own wenches," Mr. Summers said. "But just because I don't do it don't mean I see somethin' wrong with it. Why, some of them younguns has growed up to be mighty fine-lookin' darkies. Over at Cragfont, the Winchesters have a house wench named Fanny who's near white as you an' me, an' a dern sight prettier. An' everybody knows she's a Winchester, 'cause she's the spittin' image of all them Winchester girls."

"What do the Southern women think, knowing that their men are siring yard children?" Clayton asked as Mr. Summers strode toward the house.

"I ain't never inquired!" returned Mr. Summers heatedly. "It's just the way the South is. Wenches have always been pestered by their masters. Hell, we own 'em. An' ever'body knows hot-blooded black women enjoy a man's dallyin' a whole lot more'n cold-blooded white women do. I reckon that's the reason black men are hung like well ropes, so they can accommodate them wenches."

Mr. Summers slowed his stride and faced Clayton. "Look here, son," he said. "We're back to what we was talkin' about yesterday. You are outraged over somethin' you don't approve of, or understand. An' the truth is, while you might never like what us Southerners do concernin' our property, one of these days, if you stay in the South long enough, you'll understand why we do it . . . an' that's what's important."

"I don't think so, Mr. Summers. I don't think I'll ever

understand a society that places human beings, no matter their color, in the same category as cattle or horses." Clayton took a deep breath, then looked at the old man squarely. "And don't you ever yell at me again either . . . sir."

Mr. Summers and Clayton had just reached the main house when Butler arrived. He was a big man, dressed in woolen trousers, a blue-cotton, long-sleeved shirt, and worn knee boots so scuffed that one would be hard pressed to tell they had ever been black.

Ignoring Clayton, he informed Mr. Summers that he had been unable to locate a mowing machine in Gallatin, so he had ordered one from Nashville that would be delivered by boat to Cairo within the week.

Mr. Summers waved his words aside, commanding the overseer to join him in the library. A few minutes later Butler emerged, red-faced and angry.

"Git one of the niggers to hitch up the wagon," he ordered Clayton. "Mr. Summers says you and somebody named Cotton need to learn your way around the country. So he aims for you to go to Cragfont with me to fetch ol' Chatty. A damned waste of time if you ask me."

Clayton appraised the man closely, not liking what he saw. "With all due respect, Mr. Butler," he said, "if you want one of the 'niggers' to fetch the wagon, tell him so yourself."

Although it was only two miles to Cragfont, an hour had passed when they rode up the winding lane that skirted the bluff overlooking Bledsoe's Creek and came into view of the mansion. Clayton was awed.

Built of chiseled limestone, Cragfont loomed up out of the earth two and a half stories high, its Roman Gothic facade as imposing as that of an ancient feudal castle. In a word, Cragfont, in its dignified simplicity, was imposing.

They drove the wagon past the front gate, where a horse and buggy were tied, and on toward the west entrance gate. A young Negro gate-watcher rose from a bench beside the doorway of a nearby slave house and ran to meet them.

"We've come to have a word with Mizz Winchester," said Butler, handing the bridle reins to the boy.

"Yes, suh," the young Negro said while tying the horses to the gate. "I'll run an' tell ol' Miss you's here."

He was back in an instant. "Ol' Miss say fo' you to wait in da kitchen, she'll be 'long directly."

Instructing Clayton to stay with the wagon, Butler told Cotton to come along with him to fetch Chatty's bags, and together they walked up the driveway that led to the back of the house.

Clayton squatted at the edge of the gravel drive and scooped up a handful of stones. Allowing them to trickle through his fingers, he speculated on the amount of back-breaking labor it had taken to cart enough gravel up the hill from Bledsoe's Creek to pave the entire drive.

He looked up to see a small, blond-haired girl, whom he guessed to be six or seven years old, step gingerly through the double doors that dominated Cragfont's front facade. With arms stretched rigidly before her, as though the saddlebags she carried were filled with eggs, she carefully descended the front steps and picked her way down the brick walkway toward the front gate where the horse and buggy were hitched.

Halfway down the walk, the child stumbled and the saddlebags hit the bricks with a resounding thud. The girl's hand flew to her mouth, the knuckles pressed hard against her teeth. Then Clayton saw tears well up in her eyes and break free to slide down her cheeks and drip from her chin. He was up in an instant, sprinting across the lawn.

"Are you hurt?" he inquired, kneeling before the child and searching her horrified face intently.

"Come on now," he urged, thumbing the tears from her cheeks. "Tell me what has upset you so."

The child pointed to the saddlebags at her feet. After several attempts to catch her breath, she wailed, "They're Dr. Mentlo's! He trusted me to carry them to his buggy!" With that, her sobs became even more racking.

"Well," Clayton said, taking her into his arms, "I saw you stumble and nearly fall." His eyes quickly searching the walkway, he pointed to a loose brick. "See here. Here's the reason you dropped the bags. It was not your fault at all."

The girl cried even harder. "You don't understand."

Clayton fished his handkerchief from his pocket and dabbed at her cheeks. "What is it that I don't understand?"

The child sniffled and wiped her nose with the back of her hand. "Dr. Mentlo brings babies to folks' homes in his saddlebags. Grandma told me he even brung me to my mama in these very same saddlebags."

Clayton nodded uncertainly and offered her his kerchief, which she accepted. "Go on, tell me the rest," he coached.

Taking a deep breath and dabbing at her eyes with a corner of the kerchief, she said, "Dr. Mentlo came by to see if my mama needed a new baby . . . and she does, but the doctor told her that she wouldn't be needin' it for a few more weeks. He allowed me . . . to carry the babies back . . ." The girl flung her arms around Clayton's neck and buried her face against his shoulder.

"I dropped the babies," she wailed, "an' probably killed one or two of them. Some mama will hate me." Her sobs touched Clayton's heart, yet it was all he could do to keep from laughing aloud.

"Let me take a look," he said. "Perhaps the babies aren't hurt too badly."

Climbing to his feet, he opened the saddlebags and peered inside at the array of instruments, bottles, and various items that he would not even venture to identify.

Squinting his eyes in serious thought, he eased his hand into the bag and moved the contents around.

"There doesn't seem to be any damage done," he said. "There're lots of babies in here, but they're all happy and well."

The child smiled with relief.

"Just to be on the safe side," he continued, buckling the flaps, "we'll both carry these bags to the doctor's carriage."

The girl cautiously took one bag while Clayton carried the other. Together, they walked to the buggy.

As they deposited the saddlebags on the floorboard, she told Clayton that her name was Susan Black Winchester but that everyone called her Susie, and that "Susie" was even inscribed on her silver drinking cup. Clayton told her his name and said he was pleased to make her acquaintance.

With Susie holding his hand and talking constantly, they had started back toward the house when a lovely young lady, her long golden hair piled in disarray atop her head, stepped onto the front stoop. Clayton was startled; the young woman was an older version of the girl who held his hand. She had the same finely chiseled face and thin, straight nose, and lips that were fully formed into a provocative pout.

"Cousin Lettie! Cousin Lettie!" called Susie. "Come see who I've met. Isn't he just the handsomest man? He helped me put Dr. Mentlo's babies in the buggy."

Clayton squeezed Susie's hand and whispered, "A lady doesn't say such things in the presence of a gentleman."

Susie pulled away, scampered up the steps and clutched a handful of Lettie's skirt. She dragged the startled girl toward Clayton. "Come meet him, Lettie. You'll like him."

Embarrassment, followed by anger, sent roses into Lettie's cheeks. Seizing Susie's long braid, Lettie yanked hard, causing the child to let out a wail of pain. "Serves you right," Lettie snapped, smoothing her dress while avoiding Clayton's eyes. "Young ladies do not shove people around and scream at the top of their lungs. Nor do they embarrass young gentlemen by paying them such brazen compliments."

"I know," the child pouted. "Clayton done told me."

"Well, obviously you didn't pay any attention . . . as usual."

"Oh, fiddlesticks, Lettie," Susie said. "Ever since you came back from Miss Miers' School in New York, you've been so uppity that you about make me sick."

"That's quite enough!" Lettie cried.

Clayton ducked his head and grinned, for Lettie had just admonished Susie for screaming only half so loud.

Lettie regained her composure and curtsied to Clayton. "I'm Lettie Billingsly, Susie's first cousin."

Clayton bowed. "I'm very pleased to make your acquaintance, Miss Lettie. I am Clayton Harris, from Ohio." He almost blurted out that he had been engaged by Mr. Summers as schoolmaster for his slaves, but an inner voice warned him to be cautious. He said instead, "I am a guest at Summerset."

"Lettie's promised to marry Bailey Peyton, Jr.," Susie offered importantly. "They been engaged forever, an' they even kiss."

Lettie's face flamed and she cast Susie a killing look. Then, smiling at Clayton, she inquired, "And how are Aunt Helen and Uncle Jonathan?"

"They're fine, ma'am. Mr. Summers didn't tell me he was related to the Winchesters."

"Oh, he's not, really. We call all our elderly neighbors 'uncle' or 'aunt' whether they are kin or not. If the truth were known, however, just about everybody in Sumner County is a distant relative somewhere down the line."

"It surely is different from Columbus, where I come from," said Clayton. "People don't even know their next-door neighbors, nor do they want to."

"Isn't that the truth?" agreed Lettie. "In New York City, where I attend school during the winter, no one even bothers to get acquainted with anyone else. They just ignore a body as though they don't exist."

"I'll wager you didn't have that problem," said Clayton with a confidence inspired by Lettie's friendliness.

"Are you insinuating that I am easy to approach, sir?"

"Not at all," Clayton returned, taken aback. "I only meant that someone with such obvious intelligence and beauty should attract many new friends."

The girl's face became animated. "Mr. Harris, the New Yorkers were very standoffish. I do believe, sir, that they were intimidated by my beauty and my social background."

Clayton was awestruck. Never had he encountered such a creature. She was beautiful—and knew it—and was neither overly modest nor falsely coy about her comeliness. He wasn't sure that he approved of such self-assurance in a young lady, especially one who could not possibly be a day older than himself.

"She thinks all the boys are in love with her," said Susie.

"Susie!" Lettie caught the girl by her shoulders and steered her toward the house. "Children are to be seen, not heard. Run along and tell Grandmother that Mr. Harris and I will take a julep in the parlor."

"You know you're not 'llowed to drink juleps yet," Susie said. "You're just tryin' to trick me into leavin'."

"I am so," Lettie said, casting Clayton a smile that apologized for her cousin's behavior. "Grandmother said that now I am fifteen, I can drink juleps as long as they don't have white liquor in them. After all, Grandmother was just my age when she had my mama."

"She did not!" Susie cried, shocked. "Dr. Mentlo brung Aunt Maria to Granny in his saddlebags."

Clayton cleared his throat. "Miss Susie," he said, "I surely am thirsty. Do you think your grandmother would be so kind as to invite a weary traveler in for refreshment?"

"She just might if I ask her," the girl said, glaring at Lettie.

"Well then, go ask her," commanded Lettie.

CHAPTER 6

Cotton and Butler waited in Cragfont's large kitchen which, unusual for a Southern house, was attached to the main structure.

A Negro woman, whom Cotton guessed to be in her early thirties, was bent over a mortar grinding dried mint leaves into a powdery dust with a stone pestle. The aroma wafted about the room with a richness that made the boy's mouth water.

"Smells mighty good," he said to the woman, who smiled and bobbed her head, the stone grinder rhythmic as she pounded the leaves.

Butler strode over to her and caught her chin in his palm. Forcing her head up until she was looking into his eyes, he asked, "Ain't you goin' to respond to the boy, Sylla?"

Sylla twisted her face away.

"Well now, Sylla," Butler said, "you sure are an unfriendly wench, an' I don't take kindly to unfriendly wenches."

"I's not unfriendly, Mista' Butler," she said. Ducking her head, she continued her grinding.

A moment later Cotton heard the woman suck in her breath. Butler had pulled the neck of her shift low and was fondling her breasts.

"While Chatty's getting ready to travel," Butler said to her, "you go up to your cabin. I'll be 'long directly. You understan' me, Sylla?"

"This be Sat'day, Mista Butler," she said, pushing his hand away, "an' my husban', he be gettin' a pass tonight . . . an' be a-comin' over from Summerset."

"Sam won't be a-comin' lessen I say he can come," Butler said. "You know that, Sylla. An' if you ain't nice to me, I'm goin' to tell Mr. Summers that Sam didn't work hard 'nough this week an' don't deserve no pass to come visit his wife. Is that what you want, Sylla?"

"No, Mista Butler, suh," Sylla whispered, staring listlessly at the man. "You knows I want to see my husban' powerful bad."

Butler grasped a handful of Sylla's crisp hair and snapped her head back so that she was forced to look up at him. "Then you get yourself over to that cabin, Sylla."

Stifling a sob, she nodded.

A ponderous Negro woman with a silver teapot in her hand came through the door.

"Lawd! Lawd! Sylla!" she cried. "Ain't you' got dat mint groun' yet?"

Stopping abruptly, she looked from Sylla to Butler, her eyes barely pausing at Cotton. "Lawdy be, Sylla," she continued hesitantly. "Ol' Miss done want mint tea in de parlor right dis instant."

Sylla sprang to her feet and with the mortar clutched tightly to her bosom, backed slowly away from Butler.

The portly woman fixed Butler with a hostile glare. "Yo' leave po' Sylla 'lone, Mista Butler. She be a married woman, and yo' knows it. What fo' you always a-tryin' to pester her? Dey's lot of unmarried wenches over to Summerset."

"Mind your own business, Delphy," he warned, not taking his eyes off Sylla. "Sylla wants me to pester her, don't you, Sylla?"

Sylla's eyes filled with tears.

"Mista Butler," Delphy said, "yo' a mean white man. An' de debil gonna git you one o' dese days."

"I 'spect you're right, Delphy." He grinned.

Hastening past Butler, Delphy set the teapot on a table in the center of the room. "Gimme dem mints, Sylla," she said, taking the mortar and pestle. "Ol' Miss be in here any minute wonderin' where de tea be."

Butler motioned Sylla toward the door. "Get on up to that cabin like I told you to, Sylla."

Cotton stepped aside to let the woman pass.

Clayton stood in the Cragfont parlor trying to conceal his amazement. The room seemed to be an illusion. The hand-painted stenciling that adorned the walls imitated wallpaper, and the fireplace was not marble; it had simply been painted to look like marble.

Reading his face, Lettie said stiffly, "I'm sure this is not as elegant as the mansions in Ohio, Mr. Harris. But when Cragfont was built, my ancestors had to make do with what was available on the frontier."

Clayton blushed. "Excuse me for being so transparent, Miss Lettie. I've never seen anything quite like this. It's ingenious . . . and very beautiful."

Lettie's animosity vanished. Smiling, she went on to tell him that much of the furniture had been brought over the mountains in the late 1700's by her late grandfather, General James Winchester.

"That was during the years when the Indians were still hostile, wasn't it?" Clayton inquired.

Lettie nodded proudly. "Tennessee was just a raw frontier." Then she added, "Perhaps you would care to visit Cragfont some evening and listen to the stories Grandmother can tell about her childhood days at Bledsoe's, and about Greenfield Fort and the Indian battles that were fought there. I'm just purely certain you would find her stories fascinating."

"I would be honored, Miss Lettie," he said, bowing.

"Honored to do what, young man?" came a crisp voice from the doorway.

Clayton turned to find the widow, Susan Black Winchester openly evaluating him. Her unwavering scrutiny caused him to study her with equal candor.

It was plain that she had once been a rare beauty, because even at the age of eighty-two, she still possessed a regal dignity and a proud carriage that were sufficient to demand attention and respect from all observers, be they old or young.

"I was just agreeing with Miss Lettie, ma'am," Clayton said, bowing from the waist, "that it would be an honor to learn from you firsthand about the early history of Sumner County, and indeed, of Tennessee itself."

The old lady arched her eyebrows in pleased surprise.

"Very well put, young man," she said, entering the room and extending her hand for Clayton to kiss.

"I apologize for my tardiness," she continued as he bent over her hand, "but my daughter, Malvinia, is . . . delicate. Doctor Mentlo and I have been attendin' her."

Clayton knew that no comment on a lady's pregnancy was permissible. He merely nodded that he understood.

The old lady crossed to the sofa and settled herself comfortably on the horsehair seat. Susie plopped down beside her, but Lettie moved to the large front window and nervously drew the drape aside.

"Your fiancé won't be here for hours, Lettie," Susie said.

"I wasn't looking for Mr. Peyton," Lettie snapped.

"Oh, yes you was."

"Hush, you two," the old woman commanded. Then turning to Clayton, she indicated that he was to take the wing chair next to the fireplace.

"I'm sorry, ma'am," he said politely, "but I'm afraid I haven't the time. Mr. Summers sent Mr. Butler over here to borrow a midwife—"

"Young man," the widow said, "company is much more important than a wench who is fixin' to birth. Birthin's happen nearly every day, but guests, especially Northern, as I can tell by your speech, are a rarity that is indeed a treat. However, ease your anxiety. I have sent Susie's nurse, Fanny, to fetch old Chatty, who is a mile or so down in the woods diggin' ginseng. They should be back directly. 'Til then, please sit down and tell a nosy old woman what's goin' on in the world outside of Sumner County, Tennessee."

When Butler reached Sylla's cabin, she had already stripped off her shift and was standing beside the bed, her back to the door.

"You're a mighty shapely wench to be full-stock Afric'n," he said, pausing in the doorway to appraise the sweep of her buttocks and muscular thighs.

Without a word, Sylla turned and sank down on the edge

of the bed, then lay back, her widespread legs dangling over the side.

Cotton leaned against the kitchen doorjamb and watched Butler disappear into Sylla's cabin. A nerve at the corner of one eye twitched spasmodically, and his perpetual grin faded. He had seen men like Butler before—plenty of them. All he had to do to remember what they looked like was to conjure up the faces of his thirteen brothers and sisters, for not one of them favored the other.

Cotton's throat tightened. After his sharecropper father was killed, his mother, having nowhere to go and no one to turn to, had survived in the only manner possible.

How many times, just to keep a roof over their heads and food on the table, had she, like Sylla, been pressured or blackmailed into a man's bed? More times than he could remember. But he did remember that as the years dragged by, she had finally accepted her lot in life, and even learned to embrace it . . . and then, as now, he had been powerless to intervene.

Cotton became aware of movement in the distance. Blinking several times to clear the tears of memory, he saw a Negro girl carrying a bucket of water toward Sylla's cabin. As she entered, Cotton pushed himself away from the door frame and struck off in a fast walk toward the same cabin.

Clayton sipped his mint tea and told Mrs. Winchester of the steamboat trip down the Ohio. The old woman listened with rapt attention, then explained that her late husband, General James Winchester, had been in the steamboat business, having owned one of the first paddle-wheelers, the *Cumberland,* to run from Cairo—which, and she laughed, had been a thriving metropolis in 1819—to Memphis, Cincinnati, and New Orleans.

The old lady sighed. "The *Cumberland* ran aground and sank in eighteen twenty-five. I do believe that my husband never got over the tragedy. He died the very next year."

"I'm sorry, ma'am," Clayton murmured. "I'm sure that General Winchester was a fine man."

The old woman laughed. "Mr. Harris, the general was a rogue! But I must admit, I would have been happy with nothing less."

"Grandmother!" Lettie wailed, refusing to meet Clayton's gaze. "Grandfather was a gentleman! Why, Mr. Harris will think—"

"I have Grandpa's silver shoe buckles and his Revolutionary War tricorn hat," interjected Susie proudly.

The old woman shook her finger in the child's face. "Have you been in the attic again?"

"Just for a little while," the girl hedged.

"Upstairs! This very minute." The old woman pointed toward the great hall. "To your room, young lady, and don't you come down until you're told."

"Aw, Grandma, can't I stay a while longer? I promise I'll stay out of the attic. Please?"

The old woman's face softened. "You try a person's patience, Susie. Always snoopin' around and gettin' into things that don't concern you."

"I'll be good," the girl said, hugging the old lady and kissing her cheek. "Let me stay a little longer, please."

Clayton could not help smiling as the old lady said, "Oh, very well. But in the future, stay out of the attic."

"Grandmother," Lettie said, "just because Susie is your namesake, you absolutely spoil her. It's no wonder she's so rotten."

Susie stuck out her tongue at Lettie, who glared back at her and would have retorted had not a lovely girl, followed by an ancient blue-black crone, stepped into the room and curtsied to Mrs. Winchester.

"Fanny, Chatty, come in, come in," the widow said. "I was beginning to wonder what had become of you."

Clayton gaped at the girl. Mr. Summers had told the truth . . . up to a point. The distinct Winchester bloodline was undeniable in her facial features and thick blond curls, but what the old man had failed to say was that she was not only beautiful, she was exciting. Mrs. Winchester instructed Fanny to inform Mr. Butler that Chatty would be ready to travel momentarily. Fanny curtsied and left the room, but not before her bold eyes had appraised Clayton from head to toe.

Lettie observed Fanny's evaluation of Clayton and noticed the flicker of approval in the slave girl's eyes. Turning quickly to Clayton, she said, "Fanny is married to Eli, one of the Barr Plantation slaves."

Clayton nodded, not sure of a proper response.

"Fanny's still got a rovin' eye," said Mrs. Winchester, having also seen the girl's appraisal. "But she comes by it honestly, for it's naught but the natural lustiness she inherited from—"

"Grandmother!" Lettie's hand fluttered to her throat.

"Yes," Susie said, paying no attention to Lettie, "Fanny's eyes rove all the time. They even roved over Clayton."

"To your room, young lady," the old woman commanded. Obviously Susie knew that she had overstepped her boundaries, because without a word, she marched into the hall. Clayton could hear her mumbling to herself as she stomped up the stairs. He could have felt sorry for the child, for she, as most children are want to do, was merely mimicking her elders. Instead, he was shocked at the seven-year-old's mature perception of adult sexuality.

"Chatty," Mrs. Winchester said to the midwife, "pack a satchel. Mr. Butler will carry you to Summerset to attend a wench in labor."

"Yas 'um. An' how long is I 'posed to stay ober dare?"

"Until the girl births—unless she's in false labor, which is doubtful. Stay as long as you are needed, Chatty."

When Cotton reached Sylla's cabin, Butler, drenched from head to toe, was standing in a puddle of water hitching up his breeches. Sylla, who was hastily donning her shift, said, "Mista Butler made me do it, Mandy. He say yore daddy ain't gwine to git to come visitin' dis evenin' lessen I pleasured 'im. I wants to see yore daddy parful bad . . ."

"I's been a-pleasurin' Butler fo' months, and yo' knows it!" Mandy cried.

She was not a pretty girl at best, but as she glared at Butler and her mother, her nostrils flared and her lips drew across her teeth in a snarl that raised the short hair on the back of Cotton's neck.

"I did'n hab no choice," Sylla said. "Mista Butler weren't gwine to 'llow Sam to come—"

"You's jist a liar!" Mandy yelled. "You was a-wantin' to lay wif Butler. An' I's gwine to tell my pappy what you is been a-doin'."

"Girl," Butler warned, pointing his finger at Mandy, "you better keep your mouth shet about all this."

"Yo' can kiss my black ass!"

Mandy flung the water bucket at Butler's head, then launched a scratching, kicking, biting assault on the overseer.

Butler cocked his fist and smashed it into Mandy's face, propelling her across the room. When she slammed into the brick wall, it sounded as though a sack of eggs had been hurled against a stone. The girl crumpled to the floor with great shuddering sobs.

"Yo' knows I love you, Massa Butler," she wailed, attempting to catch her breath. "Yo' knows I done ever'thin' yo' ast me to. Yo' said I pleased yo' . . ."

"You're a mean, ornery bitch," he said, dabbing with his sleeve at the lacerations Mandy's fingernails had left down the side of his face.

"Yo' said yo' was gwine to buy me," the girl sobbed. "Said yo' was gwine to free me."

"Buy you? Why would I want to buy a stenchy nigger field hand like you? Why, if I was goin' to buy me a wench, it would be one like Fanny . . ."

"Dat ain't da way yo' talk when yo' is pantin' 'tween my legs," the girl said, pushing herself to a sitting position.

"Ain't nuthin' worse than a jealous nigger," Butler said, drawing back his foot and kicking Mandy hard in the thigh.

Crying out in pain, the girl scrambled backward until brought up short against the wall.

"Don't you ever back-talk me again," Butler said, his chest heaving as he stared down at the girl. "Not ever again, damn you."

"Why don't you kick 'er to death, Mr. Butler?" Cotton asked, stepping into the room. "I don't imagine Mrs. Winchester would mind one whit that an overseer from Summerset mistreated one of her slaves. Go on, kick her again."

Butler spun on his heel. "What in hell are you doin' here? You spyin' on me, boy?"

"Don't call me 'boy,'" Cotton said. "I ain't no slave."

"Then why are you takin' up for this wench? You a nigger-lover?"

"Naw," Cotton said, "but I wouldn't beat a mule the way you did her." He gestured toward the girl's bloody mouth. "You can ruin a animal that way, Mr. Butler."

Nudging Mandy with the toe of his boot, Butler said, "Ever' now and again you got to teach these wenches to stay in their place. An' it don't make a damned bit of difference to me who they belong to."

A gasp from the doorway brought both men's heads around. Fanny was standing in the opening.

"Masta Butler," she whispered, her eyes riveted on the crumpled heap of Mandy, "ol' Miss say dat Chatty be 'bout ready to go to Summerset wif yo'." Backing from the doorway, she turned and fled toward the big house.

Pushing Cotton aside, Butler hurried to the door and looked after Fanny.

Turning abruptly he pointed his finger at Sylla. "Get up to the big house an' tell Fanny she better keep her mouth shet about what she seen in here. Tell her if she don't, she'll regret it to her dyin' day. Now git!"

Sylla gave a final tug to her dress and rushed out the door.

Turning to Cotton, Butler said, "An' that goes for you too."

"Don't threaten me, Mr. Butler. I ain't no field hand who has to put up with your crap." Cotton brought his hand out of his pocket thumbing the blade open on his jackknife, he began paring his nails.

"Boy," Butler grated, "if you ever even act like you're goin' to cut me, I'll kill you."

Cotton burst into laughter. "If I was you, Mr. Butler," he said, indicating Mandy with a thrust of his chin, "I'd be a-worryin' 'bout gettin' that girl cleaned up. You won't be killin' nobody if the Winchesters see that blood on her face."

Still laughing, he stepped out the door and walked toward the house.

Even though it was seven o'clock in the evening, the sun was still high when Butler delivered Chatty to Summerset. Leaving the wagon at the barn, he mounted his horse and ruthlessly spurred the animal toward the tobacco field where Sam, Sylla's husband, was hoeing weeds.

He rode up to the big Negro and gazed down the long row the black man had cleared.

"Sam," he said, noting with irritation the arrival of

Cotton, who had wasted no time in following him, "you been a mighty lazy nigger this week."

Sam leaned on his hoe handle and pushed his straw hat to the back of his head. "Marse Butler," he said, squinting up at the man, "if'n yo' find one weed in dem dare rows, suh, it growed dare since we been talkin'."

Butler reset his hat, drawing the brim low over his eyes. "I didn't give you permission to speak, Sam."

Sam's mouth drew into a thin line. "Why yo' a-pickin' on me, Marse Butler?"

"'Cause you're a lazy nigger who ain't doin' his share of the work. An' until you do, you won't be gettin' no more passes to visit Cragfont." He didn't want Mandy to have a chance to talk to Sam. Not tonight.

Sam's hands tightened on the hoe handle. "I done weeded fo'teen acres dis week, Marse Butler."

Cotton edged his horse closer to the overseer.

"Mr. Butler," he whispered, "Sam worked hard this week. You know it, I know it, an' so does ever' slave on this plantation. If you don't allow him to visit his woman, ever'body is goin' to be pissed off."

"You tryin' to tell me my job?"

"Naw, Mr. Butler, I ain't. I'm just pointin' out that what you're worryin' about preventin' might be a better move than if you don't let Sam go to Cragfont. Hell, ain't no slave goin' to give you a good day's work lessen he's got somethin' to work toward."

"Mind your own business, boy. I run this plantation the way I see fit. Now get out of the way. I ain't finished tellin' Sam he ain't gettin' no pass tonight."

Cotton looked across the field in the direction of the slave cabins. He longed to tell Mr. Summers about what was taking place, but he just couldn't bring himself to inform on the overseer.

Sighing in disgust, he turned his horse in the opposite direction and galloped toward the river. He needed some fresh air.

Candlelight flickered off Pauline's sweat-stained face as Chatty gently drew the girl's legs up against her swollen abdomen.

"Now yo' jist strain hard, Pauline, an' keep on a-strainin'," instructed the old midwife, "an' dat baby'll jist pop right out'n dare."

Pauline's lips flattened into a grimace as she emitted a long, high-pitched scream. Then turning her glistening face to Mrs. Summers, she said, "I's sorry fo' hollerin', Missy. I's tryin' real hard not to."

Mrs. Summers patted Pauline's raised knee. "You're doin' fine, Pauline. Just do ever'thing Chatty tells you. An' don't worry 'bout hollerin'. You holler all you want to."

The girl nodded, her face drawing into a contortion of pain.

Mrs. Summers drew Chatty aside. "How is she?"

"Dat girl gwine to die, Missus Summers," the old midwife whispered, her eyes angry and frightened. "Dat oberseer be to blame. He be a sucker. I done hear't 'bout him. Yas, ma'am. He be a sucker, an' he done kilt po' Pauline."

"Hush up that Africa talk, Chatty," Mrs. Summers said. "The baby's too big to come, an' you well know it."

Chatty's eyes drew to mere slits. "If'n Pauline hab da strength, Missus Summers, she could spit dat baby out'n dare, but she be sucked . . . I done tolt yo' so."

Mr. Summers and Clayton, standing outside the closed door, heard old Chatty's words plainly. Mr. Summers turned and stared at the sunset. Then, doffing his hat and running his fingers through his hair, he said to Clayton, "Some of these old Africans have the silly notion that if a grown man sucks a wench's tits, he draws the strength right out of her body through her nipples." He smiled sheepishly. "If that was true, half the women in the world would be dead by now."

"How weak is Pauline?" Clayton asked, blushing.

"She's goin' to die."

"Isn't there anything we can do, Mr. Summers? Maybe get Dr. Mentlo?"

The old man shook his head. "Mentlo is a fine physician, but he won't treat slaves. If he did, he'd be busy mornin' 'til night. Anyway, Chatty's pret' near as good a doctor as Mentlo . . . better sometimes, 'cause she don't mind callin' upon that voodoo nonsense that the darkies put so much stock in. I think she terrifies 'em into gettin' well." He shook his head again. "Voodoo won't work this time."

Clayton realized that the note of sadness in Mr. Summers' voice was not that of a man losing a valuable piece of property, as he had earlier believed, but that of a man who felt genuine sorrow for a young woman who was dying in childbirth. He was surprised at the difference that the realization made in his estimation of Mr. Summers.

They buried Pauline on a hill that overlooked Bledsoe's Creek. Only Mr. Summers, Clayton, Cotton, and the grave-diggers were present. Butler had refused to allow the other slaves to attend, using the excuse that it would upset their daily routine, and Mrs. Summers had come down with a severe case of the summer ague, presumably because of the stifling heat she had suffered while in the slave cabin attending Pauline.

The grave-diggers lowered the blanket-wrapped body into the pit. Then they dusted it with lime and quickly shoveled the soil back into the hole.

In a few years, thought Clayton, taking in the wild beauty of the hillside, nature will reclaim this plot. There will be no gravestone. No one will ever know that the remains of a woman and a half-born child lie here. Sighing, he thought that perhaps that was as it should be. Pauline owned nothing in life, so why should she own anything in death? "It's just not right," he said aloud.

"What ain't right?" Cotton asked. He was using his bare toes to dribble dirt into the grave.

"At the least, someone should read over her."

"No white man's goin' to read over no slave, Clayton," Mr. Summers said. "But if it really bothers you, why don't you get busy and start teachin' the Summerset blacks their ABC's? Then they could read over their own."

"Now wait a minute," Clayton said. "I'm not the one who's abusing the blacks . . ."

"Hell, Clay," Cotton said, "you get all pissed 'cause they're mistreated, but it appears to me that a fella who has the know-how to make their lives better and don't do it is mistreatin' 'em a damn sight more than us who don't know no different."

Clayton stared hard at Cotton, then frowned. "Cotton, sometimes you amaze me."

Cotton grinned from ear to ear.

The two boys walked to Cotton's horse. Clayton gave Cotton a foot up and then handed him the reins. "Are you going back to the fields?"

"Yeah. Ol' Butler hates my guts, an' I want to get back over there just to aggravate 'im."

Swinging his mount around so that it was between Clayton and the small group of people at the grave, Cotton leaned from the saddle and said in a voice too low to be overheard, "Butler's trompin' on eggs right now, what with Pauline a-dyin' and Chatty over here at Summerset talkin' to the field hands an' all."

"It's not Butler's fault that Pauline died," Clayton said. "Why is he worried about Chatty conversing with the Summerset slaves?"

"Well," Cotton said, scratching his chin where a fine blond fuzz was fighting its way to the surface in a manly attempt to become a beard, "I ain't one for carryin' tales, but when we went to Cragfont to fetch ol' Chatty, Butler stirred up a passel of shit . . ."

"What are you talking about, Cotton?"

Cotton glanced beyond Clayton to see Mr. Summers and the diggers fast approaching. Touching the horse with his heel, he broke the animal into a fast trot. "I'll tell you later," he called over his shoulder.

"Slow that horse down to a walk," Mr. Summers yelled to Cotton's retreating back. "It's too hot to be runnin' a horse on a day like this."

The old man and Clayton climbed onto the wagon seat and waited while the diggers threw their picks and shovels into the back and then parked themselves comfortably on the open tailgate.

Clucking the animals into motion, Mr. Summers said, "I sure do hate to lose a fine wench like Pauline. She was a good, even-tempered girl, and smart as a whip. I was lookin' forward to seein' what you could teach her."

Clayton remained quiet. Mr. Summers said nothing more.

As the wagon creaked and rattled across the fields, both men drew into themselves. The old man wondered about the future of his slaves; the young man wondered if planters such as Mr. Summers even had a future.

CHAPTER 7

The wagon had just topped a rise when Mr. Summers
kicked forward the brake and snatched the mules to a halt,
nearly throwing Clayton from his seat.

Jumping to his feet, the old man peered angrily at a dust
cloud racing toward them across the plowed field where
slaves were working. "I told that boy it was too hot to be
a-ridin' that horse like a wild Indian. He'll wind it for
certain!"

"Something's wrong, Mr. Summers," Clayton said, making a visor of his palm while watching Cotton whip the
horse into an even faster pace, its hooves kicking up clouds
that swirled and eddied like miniature dust devils.

When Cotton skidded his lathered mount to a halt
alongside the wagon, the horse's head dropped between its
knees and its sides heaved like a great bellows.

"Dern it, Cotton!" Mr. Summers shouted. "You done
winded—"

Cotton flung his bridle reins to Clayton and leaped from
the saddle into the wagon bed. "Ol' Sam's gone an' laid
Butler's head wide open. Better build a fire in them mules'
ass an' get over there quick as you can, Mr. Summers, 'cause

Butler is bleedin' like a stuck hog."

Kicking off the brake, Mr. Summers lashed the startled mules into a dead run. The winded horse nearly jerked Clayton out of the wagon before it, too, broke into a lumbering cantor. "Is Butler dead?" Mr. Summers shouted above the rumbling of the wagon.

"Not yet," Cotton returned, "but he's layin' in the broilin' sun, which ain't helpin' none. I put some of the women to fannin' the blowflies away, 'cause he's bleedin' purty bad. Hell, Mr. Summers, I don't rightly know if he'll live or not."

"What about Sam? Did he run?"

"Naw. I talked him out of it."

Cotton's certainty, coupled with the tension the news brought, was almost too much for the old man. "Sam's been a troublemaker ever since I've owned him," he exploded. "He's a fine worker, but he purely hates white authority. Now just what in hell's name makes you so cocksure that you kept him from runnin'?"

Cotton grinned. "I told you, Mr. Summers, I can handle slaves an' mules. I just talked to Sam slow an' easy an' explained that if he run, the law would catch him an' the high sheriff would break his feet off like they did Mr. Jameson's houseboy, an' then they'd hang him by his ears 'til all his blood run out the end of his legs. I told him that if he stayed put, you'd see to it that nothin' like that happened to 'im . . . so he just plopped hisself down 'tween the tobacco rows an' said he'd wait for you. I also sent Rufus to Gallatin for the sheriff."

Mr. Summers shook his head. "Sounds like you did real good, son. But don't get your feelin's hurt if Sam's gone when we get there."

"He won't be."

When the wagon rumbled to a halt, Clayton breathed a sigh of relief; Sam was walking to meet the wagon. Butler lay where he had fallen, and several slave women were using their bodies to screen the unconscious man from the sun. Others kneeling beside him were fanning away the flies. Still others were milling about aimlessly, their eyes large with fear, their nervous chatter a steady drone.

Mr. Summers climbed down from the wagon and instructed the diggers to lift Butler into the wagon. "You get in there too, Sam," he ordered, taking the man by the arm and leading him to the tailgate.

Clayton jumped to the ground and tied Cotton's horse to the coupling pole, then resumed his seat. Sam crawled in beside Butler and squatted against the sideboards. "What's goin' to happen to me, Massa?"

"I don't know," the old man admitted. "I suppose it depends on whether Butler dies."

"He done messed wif my wife, Massa. He been foolin' wif my daughter too—but she unmarried and right lusty—but I ain't wantin' him t' be messin' wif my wife, an' a-knockin' her up an' her a-dyin' like po' Pauline done."

Mr. Summers didn't answer. Sam's voice raised in anger: "Massa, you knows me and Sylla jump de broom. You knows we don't fool around none after we's married." Mr. Summers shot the man a look of genuine pity. "Massa," continued Sam, "my marriage to Sylla, an' hers to me, is all I rightfully own in dis world . . . an' now Butler, he done took even dat away."

Mr. Summers climbed onto the wagon seat and picked up the reins. Looking down at Cotton, standing beside the wagon, he said, "Keep these people busy. I don't want 'em dwellin' on what's happened here today. You understand?"

Cotton nodded. "They'll be too damn wore out to even remember what their names is, Mr. Summers."

The old man slapped the reins against the mules' hindquarters. "Git up!" The team broke into a tired walk.

Cotton picked up Butler's wide-brimmed panama hat and fingered the slash made by Sam's hoe. Grinning, he plopped it on his head then slanted it arrogantly over one eye. That the hat was too large bothered him not at all. Striding to Butler's horse, he swung into the saddle and seated himself as straight as a ramrod. Surveying his domain, he took a deep breath of prideful accomplishment. Then it vanished. He had not intended for Sam to kill Butler—if indeed Sam had. Cotton had only hoped that when he told the big man what had happened at Cragfont, the slave would raise such a howl that Butler would be dismissed.

Cotton shrugged. Either way, he had done what he set out to do: He had gotten rid of Butler.

"All right!" he cried, riding among the milling Negroes.

"Ever'body back to work. They's a lot o' rows needs hoein'."

Mr. Summers, Dr. Mentlo, and Clayton were waiting in the Summerset yard when the sheriff arrived. Stepping down from his horse, the lawman handed the reins to Rufus, who had ridden double with him from Gallatin.

"Rufus tells me Sam killed Butler with a grubbing hoe," the sheriff said, shaking hands with Mr. Summers.

"Butler's not going to die. Mentlo had to do some right smart sewin' on his scalp, an' he'll be laid up for a week or so, but he'll live. Soon as he's able to travel, I'm goin' to discharge him."

The sheriff took a plug of tobacco from his shirt pocket and cut off a large chew. "What is it you want me to do here, Jonathan?"

Clayton detested the decision Mr. Summers made, but he could understand it; Sam's belligerent attitude was as much an open wound in the life of Summerset as was the terrible slash the slave had left in Butler's scalp. "I reckon you'd better take Sam to Gallatin and hold him 'til I can find a buyer," Mr. Summers said. "My darkies are rightly upset by this mornin's doin's. The quicker I get Sam away from here, the quicker things'll settle down."

The sheriff nodded, then spat a stream of amber into the dust at his feet. "Where you got Sam locked up?"

"In the corncrib. An', Sheriff," Mr. Summers added as the lawman started toward the barn lot, "you might carry Sam over to Cragfont . . . to say good-bye to his wife."

When the sheriff was out of earshot, Mr. Summers turned to Clayton. "If you'd accompany him, I'd be obliged. I'd like you to carry a note to Mrs. Winchester, apologizin' for Butler's . . . indiscretion. She might want to send an answer."

Despite his dismay over Sam's plight, Clayton was elated. Perhaps he would see Lettie again.

The sun was twelve-o'clock high when Clayton and the sheriff, with Sam in tow behind, rode up to the Cragfont gate. A score of slaves had already gathered. Their frightened eyes darted from Sam, whose wrists were secured in heavy iron manacles, to the sheriff, who sat slouched in the saddle, holding a coil of rope whose other end was tied loosely around Sam's neck.

Mrs. Winchester, regal in manner and bearing, arrived at the gate with her grandchildren and house servants.

"We've already heard about the trouble at Summerset, Sheriff," she said. "Sylla's waitin' for you at her cabin."

The sheriff nodded. "Thank you, ma'am." Then, tipping his hat to her, "With your permission, we'll mosey on over there."

Clayton frowned. How had the news of Sam's attack on Butler reached Cragfont so quickly? Especially since Chatty had returned to Cragfont early in the morning, before the burial.

Mrs. Winchester said, "Fanny, show the sheriff to Sylla's cabin. The rest of you go on about your chores."

Clayton dismounted and handed his bridle reins to the gate-watcher. "Mrs. Winchester?" She turned. "Mr. Summers sends his apologies, ma'am."

The old woman accepted the paper he offered her and hastily read it.

"Things of this nature happen occasionally, Mr. Harris," she said, refolding the note. "Thank the good Lord they are few an' far between." Then, linking her arm through his, she guided him toward the main house. "I've lived among slaves all my life, young man, and nine times out of ten when a slave rebels, it's because a white person is guilty of breaking the rules."

"Breaking the rules? I'm afraid I don't understand, Mrs. Winchester."

"Plantations are cities unto themselves, Mr. Harris. We have a community here at Cragfont made up of persons, places, an' things . . . much as one would find in any large town. We have carpenters, blacksmiths, cobblers, laborers, cooks, nannies, housekeepers . . . I could go on an' on. And like any city, we have our own social structure, which in many ways parallels the better features of the old feudal system in Europe that worked so well for centuries.

"The owners and their children are the lords an' masters; they set down the laws that govern the domain. The overseer enforces those laws. Then there are the house servants, who are the slave elite." She laughed and squeezed Clayton's arm. "You have never witnessed class distinction until you have seen it practiced by blacks upon blacks. They are far more arrogant and obsessive where power is concerned than the whites ever thought about being."

Clayton let that remark go in one ear and out the other. Mrs. Winchester continued: "Next in line are the tradespeople: the carpenters, blacksmiths, seamstresses, cooks, and so forth. And last there are the field hands, who are equivalent to the poor white trash of the white society. Yes, Mr. Harris, a plantation—in fact, sir, the entire South—is just one big community . . . one big plantation, if you will . . . And the people, including the whites, are governed by rules an' regulations—unspoken laws that ensure domestic tranquility. One of those laws plainly states that there are to be absolutely no . . . shall we say, intimate overtures, made toward a married slave woman. Butler knew that slaves practice their nuptial vows with serious religious feelings, yet he broke the rule. As far as I'm concerned, Mr. Harris, he got exactly what was comin' to him. The sad part is, we owners can't allow our slaves to enforce the very laws that we insist they live by."

After seeing Mrs. Winchester safely inside the house, Clayton hurried to Sylla's cabin.

There in the yard, silence hung in the air like a heavy weight as Sylla tied Sam's extra clothes into a tight bundle, which with shaking hands, she presented to her husband.

Not a word passed between them, but tears suddenly filled Sylla's eyes as the sheriff led Sam back to the horses.

The moment the sheriff was out of sight, Mandy, Delphy, Chatty, and several of the other slaves crowded around Sylla. "What dey gwine to do wid Sam?" cried Delphy. "Will yo' ever see him again? What fo' did he try to kill dat oberseer wid a hoe? He knowed better'n dat."

Old Chatty, her head in her hands, sank to her knees and moaned aloud. "Now I knows why I drempt 'bout muddy water las' night. Lawd, yes, it mean trouble a-comin' in de mornin'! I knowed it! Yes, Lawd, I allus knowed dat Sam wuz a mean nigger. I knowed he'd come to no good." The other slaves groaned and wrung their hands.

Mandy glared at her mother. "I hope dey hang de bastid, him a-hittin' my man wid a hoe. I hope dey hang 'im."

Then, startling the group even more, she spat in Sylla's face and darted around the cabin to disappear into the orchard behind the slave quarters.

"Sylla," whispered Susie, her large eyes glistening with tears not yet fallen, "why did Mandy say such a terrible thing 'bout her own papa?"

Shaking her head, Sylla did not respond but walked into the cabin; she had not uttered a sound during the entire episode.

Susie flung her arms around Clayton's waist.

"I'll never own any slaves," she sobbed. "It's just not right, breakin' up families like this. Sylla is a good and sweet woman. An' even if Sam is a mean nigger like Chatty says, it's still not right."

"Hush, Susie," Lettie said sharply. "Sam tried to murder a white man. If he had been owned by anyone except Uncle Jonathan Summers, Sam would have been hanged." Turning to Fanny, Lettie reprimanded the girl harshly for having allowed Susie to witness the event, and Clayton could not help but wonder at the ease with which Lettie shifted the burden of responsibility to the slave.

Fanny's eyes flashed with anger, but then the spark was gone, veiled by her long lashes. "Yes'm," she murmured, taking Susie's hand. "I's sorry, Miss Lettie. But wif the high sheriff a-bringin' Sam here an' all . . . I jist wasn't thinkin', ma'am." Fanny smiled timidly at Clayton; then, with Susie in tow, she walked toward the big house.

"Come, Clayton," commanded Lettie. "The pond is absolutely gorgeous at this time of day."

Not waiting for a response, she slipped her arm through his and raising her long skirts with her free hand, led him toward the formal gardens and a small lake bordering their north side.

When Fanny reached the house, she turned and watched the couple stroll toward the garden. Then, pushing Susie before her, she undulated her hips as she followed the child into the house, for she was determined to learn to imitate Lettie Winchester's sensual stride.

Clayton and Lettie wandered leisurely down the brick walkway, stopping often to breathe deeply of the aroma of the flowers. It was the virgin's bower around the gazebo whose perfume was the best. Lettie referred to the small, airy structure as "the Tunnel of Fragrance." Clayton thought the description appropriate and said so.

Hand in hand, they strolled to the lake, where Lettie sank gracefully into the soft grass beneath a huge weeping willow tree, her broad, pale-pink skirts billowing out around her so that Clayton was forced to sit several feet away, beyond arm's reach. He wondered if she had planned it that way.

Lettie's conversation dwelled mostly on New York and her schooling there. But each time she raised her lovely eyes to Clayton, or readjusted her full-figure body, his pulse raced to such a fever that it made little difference to him what she talked about, or even if she spoke at all.

Finally he interrupted her chatter and asked the question that had been foremost in his mind since their first meeting: "Are you really engaged, Miss Lettie?"

Lettie pursed her pouty lips and leaned toward him. "Well, I do declare, Mr. Harris. I am here with you this very minute . . . isn't that answer enough?"

Clayton smiled. "That isn't any answer at all, Miss Lettie."

Irritation flicked across Lettie's face. Then, looking beyond Clayton, her eyes grew wide; the Widow Winchester, leading Susie by the hand, was walking toward them. Quickly Lettie snapped back into her prim posture.

"I just had to get out of that stiflin' house," the old lady said as she approached.

"No you didn't, Grandma," Susie piped. "You saw Lettie an' Clayton from the balcony an' said it wasn't proper for a young woman to be alone . . ."

The old lady gave Susie a look that caused the girl to catch her breath and close her mouth in a tight little line.

Clayton jumped to his feet. "I apologize, Mrs. Winchester. I am well aware that I have flouted etiquette, and you are quite correct to—"

"Don't get carried away, young man. One might think your intentions were other than honorable. You know the old saying: 'He who protests too much . . .'" Laughing lightly, she seated herself in the spot Clayton had just vacated.

"Grandmother!" Lettie's face was a deep crimson. "You

are deliberately embarrassing me in the presence of a guest."

The old woman smiled at her. "Perhaps it would be best if you took Susie and returned to the house, Lettie. I wish to speak with Mr. Harris alone."

Clayton shifted uncomfortably. He did not know whether to be insulted or amused.

"Oh, my goodness!" Lettie exclaimed irritably. Jumping to her feet, she caught Susie's hand and walked quickly toward the house.

Clayton gazed at his riding boots, and a drawn-out silence ensued, punctuated by the slamming of the door as Lettie entered the house.

"Mr. Harris," Mrs. Winchester said, "times have changed since I was Lettie's age. Back then we were fighting Indians, the British, nature, and each other. A person lived life one day at a time. Social niceties meant little on the frontier, and certain . . . situations were not frowned upon. Civilization in the backwoods, sir, was measured in two ways: by how quickly a man could reload his rifle, and by how quickly he could get his woman in the family way." The old woman's penetrating blue eyes gazed steadily at Clayton. "Those days are gone, Mr. Harris. Do I make myself plain?"

"I assure you, ma'am—"

"Do we understand each other, sir?"

Clayton bowed to the old lady. "You leave very little room for a misunderstanding, Mrs. Winchester."

The mid-July sun was a fireball that turned the one-room log cabin into a sweltering furnace. With sweat plastering his shirt to his body like a second skin, Clayton, along with Rufus and a score of young slaves, worked feverishly to clear the room of twenty years' accumulation ranging from broken furniture to worn-out horse collars.

Clayton held up a double-handled crock that had both handles missing. "Don't Southerners ever throw away anything?"

Rufus shrugged. "It'll still hold water, Massa."

By the end of the week they had cleared the cabin, whitewashed the walls, and smoothed the dirt floor. Then they placed rough-hewn benches—hurriedly constructed by Otis, Mr. Summers' carpenter— in rows that gave the room the appearance of a church house.

Clayton fashioned a two-foot-square chalkboard from a slab of slate pried from a dry creek bed and hung it on the wall behind the table that served as his desk.

He was looking at the schoolhouse interior with pride when Mr. Summers stepped inside.

"Comin' long real nice, son, real nice indeed," the old man said. He propped a booted foot on the nearest bench. "I need a favor, Clayton. Butler's fired. He left this mornin'. An' Cotton's got his hands full in the fields. What I need is somebody to go with Rufus into Cairo and pick up my mowin' machine at the wharf. The steamboat just docked and they sent word that it's there."

Clayton said he would be glad to go to Cairo and that he needed to pick up some chalk and pencils and paper anyway.

Mr. Summers shook his head. "If you go into town an' start buyin' school supplies, we're goin' to be up to our necks in a hog trough, son. I been plannin' this school for a long time, an' ever' trip I made East, I bought such things as I thought a schoolmaster might need. I'll have 'em brought out here for you when you get back from Cairo."

"Sho' is a purty thing." Rufus walked around the haymower, smiling proudly.

"And heavy," Clayton said. How were the two of them to get the cumbersome piece of machinery onto the wagon?

The dock clerk snapped his ledger shut and slipped his pencil behind his ear. "I'll have a couple of roustabouts give you a hand loading it."

"Much obliged," Clayton said. Then he grinned at himself. He had been in the South less than a month, yet he was already beginning to speak like a Southerner.

Rufus removed the wagon's tailgate and he and Clayton raised the ends of two heavy planks onto the opening, creating a loading ramp.

They had just finished setting the ramp in place when two boatmen and the clerk arrived. "Damnedest thing I ever saw," one boatman was saying to the clerk. "People were everywhere—on the boat, in the river, clingin' to flotsam. It was a sight. Hell, it didn't take ten minutes for the *Princess* to sink."

"What's that?" Clayton rounded the end of the wagon in long strides. "You said something about the *Princess* sinking?"

"Yeah," the man said. "Boilers blew sky-high down near Baton Rouge. Lotta folks were killed outright. Others drowned tryin' to swim ashore. Hell, I was thrown forty feet into the river myself. Only reason I wasn't killed was that I was standin' on the texas deck when it blew. The folks that didn't drown was so badly scalded that the people on shore dumped barrels of flour on the ground an' rolled 'em in it. Didn't help much, tho'."

Clayton's insides twisted into a tight knot. "There was a lady on board the *Princess*. Her name is Claudette LaBranche . . ."

The man guffawed. "Lady, you say? Hell, you're talkin' about the highest-paid whore on the Mississippi."

"Do you know what happened to her?"

The roustabout nodded. "She was in a cabin over the boilers with some bigwig from St. Louis, plying her trade, when the boilers blew. She took the full blast. Her body was damned near unrecognizable, she was burned so bad."

Clayton turned his head and fought down a wave of nausea. "Were you a friend of hers?" the clerk asked.

Clayton didn't answer. He was remembering something Claudette LaBranche had said to him: "I dream about being burned to death in a boiler explosion."

Was her dream a prophecy? He recalled her parting words to him: "Allow no woman, and especially not the gorgeous seductress, the South, to change who you are and what you believe in. For beneath the beautiful and elegant ball gown that the South wears, you will find nothing but a tattered chemise." Was that a prophecy also?

"Was she a friend of yours, mister?" the clerk asked again. Clayton shook his head. "I only met her once or twice."

The second boatman stalked up to the wagon. "If you want this goddamned machine loaded, then you an' your nigger get over here an' lend a hand."

It was a dangerous, cumbersome job to maneuver the iron-wheeled haymower up the makeshift ramp. Even the clerk was obliged to lay his ledger aside and put his shoulder to the task.

As the machine rolled heavily onto the wagon bed, Rufus' sweaty hands slipped on the cleated wheel, allowing the mower to slam against the sideboards. "You damned, lazy nigger, you nearly pinned my hand!" the second boatman shouted at Rufus.

"I's sorry, Massa," the boy stammered. "My hands done got slick . . ."

The boatman backhanded Rufus across the mouth, knocking him out of the wagon. The boy hit the ground hard and for a minute lay there, not moving. Then, pushing himself painfully to a sitting position, he burst out crying.

Clayton vaulted over the side and knelt by him. "Are you all right, Rufus?"

The boy wiped his eyes. "My hand slipped, Massa Clayton. I never meant to turn loose o' dat wheel. It was a accident."

The burly boatman climbed down over the wheel and towered over Clayton and Rufus. "Accident, hell. You're just a triflin' nigger who wanted us white men to do all the work. I got a good mind to take a snake to you."

The man unbuckled his wide leather belt and jerked Rufus to his feet.

"Thanks for the help with the mower, mister," Clayton said quickly. "Come on, Rufus. Let's get back to Summerset."

Ignoring Clayton, the boatman drew back the belt. "I ain't through with this nigger."

"Yes you are." Clayton stepped in front of Rufus.

The boatman's eyes narrowed. "I remember you. I couldn't place you at first, but you're the bastard who helped that stowaway come over the rail on the *Princess.*"

Clayton grinned at the man. "You're that bull, and you haven't changed. You still pick on defenseless children."

Before the boatman could blink, Clayton's fist caught him hard in his mouth. It was a short punch straight from the shoulder, but it snapped the bull's head back as though he had been hit between the eyes with a hammer, leaving his chin exposed to Clayton's other fist, which exploded there, dropping the man flat on his back in the sun-scorched dust of the loading area.

The bull drew himself to a sitting position, his head hanging between his knees. Blood dripped from his nose and mouth, creating small geysers in the powdery dust.

Rufus had ducked under the wagon and was peering out between the wheel spokes.

The other boatman leaned casually against the same wagon wheel; he liked a good fight, and in truth, he was impressed with Clayton's expert fisticuffs. "Well, Ben," he said, grinning at the bull, "are you jist gonna sit there all day?"

"Shut up." Ben shook his head, scattering thick droplets of blood in all directions. With measured slowness, he climbed unsteadily to his feet and turned his back to Clayton.

Clayton dropped his guard and looked toward the wagon. "Come out from under there, Rufus. Let's get started toward home."

The bull erupted into action. Spinning toward Clayton, he caught the youth with a roundhouse blow that opened his cheek to the bone. Before Clayton could react, Ben hit him just above the heart with such force that he was plummeted backward over a stack of empty wooden crates and onto the dusty ground beyond.

Store owners and patrons, having heard the commotion, stepped into the street, and passengers on board the docked paddle-wheeler gathered at the rail, all of them hoping to witness a real knock-down-drag-out fight.

Clayton lay there, stunned, and indeed thinking that every bone in his body had been shattered. Above the roar in his ears he could hear Rufus crying for him to get up, and the boy's voice spurred him to move.

Using a crate for leverage, he pulled himself to his feet and shook his head to clear the cobwebs.

Ben had skirted the pile of boxes and was advancing with the confidence of a man certain of conquest.

When he made his lunge, intending to pound his opponent into the dirt, Clayton ducked inside the punch and slammed his rock-hard knuckles into the man's temple, splitting the delicate skin at the corner of his eye and raising a welt that instantly reduced Ben's vision to a mere slit.

Taking his advantage, Clayton followed with a hard left to

the man's midsection that burst the breath from Ben's lungs, then with a quick right to the chin that dropped him in the same dust in which Clayton had just groveled.

Breathing hard, Clayton leaned weakly against a crate and wiped his hand across his lacerated cheek, smearing the blood into a grotesque pattern that caused the wound to appear worse than it was.

Rufus thrust his head between two of the wagon spokes. "Massa Clayton, you is hurt bad. You is a-bleedin' all over yo'self, you is."

Ben rolled onto his back and gulped in great breaths of air. His face was plastered with blood and sweat-saturated dust. Slowly, as though each movement were a painful chore, he climbed unsteadily to his feet. In his hand was a dirk, its eight-inch blade flashing in the sunlight. He wobbled toward Clayton, the knife weaving dangerously from side to side. Clayton inched backward toward the wagon. The mules, already spooked by the uproar, pranced in their traces and gnawed at their bits.

"He got a knife, Massa Clayton!" cried Rufus. "Run, suh, run fast as yo' can!"

Rufus' shrill shout was more than the skittish animals could endure. The left mule reared and fell backward over the wagon tongue, tangling itself and the off mule in a melee of horse collars, harness, trace chains, and singletrees. The wagon lurched backward. And as the massive wheels turned, Rufus' head slipped into the vee of the wooden-spoked hub; his neck was pinned as surely as if it had been secured in a vise.

The big wheel continued to turn, and the boy was flipped into the air with such force that the slapping of his backside against the undercarriage sounded as loud to Clayton as a shotgun blast—which was, in fact, exactly what he had heard. Mr. Higher, the shopkeeper, having observed the fracas from the beginning, had raced into his store and emerged with a sawed-off, double-barreled fowling piece. He had just unloaded one barrel into the air. And if Rufus' head had not been jarred from between the wagon spokes when his buttocks smashed against the undercarriage, he would have, without a doubt, been beheaded by the churning of the wheel as the terrified mules went berserk.

Mr. Higher marched over to Ben and Clayton, neither of whom had taken his eyes from the other for the briefest instant.

"There ain't goin' to be no cuttin' in this town, boat-man," Mr. Higher said. "So you put that knife away an' go on about your business. An' you, Harris. Get them mules settled down."

"I'm not through with this bull," Clayton said. "He owes Rufus an apology."

"Go straight to hell," Ben said, slipping his knife into a sheath in his boot.

Mr. Higher cocked the hammer of the second barrel. "No white man's goin' to apologize to a slave, Harris. Not while I hold this gun, he's not."

Ben grinned. Straight-arming Clayton aside, he stomped off toward the boat.

"Harris"—Mr. Higher eased the hammer down on his shotgun—"don't never butt in when a white man is correctin' a black . . . no matter whether you think he's right or wrong, or whose slave it is. All that does is confuse the niggers into thinkin' that white folks might not be supreme an' justified in everything we do."

He draped his arm across Clayton's shoulder. "C'mon inside the store an' let me clean up that face of your'n. Your head looks like that boat feller shoved it through a sausage grinder. 'Course, I'd not be fair if I didn't add that he looked a whale of a sight worse."

The first half of the drive back to Summerset found Rufus complaining that his neck was broken or, at the very least, stretched several inches longer than normal.

The last half of the trip was filled with questions: Wasn't Clayton afraid of the boatman? Would the man really have stabbed him? What would Clayton have done if he had? And finally, where did Clayton learn to fistfight so well?

"They call it boxing, Rufus," Clayton said through the dull throbbing in his head. "I was taught boxing and fencing at Ohio University." He grinned painfully at Rufus. "Obviously I wasn't taught brawling, or I would never have let that man get up; I'd have kicked his teeth in. Next time I'll know better."

* * *

Clayton stood behind his desk and counted the silent group of Negroes who sat on the benches, stood in the aisles, and lounged against the walls of the schoolroom. Thirty-seven of them, not counting babies. Some faces showed interest, others wonder, and a few open boredom. But all eyes were upon him, waiting.

Self-consciously he pushed a lock of unruly hair off his forehead. A moment later it was back, accenting the partially knit, half-moon gash on his cheek and lending him a rakish look that barely missed being sinister.

"I called you here tonight to explain about the school—your school—that Mr. Summers is opening, with me as your teacher." A baby began to wail. Its mother unbuttoned her blouse and fed her nipple into the infant's mouth. Clayton continued: "I intend to teach you to read and write, and to understand simple mathematics."

A murmur rippled across the room.

Clayton leaned on his desk and watched them closely. "The first step toward true freedom is an education." He hesitated. The expected applause did not come. Instead, he saw fear, disbelief, and very real hostility on their faces.

Clayton swung his gaze to Mr. Summers, who was sitting in a cane-bottomed chair in a front corner. The old man stood, and the room became quiet.

"That's enough for tonight. You folks go on back to your cabins."

When the room emptied, Mr. Summers walked across to Clayton's desk and seated himself on the edge. "That was a mistake, Clayton, talkin' about freedom. You scared those folks. They thought you was advocatin' insurrection."

"All I was talking about was freeing their minds, Mr. Summers."

"I know that. But be a bit more careful in the future; slaves don't trust many white people, especially not a stranger who might get them killed. You're goin' to have to win their confidence, Clayton, or you ain't goin' to be able to teach 'em nothin'. An' gettin' their confidence may be a real trick . . . now."

Clayton was careful not to mention freedom again during class. In fact, he spent the remainder of the school week reading stories, asking questions, and generally making himself known to the slaves. During the morning hours, he held class for the very young, ages four through six. The older children and adults came in the evening after the day's work in the fields was completed.

Many of the younger slaves displayed an eagerness for knowledge, and Rufus would have been a delight to any educator. The boy's mind was quick and agile, and his ability to grasp and retain information was remarkable. But the adults, after the novelty had worn thin, quickly lost interest. And the truth was, Clayton didn't blame them; after a back-breaking day in the sun, sitting in a hot, stuffy classroom was more an aggravation than an opportunity.

Clayton explained his dilemma to Mr. Summers. "I know they're intelligent, sir. Rufus is extraordinarily bright, and some of the smaller children show a lot of promise. But for some reason, I'm not getting through to the older people. It's the first of August and we've been studying for nearly a month now, but not over four or five can count to twenty, and fewer than that can recite half of their ABC's."

The old man took a thoughtful stroll around the empty classroom. "In eighteen twenty-six," he said, "the Presbyterians in Cairo opened a school to teach Negroes to read an' write. It didn't last no time a'tall. The schoolmaster said that darkies haven't got the mental capacity to learn nothin'." He placed his foot on a bench and leaned on his knee. "The man didn't know what he was talkin' about, Clayton. Niggers are smart. In fact, they're a derned sight more intelligent than they want us white folk to believe. I've seen 'em conjure up more ingenious ways to git out of doin' a day's work than you could ever imagine. An' they ain't lazy. They'll work their fingers to the bone if it's somethin' they want to do."

"That's exactly the point I've been trying to make, sir. They have to want to learn."

"Well, if four or five have come along as good as you say they have, you're doin' fine. Heck, son, that's one-tenth of my darkies, an' that's not a bad average."

The old man started toward the door, but Clayton stopped him. "It's not good enough, Mr. Summers! You hired me to teach these people to read and write . . . and I'm not doing it."

"You'll do it. Just don't be in such a hurry."

Clayton grimaced. "I guess I do have a rather high opinion of my ability, haven't I?"

Mr. Summers smiled; Clayton was learning. He walked to the door, then hesitated. "There's nuthin' wrong with self-confidence, Clayton, as long as it's moderated with a pinch of common sense and a cupful of humility." He stepped outside and walked toward the house.

Clayton lay awake that night considering how to awaken the minds of human beings who had never been required, or indeed allowed, to think for themselves.

He fell back on a basic truth: Man must have a personal and/or a selfish reason to justify any kind of exertion, mental or physical. He drifted off to sleep with that thought in mind.

It was with renewed vigor that he approached Mr. Summers the next morning and presented a new and, to him, exciting strategy: Allow the field hands who were his students to cease work two hours before sundown on weekdays, and at twelve-o'clock noon on Saturdays.

"Well, I don't know about that," the old man said, scratching his chin. "We've got a world of work to do on that tobacco crop. Still, I know what you're drivin' at. You want to give 'em a reason to go to class."

"Yes, sir. If they have a tangible incentive, they might be more inclined to study. And the ones who don't put forth a certain effort will be sent back to the fields."

The old man nodded. "Tell Cotton I approve of your plan."

Cotton was irate. "Yore askin' for trouble, a-pamperin' them slaves, Clay. You give 'em a inch and they'll take a mile."

"Maybe so," Clayton said. "But a mile is a short distance when you consider that a man's mind can span continents."

"Damn it, Clay! Don't throw that school-learned shit at me. You know I don't understan' a word you say sometimes."

Clayton grinned at his friend. "Perhaps you should come to class too."

"I ain't a-goin' to school with no bunch of ignorant slaves, Clayton."

Seeing the anger that flushed Clayton's cheeks, Cotton said, "I'll have the slaves at the schoolhouse two hours a'fore sundown, all a-shinin' an' sassy. But I still think yore pissin' into the wind, Clay. I jist want you to know that."

Clayton nodded.

"One more thing, Clay," Cotton said, frowning, a phenomenon that sobered Clayton instantly. "Butler was here this mornin', an' he tried to get mean with Mr. Summers. He's blamin' the old man 'cause they ain't a plantation owner in Sumner County who'll allow him to set foot on his property. He says Mr. Summers has done ruin't his reputation, an' a lot more stuff, an' he's aimin' to get even."

"Butler's nothing but a loudmouthed blowhard, Cotton. He won't come back here, but if he does, we'll put the sheriff on him."

"That's a crock o' shit, Clayton. Me an' you ought to run him out'n the county—right now, a'fore somethin' bad happens."

"Let the law handle it," Clayton said, dismissing the subject.

A week later the overseer's house mysteriously burned to the ground. Cotton swore to Clayton that Butler had fired the house because he assumed that he, Cotton, was living in it. Clayton didn't believe it.

The next morning the sheriff stopped by and informed Mr. Summers that Sylla's daughter, Mandy, had run off during the night with Butler. Cotton leaned toward Clayton and jeered, "I told you so. But hell no, you didn't think the son-of-a-bitch would do nuthin'. We should have hunted Butler down and killed him, Clayton. But you wouldn't listen . . . hell no!"

"Of course I wouldn't listen, Cotton. That's murder. We've got no proof that Butler started the fire."

"He started that fire. You know it as well as me. An' I'll tell you somethin' else, Clay. We ain't seen the last of Butler. An' it scares me, 'cause once a dog starts suckin' eggs, the only cure is to put 'im out of his misery."

Clayton's school incentive was working, although not as well as he had envisioned. The slaves who attended class appeared to be putting forth a sincere effort to learn. But other than a dozen of the girls and only half that many of the boys, the overall results were disappointing. There was, however, a bright spot: Cotton, feigning disinterest, had begun appearing at the classroom—"just to see what my field hands are learnin'."

But as the days wore on, he became an apt pupil, and even though his learning ability was not as keen as Rufus', his enthusiasm ran the slave boy's a close race.

Despite the drawbacks, Clayton was proud of his school. He did, however, detest the law that necessitated his keeping the scholastic accomplishments of his scholars hidden from the world, or at least from the Southerners.

That thought prompted Clayton to pen his first letter to his father since leaving college.

Summerset Plantation
Cairo, Tennessee
September 25, 1859

Dear Father:
I am sure you have learned by now that I quit college. I can only pray that you will find it in your heart not to be overly disappointed in my decision to find my own way in life. It is not that I rebel against following in your footsteps, sir. It is simply that I wish to see the length of my own stride. I have at present taken a position as schoolmaster on a plantation near Gallatin, Tennessee.

We have set up classes in a log building that was the original home of the owner, Mr. Jonathan Summers. I thought you would find that interesting: a Southerner who promotes slave education. I have thirty-eight scholars, all of them slaves except one.

Many things about the South appear to be different than we Northerners have been led to believe. I will explain further in future correspondence.

I sincerely hope this letter finds you in good health.

Your affectionate son,
Clayton Harris

At Cragfont a hot and heavy argument was in progress. George Winchester, the youngest son of the widow and

father of Susie, was an attorney whose law office was in
Gallatin. While he had little to do with the physical running
of Cragfont, which was ruled by the iron hand of his
mother, he nonetheless pleaded his case with the same
heated enthusiasm that he employed in the courtroom:
"The school at Summerset will do nothing but stir up
resentment among the slaves of every plantation around,
including this one! Why, every darky within a fifty-mile
radius of Gallatin has known about the classroom at
Summerset since the day it opened. And God knows, unrest
is already at a peak throughout the country."

"Unrest is at a peak throughout the nation," said Mrs.
Winchester, unimpressed.

George cast a glance at Fanny, who sat quietly in a corner.
He wished she were somewhere else. "Educating slaves is
against the law, Mother. Have you forgotten the Nat Turner
uprising of eighteen thirty-one, and the laws that were
enacted because of it? Hell, that's why they did away with
the slave school at Cairo."

Mrs. Winchester rose to full height. "If you ever use
profanity in this house again, George, I'll take my walking
cane and give you the hiding of your life. Not even the
general used profanity within these walls!"

"I apologize, Mother. But educating slaves is against all
that's holy. Mr. Summers is breaking God's laws!"

"Spare me the courtroom drama, George," the old lady
said. "You know as well as I that the laws governing the
slaves were enacted by greedy, cowardly men and have
nothin' whatsoever to do with God. Furthermore, they
discontinued the school at Cairo because the white schoolmaster we hired didn't have sense enough to stick his thumb
in his ear."

Lettie rose to stand beside her grandmother. Facing her
uncle, she raised her chin defiantly. "I think it is an
honorable and decent thing that Mr. Harris is doing. I think
that every slave owner in the South should follow Uncle
Jonathan's example. Do you realize that not one of
Cragfont's eighty slaves can read or write?"

"It is the law!" George fumed. "It is not a moral
issue . . ."

"Well, it should be!" the widow said. Then, with an angry
slice of her hand, "Now, I'll hear no more about it. What

Jonathan does with his slaves is his business."

George's face darkened, but he bowed to his mother. "As you wish," he said. "May I be excused, Mother?" Without awaiting her answer, he left the room and headed toward the kitchen, calling for Delphy to prepare him a toddy.

Mrs. Winchester turned to Lettie. "Would you be so adamant in your support of the school if Clayton Harris were not the schoolmaster?"

Lettie's face tightened with annoyance. "Grandmother, you know perfectly well that I have absolultey no interest in Mr. Harris. Why, I hardly even know the man. Furthermore, I am engaged to Mr. Peyton."

"Hogwash!" Susie said. "You was a-fixin' to kiss Clayton when me an' Granny got to the pond that day."

"Must she always be present?" Lettie demanded. "Everywhere I step, she's underfoot. Everything I do, she has her long nose stuck right in the middle of it! I am sick to death of her, Grandmother, just sick to death."

"Well," Mrs. Winchester said, "it did look as tho' we were interrupting something."

"I only flirted . . . just a little. Oh, Granny"—the girl flung her arms around Mrs. Winchester and burst into tears—"I'm grown up now, and I'm pretty. Is it a sin to tease my admirers?"

"No, child," said the old lady. "But it's a sin to worry your old grandmother, who promised your ma and pa in New Orleans that she would see to it that no harm comes to you."

"Yes," Susie said, big-eyed. "You might mess 'round an' get knocked up . . ."

"To your room!" shouted Mrs. Winchester, pointing toward the hallway. "An' don't you come down 'til I send for you."

Startled by her grandmother's anger, Susie walked toward the door, but the old lady called her back.

"Susie," she said, taking the girl by her shoulders and peering into her upturned face, "do you know the meaning of what you just said?"

Susie nodded. "Of course I do, Granny. I heard Fanny an' Eli talkin', an' Eli was mad. He said he was goin' to knock her up."

"What did he mean by that?" Mrs. Winchester asked.

"Why, Granny, you know that when men get mad at other men, they knock 'em down . . . but when they get mad at women, because we're delicate, they knock us up 'cause it don't hurt near as bad."

The old lady sighed and hugged Susie. "Run along to bed, sweetie. I'll send Fanny up to tuck you in."

Upon hearing Susie's steps on the stairs, Mrs. Winchester turned to Fanny. "You are allowing Susie too much time around the slave quarters, Fanny. If I hear one more outburst such as I just heard, it's your mouth that will be washed out with lye soap. And I'll use a hog-bristle brush to do it with."

Fanny's dusky complexion drained to a sickly gray. "Eli stays mad all the time, ol' Missus. He done say he ain't never gwine to knock me up if'n the only times he ever gits to pester me is on Sat'day nights. He always be a-talkin' 'bout knockin' me up."

"Your husband knows better than to talk that way in front of a child," returned the old lady sternly.

Fanny shook her head emphatically. "He didn't know she were there, ole Missus. Hones' he never. It be like Miss Lettie say: Miss Susie can slip 'roun' quiter'n a 'possum . . . an' she got ears like a number-fo' washtub. She hears ever' word folks say from a hunnert acres away."

"You tell Eli when he comes this Saturday that he better be sure you're alone before he starts talkin' filthy to you."

"I will, ol' Miss. I sho' will." Fanny nodded her head vigorously. "Eli wouldn't want my mouth all blistered from no lye soap, no, ma'am. He say I done got the sweetest mouth he done ever kissed."

The old lady studied Fanny's lovely face. Eli is perfectly correct, she thought, you are a rare beauty. "Run along an' tuck Susie in," she said, dismissing the girl.

"Grandmother," Lettie said, after Fanny started up the stairs, "I wish you would sell Fanny."

"Well, for heaven's sakes, child, why would I want to do that?"

"She . . . she is an embarrassment."

"I do believe you are jealous," the old lady said, amused.

"I am not! I would never be jealous of a slave, no matter how pretty she might be. It's just that Cragfont has problems enough without an arrogant, light-skinned hussy adding to them. You must admit that she's a bad influence on Susie. Why, there's no telling what that poor child has heard and seen. I've even been told that Fanny keeps her drawer strings untied so she can get her drawers off in a hurry. We certainly don't want Susie witnessing an . . . indecent act between our slaves. Oh, how utterly disgusting!"

Mrs. Winchester pursed her lips. George wasn't the only member of the family capable of courtroom drama.

"Fanny is a bit uppity," she agreed, "but that's because all her life she's been the envy of our blue-gummed purebloods. And as for the rumor that Fanny's drawers are loose, your worries are unwarranted, my dear. Fanny doesn't wear drawers."

Mrs. Winchester tucked her shawl more tightly about her shoulders. "I'll bid you a good night," she said, bending to kiss Lettie's startled, upturned lips. As she drew away, she said, "Everything will work out fine. Folks will complain about Clayton's school, but after a while they'll accept it. An' as for Fanny, you are more beautiful than she . . . and she's married." The old woman smiled fondly at her granddaughter. "Methinks you worry too much."

Lettie wanted to tell her that it wasn't Fanny's husband that she was concerned about. But she didn't. In truth, she considered it beneath her dignity to admit, even to herself, that Fanny's interest in Clayton Harris bothered her even a little bit.

CHAPTER 8

Clayton was pleased. It was October twenty-sixth, and his school was showing a definite improvement. Rufus, along with several of the female children and a few of the younger boys, could recite his ABC's with a minimum of mistakes, and nearly half of the children, and adults as well, could count to twenty.

Clayton was explaining to the class the process of assembling letters into words when Mr. Summers entered and asked if he could speak to him privately.

He followed the old man outside and caught sight of the sheriff leaning leisurely against the log wall. Clayton's mouth set into a defensive line. "I suppose you've come about the school?"

"You might say that." The sheriff handed Clayton a newspaper.

Clayton glanced at the headlines: "Fugitive Abolitionist John Brown Captures Federal Arsenal at Harpers Ferry, Virginia."

The paper told of the capture, then went on to say that two days later, on October eighteenth, Colonel Robert E. Lee with a detachment of Federal troops stormed the arsenal and forced Brown and his eighteen followers to surrender. Brown was being held by the State of Virginia for trial, not only for the insurrection, but for the brutal murder of five slave owners at Pottawatomie Creek, Kansas, in May of 1856.

Clayton returned the paper. "What does this have to do with us?"

The sheriff shifted his cud of tobacco from one cheek to the other and spat a stream of amber from the side of his mouth. "I don't believe you fully understand what John Brown was up to. He figured on usin' them weapons at the arsenal to arm the slaves thereabouts so he could declare war on Southerners."

Clayton scowled; he was aware of John Brown's fanatic hatred of slavery. The sheriff went on: "The slaves didn't rally to Brown's drum, but the music sure stirred 'em up. An when slaves get stirred up, white folks just naturally get a mite nervous."

"Get to the point, Sheriff."

"I'm gettin' there."

Clayton gritted his teeth, wondering if the man was deliberately dragging out the conversation.

"It ain't no secret that you been teachin' these darkies to read an' write," the sheriff said, watching Clayton's face, "an' chances are, nobody'd ever have opened their mouth about it if John Brown had stayed in Kansas." The sheriff sighed and shook his head. "The truth is, Mr. Harris, folks around here are plumb terrified by the possibility of a slave uprisin'."

Clayton nodded toward the schoolroom door. "Take a look in that room and tell me those children are plotting an insurgence. Go ahead, take a look."

The sheriff ducked his head. "It ain't the younguns that's botherin' folks, Mr. Harris. Leastways not right now. Hell, them pickaninnies won't be a threat for maybe ten, fifteen years down the road. Naw, son, it ain't the younguns. It's the full-grown slaves what's got the folks edgy. I reckon they just ain't about to forget Nat Turner's revolt back in thirty-one. He was an' educated nigger preacher. He used that education to whip sixty or seventy of his male congregation into such a frenzy that they went on a rampage an' slaughtered fifty-one white men, women, an' children." The sheriff's face turned to stone as he detailed the hideous murders and rapes of the victims.

"Yes," he said when he had finished, "it was unbelievable what them educated niggers did to those white folks. So I don't reckon as how I can blame a body for bein' a bit upset about your school here."

Clayton's stomach had drawn into a tight knot as he listened to the sheriff's account of the uprising. Was he, in essence, nurturing a monster such as Nat Turner? Rufus had a quick, intelligent mind. But what of his soul? In the deepest, darkest recesses of his being, was Rufus diseased with murder, hatred, revenge?

"Sheriff," said Mr. Summers, "I trust my darkies. They are fine people, and would give their lives to protect me and my family. An' no education is goin' to change that."

"That's what folks said 'bout Turner, Jonathan. An' you know damned well I had to sell Sam in Memphis 'cause ever'body around here was afraid of him."

Mr. Summers grimaced. Still, he knew in his heart that Sam had been in the right. That had been no insurrection.

"I know folks is scared," the old man agreed. "They got a right to be. But I don't think they'll panic just 'cause John Brown was arrested . . ."

"They already have, Jonathan. The Barrs are down at Nashville now, bookin' passage for their slaves on a steamboat bound for a place called the Republic of Liberia."

Clayton's mouth fell open. "They're sending them back to Africa?"

The sheriff nodded. "Barr said that was where they come from an' he was sendin' 'em home where they belong."

"Did they want to be returned to Africa?" demanded Clayton. "After all, there hasn't been a new slave brought into America legally since early in the century. So most of these slaves are second and third generation. Chances are, the young ones have never even heard of Africa."

"It don't make no difference whether they want to go or not, Mr. Harris. Slaves ain't got no say-so in the matter."

"Well, that's a fine kettle of fish!" interjected Mr. Summers. "Old Anderson, my blacksmith, has a wife over at Barr's. And my Pompey, too. And Rose's husband, and Sukey's. An' Fanny, at Cragfont, her husband, Eli, is a Barr slave. There's goin' to be a passel of broken families, Sheriff."

The lawman shrugged. "Can't be helped, Jonathan." Then he said what he had come for: "I've got to shut down your school, Mr. Harris. I'm sorry about it, but feelin's is runnin' high right now."

Clayton angrily waved the apology aside; the tattered chemise of the South was beginning to show.

The Barrs wrote passes so that their married slaves could visit their families one last time. With chagrin Clayton observed the sad farewells of husbands, wives, and children, remembering the Saturday nights when they had gathered at the cabins after a hard week's work to sing, to dance, to make love . . . to enjoy the simple pleasure of belonging to someone other than their masters.

A fanatical white man, who had never worn the fetters of bondage, had taken it upon himself to use terror and violence as a means to force the freedom issue. Well, it had worked, Clayton thought bitterly. Mary, who was married to old Anderson, was down on her knees pleading with Mr. Summers to tell Mr. Barr that she would rather remain a happy servant at the Barr Plantation than to be a free woman thousan's o' miles from her husban'. Then she clung to Anderson and wept her heart out.

Clayton bit his lip and tears danced in his eyes. Turning quickly from the scene, he went to the main house and straight to the library, where he poured himself a full glass of whiskey. Gulping it down, he raised the empty glass in a toast to John Brown. Then, with an obscenity in keeping with Cotton's vocabulary, he hurled the glass against the wall.

At Cragfont, Eli stood in the open doorway of Fanny's cabin and stared angrily into the gathering twilight. "I jist don' understan' you, Fanny," he said. "I got the right! I's your husband."

Fanny plopped down on the bed and pushed out her bottom lip. "You'll be gone in the mornin' fo'ever. I ain't never goin' to see you again, Eli. So why should I 'llow you to pester me?"

"I thought I been a-pleasurin' you!" He turned and walked to her. "What you mean, I been a-pesterin' you?"

"It was a-pleasurin' a'fore. But you ain't goin' to be my husband no more, an' I got to think 'bout startin' me a new life."

"That don't make no nevermind! Long as I's here, I's your husband an' you's my wife." He snatched her skirt to her waist and attempted to force himself between her thighs.

Fanny rolled onto her side and flipped her skirt down over her knees. "I done told yo' no, Eli. So yo' can jist button up your ol' pants, 'cause you ain't gettin' none, an' that's final! You a-wantin' to do it to me an' then run off to some place that ain't even in Tennessee, an' prob'ly leave me with a pickaninny inside o' me. No, Eli. No! No! No!"

Eli clenched his fists. "I ain't a-runnin' off. I's bein' shipped to Africa. I ain't a-wantin' to go an' leave you, honey."

"No, Eli."

Eli's eyes narrowed. "You think you foolin' me. But I been a-hearin' clear over to the Barr Plantation how you been twitchin' your ass ever' time that schoolteacher come over here. You jist like a mare in heat when he be around. He prob'ly been a-pleasurin' you right along."

Fanny jumped to her feet. "No he ain't! But if'n he wanted to, I'd let 'im. He treats me like a fine lady . . . jist like he do Miss Lettie."

Eli's face contorted. Flinging Fanny onto her back, he caught her by the ankles and yanked her feet toward the ceiling. Her skirt fell in rumpled folds over her face and shoulders, revealing her shapely legs and buttocks to his prying eyes.

Fanny squirmed and kicked, but Eli's work-hardened hands tightened their grip. "You is hurtin' my ankles," she whimpered.

Eli spread her legs and forced his way between her thighs. Working his way into her, he said, "Yo' ain't no white woman, Fanny. You ain't Miss Lettie, you's a black slave. An' no matter how hard you tries to be white, you is a nigger. An they ain't no white man ever goin' to look at you twice, 'cept when he wants some nigger ass."

Fanny winced as he entered her and began his rhythm. "Ol' Mizz Winchester's firstborn, Marcus Brutus," she grated, wishing he would finish, "took him a black wife, an' she weren't nearly as pretty as me."

"That were years ago, when they weren't no white women in Tennessee." Then, with a long, low groan, he collapsed on her.

Fanny rolled from beneath him and straightened her skirt. "Well, that don't make no difference. I's seen the way white men look at me. And they likes what they sees."

Eli swung his legs to the floor and buttoned his trousers. Rising, he walked to the door, where he turned and appraised her for the final time. "You jist a highfalutin' bitch, Fanny. An' you sho' nuff is jist like a white woman in one r'spect." He had Fanny's attention. "Jist like white men says about white women, you's as cold as ice 'tween yore legs."

Eli's mocking laughter drifted behind him as he headed across the field toward the Barr Plantation.

Fanny sprang to the floor and ran to the doorway. She took a deep breath and spat contemptuously toward his retreating back, soon lost in the darkness. "I is a Winchester! An I'll have me a white man someday. An' . . . an' I'll have white babies, an' they won't be slaves. Jist you wait an' see . . . you . . . you nigger!"

Then she cried.

Since the closing of the school, Clayton was at loose ends. His limited knowledge of crops and livestock was of little value to Summerset. He began to envy Cotton, who was proving to be a fine overseer, blessed with the inborn ability to communicate with animals and to understand people. He reluctantly admitted that Cotton was one of those rare mortals who bragged loudly of his capabilities, then did exactly what he bragged about, and did it well.

On the first of November, as he and Cotton walked back from Bledsoe's Creek, where they had taken a frosty dip after putting in a hard day overseeing the harvesting of the corn crop, he told Cotton that he had decided to go on to Texas as he had originally intended.

Cotton palmed his wet hair off his forehead. "You start runnin' now, you'll never quit, Clay."

"Don't talk to me about running. What do you think you were doing when you climbed over that railing on the *Princess*?"

Cotton grinned widely. "Hell, Clay, I weren't runnin' from nothin'. I was runnin' to somethin'. They's a difference."

Clayton ignored that. "Mr. Summers hired me to teach school. Well, there isn't any school. And I have no desire to wait and be discharged from my first job. I'd rather go ahead and quit."

"Mr. Summers ain't goin' to fire you. Hell, he likes you."

"I won't take a handout."

"Then quit bitchin' an do what he hired you to do."

Clayton shook his head. "The sheriff—"

"Piss on the sheriff! He can close our school, but he sure can't close our minds. Me an' Rufus been talkin' it over. Us an' some of the others could come to your room at night. You could teach us there."

Clayton stared at his friend. "I'm not believing what I'm hearing."

"Me neither, but it's true. An' if anybody asks about it, you can tell 'em you're teachin' me to read an' write . . . an' Rufus an' the others ain't doin' nothin' but learnin' to be good house slaves."

"What changed your mind about an education?"

Cotton beamed. "I didn't know I was so damned smart 'til I went to school."

Clayton paced the length of Mr. Summers' study, then retraced his steps. The old man made a tent of his fingers. "Somethin' botherin' you, son?"

Clayton stopped and took a deep breath. "Yes, sir, there is. The evening classes are going well enough, but it galls me to lounge around all day with nothing to do."

When Mr. Summers didn't answer, Clayton said, "What I had in mind, sir, was possibly taking over the bookkeeping and paperwork of Summerset. I am familiar with accounting and management. And I feel that I can be of service to you."

Mr. Summers leaned back in his chair and thought about the proposal. He despised keeping records; it went against the reason the good Lord had given him a memory. "All

right, son," he said. "Go right ahead an' do whatever it is
you think this plantation needs." Clayton smiled at the
patronage.

That evening he turned the former schoolroom into an
office and threw himself into the slow and painstaking work
of initiating an accounting system for Sumerset and an
inventory of the plantation's assets.

In late November Clayton was both shocked and pleased
when he received an invitation to a party at Cragfont.
He was shocked because he realized how very much he
longed to see Lettie Billingsly again, and he was pleased
because the invitation was signed by none other than
herself.

When he asked Cotton to accompany him to the festivi-
ties, Cotton shook his head. "Hell, Clay. You know as well
as me that I ain't welcome in that crowd. The owners
tolerate me 'cause I'm Mr. Summers' overseer, but they sure
as shit don't accept me." Cotton pointed his finger at
Clayton. "I been a-readin' one of them books of yours. An'
some feller named John Randolph, from Roanoke, Virginia, said it all: 'I am an aristocrat. I love liberty. I hate
equality.' I know my place, Clay, an' I'm goin' to stay in it."

"Randolph said that in the seventeen hundreds. This is
eighteen fifty-nine."

"Nothin's changed."

Clayton frowned at Cotton. "The sheriff was right; a little
education can be a dangerous thing for some people."

"Anyhow," Cotton said, "the real party will be at the
slave quarters, not up at the big house. Miss Malvinia
inherited some slaves from Virginia, an' them Cragfont folk
are gonna' welcome 'em right proper."

"How do you know that? Lettie didn't mention it in her
invitation."

"Old Anderson told me. Hell, Clay, slaves know everything that happens hereabouts." Cotton snapped his fingers.
"On second thought, I believe I will ride over there with
you."

"Why?" Clayton asked, curious.

Cotton grinned. "'Cause if them slaves will let me join
their party, that's about as close as I'll ever come to bein' a
nigger on a Saturday night."

"Looks like the entire county is here," Clayton said, eyeing the carriages, buggies, wagons, and saddle horses that ringed the Cragfont driveway. He and Cotton rode on to the west gate and dismounted.

Cotton passed his bridle reins to the Cragfont groom. "You can bet that Bailey Peyton, Jr., is in there, Clayton. So no matter that Miss Lettie appears to be sweet on you, keep in mind she's an' en-gaged woman." With that, Cotton headed off around the house toward the slave quarters.

Clayton straightened his coat and brushed a few strands of horsehair from his trousers. Satisfied with his appearance, he strode up the walkway to the open front doors and the awaiting gaiety.

Unlike most Tennessee homes, Cragfont boasted a second-story ballroom. So it wasn't until Clayton had topped the stairs that he came face-to-face with the aristocratic gathering.

The splendid ballroom was a fitting backdrop for the elegant guests who graced its floor. The young women wore magnificent, low-cut gowns of chintze and silk, with many hoops and petticoats, while the not-so-young sported less daring creations, if not less elaborate. The men were cocks-of-the-walk in their tight-fitting breeches and white-ruffled shirts accented by black cravats and neatly tailored, claw-hammer coats.

Clayton was immediately collected by Lettie and paraded to the punch bowl. He filled her glass, then touched it with his; the fine crystal rang clear in the noisy room. "To a lovely party," he said.

"Just about everyone in the world is here," Lettie said breathlessly. "Or at least everybody who is somebody. I only pray we haven't forgotten anyone. Wouldn't that simply be a travesty?" Then she smiled, her gaze roving boldly over his new plum-colored waistcoat, tight fawn breeches, and highly polished black riding boots.

"You look absolutely rakish, Mr. Harris. If a lady wasn't already practically engaged, she would be hard pressed not to walk in the moonlight with you . . . especially since her finacé has not yet arrived."

"Thank you," he murmured, wondering if she had intentionally opened the door for an invitation.

Lettie eyed him expectantly. When no words were forthcoming, her lips tightened with annoyance. "Well, at the least, Mr. Harris, you could return the compliment and say something nice about my dress. I had Sylla and Fanny work night and day on it so it would be ready for this evening. Isn't it just ravishing?"

Lettie made a slow pirouette so that he might appreciate both the front and the back of the gown. The emerald-green silk was low-cut, exposing her graceful shoulders and a goodly portion of her milk-white cleavage to their best advantage. The waist was close-fitting, and the overskirt belled out voluminously, the underskirt hiding the hoops and stays. Indeed, the effect was breathtaking—and so, thought Clayton, was Lettie.

Bowing, he kissed her hand. "The dress, Miss Lettie," he drawled in his best Southern style, "is nothing but a primrose . . . when worn by a magnolia blossom such as yourself."

Lettie's face broke into a pleased smile. "Why, Mr. Harris, we might make a true Southern gentleman of you yet, despite your Yankee upbringing."

The musicians struck the opening chords of a waltz.

"Would you care to dance?" Clayton set his glass on the windowsill. Smiling saucily, Lettie moved into his arms.

As the last notes died away, Lettie guided Clayton through the side door and onto the east balcony. They stood at the rail and gazed down at the gardens, where the full moon silhouetted several couples strolling arm in arm.

As they watched, a young man and woman embraced for an awkward, yet ardent, kiss. When they parted, Lettie sighed and pushed herself lightly against Clayton, turning her face up to him expectantly. Clayton hesitated, remembering his pledge to Mrs. Winchester. The delay sent Lettie to her tiptoes as she impatiently sought his lips.

It was more than Clayton could stand; spanning her slender waist with his hands, he drew her against him in a long and searching kiss.

A moment later Lettie was wrenched from Clayton's embrace and shoved toward the ballroom. "Go inside, Lettie." Bailey Peyton, Jr., was so angry he was shaking, yet his voice was perfectly controlled.

Lettie stood frozen, her fingers weakly dabbing at her lips as though to wipe away Clayton's kiss. Clayton sized up the man standing before him. Peyton was of average height and slender build. His features were not perfect, but at twenty-one, he had a mature look of assurance that Clayton envied.

"Go inside, Lettie," Peyton said again.

"Stay where you are, Lettie," Clayton ordered. Lettie hesitated, still staring at Peyton. Clayton said, "I believe this gentleman has the wrong impression as to what has occurred here."

"Wrong impression?" echoed Bailey Peyton. "I suppose you're goin' to tell me you weren't kissin' my fiancée."

Clayton looked at Lettie. Her eyes pleaded for him not to tell the truth. "Of course I was," he said. "I've wanted to kiss her since the first day I met her, but Miss Billingsly was unapproachable, sir. A moment ago I lost my head and took advantage of her." Turning to Lettie, he said, "I beg your forgiveness, Miss Lettie."

Color seeped into Lettie's cheeks and she inclined her head, unable to meet Clayton's steady gaze.

Bailey Peyton removed his coat and draped it over the balcony rail. "I told you to go inside, Lettie," he said with quiet self-assurance. "I won't tell you again."

"I will not," the girl cried. Then as Bailey Peyton turned up his sleeve cuffs, she demanded, "And just what in the deuce do you think you are doing, Bailey?" He continued rolling up his sleeves. She sucked in her breath. "Surely you don't intend to fight Mr. Harris? He has apologized, Bailey."

"I am going to teach Mr. Harris that he can't jeopardize an engaged lady's reputation, apology or not."

"You do intend to fight," Lettie breathed delightedly.

"I have dishonored nobody," Clayton said, his temper flaring. "And you, sir, are a total jackass to suggest such a thing."

"Although I would prefer pistols at dawn, Mr. Harris," Peyton cooly said, "I have heard that you lean more towards fisticuffs."

"This is ridiculous," Clayton said. "I'm not going to fight you, Peyton. That would truly be an embarrassment . . . especially for Miss Lettie."

Lettie was outraged by Clayton's declaration. But before she could voice her indignity, a group of young men stepped onto the balcony. One of them whisked her into the ballroom and twirled her away across the floor.

A second man thrust a flask into Bailey Peyton's hand with an order to drink.

A third told Clayton to go back to Summerset where he belonged.

Clayton longed to wipe the arrogance from the face of the man who had ordered him off Cragfont, but instead he looked for a way from the balcony that would not take him through the ballroom, where Lettie was dancing. The only other exit was through a bedchamber. Clayton walked to the door and stepped inside.

Several young ladies in various stages of undress immediately set up a howl. He retreated hastily onto the gallery. Peyton, standing with his friends, eyed him with amusement.

"Latecomers, Mr. Harris. They change into their ball gowns after they arrive. Any Southerner knows that."

The barb struck home. Looking neither to the right nor to the left, Clayton crossed the dance floor and descended the stairs two at a time.

Once outside, he stalked furiously toward the slave quarters. The very act of being forced to search out Cotton in such surroundings gave credence to Bailey Peyton's unspoken accusation that he didn't belong with the gentility.

"Clayton!" He looked back. Lettie, her skirts above her ankles, was racing after him. Clayton continued on.

Lettie caught him by the arm. "Clayton, don't be mad."

Shaking off her hand, he said, "Excuse me, Miss Billingsly, but right now I feel very angry and very foolish. I'm sure that by morning it will be all over Sumner County that one of Bailey Peyton's friends ran me home to Summerset."

"Oh, fiddlesticks. Let them think what they will. You and I know the truth."

Taking his hand, she led him into the blackened shadows of a lilac bush and kissed him soundly. "There, does that make you feel better?"

"No, Lettie," he said, stepping back. "It makes me feel cheap, that you would kiss me only in the dark."

Stepping to the path, he turned toward the slave cabins. Lettie caught his arm again and spun him about. "I'll have you know, dark or not, my kisses aren't cheap."

Clayton disengaged her hand. "If you'll excuse me, ma'am, I've been ordered off Cragfont."

Lettie stamped her foot angrily. "You are the most childish man I've ever met." The words were no more than out of her mouth when Clayton crushed her to him in a kiss that left her breathless. Putting her hands against his chest, she pushed him away. "Stop it, Clayton."

"Why? Because we're standing out in the open where someone might see us? Or because you enjoyed it?"

"Neither! It's because . . . I am an engaged woman."

Clayton laughed. "When, might I ask, do you intend to start acting like one?"

Lettie's eyes narrowed. "Right now," she breathed, slapping Clayton hard across the mouth. Then, raising her chin arrogantly, she drew her ball gown above her ankles and marched toward the big house.

Enraged, and consumed with the burning urge to destroy something, Clayton spun on his heel and struck off in a fast walk toward the slave houses.

Fanny, who had slipped away from Lettie's party to enjoy a few minutes of revelry at the slave quarters, had let time get away from her. Holding her cotton dress above her knees, she sped up the darkened path toward the big house.

It was inevitable that they should collide. Fanny careened off Clayton and sprawled headlong into the shrubs that lined the walk.

Clayton, clutching his side where Fanny's elbow had cracked against his rib cage, knelt beside the dazed girl lying in tangled, unladylike disarray. His eyes roved the length of her long legs where her skirt, having been snagged on a bush when she fell, was snatched nearly to her waist.

Fanny moaned and rolled slowly onto her back. When her eyelashes fluttered open and she saw Clayton bending over her, she jackknifed to a sitting position and quickly smoothed down her dress.

"Are you hurt?" he asked uneasily, aware that she had caught him staring at her.

"No, Massa," she whispered. "I isn't hurt."

For a long moment they searched each other's face. Then Clayton offered her his hand and assisted her to her feet.

As Fanny tried to stand, she lurched against him for

support. Instinctively, he put his arm around her.

"I's twisted my knee, Massa," she said. "I's sorry, sir. I didn't mean to be no bother."

The memory of her naked legs brought a deeper flush to his face than had Lettie's stinging slap. "Don't apologize, Fanny," he said, steadying her. "It was my fault. If I hadn't been—"

At that moment, Lettie's laughter, clear and distinct, floated down from the balcony. Clayton's head snapped up. The soft light filtering from the ballroom onto the balcony silhouetted Lettie in bold relief as she stepped into Bailey Peyton's arms and raised her lips to his for a long and arduous kiss.

Fanny felt Clayton's body stiffen, and she heard the sharp intake of his breath. She too looked toward the balcony. A sensation she never expected to feel for a white person, much less a white man, welled up inside her, and she said, "I'm so sorry, Massa Clayton."

With a curse, Clayton crushed Fanny against him and covered her lips with his.

"Do you live alone?" he asked harshly when they parted. Not trusting her voice, Fanny nodded.

"Can you walk?" Again she nodded.

With one last, bitter look toward the upper veranda, Clayton followed Fanny to her cabin.

CHAPTER 9

For two weeks following the Cragfont party, Fanny kept her fingers crossed. But on Monday of the third week she was spotting, and by Tuesday she was in full flow.

"Chatty," she said angrily upon entering the kitchen, "you done told me I was probably catched good an' proper . . . but I ain't. I's ridin' the cotton pony somethin' fierce."

Old Chatty swung the fireplace crane away from the flames and hung a black iron pot on it. Swinging it over the fire, she said, "I never said it were yo' who I drempt 'bout. I said I drempt 'bout a white man plantin' seeds in new groun' and a crop a-springin' up, dat's what I said."

"Well, why couldn't it be me? I done been pleasured by a white man."

Chatty cocked her head toward Fanny and pursed her lips. " 'Cause your furrow been plowed befo', and mo' times 'n once. Yes'm, the man who plows yo' furrow ain't gwine to be turnin' no new groun', an' dat's a fact."

Old Chatty dipped up a spoonful of stew, tasted it, then dropped the spoon into the pot. "Anyway, it weren't no slave wench what I drempt 'bout."

Frowning at Fanny, she continued: "Why you a-wantin' to get knocked up so bad no how? You's mighty thin an' delicate to be a-carrin' a baby inside of yo'."

Fanny thought of Clayton and smiled wistfully. "I's wantin' . . . a white baby. An' pretty as the daddy be an' lovely as I be, why, we'd have a beautiful baby for sho'."

Chatty cackled loudly. "Massa Cotton mus'a done laid some mighty fancy pleasurin' on yo' to make yo' believe dat ugly white boy done turned purty. Yes, 'deed, some mighty fine pleasurin'."

Fanny almost snapped out that it wasn't Cotton. But a voice inside her warned her to remain silent.

Still cackling, Chatty handed Fanny a blue stone pitcher. "Now, go on, get yo'self down to de springhouse an' fetch me a jar o' buttermilk. Ol' Miss be wantin' supper a'fore long."

"Chatty," Fanny said, turning at the door, "if'n it weren't no slave girl you drempt 'bout, then who were it?"

"It ain't none o' yo' affair, girl. Now do like I tolt yo', git on down to de springhouse."

As Fanny approached the limestone building—constructed over a pool near Bledsoe's Creek, where crystal-clear water bubbled up out of the ground—Patrick, one of the slaves Malvinia had inherited from Virginia, stepped from behind a sycamore tree and hastened to open the springhouse door. Pushing Fanny inside, he swung the heavy door shut behind them and caught her by her shoulders.

"Why you been 'voidin' me, Fanny? Befo' the big party, you was real friendly. Now you won't 'llow me to come near you."

Fanny pushed him away. "Why ain't you in the field where you b'long, Patrick? If'n you's caught here wif me, we both'll be whipped."

Patrick tightened his grip on her shoulders. "It would be worth it to pleasure yo' again."

"Not to me, it wouldn't. Now you git on out'n here. I got to get a pitcher of buttermilk an' fetch it to the house."

Patrick pulled Fanny against him and kissed her hard.

Fanny beat at his broad chest with her free hand, but that excited him even more, and holding her mouth with his, he backed her against the damp stone wall, caught up a handful of her skirt and began raising it to her waist.

Breaking free of his ardent kiss, she cried, "It be my time o' the month, Patrick!"

"That don't make no difference. I's crazy fo' you, Fanny!"

Fanny lifted the heavy pitcher as high as she could and slammed it down on Patrick's head.

With a sigh of escaping breath, Patrick slumped into the icy pool of spring water.

"You ain't crazy for me," Fanny cried. "You jist plain crazy!"

Holding his head and moaning, Patrick crawled out of the water. "What fo' did you go an' hit me? You done cracked my skull."

Fanny threatened him again with the crock. "Jist 'cause I took a fancy to you when you first come here from Virginia, it don't mean I fancy you now. A girl done got the right to change her mind."

Patrick drew himself to a sitting position. "You was mighty lovin' 'til the night o' the party . . ."

"Well, I ain't no more! I done been pleasured by a white man from over at Summerset . . . an' he make your lovin' seem plumb puny. So don' you go tryin' to raise my dress tail, 'cause I ain't gonna pleasure nobody but him, ever again."

Tossing her head, she stepped around Patrick and lifted a gallon jar of buttermilk from the spring. After pouring her pitcher full, she raised her dress above her ankles as she had seen Lettie do and stalked back to the big house.

In the kitchen, she blurted out to Chatty what had happened.

The old Negress clucked her tongue. "I jist knowed som'pin' bad goin' t' happen. Las' night I drempt o' walnuts a-fallin' a-fore dey was ripe. An' when de hulls hit da groun', dey busted open, but dey wasn't no nuts inside!"

Every time Patrick saw Fanny, her rejection burned into him anew, leaving him mean, unmanageable, and determined to prove his manhood.

A week after the incident in the springhouse, Fanny entered her cabin to find Patrick standing by the hearth. Fear ran the length of her as she gazed into his furious face.

Turning quickly, she hastened through the door, but Patrick caught her wrist and flung her back into the room. Slamming the door, he advanced on her, stripping off his shirt as he came.

Fanny took a step backward, then another, until she had flattened herself against the far wall.

"Don't you touch me," she warned, wishing her voice carried more conviction.

Patrick came on, and his silence was even more frightening than his appearance. When he reached out and caught a handful of her blouse, Fanny locked her hands around his.

"Please, Patrick." She tried to smile. "They's no need to d'stroy my clothes . . . I'll take 'em off."

For a long second Patrick was undecided. Then, moving to the door, he blocked the exit and crossed his arms. "Go 'head."

Fanny's heart sank. With trembling fingers, she removed her blouse.

"All of it," he shouted when she hesitated.

Terror added wings to her fingers, and a moment later she stood naked before him.

He pointed to the bed. Fanny climbed upon the cold feather tick and lay there. Patrick kicked off his trousers and flung himself on top of her.

She sucked in her breath and waited.

Patrick pressed his body tightly against her. Still Fanny waited.

Minutes went by; then Patrick pushed himself to his knees and clamped his hands over his limp genitals. With a cry of rage, he rolled to the far side of the bed and drew himself into a fetal position.

For a moment Fanny lay there, wondering why he had not taken her.

Then she snickered, and the snicker became a giggle and finally a burst of full-throated laughter. Springing from the bed, she hastily donned her clothes and bolted from the cabin.

Patrick lay there naked, yet oblivious to the December cold, and wept like a child.

Finally, not bothering to clothe himself, he left the cabin and ran to the blacksmith shop, where he wrenched a heavy spoke from a damaged wagon wheel. Heedless of the frost

that burned his bare feet, he struck out in a fast walk toward
Summerset.

Cotton bade old Anderson a good night and climbed the
ladder to his loft room. Shedding his clothes, he slipped
under the heavy quilt, tired, but pleased. It had been a good
day. The men had butchered and salted down ten hogs and
three beeves, while the women had rendered the lard and
tallow, and the children had carried hickory wood for
replenishing the fire in the smokehouse, where the meat was
hung to cure.

Locking his hands behind his head and crossing his feet,
Cotton smiled contentedly. He was satisfied with himself,
with the plantation, and with his room at the barn. He even
liked the smell of well-oiled harness leather, hay, and grain,
and especially the pungent odor of horses that wafted
upward through the cracks in the floor. Closing his eyes, he
thought that everything was fine, just downright fine.

Anderson blew out the lantern, casting the corridor of the
barn into darkness, and sat down on the cot that he used for
a bed. Dropping his elbows to his knees, he rested his chin
in his hands. Tears filled his ancient eyes as he thought of his
wife. He missed her.

He reached down and absently stroked the ears of the
mongrel dog that also slept in the barn. "Ah's me, Blue," he
said. "I sho' nuff do miss my wife. Yes, suh, I needs her in
my ol' age."

Blue licked the old Negro's hand, then pushed his head
against Anderson's palm, looking for a pat. But suddenly
the dog jumped alert then darted out the barn door, barking
loudly.

Anderson climbed to his feet and shuffled after him.
"What yo' got out dar, Blue, a 'possum?"

With one savage blow of the wagon spoke, Patrick killed
the dog. And that was what old Anderson witnessed as he
stepped into the moonlight.

In two strides Anderson caught Patrick by the neck. The
smith's fingers, although gnarled and twisted, were like
bands of steel as they closed around the young slave's
throat.

"What fo' did you kill Blue?" Anderson lifted Patrick
slowly off the ground. Patrick's eyes bulged in their sockets,

and his tongue rolled between his lips. Anderson added more pressure to his grip.

Patrick raised the spoke and brought it down with all his remaining strength across Anderson's head, splitting the old man's skull as neatly as if he had used a dull broadax.

Inside the barn, Cotton, awakened by the commotion, clambered down the ladder and ran to the door. The horse lot was eerie in the moon-glow, and the shadowy figure of Patrick bending over Anderson's body made Cotton's scalp tingle.

In eerie slow motion, Patrick turned and peered toward the barn. Then with a screech that nearly stopped Cotton's heart, he sprang toward the door. Cotton made a desperate lunge toward the loft ladder, but he had not climbed more than three rungs when Patrick was on him. Again Patrick raised the bloody spoke and brought it down.

The darkness, however, was deceptive, and the wagon spoke slammed solidly against the seasoned oak beam supporting the loft. The shock of the impact momentarily paralyzed Patrick's arm from his fingertips to his shoulder, and the spoke fell clattering to the floor.

That one moment was all Cotton needed. Springing past Patrick, he darted to the far wall and snatched a pitchfork from its holder.

"Now, you son-of-a-bitch," he shouted triumphantly, advancing cautiously toward Patrick, the needle-sharp tines of the pitchfork held low, "I'm goin' to spike your black ass to a stall door!"

The lethal weapon and the deadly intent on Cotton's face sent Patrick to his knees. Forgotten was the bloody wagon spoke. Forgotten were the bodies of old Anderson and his dog. All that mattered to Patrick was the fear that he was about to die.

"Don't kill me, Massa," he begged, burying his face in his hands. "Please don' kill me . . ."

Cotton's hands trembled as he drew the pitchfork above his head. Then with a cry of frustration, he lowered the weapon.

"Get up," he said through clenched teeth. "But if you so much as allow your stomach to growl, you're a dead man."

* * *

Mr. Summers sent Rufus for the sheriff. Still, it was well after daybreak before a deputy and four self-appointed constables showed up to collect Patrick.

Cotton related the night's events to the deputy and then said, "The only thing I can't figure out is why he wanted to kill a fine ol' man like Anderson. It just don't make no sense."

Patrick, who was manacled to the hitching ring in the mounting block, said, "I didn't mean t' kill ol' Anderson. He done tried to choke me to death. Was an accident."

The deputy eyed Patrick. "And I reckon it's just an accident that you was runnin' around the countryside in the middle of the night naked as a jaybird an' carryin' a wagon spoke?"

Patrick pointed his chin at Cotton. "He been a-pleasurin' hisself wif Fanny, an' she be my woman. I done come over to ask 'im to stay 'way from her."

Cotton's mouth fell open. What was the man talking about? Had Cotton been looking at Clayton, however, the sudden flush of guilt on the young Northerner's face would have answered the question.

"You come over here to kill a man is what you done, nigger," one of the constables said. "You didn't bring that wagon spoke 'cause you wanted to talk to him."

"Naw, sir." Patrick shook his head. "I never come here to kill nobody. I done brung dat spoke in case I run upon a bear or sumpin'."

"They ain't been no bears in these parts for nigh onto fifty years," the constable scoffed.

"Who told you I been a-cuttin' Fanny?" Cotton demanded.

"She done tole me," the slave said. "Tole me she done fall in love with a white man over to Summerset. An' you's the only white Summerset man what visits the slave quarters at Cragfont." Cotton's face drained, and his eyes swiveled to Clayton.

"You mean to say," the deputy broke in, "that you came over here after Cotton 'cause he done dallied in a slave wench's drawers? Well, I reckon I done heard it all!"

"Git him off my place, Deputy," Mr. Summers said with disgust. "We got a buryin' to attend to."

"If you say the word, Mr. Summers, we'll hang the bastard right here an' now. You can bury both them niggers in the same hole."

"He ain't fit to lay next to Anderson," Mr. Summers said, handing the deputy a pair of Anderson's pants and a shirt. "Get this man clothed, and get him off my property."

The deputy unfettered Patrick, then placed a noose around his neck and passed the rope to one of the constables.

"Yo' ain't gwine to 'llow them to hang me, are yo', Marse Summers?" asked Patrick, a note of pleading in his voice.

"Hush up that whinin', boy," the deputy said, handing Patrick the clothing. "Get yourself presentable. We're goin' to take you to Gallatin an' let the judge d'cide what to do with you. But if'n it was up to me, I'd hang you for just thinkin' about killin' a white boy. Yes, sir, I would."

The deputy and his party were halfway to Gallatin when a heavily loaded wagon, on its way to Cairo Landing, forced them to the side of the narrow road so that it could pass.

"Mornin', sir." The deputy tipped his hat to the driver as the wagon rumbled past.

The four-horse team of Belgians plodded to a halt. "Where you goin' with that nigger?" asked the driver.

"Takin' him to jail."

"What'd he do?"

"Tried to beat a white boy to death with a wagon spoke. Claims the fella been a-layin' with his wench."

"The hell you say!" The driver gave Patrick a once-over. Then, reaching under his wagon seat and dragging out a one-pound lard bucket, he said, "Back in Alabama where I hail from, we got a way of dealing with bucks who got too much sap in 'em."

The five riders looked at the bucket. It was filled with pine tar that the driver used for greasing the wagon axles; but the riders knew that upon occasion pine tar was also used as a disinfectant for freshly castrated animals. Then one of them laughed. "He's right, boys. We've got to teach these niggers that it's the white man's right to service any slave wench he wants."

The deputy scowled at the constable who had spoken. "You ain't never owned a slave in your life, Lassiter. So what in hell do you know about rights or wrongs where niggers are concerned?"

"Well," the wagon driver drawled, "whether he's owned no slaves or not, he's right, Deputy. Bucks ain't got no say-so in who pleasures their women."

"Maybe not in Alabama, mister. But around here we don't fool with a married woman, an' that includes slave women."

The wagon driver dropped his head back and hooted. "Mighty upright bunch of folks in Sumner County. An' I don't believe one word of that bullshit. Men have been dallying with married women, white or black, since time began, an' I don't 'spect that folks around here are any different than anyone else."

The deputy blustered. "I never meant we didn't fool with married women. I meant that we—"

"Well, this here buck ain't married to that wench," interrupted another constable.

"Then what are we waitin' for?" The wagon driver climbed down and walked to Patrick.

The riders dismounted and two of them pinioned Patrick flat on his back on the icy ground. Two others snatched off Patrick's trousers and spread his legs. The deputy reached between the slave's thighs and cupped Patrick's testicles in his palm.

Patrick went berserk, and it was all the men could do to hold the bucking, kicking man down.

The wagon driver pulled a long-barreled, revolving pistol from his coat pocket and slammed its butt against Patrick's temple.

Then, kneeling beside the semiconscious slave, he dug into his overall pocket and withdrew a large clasp knife.

By the fifth of December, the major portion of the autumn's work at Summerset was finished. The fields and gardens had been harvested, and all manner of vegetables, fruits, and meats had been canned and shelved, both in the main house and the slave quarters. Nuts and berries had been gathered and stored in the cellar, and hams, shoulders, and skins of sausage hung from blackened beams in the smokehouse.

The winter had begun. The young male slaves were busy chopping, sawing, and stacking cord after cord of oak, hickory, and ash, while the older men repaired barns and outbuildings, split fence rails, and mended harnesses and machinery. The women carded and spun, wove fabrics, sewed, churned, and cooked—all in preparation for survival should the approaching winter prove long and hard.

Mr. Summers was pleased. In spite of the drought, 1859 had turned out to be a surprisingly good year. And 1860 showed even greater promise, for only a month ago the last rails had been laid connecting Louisville to Nashville. A steam engine had already puffed its way across Sumner County, guaranteeing Summerset and the other plantations a speedier, safer, and less expensive way to ship their produce; the day of the slow, cumbersome, costly steamboat had come to an end.

"If your receipt and disbursement sheets are correct, son," the old man told Clayton, "Summerset has had a golden year. Yes, sir. It just goes to show that my ol' pappy was right. He told me years ago, 'Boy! Don't never take nothin' from the soil that you can't put back. If'n you follow that rule, the earth will be good to you forever.'" The old man fished a cheroot from his pocket and fired it up. "Our greatest losses this year were the deaths of Pauline and Anderson . . . an' I done notified the insurance company. We should be hearin' somethin' soon."

"Insurance?" Clayton was astonished. "Your slaves are insured?"

The old man blew a puff of smoke toward the ceiling. "'Course they are. Ain't a planter in the South—one of any size, that is—who hasn't got his slaves insured against death and escapement."

Mr. Summers opened a desk drawer and withdrew a handful of papers. Thumbing through them, he selected one and passed it to Clayton. "The United States Life Insurance Company, in New York City." He pointed at the bold script at the top. "I've been doin' business with them for years."

Clayton opened the policy and scanned it. Mr. Summers said, "They used to charge me eight dollars per slave. But they done notified me that they're goin' up on the premiums. Hell, they're just usin' the Northern carryin'-on for an excuse. Them crooked folks are tryin' to gouge us owners ever' way they can. The darned fools are goin' to keep on 'til they price themselves out of business."

Clayton handed the policy back to the old man. "The

insurance companies are gambling on the future, Mr. Summers. And right now the future doesn't look too good. A group of Washington politicians are trying to make a martyr of John Brown. And if they succeed, slavery will be even more unpopular in the North than it is now. If that's the case, public opinion will probably force the insurance companies to cancel their policies. I'm surprised they haven't done so already."

"It was the Federal government who hung John Brown," Mr. Summers said hotly. Then more calmly, he added, "Them insurance companies have been makin' good money off'n Southern planters for years. They ain't about to let no Yankee politicians ruin their industry. No, son. Slaves are big business, an' nothin' is goin' to change that . . . not for a long time yet."

Clayton shook his head. "You are contradicting yourself, sir. You told me when I came here that trouble was brewing between the North and the South . . ."

"And it is! An' I agree that the John Brown incident didn't help matters none. But folks will simmer down, wait an' see."

Clayton wondered.

Clayton and the Summers were invited to visit Cragfont during the New Year's holidays.

Cotton would not be going. He had told Clayton that he wasn't welcome there anymore; Mrs. Winchester had made that plain when she came to apologize to Mr. Summers for the murder of old Anderson.

Clayton had offered to tell Mrs. Winchester the truth, but Cotton wouldn't hear of it. He had said, "Do you know, Clayton, that not one person, not even Mr. Summers, as't me if I laid with Fanny? Hell, no. Ever'body just naturally believed that I did. I'm white trash, see? An' nobody expected nothin' better out o' me. So they wasn't disappointed."

Clayton had started to protest, but Cotton cut him off. "It's different with you, Clay. You done gained the respect of most folks hereabouts. Why, Mr. Summers has bragged so much about your bookkeepin' that planters all over the county think you're some kind of wizard or somethin'." Cotton had looked at his friend and grinned. "Naw, Clay. I

thank you for worryin' about me an' all, but the best thing
you can do is leave well enough alone. Furthermore, it don't
bother me none a'tall for folks to think that a girl as purty as
Fanny jumped into the shucks with me." He hooked his
thumbs in his overall bib and reared back on his heels. "Just
in case anybody asks, was she as good as she looks?"

A big disappointment awaited Clayton at Cragfont. Lettie
was gone. The day after the November party, she had
packed her trunks and returned to New Orleans.

Yes, Mrs. Winchester agreed, Lettie's hasty departure had
been unexpected, for she had been intending to stay at
Cragfont until mid-January.

No, Mrs. Winchester said, she had no idea what had
changed Lettie's mind. Clayton wasn't sure that he believed
her.

"Did it have anything to do with Fanny?" Clayton asked
before he caught himself.

"No," Mrs. Winchester said, then excused herself to
attend to her other guests.

Susie, who had been listening to the conversation, said,
"Ever since the sheriff brought Patrick home, he just mopes
around. An' on Saturdays he gets plumb sullen an' don't
talk to nobody. Just sits an' ponders an' reads his bible."

"I wasn't aware that Patrick could read and write,"
Clayton said.

"Oh, yes. Most all of them Virginia slaves that Mama
inherited is educated. Papa says that's what brought on
Patrick's trouble, him bein' able to read an' write. Papa told
Mama that Patrick would still be a fine, randy buck if he
hadn't been too smart for his breeches." The little girl
looked questioningly at Clayton. "What did Papa mean,
Clayton? Patrick looks fine to me."

Clayton took a deep breath, wondering how he was going
to deal with her question. Luckily, Susie did not wait for an
answer. "Well, whatever it is that's wrong with him," she
said, "sure stirred up a passel of trouble in the quarters. Our
Cragfont slaves don't like them Virginia darkies at all. The
day they brought Patrick back from Gallatin, ol' Chatty said
to my mama: "'Good mornin', Miss Mally,'"—the child
mimicked perfectly—"'I sho' is sorry 'count o' what done
happen. 'Course it's yo' nigger what you' ma give yo', and I

knows yo' feel awful bad 'bout it. Yes'um, I knows yo' does. I knowed somp'n awful goin' happen. Yes'um, I did, 'cause las' week I drempt I see 'taters growin' an' grapes hangin' on de vines. I knowed somp'n awful goin' happen 'cause o' de ol' sayin', Dream o' fruit outten season, sign o' trouble outten reason. I sho' is sorry fo' yo', Miss Mally, de Lawd bless yo.' "

Susie was going on, but Clayton wasn't listening; Fanny was crossing the room toward him, carrying a tray of drinks, and the look he threw her said plainly that if she had kept her mouth shut, none of this would have happened. Fanny quickly did an about-face and served the guests on the far side of the room.

CHAPTER 10

Lettie Billingsly returned to Cragfont in mid-May of 1860, only to lose her temper when she found that Bailey Peyton had gone to Kentucky in search of blooded horses with which to stock his father's breeding farm.

Lettie's temper was not the only one aroused that spring. Mr. Summers ranted and raved because after the Republican nomination went to Abraham Lincoln on May sixteenth, the Democratic Party had gone berserk and split itself into three factions: the Northern Democrats, who nominated Stephen A. Douglas of Illinois; the Southern party, which nominated John C. Breckenridge of Kentucky; and a third group, calling itself the Constitutional Union Party, which nominated Senator John Bell of Tennessee. This idiocy guaranteed that Lincoln would be a shoo-in, regardless of the fact that the American voters were against him nearly two to one.

Clayton grinned at the old man's tirade. "Well, Mr. Summers, there's one bright spot you've overlooked."

Mr. Summers scowled. "What's that?"

"For the first and probably the last time in the history of

this country, Southerners and Northerners are united; neither side wants Lincoln for President.

Mr. Summers pointed a finger at Clayton. "You can laugh if you want to, but South Carolina has publicly stated that if Lincoln gets elected, she's goin' to sever her connections with the United States."

Clayton shook his head; nobody believed that.

Lettie sat in the Cragfont parlor and seethed. If Bailey Peyton assumed that she would spend the summer in solitude, he was badly mistaken. Angrily she snatched up paper and pen and hastily scribbled a note.

Clayton leaned back in his office chair and again contemplated Lettie's curt invitation to Cragfont. Although he tried to tell himself that he really didn't care if he saw Lettie or not, he knew it was a lie: He longed to see her, and that was humiliating. Also, the thought of facing her brought on a nagging apprehension: Had Fanny told Lettie that he had seduced her? Fanny. In spite of himself, the thought of her stirred his blood; she had been wonderful that night. Clayton's face hardened. It'll never happen again, he vowed. He pushed the thoughts aside, praying that Fanny had not told Lettie, and concentrated on his ledgers.

Lettie paced her bedchamber like a caged tigress.

"I assume that Mr. Harris is still employed at Summerset?" Fanny, ironing Lettie's dresses that had been carelessly packed in her travel trunk, said, "Yes'm, Massa Summers done made him plantation manager."

"Well, manager or not, he could show enough respect to answer a lady's summons. It's been ten days!"

"Yes'm," Fanny said, leaning on her iron. She too, wished that Clayton would come. He had not set foot at Cragfont since New Year's, six months ago.

"Stop daydreaming, Fanny!" Lettie ran to the ironing board and snatched her dress from beneath the iron. Holding the garment up to the light of the window, she inspected it thoroughly. "If you have scorched this gown, Fanny, I'll have your lazy backside blistered."

Fanny moistened her finger with her tongue, then lightly touched the bottom of the iron. It was only lukewarm. "I ain't scorched yo' dress, Miss Lettie," she said. "No ma'am,

I ain't burnt it a'tall."

Lettie flung the dress onto the bed. "Fetch me Grand-mother's pen and ink. I'll write Mr. Harris another note . . . and when Fleming delivers it, have him wait for a reply. I should have thought of that in the first place."

Cotton glanced out of Clayton's office door. The Cragfont valet, Fleming, waited patiently beside his horse.

"You're goin' to have to tell Fleming somethin', Clay. He'll stand there waitin' for an answer 'til he turns to butter."

Clayton leaned back in his chair. "I don't know what to do about Lettie, Cotton. To tell the truth, I'm about halfway afraid to go over there . . ."

"You can't hide from her forever."

"I don't intend to. Not forever . . ."

"Hell, Clay." Cotton walked to the desk and picked up the note. "She even said 'please' call this time."

When Clayton made no reply, Cotton continued, "If'n Fanny had spilled the beans, Clay, you'd a-heard about it long before now. Hell, Fanny's no dunce. She knows when to keep her mouth shut."

She didn't before, thought Clayton. He stood up and walked to the door. "Fleming, tell Miss Lettie I'd be honored to call on her Saturday morning."

Susie met Clayton at the Cragfont gate. Taking his hand, she skipped beside him up the front walk.

"So much has happened, Clayton, since you was last here!" She laughed up at him. "For one thing, Dr. Mentlo brought Mama a new baby girl on April Fool's day. We just call her 'Babe.' Mama said she would let Babe pick her own name when she's three years old . . . like she did with me."

"I'll have to congratulate your mother and father," Clayton said.

"An' Dr. Mentlo too. He surely did pick us a pretty one. An' she don't hardly cry at all."

Fanny met them at the door. Her curtsey was a quick bob that did not require the removal of her eyes from his face for even an instant.

Clayton scowled at her. The happiness in her smile wavered, and she quickly looked away. "It's nice to see you 'gin, suh," she murmured. Clayton nodded coldly. Regardless of Cotton's reassuring words, Fanny had betrayed a confidence once, with catastrophic repercussions, and he could not help but wonder if she would do it a second time. "I'm here to see Miss Lettie," he said.

Fanny's heart twisted. If only he would say hello, she silently cried. If only he would not look at me so hatefully. "Yes, suh," she said. "Miss Lettie's in the parlor."

When Clayton and Susie entered the room, Lettie was standing by the harp absently strumming its chords. He paused to study her from the doorway.

Her hair hung loose in soft, golden ringlets, made all the richer by the deep-blue dress she wore. My God! he thought, she's more lovely than ever.

Crossing the room, he caught her outstretched hand and brought it to his lips. "You are breathtaking, Lettie," he murmured.

Fanny, standing in the doorway, fought to control sudden tears. My husband, Eli, was right, she thought. The only time Clayton ever told me I was beautiful was when he . . . Fanny closed her eyes, refusing to finish the thought.

"Time seems to have improved your manners, Mr. Harris," Lettie said, nearly forgetting how angry she had been at him for the past two weeks.

"Well, I declare, Lettie," Susie said, her hands on her hips. "You said just the day before yesterday that Clayton didn't have no manners at all 'cause he didn't come runnin' when you sent for him."

Lettie's face flamed, but her voice was undaunted. "You were a trifle tardy, Mr. Harris." She smiled at Clayton, thinking that he had changed during her absence. His face had thinned, was more mature, more handsome. And a new air of self-assurance was very apparent.

"You have my apologies, Lettie," he murmured. "But, as you well know, we parted on less than . . . a desirable note last November." He cut a quick glance at Fanny. "I wasn't sure of how I would be received."

Fanny stared at him.

"That horrid party was long ago," Lettie said, taking his arm and guiding him through the door. "Let's walk by the creek. I simply must hear of all that's happened while I was away."

With Fanny and Susie following, Clayton and Lettie picked their way down the bluff that overlooked Bledsoe's Creek. The path that skirted the stream was cooly shaded by tall sycamores, elms and beeches, and the soft June air was scented with the fragrance of wild mint.

They stopped in a small clearing covered with fern intermixed with bluebells and bloodroot. Lettie leaned back comfortably against the smooth trunk of a beech tree and gazed at Clayton. "I love this spot. It's like the enchanted forest in the storybooks."

Clayton silently agreed, thinking that she fit into the surroundings perfectly.

"Did you miss me, Clayton?"

Clayton frowned at her. "Have you forgotten the last time we were together, Lettie? I was not aware that I had the right to miss you."

"Don't be boring, Clayton," she said, bending to pluck a mayapple bloom, which she tucked into her hair.

"You didn't answer my question, Lettie."

Lettie arched her eyebrows at him. "It's really none of your business, Mr. Harris, but . . . Mr. Peyton will not be calling at Cragfont this summer."

A nearly inaudible sigh drew Clayton's attention to Fanny, who was staring at him with a look of . . . was it pity? She quickly turned away and knelt down beside Susie. Choosing a small, flat stone, she sent it skipping across the placid surface of Bledsoe's Creek.

Each time the stone kissed the water, sending out ever-widening ripples, Fanny whispered, "I love him, I love him not," until, finally, the stone sank.

"Who do you love, Fanny?" Susie asked.

Fanny swatted Susie's bottom. "I love you," she laughed, hugging the girl to her.

"So," Lettie said, taking Clayton's arm and strolling on down the path, "let's not talk of Mr. Peyton, nor of last fall. This is a new year, a new world. Everything is young and alive. We're young and alive!"

Susie left the creek and trotted after them. "You're not young, Lettie," she said. "You're sixteen. You're an old maid." Then, jeeringly, she cried, "Old maid, old maid, won't get married 'cause she's afraid."

"You are insufferable!" Lettie pointed up the bluff toward

the house. "Get out of my sight before I snatch a switch off one of these willows and wear you out with it."

"I don't have to!" Nevertheless, Susie turned and marched up the hill. "Come on, Fanny," she said as she passed the slave girl. "I'm goin to tell Granny on Lettie."

Fanny looked at Lettie. "Go on," Lettie said. "Take Susie back to the house. Mr. Harris and I will be along directly."

For a long moment Fanny didn't move. Then, curtseying to Lettie, she hurried up the hill after Susie.

"Fanny's getting too bold for her own good," Lettie said. "Why, I would have sworn she was about to disobey me." Then, grinning impishly, she leaned close and peered into Clayton's face. "Fanny has been watching you as though she has some kind of claim on you. You haven't been pestering the slave girls while I've been gone, have you, Mr. Harris?"

"Of course not," Clayton said too quickly. Then, more slowly, "I don't think we should be discussing such an indelicate subject, Lettie."

"Why, I do declare, Mr. Harris," she teased, "if I didn't know better, I would be inclined to think it was you and not Cotton who amused himself at Fanny's expense. Furthermore, we are adults; we should be mature enough to discuss certain matters privately . . . especially after what you attempted the last time I was with you."

Without a word, Clayton snatched her into his arms and lowered his lips to hers. For a split second, Lettie tensed, then she answered his demanding kiss with her own.

Up the hill, in the shadows of a tall elm, Fanny stood and watched them embrace. After a moment she took a deep breath to still the aching in the pit of her stomach, stepped into the open, and hastened noisily toward them.

Lettie heard her approach and instantly pushed Clayton away. "You were spying on us, Fanny," she said angrily when the girl reached them. "You slipped down here just so you could see what we were doing."

"No, Miss Lettie, honest I weren't," lied Fanny. "I's jist doin' what ol' Miss tolt me to do. She say fo' me to hurry back down here an' tell you-all to come on up to the house, 'cause it ain't proper fo' you to be a-walkin' by the creek without no chaperone. That's what ol' Miss say."

"I don't care what Granny said! You were still spying on us. You were hiding behind that . . . that tree."

Clayton fidgeted. "I don't think Fanny was watching us on purpose, Lettie."

"Oh, yes she was. You don't know these darkies, Clayton. They sneak around and watch every move a white person makes. Then they go to their cabins and talk about us, and laugh at us . . . and make voodoo."

"No, ma'am," Fanny protested. "I wouldn't do no such thing as that . . ."

"Horsefeathers!" Lettie cried. "And if you mention one word of . . . of what you just saw, I will see to it that you are buggy-whipped, Fanny."

"Oh, no, Miss Lettie. I didn't see nuthin'. Honest, I never."

Clayton said, "Lettie, the girl meant no—" but Lettie was going on.

"You'd best heed my warning, Fanny. Or, so help me, your back will look like a washboard." Taking Clayton's arm, Lettie strode up the incline that led to the house.

Fanny followed. But upon reaching the house, she immediately raced to the kitchen, where Chatty was roasting coffee beans on a tin in the fireplace.

"Don' bodder me, chile," the old woman warned. "If'n I burn one of dese here beans, Massa George will stripe my bucket."

Fanny walked to a three-legged stool and straddled it, cupping her chin in her hands.

"What fo' is the matter wid yo'?" Chatty asked a minute later. "You looks plumb down in de mouth."

"I's got sumpthin' I wants you to do."

"Sumpin' magic?"

Fanny nodded.

"I ain' gonna grow no balls on Patrick," said the old slave, wagging her head from side to side. "Yo' the one what got 'em cut off, yo' the one what gwine to have to do wid out his pesterin'."

"I don't want you to grow no balls on Patrick," said Fanny. Then she shrugged. "Well, I maybe do want you to grow one ball on Patrick, 'cause I feel real bad about what done happened to him. But that ain't why I's here."

"Well den, spit it out. What fo' are yo' a-wantin'?"

"I's wantin' yo' to . . . to put a big canker on mean old Miss Lettie's mouth."

Angrily, the girl told the old woman of what she had seen by the creek, and of the threats that Lettie had made.

Chatty's aged face narrowed in thought. "Dat girl don' like yo' none, an' dat a fact. An' she mean what she say about havin' yo' whipped. Maybe it be time I done brung her down a rung o' two. Yes'm, I believe I'll gib her sumpin' else to worry her po' head 'bout fo' a while."

"Make it a big, runny ol' canker. Put one on her top lip too."

"Yo' goin' t' make me burn dese beans. Now you git on out'n here an' let me think."

As Fanny flounced toward the door, Chatty's voice halted her. "Yo' fetch me a toad frog . . . an' some slimy, green stump water . . . an' a spoonful o' blood from a wench who be endin' her moon. An' bring me a dab o' Lettie's lip rouge."

Fanny hurried out through the door, the rhythm of her heart in time with the old woman's chanting cackle.

Lettie was miserable. A terrible cold sore had mysteriously appeared at the corner of her lower lip ten days ago. She had barricaded herself in her bedchamber and refused to see anyone, but the sore showed no signs of diminishing.

During the second week of Lettie's seclusion, Clayton sent Rufus to Cragfont to see if Lettie were receiving guests. Rufus was lounging on the wooden bench by the kitchen door, awaiting Lettie's answer, when Fanny stepped out, carrying a skillet and pitcher.

"I's sorry, Rufus," she said, "but yo' goin' to have to tell Massa Clayton that Miss Lettie ain't r'ceivin' guests." The girl smiled at him. "Howsoever, I did bring you some cornbread an' buttermilk 'cause you look hungry . . . an' it be a long walk to Summerset." She took a wooden bowl and spoon from her apron pocket and handed them to him.

Rufus took a wedge of cornbread from the skillet and crumbled it into the bowl. "When do you suppose Miss Lettie will be well?"

"Oh, it'll be 'nother week o' two fo' she'll r'ceive callers." Fanny poured milk into the bowl. Then casually she asked, "How's folks at Summerset?"

"Doin' fine." Rufus spooned bread and milk into his

mouth. "We got the fields planted. Why, Cotton even had us whitewash the slave house. Looks real pretty, too."

Fanny bit her lip; she wanted to hear about Clayton. "Rufus, you sho' nuff do talk fine," she said, pouring more milk into the bowl.

Rufus grinned. "Masta Clayton been teachin' me at night. He says I am highly intelligent. Why, I can already read an' write an' do a little 'rithmetic. Masta Clayton keeps me with him all the time. He says I'll learn from the 'power of association'."

"What in th' world is dat?"

"That means a body can learn a heap by just watchin' an' listenin'."

Fanny pursed her lips. "Yo' reckon I could do dat with Miss Lettie? Yo' reckon I could learn to be just like her?"

Rufus laughed. "You already walk just like her, a-swayin' your hips the same way she does."

"I mean, you reckon I could learn to be a real lady like she be?"

Rufus frowned. "Naw, Fanny. No matter how smart I learn to be, I ain't never goin' to be no gentleman. We's slaves. Ain't no schoolin' goin' to change that. Ain't nothin' goin' to change that." He looked at her appraisingly. "Niggers at Summerset say yo' already act too 'lady.' Say you're too uppity for your own good."

"I jist tries to be like Miss Lettie," Fanny said.

Rufus spooned more mush into his mouth. "Why you want to be like Miss Lettie? Mista Cotton shore don't like her none. He says she's stuck up higher'n a church steeple."

"Cotton don't know nothin' nohow! Why, he ain't nothin' but an oberseer. But Massa Clayton, he be a real gentleman, an' he sho' nuff likes Miss Lettie."

"Yep, he does. He told Mista Cotton that he believes he done fell in love with her."

Fanny's hand tightened on the handle of the pitcher.

"'Course," Rufus continued, "Mista Cotton told Masta Clayton that was a crock o' shit. He said Miss Lettie was just stringin' Masta Clayton along. He say Miss Lettie is goin' to marry Masta Peyton, 'cause he's rich and powerful."

"Cotton might not be so dumb as I thought," Fanny said, "'cause he's right. Massa Clayton be blind as a bat where Miss Lettie's concerned."

"Well, it's none of your business," Rufus said. "What he does ain't nobody's business but his'n."

The minute Rufus left, Fanny went to find Chatty in the quarters. Upon hearing Fanny's plea, the old slave chased the girl from her house.

"Very idea," mumbled Chatty, returning to her herbs gathered that morning. "Dat girl a-wantin' me a-voodooin' Miss Lettie into lettin' young Marse Peyton knock her up when he gits back off'n his trip. Very idea!" Then, showing a thin smile, she muttered, "Voodoo ain't necessary . . . ain't necessary a'tall."

The moment that Lettie's lip mended, Clayton was summoned to Cragfont.

When he arrived, he found Lettie walking in the garden.

"Oh, it feels good to be out of the house," she said, removing her straw bonnet and tilting her face toward the sky. "Doesn't the sun feel marvelous, Mr. Harris?"

Clayton caught her hand and brought it to his lips. "I thought ladies never allowed the sun to touch their skin."

"A touch of sun feels wonderful. But it is true that a sun-browned skin is the mark of a low-bred white woman, one who has worked out of doors . . . a field hand."

Or a slave, Clayton added to himself. "How are you feeling?" he asked.

Lettie patted her bonnet into place and tied the ribbon beneath her chin. "I'm fine. Please don't be a cad and ask what was ailing me."

"I wouldn't think of doing such a thing," he lied.

Lettie flashed him her most alluring smile. "I want you to escort me to Gallatin this coming Saturday. It's the day of the county fair . . . and I adore the horse races. Do you like racing, Mr. Harris?"

"I've never been to a race."

Lettie took his arm and led him toward the lake. "Well, I'm positively certain that you will find it exhilarating."

Her touch set Clayton's pulse to hammering. Quickly he glanced at the big house to see if old Mrs. Winchester were watching from the balcony. She wasn't. Drawing Lettie to him, he bent his head to hers. At the last moment she turned her face aside and spun from his arms. "You didn't answer my question, Mr. Harris. Will you escort me to the fair?"

"I wasn't aware that was a question, Lettie," he said dryly.

"Of course it was, silly. No self-respectin' lady would *order* a gentleman to escort her to a social function, Mr. Harris."

"In that case, I would be honored by your company, Miss Lettie." He drew her to him and kissed her soundly. She didn't resist.

Rufus, with Fanny and Susie perched beside him on the driver's seat and Clayton and Lettie in the back, drove Mr. Summers' scrubbed and polished phaeton up the fairgrounds drive.

Scores of buggies and saddle horses were tied to every available tree or bush, their grooms squatting in the shade awaiting the owners.

"Look!" Susie cried, pointing to a boy a year or two older than she who was walking down the road toward them. "It's Opie Reed." Standing up in the chaise, she waved at him.

Opie's pudgy face broke into a smile. "Y'all goin' to the fair?" he yelled as they drove past.

"Yes," shouted Susie, bouncing up and down. "I want to see the sheep, an' the chickens, an' the hogs."

Opie nodded. "Be sure to see them prize oxen of ol' man Bate, too."

"I will, I will." But they had rounded a curve and Susie wasn't certain that Opie had heard.

"You see all those things at home, Susie," Lettie said. "I would think you would want to see the thoroughbreds."

"The only reason you want to see the races," Susie said, "is 'cause Bailey Peyton is off buyin' horses for his father's farm."

Clayton whipped around, his eyes searching Lettie's face. "Is that true, Lettie? Is that the reason Peyton won't be calling at Cragfont this summer? Because he's out of town?"

Fanny cocked her head a hairbreadth to the rear.

Lettie blushed deeply. "That's one reason. But the main reason is because he and I had a . . . a misunderstanding on the night of the ball after you left. We agreed that perhaps it would be better if we didn't see each other for a while." Lettie took Clayton's hand and smiled disarmingly at him. "The arrangement was my idea, Mr. Harris, because I wanted to spend the summer with you."

That's a lie! Fanny screamed silently. You never even knew Massa Peyton was gone away 'til you got back from New Orleans. Oh, Massa Clayton, don't you believe nuthin' she says.

"But if you don't believe me," Lettie went on, raising her chin as though she had heard Fanny's thoughts, "you can turn this buggy around and carry me right back to Cragfont."

Susie broke the tense moment by quickly moving away from Fanny. "Have you got to go to the privy?" she cried. "The way you're a-moanin' under your breath an' a-twitchin' on the seat—"

"Yes'm," Fanny said, turning to Lettie. "I's got to go awful bad."

"Stop the carriage, Rufus," Lettie commanded. "You may use those bushes, Fanny." She pointed to a thick stand of cane and honeysuckle growing in a ditch near the roadside.

Fanny climbed from the phaeton and hurried behind the cane. Screened from view, her hands balled into fists, she kicked angrily at a clod of dirt with her bare toes. "He's a fool," she whispered, snatching aside some cane and peering out at the carriage. She frowned. Rufus was turning the vehicle around.

Catching up her long skirt, Fanny hastened around the bush and ran back to the phaeton.

"Clayton is takin' us home," muttered Susie sourly as Fanny climbed aboard. "He don't believe what Lettie said about Bailey Peyton. I wanted to see the pigs, an' mules, an' chickens, an' Mr. Bate's oxen."

Fanny threw a sidelong glance at Lettie and Clayton. Lettie was sitting ramrod-straight, her chin high and defiant. Clayton was slouched in his seat, staring at nothing.

As the chaise picked up speed, Fanny settled herself comfortably into the upholstery. "We'll go to the barn lot when we gets to Cragfont," she told Susie. "I believe I knows where an' ol' settin' hen done hid her nest, an' it wouldn't s'prise me none if dem chicks ain't done hatched."

When two weeks had gone by and Lettie had not seen or heard from Clayton, her confidence began to waver. When a third week slipped into oblivion, she nearly panicked.

"Fanny," she said, pacing her bedchamber, "have Fleming saddle a horse for me . . . and one for you. We are going calling."

"Why, Miss Lettie," Fanny gasped, "you know I don' know how to ride no horse!"

"Well, then you will learn. Now do as I say. But first lay out my green riding habit."

It was a queer sight that met Clayton as he walked from his office to the main house that afternoon. Stopping, he shaded his eyes from the July sun and stared at Lettie, riding sidesaddle, and then at Fanny, trailing along behind on a Percheron plow horse, riding not only bareback, but astride. Her long legs were bare to the thigh. He dropped his eyes hurriedly.

Lettie lifted her horse into a canter and rode toward Clayton, leaving Fanny in the stifling dust kicked up by her mistress' horse's hooves.

Lettie reined in beside Clayton, enjoying the fact that he was forced to look up at her. "We're going riding," she said. "I wondered if you would care to join us."

Clayton shifted his gaze to Fanny, who had stopped some yards away and slipped to the ground to lean wearily against her horse.

"Fanny doesn't appear to be up to a ride."

Lettie glared at him. "Mr. Harris, I rode over here to . . . to . . . you are making it very difficult, sir."

Clayton tilted his head back and appraised her. "Why don't you just try being honest, Lettie?"

"Very well. I rode over here to make amends. I would like for you to come calling again."

"What about Bailey Peyton?"

Lettie stiffened in the saddle. "Mr. Peyton is in Kentucky. I have no idea when he will return, and at the moment, sir, I don' really—"

"Well! well!" Mr. Summers cried happily as he descended the porch steps two at a time. Over his shoulder he called, "Mrs. Summers, come out here an' see who's come a-visitin'. Get down, Lettie, an' come in out of the sun." He reached up to give her a hand.

Lettie slipped her knee over the horn and, with Mr. Summers' assistance, dropped lightly to the ground.

"Thank you, Uncle Jonathan," she said, smiling wickedly at Clayton. "Some people have no manners . . . no manners at all."

"Lettie," Mrs. Summers called from the porch, "come in, child. Lord, you haven't been to see us in I don't know when."

"It's been a coon's age, sure 'nough," agreed Mr. Summers, escorting Lettie up the steps.

Leading Lettie's horse, Clayton walked over to Fanny, who was still leaning against her mount. "You're an awful little girl to be holding up that big heavy horse, Fanny."

Fanny smiled sickly, even though her heart fluttered from his nearness. "This be the first time I ever rode a horse, Massa Clayton. I's scared plumb silly . . . an' my backside done been rubbed raw."

Laughing, Clayton said, "I'll take these horses to the barn and see that they're fed and watered."

"I'll do it, Massa Clayton," Fanny said, wishing he would laugh again. From under her lashes, she glanced toward the house. "I believe Miss Lettie be a-waitin' fo' you on the porch."

Clayton turned. Mrs. Summers was hugging Lettie and exclaiming over how wonderful the girl looked. And although Lettie was laughing and returning the old lady's embrace, her eyes kept sliding to Clayton and Fanny.

Handing Fanny the reins, Clayton struck off in a fast walk toward the house; indeed, Lettie did look wonderful.

Clayton and Mr. Summers followed the women into the parlor, where Lettie and Mrs. Summers seated themselves on the sofa. Trillie appeared carrying a tray with four tall glasses of lemonade.

Clayton accepted a glass and sat down in the wing chair across from Lettie.

"Lettie rode over to inquire if you would escort her to church on Sunday," Mrs. Summers said to Clayton. "I told her you would be honored."

"Well, I . . ." Clayton's eyes narrowed at Lettie. "Actually, Cotton and I have plans to go fishing."

"Nonsense," the old lady said. "You can fish after church."

"Really, Aunt Helen," said Lettie coldly, "I wouldn't want to impose on Mr. Harris. In fact, if you'll have my horse brought around, I must be getting back to Cragfont."

"Clayton an' I will get your animal," said Mr. Summers, indicating that Clayton join him.

As they walked toward the barn, the old man said, "You embarrassed that girl, Clayton. Why?"

"I've got my reasons, Mr. Summers."

The old man studied Clayton out of the corner of his eye, wondering what had come over the boy. "They'd best be derned good reasons, Clayton, because a gentleman don't embarrass a lady . . . it just ain't done."

"She lied to me about being engaged to Bailey Peyton, Mr. Summers."

"So?"

"I don't like being lied to."

The two men walked on in silence. At the barn door, Mr. Summers stopped. "Lettie Billingsly ain't no fool, Clayton. She ain't about to give up Bailey Peyton for you. Leastways not 'til she has a chance to see what you're made of."

"Well, I'm not made of green hickory, Mr. Summers. Not if it means bowing down to a woman no matter how bad she treats you."

Mr. Summers smiled at that.

"Old Andy Jackson was made of seasoned hickory," he said. "Why, he'd cane a man quicker'n he'd spit. But when it came to Rachel Donelson, he'd a-kissed her ass in public if she'd asked him to."

"I'm not Andrew Jackson, Mr. Summers."

"No, an' sometimes you ain't half bright."

Clayton started into the barn, but Mr. Summers laid a restraining hand on his shoulder. "Answer me somethin', Clayton, an' answer me truthful." Clayton turned and pierced Mr. Summers with a hard gaze. "Do you want to court Lettie Billingsly or not?"

Clayton paused for a moment, then said, "Of course I do, sir, but—"

Pushing Clayton ahead of him into the barn, the old man said, "But you don't want to call on her 'cause she fibbed about Bailey Peyton."

Clayton nodded.

"Well then," Mr. Summers said, catching up the reins to Lettie's horse, "enlighten me on somethin' that has me puzzled. How in the world are you goin' to beat Bailey's time if you don't call on her?"

Clayton escorted Lettie and Fanny back to Cragfont. And on Sunday he sat in the Winchester church pew. And on Wednesday he rode with Lettie and two dozen other young people to the bay of the hounds as they chased the fox in a five-mile run. He and Lettie attended prayer meetings and church socials; they even danced at the "Fiddlers' Carnival" in Gallatin.

He escorted her to a basket supper, given by the church to raise funds for a new church bell, where the minister auctioned off covered baskets to the highest bidder; the lucky winner was privileged to share the basket with the lady who prepared it.

It appeared that all of the young men knew when Lettie's basket went on the block, for Clayton was forced to bid an astounding twenty dollars for the honor of dining with her.

Indeed, it was a whirlwind summer of gaiety and laughter.

Beneath Sumner County's euphoric surface, however, the controversy concerning Lincoln's nomination had erupted into such a heated debate that for the first time in the history of the State of Tennessee, congressmen and senators were carrying guns to their meetings. Added to that, longtime friends were quarreling at dinner parties, and next-door neighbors were snubbing one another on the streets.

And on a broader scale, the same behavior in Washington, D. C., was fast bringing the Federal Government to a point of paralysis.

CHAPTER 11

On November 1, 1860, Mr. Summers sat across the kitchen table from Clayton and Cotton sipping a cup of black coffee. "I guess you boys wonder why I called this meeting."

Clayton settled his elbows on the table and waited; Mr. Summers never called them in unless it was important.

The old man appraised the two openly. "I want to know what you-all think about the mess this here United States has gone an' got itself into."

Clayton took a sip from his cup. "I don't believe the Southern states will secede. I think the threat is meant only to force the North to take a long look at the consequences should the Federal Government continue to abuse the Constitution by disregarding the rights of the individual states."

"Bullshit," Cotton said.

Mr. Summers' face clouded. "Cotton, I'll have none of your cussin' at my table, none a'tall."

"I'm sorry about the cussin', Mr. Summers. But I think the South will secede. And it'll go to war again the Yankees if it comes down to it. Clayton is foolin' hisself. Hell, most of the young fellas around here is chompin' at the bit to fight the sons-of-bitches—"

"Dern it, Cotton!" Mr. Summers shouted. "I told you to quit cussin' at my table!"

"Sorry, sir."

The old man nodded his acceptance of the apology, then said, "Southern men are fighters. But, like Clayton, I don't believe the South will secede. Most of us, the old folks, worked too hard to build this country into a union to want to see it divided. But if Lincoln's elected—"

"He's going to be elected, Mr. Summers," Clayton said. "The Southern Democrats killed themselves when they split the party. Breckenridge and Bell have got to beat a hundred percent of the Republican vote, while Lincoln has to beat only a third of the Democrats'. The South guaranteed Lincoln the Presidency, sir."

Cotton looked at Clayton with something akin to awe. Although he had learned a great deal over the past months of evening tutoring, he wondered if he would ever learn enough to follow his friend's conversation.

"That's true," Mr. Summers sighed. "But like most Southerners, I won't admit defeat until the last vote is counted."

On November 6, 1860, even though more Americans voted against Lincoln than for him—1,865,593 for, 2,823,975 against—Abraham Lincoln became the sixteenth President of the United States, and the entire world held its breath waiting to see what would happen next.

It wasn't long in coming. On December 20, 1860, South Carolina passed an Ordinance of Secession, declaring itself independent of the United States of America. Mississippi, Florida, Alabama, Georgia, Louisiana, and Texas immediately followed suit, organizing themselves into the Confederate States of America, with Jefferson Davis as President.

Virginia, Arkansas, and North Carolina elected to remain in the Union. Tennessee, however, decided to hold a statewide referendum on February 9, 1861, to determine whether a convention should be held on the question of secession.

Mr. Summers quickly wrote to every prominent family in Sumner County inviting them to a Christmas open house at Summerset on December twenty-third.

To Lettie's disappointment, the Summerset party was

more a political gathering than it was a social event. And she fumed at Clayton, accusing him of being more interested in the boring conversation of the menfolk than he was in her.

"All the talk," she complained, "is about secession, secession, secession. I'm sick of it."

"Do you want Tennessee to secede, Lettie?"

"I don't care what Tennessee does," she retorted. "I just want things to get back to normal."

"So does Mr. Summers, Lettie. That's the reason for this party . . . to try to see to it that Sumner County votes not to secede."

"If you had told me that beforehand," she snapped, "I would have stayed at Cragfont."

After the last guest had left, Mr. Summers poured Clayton and himself stiff shots of whiskey. "What do you think, Clayton? Did I accomplish anything?"

Clayton smiled at the old man. "Well, you made Lettie mad."

Mr. Summers laughed softly. "Her an' all the other women, includin' Mrs. Summers. But I'd rather have 'em mad now than sorry later."

Mr. Summers' ploy didn't work: Six weeks later, on February 9, 1861, although the State of Tennessee voted unanimously to reject the convention and stay in the Union, Sumner County voted 1,535 in favor of secession, 770 against.

And on March 23, 1861, an event took place that stirred the Sumner County populace to such fury that it clamored even more loudly for secession: Just outside Gallatin, slaveholder William C. Moore was murdered by one of his field hands.

On that same day, Clayton drove the Cragfont buggy down a little-used lane that skirted the north bank of the Cumberland on the far side of Summerset.

"I just love the month of March," declared Lettie, drinking in the crisp, clean air. "Winter's over for good and spring's just around the corner. Oh, it's so warm and lovely."

Clayton agreed. It was unseasonably warm, even for March.

"That looks like a fine spot fo' a picnic," Fanny said,

pointing to a big oak tree whose newly leafed-out branches swooped nearly to the ground.

"Yes," cried Lettie, "let's do stop there, Clayton. Spread the cloth in the sun, Fanny."

Fanny had just spread the quilt and opened a basket of fried chicken when the excited baying of hounds came into hearing.

"Someone must be riding to the fox," Lettie commented, settling herself leisurely upon the quilt while Fanny filled china plates with delicacies and poured sweetened tea into crystal goblets.

"I hadn't heard that a fox hunt was planned," said Clayton, seating himself next to Lettie.

"Them ain't foxhounds," Fanny murmured, gazing toward the sound of the dogs.

"If they're not foxhounds," Lettie demanded, glaring at Fanny for contradicting her, "then what are they?"

Fanny's face was ashen, and her hands trembled as she handed Lettie and Clayton their tea, but it was the stricken look in the girl's eyes that caused Clayton to jump to his feet and demand to know what was wrong.

"They be bloodhoun's, Mista Clayton," Fanny said quietly. "An' you know well as me what dat means."

Lettie rose and put a shaking hand on Clayton's arm, for the baying hounds were drawing nearer.

A movement near the buggy caught Clayton's eye. A young black man had sprung onto the buggy seat and was whipping the horse into motion.

Clayton lunged headlong toward the team. Catching the horse's headstall, he threw himself against its chest, causing it to miss its stride, which brought it up sharply against the breeching and traces.

The horse reared, flinging Clayton into the air. The buggy raised on two wheels, then toppled over onto its side.

The slave rolled free and was up in an instant, sprinting to the floundering horse. Using a bloodstained corn knife, he began hacking at the harness to free the animal. He had nearly succeeded when Clayton caught him with a hard right fist to the temple that dropped the slave to his knees.

The blow should have rendered the man unconscious, but he lunged erect and drove himself at Clayton with desperation. Clayton caught the slave's wrist and tried to wrest the knife from him. The dogs' baying sounded no more than two hundred yards away.

Lettie stood as though rooted to the earth, terrified. Fanny, on the other hand, was anything but intimidated. Even though she longed for the slave to escape, she loved Clayton Harris and would not see him maimed or killed to serve that purpose. With a cry, she flung herself on the slave's back, scratching her nails and raking her teeth across his flesh.

Locked together like two bull mastiffs, the men struggled over the uneven ground, Clayton trying desperately to gain possession of the knife, the slave trying just as hard to wrench it free.

All the while, Fanny continued to pummel the slave's back with her fists until, with a bellow of rage, he caught her by the nape of the neck and flung her headlong into the trunk of the giant oak tree.

Fanny slumped down among the gnarled tree roots and lay there unmoving.

Clayton's eyes flicked to the girl and searched for signs of life. He saw none. Although his concentration was broken for only an instant, it was enough. The slave hit him a blow that sent him reeling, then followed with a kick to the groin that dropped Clayton to his knees.

The Negro twisted his fist in Clayton's hair and snapped his head back, exposing his throat to the blade.

Above the dull ringing in his ears, Clayton could hear the distant screaming of a woman; almost as in a reverie, he was saddened by the thought that Lettie would witness such an undignified death. His death.

It took Clayton nearly a full minute to realize that the roaring in his ears was not the sound of his life escaping through a slit throat. When he forced open his tightly clenched eyes, he almost cried out with relief; Cotton, with pistol in hand, was swinging down from his horse.

"I told you to drop the knife," Cotton shouted, recocking the revolver and aiming it between the slave's eyes, "or I'm goin' to shoot you dead as a mackerel."

The black man's militant eyes moved from Cotton to the cocked pistol. There was no trace of fear. With a shrug, he let the knife clatter to the ground.

"Clayton," said Cotton, his revolver unwavering as he

edged around the slave to give Clayton a hand up, "Mr. Summers has told you time an' again to never go nowhere without a pistol. Damn it, man, don't you never pay attention to nuthin' nobody says?"

Without answering, Clayton walked to Lettie and took the nearly hysterical girl in his arms.

Fanny regained her senses. Using the tree for support, she painfully worked her way to her feet. Blood trickled from her nose onto her blouse, and her chin looked as though the top layer of skin had been ripped away. But she felt none of that as she watched Clayton console Lettie, for the pain in her heart made her physical hurts seem trifling.

The bloodhounds burst through the underbrush and raced toward the slave, barking and baying. He quickly scrambled to the top of the overturned buggy and kicked at the dogs as they sprang toward him. Moments later, forty men galloped up.

Bailey Peyton swung down from the saddle, his gaze roving from the picnic blanket to the overturned buggy, and finally to Lettie. With a wail, Lettie broke free of Clayton and rushed to Peyton.

"Oh, Bailey," she cried, throwing herself into his arms and kissing his lips. "It was horrible, just horrible. We were going to picnic, but that runaway tried to steal our buggy . . ."

Peyton tightened his embrace. "The man's not a runaway, Lettie. He's a murderer."

Clayton caught Bailey Peyton's shoulder and spun him around. "What are you talking about, Peyton? Who's been murdered?"

"You're lucky to be alive, Harris. That man just cut old man Moore's throat."

Lettie was aghast. She knew Mr. Moore to be a kind and gentle man who never mistreated his slaves. "Why?" she cried. "Why would he do such a horrible thing?"

Peyton shrugged. "Who knows what goes on inside a nigger's head?" He eyed Clayton. "Or for that matter, a white man's either."

"You can talk plainer than that, Peyton," Clayton said. "Why don't you say what you mean?"

"I want to know what you're doin' out here with my fiancée, Harris."

"Picnicking." Clayton answered, stepping toward Peyton. "Furthermore, she isn't your fiancée."

Lettie rushed between the two men. "Stop it, Clayton," she said. "You know I'm promised to Bailey. You've known it from the beginning."

Incredulity and disbelief whipped across Clayton's face.

Fanny, watching from where she leaned against the tree, was sure that she would be sick to her stomach, for it was plain that Clayton was as hopelessly entangled in Lettie's web as she herself was in Clayton's.

Bailey Peyton pushed Lettie toward his horse. "Get your things together. As soon as we finish up here, I'll see you home."

"No," Clayton said, "it doesn't work like that, Peyton. Lettie came with me and she'll leave with me."

Bailey Peyton began unbuttoning his coat. "Harris, I should have whipped you at Cragfont that night. Well, I sure aim to do it now."

"Fine," Clayton said, following Peyton's lead and taking off his coat.

The sheriff rode up. "What do you two think you're doin'?"

"This is personal, Sheriff," said Peyton.

The sheriff leaned from the saddle and spit a stream of tobacco juice on the ground. "Not now it ain't. We got a murderer to dispose of. So whatever it is you got in mind can wait. You hear me?" When Peyton didn't answer, he said, "We owe Mr. Harris a debt. If that darky had got away with that buggy, we never would have caught him."

When Cotton was certain that the sheriff had indeed postponed the confrontation between Clayton and Bailey Peyton, he walked to the tree where Fanny stood.

"I saw what you was a-tryin' to do when I rode up, Fanny," he said, grinning widely. "An' I want you to know that that was about the dumbest damn thing you ever did in your whole life. Don't you know better'n to attack a tree with your chin? Normal folks don't use nothin' less'n a double-bitted ax."

Fanny lay her head on his shoulder. "I thought it were a cottonwood, Massa," she murmured. "But it were a damned ol' oak."

Cotton laughed, then sobered. "Why'd you take a chance

like that, Fanny? An' don't talk none of that African crap to
me, 'cause I know that under that dumb act, there's a
mighty smart girl."

Fanny raised her lips to his cheek; it was a thank-you kiss
that left a red streak on his skin that was not lip rouge.

"I did it fo' the same reasons yo' took the blame fo' what
Patrick done. I love Mista Clayton too, Cotton. An' as fo'
talkin' African crap? You an' me act exactly the way white
folk 'spect us to."

The posse members dragged the slave down from the
buggy and then lent their shoulders to the vehicle in an
effort to set it back on its wheels.

"Roll the buggy over to that oak tree," said a man
guarding the prisoner. "And somebody bring a rope."

The sheriff took a coil of rope from his saddlebags and
began fashioning a noose. Two other men caught the buggy
horse by its headstall and led the skittish animal toward the
tree where Fanny stood.

"Hold it right there," Clayton commanded, stalking over
to the horse and catching its bridle. "You're not intending to
use this buggy as a scaffold, are you?"

"Well, that's what we was figurin' on doin'," the sheriff
said. "He killed old Mr. Moore in cold blood. Near cut his
head off."

"You're not going to hang the man without a fair trial,"
Clayton said, "and that's final."

"Mr. Harris," the sheriff said, "you are beginning to try
my patience. This man had his trial the moment he picked
up that corn knife." The sheriff nodded for the men to
proceed.

"Listen to me, Sheriff," Clayton said, following him as he
walked toward the tree. "Let a judge and jury convict that
slave according to due process of the law. Lynching is
nothing but murder."

The sheriff stopped, and Clayton was sure he saw indecision on the man's face. A moment later, however, the
question was answered forever. The captured slave cried,
"Ole Marse Moore was a-goin' to cart us niggers to Alabama 'cause Tennessee didn't secede. I done told him I
weren't a-goin' to no Alabama. I told him Marse President
Lincoln done say it was wrong fo' white folks to own us

slaves. I done told him I wanted to be free! Yo' hear me?" He stared belligerently at the men. "Us slaves wants to be free, an' if we has to kill all of you-all, we's goin' to be free—jist like Marse Lincoln say."

An angry roar erupted from the mob. Clayton jumped in front of the men as they dragged the slave toward the tree.

Raising his hands, he shouted, "Don't do this . . ."

Someone snatched a pistol from a coat pocket and clubbed Clayton to the ground. Stepping over him, the men forced the kicking, bucking slave up onto the buggy seat.

But even then, as they placed the noose over his head and drew it tight around his neck, his cries of "We's goin' to be free!" rose above the din and seemed to hang there, suspended in time as they echoed up and down the peaceful Cumberland Valley.

The buggy ride back to Cragfont was anticlimactic; Bailey Peyton had ridden off with the posse, Cotton had gone back to the fields, and Clayton, Lettie, and Fanny sat immersed in their private thoughts.

Fanny was seeing again the execution of the slave. She had not known that hanged men often formed an erection, and even ejaculated as they strangled to death. This hanging had been a revolting spectacle, made all the more sickening because the man's thin cotton breeches did little to hide his final indignity.

Fanny's mouth drew into an angry line. She didn't know who she hated the most: the men who coldly and methodically disposed of a human being with no more thought than they would give to a wild animal; or herself, for experiencing not compassion, not pity, but an overwhelming sense of shame for her race. She was certain that had the hanged man been white, he would have died with pride and self-respect.

Then she remembered his final words: "We's goin' to be free! Free! Do yo' hear me? Free!" Her anger abated. The slave had not begged for his life. She could be proud of that. Perhaps he had died with dignity after all.

Lettie sat slumped in her seat, her chin resting on her chest; she was still trembling. She blamed Clayton Harris for having chosen that particular place for a picnic. What a nightmare the day had become. She shuddered. Oh, God, never in my life do I want to witness another hanging!

Lettie longed to return to Cragfont and forget the event ever happened, but that was an impossibility. She knew she would take the memory to her grave. Pushing the incident to the farthest recesses of her mind, she thought of Bailey Peyton. Surprisingly, she was sincerely glad that he was back.

Clayton's head was splitting, and each time the buggy wheels hit a rut, he felt as though his skull was coming apart.

Although he tried not to think about the lynching—nothing could change that now—he could not put it from his mind. Nor could he forget Fanny's bravery . . . and Lettie's lack of it. Glancing at the slave girl, he knew a moment of resentment because it was she, not Lettie, who had placed herself in danger on his behalf.

He refused to look at Lettie. She had toyed with his affections for nearly a year, and he had been too blind to see it. Clayton shook his head; Cotton had tried to tell him months ago that Lettie was in love with Bailey Peyton.

And Cotton had also tried to tell him something when he had helped him into the buggy. "Law an' order work fine in Ohio, Clayton, but they ain't worth a hoot in hell on a riverbank in Tennessee. Damn it, Clay, you'd better get it through your thick skull that this here United States is *not* one big country! Hell, man, the North an' the South are as different from one another as night and day. An' the fact that the good Lord saw fit to have 'em geographically attached don't do nuthin' but muddy the water."

Was Cotton right this time too?

On March 24, 1861, *The Gallatin Courier*, a newspaper that had been strongly opposed to secession, published an editorial about the murder of William C. Moore and the lynching of his murderer: "Opposed as we are to everything in the shape of a mob, we are yet inclined to think that the courts of the county should not be troubled with such cases as this. They [the murderers] deserve a summary disposal."

Clayton wadded the newspaper into a ball and threw it into the fireplace. Men did not have the right to take the law into their own hands. And it was beyond his comprehension that the Southern judicial system—and the newspapers—

openly applauded, even advocated, such actions by its citizens.

Clayton was not only outraged, he was saddened, for as much as he was growing to like the South, he knew that he could never accept its eye-for-an-eye attitude. And that knowledge left him feeling as much an outsider as he had on the first day of his arrival in Sumner County.

On April 12, 1861, the question of secession was settled once and for all: Union-occupied Fort Sumter, in the Charleston, South Carolina, harbor, was fired upon by the newly formed Confederate Army, General P. G. T. Beauregard commanding. The next day Fort Sumter surrendered.

The Sumner County populace was jubilant, and Beauregard was a hero.

And then the new President, Abraham Lincoln, foolishly misjudged Tennessee's deep-seated Southern spirit. He demanded that the state put 75,000 men in the field against the Confederacy.

One result of Lincoln's mistake was that at the Gallatin courthouse on April 18, 1861, with hundreds of Sumner County citizens looking on, the American flag was dragged down the pole and the Confederate Stars and Bars, which had a circle of seven stars on a field of blue and three wide red and white stripes, was raised.

Susie Winchester, standing with Lettie, Bailey Peyton, and her young friend, Opie Reed, tugged the brim of her bonnet lower to shield her eyes from the morning sun and said, "That flag isn't near as pretty as the ole one."

"Naw," agreed Opie Reed. "The stripes are too broad."

Whether the flag was ugly or not, a reporter with *The Nashville Daily Gazette* watched the banner pop and flutter in the breeze and then scribbled on his pad: "The flag was hailed with a great demonstration of joy and cheers for the South."

In the midst of the crowd, Mr. Summers turned to Clayton and said bitterly, "I don't think I ever really believed it would come to this."

CHAPTER 12

On April 25, 1861, a second extra session of the Tennessee legislature convened in Nashville. And on May sixth, it adopted "a Declaration of Independence . . . dissolving the Federal relations between the State of Tennessee and the United States."

In Sumner County every road to Gallatin teemed with eager young men bent on joining the Confederacy. Gallatin itself was swarming with would-be soldiers awaiting trains to transport them to Nashville, forty miles away.

And when the trains did arrive, the entire county turned out to cheer its boys off to war. Bands played, speeches were made; indeed, the event was a holiday.

The Cragfont ladies presented Captain Humphrey Bate with a company flag made by Sylla. Then Fanny Trousdale, daughter of the former governor of Tennessee, presented Bate with a silk flag made at her home in Gallatin. And although the recruits had no arms or uniforms, they proudly displayed their new "colors" from the top of the engine when it puffed out of town that evening.

No one was surprised, least of all Clayton Harris, when on June 8, 1861, Sumner Countians turned out en masse to

vote more than a hundred to one in favor of ratification of
the Declaration of Confederate Independence.

Ignoring Abraham Lincoln's assurance to the South that
he would not be drawn into a conflict over the slavery
question, nor would he ever allow Union troops to invade
one inch of Southern soil, Sumner County men prepared for
war. Even the ladies were swept up by the fever; parties,
socials, and suppers to raise revenue for the cause were an
almost nightly event.

By the middle of June there were over six thousand men
at Camp Trousdale, a hastily erected training facility near
Richland, sixteen miles north of Gallatin.

Clayton, along with Cotton, Rufus, and Mr. Summers,
rode to Richland to see the camp.

They were appalled by the sight. Almost as far as the eye
could see, not a living sprig of vegetation had survived the
soldiers' axes, shovels, and spades. In the place of trees and
fields stood thousands of tents and other shelters of every
description. Clotheslines were stretched from tent pole to
tent pole, and cook fires stoked with green wood created a
haze so thick that one could not see from one end of the
camp to the other. Indeed, it appeared that chaos prevailed.
But the worst of it, by far, was the odor.

"Masta Summers," Rufus said, attempting to hold his
breath, "this is the most awful-smellin' place I have ever
been to. A hog pen smells like a bouquet of roses next to this
army camp."

The Summerset party turned its horses toward home.

The following Sunday, Clayton crossed his legs and
attempted to settle himself more comfortably on the hard
pew in the rear of the Presbyterian church in Gallatin.

For over two hours the Reverend D. B. Hale had been
raining hellfire and brimstone upon the heads of Abraham
Lincoln and his Northern warmongers.

Clayton's attention wandered to the front of the church,
where Lettie sat in the Peyton family pew next to Bailey
Peyton; she looked radiant.

As though she felt his gaze, Lettie glanced over her
shoulder and her eyes met his. Then they were gone, locked
again on the irate pastor as he pounded the pulpit and

damned those Republicans who would interfere with God's plan for a Democratic South.

A moment later Lettie raised her hand to her hair to pat a loose ringlet back into place. A diamond ring sparkled like a million tiny sunbursts.

"Clayton," whispered Mrs. Summers, fanning herself with a cardboard fan that did little more than move the sticky air back and forth across her face, "stop staring at Lettie and pay attention to the sermon."

Clayton faced the preacher, but he didn't hear a word the man was saying. When the service finally ended, many of the congregation dashed out of the stifling building, but Clayton forced himself to walk with Mr. and Mrs. Summers to the pulpit and shake the pastor's hand and mumble something nice about the sermon—a duty that made him nervous, for he purely hated lying in God's house.

Even though the June heat outside the church was sweltering, the air felt cool when he followed the old couple down the gravel walk to the phaeton and handed Mrs. Summers into the carriage.

Behind them, Bailey Peyton, Jr.—in a new, tight-fitting, blue-gray uniform with highly polished, knee-length black riding boots, a black felt hat complete with plume, and his father's saber jingling at his side—strode from the church. On his arm, with head held high, Lettie was equally splendid in a pale-gray, high-necked dress that accented her fine figure.

"Well, now, Bailey," said Mr. Summers as Peyton and Lettie passed the phaeton, "I see that you've done been made an officer in the infantry. That's mighty fine, son."

"Thank you, sir," Peyton said, shaking Mr. Summers' hand. "I'm a lieutenant in General Zollicoffer's command at Camp Trousdale." Then, casting a look at Clayton, he asked, "Are you not intendin' to join up, Mr. Harris?"

Clayton shifted uncomfortably on the phaeton's seat. He had not missed the challenge in Peyton's question, nor the expectation of the correct answer in Lettie's eyes.

Mr. Summers nudged Clayton to keep silent and said, "Bailey, I'm goin' to tell you what I told Clayton an' Cotton when they come to ask my permission to join the Confederacy." Clayton's mouth turned dry. It had been Cotton alone who had spoken to Mr. Summers about joining the army. "I told the boys that if they was bound an' determined to join the army, then they needed to know somethin' that I learned a long time ago, the hard way."

The old man smiled easily at Peyton. "Bailey, a man's a fool to walk with the infantry when he can ride with the cavalry. Heck, son, me an' Andy Jackson's Tennesseans walked clean to New Orleans and back in eighteen fourteen. An' I marched ever' step of the way to Oklahoma when we moved the Cherokee out of Tennessee and North Carolina in the winter of thirty-eight." Mr. Summers shook his head. "Yes, sir, I told Clayton an' Cotton to wait until Jeff Davis calls for cavalry, then go in style! Heck fire, Bailey, any idiot can walk with the infantry." Chuckling, the old man settled back into the upholstery. "Take us home, Rufus."

Lettie fumed as the phaeton sped out of the church-house drive and turned toward Summerset. "Clayton Harris won't fight for the South," she snapped. "He will go back to Ohio, where he belongs, and join the Union. Just you wait and see . . . and it won't be the cavalry neither!"

Peyton studied Lettie's face, made even more beautiful by the anger that danced in her blue eyes.

"Lettie," he said, handing her up into his buggy, "there's no need to get so mad. Old Mr. Summers was just needlin' me, that's all. As for Mr. Harris, if and when he joins either army, it will be of his choosing—not Mr. Summers', not yours, not anyone's but his." Climbing in beside her, he picked up the reins and snapped the horse into motion. "Anyway," he continued, laughing, "if what folks say is true, Mr. Summers was a mighty fine infantryman."

Lettie sat ramrod-straight as the buggy rattled down the road toward Cragfont. "I don't care a flitter what Uncle Jonathan was. Clayton Harris is a coward. I think folks lied when they said he fought that riverboat man. Do you hear me? . . . he is a coward. No, he's even worse than that. He's what Grandma Winchester said a Tory was in the War for Independence!"

"He's no coward or traitor, Lettie," said Peyton, slipping an arm around her, "and I had no right to badger him like I did. Mr. Summers is right; a man's got to do what's right for himself."

"Then why doesn't he join the army like the rest of the young men? It's not fair for all the Sumner County boys to go off to war and him to stay behind."

"You sound like you're afraid for him to be here with the rest of us gone." Peyton drew her hard against him and inclined his head toward hers expectantly, but Lettie turned aside, causing his lips to brush her cheek.

"You haven't answered my question, Bailey," she said.

Peyton sighed and removed his arm. "You mean about Harris joining the army?" When Lettie nodded, he said, "I've a notion that he will join the Union Army . . . when he's damned good an' ready. Is that what you wanted to hear?"

"You sound as though you approve of his cowardice," she said, moving to the far side of the buggy.

"No, Lettie, I'd never approve of a coward. But just because a man doesn't champion this so-called 'rebellion,' doesn't mean he's a coward. Shoot, Lettie, my father is a Loyalist . . . or as you so nicely put it, 'a Tennessee Tory.' So is Mr. Wynne. Yet his oldest son, Val, has joined the Confederacy and is already at Memphis and will probably see action soon." Bailey Peyton's brow furrowed. "A lot of homes are split, sendin' men to both sides. Do you think my father and Mr. Wynne are cowards, Lettie?"

She took her bottom lip between her teeth, wishing she had said nothing. "Of course not, Bailey. You know I don't think that. It's . . . it's just that they are old. They've seen plenty of wars. But Clayton Harris is young . . . an' in my mind, that makes him a coward."

Peyton smiled at her. "In my mind, you are beautiful, Lettie." He took her hand and kissed the diamond ring he had given her.

Lettie pulled her hand free. "Don't try and change the subject, Mr. Peyton."

There was a long silence. The buggy sped up the Hartsville road and then turned toward Cragfont. As they neared the house, Lettie said, "And furthermore, I'm not afraid for Clayton Harris to stay home while the rest of you are off fighting. No respectable girl would give him the time of day." Crossing her arms over her chest, she sank into an angry silence.

When Peyton drew the buggy up to the Cragfont gate and stopped, Lettie jumped down and stomped off across the lawn toward the formal gardens, her long skirts swishing on the grass. Bailey Peyton hurried to catch up with her, his father's sword making a metallic jingle as he ran. When they reached the garden gate, Lettie whirled on him. "When you and Uncle George go off to play soldier, there will be no one left at Cragfont but we women. Have you thought about that, Bailey?"

"Yes, Lettie. I've thought about that."

"You have? Well, with all the men leaving, have you also decided who is going to protect us? Has it not dawned on you that the only able-bodied men who will be around will be the Union sympathizers? And cowards like Clayton Harris? That's like asking a famished hyena to guard a newborn lamb, Bailey."

Bailey Peyton caught Lettie by the elbow and drew her against him. "Darn it, Lettie, don't you think I've considered that? Of course I'm concerned about you." Then, more softly, he said, "Yes, I am worried about you, Lettie. You've changed since Clayton Harris arrived in Sumner County."

"Of course I've changed. So have you. So has everybody. I'm not a little girl, Bailey. I'm almost seventeen years old."

"That's what bothers me, Lettie. You're a woman, a beautiful woman—"

"And you just don't like anyone who finds me attractive," the girl said. Breaking away, she bent, plucked a daisy, and raised it to her nose.

"I like everyone who finds you attractive," countered Peyton. "It's the ones you find attractive that I don't like."

"I don't find Mr. Harris the least bit appealing," she said. "He's arrogant, deceitful, overbearing . . . and a coward."

Peyton shook his head. "No, Lettie, there's something different about him, something that I don't see in other men."

Lettie busied herself with removing a small honeysuckle vine that wove in and out among the rose bushes. "And . . . just what is it that you see in Mr. Harris?"

"I'm not sure. A driving force. A determination. He intends to have you, Lettie . . . and quite frankly, I don't believe you've discouraged his advances."

She flung the honeysuckle into the air and faced him angrily. "Well, what did you expect? You were gone for more than a year, Bailey. It's not fair for you to think a girl should sit at home and waste away like a summer flower."

"Other women don't require constant attention, Lettie.
All of Sumner County is talking about you and Clayton
Harris."

"I don't give a fig what Sumner County says. Mr. Harris
was an attentive companion."

"Is that all he was, Lettie?"

"That's all he was, Bailey."

Lettie walked away from Bailey Peyton, down the brick
path and into the gazebo, where she crossed to the far side
and dropped lightly to the low wooden bench that encircled
the inside perimeter.

Bailey Peyton stopped in the doorway. His breath caught;
Lettie was unbelievably beautiful, sitting there with her full
skirts spread across the bench, her heavy hair sparkling like
thousands of tiny golden nuggets where the sun dappled it
through the vine-covered lattice.

Crossing the floor in two strides, he dropped to one knee
and took her hands in his. "I love you, Lettie. Let's get
married immediately. Today."

Lettie twisted uncomfortably. "Let's wait a little longer,
Bailey. You'll be gone for two or three days at a time when
the fighting begins." Peyton smiled, wondering if he should
tell her the truth—that he would be gone for weeks at a
time. She leaned forward and kissed his lips. "The war
won't last over a month or two, Bailey. You can wait that
long, can't you?"

He rose to his feet and stood looking down at her. "No,
Lettie, I think I've waited too long already. I think I've been
much too lenient with you. I'm going off to war, and before I
leave, I want to be your husband in the truest sense of the
word."

"And I want to be your wife," she said, "but I want a
husband who will be here with me. I want a home. I want
slaves. No, Bailey. We'll be married when you return, not
before."

Peyton measured his words with care. "No, Lettie, we'll
be married immediately . . . or not at all."

Lettie's hand fluttered to her throat. She could feel her
control over Bailey Peyton waning. A small, panicky voice
told her that she had pushed him too far. She loved Bailey
Peyton, even if she wasn't in love with him. And she
certainly did not want to lose him. For a split second, her

hand trembled against the erratic pulse that throbbed in her throat. Then she was again in command.

"Bailey," she murmured, lying back across the bench, "I want you to make love to me . . . now."

After Bailey had gone, Lettie smoothed her skirts and adjusted her rumpled petticoats. She felt sick, and bitter, and disappointed. But she had accomplished what she had set out to do: Bailey Peyton had agreed to wait until after the war to marry.

Had it been worth it? she wondered, her lips trembling. Had it been worth the risk of getting pregnant?

"What difference does it make?" she cried aloud. The war would soon be over and she would marry Bailey Peyton before she could possibly begin to show.

Then realization struck home: A child might be forming in her womb that very instant!

Tears sprang to her eyes. She turned her head and nestled her cheek into the crook of her elbow.

Oh, God, she prayed, I don't want to be a mother. Not yet, please . . . please, sir.

A week passed and Bailey Peyton did not return to Cragfont to reassure Lettie of his undying love. Lettie was despondent.

The following Monday, her cousin, Napoleon Winchester, son of George and Malvinia, who was training at Camp Trousdale, now called Camp Zollicoffer, rode to Cragfont to pick up the uniform Sylla had made for him. While there, he told Lettie that Bailey Peyton was working night and day to form the 20th Tennessee Infantry Regiment into a military command. "No easy feat," Napoleon said, "considerin' that most of our troops are down with the measles."

When a second week elapsed with no word from Peyton, Lettie began to fear; did he no longer intend to marry her?

As the third lonely week drew to a close, Lettie threw a vase of flowers against the stone hearth in her bedchamber, flung herself across her bed and pounded the feather-tick pillows with her fists.

I hate him! Oh, God, how I hate him, she told herself over and over. Then, burying her face in the plump cushions to muffle the sound, she screamed hysterically. But when she at last raised her red-splotched, swollen face from the pillows, her eyes shone with something more than anger and tears: Cold, calculating hardness glittered in their depths.

Jumping from the bed, she fled down the staircase and out the front door. The July sun beat down on her unprotected head as she raced through the formal gardens and on to the lake's edge. Wrenching her engagement ring from her finger, she flung it as far out over the water as she could, watching with bitter satisfaction as it slipped soundlessly beneath the surface.

Then, with angry determination, she marched back to her room and picked up paper and quill.

> *My Dearest Bailey,*
> *I simply must see you. Please present yourself at Cragfont on Sunday at two o'clock. Be punctual.*
>
> *Your affectionate,*
> *Lettie Billingsly*

Lettie folded the note and sealed it. Picking up the quill again, she began another letter:

> *Dear Mr. Harris,*
> *I am no longer an engaged woman. I simply must see you. Please present yourself at Cragfont on Sunday at one-thirty o'clock. Be punctual.*
>
> *Until then,*
> *Lettie Billingsly*

"What in hell's name has got you jumpin' through your ass?" Cotton inquired on Sunday as Clayton led his horse out of the stall and flipped his saddle onto its back.

"Lettie wants to see me," Clayton said, exhilaration in his voice. He tightened the cinch.

Cotton ran his hand down the animal's neck and patted its well-muscled shoulder. He gave Clayton a hand up and fitted the stirrups for him. "Lettie's engaged to Bailey Peyton," he said. "She's goin' to marry him."

"Not anymore she isn't." Clayton ducked his head and

spurred his horse through the double doors.

"She told you that same thing before," Cotton yelled, but Clayton had already jumped his horse into a hard gallop and was racing toward Cragfont.

When Clayton dismounted and walked to the house, Lettie herself opened the door. Whisking him off to the parlor, where two toddies awaited, she explained that except for the slaves, she was alone in the house. Everyone else had gone to the Barr Plantation to visit.

"I pretended to be ill," she said, and Clayton's pulse raced. "I also wanted to apologize for the way Bailey Peyton acted outside the church house last month. He had no right to put you on the spot that way. What you do is none of his business. I told him so." Lettie sipped her drink. Her eyes above the glass were warm and inviting. "Bailey and I . . . argued about you," she murmured, looking away.

"I probably should say I'm sorry, Lettie. But I'm not."

"Neither am I," she lied. "I was never in love with Mr. Peyton."

As the tall clock in the hall struck its three-quarter-hour chimes, Lettie flinched, nearly spilling her toddy.

"Is anything the matter, Lettie?" Clayton wondered at her nervousness.

"Everything is fine." But she refused to meet his eyes.

"Lettie," he said, setting his glass on a table, "perhaps it would be better if I returned at a more appropriate time?"

"No!" she said hurriedly. "No. I . . . I would rather you stayed."

For several minutes they sipped their drinks and attempted small talk. As the movements in the tall clock dropped into position preparatory to chiming, she suddenly hastened to the sofa and seated herself, indicating that he should join her.

Clayton walked slowly over to her and stared down; something was definitely wrong.

"I wanted some time alone with you," she stammered as he continued to stand above her. Then as the tall clock began its two-o'clock chimes, she drew him down and plastered her mouth to his.

Clayton broke away and pushed her to arm's length. "What's going on, Lettie?"

Ignoring the question, she embraced him tightly and flung

herself back onto the cushions, forcing him down on top of her.

Clayton tried to push himself erect, but Lettie caught his lower lip in her teeth and bit hard. A moment later, heavy footsteps, combined with the jingle of a cased saber, sounded in the hall.

For what seemed a lifetime, all that Clayton could hear was the ticking of the tall clock. Then Lettie released him and pushed him away. Gracefully, she rose to her feet and began straightening her rumpled dress. A smile hovered at the corners of her mouth as she gazed into Bailey Peyton's ashen face.

"I should kill you both," Peyton said quietly. "But neither of you are worth the effort. To kill you would be an admission of how stupid I've been. All these years, Lettie, and I didn't see you for what you actually are."

Clayton drew himself to full height. "You may have satisfaction any time you like, Peyton. But I'll not tolerate another slurring word about Miss Lettie."

"Lettie is a whore, Harris, an' I don't fight duels over whores."

"How dare you call me a whore?" Lettie cried. "You, who proposed to marry me! You, who . . ." She cast a quick look at Clayton; then, with lips trembling, she shouted at Peyton, "It was you who treated me as though I were a whore. At least you could have respected me enough to have ridden by and told me you no longer cared to see me. But no, you just left me sitting here wondering! And wondering! And wondering!"

Peyton's mouth twisted into an ugly, thin line. "I see how you were wondering, Lettie." Turning on his heel, he marched from the room. At the door, he hesitated. "Just to keep the record straight," he said, turning, "for the past three weeks, I've been in the infirmary with a severe case of the measles."

As Peyton's footsteps echoed down the hall, Clayton caught Lettie's arm and spun her toward him. "Damn you, Lettie, this whole masquerade—"

Snatching herself free, Lettie ran to the window and threw open the blinds. Peyton was at the gate.

"He's been sick!" she cried. "For the last three weeks, he's been sick."

"So?"

Ignoring Clayton, Lettie pressed her forehead against the windowpane.

"I love you, Bailey," she whispered. "I've always loved you."

Angrily, Clayton snatched the girl around. "What's going on? I expect an answer, Lettie."

"Get out of here!" she screamed. Then rushing past him to the stairwell, she caught the newel post and leaned against it for support. "Get out of here . . . and don't ever come near me again!"

CHAPTER 13

Cotton was worried about Clayton and it bothered him because he normally didn't worry about anything.

"What in hell's wrong with you, Clay?" They were riding the fields to check on the corn crop, which was promising an excellent yield.

"I'm thinking about going back to Ohio. I don't believe I'm cut out to be a Southerner."

"Well, what brings all this on?" Then, with a touch of anger, Cotton added, "You ain't been worth a damn since you got back from Cragfont the other day. What did Lettie say to put them kind of thoughts in your head?"

"She didn't say anything. I've just been thinking about leaving, that's all."

"Bullshit," Cotton said.

Clayton's shoulders slumped. "It's not only Lettie, Cotton. I got a letter from my uncle. He and my father have closed their office; they've both been commissioned as colonels in the Union Army. My uncle insists that I come home and join his command." Clayton did not tell Cotton that the letter had gone on to say that his father was threatening to disown him if he did not return to Ohio immediately.

"Well, I ain't goin' to let you leave," Cotton said. "Have you forgotten 'bout your dream? Wealth? Position? Prestige?"

"Maybe those things aren't all that important, Cotton."

"The hell they ain't." Cotton twisted in the saddle and frowned at Clayton. "Man, I believe in you. One of the reasons I come to Tennessee was to see you make it big. I can feel it in my bones, Clay. Someday you're goin' to be a powerful man." Cotton grinned sheepishly. "Damn it, Clayton, you're my dream."

"What are you talking about?"

"You came here with nuthin', same as me. An' the way I figure it, if you would stay away from Lettie Billingsly and quit meddlin' in business that don't concern you— primarily how folks treat their slaves—an' get back to thinkin' up ways to make Summerset more prosperous . . . . Hell, Clay, there was a time when planters hereabouts would have paid you highly to keep their books like you do Mr. Summers'. I heard 'em say so." When Clayton didn't respond, Cotton said dejectedly, "I reckon I figured that if you could start with nothin' an' become somethin', then maybe there's a chance for the rest of us little bastards who ain't never had nuthin' to become somethin' too."

Clayton glanced at his friend and was appalled to find that Cotton was, indeed, serious.

"Damn it, Cotton," he said. "Don't make a martyr of me. You don't understand what I'm going through."

Cotton rode his horse close and laid his hand on Clayton's shoulder. "Clay, why don't you go on over to Cragfont an' cut Lettie an' get it out of your system? You ain't goin' to be worth a crap 'til you do."

"She's a lady," Clayton said, pushing Cotton's hand aside.

"That ain't what I hear," Cotton said. "Fanny told Rufus that Bailey Peyton busted her cherry in the gazebo before he went off to the army."

Clayton's fist exploded against Cotton's chin, lifting the young man out of the saddle and tumbling him over the hindquarters of his horse to land heavily on the freshly plowed ground.

Cotton was up in a flash. And Clayton found himself looking down the barrel of a five-shot Colt's revolving pistol. Even more unsettling was the expression on Cotton's face, which chilled Clayton to the soles of his boots: Cotton was, at that instant, perfectly capable of killing him.

For what seemed an eternity, the two young men stared at each other. Then Clayton touched his heel to his horse's flank and trotted the animal down the newly turned furrow.

Cotton leaped on his own mount and caught Clayton before he had gone a hundred yards. "I reckon I was out of line, Clay, what I said about Miss Lettie. I ought not shoot my big mouth off when it ain't nothin' more'n a jealous wench gossipin' about her mistress."

Clayton faced his friend. "Don't ever pull a pistol on me again, Cotton."

Cotton grinned sheepishly. "Aw, I weren't goin' to shoot you. Hell, I got only one chamber loaded. I probably would of missed anyhow."

Clayton eyed Cotton hard. "Yes, Cotton, there for a moment you had every intention of shooting me. I saw it in your eyes."

"Well, damn it all to hell, Clay. That hurt when you slapped me off'n my horse. An' all I was tryin' to do was en-light'n you 'bout Miss Lettie."

"That kind of talk can ruin a lady's reputation, Cotton. You may not be a gentleman, but I am. And Miss Lettie is a lady, and don't you forget it."

Cotton shook his head sadly. "She was born a woman, Clay, and no matter what title she holds in between, she'll die a woman." With that, he clucked his mount into a canter and rode on down the field.

Clayton drew his horse to a standstill and slouched dejectedly in the saddle. He didn't believe for a minute that Lettie had allowed Bailey Peyton to seduce her. Still, young women all across Sumner County appeared to be smitten by men in uniform. And for some reason that escaped Clayton, they either ridiculed or outright shunned those who were reluctant to march off to a war that was as yet many miles away and many days—if not weeks—in the future.

Cotton spun his horse around and galloped back to Clayton. "You know what you need, Clayton?" he asked. "You need to get drunk. Yep! You need to forget women entirely. An that's the only way to do it, just get pig-rootin' drunk."

Clayton did not respond. Cotton insisted: "Well, what do you say?"

"About what?" He had not heard a word Cotton had said.

"About getting drunk."

"You know I don't drink."

"Well, it's about time you started."

Clayton thought it over. "You think it would help?"

"Hell, yes. Didn't you hear me tell you it would make you forget all about Lettie Billingsly?"

That night Clayton and Cotton drank themselves into a stupor that turned into a crying jag for Clayton before he finally passed out in Cotton's loft.

When Mr. Summers went in search of them the next morning, he found them dead to the world. Picking up the empty whiskey jug, he shook his head, not sure if he should be amused or angry.

"Up an' at 'em!" he bellowed. "Work's a-waitin'!"

Clayton bolted to a sitting position, then lay back, holding his head in his hands. "Please, Mr. Summers," he moaned, "just let me die."

Cotton staggered to his feet and stared owlishly at the old man. "Jesus Christ," he said. "Some son-of-a-bitch ate cat shit with my mouth while I was asleep." Setting his hat gingerly on his head, he carefully descended the ladder.

Clayton raised himself on one elbow, then dropped his legs over the edge of the bed. "Last night Cotton and I were talking about girls," he said, lifting his bloodshot eyes to the old man. "I guess we got a little carried away . . . and got drunk."

Mr. Summers nodded, thinking that it was indeed an understatement. "It's been a spell," he said, "but I reckon I know what you're meanin'. I've done it a time or two my own self."

Clayton told him the whole story, beginning with Lettie's note and ending with, "Did you ever have this kind of problem when you were a young man, sir . . . before you were married?"

Mr. Summers pursed his lips. "I suppose I did. But not often, 'cause times was different when I was young. Women was different back then, too. You see, son, white women are a complicated an' contrary lot. In times of stress, such as war years, they just naturally become more accommodatin' ... if you follow my meanin'."

Clayton felt sick, but not from the whiskey. What Mr. Summers said only strengthened Cotton's words. The old man continued, "Well, that's the way times was when I was young—always a war of some kind, be it with the British, or the Indians, or both. An' the fact is, this confounded notion that's become so popular with women over the last few years—an' I'm speakin' of the absurd idea that fornicatin' should never occur except for the purpose of childbearin'— didn't come about 'til times had been peaceful for quite a spell. Then all of a sudden the very same women who sent their men off to war smellin' like a whorehouse didn't enjoy fornicatin' no more. Hell, they didn't enjoy nothin' no more."

The old man scowled at Clayton. "Yes, sir, son. The moment women become complacent, the first thing they do is cross their legs. So I doubt if I'd believe any rumors about Lettie Billingsly along them lines. She's the daughter of a wealthy New Orleans family, an' unless I'm badly mistaken, she's mighty complacent."

The old man sat down beside Clayton and draped an arm over the young man's shoulders. "I wish that Lettie Billingsly's chastity was our only problem, son." Mr. Summers' tone brought Clayton's head up. "We've got real problems. There's been a big battle at a place called Manassas, in Virginia. On July twenty-first, P. G. T. Beauregard and his Confederates purely thrashed the Union forces. Hell, they run 'em nigh all the way back to Washington, D.C."

Clayton was stunned. His first thoughts were for his father and uncle. Mentally he raced back through the calendar to the day he had received his uncle's letter. It had arrived in the first week of July—there had been plenty of time for them to have left Ohio and reached Virginia—but it had not mentioned a mustering of troops in Virginia. Clayton sighed. The letter had specifically insisted that he come to Ohio to join his uncle's command.

Mr. Summers was going on: "It beats me how they did it. It beats me even more how the Federal Army let 'em do it! But then, maybe I shouldn't be surprised. Like I told you over two years ago, the Southerner ain't been born who would walk away from a fight."

Clayton, too, had trouble believing that the Union Army had been routed by the Rebels. All summer long, Confederate soldiers had been passing through Gallatin en route to and from Camp Zollicoffer. Not one in fifty wore a full uniform. And not one in a hundred carried a modern, big-bore caplock rifle; in fact, most of the men shouldered antiquated flintlock rifles, muskets, and fowlers.

"How in the world could that happen, Mr. Summers? How can poorly trained troops with outdated weapons face a finely disciplined, well-armed army and expect to defeat it? It just doesn't make sense."

In spite of his convictions, Mr. Summers was proud of the Southern troops at Manassas. "I know you won't believe this, Clayton, but overconfidence, belligerence, raw courage, expert marksmanship—and the belief that it's God's own will—make a mighty powerful combination."

The old man rose and began to pace. "The worst thing about the Confederate victory is the impact it's having on Sumner County. Every able-bodied man over thirteen years old is joinin' the army. Cotton's still pesterin' me, a-wantin' to go." The old man stepped up his pace. "I talked him out of it, at least 'til the harvest is in. 'Course, he ain't heard about this battle yet."

"He won't go back on his word, Mr. Summers."

"No, I don't reckon he will. But I couldn't blame him none if he did." Throwing a hard look at Clayton, he added, "Nor you either!"

Not waiting for a reply, he continued, "The nation is at war, Clayton. And I'm a-feared that Sumner County ain't goin' to take kindly to Loyalists like me, an' A. R. Wynne, an' old man Bailey Peyton, Sr. What I'm gettin' at, son, is that you might ought to think about goin' back to Ohio."

Clayton blanched. Only yesterday he had considered doing that very thing. "Are you discharging me, Mr. Summers?" he asked, suddenly realizing that now he was truly faced with it, he did not want to leave Summerset.

"No. I'm just makin' a suggestion. I'm tryin' to make it easier for you. Hell, son, you can bet your bottom dollar that on August one, Tennessee will vote to accept the Constitution of the Confederate States of America; that battle at Manassas assured it."

Clayton stood up, walked over to Mr. Summers and threw his arms around him in a bone-crushing hug that caused the old man to wince. "I'm not leaving, Mr. Summers," he said. "Whatever comes, we'll face it together."

On July 26, 1861, Bailey Peyton, Jr., along with General Zollicoffer's 20th Tennessee Volunteer Infantry, was ordered to the East Tennessee arena, some one hundred fifty miles from Gallatin.

On August 1, 1861, when Sumner County went to the courthouse to vote on the Constitution of the Confederate States, Clayton rounded a hallway corner and found himself looking into Lettie's jeering face.

"The vote was two thousand for the Confederate Constitution, Mr. Harris, and four against. I suppose I needn't ask which way you and the other three voted."

"I suppose not, Lettie," he returned, and then wondered why he didn't remind her that he was not a property owner and therefore ineligible to vote.

"I might have known," she flung at him.

"Lettie, can we go somewhere and talk?"

She stared at him. "Talk?" she said. "We have nothing to discuss, Mr. Harris. You have destroyed my engagement— and very probably my life—and you want to talk?"

Tossing her head, she opened her parasol and flounced off in a rustle of skirt and petticoats to join several young women who had gathered on benches outside the courthouse.

Spinning on his heel, Clayton stalked through the rear door of the courthouse and made his way to Mr. Summers' phaeton, where his and Cotton's horses had been left in Rufus' care.

"Well, Rufus," he said, untying the reins and climbing into the saddle, "Tennessee is no longer a part of the United States."

"What's that mean, Mista Clayton? Are we a-goin' to war?"

"We're already at war, Rufus." He swung his horse around. "Tell Cotton and Mr. Summers I'll wait for them at the Johnny Bell Hotel. I feel the need for a good stiff drink."

Rufus watched Clayton ride away. "We gonna have class

tonight, Mista Clay?" he called.

Clayton reined in and for a moment sat slouched in the saddle. Then, angrily, he said, "I'm not going to get drunk again, Rufus. Yes, we'll have class."

Cotton, having seen the exchange between Lettie and Clayton from the second-story landing, ambled down the stairway and out through the front door. Grinning at the lounging women, he tipped his slouch hat. "Mornin', ladies."

The women glanced at him, then continued their chatter, all except Lettie, who did not even look in his direction.

Cotton swaggered toward her. "Clayton sends you a message, Miss Lettie . . ."

Lettie raised her chin defiantly. "There's nothing Mr. Harris could say that would interest me in the least, sir."

The other young women stared scornfully at Cotton, but they could not hide their disappointment at Lettie's dismissal. Cotton grinned even wider.

"As you wish, ma'am." He bowed from the waist, as he had seen Clayton do, and stepped toward the door. He heard an urgent, whispered conversation commence behind him. It was obvious that the girls were pressuring Lettie to hear Clayton's words.

"Oh, what did he say?" called Lettie.

Cotton turned and glanced at the eager young women, then centered upon Lettie. "Clayton said for you to kiss his ass."

Lettie's mouth fell open. Cotton grinned from ear to ear.

Several of the girls sniggered but were immediately sobered by Lettie's angry glare. "If all the honorable men weren't off to war," Lettie said acidly, "you would be called out and shot for that remark, you . . . overseer!"

The other girls nodded solemnly.

Cotton, enjoying himself, walked back to the group. "What Clayton really said"—he laughed, looking into each girl's face—"was that you could get in line an' take turns kissin' his ass."

Lettie bounded from the bench and hit Cotton with her parasol. Ducking under the flimsy cudgel, he laughed again and dodged out of reach.

A girl, small for her age of fourteen and as slender as a rail, dressed in plain homespun, pushed her way free of the others and approached Cotton angrily. "You should be ashamed of yourself, talking like that to Miss Lettie," she said. Then, standing on tiptoe, which brought her only chest-high to Cotton, she said contemptuously, "I've a good mind to slap you silly. But it would be a waste of time, because evidently somebody has already beat me to it."

Cotton hooked his thumbs in his suspenders and inspected her. She wasn't pretty, but he guessed that she might be a late bloomer. "What are you goin' to be when you grow up? A midget?" Then, ignoring the way her face whitened with anger, he turned and sauntered off.

"You know something, mister?" she called after him. "The only time a mouth as big as yours looks good is when it's closed!"

Cotton turned and grinned at her. "When you get big enough that I can kiss your mouth without you havin' to stand on a mountin' block, you come see me."

The girl's face blanched even whiter. Then, faster than one could blink, she snatched up a stone and flung it at Cotton.

The missile caught him above the eyebrow, opening a gash that took Dr. Mentlo five stitches and the better part of an hour to close.

"Girls ain't got no sense of humor a'tall," Cotton told Clayton as they rode toward Summerset. "This little bitty one with a turned-up nose, not much taller than a butter churn, walks up an' looks me right in the belly button an' says she's gonna slap hell outt'a me."

Clayton frowned at the cut above Cotton's eye. "Looks like she did a pretty good job."

"She lied to me, Clay. She said she was goin' to slap me. She hit me with a damned rock."

"Well, she sure was upset about something when she chased you around the courthouse."

"She weren't upset; she was madder'n hell. An' all I did was try an' appease Miss Lettie for your sake . . . tried to say somethin' romantic for you."

Clayton reined his horse to a standstill and peered narrowly at his friend. "What did you say to her?"

Cotton shrugged. "I told Miss Lettie and them others, real nice an' polite-like, that they could all get in line . . .

and kiss your ass."

For a long second Clayton stared at Cotton. "I ought to kill you . . . and I believe I will," he whispered.

With a hoot of laughter, Cotton was gone, his horse's hooves throwing clods of earth into Clayton's face as the animal sprang away.

Clayton's mount reared and spun sideways, and a moment later Clayton was sitting in the dusty road watching the terrified animal follow Cotton's horse pell-mell across the fields toward Summerset.

The last day of summer was hot and bone-dry; even the air seemed preheated, and the horses' hooves stirred up dust devils as Clayton, Cotton, and Mr. Summers inspected the plantation.

Beyond the parched half-mile of open pasture, a large body of Confederate soldiers cantered toward Gallatin. The summer dust boiled up so thick around the cavalcade that the men at the rear of the column seemed ghostly silhouettes in a sepia haze.

"Bennett's Cavalry," Mr. Summers said, squinting through the shimmering heat waves. "He's been raising a company all over Sumner County. They're musterin' at old Colonel Elliott's racetrack on East Camp Creek."

"I wish I was ridin' with 'em," Cotton said.

Clayton drew his panama lower over his eyes and studied the horsemen. They were too far away for him to hear the normal sounds of cavalry on the move. Yet he could feel the earth tremble under the pounding of the hooves. It was an eerie sensation that intensified with each stride until the ground was shuddering and the three onlookers were forced to leap from their horses and grasp their bridle bits to keep the terrified animals from bolting.

"Hold on to them horses!" Mr. Summers cried as his mount reared and fell backward, snatching the old man off his feet. He got up slowly, cursing the animal with every breath. By the time his horse had staggered erect, the earthquake had subsided and the countryside was again serene.

When the dust had settled, Clayton looked for the cavalry but the troops were gone, as if the trembling earth had swallowed them. A shudder ran the length of his spine. Was the earthquake an omen? He glanced at his companions. To his disappointment, they were totally engrossed in quieting their horses.

Clayton licked his suddenly parched lips; lately he was getting more skittish than a green-broke mule. Still, it had been a strange and timely phenomenon.

As autumn lost its shape and blended into winter, Cotton seemed to go berserk. He was everywhere at once, pushing the slaves to repair the split-rail fences, to reshingle leaking barn roofs, to replace the stall door that one of the horses had kicked off its hinges, to kill and cure meat, to cut wood, and finally, to harvest the fields. By the middle of November, 1861, Summerset Plantation was in better condition than Mr. Summers had ever seen it, both financially and physically.

"You boys have done a fine job this year," said the old man at supper on the evening of the fifteenth.

"You can thank your overseer," Clayton said. "Cotton turned a much larger yield than last year's."

"It's the biggest and best crop this plantation has ever harvested," Mr. Summers said to Cotton. "You've been mighty industrious, son. It's almost like you couldn't wait to finish the fall chores . . . an' I reckon I know the reason why."

Cotton stared at his plate. He had hardly touched his food. In a way, he hated what he was about to say. "I'm goin' to Elliott Springs tomorrow, Mr. Summers, an' join Colonel Bennett's Cavalry. That is, sir, if you would make me the loan of a horse."

Clayton laid his fork quietly beside his plate. "You sure that's what you really want to do, Cotton?"

Cotton nodded. "I promised Mr. Summers I'd wait 'til the crops was in. Well, they're in."

Clayton slouched back in his chair. He had known that Cotton was leaving. Lord knows, he thought, it's all Cotton has talked about. But now that it was actually happening, Clayton was upset.

Mr. Summers cut into the silence. "Pick yourself the best horse on the place, Cotton. And while you're about it, get a couple of heavy blankets, and that double-barreled shotgun that stands in the corner of the hall. If you think of anything else, just holler."

Turning to his wife, who had sat through the exchange in quiet solitude at the far end of the table, he smiled. "I believe Mrs. Summers also has somethin' for you, Cotton."

The old lady dabbed at her eyes with her linen napkin, an act of tenderness that shocked Clayton because Mrs. Summers had never shown any feeling for Cotton.

Excusing herself, she left the room and returned shortly, carrying a newly made uniform.

"My goodness alive!" Cotton said, jumping to his feet and reverently fingering the gray cashmere coat with its small brass buttons. Mrs. Summers set a black felt hat, one of her prized, blue-egret plumes pinned to it, on his head, then tilted it rakishly over one eye.

For a split second, Cotton hesitated. Then he threw his arms around the old lady and hugged her. "Thank you kindly, ma'am."

Mrs. Summers kissed Cotton's beardless cheek. He's only a baby, she thought, tears trickling down her face. He's just seventeen years old, an' goin' to war. But she said nothing.

"Now, Helen, don't you go an' start a-cryin'," chided Mr. Summers, frowning at his wife.

She wiped her eyes, then faced her husband. "I'm an old woman, Mr. Summers, an' I'll cry if I want to."

Mr. Summers stared at his wife of nearly sixty years. He opened his mouth, but words wouldn't come. Then, rising and crossing the room in three strides, he took her in his arms and kissed her still-soft lips. "Yes, by God," he said, "you've earned the right to cry."

He hugged her even more tightly. Over her shoulder, he nodded to Cotton. "Go down to Clayton's room and put your uniform on, son. Me and the Missus want to see how you look in it."

Cotton's return into the dining room was more a parade than an entrance. He strutted, turning this way and that for all to see, and Clayton had to admit that his friend's appearance was indeed impressive.

Later that evening, after Cotton had said good night, Clayton went out to the barn. He found Cotton admiring himself in a large, badly tarnished mirror that had once graced the hallway of the big house.

"You act as though you've never seen a uniform before," Clayton said.

Untouched by the sarcasm, Cotton continued to gaze at his reflection, first this way, then that, adjusting the coat and squaring his shoulders accordingly. "You're just jealous," he said, grinning.

"And you're a show-off." Clayton returned the grin.

Cotton continued to stare into the mirror, fingering the brass buttons on his coat. "Clay," he said, "this is the first suit of clothes I've ever owned in my whole life. It's not a hand-me-down or a castoff; it's brand-spankin' new. An' it's mine—made 'specially for me—an' I'm proud of it." The boy turned his head so that his eyes were hidden. "I don't expect you to understan' . . ."

Clayton's face flamed. At that moment he wished he were half as intelligent as people thought he was. He stepped further into the room. "That uniform was worth waiting for all these years, Cotton. You look just great in it."

Cotton's face broke into its customary grin. "I sure as hell do, an' that's a natural fact! Why do you reckon I been admirin' myself all evenin'? It sure ain't 'cause I look ugly."

CHAPTER 14

Summerset was not the same without Cotton. For the two weeks since he had been gone, Mr. Summers and Clayton had had their hands full trying to keep the slaves working efficiently. But the Negroes went about their work as though they had no guidance at all. And if the two men answered the same question for one slave, they must surely have answered it for every slave: "No, Cotton won't be back until the war is over."

"I didn't realize how much they depended on Cotton," Clayton commented. He and the old man were riding the pastures, checking the herd of beeves to see if any new calves had been dropped.

Mr. Summers shifted his weight in the saddle; he purely hated riding astride. "It's like Cotton said on the steamboat, Clayton: 'Mr. Summers, I can handle horses and darkies.'" The old man's face took on a faraway expression. "The boy didn't lie, Clayton. He's the best overseer I've ever seen. Summerset is goin' to miss him sorely."

It already does, thought Clayton.

The old man fished a cheroot from his pocket and struck a match on his saddle leather. "When are you leavin', son?"

Clayton shook his head. "I'm not leaving, Mr. Summers. With Cotton gone, someone's got to look after the plantation. No offense, sir, but you are getting on in years . . ."

The old man squinted at Clayton, then blew a thin tendril of smoke that eddied up around his hat brim. "I run this plantation for nearly sixty years a'fore you and Cotton came along. I reckon I can handle it a mite longer."

"I've no doubt that you can, sir. But with your permission, I'd really like to learn planting from the ground up. And to tell you the truth, Mr. Summers, I've got mixed emotions about this war. Everybody I grew up with will be fighting for the Union—all my kin, all my friends."

The old man nodded. "It takes a strong man to hold to his beliefs when they go against the public's feelings." Then he changed the subject. "Mrs. Winchester is throwin' a big reception on Sunday. George and his son Napoleon are home on leave, but they're goin' back on the twenty-fifth. Why don't you come along? Might do you good to have some fun for a change."

"I wasn't invited."

"That don't make no difference."

"It makes all the difference, Mr. Summers." Clayton was not sure he could stand being near Lettie, but he couldn't say that to Mr. Summers.

"Well, we're goin'," the old man said flatly. "I want to see those Winchester boys before they leave. Heck, son, me and George's mother and father fought Indians together back when Sumner County weren't nothin' but tall trees. An' regardless of the fact that I support the Union, I know the Winchesters. They ain't about to let this war come between a friendship that's lasted dern near as long as this nation has."

Clayton drove the phaeton with misgivings. But it wasn't until he and the Summerses actually stepped into the ballroom that true discomfort set in: All the other men were in uniform. Clayton squared his shoulders and raised his chin defiantly.

Old Mrs. Winchester broke from a group and sped across the floor. "Jonathan! Helen!" She caught the old couple's hands in a warm salutation. "It's so nice of you to come." Her aged face was alight with pleasure.

"Clayton," she whispered, offering him her hand, "nobody believed you would show your face here after that trick Cotton pulled in Gallatin . . . telling the girls that they could perform special favors on a certain portion of your anatomy."

Clayton gritted his teeth, wishing he had his hands around Cotton's throat. "I wasn't aware that word had gotten around," he said.

The old widow threw back her head and laughed. "Oh, yes, Clayton. Word has definitely gotten around."

Then, taking Mrs. Summers' arm and guiding her toward a bevy of elderly ladies, Mrs. Winchester said, "Let me tell you what that young man of yours did. Reminds me of what the late general once told the local do-gooders who were pressurin' him to make an honest woman out of me . . . after five illegitimate children. You remember that?"

Several elderly gentlemen converged on Mr. Summers and dragged him off toward the gentlemen's smoking chamber, leaving Clayton standing alone. He glanced about the ballroom, but it wasn't until he started toward the punch bowl that he became aware of Lettie staring at him from the gallery. He nodded in recognition; she turned her back to him.

Clayton walked to the punch bowl and filled a glass. Over the rim, he noticed that all around the room the ladies' eyes above their spread fans were following his every move. He was sure that behind the fans their mouths were equally busy as they related to their companions the story of his alleged actions toward Lettie and the local girls. He nearly laughed at the shock of indignation that registered in the listeners' eyes.

The men, however, were paying him no heed. Their conversation was about the new Sumner Armory that was turning out a perfect facsimile of the United States Mississippi rifle, a percussion gun of superior quality. The armory could also convert the old-style flintlock muskets to the latest mode of percussion, commonly known as the caplock rifle.

Tiring of the constant talk of war, Clayton made his way downstairs and headed toward the gardens. The pale November moon threw just enough light on the withered flowers and shrubs that they appeared to be alive and blooming. It was there that Fanny found him.

"Mr. Clayton," she said hesitantly, "I been wishin' to speak with you for some time now."

Clayton smiled, startled by the girl's ladylike speech. "What did you wish to speak to me about?" he asked, unconsciously mimicking her formality.

Fanny forced a smile. "I's . . . I has been tryin' real hard to stop talkin' like a darky. An' I been bein' real careful 'bout how I dress an' do my hair."

Clayton studied the young woman in the dim light. Indeed, her thick tresses were done in ringlets identical to Lettie's, and her dress, while obviously finely made, was a nondescript green, paled from too many washings. One of Lettie's castoffs, he decided.

"I even been learnin' to eat like a proper lady," Fanny said, dropping her eyes.

"Well, that's real nice, Fanny. But what does that have to do with me? If you're thinking that I might teach you to read and write, well, I can't do that. The sheriff stopped me over a year ago."

"Oh, no, sir," said the girl. "It ain't that."

"Well, what is it then?" He wished she would say her piece and leave, for he was certain that everyone on the balcony was watching them.

Humiliation filled Fanny's face. "I . . . I jist been wonderin' why you . . . never wanted to pleasure yourself wif me, after that one time. I . . . I tried real hard to please you."

Clayton quickly glanced toward the balcony, wondering if Fanny's voice could have carried that far. No, the noise from the ballroom would have made that impossible.

Praying no one at the house was watching, Clayton took Fanny's arm and led her to the gazebo. Inside, he took a turn around the small room before coming to stand at her side. "Fanny," he said, looking into her upturned face, "I have been avoiding this confrontation for months. That was a mistake on my part."

"Why, Mista Clayton? Was what we done wrong?"

Clayton grimaced, wondering how to deal honestly with her, yet be sensitive to her feelings. Finally he said, "That night, the night of the party, I had been hurt very deeply by Miss Lettie. I . . . I needed someone to be with." Fanny's eyes were glued to his face, waiting. Taking a deep breath, he said hurriedly, "You just happened to be at the right place, at the right time."

Fanny turned her back on him and leaned against the latticed wall. The silence that followed was so profound that even the sounds of gaiety from the big house were drowned out. "Fanny," Clayton said, stepping toward her, "it was all wrong. I'm sorry."

Pushing herself from the wall, Fanny threw her arms around him and buried her face against his chest. "You just said it was the right place . . . an' the right time!" she cried. "Then it was s'posed to happen, can't you see that, Mr. Clayton? It was s'posed to happen! So how can it be wrong?"

Clayton pushed her to arm's length, his fingers biting into her shoulders. "It wasn't supposed to happen. It just did, Fanny. I took advantage of you, and I've regretted it ever since."

Fanny's stomach turned over, and for a moment she was sure she would be sick. "I know I ain't . . . haven't got no rights, Mr. Clayton, because I'm nothin' but a slave. An' please don't go an' think I was tryin' to assume nothin', 'cause I'm not. But you treated me so fine, like a real lady, an' I . . . an' I . . . oh, Mr. Clayton, I love you!"

Tears streamed down her face and she closed her eyes, taking a deep, shuddering breath. "I's sorry, Massa," she whispered, backing away. "I's so very sorry." Then she turned and fled into the garden.

After she had gone, Clayton walked to the gazebo bench and sat down heavily. His mind drifted to a night aboard a paddle-wheel steamboat; there he had promised another beautiful quadroon girl that he would not change; that he would always treat Negroes, no matter their status, with the same respect and consideration that he would accord any other race.

"I'm still the same person," he whispered through clenched teeth, but he knew that he lied. He dropped his head into his hands. He had changed. Circumstances had altered every living soul south of the Mason-Dixon line, himself included. He almost laughed aloud. Yes, his life had certainly done a complete turnabout.

* * *

Although she had not heard the conversation from where she stood on the balcony, Lettie had seen Clayton lead Fanny into the gazebo. She pondered that, not sure whether to be amused or insulted. Deciding that she was insulted, and determining to confront the two, Lettie started to turn from the railing when something strange occurred.

A man, whom she had not seen hiding near the gazebo until he moved, slipped quietly away and was quickly lost in the night.

"If you lean out any farther over that rail, Miss Lettie," said Val Wynne's younger brother Hall, gripping her waist to steady her, "you'll fall off this balcony for certain. What are you watchin' so intently, anyhow?"

Lettie straightened. "Probably nothing. No, I'm sure it was nothing." Turning, she smiled at Hall. "One of our slaves was eavesdropping on Mr. Harris . . ."

"Slaves eavesdrop all the time," Hall said. "But I'd say one was surely hurtin' for conversation if the best he could do was to listen to what that damn Yankee had to say."

Lettie saw Fanny leave the gazebo and run toward the house, and suddenly the incident had no significance. "You're probably right," she laughed, wondering why the fact that Clayton was alone left her feeling so lighthearted.

At the gate, the slave Patrick turned and glared at the gazebo where Clayton sat.

"I should have knowed it were yo' an' not the other'n," he whispered, his eyes alive with the fire of mania. "I's gwine to make yo' pay fo' what yo' done to me, yo' white bastard. Some day I's gwine to make yo' sorry yo' was ever born."

Clayton left the gazebo and walked to the lake. Its shimmering, inky surface, etched with gold leaf by the full moon, should have had a soothing effect, but it didn't. Fanny's honest declaration of love for him had cut him like a knife. Not once in all these months had he considered the depth of her feelings. She had given him clues, quite obvious ones—such as attacking a murderer with her bare hands because Clayton's life was in jeopardy—and more subtle ones, like the way her face lit up when he was near.

Why hadn't he noticed? He knew the answer: Lettie. Clayton sighed. That wasn't entirely true either. Whether he wanted to admit it or not, one of the reasons he had shunned Fanny was because she was a slave.

"Did you really tell Lettie an' them to kiss your . . . bottom?"

The question snapped Clayton back into his surroundings. "Susie, darn you," he said as the girl flounced up to him. "What are you doing up this time of night?"

"It's early, and there's a party goin' on. Well, did you?"

Clayton knelt down. "What do you think?"

Susie perched herself on his knee and looked thoughtfully into his face. "I don't think you said it. I think Cotton made it up."

"Thank you," he returned, wondering why her opinion mattered, but knowing that it did.

"I think you should have said it, though," she added quickly. "I've wanted to say that very same thing to Lettie a bunch of times. But Mama would tan my britches if I did. An' Papa would scold me for not bein' a 'little lady.'" She mimicked her father's voice perfectly.

Clayton gave her a hug. "You are probably going to grow up being the finest lady of them all."

The little girl giggled and dropped her eyes. Clayton nearly laughed aloud, so pure and sweet and feminine was the gesture.

"Yes," she said seriously, "I think you are right. I will be a fine lady, just like Granny Winchester."

You may never get the chance, thought Clayton sadly. It's the very young and the very old who will suffer most in this war, for they are the ones with the least strength. Clayton drew Susie closer. Instinctively, she put her arms around his neck and held on tight.

With a sigh, Clayton stood. Then, laughing, he flipped Susie around his hip and much to her delight, carried her piggyback up to the big house.

Lettie, standing on the balcony with several friends, saw him trot up the walkway with Susie on his back. The little girl was laughing gleefully and Clayton was making whinnying noises as though he were a horse.

In spite of herself, a smile dimpled Lettie's cheeks.

"Look at him," Hall Wynne said, standing beside her. "He ain't got the guts to come up here. He would rather play with children."

"They say he whipped a riverboat man, and you know how tough they are," someone commented.

"Did any of you-all see him whip a riverboat man?" Hall Wynne asked.

"No, but too many folks say they saw it for it not to be true."

"Well, I don't believe it," Hall insisted. "He wouldn't fight Bailey Peyton . . . twice!" Pushing himself from the rail, Hall walked into the ballroom, returning moments later with the punch bowl cradled in his arms.

Clayton knelt and helped Susie to the ground. He was aware of the faces above the balcony handrail and he had heard their idle chatter. It was time to leave.

"Don't pay no nevermind to them, Clayton," Susie said. She had heard it too.

Clayton smiled at her. "Didn't I see your friend, Opie Reed, when I arrived? I'll bet he's looking everywhere for you."

"Aw," moaned the girl, "Opie Reed ain't no fun. Even if he is only nine, all he talks about is shootin' Yankees."

"Well," Clayton said, "this is one Yankee I sure hope he doesn't shoot. In fact, I'm going in and see if Mr. and Mrs. Summers are ready to go."

"Oh, heck," Susie sighed. "I was havin' such a tall time with you." Then she brightened. "If you'll stay, I'll tell Granny to send them snots on the balcony home. She'll do it, too!"

Clayton laughed. "She probably would. Now, go on and find your friends."

Susie darted up the steps of the lower veranda, turned and blew him a kiss, and went into the house.

Clayton bent to brush bits of twigs and leaves from his trousers' knees. As he straightened, the contents of the punch bowl drenched him from head to toe.

Amid laughter from the balcony, he calmly flicked pieces of berries and fruit from his clothing, then pushed his wet hair off his forehead. Raising his face to the people above, he smiled a slow, even smile. "Would the person who felt that I needed a drink please come down here so I can thank him properly? Or is he too much a coward?"

A hush rippled across the upper deck. "It was done in fun, Mr. Harris," Lettie said.

"I'm not laughing."

The crowd milled uneasily; the joke had suddenly taken a wrong turn. All heads swung toward Hall Wynne.

"I told you not to do it," Lettie whispered fiercely.

Hall thrust the bowl into the hands of the young man nearest him. "Nobody calls me a coward," he said in a loud voice. "And definitely not a yellow-bellied Yankee."

With that, he swung his legs over the handrail, caught the edge of the decking and dropped lightly to the walkway below.

Approaching Clayton with the fearless swagger assumed only by one without the slightest experience in physical combat, the boy brought his fists up and danced around Clayton. "Try and hit me!" he commanded.

The brand-new Confederate uniform Hall Wynne wore told Clayton the whole story; the young soldier was caught up in his own importance, and Clayton was merely a tool with which he could bolster his image.

"I've changed my mind," Clayton said, fighting back his anger. "I shouldn't have gotten mad over something that was 'done in fun,' as Miss Lettie said."

Hall pranced up stiff-legged to Clayton, his fists windmilling. "You're the one that's yellow, Yankee. I knew it all the time."

"Don't push your luck, Hall."

"Hogwash!" The boy danced closer, then took a roundhouse swing at Clayton's jaw. The awkward blow never landed. Clayton struck from the shoulder, a short punch to the boy's chin that left Hall flat on his back, unable to focus his eyes.

"Big bully!" Lettie cried. "You are nothing but a big bully, Clayton Harris!"

Clayton stepped over Hall Wynne and walked into the house. "Bring the phaeton around," he instructed Rufus. "The North and South just came to blows."

Rufus' mouth fell open. "Who won, Mr. Clayton?"

"Nobody."

The week before Christmas a letter came from Cotton. Clayton tore it open. Cotton's big, childlike printed characters read:

*Fort Henry on the Tennessee River,
West Tennessee*

Dear Clayton and Mr. and Mrs. Summers,
*I am as of now in Col. Forrest's Cavalry. We are at
Fort. Henry guarding the Tennessee River in case of
gunboats. We are not doing much guarding because
about the only guns we got is squirrel rifles and fowling
pieces. We have not got no caps for them. The powder in
the magazine is too coarse for them kind of guns, too.
We do have a lot of cannons, but we have not got
nobody that's trained to shoot them.*
*Would Mr. Summers please send me one pair of
thick drawers. Two checked linen shirts. Another blanket. One pair of boots lined with bladder and full
waterproof. Some socks. And gloves. And twelve twists
of tobacco.*
*Thank you. Some of the men's wives and sweethearts
is supposed to come to Fort Donelson which is only
fifteen miles across the peninsula on the Cumberland
River on Jan. 9 of next year and will leave Nashville on
the* General Jackson *on the 7th. Fannie Trousdale has a
beau in Gen. Head's 30th Regiment. He told me she is
coming to see him. Please send the package by her.*

*Yours affectionately,
Cotton Ferris*

"Lord, have mercy," Mr. Summers said when Clayton
finished reading. "Cotton will be the best-equipped soldier
in the army, both North and South."

Clayton folded the letter and slipped it into its envelope.
"I didn't think I'd miss Cotton like I do," he said with a
touch of bitterness.

"We all miss him, son," Mr. Summers said, "so don't feel
bad about feelin' bad. We all wish he was home."

"Don't pay any attention to me," Clayton said. "I guess
I'm just melancholy. It's Christmastime, and folks should
be with their loved ones, not sitting on some isolated hilltop
in West Tennessee like Cotton is."

He sighed. "Nearly everyone I know is in the army, doing
what he thinks is right, while I'm . . . Maybe the folks

around here are right to resent me." He was painfully aware
that the prominent families of Sumner County were cele-
brating the holidays almost nightly, but that Summerset
Plantation had been removed from all guest lists, except
Cragfont's.

"That's not true," Mrs. Summers said. "A lot of the
soldiers who joined up back in April are writin' home
advisin' their younger brothers not to enlist. I reckon the
spirit of adventure is losin' its attraction."

"And I'll bet you one other thing, Clayton," Mr. Summers said. "Those boys sitting in those miserable field
camps would trade places with you in a heartbeat."

"Maybe so," Clayton murmured, grateful for the solac-
ing, but not convinced.

The New Year came in quietly at Summerset. But at the
surrounding plantations no one would have guessed that a
war was in progress. Musicians played, glasses tinkled, and
laughter echoed through the high-ceilinged rooms and halls.
Yet just below the surface of the gaiety, a fine-tuned,
nervous tension prevailed. It was as though the revelers
were pushing themselves to partake of life's fullest cup, as
though they suspected it would be the last time that the
South would enjoy a carefree holiday.

To Clayton, the solitude was particularly welcome; Bailey
Peyton was home on furlough, and Clayton had no desire to
chance a conflict. Furthermore, it was rumored that Lettie
was abed and that Dr. Mentlo refused to discuss her illness.

CHAPTER 15

The moment Dr. Mentlo left Lettie's bedchamber, Fanny rushed to the kitchen to confront old Chatty.

"Dr. Mentlo be plumb closed-mouthed about Miss Lettie," she said. "He won't tell me nothin'."

Chatty, bent over the hearth where she was baking cornbread in a black iron skillet, said, "Go away from here, Fanny, 'n' don't bodder me. If'n I burn dis' here bread, ol' Mizz will bring mo' woe 'pon my head den yo' can shake a stick at."

"I don't care if'n you do burn that bread. I want you to tell me if'n Miss Lettie is catched."

The old woman removed the skillet from the fire and glared at Fanny.

"Well?" demanded Fanny.

"Well what?"

"Was it Lettie you drempt about?" the girl cried.

"Can't r'member."

"Of course you can remember."

"Nope."

Fanny quivered with suppressed anger. "I hope that bread

burns plumb up!" she shouted, stalking from the kitchen.

Upon entering Lettie's bedchamber, she found her mistress propped up among the pillows addressing an envelope.

Lettie looked up. "I want this posted as soon as possible, Fanny. Today."

"Yes'm." Fanny took the letter and glanced at the name. Oh, I wish I could read, she told herself bitterly. Hurrying down the stairs, she left the house and raced toward the slave quarters.

Fleming, walking up the path carrying a milk pail, was startled to see Fanny, her skirts above her knees, running toward him. Quickly he looked to see if the big house was on fire.

"Have you seen Patrick?" Fanny called as she neared him.

Fleming nodded. "He be down at de horse barn." Fanny left the path and sped toward the barn.

"Ain't no use in a-hurryin'," Fleming called after her. "Ol' Patrick ain' goin' nowhere. He ain't got no reason no mo'."

Fanny paid no attention to Fleming's laughter, but raced into the barn, stopping abruptly to adjust her eyes from bright daylight to the dimness of the interior. The necessary delay irritated her.

"Patrick, where are you?"

Patrick's voice came from above. "I's up here in the loft, a-forkin' hay down to t' mangers."

"Well, get down here fast!"

"I don't have to," he said sullenly. Now she could see him, peering down at her. "Yo' ain't my boss."

"Miss Lettie says for yo' to post this here letter right this minute."

When Patrick didn't respond, Fanny shouted, "Right this very minute, Patrick."

Laying his pitchfork aside, Patrick dropped down the ladder and took the envelope from her.

"Who's that letter 'dressed to, Patrick?" she asked.

"None of yo' business."

Fanny's hands doubled into fists.

"Yes it is my business, 'cause I want to know," she spat.

Patrick scowled at her and started toward the door.

"You can't tell me, 'cause you can't read," she said, following along behind him. "You's just a liar, Mr. Patrick from Virginia. You can't read one whit better'n me."

"I can so," he said, shaking the letter in her face. "So don't try foolin' me, Fanny. 'Cause it won't work."

Fanny snatched the letter out of his hand.

"I can see that it be 'dressed to Mista Bailey Peyton," she said, praying that she was right. "But I can't read where he is a-armyin' at. That's what I wanted you to tell me, where he's a-livin'."

Patrick grinned triumphantly. "I'll never say. If'n Miss Lettie wanted yo' to know where Mista Peyton was a-armyin', she'd a-tolt you her own self."

After Patrick was gone, Fanny leaned against the barn wall. If Lettie was pregnant as she suspicioned, then the letter was more than likely addressed to the father. Laughing shakily, she mouthed the words, "Thank you, Patrick, for tellin' me it weren't Clayton."

Lettie was careful to slip out of the house unobserved, even by the slaves. Her letter had asked Bailey Peyton to meet her in the gazebo at two o'clock. It was now a quarter past two, and she prayed that he would already be there.

He was.

"It won't work, Lettie," he said as she stepped into the building and quickly seated herself on the bench.

For a minute she didn't answer. She merely stared up at him, and he was struck by the dark rings under her eyes, and by her flushed complexion.

"I don't like it any more than you, Bailey," she said, turning her face aside and staring out the window.

Steeling himself against her haggard appearance, he demanded, "How do you know whose baby it is? For all I know, it could be Harris', or, hell, anyone's."

"Damn you!" she cried, bolting upright. "You know this child is yours."

"I know nothing of the kind. The last time I saw you, Clayton Harris—"

Lettie buried her face in her hands and burst out crying. "I didn't know you had been sick with the measles, Bailey. I thought you had . . . forgotten me."

"Forgotten you? Obviously, if anyone did the forgettin', it was you, Lettie."

"I never heard a word from you," she said, wiping her eyes with a handkerchief, "after . . . after that Sunday. Not one word."

"It was only three weeks, Lettie."

"That's a long time, Bailey. Especially just after . . . you know."

Wiping her nose, she said, "I wanted to hurt you, Bailey, like you hurt me. So I planned it that you would see me and Mr. Harris . . . together. But we never . . . did it. You are the only person who has ever done that with me."

Her body shook with new sobs. "I love you, Bailey. I'll swear it on a stack of Bibles."

"I'm not goin' to marry you, Lettie," he said quietly.

Lettie raised her head. Her eyes bore into his. "Oh, yes you will. This baby is yours. And you are going to do the honorable thing." She twisted her handkerchief. "I know you will never trust me. I ruined that for us, but I will be a good and faithful wife to you . . . I promise you that, Bailey."

Bailey Peyton dropped heavily to the bench and glared at her. Then his shoulders slumped. "I have no choice, have I?"

"We have no choice," whispered Lettie, praying that he would take her into his arms and hold her. But he didn't.

The wedding was set to coincide with Bailey Peyton's next furlough, the first of February. It would be a simple ceremony at Cragfont.

Fanny and Sylla began work on Lettie's wedding dress. Susie was disappointed that her cousin had chosen a very plain pattern instead of the elaborate creation that she had always insisted she would wear.

Lettie kept to herself, seldom venturing beyond her bedchamber, and a hushed atmosphere settled over Cragfont.

Clayton Harris threw himself into his work and tried not to count the days. But that was an impossibility. Near the middle of the month, it dawned on him that Lettie was but another war he refused to fight. Perhaps he was indeed the coward she believed him to be.

Throwing a saddle on his horse, he thundered toward
Cragfont, prepared to do battle. But Lettie would not
receive him, and Mrs. Winchester offered no apologies.

As he returned to the front gate, he took a last look at
Cragfont. Lettie stood in an upstairs window, partially
hidden by the heavy drapes.

Anger surged through Clayton as only the anger of
rejection can do, reducing him to a childish shell of a man.
He cried out to Lettie, "I wish to God a Yankee bullet would
find Bailey Peyton."

On January 19, 1862, Clayton's wish became reality.
General Zollicoffer's 20th Tennessee Infantry Regiment
was decimated by General George H. Thomas' Union
forces. Dead on the field: General Zollicoffer; dead on the
field, Lieutenant Bailey Peyton, Jr.; dead on the field, dead
on the field, dead on the field . . . the list of Sumner County
men went on and on.

But only one name kept pounding at Clayton's brain,
until he thought he must go insane. Even when he did find
the strength to reason with himself, he could not help but
feel partially responsible for Bailey Peyton's death. And he
knew that each time he faced Lettie, this guilt would be an
ugly, invisible barrier between them. His selfish desire to
possess her had turned out to have too high a price; for even
though Lettie Billingsly would now be more vulnerable than
ever before, and might well turn to him, he knew that he
had, unintentionally but most securely, locked himself out
of her life forever.

It was that realization that left Clayton wishing it had
been he, not Bailey Peyton, who had fallen in battle at a
place called Fishing Creek, Kentucky.

On February 1, 1862, the very day on which Lettie had
planned to wed, the General Assembly in Nashville interrupted its deliberations to follow Governor Harris and
other state officials, including the members of the House
and Senate, to the Louisville and Nashville Railroad depot
to receive the bodies of Zollicoffer and Peyton.

The procession then escorted the two heroes to the
Capitol building, where they were to lie in state so the

citizens of Nashville might pay their respects.

On February second, Bailey Peyton's casket was put aboard a train and removed to Sumner County for burial.

Clayton stood in the hushed crowd at the Gallatin depot as the Peyton family carried the casket to the waiting hearse. It was a solemn procession, interrupted only by the quiet sobs of the mourners. Standing near Clayton as the hearse rolled away, a young soldier who had arrived on the funeral train spoke to the woman next to him. The slaughter at Fishing Creek had been awful, he said. Rain and sleet had drenched the Confederates, rendering their antiquated flintlock muskets useless, while the Union late-model caplocks fired without fail.

"All we could do," said the soldier, "was to keep advancin' and wait for their bullets to find us. It was terrible."

Lettie, dressed in black and with a veil covering her face, walked behind the pallbearers. But it was not until the body had been lowered into its final resting place and she raised her veil while preparing to sprinkle a handful of earth on the casket that Clayton had a glimpse of her face. Her skin was ashen, and her normally full and provocative lips were drawn into a thin, bloodless line.

As she readjusted her veil, her eyes met Clayton's. He was dismayed by the very real sorrow in their depths. A split second later, he was even more dismayed by the pure hatred that flashed at him like a lance. If she had screamed "Murderer!" at him, he would not have heard her accusation any more loudly. He looked away.

Upon returning to Cragfont, Lettie went immediately to the kitchen and dismissed all of the servants except Chatty.

Old Chatty looked askance at her. "What yo' want, chile?"

Lettie walked to the fireplace and stared into the flames. She said, "Bailey's dead, Chatty."

The old slave nodded her head. "I know, and I's real sorry, Mizz Lettie. But I knowed some'in bad gon' happen, 'cause I drempt o' watermelons a-bustin' open on de vine an' de thick red juices a-runnin' into de groun'. Yes'm, I knowed some'in bad gon' happen."

"It doesn't end there, Chatty."

"I knows it don't," the old woman sighed. "An' I reckon I knows why yo' wants to talk to ole Chatty."

"I'm over six months along, Chatty. Can you help me?" Before Chatty could answer, Lettie flung her arms around the old woman and pressed her face against Chatty's dried-up chest.

Lawd! Lawd! thought Chatty, the world done come to an end. Miss Lettie done gone an' touched a slave! Patting the girl sympathetically, she said, "Dat be a awful long time, Miss Lettie. De baby be more'n half-growed. Yo' sure dat's what yo' want, chile, to do away wid it?"

"I have no choice," the girl said bitterly. "A scandal would simply kill Grandmother, not to mention my parents."

"Miss Lettie," said Chatty seriously, "what yo' askin' me to do . . . is mo' dangerous dan any ol' scandal. Yo' could die, chile."

Lettie's face lost its color. But after a drawn-out silence, she said, "I'd rather be dead than have everyone in the county looking down their nose at me. I . . . I couldn't live with that, Chatty."

Chatty shook her head. "No'm, I don' s'pose you could."

Still, the old woman was reluctant. "Miss Lettie," she said, "what 'bout Massa Clayton? He loves yo'. Couldn't yo' p'tend it was his'n?"

Lettie shook her head violently. "Never! I can't stand the sight of him. Besides, I've never . . . he would know the truth, Chatty."

"What yo' mean yo' can't stan' no sight of 'im?" cried Chatty. "Yo' could fo'ce yo'self to stan' the sight o' him. Least 'til after the baby be born!"

"Get rid of this baby, Chatty," Lettie said, eyeing the old slave coldly. "I don't want it. It would be nothing but a constant reminder. Oh, God, I hate it, and it's not even born!"

Old Chatty pushed Lettie to arm's length and gazed sternly into the girl's face. "Yo' come to my cabin at midnight. Don' yo' tell nary a soul. Yo' hear me, Miss Lettie? Nary a soul!"

"I won't! I promise."

Chatty looked deep into Lettie's eyes. "It ain't gon' to be

purty, Miss Lettie. An' it a-gon' to hurt powerful bad. An' yo' gwine to be awful sick fo' a long spell."

The girl dropped her face into her hands. "I . . . I trust you, Chatty."

"Den ever'thin' be jist fine. Yo' jist leave ever'thin' to ole Chatty." After the girl left, Chatty wrung her hands and wished she really believed her own words.

Lettie lay naked on Chatty's bed while the old woman examined her from head to foot.

"Even tho' yo' ain't a-showin' much," said Chatty, "yo' is carryin' a big boy-chile."

Tears swam in Lettie's eyes. A boy. Bailey would have liked that. But Bailey was dead. She must remember that, or she could never go through with this. Bailey is dead! Dead!

Aunt Delphy held the lantern close and studied Lettie. "Yo' sho' she can even have dis chile, Chatty? She sho' 'nough do look small . . ."

Chatty ignored Delphy. She picked up a gourd dipper and held it to Lettie's lips. "Yo' drink dis potion I done brung yo', Mizz Lettie, an' we'll hab dat baby a'fore yo' can say Jack Sprat."

Fear filled Lettie's eyes, but she forced herself to swallow a sip. Then, gagging, she turned her face away. "I can't drink that awful stuff, Chatty. I just can't!"

"Yo' goin' to drink ever' drop!" Chatty forced the dipper between Lettie's lips. "Drink it! Drink it all."

Lettie emptied the gourd, then hung her head over the bedside and retched up the black liquid.

"Yo's got to hol' it down," Chatty warned. "Won' do no good a'tall if'n yo' can't keep it inside yo'!"

Lettie wiped the perspiration from her brow and nodded. It took three attempts before her stomach grew too weak to rebel.

"How long is dis a-gonna take?" Delphy asked as Lettie began to quiver and shake. The writhing worsened; then Lettie convulsed with spasms that left her drenched in sweat.

"I's hopin' it ain' gwine to take long," Chatty said, spreading Lettie's thighs and forcing her hand into the girl's vagina.

Lettie screamed and tried to kick Chatty away.

"Hol' her down," Chatty ordered. "We's got to hol' her still."

"No!" cried Lettie, attempting to swing her legs off the bed. "I've changed my mind. I'll have the baby . . . I've changed my mind!"

"It be too late fo' that," Chatty snapped. Then, "Yo' do as I tol' yo', Delphy."

Delphy caught Lettie's ankles and threw her considerable weight on the girl's legs. Looking toward the door, she called, "Fanny? Is yo' still out dare?"

"I's here."

"Run up to de house and fetch ol' Fleming. Hurry now."

"Yo'all better stop Miss Lettie from hollerin'," said Fanny. "They gonna hear her plumb to the big house."

"Yo' git on up dare like I tol' yo' to," Delphy said. Then, releasing one of Lettie's legs, she quickly snatched her bandana from her head and wadded it into a tight ball. A second later, Lettie's screams were a muffled whine.

Even with Fleming's help, it was all Delphy could do to hold the thrashing girl down. As Chatty's potion took effect, Lettie's eyes rolled up into her head until only the whites showed, and even though the cabin was so cold the women could see their breath, her naked body glistened with perspiration that pooled like rivulets into the indent of her navel and the vee between her breasts.

Chatty worked steadily, kneading Lettie's abdomen with a constant, heavy pressure, until suddenly she drew back her bony fist and slammed it into the girl's stomach, again and again.

Delphy's eyes stood out as though on stems, and old Fleming turned ash gray.

"Yo' goin' to kill her, sho' nuff," Fleming whispered as Lettie's head lolled sideways and bloody black vomit forced the gag from her mouth, then splattered on the dirt floor.

Chatty's gnarled hands snaked between Lettie's thighs and worked their way into her vagina again. A minute later she held a mass of bloody pulp above her head.

Delphy went to the door and cracked it open. "Fanny?" she called.

"I'm here," answered the girl, slipping quickly into the room.

"Is that Miss Lettie's baby?" Fanny asked, her stomach threatening to revolt as she eyed the dripping matter in Chatty's hands.

"What dey is of it," old Chatty said. "It ain't fully d'veloped yet."

Fanny swallowed hard, then looked away. Delphy gestured toward a bucket of water by the door.

"Get Miss Lettie cleaned up, an' don' tarry none," she said. "It gwine'a be daylight soon."

Fanny poured cold water into a tin wash pan and began bathing her mistress' blood-splattered body.

"It be almos' too big to come," Chatty said, wrapping the fetus in a piece of red calico and laying it on the hearth. Then, in a language Fanny had never heard, the old woman began a wailing chant that made the girl's skin crawl.

Still chanting, Chatty picked up an ash shovel and began digging in the hard dirt floor.

"You ain't a-goin' to bury it in here, are yo'?" Fanny whispered, wide-eyed.

"Hush," Chatty snapped. Then, raising the bundle above her head and chanting again, she laid the calico in the bottom of the hole and quickly shoveled the dirt back into place.

Hurriedly, she snatched a broom from beside the mantel and swept the area, obliterating any sign of digging; then, crossing to the door, she cracked it open and squinted at the eastern horizon, which was showing a thin line of silver. "We got to be quick now an' git Miss Lettie up to her room a'fore daylight, or we'ns gwine be in mo' trouble dan we ever 'magined."

"How's we a-goin' to do dat?" demanded Delphy. "She ain't able to walk."

"Why, I done reckon ol' Fleming gwine to haf t' carry her up dare, if'n he still got de strength."

Fleming lifted the unconscious girl into his arms. "She don' weigh nuthin'," he said.

As Fleming, followed closely by Fanny, stepped from the cabin and started toward the house, Chatty caught Fanny's arm. "Yo' stick wid dat girl closer'n hair on a dog's back. Yo' hear me, Fanny? 'Less I's plumb m'staken, Miss Lettie gwine to be a mighty sick chile fo' a long time . . . a long, long time."

Fanny's brow puckered, causing tiny lines to form between her eyes. "Miss Lettie appears to be restin' easy an' ain't bleedin' hardly none at all, Chatty . . ."

"I ain't talkin' 'bout her body, girl!" Chatty shot back. "No'm, I wish't her body be de only thing dat's ailin' Miss Lettie. Yes'm, I purely do."

BOOK II
The Tattered Chemise

CHAPTER 16

The first major Union assault on Confederate Tennessee came on February 5, 1862, three days after Bailey Peyton's funeral and Lettie Billingsly's abortion.

Ten Union gunboats and thirty steam-powered troop carriers poured into the mouth of the Tennessee River at Paducah, Kentucky, over one hundred miles northwest of Gallatin, and ran full-throttle toward Fort Henry, some forty miles south.

Cotton sat on a moss-covered limestone outcropping high above the Tennessee River and shivered despite the patchwork quilt wrapped tightly about him. The wind whipping up the bluff was not only penetrating, it held the promise of miserable weather. Cotton hoped that it would bring snow instead of more rain and sleet, for the frozen ground was already treacherous.

Then he was on his feet, his discomfort forgotten; the northern bend of the river was alive with the enemy flotilla.

"Jesus Christ!" he breathed. "One, two, three . . ." By the time he had counted twenty boats, he was already in the saddle, and when he reached thirty, he pivoted his horse and spurred it into a hard gallop toward Fort Henry, five miles upstream.

Cotton hit the ground running while his mount was still sliding to a halt. Ignoring the sentry beside the door, he burst into General Lloyd Tilghman's headquarters.

"The goddamned Yankees are here, General," he gasped, out of breath. "I counted over thirty boats an' they was still a-comin' . . . a whole damned river full of 'em."

Tilghman propped his elbows on his desk and rested his chin on his clasped hands. "Well," he said presently, "this is a fine kettle of fish. Thirty boats will hold ten, twelve thousand troops."

Rising, he walked to the door and threw it open, oblivious to the frigid air that blasted in around him. "We can't defend this place with three thousand men," he went on as though speaking to himself. "I told those fools in Nashville that we needed more support. Told them weeks ago."

Turning to his adjutant, he said, "Evacuate the troops to Donelson, immediately. Leave me enough artillerymen to man our big guns, but get the rest of the troops out of here."

The adjutant saluted and rushed out the door.

"Hell, General," Cotton said, "Fort Donelson ain't in no better shape than this place is. They can't defend it neither, and they's fifteen thousand men over there."

Tilghman pierced Cotton with a hard stare. "I don't need you to tell me that, Private."

"Sorry, sir," Cotton said, trying to grin, but failing. "I reckon the thought of givin' up Fort Henry kinda galls me, sir."

"Well, it galls me too," Tilghman said. "But maybe my three thousand men can help buy Donelson a little time."

"General," an artillery officer said from the doorway, "we got a Union gunboat sighted, sir."

"Just one?" Tilghman asked.

"Well, yes, sir. That's all we've seen so far."

"There's over thirty more right behind it, mister."

"Thirty!"

Probably more like forty or fifty, thought Tilghman. "Man your guns and prepare for action," he ordered blandly.

Turning to Cotton, he said, "I want you to keep your

horse saddled and ready to travel. When this is over, you are to report what has transpired here to the staff at Donelson. That's all, Private."

On the sixth of February, once the Union gunboats found their range, the bombardment of Fort Henry began. It was devastating.

Cotton, alone and bitter, stood on a windy knoll west of the fort as Union cannon wreaked havoc on Confederate men and gun mounts.

And even though a hundred Confederate gunners worked their seventeen cannon like madmen, they were able to sink only one boat: the one-thousand-ton ironclad, *Essex.*

The enemy shelling of Fort Henry increased with uncanny accuracy, and gun after gun on the Confederate rampart fell silent. Cotton tried to be aloof. And when that failed, he tried indifference, but it was a useless effort. Too many of the boys—lying scattered like tenpins around demolished guns and craters that still smoldered, even though some of the shell blasts had occurred long before—were from Sumner County.

Another great blast shook the ground. It was a Confederate twenty-four-pounder cannon exploding in its emplacement on the north end of the fort. When the smoke and debris cleared, the remains of the gun lay fifteen feet from its cradle, and the entire crew was dead or dying. The gun beside it, a ten-inch Columbiad, was also destroyed—with its entire crew. Cotton choked back tears of rage.

The day wore on. By late afternoon, only two of the original seventeen cannon were answering Union fire.

Near dusk, General Tilghman walked up the hill toward Cotton. His shoulders were slumped, and he limped from a shell fragment in his left thigh.

"I'm goin' to haul down the colors, Private," he said. Then, handing Cotton a packet, he murmured, "My report is in there . . . but I expect that yours will be clearer and more detailed than this."

Tears formed in Tilghman's eyes. "Go on, get out of here," he said, looking away. "Any minute now, I'm apt to do somethin' that's embarrassin' to a grown man."

"Why, General," said Cotton, forcing a grin, "I was

a-hopin' you'd order us to sit ourselves right down on this here hilltop and cry together."

Cotton waited until the white flag fluttered over the smoking ruins of Fort Henry. Then he swung into the saddle and set off across the fifteen-mile-wide peninsula that separated Fort Henry, on the Tennessee River, from Fort Donelson, on the Cumberland.

He thoroughly detested carrying news of the first surrender in Tennessee's history.

At midnight he dismounted before the tent of Lieutenant Colonel Nathan Bedford Forrest and told the sentry to awaken the colonel. Then he walked to the fire and poured himself a scalding tin of coffee.

Gripping the cup with both hands to warm them, he looked up to find that the sentry hadn't moved.

"Boy," he said, unable to contain his anger, "if you don't rouse the colonel this goddamned minute, I'm gonna kick your ass up 'round your ears."

The young infantryman glared at Cotton, then ducked into the marquee, muttering something that sounded like: "Damned cavalry soljers, thinks their shit don't stink."

A moment later, Forrest, his dark hair and beard disheveled, and indeed resembling Satan incarnate in his red long johns, erupted from the tent.

His cold blue eyes bore into Cotton. "Well?"

Cotton was forced to look up at the six-foot, powerfully built man.

"General Tilghman surrendered, sir," Cotton said. "I have his report . . ." He shoved the pouch toward the colonel. "It was a hell of a fight, sir. They sunk the shit out'n one of them iron-covered battle boats . . . but more of 'em just kept a-comin'."

"How many boats does the enemy have?"

"I counted more'n thirty, sir."

"All of them gunboats?"

Cotton took a long pull from his coffee tin. Then grimacing as though the contents of the cup were unpalatable, he flung the tin toward the fire.

"All of 'em I seen had guns!" Then, more softly, he added, "Hell, Colonel, I don't know how to tell the difference."

Forrest untied the packet and glanced at its contents.

"See to your horse, then meet me at General Pillow's quarters," he said. "I'm sure the General will want an eyewitness report."

Cotton nodded. Leading his weary mount, he struck off across the frozen ground toward the stables.

For the next four days Fort Donelson was a beehive of activity. Trenches were opened outside of the fort perimeter; breastworks were thrown up throughout the woods on the slopes above the river; cannon were cleaned and elevated; rifles and sidearms were loaded and primed.

Cotton was sent to scout the Union flotilla on the Tennessee. He returned on Monday, February tenth, wet and nearly frozen. Sleet-filled rains had continued to plague the western part of the state.

Warming his hands over the potbellied stove in Forrest's tent, he told the colonel that the boats had headed back to the Ohio and then looped up the Cumberland. "My guess, sir, is that they'll be here 'long about Wednesday, if the river don't freeze over."

Forrest fingered his goatee. "The Cumberland hasn't frozen over in nearly a hundred years," he said. Walking to the tent door, he drew aside the flap. Cavalrymen were hunkered by their cook fires, some of them eating, some laughing and joking, some writing letters, and some just waiting.

"The men are going into Dover tonight," Forrest said over his shoulder. "I've already laid the law down to them, but you weren't here so I'll tell you now: Do anything you're big enough to handle as long as it don't wind up alienatin' the townfolk. I know you're not goin' to listen, but I'll tell you anyway—be careful of the whores. Word has it that a couple of them are burnt with the clap. Be back here, ready for duty, tomorrow afternoon." He went out.

Grinning, Cotton touched his fingers to his temple in a salute.

That same night, Mr. Summers paced the parlor floor at Summerset.

"Dern it, Clayton," he said, "I'm upset over the death of young Peyton as much as anybody. His father and I have been friends for more years than I care to count. But that ain't reason enough to make me run out an' join crazy ol' Jeff Davis' army."

Clayton released a tired sigh. He had hoped the old man would accept without question his decision to join the Confederacy. He could not tell him—or anyone—the truth about why he had volunteered his services to the South; nobody would understand his overwhelming sense of guilt over Bailey Peyton's death. The least he could do was to take the field in the dead man's stead. Even though he knew it was a childish, senseless decision, it was something he had to do.

"I knew you would go," Mr. Summers said. "I just didn't think it would be to the Confederacy. And I didn't think it would be this soon."

Walking to the hallway door, he called, "Missus Summers, would you fetch that other uniform you made . . . please."

Moments later the old lady appeared carrying a midnight-blue, knee-length coat and trousers of a lighter shade.

Mr. Summers cleared his throat. "We figured you would join the United States Army . . . so the color ain't quite right."

Clayton accepted the coat from Mrs. Summers and slipped it on. "The Confederates I've seen wear all different shades of gray and blue," he said, smiling at the old lady. "On a battlefield it is probably darned confusing to tell who the enemy actually is. This will do just fine. Thank you, Mrs. Summers."

The old man walked to the fireplace and lifted a saber from its pegs above the mantel. "I took this sword off a British officer at the battle of New Orleans. Wear it . . . with my blessing, son." His eyes bored into Clayton. "It was used against the United States then too."

At daylight on February twelfth, the Confederate troops at Fort Donelson had manned their battle stations and were awaiting the enemy. Gun crews had rammed canisters of grapeshot, nails, and pieces of iron down the muzzles of their cannon; infantry units were making nervous, last-minute inspections of their weapons and gear. Many were honing their knives and bayonets to a razor-sharp edge.

Cotton drew the cinch tight as he saddled his horse. Cursing, he slammed his knee into the animal's stomach. When the horse exhaled from the blow, Cotton drew the cinch even tighter.

"Son-of-a-bitch sucks air when I gird him up," he told the cavalry officer saddling the horse next to him. "Then he lets it out when I mount up. My saddle damn near turned with me last night."

The officer dropped his stirrup into place and grinned at Cotton. "You got drunk in Dover and nearly fell out of the saddle on your way back to the fort. It wasn't your horse's fault."

Cotton nodded. "I ain't used to hard liquor, an' that's a natural fact."

"I wish we had a jug right now," the man said. "I've a notion we'll wish we were all drunk before this battle is over. We can't defend this place any better than Tilghman did Fort Henry." His horse swung its muzzle toward him and bared its teeth. He spat a stream of amber at its head and went on. "Hell, I slipped out a while ago an' took a look at the Yanks those transports are unloadin'. I swear, Cotton, the whole Union Army is comin' ashore."

Cotton adjusted his stirrups and pulled hard at the saddle to be certain it was tight. "That evens the odds," he said. "You know as well as me that one Reb can whip ten Yanks."

Both men laughed and lifted themselves into their saddles.

For four days, eighteen thousand Confederates kept twenty-seven thousand equally determined Union soldiers from the one hundred acres of Tennessee yellow-clay hilltop called Fort Donelson.

The slaughter on both sides was terrible.

Before noon on February 15, 1862, Confederate General Simon B. Buckner called Generals Floyd and Pillow and Colonel Forrest to his headquarters.

"Gentlemen, I have sent a note to the Union commander, offering to surrender." Buckner picked up a piece of paper from his desk top. "This is his reply: 'Unconditional surrender. I propose to move immediately upon your works.'"

Buckner crumpled the paper into a ball. "They're damned ungenerous and unchivalrous terms, but we have no choice. We've disabled two of their gunboats, and according to our spotters, we hit one of those boats fifty-nine times. But even with shootin' like that, it's not enough, not with four thousand of our men layin' out there dead, or wounded, or missing." Angrily, he threw the ball of paper across the room. "Our men haven't slept in eighty-four hours. Hell! I saw soldiers fall asleep under fire on the battle line. Unbelievable!"

"Just who in Hades is the Yankee commander who would dishonor us by such terms of surrender?" Forrest demanded.

"I've never heard of him before. Somebody named Grant."

"Well, he's a son-of-a-bitch!" Forrest said.

"I expect you'll get the chance to tell him so to his face," Buckner returned.

"Not me," Forrest said quietly. "I'm takin' my men out of here."

"Nathan," Buckner said, "we're entirely surrounded. There's no chance a'tall in you and your cavalry makin' it through their lines. No, I can't permit you to sacrifice any more lives."

"I'm ridin' out, General, and I'm takin' any man who wants to go."

Saluting, he turned and left the room.

Due to the heavy overcast and spitting sleet and snow, it was as dark as night by three o'clock that afternoon.

Forrest called his hollow-eyed cavalrymen together. Pulling his hat low over his eyes to shield his face from the driving sleet, he spoke to his men as though he were addressing each one individually.

"Generals Pillow, Floyd and Buckner have determined that Fort Donelson's position is untenable and have decided to surrender. We are completely surrounded, with no avenue of escape." He gazed, hard-eyed, at his troops. "Gentlemen, I didn't join the Confederacy to surrender."

Cheers rose from the ranks of the cavalrymen, and Forrest raised a gloved hand, silencing the troops. "I knew you would feel the same as I. So I informed the generals that we would be riding out.

"You are to discard everything but your fighting gear. Keep your weapons and what clothing you are wearing, and nothing more. Leave your tents and bedrolls. Tie down every piece of gear that rattles, squeaks, or grinds. Cut your blankets into squares and make hoof covers for your mounts."

Forrest looked long at the grimy, powder-burned faces that stared back at him. "I believe we can slip out of here under the cover of darkness if we do it quietly. But if we can't"—the tall colonel gave the men a one-sided, Satanic smile—"then we'll ride over the Yankee bastards."

The men cheered and hurrahed, then slouched off to assemble their gear and care for their horses, all except Cotton, who stood with sleet pelting his sour face.

"Something wrong, soldier?" asked Forrest, stepping toward the boy.

"Not exactly, Colonel, "Cotton said. "I was wonderin', sir, if'n I could take my new clothes with me. I jist got 'em from home two weeks ago."

Forrest shook his head. "Sorry, Cotton, but we've got to travel as light as possible. No extra weight. If we have to make a run for it, I want nothing slowing us down."

Cotton's shoulders slumped. "I wish I hadn't sent for all them nice warm clothes. Hell, sir, some damn Yank will be wearin' 'em a'fore the week's out."

"Probably," Forrest returned. "But it'll be a fair trade; you'll be burying him in them nice clothes before the winter's half gone—and that's a promise."

Cotton grinned. "Much obliged, Colonel."

On February twentieth, five days after the fall of Fort Donelson, the news reached Gallatin. The city went into mourning. Clayton instructed Rufus to drive him to Colonel George Elliott's farm, Elliott Spring, on East Camp Creek.

Colonel Elliott walked with Clayton to the horse barn and opened a stall door. Leading a beautiful thoroughbred into the aisle, he said, "This young stallion is a direct descendant of Atlas, one of the finest racing horses I ever owned. He's not as heavy as a war-horse needs to be, Mr. Harris, but he's a runner, and he's not gun-shy like most thoroughbreds. His name is Leviathan."

The stout old colonel ran his hand down the stallion's back and over its rump. "If you've joined Morgan's Cavalry, you're goin' to need a fast, steady horse mighty bad."

The colonel turned his piercing gaze to Clayton. "Don't let no Yankee kill or capture this animal, Harris. There's not an officer in the Union Army who rides one half so grand . . . not even that Ulysses S. Grant, who the North is hailin' as the greatest general in the world just because he finally won a battle."

Clayton studied the graceful thoroughbred appreciatively. Mr. Summers was right to send me here, he thought; there isn't a horse on Summerset that can compare with Colonel Elliott's stock. "He's a beauty, Colonel," Clayton said. "Shall we talk about his price, sir?"

As Clayton rode Leviathan down the main thoroughfare of Gallatin, weaving in and out through the throngs of Confederate soldiers who filled the streets and walkways, he saw Lettie, Susie, and Fanny step out of a general-merchandise store and turn in his direction. He considered riding by without acknowledging their presence, but Susie slipped her hand from Fanny's and raced toward him.

"What a beautiful horse!" she cried, dancing around the skittish animal. "Take me for a ride, Clayton," she begged, attempting to pat Leviathan's muzzle.

"Well now, Susie," he said, glancing sideways at Lettie's thin, sunken-cheeked face, "I'm not at all sure that Miss Billingsly would approve." His words were more a question than a statement.

"Oh, please, Clayton," Susie wailed. "Lettie won't mind . . . will you, Lettie?"

Clayton looked into Lettie's eyes. "Well?" he asked softly, appalled by how sickly she appeared.

"Ride on, Mr. Harris," the girl returned stonily. Taking Susie's hand, she moved slowly down the sidewalk.

Fanny gave Clayton an embarrassed smile, then caught Lettie's arm to help support her mistress.

Clayton touched his fingers to the brim of his hat. "Ladies," he murmured.

"Come up to the house, Clayton," Susie called over her

shoulder. "I'm dyin' to ride your horse."

Lettie yanked the girl around and said something to her
that Clayton couldn't catch, but by the way Susie's shoulders slumped, he could guess that the little girl was being
chastised. Wheeling his mount, Clayton drew abreast of
them.

"It's good to see you up and about again, Lettie," he said,
reining in. Lettie ignored him.

"Miss Lettie," he said, leaning from the saddle, "I offer
my condolences, ma'am. Bailey Peyton was a fine man. I
admired and envied him. I was a childish lout that day at
Cragfont. I'm truly sorry, Lettie." He wished she would
look at him. "I joined the Confederacy, Lettie . . ."

The girl's face snapped up, fury causing a hint of color to
creep into her cheeks. "You'll never be half the soldier
Bailey Peyton was, Mr. Harris. Furthermore, you're not fit
to mention his name." Angrily, she dabbed at her eyes with
her kerchief. "And . . . don't ever set foot on Cragfont
property again!"

"Can't you forgive me, Lettie?" he asked, his voice as
emotionless as hers was animated. "Do you hate me so
much that we can't even be friends?"

"Yes," she flung at him. "I loved Bailey Peyton. I just
didn't realize how much until—" She turned her back on
him and slumped against the building. Her shoulders
heaved as she wept.

Clayton glanced at Fanny for confirmation, and was
shocked by her appearance for she was as worn-looking as
her mistress. Fanny said, "It might be better, Mr. Clayton, if you stayed 'way for a while."

"She's blamin' the world for Mr. Peyton's death, Clayton," Susie said, putting her arm around Lettie's waist.
"Grandmama says it will take a while for her to get back to
bein' herself again."

Clayton nodded, but he was thinking that Mrs. Winchester was mistaken. Neither Lettie nor he would ever be
themselves again. Part of each of them had been lost at
Fishing Creek, Kentucky. The ironic thing was that neither
of them had even known they were there.

With one last look at Lettie, he turned his horse and again
threaded his way through the milling soldiers who, like him,

seemed bent on going someplace but didn't quite know where.

When Clayton and the Summerses descended the front steps of Summerset at daybreak of February 21, 1862, Rufus waited at the mounting block with two saddled horses.

"Yore soldier suit shore looks purty, Master Clay," he said. "You look jist like a general, with them knee boots and sword, and that purple sash to match the plume in your hat. Yes, sir, you shore are a fine-lookin' soldier."

"He's after something," Clayton said to Mr. Summers. "All right, Rufus, why have you saddled two horses?"

Rufus kicked a frozen clod of dirt with the toe of his brogan.

"I'm a-goin' with you, Master Clay."

"No you're not," Clayton said, wondering if Rufus had lost what little sense he, Clayton Harris, had beat into his brain over the past two years. "I didn't teach you to read and write and do arithmetic so you can go off to war and get it shot out of you."

Rufus dropped his head. "Shucks, Mr. Clay, I won't mind bein' shot at long as I can be with you."

Mr. Summers said, "You might as well take him with you, son. He won't be worth a tinker's damn around here with you gone."

"He'll just be in my way," Clayton argued.

"No, sir! I shore won't, Mr. Clay," Rufus said. "You goin' to need somebody to look after yore fine new horse, an' do yore washin', an' yore cookin' . . . 'cause you know you can't do none of them things."

Clayton threw up his hands in defeat. "All right. Get yourself a blanket and some clothing, and that old pair of boots I left in the chifferobe."

Grinning broadly, Rufus reached behind the mounting block and held up a tightly rolled traveling pack. "I got me everything we're gonna need. Mizz Summers even loaned us one of her good skillets."

Clayton wheeled on the old couple. "You've been planning on him going along since the beginning, haven't you?"

"Well," Mr. Summers drawled, "even though you ain't exactly helpless, Rufus'll be an aid to you, son. Furthermore

—and you ain't thought about it, 'cause you ain't been faced with it yet—you're goin' to need somebody to be your runner. If you think we're goin' to let you go off to war and not know what's happenin' to you, you're wrong. Now, Rufus knows what he's s'posed to do. He's goin' along to keep us informed."

Rufus nodded his head. "I'm an informant."

Clayton scowled at the old couple. "I hope you know what you're doing, sending Rufus with me. If he goes around telling everyone he's an informant, they'll hang him for a spy."

Mr. Summers laughed. "Rufus will be all right, you'll see."

Clayton walked over to Mrs. Summers and caught her hand. The old lady pushed his arm aside and flung her arms around his neck. "We love you, Clayton," she said. "Please come home safely."

"I will, ma'am." He kissed her wrinkled cheek. Then, turning to Mr. Summers, he shook the old man's hand. "Thank you, sir, for everything."

Mr. Summers pushed Clayton toward the waiting horse. "I never did like good-byes. Go on, take yourself off to war."

Clayton and Rufus trotted their mounts down the lane to the first bend, where, in spite of himself, Clayton drew rein and turned for one last look at Summerset. He had the feeling that the place he had called home for over three years would never be the same again, no matter who won the war.

Mr. and Mrs. Summers, looking forlorn, and indeed ancient, waved to him. With his mouth suddenly gone bone-dry, he snatched off his hat and saluted the old couple. Wheeling Leviathan, he raced down the lane and did not look back again.

On February twenty-eighth, Clayton sat in his field tent at Murfreesboro, Tennessee, fifty miles south of Gallatin, and watched through his partially drawn tent flap as file after file of haggard, beaten infantrymen from Fort Donelson dragged their feet through the ankle-deep mud.

It was a heartbreaking sight, but even more discouraging was the news they brought. Nashville was in a state of panic. The streets there were thronged with soldiers and civilians vying for any means of transportation that might evacuate them from the city, for the Union flotilla was coming up the Cumberland to take possession of Middle Tennessee. Even more stunning and demoralizing was the Confederacy's decision to surrender Nashville without firing a shot.

The only bright spot was the fact that Colonel N.B. Forrest had escaped with his entire cavalry . . . and that the Union's conquering hero, Ulysses S. Grant, was said to be furious.

Rufus, heedless of the mud he was splashing every which way, burst through the tent flaps. "Mista Clayton! Mista Clayton!" He snatched up Clayton's coat and held it open for him. "Come quick, they's more cavalry comin' in, and Mista Cotton's with 'em!"

Clayton sprang to his feet and rammed his arms through the coat sleeves. Cramming his hat low over his eyes, he struck off in a run with Rufus, oblivious to the mud he splashed onto the weary troops who were passing.

Cotton had just pulled the saddle from his jaded horse and dropped it unceremoniously into the mire when Clayton bounded up. For a moment the two young men appraised one another. Then, with an oath, Cotton crushed Clayton to him. "Damn, it's good to see you!" Pushing Clayton to arm's length, he eyed the blue uniform. "You a goddamned prisoner, or what?"

Clayton pumped Cotton's hand, laughing with delight. Inwardly, however, he was appalled by Cotton's appearance. It wasn't Cotton's gray pallor or thin frame that bothered Clayton the most; it was the dullness of his eyes and the forced look about his perpetual grin.

"No," Clayton said, "my uniform is just a strange color of gray, that's all."

Cotton fingered one of the old brass buttons that Mrs. Summers had stolen from Mr. Summers' uniform of 1812. "What's the U.S. stand for on these buttons, then?"

Clayton grinned widely. "It stands for United South, naturally."

Cotton laughed. "How are Mr. and Mizz Summers . . . and things at Summerset? Hell, boy, I'm dyin' for information, so tell me everything, and don't leave out nothin'."

Clayton slipped his arm through Cotton's and turned him toward the tent. "Rufus will see to your horse and gear. You and I have some tall catching up to do."

As they sloshed toward the tent, Clayton filled Cotton in on the local news.

"Sorry to hear about Bailey Peyton," Cotton said. "He wasn't a bad sort. I saw a lot of our neighbors die at Henry an' Donelson. It was a goddamned slaughter, Clay. It gets easier to stomach after a while, tho'."

Clayton glanced sideways at his friend. Cotton's eyes had that same hundred-year-old look that he'd seen in nearly every young face that had marched past that morning. Lord, Clayton silently prayed, don't ever let me see the side of hell that can burn the youth out of a person in the blink of an eye. Amen.

"That's one of the reasons I'm here," Cotton continued. "Colonel Forrest sent a dispatch to Morgan. I don't know exactly what the orders are, but I've a notion that Capt'n Morgan is supposed to harass the Yankees on the north side of the Cumberland River while our army rebuilds itself. Forrest says that quick as we're strong enough, he aims to attack Nashville from the south. That's what the shit-house rumor is, anyhow."

Clayton nodded. He'd heard it too.

"You can bunk in with me," Clayton said when they reached the tent. "I'll send Rufus after your belongings."

Cotton laughed and shook his head. "Then tell him to fetch my saddle, 'cause that's all the belongings I own, 'cept for these two brand-new Navy Colt revolvers I took off'n a couple of dead Yankee officers. I figure they're a trade-out for the clothes I had to leave at Donelson."

Cotton pulled two .36-caliber pistols from his waistband and handed them to Clayton. "Them's good shootin' guns, Clay. Better'n anything we're makin' in the South."

Clayton cocked the weapons several times, observing the smooth action of the revolving cylinders.

"You keep them loaded full around?" he questioned, noticing that each nipple was capped. "I've heard that most of the men leave one cylinder empty for the hammer to rest on . . . a safety precaution."

"I ain't goin' to shoot myself, not like some of the idiots done did. And you never know when you just might need that extra ball. Hell, I've needed it a time or two already."

* * *

The first Union soldiers tramped into Gallatin on March second, their band blaring out the strains of "Dixie." They had a billowing backdrop of black, oily smoke to the north, where the Confederate recruits had burned the barracks and buildings of Camp Zollicoffer, at Richland, before retreating.

In Gallatin, church bells tolled as for a funeral. Citizens draped white bed sheets from their windows as the Federal soldiers hauled down and burned the Confederate flag.

Lettie, Susie, and Fanny, along with old Mrs. Winchester, were visiting the Trousdales in Gallatin. They stood on the front stoop of Trousdale Place and watched the crisp, neat Union troops parade past.

"All they're goin' to do is set up a telegraph office here in Gallatin," the old lady commented. "Thank the Lord they're going on to Nashville and won't be bivouacking here. Nothin' or no one would be safe." She cast a glance at Lettie and Fanny. Especially not the two of you, she thought. You would fast become the spoils of war.

"Granny," Susie said, paying close attention as the troops filed past. "I don't see no horns or tails on them devils."

Fanny clamped her hand over Susie's mouth. "Hush," she whispered. "They'll hear you."

"Well, I don't!" mumbled Susie around Fanny's fingers. "You told me that all the Yankees had horns an' tails."

Old Mrs. Winchester gave Fanny a stern look. "You should be ashamed of yourself, tellin' a child such non-sense." She pulled Susie close and hugged her. "They're only devils in their hearts, honey. That's what Fanny meant, wasn't it, Fanny?"

"Fanny's right," said Lettie. "They are the spawn of hell. Probably the same ones who murdered . . . Bailey."

Mrs. Winchester winced. She wished Lettie would release the grief that she had bottled up inside her. If she would cry, perhaps then she could learn to laugh again.

After establishing their telegraph office in the railroad depot on the northwest side of town, the Union Army continued on to Nashville and reported to the Union commander, General Don Carols Buell, that Sumner County was secure.

Secure, indeed, was how Gallatin appeared at three

o'clock in the afternoon of March sixteenth, when Captain John Hunt Morgan, Clayton Harris, Cotton, and Rufus rode slowly through the city toward the depot. Each man, including Rufus, was wearing a Union greatcoat, taken during a train raid in Kentucky. With their hats pulled low and their collars turned up, they drew no attention; Union soldiers passing through Gallatin were becoming a common sight.

The three cavalrymen dismounted and handed their bridle reins to Rufus. Then, unbuttoning their overcoats, they slipped their pistols from their holsters and walked into the train station.

The telegraph operator, a lean man wearing gold-rimmed spectacles, glanced up as the door opened, then continued pecking out a message.

"Be with you in a minute," he said, appraising Morgan's six-foot frame while his fingers drummed the key. "We just got word that Morgan's Cavalry has abandoned Murfrees-boro and might be heading this way."

"Is that so?" Morgan drawled, tipping his hat lower to hide his gray-blue eyes.

The operator looked up over his spectacles. "Where you from, mister? You've got a Southern accent."

Morgan brought his hand from beneath his coat and cocked his .44-caliber Starr double-action revolver, point-ing it directly between the operator's eyes.

"Morgan's Cavalry is here," he said, tipping up his hat brim to reveal the polished-brass C.S.A. emblem that was pinned to the underside.

"Son-of-a-bitch," breathed the operator, his face mottling with rage and shock. "Where's those idiot guards who were supposed to keep you from getting in here?"

Morgan shot a glance at Clayton and Cotton. "You boys scout around and see if you can locate them. And send Rufus to bring up the rest of our men." As the two started through the door, Morgan cautioned, "Be careful, boys. They were expectin' us."

"You want us to shoot them guards when we find 'em, Capt'n?" Cotton asked.

Morgan shook his head. "Not unless it's necessary. I'd like to do this job quietly."

When Clayton gave him the order, Rufus pivoted his

horse and heeled the animal into a hard run for the east end of town, where forty Confederate cavalrymen waited.

Clayton and Cotton rode slowly to the courthouse square, their eyes searching each walkway and window they passed. The guards were nowhere to be seen.

At the courthouse, Josephus Conn Guild, of Rosemont Plantation, was walking down the steps. Clayton knew him; he had visited Rosemont several times in the past.

"Mr. Guild," Clayton said, drawing in his horse, "have you seen any Union guards around here? We've lost a couple."

The elderly Guild leaned on his cane and studied Clayton and Cotton cautiously. Then his thin face lit up with recognition. "Well, I'll be derned!" he said. "I mistook you boys for Yankees, and I wasn't about to tell you nothin'. You-all are takin' a chance comin' into Gallatin alone; there's Federals passin' through here all the time."

"We're lookin' for the sons-of-bitches what guard the telegraph office," Cotton said, "an' we ain't alone. Morgan's got forty men here."

Guild laughed. "Those guards you're lookin' for are sittin' in the courthouse hallway playin' checkers by the stove. Insolent bunch of scalawags, they are; they think they've scared us Rebels to death." The old man hobbled to the door. "Step right in, boys. It'll be a pleasure to introduce you."

Clayton and Cotton marched the two guards into the depot.

The operator, sitting on the floor in a corner, threw the Union soldiers a murderous look before turning his face to the wall.

Morgan indicated the operator with a flip of his pistol barrel. "Clayton, this dispatcher was good enough to tell me that a train is due here momentarily. Take half the men an' hide them on each side of the tracks. We'll catch ourselves a Yankee engine and tender."

When the locomotive chugged to a steaming, hissing halt outside the depot, Clayton sprang into the cab and shoved the barrel of one of Cotton's Colts against the engineer's temple. "You, sir," he told the astonished man, "are a prisoner of the Confederate States of America."

"Christ Almighty!" the burley engineer exclaimed. "Gallatin's supposed to be Union-held."

Cotton, who had followed Clayton into the engine, reached up and pulled the whistle lanyard, producing a long, piercing wail of steam.

"I always wanted to do that," he said, grinning at Clayton.

The train crew, along with twenty carpenters who were traveling to make repairs along the railroad bed, were quickly overpowered by Morgan's men and paraded to the depot.

As Morgan stepped outside the building to take charge of the prisoners, he was met by Josephus Conn Guild and a large body of civilians, most of them elderly men armed with pitchforks, briar scythes, and a few ancient pistols.

"We'll take care of your prisoners, Captain Morgan," Guild said. "You an' your men just go on about your business an' don't worry about these Federals."

Morgan touched his hat brim. "Much obliged, sir. I was wonderin' what we were goin' to do with them."

Then, looking out over the railroad yard, Morgan said, "We can't take these train cars with us, an' we can't leave em' for the Yankees. Run all the cars an' engines together and burn them."

"You talkin' 'bout the ones on the sidetracks too?" Cotton asked.

Morgan nodded. "Anything that rolls. Keep the best engine, because we're going to need it. But burn the rest." Turning, he entered the depot, where Clayton was seated at the desk poring over several secret dispatches. "Find anything interesting, Private?"

Clayton smiled up at him. "Mighty careless man, the operator. These are confidential orders from General Buell in Nashville."

As dusk settled cold and low over Gallatin, Morgan's great train-car bonfire got underway. The glow of the sixteen cars and two engines lit the underside of the treetop-level clouds with an incandescence that had people in Goodlettsville, twenty miles away, wondering what the flickering phenomenon might be.

Before daylight the next morning, the Confederates were again at work, dismantling the high, stilt-legged wooden water tank that overlooked the depot. Without water to replenish their boilers, any locomotives coming into Gallatin would be stranded.

Morgan, Clayton, Cotton, Rufus, and ten cavalrymen boarded the remaining engine and ran it full-throttle north. They stopped the engine in the middle of a tunnel six miles out of Gallatin and walked on through the passageway to its mouth.

"According to those confidential dispatches you found, Clayton, there's a Federal mail train due to come through here this mornin' from Louisville," Morgan said, gazing up the tracks. "Reckon we'll just sit a spell an' see if we've got any letters aboard."

"Sure will be a bunch of pissed-off Yankees in Nashville when they find out we read their sweethearts' mail," Cotton said.

"You can't read," scoffed a cavalryman.

Cotton's face flamed. "I can so read. Hell, anybody with any sense can read. Even Rufus can read."

The soldiers pinned the young slave with hostile eyes. Rufus dropped his head. "Massa Cotton were jist a-funnin', sirs," he mumbled in his best slave manner.

Morgan caught Rufus' chin in his hand and tipped his head back so he could look into his face. "Can you read and write, boy?"

Rufus rolled his eyes toward Clayton; Clayton nodded for Rufus to tell Morgan the truth.

"Yes, sir. I can read, write, and do ciphers, sir."

Morgan's brows raised in surprise. "That's somethin' to store in the back of my mind. An educated slave . . . you could come in mighty handy, Rufus." Morgan turned and walked up the tracks, watching the horizon for the telltale smoke of the approaching train.

Two hours later a cavalryman galloped his horse out of the mouth of the tunnel and hailed Morgan. "Ain't no train a-comin', Capt'n. Somebody done warned the Yankees in Nashville that we're at Gallatin."

"I figured as much," Morgan said. "All right, men, stoke up the engine. We're headin' back."

When they reached Gallatin, several score of well-wishers were gathered at the depot. Amid wild cheers, they presented Morgan with a battle flag.

Clayton studied the crowd. He had entertained the romantic notion that when the news of the raid spread through the county, perhaps Lettie would come to see him. But no one from Cragfont was there. The Summerses, however, came racing down the street in the phaeton. Shouting for folks to get out of the way, Mr. Summers drove the carriage to the depot walkway. Standing up so he would tower over those on foot, he called to Clayton: "We didn't figure you'd get a chance to ride by the house, so we came on in."

Mrs. Summers also stood. But before she could speak, Clayton, Cotton, and Rufus were climbing into the phaeton.

Many of the civilians, including the Summerses, followed Morgan's detachment three miles south to the Cumberland River and helped ferry the Confederates to the opposite bank.

Clayton, with Cotton and Rufus following, broke away from the group and rode over to the phaeton. "We've been ordered back to Murfreesboro," he said, leaning from the saddle to shake Mr. and Mrs. Summers' hands. "But if all goes well, we should get a furlough before too long. We'll see you then."

Sparks from Morgan's train-car bonfire, however, had ignited a powder keg of repercussions that would keep the Confederate cavalry in the field for months to come.

CHAPTER 17

The Louisville Daily Journal reported that the surprise visit to Gallatin by Morgan's Raiders had netted "two bridges, a water tank, a construction train, and two locomotives, in addition to telegraph wires and apparatus, plus a score of prisoners."

Morgan laughed. "Damn fools can't get anything right. One of those engines was already damaged, and we didn't burn any bridges at all."

In Nashville, General Buell was furious. He immediately dispatched two companies of the 9th Pennsylvania Cavalry to Gallatin, and on the first of April, the 5th Regiment Kentucky Cavalry, consisting of 789 men, joined them. Then Ulysses S. Grant, taking the raid as a personal insult, placed the entire State of Tennessee under martial law. President Lincoln appointed Tennessee's own son, Andrew Johnson, military governor of the state.

On April ninth, the flame of joy that Morgan had lit in the hearts of Sumner Countians was doused when news came from a place called Shiloh Churchhouse, in West Tennessee, that on April sixth, General Albert S. Johnson's forty thousand Confederates had attacked Ulysses S. Grant's seventy-five thousand men.

The defeat was devastating, with over ten thousand Confederate men killed or wounded. Nearly every Sumner County family suffered a loss, for Colonel William B. Bate, of Gallatin, with the 2nd Tennessee Regiment and the remnants of Bailey Peyton's 20th Regiment, had joined with five other Sumner County companies to become the vanguard of Johnson's army.

Then, to make matters worse, on April 11, 1862, the new military governor sent orders to Colonel Haggard, Federal commanding officer at Gallatin, demanding the arrest of Josephus Conn Guild for "uttering treasonable language and using his influence during Morgan's siege to insurrect the people of Sumner County against the Government of the United States."

No one was fooled by Guild's arrest; it was intended to discourage the people from lending aid to the Confederacy. As Cotton put it, "Ol' Morgan sure stirred up a passel of shit!"

In the next few weeks many more Sumner Countians were arrested and jailed at Nashville. Included were A.R. Wynne, Robert Williamson, and Jonathan Summers. Surprisingly, all three were regarded by the local people as Union sympathizers.

Then, in May, Morgan experienced his first setback. His cavalry suffered a surprise attack at Lebanon, Tennessee, that netted the 7th Pennsylvania Cavalry, under General Ebenezer DuPont, some three hundred of Morgan's eleven hundred Raiders.

Morgan wasn't long in retaliating. Calling newly commissioned Lieutenant Clayton Harris into his field tent, he said, "We've got a job that needs doing. We are goin' to take Gallatin away from the Federals." He leaned back in his chair, lit a long, black cheroot and blew the smoke toward the ceiling while Clayton digested the news.

"We will need a spy the Yankees won't suspect, someone they hold in higher contempt than they do us Southern gentlemen. He will have to be someone sharp enough to know when he sees or hears something important. But most of all, he will have to be a man I can trust with the lives of my cavalry."

Clayton nodded uncertainly. "Who do you have in mind, Colonel?"

Morgan clamped the cigar between his teeth. "Do you trust that darky of yours?"

Incredulity filled Clayton's face. "Yes, sir. He's a loyal friend, but—"

"Would you trust him with your life?"

"That depends."

"On what?"

"On whether you're asking me if I would trust Rufus to give up his life for me. I wouldn't trust any man to do that."

Morgan settled back and appraised Clayton through the cigar smoke that hung like gauze above the desk. He understood Clayton's reluctance to send Rufus on a mission that could get him hanged, but personal feelings had to be put aside: He needed a spy.

"Would you trust him not to give information to the enemy if he were captured?" Morgan asked.

Clayton shrugged. "Who knows what a man would do?"

Morgan grinned. "Call him in here."

Rufus approached Morgan nervously. "You want to see me, Colonel, sir?"

"Rufus, I need a good man to go into Gallatin an' see what's goin' on there; I want to know every move the Federals are makin'. I can't send a cavalryman 'cause they'd spot him right off . . ."

Rufus took a step backward. "Colonel, I can't go into Gallatin an' act as no spy for you!"

"Why not?"

"Why, sir, Mr. Clay says they hang spies . . ."

Morgan nodded. "They do, Rufus. If they discover them. That's why I want you to go in. They'd never suspect a nigger, not in a thousand years." He winked at Rufus. "Why, everybody knows how stupid you boys are."

Rufus took a deep breath and turned to Clayton. "What do you think, Mr. Clay?"

"I can't make that decision, Rufus," Clayton said, avoiding Rufus' eyes. "Only you can."

Rufus turned to Morgan. "When do you want me to go down there, sir?"

Morgan gave a pleased grin. "Today. Leave your horse at

Summerset and walk into Gallatin. Pretend you're a runaway. Get as close to the big brass as possible. Perhaps a job as personal valet to the commander. Don't try to get in touch with me. I'll contact you. Trust no one, Rufus, unless he tells you Lieutenant Clayton Harris sent him." He offered the boy his hand. "Be careful, soldier."

Surprised, pleased, and embarrassed, Rufus shook Morgan's hand. "I'll get the information you need, Colonel. Don't worry about me."

Rufus shuffled down the bustling main street of Gallatin, trying hard to conceal his shock at what he saw. After four months of Union Army occupation and the arrest of many prominent Sumner Countians, the local men were sullen and aloof, and the women were openly hostile, carrying small Confederate flags and calling the Union soldiers names that would never have crossed their lips a year before.

Rufus spent three days determining the safest way to gain an audience with the Northern commander, Colonel William P. Boone. On the fourth day he made his move.

The young sentry standing guard at the door of the Johnny Bell Hotel where the officers were housed brought his rifle up to port arms at Rufus' approach.

"Move on, boy," he ordered. "This hotel is the officers' quarters. There ain't nothing here for you. If you're looking for a handout, try the back door."

"But, Cap'n," Rufus cried, attempting to sidestep the guard, "I wants to see the gen'l . . ."

Colonel Boone, his tight-fitting uniform emphasizing his paunchy stomach, stepped out the door. "What's all the commotion, Private?" Then Boone's red heavily veined face turned an even darker shade. "What in Christ's name does this field hand want?"

Rufus smiled to himself. He had timed things just right. "I's done run'd away, Gen'l Boone, Massa," he said before the sentry could speak. "The Federates done nearly worked my ol' bones to death. Look at me, suh! I's only a tintype turned sideways of what I once't was. I's a good nigger, suh, an' I work hard. I's a man's valet, and I wants to serve the gen'l!"

"Send this boy on his way, Private," Boone said, walking

widely around Rufus toward his waiting surrey.

Rufus followed him down the steps, ignoring the young sentry's orders to move on. "But, Gen'l, suh," he said, "I can shine boots, press pants, polish buttons. I's a dandy button polisher, suh. Ever' gen'l needs hisself a nigger boy to fetch fo' him . . . ain't manly not to have one."

Boone stopped and pursed his lips. "You might have something there. What's your name?"

"I's Jim Childress, suh," Rufus lied, wondering where that name had popped up from. He had never heard of anyone named Jim Childress.

The colonel nodded at Rufus. "Be at the door to my quarters tonight at six o'clock sharp. I've a supper engagement at eight, and my uniform will need pressing."

"Yas, suh, Gen'l! I be there, six o'clock. But how is I gwine to know it's six o' clock?"

"Ask somebody!" came Boone's irritated reply as he climbed into the surrey.

Rufus gave the colonel a half-wit's grin and nodded. He slouched up Main Street, turned a corner onto South Water Street, and fell against the brick wall of the closest building.

There he shook like a dog shedding water; he didn't like being a spy, didn't like it at all.

Within a week Rufus had a permanent position as the colonel's valet. He took his meals at the Johnny Bell with the cooks in the hotel kitchen and slept in the attic; he worked part-time as the hotel lackey, serving the Northern officers and their wives who patronized the establishment. And he stumbled into the most productive role of all: As a favor to one of the Federal officers billeted there, he persuaded a young and pretty black chambermaid to visit the man's room for an evening. From that moment on, Rufus became the United States Army's pimp—a position that opened doors to information where there were no doors.

Sunrise had turned the sky to rose-gold when Clayton Harris rode wearily up the Cragfont driveway. What would be his reception? He hoped that Lettie's grief had diminished enough that she might acknowledge his presence with something other than contempt. He sighed. It really made no difference, for it wasn't Lettie he had come to see. It was Fanny.

Colonel Morgan needed a runner, a go-between for Rufus and the Confederates, someone who would be above suspicion. The only people who fell into that category were the slaves, because all whites, even the Union sympathizers, were distrusted by the Federal Army.

Upon Clayton's recommendation, Morgan had agreed that if old Mrs. Winchester would consent, Fanny would act as message bearer.

Clayton appraised Cragfont as he approached. The beautiful old plantation was already taking on the subtle appearance of neglect, as though the necessary work was being accomplished but without the love and care that had been lavished in the past.

No one met him at the mounting block to take his horse. Gazing at the empty fields, puzzled by the absence of activity on a workday, he swung down and opened the gate.

He was bone-weary, having traveled for four nights, with only an occasional catnap during the daylight hours. He wanted little more than to take care of the business at hand and then make good use of one of Cragfont's bedchambers.

He led Leviathan to the barn; no grooms were there. After wiping down the horse and pouring a bucket of grain into the feed trough, he stepped outside. Full daylight revealed smoke curling lazily from the kitchen chimney. At least old Chatty was up.

Chatty cracked the door open to his knock.

"What fo' you want at dis time o' mornin'?" she demanded, gazing squint-eyed at Clayton's blue uniform. "Yo' Yankee allus' out here a-messin' 'round at God-awful hours."

"Hush, Chatty," he whispered, forcing the door open and stepping into the kitchen. Then, dropping down on the three-legged stool next to the hearth, he said, "I could sure use a cup of hot coffee, Chatty."

"My Lawd!" she cried to Delphy, who was stoking the fire, "It's Massa Clayton, his own self! My Lawd."

She quickly poured him a cup of steaming coffee.

Delphy took an iron skillet from its hook over the mantel. "From the looks of yo'," she said, eyeing Clayton from head to toe, "yo' could use some ham an' eggs too."

Clayton ran his hand across his four-day stubble of beard. "And a bath and a shave. Heck, Delphy, I could use just about everything. I don't even feel human anymore."

"Well, we can fix you right up with . . . about every-thing." Fanny was standing in the doorway that opened into the dining room.

Clayton threw her a startled glance. She was heavy-eyed and disheveled, her thick, ash-blond hair falling in cascades over a worn, faded-blue nightdress. She flashed him a sleepy smile, and he wondered if she had always been so beautiful.

Fanny walked to the hearth where Clayton sat and poured herself some coffee. "You look real good, Mr. Clayton," she lied, thinking how very tired and haggard he appeared while at the same time experiencing a strong desire to take him in her arms and rock him to sleep as she would a child.

"Yo' git on out'n here," Chatty ordered Fanny. "Yo' go turn down de guest bed fo' Mista Clayton an' tell ol' Miss dat he be here. She'll be a-wantin' to talk wif' him fo' sho'."

By the time Clayton had finished eating, the household was awake and he joined old Widow Winchester by the dining-room hearth. She sat in a Chippendale chair, sipped her coffee, and listened closely to his adventures of the past six months. She broke in occasionally with questions. But for the most part, she and Susie and Susie's mother, Malvinia—who breast-fed her two-year-old daughter while listening—let him talk uninterruptedly. Lettie had inten-tionally absented herself from the meeting. He had hoped that her curiosity, at least, would have compelled her to be present.

"Mrs. Winchester," he said finally, "I would appreciate it, ma'am, if I could speak to you. Alone."

"Of course," the old lady said. "But if it's bad news about my son George or my grandson Napoleon, I believe we should all hear it at once. We are a strong family, Clayton."

"It's not bad news, ma'am. But it is a matter that I would rather discuss only with you."

"Come, Susie," Malvinia said. "We've got mornin' chores to see to." Then, smiling self-consciously at Clayton, she explained: "Our darkies have gotten so triflin'. We have to keep after them to get them to do anything."

"Yes," Susie said. "Since the Yankees started ridin' over

the countryside tellin' them they are goin' to be free, it sure has been hard on us, tryin' to keep our land producin'."
Clayton was surprised anew by Susie's mature grasp of plantation problems. She's only ten years old, he thought sadly. He looked into her eyes; they were still young, trusting eyes, beautifully young.

When they were alone, Mrs. Winchester said, "The Yankees have been sayin' that Mr. Lincoln is draftin' a proclamation that will free the slaves. It sounds too incredible to be true! He swore on the Bible that this war had nothing to do with slavery."

"I don't believe Lincoln started out intending to free the slaves, ma'am. I think the war has snowballed into a political monster that neither side can control."

"Politicians have a way of lettin' that happen, don't they? Except that this time the American people are paying the price with their blood instead of with their money." Mrs. Winchester looked hard at Clayton. "No matter the outcome of this war, Clayton, politicians have the ability to separate themselves from reality; they are the ultimate excuse makers. But worse than that, they readily believe their own lies, for they are born without a conscience. No," she sighed, "that's not entirely true. I too believe that Mr. Lincoln bleeds for every man who is killed . . . and that human tenderness will, in the end, be the direct cause of his death, just as he is the direct cause of ours, of the South's."

Squaring her shoulders, Mrs. Winchester said, "Enough of cracker-barrel speeches. Tell me what it is that you don't want my family to hear."

"Yes," Lettie said from the doorway, "I would like very much to hear. Because if it concerns me, sir . . ."

Clayton made no attempt to hide his appraisal of Lettie. For even though it was early morning, she was fully dressed and her hair had been drawn severely to the back of her head and fashioned into a heavy bun. Although she was still underweight and pale, she was delicately lovely.

Clayton rose to his feet and inclined his head in a mock bow. Then he smiled at the girl. "If I had come here to speak either to or about you, Lettie, I assure you that I would have done so in your presence. But I didn't come for that."

Lettie took a step backward, her hand fluttering to her throat. Then she turned, and Clayton could hear her light tread on the staircase.

"She's a very disturbed young woman," Mrs. Winchester said. "She still blames herself for Bailey Peyton's death."

I know the feeling well, thought Clayton, running his hand through his hair.

"Clayton." The old lady touched his arm. "Why don't you get some sleep? Whatever it is you must say, it'll keep until you've rested."

Clayton nodded his thanks.

Shadows were stealing in through the window when Clayton awoke. It took him a moment to orient himself. Then, snuggling deeper into the feather-tick mattress, he sighed with pleasure. At last he sat up, stretched, and gazed about the room. A galvanized washtub had been placed in the corner while he slept, and he could see steam rising from it.

How long had it been since he had taken a real bath, one with hot water and soap? He couldn't remember. I must smell to high heaven, he thought, climbing from the bed and stepping into the water. Slowly he settled himself into a sitting position, his knees drawn up under his chin.

He closed his eyes. Before the war, he had never considered bathing a luxury. In fact, since he had become a soldier, many things he had previously taken for granted had become glorious extravagances.

There was a light knock on the door and Fanny stepped in, closing the door behind her. For a long moment she stood there, her eyes openly caressing him, her fingers toying with the shaving mug she carried.

Clayton blushed and slid farther down into the tub. The slave girl gave a throaty laugh.

Crossing the room, she knelt beside him and dipped the shaving mug into the water. "Don't say a word, Mr. Clay," she whispered. "I can't stay long or they'll miss me. I wants to shave you."

"I can shave myself, Fanny."

As though she had not heard, she whipped the soap into a foaming lather that bubbled over the edge of the mug, then brushed the lather onto his cheeks. With practiced hands she deftly drew the straight razor across his right cheek.

"I use' to shave Mr. George and Mr. Napoleon, before

they done went off to the war," she said.

"Did you do it while they bathed?" he asked dryly.

Fanny twisted his chin up so she could scrape his throat. "No. I had no d'sire to see them naked. Now hush, so I won't nick you."

Clayton put his hands between his thighs to cover his nudity. Fanny laughed. "Who do you think undressed you, Mr. Clay?"

Clayton groaned. "I was hoping I had undressed myself."

The girl smiled. "You was dead to the world. I don't believe your head hardly touched the pillow a'fore you was asleep. Anyways, your modesty is unnecessary, 'cause I have . . . seen you naked a'fore."

Clayton shifted uneasily. Fanny was leaning over the tub, and the coarse fabric of her blouse where it was drawn tight across her breasts caused his skin to tingle each time she brushed against him. As she moved the razor to the other side of his face, he said, "That night was a mistake, Fanny," then winced as the blade clipped his skin.

"Oh," the girl said, "I believe I have cut you . . ." Then she looked into his eyes. "A mistake is sometimes just a tiny cut, Mr. Clay, but it bleeds p'fusely . . . for a long time."

Clayton hastily changed the subject. "How in the world have you learned to speak the way you do now, and so quickly? I taught school for several months and not one of my scholars, except Rufus, speaks half as well as you do."

Fanny dabbed at the cut on his cheek with the corner of a towel. "Miss Susie been teachin' me. I talk a lot better than I can read or write. In fact, Miss Susie done say I speak better English than lots of educated folk hereabouts." Pride showed in Fanny's face, coloring her dusky cheeks a rosy hue. "Miss Susie says I talk better than her, too. An' she says slaves got no reason to talk so fine, but she teaches me anyhow."

"You've done well, Fanny," Clayton said sincerely. "But you must have worked night and day."

"I practiced all the time . . . I still do," she said, pleased by his compliment. "Sometimes I get excited, or mad, and r'vert back to talkin' like a nigger."

"What made you work so hard?"

The girl busied herself wiping lather off his face, her dark eyes veiled by her thick eyelashes. "Rufus talks so fine," she said finally. "You treat him with respect. I thought that maybe if'n I learnt to talk better . . . I's gettin' nervous, sir." She moved from the tub and turned her back to him. "I love you, Massa Clayton," she said simply. "I wishn't yo'd buy me so's I would b'long to yo', forever."

"Jesus Christ, Fanny!" he said, jumping to his feet and stepping out of the tub. Bathwater sloshed onto the wide-planked floor. "I don't believe in buying and selling people."

Fanny dropped to her knees and quickly toweled up the overflow before it could seep through the cracks between the boards and ruin the plastered ceiling below. Then, flinging her arms around his legs and pressing her face against his thigh, she sobbed, "Please buy me, Mr. Clay. I will be a good slave. I'll work hard fo' yo', an' not complain . . ." Her tears mingled with the bathwater, losing themselves on his already wet skin.

Clayton sucked in his breath. He had been without a woman for a long time, and Fanny's nearness was more than he could endure. Lifting her into his arms, he carried her to the bed.

CHAPTER 18

July 8, 1862, was an exceedingly hot day, and Rufus was in a foul humor as he struggled with one of Colonel Boone's heavy war trunks. He was taking it to the buggy and implement shop on North Water Street so the latch could be mended. Fanny caught him at the corner of the courthouse square.

"Hello, Rufus," she said. "I need to talk to you."

Startled, he quickly scanned the square. "Fanny, what are you doin' in Gallatin?"

"Lieutenant Clayton Harris sent me, Rufus," she whispered.

Rufus' face turned chalky. "You? They sent you? Doggone it, why didn't they send a man?"

"Because I can do the job better," bristled the girl. "Do you think you're the only slave who's got any sense?"

Rufus groaned. "Why, you won't even be able to remember what I tell you, an' I got important information to pass on, Fanny."

"Try me. I'll remember it."

Rufus shook his head. Then, reluctantly, he told her the intelligence, stressing the fact that she was to deliver it to

Colonel Morgan quickly.

True to her boast, Fanny remembered every word and conveyed the message without a flaw. It was the beginning of a pattern. As the weeks went by, Fanny traveled to and from Gallatin regularly.

On July thirty-first, Fanny was again in Gallatin. It was raining. She waited across the street from the Johnny B., watching the front doors, praying that Rufus would emerge. Finally, drenched to the skin, she threw caution to the wind and crossed to the hotel.

Rufus was in the lobby kneeling before an officer, shining his boots. He saw her. With a curt shake of his head indicating that she leave, he busied himself with the man's boots.

Fanny turned to the door and hesitated; the rain was coming down in sheets.

She glanced back at Rufus. He nodded his head toward the staircase and rolled his eyes toward the ceiling, indicating that she go to his room in the attic.

Taking the cue, she quickly climbed to the second floor.

It was there that Rufus found her a minute later. Ashen-faced and trembling, she was trying her best to push past three officers who had backed her against the hallway wall.

Rufus approached cautiously. "Ge'mens!" he cried. "I hates to inter'upt yo'all's fun, but Colonel Boone done be s'pectin' dis girl in his quarters, 'mediately!"

"Well, Boone's just going to have to wait," said one of the men.

Rufus' stomach churned; the speaker was a brutal man known to enjoy physically abusing women.

"Aw, ge'mens," Rufus pleaded, "de colonel, he gon' be awful mad if'n I don' bring her to his room. Please, why'n yo'all just let her go? C'mon, Fanny." He reached toward the girl. "We's got to git on down—"

Rufus saw the fist coming, but there was nothing he could do to stop it. The blow slammed him into the wall; dazed, he sank to the floor.

Pushing himself to his elbows, he tried to call out to the men as they forced the struggling girl down the hall and into a bedroom. As unconsciousness claimed him, the last thing

Rufus remembered hearing was one of the officers saying, "I'm going to change my luck."

For three days Rufus took food and drink to the officers' room. Not once did he get a glimpse of Fanny, and not once were all three of the men absent from the room at the same time.

But on the morning of August fourth he was perched on the seat of Boone's surrey, waiting for the colonel, when the three officers, resplendent in their fine uniforms and dress swords, stepped out of the Johnny Bell.

Rufus looked straight ahead, afraid of what his eyes might reveal should he face the men.

"Sleeping late of a Sunday morning, gentlemen?" asked the colonel as he too stepped out the door. "Well, you can ride to church with me. Reverend Pitts would be disappointed if we 'damned Yankees' did not attend his service."

The three officers scowled, but they followed Boone to the surrey. Rufus clucked the horses into motion and sped down Main Street toward the Methodist Church; there the colonel instructed him to wait for them.

"Yes, suh," Rufus said. "I be right here when yo'all come out." The moment the four entered the church, Rufus whipped the horses into a dead run.

Taking the stairs at the Johnny B. three at a time, Rufus ran down the hall and nervously inserted his skeleton key in the lock.

The smell of stale whiskey, tobacco, and raw sex that met the opening door was staggering. He put it from his mind and rushed toward Fanny, who lay naked, facedown, across the bed.

"Fanny?" he whispered, trying not to stare at her nudity. "Fanny? It's me, Rufus."

Slowly the girl pushed herself to her elbows and rolled onto her back.

Rufus moaned low in his throat. One of Fanny's eyes was swollen nearly shut. Her lips were puffed and had, if the amount of dried blood on her skin was any indication, been bleeding freely. Her hair was plastered to her scalp and hung in filthy disarray across her face.

Her breasts shone blue-black with bruises, as did her

thighs and legs. Then the tears came, and although she tried hard to still them, she could not. Finally she stopped trying.

"Sons-of-a-bitches," Rufus choked, taking Fanny into his arms and weeping along with her. All of his life he had heard white people say that black people weren't human and white people were. Bullshit.

Wiping his nose with the back of his hand, he drew Fanny to her feet and helped her slip her dress over her head.

"We ain't got much time, Fanny," he said. "I've got to get back to the church an' pick up the colonel." Clutching Fanny's shoulders, he asked, "Are you in good 'nough shape to ride?"

Fanny nodded, but she refused to meet Rufus' eyes.

"Look at me!" he grated. "Speak to me! Are you all right?"

"Yes!" she cried. "I can walk, an' I can talk, an' I can ride . . . but am I all right? Well, what do you think, Rufus?" Then, with a sob, "What do you think?"

Rufus gritted his teeth. There wasn't even time to apologize. "Did you leave your horse at Mr. Ring's place like you always do?"

The girl nodded.

"Good!" he said. "Colonel Morgan's at Sparta; find him. Tell him that if he 'tends to take Gallatin, it better be quick, 'cause Boone's askin' for reinforcements. Tell him Boone's got pickets an' spies watchin' the Hartsville road day an' night, so's he better be careful. Tell him I'll be at the Levy Ring place one hour 'fore dawn ever' day 'til he comes."

Rufus pulled a handful of rumpled currency from his pocket and pressed it into Fanny's hand. He did not tell her how he had earned it. "Can you remember all that I told you, Fanny?"

"Yes," said the girl. Then she said in a low voice, "Be careful, Rufus. These Yankees are awful people. Oh, God . . ." Then she was gone.

Before sunrise on the morning of August twelfth, Colonel Morgan and eight hundred cavalrymen rode quietly through the sleeping streets of Gallatin. He had covered an incredible eighty miles in less than two days.

It was eerie, the way the army of gray ghosts filtered soundlessly in and out of the pitch-black shadows, causing

Rufus, who had watched them ride into the Levy Ring yard, to jump when Colonel Morgan halted the column and quietly called his name.

Darting into the open, Rufus whispered, "I wasn't sure Fanny would get through to you."

"She slipped right past the Federal lines like she'd been doin' it all her life," Morgan said. "That girl's got spunk." Turning in his saddle, he said, "Love?" Cavalryman T.R. Love rode closer to Morgan. "Canvass the town, will you?" Silently Love rode off.

"Was Fanny all right?" Rufus asked Clayton.

Clayton detected hesitation in Rufus' voice. "She was hurt a little," he said. "Mostly cuts and bruises . . . she said her horse had thrown her." Clayton didn't add the other thing he had noticed: She was nervous, almost as though she were afraid to be around white men, including himself. That bothered him, because even though he and Fanny had not made love since that last time at Cragfont, an easy comradeship had existed between them; now it was gone.

Rufus looked away. Then he asked, "You-all a-plannin' on killin' anybody, Mr. Clay?"

"Not unless it's absolutely necessary," Clayton answered, trying to read Rufus' face in the gloom. Failing, he said, "Why do you ask?"

"I've got my reasons, sir. But if it's all right with you, I'd rather not say . . . leastways not right now."

T.R. Love trotted his horse back up the dark street. The clop of the hooves sounded loud in the silence.

"Colonel," he whispered, "I checked the town like you said. If anybody saw us ride in, they are well hid, 'cause I didn't see nothin' out of the ordinary."

Morgan nodded. "Maybe we got lucky, but I wouldn't bet on it." He turned to Captain Joseph Desha. "You an' your men take care of Boone; I'll disperse the rest of the troops at strategic points, then ride to the telegraph office an' wait for your signal. If anything goes wrong, get out of town any way you can an' meet me at the old Tillman Dixon place the other side of Hartsville."

With T.R. Love and his sawed-off, double-barreled shotgun leading the way, Rufus, Clayton, and Desha slipped up the back stairs of the Johnny Bell. Rufus' passkey did its job; the door of Colonel Boone's room swung open.

Meanwhile, Morgan posted his troops throughout Gallatin, then rode on to the telegraph office.

"Good God!" the operator cried when Morgan and Cotton stepped into the room. "You can't come in here and ruin this place again!"

Cotton drew his revolver and smacked its barrel against the operator's forehead. The man dropped, limp as a sack of corn.

Morgan looked at Cotton, who shrugged and said, "I just didn't want to listen to his whining again."

The telegraph clattered.

Morgan scanned the men outside the door. "Where's Ellsworth?"

"Here, Colonel." The man pushed his way to the front.

"Get on that telegraph, George. I want to know what's bein' said."

A moment passed, and Ellsworth looked up at Morgan. "It's that Yankee general at Nashville. He wants confirmation that you're here in Gallatin. Now how the hell did he know that?"

"Buell's got more spies than we have," Morgan said. "Deny the rumor. Tell Buell that I've been sighted in Adairville, Kentucky."

Ellsworth pounded the keys, then waited.

Shortly another message rattled the keys.

He looked up at Morgan and grinned. "Affirmative!"

The four Confederates surrounded Colonel Boone's bed. Clayton nodded to Rufus. "Wake him up."

Rufus shook the colonel's shoulder. Boone rose sleepily to a sitting position.

"Massa Gen'al! Massa Gen'al!" Rufus cried, wringing his hands. "Don't let 'em kill me. Please, Massa Boone."

"What in God's name is wrong with you, Childress?"

"I done pee'd my pants, Massa Boone," Rufus whined. Then, clutching the Colonel's hand tightly, he drew it against his crotch.

"Goddamn you, nigger!" yelled the officer, coming fully awake.

"You, sir," Clayton said, shoving the muzzle of his pistol

into the colonel's gaping mouth, "are under arrest."

Boone's eyes bulged as he took in the weapon that protruded from his mouth, then the grinning faces of his captors. With a groan, he squinched his eyes shut.

"We have Gallatin surrounded, Colonel," Clayton continued. "Our men are watching your hotel window at this very moment. If we don't show a white flag immediately, there's going to be a hell of a war in this town and a lot of men are going to die. And it's going to start right here in this room." Clayton eased back the hammer of his Navy Colt. The sear clicking into position echoed loudly in the silent room.

Boone opened his eyes wide and nodded vigorously.

"Does that mean you surrender?" Clayton asked. Again Boone nodded.

Clayton removed the pistol muzzle and wiped it on the colonel's nightshirt. Shoving a paper under Boone's nose, he said, "Sign it."

Without reading the document, Boone scrawled his name across the order for his subordinates' immediate and unconditional surrender. By ten o'clock that morning every Union soldier, picket, and guard in or near Gallatin was a prisoner of war.

And thanks to the capture of the telegraph, two Union trains, one of forty cars full of government stores, pulled unsuspecting into the Gallatin yard to refuel. They were quickly seized by the Rebels, unloaded, and burned.

Ellsworth, the Confederate operator, caught an incoming message on the wire. Grinning as wide as Cotton, he reassured the Franklin, Kentucky, operator, thirty miles north, that all was well in Sumner County. Shortly a freight train arrived loaded with seventy cavalry horses, which were immediately pressed into Confederate service.

Rufus, wearing new trousers, shirt and coat, compliments of the trainload of confiscated stores, walked among the prisoners, scrutinizing each Union officer with infinite care. He stopped in front of one. "Colonel Morgan wants to see you, sir," he said.

"What the hell for?"

Rufus shrugged. "He jist sent me to fetch you, sir. An' he also says he wants the two officers you bunk with."

The man looked at Rufus. "Ain't I seen you somewheres before? Ain't you Colonel Boone's boy?"

"No, sir, I'm not. But don' feel bad, us niggers all look alike to white folks. No, sir, I'm not nobody's boy. I'm Lieutenant Harris' body servant. Now, sir, if you'd get your friends an' come with me . . ."

The officer called out for Captains Tate and Wells. The two men made their way through the crowd of prisoners. Rufus smiled to himself.

"Morgan wants to see us," the first officer said as Tate and Wells approached.

"If he's smart, Wilson," said Tate, "he'll parole us and get the hell out of Gallatin as quick as he can."

"What about it, nigger?" Wells asked. "Is Morgan intending to parole us?"

Rufus shrugged.

"Well, let's go find out," Wilson said, pushing Rufus aside and striding toward the railway office.

Upon reaching the depot, Rufus told the three officers to wait outside until he could announce their presence. Once inside, he went to the table where Clayton was going over papers with Morgan.

Clayton looked up as Rufus approached. "What is it, Rufus? You look excited."

"I need to talk private, Masta."

Clayton rose and followed Rufus to a corner of the room.

"Masta," Rufus said, his eyes on the floor, "I's got a big favor to ask."

"What's gotten into you, Rufus?" Clayton asked. The boy had long since abandoned this kind of subservient behavior when they were alone.

"I got a chore to do, sir. It's personal, 'tween me an' three Union officers."

Clayton studied Rufus. "Have they mistreated you?"

The Negro shook his head. "No, Masta, it weren't me who they hurt. It was a friend."

"What kind of 'chore' do you have in mind? If you intend to kill them, I'll have to refuse. Morgan wouldn't approve of a black man killing three whites, even if they are enemies."

"I don't 'tend to kill them, sir. I jist want them to suffer a bit."

Clayton hesitated. Rufus had never before asked a favor.

And Rufus was accustomed to nearly every known form of abuse. Whatever had been done to the "friend," it must have been awful.

"What have you got in mind, Rufus?"

"There's a woodshed behind the depot, sir. I want those three men brought to the shed, one at a time, ten minutes apart—"

"Rufus"—Clayton shot him a stern look—"you're not to kill them. Do you understand?"

"Masta Clayton," smiled the boy, "I promise you, sir, I won't kill them."

Rufus' eyes slowly adjusted to the dark room. He hefted the hickory mattock handle and took several swings, testing its weight; it would work fine. Sweat beaded his brow. He had never raised his hand in anger toward another human being, and especially not toward a white man. Would he be able to do it when the time came?

"Hey, you in the shack," called a Confederate. "We got this Yankee out here. What do you want us to do with him?"

"Send him in." Rufus gripped the mattock shaft tightly and wished his sweaty hands would stop trembling.

The door opened and Wilson walked hesitantly into the room. He whirled as the door was closed and barred behind him.

"What in hell is going on here?" he demanded as Rufus stepped silently out of the shadows.

"Now listen here, nigger," Wilson said when his eyes grew accustomed to the dim interior and he saw the mattock handle that Rufus carried. "You're making a big mistake—"

"No, you listen here," Rufus interrupted, "an' you listen real good."

"Like hell I will." Wilson backed toward the door. "I am an officer of the United States of America, and no nigger slave is—"

Rufus rammed the butt of the mattock handle into the man's solar plexus. "Shut your mealy white mouth," he whispered, his tone so dangerous that the officer stared mutely, afraid even to try and regain the breath that had been driven from him.

Rufus raised the handle and Wilson cowered backward

until he was brought up against the wall. "What did I ever do to you?" he gasped. "I'm here to set you free!"

"I'll tell you what you did." Rufus again drove the mattock handle into the man's stomach. The officer doubled over, fighting for breath. "You an' your two friends took a slave girl to your quarters and kept her there for three days." He jabbed Wilson again. "You bragged about how she cried every time you . . . hurt her. You thought it was funny." He could still hear Fanny's voice telling him this. Again the handle punched into Wilson's stomach.

Then Rufus took a good, double-handed grip on the sweat-slippery wood, drew the handle over his shoulder, and brought it around to smash the officer's rib cage. It was a blow that lifted Wilson completely off his feet before dropping him into a crumpled heap on the dirt floor. Not a sound escaped the man's lips as his mouth opened and closed spasmodically. Then Rufus turned the mattock handle flat side out and caught Wilson with a roundhouse swing that crushed his nose, drove six of his front teeth into the roof of his mouth, and splintered both of his jawbones.

Rufus dragged Wilson to the back of the room and propped him in a sitting position against the wall. Then he retrieved his mattock handle and called for the sentry to send in the second man. He was no longer sweating.

Morgan, who had been pacing the room angrily, swung toward the door as Clayton and Rufus entered.

He stared silently at the two. Then he roared, "What in hell's name took place in that goddamned woodshed?"

"Rufus had a personal vendetta to settle, sir," Clayton said.

"I pray you found satisfaction?" Morgan's eyes bore angrily into Rufus. "You've beaten three Union captains nearly to death. What in the name of God came over you, Rufus? And you, Harris, for allowing it?"

Rufus dropped his head and stared at his feet. "They had it comin', sir."

"Speak up, Rufus, an' look at me, damn it. You're no field hand who's afraid to look a white man in the eye." Morgan slammed his fist on the table. "Why the devil did you beat those men to a pulp? I want to know."

Rufus raised his head and faced Morgan squarely. "Can I

speak freely, Colonel?"

Morgan nodded. "Tell me the truth, Rufus. I've got several hundred prisoners out there who are outraged over what you've done. Hell, even my own men won't stand still for it. Not without a reason."

Rufus took a deep breath. "Them officers forced a . . . Southern girl to go to their quarters, sir. They pleasured themselves with her, over and over. When they turned her loose after three days, she could barely drag herself through the door."

Morgan glanced at Clayton. "I haven't heard any complaints of rape, have you?"

Clayton shook his head, frowning. "Who was she, Rufus?" he asked.

Rufus dropped his eyes. "Masta, she begged me never to tell."

"Well, I've heard enough," Morgan said. "I'll order a public hangin'. We'll make an example of the three. Raping a Southern woman, indeed!"

Clayton studied Rufus, who had gone suddenly ashen. "Who was the girl, Rufus?"

"Masta," cried the boy, "I promised, sir . . ."

"All right," Clayton said. "Just answer this. Is the girl white?"

Rufus gritted his teeth, then shook his head, no.

Morgan raised his eyebrows. "Well, much as I hate to say it, that puts a different light on the matter. We can't hang men, not even damn Yankees, for raping a slave."

Rufus' hands balled into fists. He liked Morgan, but he wanted to hit him, hit him hard. After a long, tense moment, he unclinched his hands. "I believe I done made an example of 'em, Colonel,"

Morgan fingered his goatee and studied Rufus thoughtfully. He wondered if, had the situation been reversed, he would have been man enough to tolerate the statement he had just made. He thought not. "You're a good man, Rufus," he said with a sigh. Almost as an afterthought, he added, "We've got to come up with a story as to why you maimed those men with a pick-ax handle . . . somethin' the soldiers will understand."

Clayton felt his bunched muscles relax; it had been touch and go there for a minute. "Sir?" he said. "Why don't we twist the truth a bit? Why not tell the men that Rufus caught the three . . . seducing one another?"

Morgan burst out laughing. "I believe you have hit the nail on the head. Nobody has any sympathy for a nancy, not even the Yankee soldiers. Yes, sir. That just might work." Turning to Rufus, he said, "You keep a low profile until I can get the rumor circulatin'."

As Clayton and Rufus left the depot, Clayton said, "Rufus, that girl . . . it was Fanny, wasn't it?" Rufus' face could not hide the answer.

Morgan eliminated any chance of a Union railroad approach by ordering Cotton and a detachment of cavalry to the tunnel six miles north of Gallatin; they were to destroy the roadbed and block the passage.

Upon hearing Cotton's report that he had collapsed eight hundred feet of the thousand-foot tunnel, Morgan laughed heartily, then directed him three miles downtrack to Pilot Knob to burn a trestle that spanned a deep ravine. When Cotton returned, Morgan paroled Colonel Boone and his soldiers and sent them trotting down the pike toward Nashville, some forty miles distant.

"It's been a good day, Clayton," Morgan said, sitting at the telegraph operator's desk in the depot sipping Colonel Boone's bonded whiskey. "The local folks have carted off tons of Union supplies. Gallatin is free of Federal soldiers . . . and it will take months to repair the tunnel. We've accomplished nearly everything we set out to do."

"You still planning to withdraw the men at midnight, sir?"

Morgan refilled their glasses. "It's seventeen miles to Hartsville. I intend to be there by sunup to establish a new base camp. But not you. I want you to stay until morning and see to the destruction of that Federal campsite a mile northwest of town. Keep Cotton and twenty men."

Clayton nodded, pleased. He didn't envy the cavalry their long night ride.

"What are we gonna do with all this shit?" Cotton wondered aloud as he and Clayton surveyed the hills of pots, pans, bedding, canteens, and other accoutrements they had confiscated from the Federal camp.

"I suppose we'll have to burn it or bury it," Clayton said. "The only thing we're going to salvage is the wagonload of guns we collected."

"Hell, Lieutenant," said one of the cavalrymen as he rummaged through the Union solders' personal belongings, "this stuff is better'n what my folks have at home. I shore wish they was some way we could—" A soft plopping sound, and the man staggered backward. Then the report of a rifle echoed across the valley. The soldier collapsed and lay unmoving, as though he were a discarded rag doll.

For a moment all eyes were on the dead man. Then, "To your horses!" Clayton bellowed, drawing his pistol and racing to his mount while scanning the woodlands to the west, from whence the shot had come.

"Get that wagonload of weapons moving!" he yelled, swinging into the saddle. Spurring Leviathan into a gallop, he raced north in an effort to flank the enemy and gauge its strength.

A cavalryman sprang onto the wagon seat and whipped the mules in a hard run toward Gallatin. Hundreds of blue-clad men broke from the distant tree line and quickly ranked in battle formation, the front line kneeling to fire, the rear rank ready to move up when needed. Moments later a hail of bullets ripped into the sideboards of the fleeing wagon, killing the driver instantly.

Spinning his horse around, Clayton leaned low over its neck and flayed the animal savagely across the rump with his hat. "Retreat!" he yelled. But the cavalrymen had spurred toward Gallatin the moment Clayton turned.

Cotton held back until Clayton had galloped abreast. "We've got five or six men down," he cried.

"Leave 'em!"

Amid a barrage of whining bullets, the two Confederates lay low on their horses and raced toward Gallatin.

In Gallatin, shopkeepers hurried to lock and bar their doors, while pedestrians ran home to hide their valuables, many of which had been retrieved from secret places just that day. Minutes later, Confederate cavalrymen thundered up Main Street, through the courthouse square and out the other side of town toward Hartsville.

The dust from their flight had hardly settled when, with

bugles blaring, drums rolling, flags fluttering, and bayonets fixed, the Union infantrymen marched into town.

The Federal officers sat their horses and turned a blind eye while their troops broke into stores, looted houses, and robbed the citizens at gunpoint. Every man, woman, and child in Gallatin was placed under arrest for having aided the Confederates.

CHAPTER 19

On the evening of August nineteenth, six days after the Union Army had retaken Gallatin, Clayton, Cotton, and Rufus lounged idly in their field tent at Hartsville. Clayton looked up from *The Nashville Daily Union* he was reading and laughed aloud. "Listen to this: 'Colonel Boone was arrested when he reached Nashville for surrendering without firing a shot.'"

Cotton chuckled. "Wonder what the brass in Nashville would have done if'n they woke up with a pistol barrel stuck between their teeth."

Clayton continued reading: "'Gallatin, Tennessee, is a notoriously violent Rebel hole, where nearly the whole population are traitors. The people of Gallatin are malignant, turbulent and insulting Rebels, and should have felt the weight of the hand of the Federal Government long ago. The Rebels around Gallatin cannot be won over by conciliation or gentle means."

Cotton cocked his pistol and spun the cylinder. "They goin' to spank our asses? Is that what that silly editor thinks will end this war?" Shaking his head, Cotton closed one eye and sighted down the pistol barrel. "They just ain't got it figured out yet, have they?"

"What?" Clayton laid the paper aside.

"That the Confederacy ain't fightin' nobody but the damned Union Army, while the Yankees— Hell, man, the Yankees are fightin' the entire South! Every man, woman, an' child of us."

"They've got it figured out, Cotton," Clayton said. "They're making life as difficult as possible for the women and children, knowing that a soldier can't concentrate on war if he's worried about his family and home. It's a cheap shot, but the Federal Government doesn't care who it hurts so long as it triumphs in the end."

"Well, if that's the case," offered Rufus, "the Confederacy ought to march up North and show them Yankees what it's like to see their women—" He stopped himself and bowed his head.

"Southerners aren't turned that way, Rufus," said Clayton. "There's still too much honor in the South for it to ever allow its men to make war on those who can't defend themselves. The Federal Army knows that and uses it against us."

"Bullshit, Clayton!" Cotton cried. "I believe in fighting fire with fire, 'cause if you turn the other cheek, somebody's gonna knock your face off."

"Mount up! Mount up!" The urgent call brought the three racing from the tent. All over the camp, cavalrymen were emerging from their shelters in wild disarray. Only half of them were fully clothed, while others were still stuffing food into their mouths. Many of those whose wives or lady friends were visiting were trying to get into their trousers while streaking for the horse pen.

In fifteen minutes Morgan's men were ready to ride.

Clayton trotted Leviathan up beside Morgan, who was leaning from the saddle talking to an elderly woman whose dusty, tear-streaked face showed signs of hard travel.

Morgan glanced up, his face furious. "This lady just came from Gallatin. The Yankees have rounded up every male in town over twelve years old and are marching them to Nashville to be imprisoned."

"Why, for God's sake?" Clayton asked.

The old lady dabbed at her eyes with a kerchief. "They

said the townspeople aided and abetted Colonel Morgan when you-all captured Colonel Boone." She raised an embittered face to Clayton. "My husband is eighty-seven years old, sir. He's crippled. Why are they doin' this to us? He's all I got left in the world."

"Don't worry, ma'am," Morgan said, locking eyes with Clayton. "We'll get your husband back, safe and sound."

As the Confederates rode through Gallatin at eight o'clock on the morning of the twentieth, their faces became even harder and more resolved. Grieving women and children lined the streets from one end of town to the other, and the mournful dirge of weeping anguish seemed to blot out every other sound, even the ground-jarring slam of eight hundred horses' hooves.

A woman pushed her way through the crowd and ran alongside Clayton's horse. She told him that the Federals had taken her son.

"He's big for his age, Lieutenant," she said, "but he's just a baby . . . just a baby."

"What's his name, ma'am?" Clayton leaned toward her so he could hear her answer.

"Opie!" cried the woman. "Opie Reed."

"I know Opie, ma'am," Clayton said. "Rest assured, we'll bring him back." Tipping his hat to her, he spurred Leviathan ahead.

At Saundersville, six miles southwest of Gallatin, Morgan's Cavalry overtook the Union force that was escorting the prisoners. Topping a rise, the Confederates fanned out in battle formation. Emitting the long Rebel yell, they came off the hill like a churning gray whitecap and flowed over the startled Federals before they could even muster a line of defense.

The battle proved to be a disappointing skirmish to Cotton, for that very same Federal force that with grand braggadocio had just overpowered a town full of old men, women, and children, threw away its weapons and ran in panic toward Nashville. Morgan's men captured only one hundred sixty-three of the three hundred Federals.

Clayton rode among the milling townsmen. "I'm looking for Opie Reed," he yelled above the din of laughter and joyful commotion. "Has anyone seen Opie Reed?"

"Here I am, Lieutenant." The boy caught Clayton's

stirrup and looked up at him proudly. "The Yankees said I was a Confederate soldier an' brung me along with the men."

"Well, soldier," Clayton said, grinning down at the pint-sized Rebel, "your mother told me to tell you that you'd better get yourself on home, or she's going to tan your hide good."

"Aw, heck," Opie said, kicking a clod of dirt. "I wanted to fight."

"You'd better get a move on. She was headed this way with a tobacco stick about four feet long the last time I saw her."

The boy's face drained. "Was she as mad as a wet hen?"

Clayton nodded.

With a treble imitation of the Confederate yell, Opie loped up the road toward Gallatin.

Before the cavalry and townsmen were halfway back to Gallatin, they were met by a procession of surreys, buggies, wagons, carts, and coaches. The women had come for their men.

That night the people of Gallatin celebrated; every man in Morgan's command was a hero.

Morgan, Clayton, and several other officers were in the middle of an elegant supper at the Johnny Bell Hotel when one of Morgan's camp guards from Hartsville came running into the dining room and shouted that a Yankee army had ridden through Hartsville and destroyed the whole Confederate camp. They had bivouacked at A.R. Wynne's place for the night and were planning to attack Gallatin in the morning.

"How many are there?" Morgan asked, laying his fork aside.

"I'd guess maybe twelve, fourteen hundred men, sir."

"Well," Morgan said, picking up his fork again, "the odds aren't too bad. They outnumber us by only three, maybe four hundred men."

"That's no contest, Colonel," laughed one of his officers.

Morgan turned to Clayton. "Lieutenant, I would appreciate it if you would ride out to Wynnewood and see what the Federals are up to."

Clayton wiped his mouth with his napkin. "You want us to take a few prisoners while we're there, sir?"

"No need. But on your way out, tell the sergeants to round up the men and have them turn in and try for a good night's sleep. The party's over."

At daybreak on August twenty-first, as Morgan's Cavalry rode out of Gallatin toward Hartsville, Clayton, Cotton, and Rufus cantered up and reined in beside Morgan.

"They're about two miles behind us and moving this way, sir," Clayton said. "And they mean business, Colonel. They've got several field pieces."

"I've always wanted to own a cannon," Cotton said, grinning.

Spurring his horse ahead to a small knoll, Morgan took out his brass telescope and studied the terrain ahead. To the right was a mile-long level field, a half-mile wide, flanked on the far side by a zigzag, split-rail fence that was nearly five feet high. The field would make a perfect battleground.

Morgan deployed his cavalry in an irregular line across the pasture.

Orders were not necessary: Pistol and rifle primings were already checked, shotguns loaded with buckshot and ball, sabers loosened in their sheaths. Saddles were hastily recinched; unnecessary equipment, such as food and bedding, was discarded. Nearly eight hundred anxious, arrogant warriors prepared to meet the enemy.

Morgan called his commanders to him. "Well, gentlemen, this is the chance we've been waiting for." He swept his eyes across the men. "No surrender, not from either side; this is a fight to the finish. We can whip them if we're half as brave as I believe we are." His smile touched each officer individually. "Have your men prepare to charge."

Clayton raised his spyglass and studied the Federals as they quickly formed at the opposite end of the field. The blue line was unwavering, their standards slapping silently in the breeze, their sabers sparkling in the morning sun. The 2nd Indiana Cavalry was there, as well as detachments from the 7th Pennsylvania Cavalry, the 4th Kentucky Cavalry, and the 5th Kentucky Cavalry.

Clayton wondered if the Northern cavalrymen were as afraid as he. Probably they were, he decided.

Morgan trotted his mount to the center of the line. Raising his saber above his head, he made a downward slash. Slowly, almost shoulder to shoulder, the Confederates walked their horses toward the enemy.

The Northern cavalry, employing the same formation, started to move forward from the far end of the field.

Morgan's mount broke into a trot, and over seven hundred cavalry horses followed suit.

"Bugler," he called. "Sound the charge!"

The boy brought the horn to his lips, and as the notes pierced the morning stillness, the earth shook to the rhythm of thousands of galloping hooves.

As Clayton leaped Leviathan into a dead run, he remembered the day, so long ago, when he, Mr. Summers, and Cotton had experienced the same ground-trembling sensation in the field at Summerset. Was the omen of that earthquake about to be fulfilled here?

Clamping his bridle reins between his teeth, he cocked his Navy Colt with one hand and drew his saber with the other.

A sense of peace swept through his being. This will be my one and only battle, he thought, wondering how he knew that. Why was he so sure of it? Then he thought of nothing except the enemy racing toward him.

Cotton, with a double-barreled shotgun in one hand and a pistol in the other, drew alongside of Clayton and shouted something, but his words were snatched away by the wind.

Cotton grinned from ear to ear and lay over his horse's neck, his guns thrust out past the animal's head. With a piercing Rebel yell, he spurred his mount to even greater speed, trying to keep abreast of Clayton's finely bred racehorse.

The initial collision, when the two armies met, came at full speed. Men and horses went down under the impact, and the screams, whinnies, and shouts of passion and pain that shook the countryside were awesome. Clayton had never imagined that men and animals were capable of such bone-chilling noises. Across the entire battlefield a carpet of thrashing men and horses lay entwined, forcing those behind them to jump their mounts over the living and the dying in order to engage the enemy.

Leviathan was bowled sideways by a Northern cavalryman's heavy charger and knocked to his knees. Clayton locked his thighs to his floundering horse and pulled hard on the reins, drawing Leviathan to his feet. The

Federal cavalryman spun his mount around and drove at Clayton again, slashing with his saber as he came.

Gritting his teeth, Clayton steadied his pistol and shot the man twice through the chest, driving him headfirst over the rump of his horse to fall heavily beneath the churning hooves of the horses around him.

Lying over in the saddle, Clayton thrust his sword at the closest blue uniform, but the moving target swept past without a scratch.

Something ice-cold, then white-hot, burned itself along Clayton's rib cage. In front of him, a cavalryman drew back his sword for another blow. But Clayton arched an overhead slash that sank his blade in the forehead of the attacker's horse. The animal went down as though poleaxed.

Clayton jerked his sword free and, not waiting to see if the man rolled clear, charged into another blue-clad soldier, hammering him from the saddle with his pistol barrel.

Smoke and dust roiled thickly around the combat, blinding and choking both men and beasts.

Cotton charged on with wild abandon. The young bugler beside him pitched from the saddle and fell beneath the hooves of Cotton's horse, but not even that diminished Cotton's exhilaration. He touched both triggers of his double-barreled shotgun, and ten yards ahead of him a gap opened in the Federal line as screaming horses and men went down in a heap.

Flinging the empty shotgun at the nearest bluecoat, Cotton pulled both of his revolvers and rode straight into the gap, firing first one pistol, then the other, at point-blank range.

The Confederate guideon bearer's horse collapsed without warning, propelling the man and flag into a mangled heap of flailing men and animals. Rufus spurred his horse toward the bearer, who was trying without success to gain his feet.

"My leg's shot off," shouted the man as Rufus reined in. "Derned cannonball . . ."

Rufus stared at the bloody, mangled flesh that protruded from the soldier's trouser leg. Bile rose up in his throat and leaning from the saddle, he retched, and retched again.

Propping himself against his dead horse, the guideon bearer poked Rufus with the stave. "Rufus, quit your pukin' an' take this flag."

Rufus straightened and wiped his mouth with the back of his hand.

The soldier took a twist of tobacco from his pocket and bit off a large chew. "Keep our colors flyin'." Then he laughed. "The colored carryin' the colors. Now don't that beat all!"

Gripping the stave and raising the banner, Rufus rode on.

All too soon it was evident that the Federal cavalry was gaining ground and pushing the Confederates back toward Gallatin. But for two hours on that hot summer morning, Morgan's Raiders charged again and again into the teeth of the enemy until by eight-thirty, the Federals found themselves being forced back across the same body-strewn terrain they had just taken.

At Cragfont, five miles away, the noise of the battle was loud. Old Mrs. Winchester, standing on the second-floor balcony, turned to her family and said quietly, "Ladies, start boilin' water, rippin' sheets into strips, and fixin' pallets on the floor. Our boys are goin' to need some nursin' before this day is through."

At Summerset, Mr. Summers, who had been released from jail the week before, listened to the clash of the two armies. "Clayton and Cotton are out there, Helen," he said gravely, slipping his arm around his wife's waist and drawing her close.

Mrs. Summers laid her head against his shoulder. "You love those boys, don't you?"

For a long moment the old man didn't answer. Then, softly, he said, "They're the closest we'll ever come to havin' children of our own . . . if they live through that holocaust."

"They'll survive, Jonathan," she assured him, patting his hand gently.

Clayton parried a sword thrust from a passing cavalryman and pivoted in the saddle to catch the rider from behind. As he turned, a sight caught his attention that caused him to forget his target, who was also wheeling his mount for a counterattack.

Throwing spurs to Leviathan, Clayton charged toward what he had seen: Opie Reed, sat frozen on his father's large Percheron workhorse, not a saber's length away from the heart of the action where men and horses, in their life-and-death struggle, were churning dust too thick to breath. Miraculously, the boy had been touched by neither ball nor steel.

As Clayton neared Opie, he was forced to duck under a saber thrust and slam his horse into the Union cavalryman's mount, pinning the soldier's leg against his McClellan saddle and shattering the bone just above the knee.

Without looking to see if the soldier followed, Clayton galloped past Opie Reed, snatching the boy into his arms. Spurring Leviathan savagely, he raced toward the split-rail fence that served as the unofficial boundary line of the battle.

Sliding Leviathan up to the rails, he flung the youngster into the field beyond.

"Go home, Opie," he shouted, pointing toward Gallatin. "Go on, get the hell out of here!"

"I didn't know it would be like this," wept the boy. "All this killin' an' blood . . ." Then he was running toward Gallatin faster than he had ever run in his life.

That brief interval of flinging Opie Reed over the fence provided an opening for the enemy. When Clayton pivoted Leviathan away from the rails, he found himself hemmed in by several Union cavalrymen. They jumped their mounts toward him, forcing him to back Leviathan into the vee of the zigzag fence and deploy the rails as a barricade to keep them from flanking him.

His expert swordsmanship was all that kept his foes from immediately cutting him to pieces; but even then, as he thrust and parried like a madman, he could feel their blades slipping past his defense, nicking and slashing at his flesh like the teeth of a vicious animal.

The third cavalryman forced his horse into the small enclosure and with a howl of victory, raised his saber for a killing blow. Before the blade could fall, however, Rufus, who had been fighting his way toward Clayton, slammed his horse into the haunches of the cavalryman's mount and clutched the naked saber blade with his hand.

The man attempted a slash downward; Rufus hung on. With an oath, the cavalryman snatched the razor-sharp blade free. And as the cold steel slipped through Rufus' grip, four of his fingers were severed at the second joint.

Enraged, the cavalryman hacked down at Rufus, the

blade catching his chest and knocking him from the saddle. Rufus fell heavily across the fence rails. I'm dyin', he thought. His blood poured over the bone-dry chestnut wood and dripped onto the parched ground below.

Clayton sent his blade through the abdomen of one opponent, then arced the bloody weapon into a roundhouse swing that caught the second across his upper arm. The man who had slashed Rufus raised his sword and jumped his horse at Clayton, but a Confederate cavalryman charged past and whipped a shot at the man, hitting him in the thigh. The soldier screamed and fell from his saddle, clutching his leg with both hands.

Clayton jumped down and snatched up the flag Rufus had dropped. As he slipped his boot into the stirrup to remount, Leviathan dropped to his knees. His head slowly dipping to the ground, the superb animal rolled onto his side, his trim legs thrust straight out in the trembling quiver of death.

It was then that Clayton saw the U.S. saber blade protruding from the horse's neck.

Driving the flagstaff into the ground, Clayton made a lunge at the headstall of a wild-eyed, riderless horse that was running the fence line in search of an escape from the terrible noise, confusion, and stench of death.

Clayton caught the bridle and swung into the saddle. Snatching up the guidon, he gave the Rebel yell and drove the mount headlong into the thick of the battle.

At nine-thirty that morning, the Union commander, General R.W. Johnson, sent a courier with a protective white flag to Colonel Morgan, asking that a truce be called to bury the dead. Morgan refused.

Johnson immediately ordered his men to fall back to Cairo, hoping to escape across the Cumberland River. Morgan fought him every step of the way; the Federals were unable to regroup or, for that matter, to take a deep breath that was not filled with acrid powder smoke and choking hot dust.

With its back to the river, the Northern army made one last stand. But by noon, the battle of Gallatin was over. Morgan disarmed General Johnson and his surviving cavalry and marched them toward Hartsville.

Bloody, powder-burned, and so battle-weary they could hardly sit their horses, Clayton and Cotton rode back to the battlefield. For a long few minutes they sat in silence and watched the medics move from body to body in search of those who were still alive.

Teams and wagons bringing slaves were arriving from the surrounding plantations. The black men unloaded spades, picks, and mattocks and set to opening a deep trench that paralleled the Hartsville road and the battlefield. While the slaves labored, the teamsters drove among the dead warhorses and looped the animals' necks, legs, or bodies with log chains or rope and began dragging the carcasses toward the trench.

"I ain't never seen nothin' like it," said a teamster as he dragged a dead horse past Clayton and Cotton. "They ain't a blowfly anywhere else in the county, 'cause they're all here in this field."

It was true. The green flies were so thick on the already bloated bodies of the animals that their whining and buzzing carried incessantly over the field of the dead.

"My God, Cotton," Clayton whispered hoarsely, "what have we done here today?"

Dragging his hand over his already grimy face and smearing black-powder residue even more grotesquely across his freckled skin, Cotton said, "We won a battle here today, Clayton. Nothin' more, nothin' less."

"I hate it, Cotton." Clayton eyed the battlefield with the purest form of disgust, the kind known only to those who have participated in total destruction.

"Lord God! I hate it!" he yelled. A moment later the anguished cry bounced back from the distant hills.

Cotton studied Clayton from the corner of his eye. He himself found battle exhilarating, an experience that allowed a man the truest form of freedom: that of releasing him from any commitments on earth, except to live each split second of life to its fullest potential. He knew that Clayton was no coward, so he wondered why he didn't feel the same. Turning his horse away from Clayton, whose red-rimmed, bloodshot eyes were still fastened to the battlefield, he said, "Let's get Rufus' body an' take it home."

They found Rufus where he had fallen, across the fence from Clayton's racehorse.

Cotton dismounted and knelt beside the young slave. Clayton remained on his horse, refusing to acknowledge his

fallen friend. The pain of death was too new, and too raw, to
be dealt with.

"Hell, Clayton!" Cotton cried. "Rufus ain't dead! He
probably ought to be, but he ain't."

Clayton's head snapped toward Cotton, who grinned
widely, his teeth showing a brilliant white in his blackened
face.

"Well, don't just sit up there lookin' stupid," ordered
Cotton. "Get down here an' give me a hand. I believe we can
save ol' Rufus' life."

Clayton and Cotton tried to stanch the flow of blood from
the gash in Rufus' chest, but could not. They hoisted the
unconscious boy onto Clayton's horse and tied him to the
saddle. With Clayton riding double with Cotton, they struck
out for Summerset.

Clayton glanced over his shoulder. A farmer had backed a
team of mules to Leviathan and fastened a chain around his
neck. Bile rose up in Clayton's throat as the man whipped
the mules and they began dragging the beautiful racehorse
toward the burial trench.

Now Susie Winchester would never get to ride that horse,
Clayton thought sadly, then wondered why that realization
had crossed his mind, or why it even mattered. But it did.

At Summerset, strong hands lifted Rufus down and
carried him into the main house, where following Clayton's
orders, they placed him in Clayton's bed. Upon examina-
tion, Mr. Summers declared that Rufus' chest would require
immediate sutures and that his severed fingers would have
to be cauterized.

"I'll ride to Cragfont for Chatty," Clayton said. "If
anybody can save Rufus, besides Dr. Mentlo, she can."

"I'll send one of the slaves for Chatty," Mr. Summers
offered. "You look about all in, son."

Clayton shook his head. "Rufus saved my life, Mr.
Summers. I'm going to do everything I can to return the
favor."

At Cragfont, the house was teeming with wounded men
from both armies; many of them would need long weeks of
convalescence.

Stepping over and around men sprawled on the floor of
the great hall, Clayton hailed Mrs. Winchester as she was

leaving the parlor with a dishpan of bloody water.

"Just a moment, soldier," she said, hurrying to the open front doors and flinging the contents of the pan into the yard.

"Ma'am," Clayton said, removing his hat.

"Clayton! Lord, I didn't recognize you. Are you wounded?"

"No, ma'am. But Rufus is in a bad way. Needs a few hundred stitches . . ."

"Well, sew him up!"

"We're trying, ma'am, but Mrs. Summers' has got rheumatism in her hands. We need old Chatty real badly."

Lettie rushed into the hall carrying a bundle of bloody rags. "It's awful, Granny, these poor men—"

Her eyes widened as she looked into Clayton's blackened, blood-splattered face. "I don't suppose you got a scratch, did you, Mr. Harris?" she said coldly.

"No, Lettie, I didn't," he lied, feeling blood trickle down his side where a saber blade had slipped between two of his ribs.

"I might have known," the girl said.

"Hush, Lettie," Mrs. Winchester commanded. "I'm sorry, Clayton, but we can't do without Chatty." The old lady gestured toward the yard where men were standing, lying, or sitting while awaiting their turn for medical assistance.

Clayton sighed, unable to hide his disappointment. "I'd better be returning to Summerset then. It's good to see you again, ma'am. You too, Lettie."

As he turned to leave, Lettie asked offhandedly, "Who's hurt? Did Cotton finally get what he deserved?"

Clayton took a deep breath and released it slowly. "Rufus is dying, Lettie. He took a Federal blade that was meant for me."

Old Mrs. Winchester hurried back into the parlor, giving orders to the slaves to get more bandages, draw more water, find more blankets . . . .

Lettie followed Clayton outside and watched him mount his horse. Then it dawned on her that it wasn't his horse.

"Where is your beautiful racehorse, the one you flaunted around town . . . ?" She stopped, and her mouth drew into a thin line. "Well, I should say I'm sorry, Clayton, but I'm not. He was a fine animal, and I know how proud you were of him, but everybody needs to lose something they love in this war. Don't you agree?"

"Lettie," Clayton said, catching the pommel of his saddle and drawing himself up, "I lost what I loved before the first shot was ever fired."

Spinning on her heel, Lettie hurried back into the house.

From an upstairs window, Susie called, "Clayton! Clayton! Are you all right?"

Clayton doffed his hat and waved it at her. "Fit as a fiddle, Susie."

"Did they kill Leviathan?"

"Yes."

"Shucks."

That sums it up nicely, thought Clayton.

"So long, Susie," he called, turning his horse toward Summerset.

"Clayton," she cried, "don't get yourself shot! We're 'bout out of bed sheets to use as bandages."

Mrs. Winchester stopped Lettie in the hall. "Is Clayton gone?"

Lettie nodded.

"Damn!" Mrs. Winchester handed Lettie another pan of bloody water. "We need more medicine. I'll have Fleming harness the team and carry me to Summerset. Maybe they're not knee-deep in wounded like Cragfont is."

"No, Grandmother," Lettie said. "I'll have Fleming saddle a horse. Perhaps I can catch Mr. Harris before he gets too far away. What medicine do we need?"

"Alum, sulphur, liniment, pine tar, coal oil, anything they can spare."

CHAPTER 20

When Lettie reached Summerset, she found that Mr. Summers had sent his wagon to the battlefield; wounded men of both armies were strewn about the yard and porch.

Jumping from her horse, she started up the porch steps, but a young soldier lying on the ground beside the walkway called to her. "Ma'am, would you fetch me a dipper of water?"

Lettie ran to the well and hastily drew a bucket of water. She searched for the dipper—it was gone. Quickly she cupped her hands and thrust them into the bucket then hurried back to the lad.

"Here," she said, bringing her cupped hands to his powder-blackened lips, "I've brought you water. Come on now, drink up."

The soldier stared at her. "Please hurry," she cried. "It's seeping between my fingers."

"He's dead, ma'am," said a soldier lying a few feet away. "But I sure would thank you kindly for his water."

Lettie closed her eyes and breathed deeply.

"Miss," the soldier asked, "are you all right?"

"Yes, yes I am," Lettie whispered. "I . . . I'll run and get you some fresh water." When she returned, the man drank what little water she carried, then licked her palms and fingers until every drop was gone.

Clayton, walking back from stabling his horse, had seen Lettie at the well. He had altered his course and headed for her, but by the time he rounded the house, she was gone.

"Where'd that lady go?" he asked a soldier who lay beside the walkway. Then he saw that the man's eyes had glazed over in death.

"She went inside," the other soldier said. "She gave me water, then she just up an' ran. I reckon she couldn't stomach me a-lyin' here with my arms damn near blown off."

"Are you in pain?" Clayton asked, wondering at the man's casual attitude.

"Not yet. Everything's still numb, but it'll come. When it does, stuff a rag in my mouth. I sure don't want these Yankees to hear me scream, Lieutenant."

Inside the house, Lettie stood with Cotton by Rufus' bed and inspected the sutures Mrs. Summers had painstakingly administered. Lifting the boy's hand, she examined the seared stumps of his fingers. The stench of charred flesh was nauseating. She raised a questioning eye to Cotton.

"We didn't have no choice," Cotton said defensively. "We had to cauterize the fingers an' hope to hell gangrene don't set in."

Lettie laid Rufus' hand back on the bed. "I suppose it was all you could do."

"Come outside with me for a minute, Lettie," Cotton said.

The girl started to refuse, but Cotton's fingers tightened on her arm. He guided her toward the great hall, which was crowded with wounded.

"What do you want?" she demanded when they reached the back stoop.

"First off," he said, "Clayton never said what I told you he said that day at the courthouse. So if you're blamin' him for that, don't."

"You fool! I know he didn't say that. I've always known it. If you'll excuse me—"

"I ain't through," Cotton said. "I wanted to set the record

straight, Lettie. It seems so damned childish now . . . but
we all did some pretty foolish things before this war. Hell,
we were just kids, but we didn't know it. You can't keep on
blamin' folks for things that happened . . ."

"You don't have the least idea of what you are talking
about," she said with a venom that rocked Cotton. "You're
just stupid white trash! You never had a thought in your
life."

"Well, I've got a thought now," he said thinly. "Clayton's
been wounded. He don't think anybody knows it but . . .
look here." Cotton pointed to several reddish-brown stains
on the front of his tunic. "See how these have dried?"

Lettie nodded.

"I been a-watchin' Clayton's coat," Cotton continued,
"an' the blood on it ain't dryin', not one damned bit."

"Well, if he's trying to be a hero for my benefit," Lettie
snapped, "the idiot can bleed to death!"

Cotton's face flushed angrily. "He is a goddamned hero,
Lettie. He saved Opie Reed's life today. An' he brung our
colors up out of the dust. Hell, I could go on an' on, but I
won't."

"All right!" Lettie was as angry as he. "I'll see to Clayton's
wound. Grandmother sent me over here to get some more
medicine, but while I'm waiting for Uncle Jonathan to
divide what stores he has, I'll see to Clayton. What about
you? Are you shot, or stabbed?"

"Hell, no." Cotton grinned. "Mr. Summers says I'm
tough as green hickory. In fact, I got to be gettin' on back to
Morgan's command tonight, a'fore the colonel takes the
notion me an' Clayton has gone over the hill."

The saber blade had gouged out a sliver of Clayton's rib
bone and the wound required a compress to stop the
bleeding. As Lettie tended to him, she scolded him for not
making his condition known at Cragfont. Clayton smiled at
her. "You have people over there who are really wounded,
Lettie. They would rightfully laugh at a scratch such as
this."

Lettie bound his rib cage tightly. Tying off the knot, she
told him that like it or not, he would be forced to lie abed for
a few days to allow the wound to knit.

Clayton's hand closed over hers. "Lettie," he said, "we

need to talk. There's so much that needs saying."

Lettie hesitated, then disengaged his hand. "We have nothing to talk about, Clayton . . . nor will we ever."

Lettie rode to Summerset every afternoon, helping with the wounded until nearly sundown, but her cold aloofness left Clayton feeling more a stranger than ever before. Still, he looked forward to her presence.

On the twenty-sixth of August, Lettie entered his room and handed him a copy of *The New York Times.*

"Read that," she said, seating herself beside him. "You will probably enjoy it." She ran her finger down the page. "Here. 'Defeat of the National Forces Under General Johnson.' Read the last line. That's the one you'll be the most interested in."

Clayton scanned the article. "'It does seem,'" he read aloud, "'that our various detachments of troops in Tennessee might do something else than surrender.'" Clayton laughed. Then he clutched his side and grimaced. "I can't do too much of that yet," he admitted.

"The whole country is laughing at the Yankees," Lettie said. "Morgan's Raiders have made fools of them at every turn. Lord, how they must hate you."

Clayton frowned. The Union Army did not take defeat lightly. At that moment it was no doubt planning retaliation. And unless he was very wrong, the people of Sumner County would again be a target.

"Well, you don't have to look so upset about it," Lettie said. "Isn't that what Morgan wanted, to show the Yankees for the fools they are? A few more battles like that one and they will evacuate Tennessee."

"They won't leave Tennessee, Lettie." Clayton laid the paper beside him on the bed. "The newspapers have ruined that possibility."

"What do you mean?" Lettie's smile of a moment before wavered uncertainly. "The newspapers say that the Yankee army fears Morgan as though he were a rattlesnake."

"That's just the point, Lettie. The newspapers have made a laughingstock of the Federals, thus forcing them to retaliate. The North has got to save face, no matter who it hurts in the process."

"Oh, pooh," the girl said. "You're just a spoilsport, because deep down inside you're still a Yankee and you can't stand to see your side bested."

"Lettie," he said, aware that she was deliberately provoking him but unable to restrain his anger, "I've killed Union men, any one of whom might have been a friend, or . . . or family."

Lettie rose from the bed and walked to the window. Her face was stony when she turned to him. "It might have been one of your 'friends or family' who deprived me of ever having a family, Clayton."

Over Lettie's and the Summerses' heated objections that he wasn't healed yet, Clayton escorted Lettie back to Cragfont that evening. They rode slowly, so it was late by the time he returned to Summerset. Mr. Summers was waiting at the mounting block to help him into his bedchamber.

"Don't try to do too much too quick, son," the old man warned. "I know that gal is on your mind, but you'd best take care of that wound in your side before you try and heal the one in your breast."

Clayton sat down on the bed and released a weary sigh. "I can't seem to reach her, Mr. Summers. She has raised a wall around herself. Furthermore, she's planning on returning to New Orleans as soon as the blockade is lifted, or when the railroad is opened up again. She says there are too many unpleasant memories for her here in Sumner County."

"She'll get over that, son."

"I'm not so sure, Mr. Summers. Her bitterness goes too deep." Then he added silently, Bailey Peyton's ghost will haunt her—and me—for the rest of our lives. "Right now, sir," he said, "I would settle for just being friends with Lettie. But she doesn't even want that."

"Is that really what you want? Just to be her friend? I kinda thought you two might . . ." Mr. Summers shrugged his thin shoulders.

"What I want has nothing to do with it, Mr. Summers. Lettie has a problem that only she can work out."

The old man looked down at Clayton soberly. "There's one thing about life that a body can't change." Clayton waited, sure that Mr. Summers would tell him to be patient, or some other such nonsense. "Whatever the good Lord intends to happen, son, will happen."

On September fifth, a detachment of Federal troops rode up to Cragfont and dismounted. Mrs. Winchester met them at the front gate.

The young lieutenant in charge bowed and removed his hat. "We are looking for Rebel soldiers, ma'am."

Mrs. Winchester stared at him incredulously. "Which ones do you want, sir? The ones without arms, or the ones without legs?" The lieutenant flushed, but before he could speak, Mrs. Winchester went on: "We have Rebel soldiers and Yankee soldiers inside this house, Lieutenant. And if you think you can walk in here an' take our boys and expect us to continue to nurse yours, you are badly mistaken."

The lieutenant cleared his throat. "No, ma'am. That was not my intention at all. We appreciate what you are doing for our wounded. I'm looking for able-bodied Confederates, ma'am."

"You'll not find any here," she returned stonily. "But if you doubt my word, sir, you're perfectly welcome to search my home."

The lieutenant touched his hat brim. "That won't be necessary, ma'am."

Lifting himself to the saddle, he looked past the old lady to the solemn group of slaves who had congregated in the yard. One of them had sent a message to the commander in Gallatin stating that a Confederate lieutenant could be apprehended at Cragfont. The officer wondered idly which slave was the informer. Turning abruptly, he ordered his troops to mount up. Then, to the rattle of sabers and the squeak of saddle leather, he tipped his hat to Mrs. Winchester and cantered down the driveway.

Mrs. Winchester watched the soldiers until they were out of sight. Turning, she shouted, "Back to work! Go on now. It was nothin' but a Yankee patrol searchin' for some of our boys. You've seen them before and you'll see them again. Now go on about your chores."

Talking excitedly among themselves, the slaves walked away, some toward the house, others toward the fields.

"Fanny?" she called. When the girl appeared, Mrs. Winchester said, "You go to Summerset. Warn Mr. Clayton that there are Yankees in the neighborhood. You'll have to cut across the fields, because they're guardin' the road. Tell him to wait until dark, then bring Lettie home by boat. They won't think of watchin' the creek."

As Fanny set out across the fields, Patrick slipped through the woods that bordered the Hartsville Pike and ran hard to overtake the Union patrol.

The lieutenant reined in his horse as Patrick burst from the timber that lined the road. "Are you running away from your master?" he demanded.

"No, suh!" Patrick wondered if he had made a mistake in searching out this fool. "I come to tell you that I overheard my Missus say that the 'Federate lieutenant you was a-searchin' for will be bringin' a boat up Bledsoe's Creek sometime afta dark tonight. He'll have two women with him."

"You sure of that?" The lieutenant frowned at the Negro. "How do you know so much about the Confederates?"

Patrick grinned tightly. "'Cause I's the one what sent you the message. I's the one informin' you folks what's been goin' on around these here plantations."

"Well, I'll be damned," returned the officer. "All my life I've been led to believe that slaves couldn't read or write."

"Ain't many who can," Patrick said.

The officer considered Patrick thoughtfully. "All right, we'll watch the river tonight. You'd better be telling me the truth."

"I want t' go along with you, suh," Patrick said. "I can 'denify the 'Federate soldier."

"Mister," the officer said, "I wouldn't let you out of my sight for a million dollars."

Fanny ran all the way to Summerset, all two miles of it. She was so exhausted by the time she reached the house, she could barely speak. "I's 'fraid I wouldn't get here in time," she gasped, clutching a porch column for support.

Cotton, who had just arrived from Morgan's camp at Lebanon, picked Fanny up in his arms and carried her inside to the parlor sofa. The entire household gathered as the girl gulped down a full dipper of water and asked for another.

"In time for what?" Mr. Summers asked. "Somethin' wrong over to Cragfont?"

"Let her catch her breath," Mrs. Summers said, holding the jaded girl's head as she drank again.

"What's wrong at Cragfont, Fanny?" Lettie cried.

Fanny shook her head. "Miss Lettie, a Yankee patty-roller was up there a-searchin' fo' Confederate soldiers . . ."

Then she told them about the Union patrol that was guarding the Hartsville Pike in hope of apprehending Confederate soldiers en route to and from Morgan's camp.

Fanny turned to Clayton. "Ol' Mizz Winchester says for you to bring Miss Lettie home in a skiff. She says the Yankees won't be watchin' the creek."

"Maybe we ought to ride out of here right now, Clayton," Cotton said.

Fanny nodded her head. "Mr. Cotton's right. Miss Lettie and me can make our way back to Cragfont."

"No," Clayton said. "The roads are too dangerous for unescorted women after dark. I've heard too many stories . . ." He hesitated, looking into Fanny's eyes. "Some of these Yankee soldiers are not gentlemen," he finished softly.

"Stay the night, Lettie," Mr. Summers said. "Y'all can go home in the morning."

"Grandmother is expecting us tonight," Lettie pointed out. "She'll be watching the creek, and she'll worry herself sick if we don't show up."

Clayton frowned. "Lettie's right. The Winchesters would be all to pieces by morning. Cotton and I will take you home tonight. After the moon sets." He smiled. "I've always wanted to take a night voyage with two beautiful girls."

"That seems mighty foolish to me," Cotton said. "If we get took, we could wind up in some Yankee prison."

"How many prisoners have Morgan's Raiders taken, Cotton?" demanded Clayton.

Cotton thought for a moment. "I don't know. Several hundred, I reckon."

"And how many have we sent to prison?"

"We've paroled every one of 'em. But the Yankees ain't returnin' the favor, Clay. They're sendin' our men off to

Northern penitentiaries, to die. The war has turned meaner'n hell . . ."

Clayton and Cotton pushed the johnboat into the inky waters of Bledsoe's Creek and quietly rowed upstream toward Cragfont. The waning moon was shimmering on the rippling water. Clayton gazed at Lettie and Fanny in the soft glow, two young women so alike in appearance, yet so different in nature. He wished that a few of Fanny's good qualities would rub off on Lettie, instead of the other way around. He was startled by the thought. Then he became angry, not only with himself, but with Fanny. He could not imagine why he had allowed himself to compare Lettie to her. The fact that he had, left him feeling that he had somehow been unfaithful to Lettie.

He stared into the darkness, listening to the croak of the frogs, the cry of the night birds, the sound of the breeze rustling the leaves, and found himself wishing he were back in Hartsville with Morgan and the cavalry.

Morgan and the cavalry; it only meant more terrible killing, more maiming, more widows, and more orphans. For a split second, Clayton's body shook as though it were chilled.

"Are you all right, Mr. Clayton?" Fanny touched his arm.

"A rabbit jumped over my grave," he returned somberly.

"Aunt Chatty believes those sayings come true," the girl whispered, the whites of her widened eyes reflecting the last of the moonlight.

"Chatty is just a superstitious ol' bat," Cotton said. Fanny looked pityingly at him.

As they neared the Hartsville Pike bridge, they fell silent. On that particular stretch of open water, they would be the most vulnerable if the enemy were near.

Lettie and Fanny searched the darkness of the shore for movement while Clayton canvassed the bridge. "Stop rowing, Cotton," he whispered suddenly.

Without a word, Cotton stayed the oars. Slowly the boat began to backtrack with the current.

Lettie put her lips to Clayton's ear. "What is it?"

"It's too quiet," he mouthed back.

She turned her head and listened. No frogs croaked, no

night birds chirped. Nothing. The totality of soundlessness was eerie.

"It sounds fine to me," she said. Then, "Continue rowing, Cotton. There are no Yankees here . . ."

"Hush!" Cotton said. For what seemed an eternity, the only sound they heard was the tiny splash of water dripping from Cotton's oar.

Then out of the darkness there came the jingle of harness and the clopping of shod hooves. A file of shadowed riders moved down the bank to the water's edge.

"You are under arrest," a voice shouted.

"Paddle hard, Cotton!" whispered Clayton. Flinging Lettie to the bottom of the boat, he dug his oar deep.

Shots rang out, and geysers of water spouted up in front of the skiff.

"You can't escape, Lieutenant Harris," shouted the Union officer. "I have men posted for a hundred yards along the creek bank. Row the women ashore."

Cotton drew his pistol and cocked it. Aiming down the barrel, he said, "I believe I can hit the bastard from here."

"We can't shoot with women present," Clayton said.

"Yes you can," urged Fanny. "Give us guns an' we'll help you."

"Hush up, Fanny!" cried Lettie. "They'll shoot us all if we don't surrender."

Fanny shuddered. "Some of the things they do to . . . people . . . is worse than death, Miss Lettie. Please, Clayton, give me a gun."

Clayton shook his head. "They'll blow us right out of the water, Fanny."

"I'll take my chances," the girl said.

Lettie sprang up from the bottom of the boat and raised her hand threateningly. "Do not say one more word, Fanny!" she ordered.

"Stop it, Lettie!" Clayton caught the girl's wrist and drew her away from Fanny.

"If the three of you are afraid to surrender," Lettie said, struggling to break Clayton's grasp, "then dive overboard and swim to the far bank."

"You've got one minute to row those ladies ashore, Harris," shouted the officer. "One minute before I give the order to open fire. One minute, Harris."

"Well, what do you say, Clay?" Cotton asked. "Do we give up or start shootin'?"

Clayton was studying the Union force on shore. "There's something wrong here, Cotton," he said.

"Hell, yes, there is," Cotton agreed. "We're sitting ducks."

Clayton scowled. "Didn't you hear what that Union officer said? He called me by my name, and he knows that Lettie and Fanny are aboard."

"What difference does that make?" Lettie asked. "Time is running out, Clayton. We must surrender."

Fanny touched Clayton's arm. "Old Mizz Winchester sent me to warn you. She's the one who suggested the boat."

"Well, she didn't send the Yankees after us," Lettie cried angrily.

"No, Miss Lettie," Fanny said. "I didn't mean that. But somebody at Cragfont did."

"Both of you keep quiet," Clayton commanded. "Cotton," he said, "the Federals obviously don't know that you're with us."

Cotton pushed himself close to Clayton. "What are you gettin' at?"

"Those soldiers can't see us well enough in the dark to tell how many people there are in this boat, or whether we are men or women. It means that, as Lettie suggested, you can slip over the side and swim to shore."

"Well, I ain't leavin'," Cotton returned. "I still think we should shoot our way out."

"Don't be foolish," Clayton whispered fiercely. "Get your butt over the side of this boat and swim to shore. Or would you rather see the inside of a prison camp?"

"Damn it, Clayton, I don't want to leave you-all!"

From the bank, the officer shouted, "You've got ten seconds to bring that boat ashore, or we shall open fire!"

"Move to the far side of the boat, ladies," Cotton said angrily. "I'm going over the rail an' I don't want to swamp this son-of-a-bitch." With that, he clambered over the side and slid into the blackened water. For a moment he clung to the rail, looking up at Clayton. "I reckon one hero is all this boat can handle. Take care of yourself, Clay." Then he was gone, slipping quietly beneath the surface.

"Paddle loudly, Fanny," Clayton said, handing Cotton's

oar to the girl, "and pray that the noise covers Cotton's escape." Then he called out, "I'll make a bargain with you, Yank."

"You are in no position to dicker," came the officer's voice. "But go ahead and try."

"I'll give myself up if you'll guarantee safe passage for these ladies to Cragfont."

"And if I don't?"

"Then you are a dead man, mister. I've got a rifle aimed right at your guts. One move on your part will be your last."

For a long second not a sound was heard. Then the officer laughed. "You can't even see me, Harris. But I like your nerve. All right. Safe passage for the female Rebels. You have my word."

The moment the boat touched the bank, Lettie and Fanny were snatched ashore and without ceremony marched up the path toward Cragfont.

Clayton was seized and thrown to the ground. He gritted his teeth; new blood trickled down his side as the freshly knitted wound reopened.

The soldiers drew Clayton's arms behind his back and tied them securely, then jerked him to his feet. The ground spun and he swayed nauseously, willing himself to remain erect.

The Union officer asked, "Are you Lieutenant Clayton Harris of Morgan's command?"

"Captain Clayton Harris, sir. Confederate States of America."

"Well, Captain Harris, you are a prisoner of war of the United States of America." Then, in a more friendly tone, "When were you promoted, sir?"

"Directly after the battle, Lieutenant," Clayton answered honestly. "You boys left several open commissions . . ."

"Not as many as Morgan left on our side," returned the officer grimly.

"I am curious, sir," Clayton said. "How is it that you know who I am, and that I would be bringing the ladies home by boat?"

The lieutenant shook his head. "I'm sorry, Captain. I'm not at liberty to divulge that information."

Patrick stepped into the moonlight. "It was me, who told 'em." Then, without warning, he slammed his knee into

Clayton's groin, dropping him to the ground wretching in spasms of uncontrollable nausea.

Snatching a rifle from a startled soldier, Patrick hurriedly thumbed back the hammer and pointed the weapon at Clayton's head. But as he pulled the trigger, the Federal officer kicked the barrel aside. The ball plowed harmlessly into the creek bank.

"You black son-of-a-bitch!" shouted the officer, wrenching the rifle from Patrick and smashing him in the face with its butt plate. "I've a good mind to kill you."

Patrick staggered backward, blood gushing from his crushed nose and mouth. The officer pushed his face close to Patrick's. "If we didn't need every informer we can get, you'd be dead. Now get out of here before I change my mind."

Clamping his hand to his nose and mouth in an effort to stanch the blood-flow, Patrick raced into the night.

When the shot sounded, Fanny and Lettie, halfway to the house, looked at each other in horror. "Oh, God," Lettie cried, twisting and turning in an attempt to break free of her escorts. "Oh, God, they've killed him!"

Fanny broke from her astounded guards and ran to the edge of the bluff. "Clayton!" she cried into the darkness below. "Clayton, answer me! Clayton! Clayton!" Fanny's cries echoed up and down the creek, reverberating with the timbre of despair.

CHAPTER 21

On September seventh, while Clayton Harris was being interrogated by Federal officers in Nashville, Major George Winchester hid his horse in Chatty's cabin and slipped into the main house. He had ridden fifty-three miles in one day; it was the first time he had seen his family in over five months.

Taking his wife, Malvinia, to his mother's bedchamber where they could be alone, the two talked of the wounded who occupied nearly every downstairs room in the mansion; and they talked of the war and how poorly it was going; and they talked of themselves and the family.

Malvinia laid her cheek against the rough fabric of his uniform. "There's a silent rebellion goin' on all across the county, George. In many ways it's more devastatin' than open war. The slaves won't work, they're becoming more belligerent daily, and they openly steal whatever they want. It's gettin' out of hand . . . and it scares me. With our menfolk gone, there's little we can do to stop them."

"This war won't last forever," George promised, drawing Malvinia into his arms. "And when it's over, those niggers will be dealt with. You tell them that."

"I have told them that, George. At first it worked. But now they believe that the South will lose the war. The Yankees keep stirrin' them up, promisin' to free them. Every plantation around has informers. Includin' Cragfont. That's how Clayton Harris got murdered."

Malvinia reached up to stroke her husband's dark hair. "Let's not talk of such depressin' things," she said. "I haven't seen you for months." She blushed and looked toward the bed. "I am not a bold woman, George, but . . . I am your wife. It's been so long. An' I am so lonesome. Make love to me, dear. Make me happy, if it's only for a while."

"In broad daylight, on my mother's bed?" he asked.

"Yes!" she cried. Then, "Oh, George, you must think I'm absolutely trashy, don't you?"

He grinned as he drew her down on the bed. "War has a way of bringin' out the truth, Malvinia—you're just naturally a passionate lady."

"Oh, George," she cried, "don't embarrass me more than I already am."

George laughed. "Well, there's one thing for sure, darlin'. A person can get farther behind, and caught up quicker, with lovin' than with anything else in the world."

Patrick, having seen George Winchester slip into the house, raced down the path leading to the Union encampment that guarded the Hartsville Pike. Unknown to the slave, however, old Mrs. Winchester had stationed Fanny and Susie on the promontory overlooking the road: No Federal patrol would take her son unawares.

So when the Union soldiers reined in at Cragfont and demanded to search the house, George Winchester, leaving a very frustrated wife crying into her mother-in-law's pillow, was galloping his horse in the direction of Tompkinsville, Kentucky, where his command was bivouacked.

That same afternoon, Clayton Harris was put aboard a steamer bound for Johnson's Island, Ohio, where the death rate for Confederate prisoners was reputed to be an outrageous hundred men per day.

Once at Johnson's Island, he was marched directly to a dungeon-like cell so filled with men that after the door was closed, he was afraid to move for fear of stepping on another human being. The stench of unwashed bodies, feces, vomit, and urine was deadly.

"Where you from, soldier?" asked a young man lying propped against the wall.

"Sumner County, Tennessee," Clayton returned.

"Sumner County!" The boy pushed himself to a sitting position. He extended his hand toward Clayton, but a spasm of coughing doubled him over. He lay back against the wall and stared up at the ceiling.

"He's from someplace called Bledsoe's Lick," offered the man next to the boy. "Got took at Chattanooga back in January." The man shook his head sadly. "He's come down with consumption. Gettin' worse every day."

"Who is he?" Clayton was surprised that he had not recognized someone who lived within three miles of Summerset.

"His name is Hall Wynne."

Clayton's head snapped toward the boy. Hall was a living skeleton, not at all the arrogant young man he had knocked down at Cragfont less than a year before. Kneeling beside Hall, he took the boy's cold hand in his. "Hall, it's Clayton Harris . . . remember me?"

Hall's glazed eyes swiveled to Clayton's face. "Harris?" His voice was weak. "The same one what knocked the stuffin' outta me?"

"Yes," Clayton said uncomfortably. "That was me."

The boy's eyelids fluttered; then he whispered, "You think you're man enough to try it again?"

Clayton squeezed the boy's thin hand. "Not on your life, soldier. I sucker-punched you that night. You'd have whipped me to a fare-thee-well if I hadn't."

Hall Wynne coughed deep in his chest, a hacking rattle that left spots of blood on his sallow lips. He motioned Clayton closer. Even then Clayton could barely hear the word: "Thanks."

For the rest of the night Clayton held Hall's hand, but near daylight weariness took its toll: Clayton's chin dropped to his chest and he slept.

A rough hand shook him awake. "Let go of him." A soldier in a crisp blue uniform was peering at Hall Wynne.

Then, turning, he yelled, "There's another one over here."

Clayton looked down at Hall Wynne's bloodless face. At least he looks peaceful, he thought. Unwinding Hall's stiff fingers from his own, Clayton pushed himself erect. The guards caught Hall's wrists and began dragging the body toward the door. "Will you notify his family that he's dead?" Clayton asked.

"Naw, Reb," said one of the guards. "We don't know who he is, and we don't care. If we wrote letters to the families of every Confederate who died here, we'd run out of paper and pencils in three days."

The inmate who had spoken to Clayton the night before shook his head. "You're wastin' your breath, mister. These Yanks ain't about to do us no kindnesses."

"It was just a thought," Clayton said.

A guard who had been listening pushed a Confederate soldier aside with the butt of his rifle and walked over to Clayton. "If you're smart, Reb," he said, eyeing Clayton up and down, "you won't think. You haven't got the right to think. You haven't even got sense enough to think." He prodded Clayton with the gun barrel. "Do you understand?" Clayton stared at the man. "I asked you a question," shouted the guard.

"I haven't got sense enough to answer," Clayton said, turning his face aside.

The guard smiled crookedly, then drove the butt of his rifle into Clayton's unhealed ribs. Clayton sagged to the floor, to wallow in the human filth that carpeted the flagstones. The guard caught him by his hair and lifted his face out of the excrement. "You won't last a month in here," he promised.

Although October was a quiet month for Sumner County, the adjoining countryside was shattered by the deafening sounds of war. In Davidson County, not far from Nashville, Confederate General S.R. Anderson was routed, leaving hundreds of dead and wounded lying on the field. Then at Perryville, Kentucky, just north of Sumner County, Confederate General Braxton Bragg's entire army was nearly annihilated.

Major George Winchester, outraged, wrote to Malvinia:

"Bragg is a humbug. He has no brain and is unfit for his position. His Kentucky campaign should cost him his head."

Cotton had been dispatched by Morgan to Wheeler's Cavalry, a component of Bragg's army, to observe the Perryville battle. He thought much the same as Winchester as he gazed across the hundreds of dying soldiers Bragg had deserted on the battlefield. When Bragg fled to Tullahoma, Tennessee, Cotton headed for Hartsville to report the man's cowardly retreat to Morgan.

Three miles north of Richland Station, near the old Zollicoffer training camp, Cotton's horse threw a shoe.

Dismounting and leading his lame horse, he struck off across a field toward a barn whose aged roof shingles shone silver-gray in the distance.

From behind a thicket of bushes near the barn lot, Cotton canvassed the area. The barn and outbuildings were in good repair, but the door hinges were rusted, whitewash was peeling, and occasional roof shingles were missing; the house, sitting beneath a canopy of tall maples two hundred yards beyond, appeared to be in good condition.

An old Negro woman stepped from the back door and walked to the well. A moment later Cotton heard the door slam as she reentered the house. Nothing else moved, not a chicken or a hog, not even a watchdog.

"You a deserter?" The unexpected question spun Cotton around, his revolver cocked and ready. "Well, are you?" A small girl, barely five feet tall, steadied the butt of an ancient flintlock fowling piece against her slender shoulder. The yawning bore was aimed at his stomach.

Cotton laughed. "Why, hell, no. My horse threw a shoe an' I was kinda hopin' there might be a forge around here somewhere." He indicated the barn with a sweep of his pistol barrel. "Furthermore," he continued, "I heard that the purtiest woman in all Sumner County lives here."

The girl flushed, and a skeptical smile dimpled her cheeks. "She used to . . . but she died giving birth to the ugliest."

Cotton looked her over. Although her homespun dress fell in a straight line from her neck to her bare feet, there was the intimation of budding breasts and gently flaring hips beneath the coarse fabric. Raising his eyes to her face, his breath caught; she was the same turned-up-nose girl who had opened his head with a rock on Election Day in 1861. A year had changed her into a young woman. "Jesus Christ," he breathed. "It's you!"

"You're goin' to go to the devil if you don't stop takin' the Lord's name in vain," she said.

Cotton pointed to the scar above his eye. "You ruin't my handsome face."

The girl looked at him; then, as she recognized him, she blushed prettily. "Sorry about that." She dropped the butt of her shotgun to the ground. "But you had it coming."

Cotton slipped his revolver into his holster. "Like hell I did."

The girl laughed. Her teeth were white against her pale pink lips. "You know you deserved it, so stop playacting."

She was not as homely as Cotton remembered her; he said so. Again the girl laughed. "You've changed too. I can tell that you've missed a few meals . . ."

"Ain't we all?" agreed Cotton. He nodded toward the weed-infested garden plot. "It don't look like you folks are eatin' none too high on the hog."

"We were doin' fine," she countered, "but between the Yankees and the Confederates helpin' themselves to our stock and produce, there's not much left."

"I'm sorry," Cotton said.

"Don't be. Every farm in Sumner County has lost something to both armies. At least the soldiers haven't used our fence rails for firewood, or ransacked the house . . . yet."

"I know what you mean," Cotton said. "I've done a little thievin' myself. Chickens, pigs—"

"And you told yourself that if the army was well fed, it could protect us folks better, right?"

Cotton nodded.

The girl smiled pityingly at him. "I don't believe that anything, not even war, gives a person the right to disregard the Ten Commandments, and especially not where civilians are concerned."

"Sometimes it can't be helped."

"I suppose not."

Cotton fidgeted uncomfortably, wishing she wouldn't

look at him that way. "What about that shoe my horse throwed? Do you have a forge, or an anvil, or any tools I might borrow?"

"In the second shed left of the barn." She pointed. "My father hid his blacksmith tools under a pile of sawdust when he went off to the war. He told me to hide everything of value, or the Yankees would steal it. He didn't tell me our boys would steal it too." She searched Cotton's face. "You don't look like a thief, yet you said you are."

Cotton blushed. "I ain't, not a real one. Damn it, girl, don't look at me like that." He led his horse toward the shed. "Furthermore," he said over his shoulder, "I've got dispatches for Colonel Morgan from Colonel Wheeler. So I ain't got the time to steal nothin' even if I had a mind to."

The girl fell in beside him. "Colonel Wheeler of the cavalry?" she asked. Cotton nodded. "I have a cousin in his command," she said.

"Who is he? Maybe I know him."

"He's Private Ellis Harper." She looked hopefully at him.

"No, ma'am, the name doesn't ring no bells."

"Well, it's of no consequence," she said. "He probably doesn't know you either."

Stripped to the waist despite the late-October chill, Cotton hammered the last nail into the horseshoe and dropped the animal's hoof from where it had been pinned between his knees. "That about does it, ma'am," he said, nodding at the girl. "I thank you kindly for the loan of the tools."

"My name isn't ma'am," she said. "It's William Harper."

"William?" Cotton guffawed.

She raised her chin. "My papa thought I was a boy. In the room where I was born, it was too dark for him to see me good. He saw my navel sticking out, because it was ruptured, and he . . ." The girl's face flamed. "He . . ." Cotton sat down on the anvil and howled with glee. "My friends call me Willie," she finished testily.

"Now don't go gettin' mad," Cotton said, snickering. "I just ain't never heard of no girl being named William before."

"What's your name? Maybe I'll find *it* funny."

"Cotton." He continued to chuckle.

"Cotton what?"

"Cotton Ferris."

"Why'd you have to be asked twice?"

Cotton stood up. "Now listen here, girl. You ask too damned many questions. That ain't none of your business."

Willie's eyes narrowed. "You don't like to say your last name, because your father never married your mother, did he?"

Cotton glared murderously at her. "I should make fun of you for bein' a bastard," she continued tartly. "But I can't do that, because it's not your fault, no more than my name is my fault. Actually, I feel real bad for you."

"Don't go feelin' sorry for me," he warned.

"Now look at who's gettin' angry!"

They stared into each other's face, then burst out laughing. "I haven't had so much fun since old Lem fell in the well," Willie said, giggling.

"What happened to him?" Cotton asked, wondering who Lem was and, more important, where he was.

"Papa was all for leavin' him down there, until I reminded him that Lem would probably pee in the water and it wouldn't be fit to drink." Again they went off into a gale of laughter, and the tension of the past months of war subsided. Two young people faced one another with a kinship born of sharing the simple gift of mirth.

"Miss Willie?" An old Negro man, his eyes glued to Cotton's naked upper torso, was peering around the shed door.

"Yes, Lem?" said Willie.

"I done come to tell you that supper's near ready."

Willie smiled at Cotton. "Tell Lena to set an extra plate. We're havin' company, Lem."

"Yes'm." Lem glanced suspiciously at Cotton, who was hastily slipping into his shirt.

"It ain't what you think," Cotton said, seeing the old man's dark look. "Ain't nothin' like that goin' on in here."

Lem's eyes lifted to Cotton's, and he quietly hung a curved-blade briar sickle on a nail by the door. "If'n it were, Mista soldier-boy," he said, "you'd done be daid, 'cause Miss Willie ain't that kind o' girl." The old Negro turned and shuffled toward the house.

"Crusty ol' bastard, ain't he?" Cotton said. "Don't act

like no slave I ever met."

"Lem's not a slave," Willie said. "My daddy freed him and Lena years ago, before I was born. They're my family now that Daddy's gone to the war. And they're awfully protective, Cotton."

Cotton sat his horse, looking down at the small girl who stood at the yard gatepost gazing up at him earnestly. Lem and his wife, Lena, stood on the porch, all but invisible in the darkness, but Cotton knew they were there, so he considered his words carefully before he spoke.

"Miss Willie," he said, touching his hat brim, "I surely did enjoy real food for a change. I appreciate you invitin' me to supper, an' I thank you for lettin' me borrow your pappy's forge."

Willie stepped close to Cotton's horse and extended her hand to him. "The food wasn't much," she said.

Cotton grasped her fingers and shook them formally, surprised by how rough and callused they were. Farm work is too hard for her, he thought. She's too frail to try to keep this place goin', and her darkies are too old. "Miss Willie," he said, "if I'm up this way again, may I come a-callin'?"

"Please do."

Cotton swelled with pride; he had not expected his proposal to be met with sincere warmth and pleasure. Then it dawned on him that she was as lonely as he. "Christmas," he said, pivoting his horse. "I'll come at Christmas."

With a wild Rebel yell, he spurred his horse into a dead run and lifted the animal into a beautiful jump that cleared the rail fence by a good two feet.

Willie sucked in her breath. Then, shaking her head, she turned and walked to the house. "He's as wild as a March hare," she told Lem and Lena. "But he's nice." Then, pursing her lips, she murmured, "Christmas. That's such a long time away."

The old people looked at one another knowingly; Miss Willie was growing up.

CHAPTER 22

Although it was only late October, the slime on the stone floor of Clayton's cell was frozen solid. Clayton's teeth chattered, and he pushed himself even closer to the man sitting next to him, but it did no good.

"You're colder than I am, Harry," he said, crossing his arms and slipping his fingers beneath his armpits. When Harry failed to respond, Clayton looked into his face; then his lips drew into a bitter line. It was the closest thing to emotion that he could summon.

An hour later when the guards opened the door and came for the dead man, they had in their midst a tall, well-built Indian who without a doubt was the most handsome man Clayton had ever seen. His hair was blue-black, and his high cheekbones were chiseled to perfection. But it was his eyes that demanded attention; they were a pale yet vivid blue that contrasted strikingly with his copper-hued skin. He wore a red-checked woolen shirt and gray canvas breeches that were tucked into knee-high riding boots.

While two privates dragged Harry's body toward the door, the sergeant in charge turned to the Indian. "Take them off." He indicated the man's boots with a dip of his head.

"Well, now, Yank," said the Indian, "it's colder than the North Pole in here. I believe I'll keep them on."

The sergeant leaned toward the man. "Listen to me closely, Injun. You either give us them boots or we'll cut your feet off and take them. It's as simple as that."

"Nice bunch of fellas, aren't you?" The Indian slipped the boots off and handed them to the sergeant.

Appraising the boots grudgingly, the sergeant asked, "Where did an Indian get a pair of boots like these—made of fine English leather?"

"I had them made in England, naturally. Where do you think English boots come from? China?"

Without warning, the sergeant smashed the boots across the Indian's face, knocking him to his knees. Looking up at the man, the Indian wiped the back of his hand across his bloody mouth. "I'll bet you're bald-headed," he said, his voice deep and resonant.

The sergeant's eyes narrowed. "How did you know that?"

The young Indian grinned. "I just guessed that there wouldn't be a thing about you worth taking."

The sergeant hit the Indian again. Clayton pushed himself to his feet. "There's a dead man over here you can beat all you want, Sergeant. He's more your style."

The sergeant eyed Clayton's skeleton-like face. Then he put his foot against the Indian and sent him sprawling toward Clayton. "This one can take your friend's place, and be damned to you."

The Indian pushed himself to a sitting position beside Clayton. "Nasty place we have here," he said, frowning at his soiled breeches and shirt.

"You'll get used to it," Clayton said dryly.

"I doubt it." He sniffed the air. "My grandfather says that a man can get used to the smell of shit, but I don't believe it."

"Does this place smell like shit?"

The Indian stared hard at Clayton, then laughed. Offering his hand, he said, "I'm Montclair Drew, formerly of Standwait's Brigade of Cherokee Mounted Rifles."

Clayton shook his hand. "Clayton Harris. I rode with Morgan."

"Morgan's Raiders?" Montclair Drew pumped Clayton's hand. "Man, it's a real pleasure to meet you. Morgan's Raiders are the talk of the Cherokee Nation. You boys are legendary."

Drew's enthusiasm was contagious. Despite himself, Clayton found himself smiling. "Are you really an Indian?" he asked, taking in the man's fine features. "You look like one, but then again, you don't."

"I'm an eighth Cherokee and a whole lot of something else. But, yes, I'm Indian. John Ross, chief of the Cherokee Nation, is my uncle, and he's almost a full-blooded Scotsman." He grinned at Clayton. "Are you really a Southerner? You sound like one, but then again, you don't."

Clayton laughed. It felt good to laugh. "No, I'm from Ohio."

"Do I detect a little college in your speech?"

"Ohio University."

"I'm a Harvard man. I would have been a lawyer by now if the war hadn't broken out."

Clayton stared at Montclair Drew.

"Yes," the Indian said patiently. "We savages go to college too. My sister even went to a fancy female academy up North. She was tops in her class. We're trying to change our image, Mr. Harris." He reached up and ruffled his shoulder-length hair. "No feathers. Did you notice?"

"I apologize," Clayton said. "I've read about Indians, but you are the first I've met. I assumed—"

"That we were all dressed in buckskins and carried scalping knives? Well, you're not far wrong. At the battle of Wilson's Creek, Missouri, in sixty-one, we took a few scalps."

Clayton nodded. "Word has it that the Cherokees acquitted themselves very well in that battle."

Montclair Drew waved the statement aside. "We let loose with a Comanche war cry and the Yankees crapped all over themselves."

Clayton grinned. "We took your cue and patterned our Rebel yell after you folks. It put the fear in the Federals, sure enough."

The young men talked on. Clayton told Drew about Lettie, about how thoughts of her made prison more bearable. Montclair Drew laughed. "I don't have a lost love to dream about, so I suppose I'll have to think about my sister. Angel's a real beauty, Clayton. But I always told her she was so ugly that she had to slip up on a spring just to get a drink of water. She's spoiled rotten, but she's a good girl."

Clayton listened with impatient politeness, anxious to talk about Lettie and the war, but Drew droned on about his sister.

Even though it was ten o'clock at night, November 6, 1862, the falling snow glistened against a polished-pewter sky that gave the illusion of daylight. Cotton, along with a small detachment of Morgan's cavalrymen, rode up to Cragfont's west gate; it was open and unattended. They rode through, skirted the house, then headed to the stock barn, where they rubbed down their steaming mounts with dry hay before helping themselves to the meager grain in Cragfont's bin.

Cotton fed his horse lightly, remembering Willie's theory concerning war and the Ten Commandments. He smiled, his cold face creasing stiffly with the effort. He wasn't at all sure she was right, but then again, he wasn't convinced she was wrong. Either way, she had sure piqued his conscience.

Leaving the others at the barn, he broke a trail in the snow to Cragfont's front door and pounded loudly, anxious to learn whether or not the Winchesters had any word of Clayton, who had not been seen or heard from since the night of his capture.

Lettie answered the door. For a moment she stood in silence, then smiled sarcastically. "Why is it that only the good die young?"

Cotton formed a cutting remark but decided against it; there was a harsh glitter in Lettie's eyes that caused him to shiver as though he had been thrust naked into a pool of ice.

"Won't you come in, Cotton?" she asked.

He doffed his hat. "No thanks, Miss Lettie," he said, forcing a smile. "I'm too wet an' icy to come inside. Snow's nigh hip-deep, an' gettin' worse."

"Nonsense." She drew him into the hall and closed the front doors. "This house is already icy, and has been ever since . . ." She didn't finish the sentence, but Cotton did, under his breath. ". . . ever since Bailey Peyton died."

"So come right in," she said after an uncomfortable

pause. "It wouldn't be neighborly to leave you standing outside."

"No, ma'am, I guess it wouldn't." Her unblinking gaze made him nervous. "Miss Lettie, have you-all heard anything . . ."

She pierced him again with her glittering eyes. "About what?"

Cotton stared at her. "Nothin', ma'am. It was nothin'."

Fanny came into the hall and covered Lettie's shoulders with a woolen shawl. "You need to go back to the fire, Miss Lettie," she said. "It's too cold for you to be out here." Lettie flung the wrap aside and walked into the parlor, closing the hall door behind her.

Fanny threw her arms around Cotton and hugged him. "Lord, it's good to see you, Cotton. We never knew for sure if you got away, or drowned, or what."

"Never was no chance of me drownin'." Cotton grinned. "Hell, I swam in the Ohio River a'fore I could walk." Then he turned serious. "Fanny, what's wrong with Miss Lettie? She's always been a bitch, but now she seems cruel an' bitter . . . an' . . . an' crazy."

"I don't know, Cotton," Fanny lied. "Mrs. Winchester says Lettie is a little imbalanced because she blames herself for Bailey Peyton's death. And now that Clayton's missin', old Miss believes that Lettie feels guilty for that too." But Fanny knew better. Old Chatty had said it weeks ago; the abortion of Bailey Peyton's baby was driving Lettie insane.

"Jesus Christ," sighed Cotton, walking to the front door. "What else is this goddamned war goin' to cost us?"

When the Confederates rode from the barn, Mrs. Winchester left the house and walked gingerly through the snow to meet them. She hated wintertime; it reminded her of death. "Would you boys care to come in for a cup of sassafras tea?" she inquired. "I would offer coffee, but we haven't had any for six months."

"No, thanks, Mrs. Winchester," Cotton said. "We've got to meet up with Colonel Morgan and two hundred of our men near Tyree Springs. There's a Yankee infantry unit due to pass by there tomorrow and the colonel wants to be waitin' for it."

"That's fifteen miles from here!" exclaimed Mrs. Winchester, drawing her shawl closer about her throat and shivering with the cold. "It will take you all night to reach Tyree Springs in weather like this."

Cotton nodded. "Yes, ma'am. We're going to have to push hard to get there by daylight." As Mrs. Winchester turned toward the house, Cotton handed her a one-dollar gold piece. "It's for the horse feed," he said, reining away. It was all the money he had.

The tracks made by Cotton's horse were still melting when a new set of tracks overlaid them; Patrick was on his way to Gallatin to relay the intelligence he had just overheard.

As a result of Patrick's warning, Morgan's plan of ambush was all but defeated before it began.

After a short but furious clash, Morgan retreated his men toward Gallatin, but upon learning that a large detachment of Federal troops awaited him there, he crossed the Cumberland River at Cairo and rode through the knee-deep snow to Lebanon, nearly eighteen miles away.

The Union commanders at Nashville ordered troops to every strategic location in Sumner County. Then they sat back, waiting for the Confederate colonel to make one mistake . . . just one.

Even then, with all of Sumner County swarming with Union soldiers, Morgan's Raiders continued to harass every Federal outpost within a fifty-mile radius of Gallatin.

General Rosecrans, commanding officer in Nashville, advised his field personnel in Sumner County that should they capture any man of Morgan's, they were to "shoot or hang him on the nearest tree."

CHAPTER 23

In mid-November, the controversial Brigadier General Eleazer A. Paine won the appointment as "commander" of the Sumner County district, with immediate orders to establish his headquarters at Gallatin.

Upon arriving in Gallatin, the handsome, prematurely gray general called a mass meeting of the town's citizens. Standing on a podium in front of the courthouse, he addressed the assembly:

"You are the scum of the earth. You have aided and abetted the enemy since the beginning of the war. You have done everything in your power to destroy the Union." His hard gaze moved from face to face. "I am here to preserve that Union! I am called the 'Hanging General.' The reason I have gained that title is because, in the past, I have made it a practice to hang one Rebel for every Union man murdered." He smiled at the surly crowd. "I am not going to do that during my stay in Sumner County. No! While I am in this festering hellhole, I shall hang two of you for every Union man murdered."

A howl of anger arose from the citizens. But Paine turned his back, dismissing them.

Paine requisitioned 500 men to open the tunnel that Morgan's Raiders had collapsed the year before. Working night and day, seven days a week, the laborers dug their way through the fallen debris. And on November 26, 1862, the railroad between Louisville and Nashville was again transporting Union supplies and Union soldiers across Southern soil.

The night of December sixth was worse than miserable. Snow, sleet, and subfreezing temperatures pelted at Morgan's 1,800 near-frozen troops as they crossed the Cumberland River. They were en route to Hartsville to attack the Union army encampment there.

After urging his mount up the slippery, ice-covered riverbank, Cotton dismounted and began scraping encrusted ice from his horse's legs and stomach.

The man next to Cotton tried to dismount also but found that he was frozen to the saddle. Ripping his clothing free, he dropped heavily to the ground, his numb legs buckling and pitching him face-first into Cotton's horse. The animal reared, slipped on the icy turf, and fell backward.

Cotton threw himself sideways, away from the thrashing hooves. Jumping to his feet, he cried, "You damn near got my head kicked off, Tom. What in hell's the matter with you?"

Tom pushed himself to a sitting position, but when he attempted to stand, he again sprawled headlong on the frozen snow. Ignoring Tom, Cotton gripped his horse's bridle in both hands and dragged the floundering animal to its feet. Then, talking soothingly to it, he ran his hands down its front and rear legs.

"Your horse all right?" Tom was still sitting where he had fallen.

"Seems to be," Cotton said. "What about you? You all right?"

"This is as far as I go, Cotton . . ."

Cotton knelt beside Tom. "Come on, I'll help you up."

The soldier shook his head. "Ain't no use, Cotton. I froze my legs crossin' the river . . . ain't no feelin' in 'em, none a'tall." He managed a feeble grin. "You know as well as me what that means."

Morgan rode up to the two and reined in.

"Cotton, I've dispatched J.D. Bennett's Ninth Cavalry into Hartsville to secure the town and all escape routes. I want you to take a patrol and scout the enemy camp. If they have pickets out, silence them. When we hit the Federals tomorrow mornin', it's got to be a surprise."

Cotton stood up. "Colonel," he said through chattering teeth, "we got some trouble here, sir. Tom's legs is froze."

Morgan sighed. When the man's legs thawed, gangrene would kill him. "Tie him on a horse and detail a man to take him to the nearest farmhouse. That's the best I can do." Morgan laid a gauntleted hand on Cotton's shoulder. "I would send you with him, Cotton; I know you an' Tom are friends. But dern it, tomorrow won't wait."

Cotton nodded, then moved off in search of a man who could be left behind to tend to the fallen soldier.

Morgan reached into his saddlebags and withdrew a bottle of whiskey. Swinging stiffly from the saddle, he walked to Tom and handed him the bottle. The man took a pull, then offered the bottle to Morgan. Morgan shook his head. "Drink it all, Tom. Maybe it will help a little." But he knew better.

Morgan waited with Tom until Cotton returned; then he mounted and reined in close beside the boy. After a minute he cleared his throat. "It's harder to see a friend die than an acquaintance, Cotton," he said. "Keep that in mind."

Cotton stared at Morgan. What in hell was the man talking about?

On December seventh, as false dawn brightened the heavily wooded landscape outside of Hartsville, two inches of new snow, fallen during the night, muffled the sound of the approaching Confederate vanguard.

Cotton and a half-dozen handpicked men left their horses with a holder and crept through the thickets toward the sleeping Federal encampment. They were no more than flickering shadows among the blackened tree trunks as they filtered soundlessly toward the enemy sentries, who were walking their posts with blankets wrapped securely about their greatcoats.

As Cotton crawled toward the picket nearest him, he slipped his hunting knife from his belt and gripped the handle tightly in his numbed hand. The guard, five feet away, had his back to Cotton; it was perfect.

The knife felt like a deadweight in Cotton's hand, and he found himself hesitant to move closer to the sentry. He shook his head, wondering what had come over him. He had never been squeamish before. Then Willie Harper's pixie-like face penetrated his thoughts and he heard her words again: "Not even war gives a person the right to disregard the Ten Commandments."

Damn her! This is war, an' if I listen to her, she's goin' to get me killed.

In two quick strides, Cotton clamped his hand over the guard's mouth and snapped his head back, putting the razor-sharp edge of his blade against the soldier's throat. In his mind, Willie Harper's voice shouted at him: "Thou shall not kill! Not in cold blood."

Cotton's hand trembled, causing the knife blade to nick the soldier's skin. "Yank," Cotton whispered into his ear, "if you make one sound, the snow ain't goin' to be nothin' but red mush." The guard rolled his eyes as far toward Cotton as possible and blinked rapidly. "I want you to lay facedown," continued Cotton, "and stay there until I tell you different. If you so much as wiggle, you're a dead man. You understand?" Again the boy blinked.

The moment the knife was removed from the sentry's throat, the lad dropped face-first into the snow and lay there unmoving.

When Cotton got back to the horses, several of the men were wiping their bloody knives in the snow. One of them looked at Cotton and grinned. "Easy as pie, wasn't it?"

Wondering if he had played the fool, Cotton swung into the saddle, then stood in the stirrups and strained his eyes toward where the guard lay; he could see nothing through the swirling snowflakes. Praying that the boy had been too scared to move, he pivoted his horse and counted the men. One was missing. "Anybody seen Hawkins?" he asked quietly.

No one could remember having seen the man.

Cotton gritted his teeth. He did not want to leave anyone behind, but time was of the essence; it was nearly daylight.

"Here he is," came a whisper.

Hawkins swung into the saddle, then leaned close to

Cotton. "Somebody missed a picket, Cotton. A kid, maybe eighteen, a-hidin' in the snow. I took care of him, tho'. I even warmed my hands on his body a'fore it got colder'n me. Funny how fast a dead body chills out."

Cotton felt sick.

Even though the snow had stopped and the visibility was clear, Morgan's men were within easy pistol range of the Union Army when discovered. The battle that followed turned a serene, snow-covered field into a dirty, ragged, red-and-white patchwork of death. The victory for the Confederates was complete. Federal losses were 58 killed, 204 wounded, and a staggering 1,761 captured or missing; Morgan's losses were 21 killed, 104 wounded, and 14 missing.

But there would be no rest for the Confederates. No sooner had the men dismounted and kindled their fires than a scout galloped in. "Five thousand Union infantrymen are comin' from Bledsoe's Lick!" The lick was only eight miles away.

"No wonder we're as skinny as bean poles," complained a soldier, pulling himself back into the saddle. "The damn Yanks never give us time to eat."

"Well, there's one bright spot that you ain't thought about," Cotton said, settling gingerly on his icy saddle. "As long as they're chasin' us, they ain't gettin' to eat either."

Morgan stood in the stirrups and shouted, "Move those prisoners out of here. I want to be on the south side of the Cumberland by the time those Federals arrive."

Confederate Surgeon John O. Scott rode up to Morgan and touched his hat brim. "With your permission, Colonel, I'm staying behind. We have too many wounded who can't be moved, and . . . well, heck, Colonel, the Union surgeon was killed . . ."

Morgan shook his head. "I'm sorry, John. We can't take a chance on losing you."

"There's three hundred wounded men out there who need doctorin', sir. A lot of them, ours included, won't last 'til a Federal surgeon can be brought up from Gallatin."

Morgan scanned the wounded Confederates who had been carried close to the fires and covered with blankets. Several faces were familiar; others were such grotesque masks of suffering that their own mothers would not have recognized them. "Friends . . ." he murmured, thinking of his words to Cotton not three hours before. "A good commander does not make friends."

"What's that, sir?"

"Nothing, John," Morgan said. "I was just thinkin' of something I told a soldier this very morning." Then, inwardly raging at the softness that he considered a sign of his own inferior leadership, he said, "You can stay until the Federals are within a half-mile of here, no longer. At that time you will withdraw." Morgan's eyes bored into the surgeon. "I mean that, John. You're not to stay one minute longer, no matter who you're working on. Is that understood?"

"Yes, sir." Ignoring the icy temperature, Scott shucked off his overcoat and rolled up his sleeves. "I understand perfectly, sir."

Spurring his horse into a canter, Morgan rode to the south end of the field where the Confederates were hurrying their Federal prisoners toward the river. Reining in beside Cotton, he said, "Dr. Scott's staying behind. I want you to ride a mile or so out the Hartsville Pike and watch for the Union troops. The minute they come into view, you get back here and load Scott on a horse and get his butt across the river."

"No problem, Colonel. I'll have him on the other side of the river a'fore the Yanks get within five mile o' here."

Cotton galloped to the field hospital tent and swung down off his horse. Soldiers of both armies lay, sat, or stood near the entrance, waiting their turn. It'll take days to doctor all these people, he thought.

"Well, Cotton," said one of the wounded Confederates sitting on the ground, "you came out without a scratch— again."

Cotton knelt to see who the man was. Then, "Just plain ol' luck, Haynes," he said. He tried not to stare at Haynes' blood-soaked face.

"Guess I'll be goin' home now," Haynes said. He laughed bitterly. "Won't my wife be proud to see me . . . half my face shot off?"

Cotton remained silent. There was nothing to say, nothing at all.

Leaving his horse ground tied, Cotton climbed to his feet and stepped through the tent flaps. Dr. Scott was amputating a man's hand at the wrist. Two wounded infantrymen were holding the screaming patient down on the makeshift operating table. "When I stick my head in here again, Doc," Cotton said, "you be ready to go, 'cause the Yanks'll be workin' plaits into my horse's tail."

As Cotton left the tent, a well-dressed woman brushed past him and walked to the doctor. He heard her tell Dr. Scott that she was Mrs. Halliburton and that he was welcome to use her house—just three hundred yards away—as a hospital.

Cotton stayed just long enough to hear the doctor agree.

Cotton tied his horse to a bush, then climbed to the top of a cedar tree that commanded a view of the Hartsville road for a mile or more. He hoped for the wounded's sake that the Federals would be a long time in coming; but he knew better. For even as he made the wish, the wind shifted and he heard the faint roll of drums in the distance.

He drew his overcoat more tightly about him and tried to make himself comfortable; he would give the doctor every minute possible. But in less than an hour the Union advance guard came into view, moving carefully up the icy road.

Cotton dropped down out of the tree and sprang onto the saddle. Ten minutes later he was at the Halliburton house. "Time to go, Doc," he yelled upon entering. "The Yanks'll be in rifle shot of this place in three minutes!"

"Help hold this man down," ordered the doctor, not looking up.

"Damn it, Doc!" Cotton shouted as the surgeon made another swipe at the leg with his saw, the small, jagged teeth powdering the bloody floor with dustlike bone fragments. "If we don't leave here this goddamned minute, we're goin' to find ourselves prisoners of war."

The patient emitted a bloodcurdling scream, and even though the two soldiers assisting threw all their weight on the man, he arched his body off the table and flung the pair aside. "Hold on to him!" cried the surgeon.

Cotton drew his pistol and slammed the barrel across the man's head. With a long sigh, the patient fell back upon the table and lay there quivering. "Sorry, Doc," whispered Cotton, his face deathly pale as he stared at the dying soldier. "I didn't mean to kill him. I jist meant to knock him out . . ."

"He was a dead man anyway," the doctor snapped. "You simply cut his death throes short. Get him off the table, there's another one waiting."

When Cotton didn't move, the surgeon caught the dead man by his coat lapels and jerked him off the table; the corpse fell with a sickening thud onto the blood-soaked floor.

"Get this body out of here!" shouted the doctor at the two attendants. Spinning toward Cotton, he said, "If you're goin' to puke, get it over with; I've got to have your help. Those two boys yonder," he indicated the two who were now dragging the body through the back door, "are doin' their best, but both of them are gunshot all to hell!"

"I ain't goin' to puke." Cotton flung his coat off and lifted another wounded soldier onto the table.

It wasn't until they had pushed the man's intestines back into his body and sewn his stomach shut that Cotton realized they were no longer alone.

When the Federal troops marched onto the Hartsville battlefield, they fell silent. The camp was intact, the dead lay where they had fallen, the wounded were being carried to a house not far away, but an entire Union brigade, nearly two thousand strong, had vanished. And the quiet was nerve-racking.

Colonel John M. Harlan, the Union officer in command, went to the Halliburton house. Perhaps the wounded soldiers could explain such a strange phenomenon. He certainly hoped so.

But the sight that met him when he entered was equally peculiar. A Confederate doctor was operating on an injured infantryman—a Union infantryman.

Colonel Harlan positioned himself just inside the door and watched in silence. His officers began to join him.

The doctor was finishing the sutures when Cotton glanced up to find the room lined with Federal officers and noncoms. Grinning, Cotton hooked his bloodied thumbs in his suspenders and said, "I place you men under arrest. You are, as of this minute, prisoners of the Confederate States of America."

The officers stared at him.

"Why is it," he asked, frowning, "that Yankees never laugh? I seen thousands of 'em, some of 'em real close-up, but I ain't never seen one laugh."

"Dern it, Cotton," cried the doctor, assisting the attendants as they laid the sutured soldier on a litter, "hush your mouth an' give me a hand here."

The doctor saw the Yankee soldiers and ran a bloody hand across his forehead. "If you brought a surgeon," he said to the colonel, "we can certainly use him."

Colonel Harlan shook his head. "Sorry, sir. Three or four half-trained medics are the best I can offer. But I do have some ambulances."

Another broken body now lay on the operating table. "Medics are better than nothin', I reckon," the doctor muttered.

Harlan watched the surgeon probe the soldier's chest for a bullet. "I find it a bit awkward praising the enemy," he said, "but I commend what you've done here, Doctor. Obviously the color of a man's uniform is not an issue."

Dr. Scott raised his eyes for a moment. "Uniforms covered with blood are all the same color, Colonel."

As the afternoon shadows began to lengthen, the temperature again fell below zero, turning the partially melted snow to a solid sheet of ice.

Under Dr. Scott's supervision, Colonel Harlan had the wounded who could travel loaded onto ambulance wagons and transported into Hartsville, where the citizens had opened their doors to the battlefield casualties.

After seeing to it that the wounded were settled as comfortably as possible, Harlan returned to Mrs. Halliburton's, where Dr. Scott and Cotton were still busy with the critically injured. Bidding Cotton to accompany him, Harlan walked to the battlefield. The Union troops were using pick and mattock in a futile effort to open a trench in the frozen ground. On the far side of the field, where the Confederate bodies had been taken, the townsmen were having like difficulty.

Harlan watched the progress for a thoughtful minute,

then said, "There's no sense in those townspeople breaking their backs trying to dig a separate grave. I believe I'll suggest that they bury the Confederates with our soldiers."

Cotton shook his head. "That's mighty kind of you, Colonel, but I don't think I'd do that if I was you."

"Why not?"

"Well, sir, it ain't my intention to hurt your feelin's, but our boys would rather let the buzzards pick their bones than be buried next to a Yankee, sir."

Colonel Harlan blushed. "Dr. Scott's unselfish help to my wounded reminded me that we are men as well as soldiers. I was merely trying to repay the generosity."

Cotton nodded, but said, "We'll bury our own dead, sir."

Later, in Mrs. Halliburton's kitchen, Cotton slumped into a cane-backed chair and thankfully accepted a mug of steaming coffee, compliments of Colonel Harlan, who had commandeered the coffee beans from the Union chow wagon. It was the first real coffee Cotton had tasted in a year.

When Colonel Harlan went again to check the progress of the burial detail, Cotton begged off, saying that Dr. Scott needed him. But the moment Colonel Harlan was gone, Cotton borrowed paper and quill from Mrs. Halliburton and quickly scribbed off a detailed report to Morgan, informing him that it was not the intention of the Federals to give pursuit, but instead to return to Bledsoe's Lick. He gave the Federal strength and armament, and finished by saying that although his and Dr. Scott's fate was undecided at present, they were being treated kindly.

Folding the paper, he passed it to Mrs. Halliburton and asked her to deliver it to John Hinton, in Hartsville.

As a result of Cotton's dispatch, Morgan started a rumor that he, along with ten thousand men, was marching on Gallatin. He hoped the ruse would create such a hasty withdrawal of the Union Army from Hartsville that Cotton and Dr. Scott might escape.

At three o'clock on the morning of the eighth, after the last man had been ministered to, the weary doctor slumped down beside Cotton in Mrs. Halliburton's parlor. "It's over," he said, dropping his head into his hands. "I've done all I can do."

Colonel Harlan entered the room and knelt beside the two Confederates. "I believe you men could use a bit of this." He handed a bottle of bonded Kentucky bourbon to Dr. Scott. The doctor took a long pull, then passed the bottle to Cotton.

The boy nodded appreciatively. Tipping the bottle, he drank deeply, then wiped his mouth with the back of his hand. "Lord, that's fine stuff. I ain't tasted whiskey like that since I left home in fifty-nine."

"You a Kentucky boy?" inquired Harlan.

Cotton shook his head. "I once was. But I'm a Tennessean now. Sumner County is my home." He took another pull, then passed the bottle to Harlan. "You a Kentuckian, Colonel?" Harlan nodded that he was.

The three of them—a Union colonel, a Confederate doctor, and a Rebel private—warmed themselves by the fire and shared the bottle of fine whiskey. They talked of the universal subject of soldiers everywhere: home.

As daylight drew near, Harlan ordered three horses saddled and ready to travel. After a hasty breakfast of cornbread, grits, and buttermilk, the colonel personally escorted the two Confederates through the Union lines to the Cumberland River. The snowfall had picked up again, making travel as treacherous as it was miserable. The three men stood on the northern bank and stared through the blizzard toward the invisible southern shore. Harlan shook his head. "Well, gentlemen, this is as far as I go. Good luck to you . . . you're going to need it." He indicated the icy river with a nod. "I surely don't envy you, crossing that."

"We're used to it," Cotton said, smiling. "You Yanks won't let us cross in pretty weather."

Harlan grinned. "You've never paid the least bit of attention to what we Yanks want or don't want."

"Ain't it the truth," Cotton said.

Dr. Scott offered his hand. "I can't say it's been a pleasure, Colonel Harlan, for that would be heresy. But I am glad to have met you, sir."

Harlan shook the doctor's hand and then Cotton's. "Godspeed to you both."

The two Confederates walked their horses gingerly into the river. As they disappeared into the swirling snow and icy water, Harlan absently ran his hand across his cold face. If

General Paine hears that I pardoned a Confederate surgeon, he thought, I'll be drummed out of the service.

He turned his horse toward Hartsville. I really don't care.

That same day, news of the Union defeat at Hartsville reached General Paine at Gallatin.

Immediately he telegraphed the information to General Rosecrans at Nashville, who fired back a one-sentence query: "Do I understand that Morgan has captured an entire brigade of our troops without our knowing it, or a good fight?"

Paine wired back that Rosecrans would have a complete report on the disgrace within twenty-four hours.

Near midnight, unable to eat or sleep, the distraught Rosecrans sent another dispatch to Paine: "It seems to me impossible that the entire brigade could have surrendered. Are there none left?"

Paine stalked to the stove and stuffed the dispatch into the flames. His passive face revealed none of the intense hatred he harbored toward Morgan, his cavalry, and indeed, toward Southerners in general, military and civilian.

Furthermore, he had just heard a rumor that Morgan, with ten thousand troops, was marching on Gallatin.

Snatching his quill from its holder, Paine scribbled a message to Colonel Harlan ordering him to leave Hartsville and return to Gallatin immediately. Then he penned a letter to General Rosecrans requesting that Gallatin's military strength be increased to twenty-five thousand men.

To add insult to injury, on December ninth, *The New York Times* wrote: "The guerrilla Morgan appears to have everything his own way. . . . Nothing could be more disgraceful than the capture of the brigade of troops in Tennessee."

Disgrace for one is often glory for another.

On the fifteenth of December, while President Abraham Lincoln waited for a report as to "why an isolated brigade was at Hartsville, Tennessee, and by whose command; and, also, by whose fault it was surprised and captured," Confederate President Jefferson Davis met with Colonel John Hunt Morgan at Murfreesboro, Tennessee, and to deafening roars of approval from Morgan's cavalrymen, commissioned

Morgan a Brigadier General of the Confederate States of America.

Other promotions soon followed. The men laughed and clapped Cotton on the back. "From now on," they said, "we'll have to call you by all your names: Captain Cotton Ferris, sir!" But the promotion to captaincy carried sadness also: He was replacing Captain Clayton Harris, who was now officially listed as "missing in battle."

On December 22, 1862, at Murfreesboro, General Morgan called his Sumner County men to his field tent. "Well, it's almost Christmas," he said, "and I know that many of you would like to spend a day or two with your families. So I've decided to send Colonel Boyers here to the Union camp at Cage's Ford to ask permission for you boys to pass through the Union's lines." The men shouted and clapped one another on the back. "I thought you would like that," Morgan said dryly. "I want a squad of volunteers to accompany Colonel Boyers."

Every man stepped forward.

Morgan smiled at them. "I also thought you would do that." Then, motioning Boyers forward, he said, "Thom, take the whole darned bunch with you. When you get to the Federal camp, pick two men and ride in—two men only." Turning to the soldiers, he said, "The rest of you hang back and wait. If anything should go awry, you are to attack immediately."

Boyers, Cotton, and a man named James McKoin, under a flag of truce, rode through the Union pickets and drew rein before the tent of the Federal commanding officer.

A very young captain threw back his tent flaps and stepped outside. Astonishment drew his face into a ludicrous mask. "Well, I'll be hanged," he breathed.

"We was kinda worryin' about that ourselves," Cotton said, grinning widely. "You got a thousand men here with guns pointed at us. Are they afraid the three of us might surround them?"

The captain glanced uneasily toward his troops. Then raising his face to Colonel Boyers, he asked, "Are you Morgan?"

"No, Captain," returned Boyers. "I've never heard of

Morgan. However, we do have a General Morgan, who commands us."

The officer blanched. "I meant no disrespect, sir."

"Apology accepted," Boyers acknowledged. Then, shifting himself more comfortably in the saddle, he said, "I'm Colonel Thomas Boyers, Captain. I rode over here to obtain your written permission for my men to visit their families in Gallatin durin' Christmas."

The captain's mouth fell open. "You can't be serious, sir?" Boyers stared at the man. The captain shook his head unbelievingly. "I'll have to send your request to General Paine for his approval, sir, but meanwhile, you and your men are welcome to warm yourselves by my fire and have some coffee while you're waiting."

"Well, that's mighty kind of you, Captain," Boyers said, nodding at Cotton and McKoin to dismount. "I haven't had any real coffee since I can't remember. But I have got some mighty fine chewin' tobacco."

"Well, hallelujah!" the Union officer cried. "We've been out of tobacco for weeks. You've got yourself a trade, Colonel."

They had just finished their fourth cup of coffee when the courier returned from Gallatin. Out of hearing of the Confederates, he spoke at length to the captain.

Cotton traded apprehensive glances with Colonel Boyers and McKoin. Then he slowly loosened his pistols in their holsters.

The Union captain returned. "I'm sorry, sir," he told Boyers. "General Paine . . . he says, sir, to inform you that he not only finds your proposal asinine and brash, but a direct insult to his intelligence. He also says, sir, that because of General Morgan's conduct at Hartsville, he is withdrawing all Christmas passes issued to Confederate women. He . . . well, sir, he considers the women more insidious and far more dangerous than the men."

"The no-account son-of-a-bitch," Cotton muttered. "Everybody knows that our belles are simperin' little things—"

"Who will shoot your eye out if given half a chance," the captain said, smiling. "Do you know that one spit on me the other day?"

"I don't doubt it," Boyers said.

"Shoot fire, Captain, it's Christmas!" McKoin said. "Paine must surely be a sanctimonious ol' bastard. All we want to do is honor the Christ child's birthday with our families."

With an embarrassed shrug, the captain said, "You have my apologies, gentlemen, but orders are orders."

"Well." Colonel Boyers set his coffee cup aside. "We thank you for your hospitality, sir. Merry Yuletide to you."

On the return trip Cotton rode alongside of McKoin. "What in hell does sanctimonious mean? Even Clayton Harris never used a word like that."

McKoin grinned. "It means that Paine is a no-good son-of-a-bitch."

"Hell." Cotton was disappointed. "I already said that."

"Yeah," returned McKoin, "but I said it with eloquence."

General Morgan retaliated for Paine's refusal by rolling a half-dozen cannon to the riverbank and shelling the Union camp on the far side.

Colonel Boyers was on a hill overlooking the river, directing fire, when Morgan reined in beside him. "Is there a reason why you are making no direct hits on that camp, Thom?"

Boyers, watching the shelling through his telescope, threw Morgan a slow smile. "It's Christmastime, John. Goodwill toward men . . . an', well, that little Federal captain wasn't a bad sort."

Cotton took a three-day furlough and spurred his horse toward Richland. At the river he stripped naked, rolled his clothes in oilcloth, tied his wrist to his saddle, and swam beside his horse across the choppy Cumberland.

The animal dragged him blue and shivering up the bank on the Gallatin side. It was all Cotton could do to pull himself erect once he was on dry ground. He slapped his body with his numb hands until the friction sent a thousand needle-like pains surging up his forearms. Then, with dogged slowness, he donned his dry clothing. It seemed as though it took forever before he thawed out. But finally he lifted himself into the saddle once more and pointed his horse north toward the highland rim . . . and Willie.

Willie was chopping kindling beside the woodshed when Cotton rode out of the woods. Driving her ax into the chopping block, she ran to open the gate for him.

Her cheeks were flushed with pleasure as he dismounted and shook her hand. "I was beginnin' to think you had forgotten about coming," she said happily.

Snatching his hat off, he placed it over his heart. "A man would have to be crazy as hell to forget a promise made to a girl as purty as you, Willie."

Her cheeks flushed even more deeply. "A person could listen to that kind of flattery all day long."

Drawing him through the gate, she escorted him to the house and into the front room that was both parlor and bedchamber during the winter months.

Inside, Cotton removed his spurs and hung them along with his pistols on a peg beside the door. Willie told him to take off his boots and set them by the fireplace to dry, which he did. His naked toes protruded through the holes in his heavy woolen socks.

"Can you stay long enough for me to darn those?" she asked.

Cotton wiggled his toes. "Can you do it in three days?"

Willie clapped her hands with glee. "You can spend three days with us?"

Cotton nodded. He had intended to pass part of Christmas Day at Summerset but decided against it because Federal troops were encamped at Wynnewood, just above the plantation, and at Cairo, just below it. And upon seeing the sheer joy in Willie's face, he was glad for the change in plans. Tipping back the cane-bottomed chair, he thrust his feet toward the radiant hearth.

Willie whisked off to the kitchen, calling for Lena to fix Cotton something warm to drink and for Lem to take Cotton's horse to the barn.

Clayton Harris dug angrily at his filthy, matted beard, wishing that the lice would freeze to death or become dormant for the winter, anything to ease the constant biting and crawling that was slowly driving him insane.

He could not believe that he had been incarcerated for only four months. It felt like a lifetime of agony.

Montclair Drew raised his bloodshot eyes to Clayton. "Quit scratching, Clayton. Your face is bleedin' again."

"I can't help it." Clayton clawed at his shaggy hair.

"These bugs are getting worse. Every time someone dies, his lice head straight for me."

"They do that for a fact, but you've got to quit scratching the skin off your face, or the rats will smell the blood and come running."

Clayton's stomach tightened, but not with revulsion; he would have welcomed anything edible, rodent or not.

A disturbance near the door drew both men's attention. A sixteen-year-old, named Eddie, was being dragged, screaming and kicking, toward the entrance by two Union soldiers.

Clayton dropped his gaze, wondering what he would do if the guards decided to take him for a mate. They would have to kill him first, he decided.

"Why don't they find themselves a woman, like God intended?" Drew murmured. Then he lurched to his feet and staggered toward the guards.

Clayton pushed himself up to follow, but the man next to him clutched his arm. "Stay put," he whispered. "They'll kill you."

"Drew!" Clayton rasped. He coughed in an attempt to clear his congested throat, then cried again, "Drew!"

But Drew wobbled on toward the soldiers, who were still struggling with the frightened boy. They were unaware of the Indian's presence until he caught one with a hard right fist to the temple. The man dropped face-first onto the frozen floor. The remaining guard released Eddie and bounded toward the door, bellowing for help. Instantly several soldiers rushed into the building.

Clayton struggled to his feet and staggered toward Drew.

An inmate kicked Clayton's feet out from under him, causing him to fall heavily. Two more inmates pinioned him to the floor, whispering for him to lie still.

The guards dropped their bayonets to the ready position and formed a half-circle around the Indian.

Drew took a step backward, then another, calculating his chances.

The soldier he had struck climbed to his feet and snatched a musket from the guard nearest him. With the look of murder, he advanced on Drew. The Indian retreated another step. Then he took a deep breath and squared his shoulders.

"I never ran from a man in my life," he said, "and I sure

won't run from some sodomite who molests little boys."
Crossing his arms over his chest, he spat contemptuously on
the floor.

The soldier's face twisted into a sardonic smile. "You've
bought yourself a peck of trouble, Indian." Turning to the
guards, he said: "Put him in irons. Take him to cell number
four."

Clayton kicked and squirmed in an attempt to break free
of his fellow prisoners, but they held him secure, releasing
him only after the soldiers had marched Montclair Drew
out of the building.

It was a quiet, uneasy cell block that awaited Drew's
return. Clayton studied the men around him. He wondered
if they were aware that by refusing to get involved, they had
condoned whatever abuse Montclair Drew was receiving.

Suddenly Eddie demanded, "What's takin' 'em so long?
Why don't they bring him back?"

No one answered.

Then a man on the far side of the room said, "Why are we
feelin' guilty about Montclair Drew? He ain't nuthin' but a
Indian."

A murmur rippled around the room.

"I was wonderin' the same thing," another voice said.
"There ain't a Southerner alive who don't hate Indians.
There ain't a one of us who hasn't lost some member of his
family to 'em during the Indian wars. My grandmother was
scalped by the Creek." The crowd voiced its agreement.

Clayton's eyes swept the room with a glare of disgust; this
hatred for Indians did not stem from the seed of the Indian
wars; Montclair Drew, by his refusal to stand aside and
allow a young boy to be violated, had unintentionally
brought to the surface that thin layer of cowardice that
nearly always lined the cloak of courage. His cell mates were
using the only true hero among them to appease their
guilt-ridden consciences.

Clayton buried his face in his hands. What manner of
calamity would it take to free the people of America,
especially the Southerners, of their hatreds and prejudices?
The current war certainly wasn't the answer. If anything, it
was only creating new problems and compounding old
ones.

The cell door opened and two guards marched into the room, Montclair Drew hanging limply between them. Without ceremony they dumped the semiconscious man on the stone floor.

The Indian's handsome features had been beaten beyond recognition.

"Lord God!" whispered someone. Eddie dropped to his knees and retched.

Clayton knelt beside Drew and lifted him so that the Indian's shoulders rested against his leg. "Can you make it to the pallet, Montie?"

Drew's mouth moved and he tried to open his eyes. "Go easy," Clayton said. "I think your jaw's broken, and your eyes are swollen shut . . ."

Drew shuddered. "I can't walk, Clay," he murmured. "They tore up my insides."

The muscles in Clayton's cheeks knotted into cords. His face a mask of stony anger, he demanded: "Is anybody going to help me carry this man to his pallet?" No one moved. "You sons-of-bitches," he breathed. Eddie rose and walked over timidly. Together, they dragged Drew to the filthy pile of straw that served him as a bed. The effort left them both spent.

Stretching Montclair Drew out as comfortably as possible was the sole care they could administer; they hadn't even a blanket to put over him. Drew lay there, the rise and fall of his chest the only indication that he was alive. Clayton could not tell whether the Indian was asleep or awake.

The prisoners talked in monotones. Occasionally a voice rose in anger and Clayton supposed that someone was feeling the sting of ambivalence; they could not help but admire Montclair Drew, even if they did profess hatred toward Indians. He sighed; what was it about war that turned men into animals? Then he sighed even more deeply; the beast was there all along; all that war did was to allow the creature to surface. Once war was over, the beast quickly went back into hiding and men walked proudly with heads erect, as though the monster had never existed.

But Montclair Drew would never forget. He would carry his hatred of Northerners—all Northerners—to his grave. Before then, he would pass that hatred down to his children, and to his grandchildren. Clayton groaned. At that precise moment it became perfectly clear to him how hatred could seep into the lives of generations yet to come. It had taken a brutal, firsthand example to bring that lesson into full focus . . . and Clayton knew that now he had seen the ravening beast for what it was.

CHAPTER 24

Willie held the iron skillet over the flames and shook it vigorously. Cotton sat on the floor beside her and watched with childlike anticipation. Shortly a "ping" rang against the tin top that covered the utensil.

"It's popping!" Willie cried, shaking the skillet harder.

"Take the lid off so we can watch it," Cotton said.

"You can't do that. It'll fly all over the floor. Have you never popped corn before?"

"Lot's of times," Cotton lied. Then he grinned. "You know I ain't never popped no corn, Willie. Hell, I ain't never even seen none before."

"Poor boy," the girl said, shaking the pan furiously. "It should be ready. It's about stopped popping."

She put the skillet on the hearth and removed the lid. A last kernel popped, causing several of the small white balls to leap onto the floor. Cotton picked one up and studied it suspiciously. "You sure it's fit to eat?" he asked.

Willie tossed one into her mouth, then took another and forced it into Cotton's mouth. She waited, watching him chew.

Cotton grinned.

"Lem! Lena!" Willie called. "Come have some corn."

The two old people hurried into the room. "Miss Willie, Mista Cotton, we could smell that corn a-poppin' clear in yonder," Lem said. "An' we was a-hopin' yo'all would 'vite us to join yo'."

"You knew we would," Willie scoffed. "It wouldn't be Christmas without the two of you."

The four of them sat before the cheerful fire and laughed and sang, and then Willie read the Christmas story from the Bible.

Closing the book, she suddenly became shy, and Cotton caught her watching him from under her lashes. "I have a present for you," she said, almost too low for him to hear. Rising, she hastened into the back room and returned with a bundle.

"I didn't have any paper to wrap it in . . ." Nervously she handed the present to Cotton. He looked at her for a long moment, then unrolled the bundle. It was a pair of finely made, dark-gray trousers.

Cotton kept his eyes on the garment. "Miss Willie," he said, "I can't accept these pants."

"What yo' mean!" Lena cried, coming to stand beside Willie. "Miss Willie done worked herself to the bone a-weavin' and a-cardin' and a-spinnin', an' a-huntin' sumac berries for to dye them britches."

"Please, Lena," Willie said.

Lena paid no attention. "Yo' soldier suit is plumb wore out, Massa Cotton. Why, them britches of you'rn is so saddle-slick, I can see yore bucket 'tween the threads."

"Lena!" Willie cried.

"Well, it's true, Miss Willie," Lena said. "His hind end shines like a baby's butt."

Willie covered her face with her hands.

"I truly need these breeches, Miss Willie," Cotton said quickly. "I just ain't never had a young lady give me a present before. I don't rightly know how to act. I'm sorry."

"Well, go try 'em on," Lena said. "That's what Miss Willie is a-wantin' yo' to do."

It was the finest Christmas Cotton had ever known.

On the rainy afternoon of December twenty-seventh, Cotton rode into Morgan's camp at Murfreesboro, Tennes-

see. It was all but deserted. A few men hunkered down in
the heavy drizzle, attempting to cook their evening meal.
Cotton pitched his saddle into his tent and joined them.
Every eye was on him as he squatted beside the sputtering
fire and poured boiling acorn coffee into his tin cup.

"Damn weak-lookin' stuff," he commented. The bottom
of the cup was plainly visible through the amber liquid.

"Them's third runs on the dregs, Cap'n."

Cotton lifted the cup and drank slowly.

"Well, damnit, Captain," said Samuel Lackey, "did you
get any?" The other men leaned forward. Cotton stared at
the flames. "Well?" demanded Lackey.

"Naw," Cotton replied, taking another sip of coffee.
"She's a real nice girl."

"Aw, come on, Captain," the man persisted. "You were
with her for three days and nights. An' we know you had
your pants off at least once 'cause you're sportin' some fine
new duds."

Cotton's face swung toward Lackey and his hand inched
inside his overcoat. "You tired of livin'?" His eyes bored
into the soldier like bullets.

"Well, I do declare," Elmer Green said. "I believe the
Cap'n's done gone an' fell plumb in love."

Nervous laughter rippled around the camp fire.

Cotton took another sip of coffee. "She's everything a
man could want, boys. An' just so you'll quit your tomfool
questions . . . I never even kissed her."

"Well, the least you could a-done was lie to us," Elmer
Green complained. "We been sittin' by this fire for four
days dreamin' up all sorts of spicy antics you was a-doin'.
You're a real disappointment, Cotton."

Cotton looked around the nearly empty campsite.
"Where's the general, and the rest of the men?"

"Gone off to Kentucky to do some damage to the
railroad," James McKoin said. "The Yankees are callin' the
rails we rip up and bend 'Morgan's neckties.'" The soldiers
laughed. "We went on sick call," he continued, "just so we
could be here when you got back. What a waste."

"That ain't true," Green said. "The general left us behind
to keep an eye on Bragg." Green motioned toward a distant
hill all but invisible in the misting rain and fog. "General
Bragg and fifteen hundred men are camped just over that

rise. We got word this mornin' that General Rosecrans is on
his way from Nashville with the intention of twistin'
Bragg's tail again . . . and he'll do it. Bragg is sorrier than
molasses when it comes to leadin' men."

"We supposed to support Bragg?" Cotton asked.

"Yeah, but Morgan won't be back in time to pull this
battle out of the fire. Bragg's on his own hook, and boy, is he
mad at Morgan."

"Serves Bragg right," Cotton said. "Morgan's saved his
ass too many times already."

On December thirty-first, the roar of cannon at Stone's
River, just outside of Murfreesboro, could be heard thirty-
five miles away, at Gallatin. And when the noise finally
subsided, the Confederates, with General Braxton Bragg in
the vanguard, were in retreat toward Knoxville. Over seven
hundred of Bragg's men had been killed, wounded, or were
missing.

"Hell," said Cotton, riding with his battle-weary com-
rades toward Lebanon, where they hoped to rendezvous
with Morgan, "the son-of-a-bitchin' Bragg did it again. It
was Perryville, Kentucky, all over."

Clayton Harris was also fighting a battle. It was a week
since Montclair Drew had been brutalized. Using his own
ration of drinking water, Clayton had cleaned Drew's
battered face and body lacerations. But there had been little
he could do to stop the seepage of congealed blood that
oozed from the young Indian's rectum. Clayton's pleas to
the guards for a doctor fell on deaf ears.

The prisoners kept their distance, offering neither assistance nor support, which infuriated Clayton. Only Eddie
seemed to care.

Drew's wakeful moments were a feverish nightmare of
pain. During long periods of unconsciousness, the Indian
would toss and turn and rave, until—even though the cell
was as cold as ice—Clayton and Eddie would find themselves sweating from the effort of holding him still.

On New Year's Day, 1863, Montclair Drew opened his
eyes and smiled into Clayton's haggard face.

"God, you are ugly," he whispered.

Clayton breathed a long sigh; Drew's eyes were clear of

fever, and the pain seemed to have abated. "It's about time you were coming around," Clayton said. "You've had a pretty rough time of it this past week."

"What day is it?"

"A guard said that it's New Year's Day, but you know how they lie."

Drew smiled weakly and closed his eyes.

Clayton laid his palm on Drew's forehead. "The fever's broke. That's a good sign."

The Indian opened his eyes. "God gives a person a repose right before they die, Clayton."

"Nonsense. You're going to be fine."

Drew groped for Clayton's hand. "Promise me that you will get word to my folks. Just tell them that I . . . died in prison. Be sure to tell my mother, or my father . . . not my sister. Don't tell Angel." Clayton looked away, bothered by the request. If he agreed to it, he was admitting that Drew was dying. "Promise me!" Drew cried weakly.

"Dern it, Montie," whispered Clayton, "fight to live. You can win. Fight a little longer."

"I've been fighting all week, my friend," the Indian sighed. "I'm tired . . . so very tired."

Clayton shook his head. "You're not going to die."

Drew clutched Clayton's hand. "Promise me you will let my family know. Promise me, Clayton."

Clayton nodded. "I promise."

Drew smiled wanly; then he screamed. The repose was over.

It took ten more hours for Montclair Drew to die—ten hours of screaming as his intestines tried their utmost to exit through his rectum.

In Sumner County the war had become a gruesome battle of survival. General Paine wasted no time in casting aside the white gloves of an officer and gentleman and getting down to bare knuckles. Captured Confederate cavalrymen suddenly, upon being taken prisoner, could not sit a horse at all. They "fell from their mounts and broke their necks." Confederate infantrymen, being marshaled to prison by a full company of Union cavalrymen, decided they could outrun the Union horses and were "shot while attempting to escape." Or so said General Paine's written reports to his superiors.

Nor did the civilians fare any better. An old man repairing his rail fence that had been damaged by a Rebel scouting party was shot to death by a Union patrol for "aiding the enemy."

Women whose husbands or fathers were away fighting for the South were accosted and abused, and many were raped. Their pleas for protection were ignored, for the sole authority was General Eleazer A. Paine.

President Lincoln's Proclamation of Emancipation became effective on January 1, 1863, freeing the slaves in those states governed by the Confederacy. Tennessee was not one of them, and hadn't been since the fall of Nashville in 1862; so the very proclamation that freed the slaves in the Confederate-held states bound them even tighter to their lawful owners in Tennessee.

Paine did not openly countermand the President's proclamation, but he did drop strategic hints that should a black person decide to declare himself independent of his master, the army would not waste its time in searching for him.

On March 25, 1863, several slaveholders banded together to confront Paine. The general declared that the insistent owners were themselves guilty of a rebellious movement to undermine the Government of the United States of America. He ordered their arrest, and himself sitting in judgment, convicted them without a trial, then marched them to the Gallatin courthouse square and hanged them.

On April 23, 1863, three bushwhackers retaliated the hanging: Thomas Norvill, a staunch Union sympathizer suspected of being an informant, was abducted and murdered. *The Nashville Daily Union* reported: "They killed him by stabbing him eleven times in the breast and belly, and four times through and through; then cut his neck from ear to ear through the bone, and left a little to hold the head on the body, and split down the right ear with a great gash, and cut the skin on top of the head across and pulled it down, and broke the skull to get a trophy, and took out some of the brains."

Willie Harper's slim shoulders were racked with silent sobs. She had liked her neighbor, Mr. Norvill. But that wasn't the only reason she wept; the fiendish murder had been committed by none other than the three soldiers turned bushwackers who stood facing her: her cousin, Ellis Harper, whom she adored, and two of her childhood friends, William Berryman and Peter Blane.

"Oh, God, Ellis," she whispered, thumbing tears off her cheeks and turning so she could see her cousin's face. "You knew Mr. Norvill. You've hunted his fields, and eaten at his table. How could you have done such a thing?"

"I didn't know they would publish it in the newspaper," said the tall, twenty-four-year-old man angrily. "I knew when we did it that we should have killed his wife too."

"You've gone crazy, Ellis!" Willie shouted. "War has twisted your brain. And you two!" She spun toward the accomplices. "It makes me sick to think I even know you!"

"Shut up, Willie," Harper said. "We didn't come here for no goddamned sermon."

"Well, what did you come for? Whatever it is, take it and get out! If you can't fight like real soldiers, then don't come back here."

"We are real soldiers," Harper said. "We're just fightin' the war our own way, an' I'll listen to no more of that talk. We need food and a place to rest, Willie. We've been runnin' for more'n a week."

"And what about your father?" The girl shouted at Peter Blane. "And yours, William Berryman? General Paine had them arrested and shot. They're dead! And so is Uncle George. Your father is dead because of you, Ellis. Don't you understand that?" Again tears sprang to her eyes. "I loved Uncle George, Ellis," she whispered.

"That's just one more reason why we're goin' to kill every Union man in Sumner County." Harper caught up a ladder-backed chair and smashed it against the parlor wall. "So shut your mouth, girl, and fix us somethin' to eat."

"I grew up with you three," Willie said, not intimidated, "but I don't know you anymore. I'll fix your food, and tonight you can sleep in the barn. But don't any of you ever set foot on my property again."

Willie pushed past Ellis Harper and walked to the kitchen, where old Lem and Lena huddled in the corner.

"Help me, Lena," she said, laying another stick of wood

on the fire. "The quicker we feed them, the quicker they'll leave."

General Paine blew a perfect smoke ring toward the ceiling. Through half-closed lids he studied the former Summerset overseer, Butler. Presently he said, "That fool, Ellis Harper, played right into our hands by killing a Union man. Yes, he has definitely opened the door for us, and we'll elaborate on his timely precedent and use it to our best advantage."

Butler took a long draw on the cigar Paine had given him. "How you plannin' on doin' that, General?"

"Simple." Paine smiled easily at Butler, inwardly seething at the man's stupidity. "There are good, loyal Union men in Sumner County who . . . shall we say . . . are becoming a thorn in my side. Thanks to Ellis Harper, if they suddenly come up dead, he and his guerrillas will be blamed." Paine fixed Butler with a hard stare. "I intend to divide this county into so many factions that a man will be afraid to trust his own image in a mirror. I'll turn the slaves against the whites, and the whites against one another. Yes"—his voice purred with satisfaction—"thanks to Ellis Harper, I can wield a heavy whip, which I certainly intend to do."

"How do I fit into all this, General?" asked Butler. "You didn't call me in here so I could watch you blow smoke rings at the ceiling."

Paine sat back. He detested dealing with people like Butler, but there were occasions when it was necessary. "I need a man who knows this county and its people. I have had you investigated, Mr. Butler. And I think you fill the bill."

Butler grinned. "I know Sumner County, all right."

"Are you still living with your black whore?"

Butler's face stilled. "You know about Mandy?"

"I know everything about you, Butler."

Butler nodded. "She's still with me, an' gettin' meaner all the time. I been thinkin' about sellin' her."

"You stole her from Cragfont, didn't you?" Paine enjoyed Butler's visible discomfort.

"Well, yes," the man stammered. "But they owed me somethin'. It was her pappy who knocked me in the head an' cost me my job as overseer of Summerset."

"Obviously you have reason to . . . dislike certain Sumner Countians," Paine observed, pleased.

"There's a few I ain't got no use for."

"Good," Paine said. "I am going to give you the opportunity to avenge yourself."

"Why, General?" Butler asked suspiciously. "You got thousands of soldiers—"

"In that respect, my hands are tied," Paine interrupted cooly. "Soldiers can only be used against legitimate Rebel sympathizers, and in a strictly military fashion. That's where you fit in. I need a band of night riders to do various jobs that fall outside of military etiquette. What do you think we've been talking about for the past hour? I need a man to stir up the slaves. And, when necessary, to pay . . . visits . . . to certain Loyalists." Paine made a tent of his fingers. "Are you that man, Butler?"

"What's in it for me?"

"Revenge. Women. Money."

Butler took a long pull on his cigar. "When do I start?"

"Tonight. I want you to accompany Mandy to every large plantation in the county, beginning with Cragfont. She is to advocate unrest and, if possible, insurrection. I want her to turn every slave in this county against his master. You will report back here in two weeks. Come at night, and try not to be seen. And Butler"—he pinned the man with an icy stare—"I expect results."

Throughout the spring Morgan's Raiders seemed to be everywhere at once, heating and bending rails, wrecking trains, attacking wagon shipments of supplies, and skirmishing with the Union troops at will. As a result, it was the first week in May before Cotton had the opportunity to visit Willie again.

He rode up at sundown and dismounted at the yard gate. Willie, who had been helping Lena with supper, saw him through the kitchen window. Snatching off her apron, she quickly patted her hair into place. Gripping Lena's arm, she asked, "Do I look all right, Lena? I haven't got cornmeal on my face, have I?"

The old woman put her hands on her hipless sides and surveyed her mistress thoroughly. "If'n that Cap'n Cotton don't say yo're the purtiest girl in Sumner County, then he ain't even halfway bright."

Willie ran through the front room and onto the porch. With a smile as wide as Cotton's, she bounded down the steps and caught his hand. "Hello, soldier-boy," she said, looking up into his face. "You're just in time for supper."

Cotton pushed himself away from the table. "Finest meal I've had in months." He winked at Lena, whose face wrinkled with a pleased smile.

"If she wasn't your woman, Lem," Cotton said, laughing, "I'd be after her for sure."

"Well, suh," Lem said, "Miss Willie can cook jist as fine as Lena. She done learnt everything Lena knows."

Cotton turned to Willie. "You ain't never talked none about your ma."

Willie shrugged. "She died not long after I was born. I never knew her."

"She were sho' nuff a lady of quality," Lena said, "jist like Massa Harper were a fine gentleman."

"Was?" Cotton asked, his gaze resting on Willie.

Willie looked away. "I haven't had time to tell you, Cotton. Papa was killed last September at some place called Antietam, Virginia. We didn't receive word until two months ago."

"I'm real sorry, Willie," he murmured, wishing there were something more he could say or something he could do, uncomfortable with himself because there wasn't.

"Papa wasn't meant to be a soldier," the girl said. "He was a schoolteacher and a farmer. He taught me to read and write before I was five years old. I've already read the Bible cover to cover four times."

Cotton longed to take her in his arms, but he was too unsure of himself to attempt even such a natural response. And Willie sat there needing above all else to be held and comforted by him . . . yet knowing that he would not make the move.

"Where are you going from here, Cotton?" she asked to relieve the tension.

"We were intendin' to attack Gallatin again," he said. "That's why I had a chance to come visitin'. But Paine sent word to Morgan that he would burn the whole town to the ground if we even came near the place. He knows we have friends and relatives there. Paine's probably laughin' up his sleeve, 'cause he's got Morgan between a rock an' a hard place where Gallatin is concerned."

The old Negroes excused themselves, saying they had to get some rest, leaving Cotton and Willie alone, each uncomfortably aware of the other as they sat in the flickering light of a solitary candle.

"Well," Cotton said, rising, "I'd best be headin' for the barn and bed down."

Willie nodded, staring mutely at him. Then she was in his arms, hugging him tightly. Protectively, he drew her close against him.

Cotton was appalled at how very thin she was, and he recalled the large supper he had just eaten with such unabashed pleasure. Then his stomach turned over: Willie and the Negroes had eaten hardly anything. "Willie," he asked, his cheek against her hair, "how is your garden doin'?"

The girl stiffened in his arms. "Just fine," she murmured.

Cotton caught her chin and tilted her head so he could see her eyes. "You haven't got a garden, have you?" She shook her head, no. "Why not?" he demanded.

Willie stared into his face. "Please, Cotton," she whispered.

"How long have you folks been goin' hungry?" he shouted. "How bad did I hurt your stores by stoppin' by here tonight? Damn it, Willie, tell me."

Willie turned her face away.

Cotton pushed her to arm's length. "I feel like an ass, Willie. I come in here an' eat like—"

"You should feel like an . . . one of those things!" she cried angrily. "But not because you honored us by sharing our table. A gentleman never puts a lady on the spot, Cotton." Then tears filled her eyes. "The Yankees took our mules, and they took our anvil . . . and our forge . . . and most everything else."

Cotton walked to the door. "I'll see you in the mornin'."

Willie watched him disappear toward the barn. Then she blew out the candle and sat for a long time in the dark. She wondered if, indeed, he would be there in the morning.

* * *

"Miss Willie! Miss Willie!" Old Lem shook the girl awake.

"What is it, Lem?" She bolted upright in her bed, clutching the covers about her, her eyes wide with fear. "Has something happened to Cotton?"

"Come an' see fo' yo'self," the old man cried.

Heedless of her thin nightgown, Willie sprang from the bed and ran onto the front porch.

The sun was just breaking the horizon, its soft warmth illuminating the morning with a rose-gold splendor. But that wasn't what made Willie's heart leap. It was row upon row of rich black earth turned in straight furrows from one end of the garden plot to the other. Cotton, with the plow lines looped about his neck, was leaning heavily on the handles of a single-shovel turning plow while his gaited cavalry horse struggled with the unaccustomed burden.

Willie's hand flew to her mouth, then she laughed and raised her eyes to the cloudless sky. "You certainly act in mysterious ways, O Lord," she said. Turning on her heel, she raced into the house. Catching the door frame, she spun about. "Get every seed of any kind that we have left, Lem. We've got a late garden to plant!"

It was a tired, happy foursome who sat at the kitchen table that evening eating sparingly of the hominy, poke greens, and cornbread that Lena had prepared.

Cotton caught Willie's hand under the table and squeezed it. They had worked relentlessly throughout the day and now had an exceptional garden started. If the late rains came, they would harvest quite a yield.

Willie raised her eyes to him. "Would you like to sit on the porch?"

Together, they walked outside. Willie seated herself on the stoop, while Cotton sat on the edge of the steps and leaned back against the porch post.

"I went down to Gallatin to see General Paine," Willie said. "I told him that his men had taken my mules. I even offered to go with him to the government corral and point them out. He told me I was a liar, that he had a bill of sale for my mules."

"I'm sure he does," Cotton said bitterly.

"It isn't only me," the girl continued. "Everyone hereabouts has lost stock. While I was in Gallatin, I saw Lettie

Billingsly and Susie Winchester. Lettie said the Yankees came to Cragfont with an order for five more of Mrs. Winchester's horses and three milk cows. They had already taken nine horses and all the corn, oats, and fodder in the barn. The Winchesters are in a real bad way, Cotton— especially Lettie, who looks like death warmed over. It seems that Cragfont has been singled out. But that's absurd. What good would it do General Paine to destroy such a fine plantation?"

Cotton shook his head. He had no answer.

In Gallatin, Butler said, "Mandy stirred the Winchester slaves up real good, General, 'cept for the house servants; they wouldn't come to the meetin'."

"What about the other plantations?"

"Most of 'em were agreeable. Hell, General, niggers are a lazy lot to begin with. Sendin' Mandy from farm to farm just gives 'em an excuse to be even more trifling."

"That's exactly what I want," Paine said. "I intend to levy a tax on the big plantations, and it's imperative that the owners, especially the Winchesters, are unable to make a crop or realize any means of raising revenue. Before this war is over, Butler, I intend to own all of Sumner County . . . starting with Cragfont."

Butler shook his head uncertainly. "You may be bitin' off a chunk of lard, General. Dern near ever'body in this county is kin to one another; goddamned blue bloods, all of 'em. They won't set back an' watch you take over their plantations."

Paine smiled. "It won't be me doing it, Butler. It will be the Federal Government. And if the owners can't pay their taxes, there's not a thing they can do to stop it."

Willie studied Cotton's profile in the moonlight, tracing his silhouette with a mental paintbrush. He is so handsome, she thought, then said it aloud.

Cotton blushed. "Lord, Willie," he stammered, "I wish I was as handsome as Clayton Harris, so you could be proud of my looks."

"Don't be silly. I like the way you look. I'd be proud to take your arm and go anywhere."

"Would you? For real?"

Willie nodded. "The girl who gets you is going to be awfully glad she did, Cotton. You are going to be a fine-looking man, except that it won't show up on you for another ten to fifteen years. Right now you still look like a little boy . . . but I can see beyond that, to the man that you will become. And he is handsome."

"I love you, Willie," Cotton blurted.

She threw herself into his arms and kissed him ardently.

"I know you do," she said matter-of-factly, looking up into his eyes. "I knew it when you left here at Christmas."

"You little devil," he laughed, holding her at arm's length. "I didn't even know it my own self 'til I got back to camp."

"Well, I guess Lena's right, after all," Willie said. "She said you weren't half bright."

"Damn!" he returned. "I can't put nothin' over on nobody."

Willie nestled herself more closely against him.

"Willie," he said, tightening his embrace, "I'll be leavin' in the mornin'. An' I ain't got no idea when I'll see you again . . . 'cause General Morgan is plannin' some raids into northern Kentucky, an' maybe even as far north as Ohio. But . . . well, what I mean is, when this war is over, would you do me the honor . . . of becomin' my wife?"

Willie leaned back in his arms and grinned impishly at him. "Of course I will, silly. How else will we ever have babies?"

CHAPTER 25

On July 20, 1863, the door to Clayton Harris' cell block was thrown open and several armed guards entered. With fixed bayonets, they pushed the inmates away from the opening and fanned out threateningly.

A trim, neatly dressed Union colonel stepped into the filthy room. His nostrils flared from the stench, and his eyes burned from the ammonia of the urine. He gazed into the haunted faces of the prisoners. Animals, he thought, nothing but animals. He tried to hide his revulsion, but the inmates saw it and began to mutter belligerently. The guards dropped their bayonets to on-guard.

"Which one of you is Clayton Harris?" demanded Colonel Charles Harris. The scarecrows eyed him silently.

"Speak up!" commanded a guard.

"Go to hell," a prisoner said.

The guard turned to the colonel. "You want us to give them a taste of cold steel, sir?"

Ignoring the guard, Colonel Charles Harris walked into the midst of the surly prisoners, studying each man's face intently.

Clayton pressed himself against the back wall and held

his breath; he had recognized his uncle the moment the
colonel had stepped through the door. His first reaction was
relief; he had been rescued at last. That quickly turned to
rage. Why couldn't his uncle have come sooner—when
Montie Drew was still alive? Then came shame; he had
never answered his uncle's letter. Clayton huddled closer
against the wall, his prison-befuddled mind attempting to
sort out the rush of emotions that engulfed him.

The colonel sighed and walked back to the door. "Get
these people some decent food," he said to the guard. The
man saluted and hastened out of the building. Turning to
the prisoners, Colonel Harris said, "I am the new comman-
dant of Johnson's Island, and I intend to make some
changes." He stared at the scarecrows before him, thinking
that anything he did would be an improvement. Clearing
his throat, he continued. "If Clayton Harris is among you, I
would appreciate it if he would step forward. If he is dead, I
would consider it a kindness to be told."

The Confederates shuffled uneasily. They had been lied
to before, and it had always cost them someone's life.

Even in Clayton's deplorable state of mind, he realized
that his uncle was leaving and that he must speak up.
Pushing himself away from the wall, he staggered to the
front of the crowd. "I'm Clayton Harris, sir," he said, trying
to hold his starved frame erect.

Colonel Charles Harris sat at his desk and studied the
stranger seated before him. As though he were an animal,
the man was tearing at the food the colonel had ordered.
The colonel sighed. Could this bearded, long-haired skeleton of a man really be his nephew? "You've been through
purgatory," he said, thinking that it was an understatement.

Clayton continued eating. Colonel Harris rose from the
desk and walked to the door. "I want some fresh clothes for
this man," he told the orderly. "And I want a bath and a
barber brought here immediately."

Returning to his desk, he said that they would talk after
Clayton had cleaned up and rested. Clayton raised the tin
plate he had been eating from and licked the grease from its
bottom. Colonel Harris frowned, wondering if prison had
deranged his nephew's mind.

* * *

After Clayton had bathed and the barber had all but shaved his head, and close-trimmed his beard, he was escorted naked to a barrack where he slept for several hours. A guard shook him awake, shoved clean clothes at him, and ordered him to get dressed. The colonel awaited him.

When he was ushered into his uncle's office, Colonel Harris greeted him with a smile. "How do you feel now, Clayton?"

Clayton was unsure if he should stand at attention or at ease. "I feel better, sir," he said. Then he added, "Better than I have . . . in a long time."

The colonel nodded. "You look more alert. The food and sleep must have helped."

Clayton didn't answer. He was unaware that after Montclair's death, he had willed himself into despair. But food, rest, and hope had begun to change his despondency.

The colonel took a deep breath and released it. "Clayton, I want to help you. If you will agree to denounce the Confederacy and join the Union Army, I can get you out of here." He watched his nephew for a reaction. None came. "Is that too much to ask, Clayton?"

Clayton stared at him, and the colonel wondered if he had understood the question. Then Clayton said, "Yes, it is, sir. I would be betraying every Confederate soldier, especially those men in my cell block"—not to mention the people in Sumner County, he thought, his mind forming an image of Lettie—"if I denounced the Confederacy, sir."

Colonel Harris drummed his desk top with his fingertips. "Clayton," he said, "in this year alone, there have been ten pitched battles in Tennessee. I'm not talking about skirmishes, I'm talking about recorded battles. The Union has emerged victorious seven times." His eyes softened as he gazed at his nephew's drawn face. "It's the same in Virginia, Georgia, Kentucky, the Carolinas . . . the North is winning the war, Clayton."

"That's all the more reason for me to remain loyal to the South, sir," Clayton said.

The colonel eyed him harshly. "You haven't asked, but I will tell you anyway. Your father was killed at Gettysburg three weeks ago. How do you feel about that, knowing the Confederacy was responsible?"

Clayton turned his face away. "I'm sorry to hear that my

father is dead, sir. In his own way, he was a good man." Try as he might, however, Clayton could not deny the fact that his father had secretly worked with the Northern firebrands to change the very existence of a people about whom he knew absolutely nothing. And Clayton wondered if his father had ever questioned his self-righteousness after the war became a reality. Whatever the truth, thought Clayton, his father lay dead in a field in Pennsylvania. Perhaps he had finally found his glory.

Clayton softened after the mental outburst. Although his father had been a relative stranger to him, and the times they had shared a true father-son relationship had been few, his father had nevertheless been proud of him, especially of his scholastic accomplishments—until Clayton quit school.

Colonel Harris broke into his thoughts. "Is that all you've got to say—you're sorry?"

Clayton nodded.

"Your father, rest his soul, is dead," sighed the colonel, "and all you can do is nod your head?"

Clayton took a deep breath. "My father was killed by his need to prove himself a man of deeds and not of words," he said. "It's one of the few things we ever had in common. I apologize, Uncle, but I have no tears left, nor would he have wanted them."

Colonel Harris sighed deeply. "Your father was badly disappointed when you left Ohio," he said. "He never quite forgave you. Actually, it wouldn't even have surprised him had he known you joined the Confederate Army. He always knew you were a Rebel at heart."

"Yes," Clayton said, "I suppose I am."

Charles Harris wished the interview to be over. He didn't know the stranger standing before him. "You are my flesh and blood, Clayton. I can't leave you in this stinking death trap. I owe it to your father—and to you—to get you out of here."

"You owe me nothing, Uncle Charles. It was my decision to join the Confederacy. I only regret that we could not have met under different circumstances. Not on the field of battle, sir, but as officer to officer."

The colonel sat back in his chair. Something—prison, he assumed—had turned Clayton to a young man of stone.

"Would you at least agree to take the Oath of Allegiance to the United States?" He reached into his desk drawer and withdrew a slip of paper.

Clayton squinted at the bold, black print: Parole of Honor. "I solemnly swear, without any mental reservation or evasion, that I will not take up arms against the United States, or furnish information directly, or indirectly, to any person, or persons, belonging to any of the so-styled Confederate States, who are now, or may be, in rebellion against the Government of the United States; So, help me, God.

"It is understood that the violation of this parole is death."

Clayton took a deep breath. "Yes, Uncle Charles," he said after a long moment of consideration. "I will sign the Oath of Allegiance. I'm sick to death of seeing men die."

Five hundred miles away, General Paine leaned back in his office chair to hear Butler's report.

"A whole passel of slaves walked off from their owners and come to Gallatin," Butler said. "But, hell, General, their owners are goin' to be right behind 'em, shoutin' to high heaven for you to round 'em up an' take 'em back to the plantations."

Paine smiled. Butler was quite right; the owners would demand their slaves. But he had anticipated that.

"I've already instructed the quartermaster to put the slaves to work on that farce of a military installation Fort Thomas that Colonel Boone began building before he was relieved of duty."

"What good will that do? The owners will still want their slaves back." Butler frowned. "You gonna hang all the owners in the county, like you did that first bunch?"

"No," Paine said. "I shall take a different tack this time. Under the Confiscation Act of 1862, any slave who leaves his owner and joins the Federal military service is legally free."

"That means they got to join the army, not go to work on Fort Thomas."

"I read it differently," Paine said. "The military service covers a wide range of positions. I believe the Confiscation Act includes all government employees . . . even laborers working on a military installation." Paine smiled smugly.

"Of course, if the owners care to bring a formal complaint to Governor Johnson, I'm sure my old friend will give them a fair hearing."

Paine leaned forward and shuffled through some papers. "So, Mr. Butler, keep stirring up trouble on the plantations, and try to entice all the blacks to come in and be 'free.'"

After Butler had gone, Paine laid the papers on his desk, lit a cheroot and took a deep, contented draw. He had told Butler the truth, but not all of it. He would put the male Negroes to work on Fort Thomas, but only temporarily. He had bigger plans for them, much bigger. Meanwhile, he had the black women and children to consider. But he had figured that out too.

Taking a sheet of paper from his desk drawer, he studied the carefully prepared document thoroughly, being sure that he had overlooked no loopholes in his tax levied against property owners for the benefit of "refugees and paupers within the Post of Gallatin, Tennessee."

Paine blew a smoke ring toward the ceiling. Not only would he rob the plantations of their workers, he would make the owners pay for the upkeep of their former slaves. He was pleased by his ingenuity.

Again Paine studied the long list of assessments, ranging from twenty-five dollars to three hundred dollars. His eyes scanned the names: then he skipped down to the final two: Cragfont and Summerset, assessed at two thousand dollars each.

Paine chewed thoughtfully on his cigar. Was he moving too quickly on Cragfont? Being too conspicuous in his quest to acquire that particular plantation?

No, he thought, putting the question from him. After all, there was absolutely nothing the Winchesters could do about it, nothing at all.

On July 22, 1863, Clayton Harris was ferried from Johnson's Island across Sandusky Bay to the mainland. He stepped onto the rich Ohio soil and breathed deep. Even the air smelled free.

But he didn't feel free—not in the new shirt and trousers the prison had issued him, nor with his hair close-cropped and his beard trimmed to half a finger's length. He still looked and smelled of prison. And even though he had been deloused with sulphur and oil, it would be weeks before the sores healed. He turned for one final look at the island. Would he ever get the stench of it out of his system? He thought not.

"Well, Reb," said the soldier who had ferried him to the mainland, "I suppose it's home for you, eh?"

Clayton didn't answer. Home? Where was home? Columbus where he had grown up? It was less than a hundred miles away, but he would be shunned as a turncoat there . . . even by family. Still, he would like to see his aunts and cousins.

He gritted his teeth; they had probably disowned him too.

"Yes," Clayton said to the soldier, "I am going home." Then, silently, he added, ". . . to Tennessee."

Lettie would be at Cragfont, he was sure. And Summerset would be bringing in another good crop. And there would be parties in Gallatin. With a spring in his step, he began walking south.

Since Lincoln had drafted nearly every able-bodied young man in the North, Clayton had no trouble in hiring on as a teamster with a train of wagons hauling military cargo from Lake Erie across Ohio to the Ohio River. It was slow progress, but at least he was moving in the right direction.

The teamsters were a wealth of information, and to pass away the long, tedious hours of driving, they brought Clayton up to date on how the war had progressed since he had been incarcerated.

"Back in September of last year," said a driver, "Stonewall Jackson killed thirteen hundred of our men at Chantilly, Virginia."

"That was just kid stuff," said another driver. "I was with Burnside at Antietam, Maryland. We fought for fourteen straight hours. A hundred thousand men met on the field. Five hundred cannon shooting at one another. It was a fight, I tell you. Twenty thousand were killed before Lee abandoned his invasion. Hell, Horace Greeley said it was the bloodiest day in American history!" He went on to tell about Fredericksburg, Virginia—a Confederate victory where twelve thousand Union men fell and he had been shot so severely that he had lain in a hospital for almost six months.

Then they talked of Chancellorsville, where Stonewall Jackson had accidentally been killed by his own men.

"Yes," said a teamster name Bentley, "it was the best thing that could have happened for the North. Lee ain't been worth a damn since."

They talked of Corinth, Mississippi, another Union victory; and of Stones River, at Murfreesboro, Tennessee. Of Vicksburg and Port Hudson, and finally of Gettysburg—all of them Union victories.

Clayton listened intently to the appalling description of the awful battle of Gettysburg, and he thought of his father. The speaker finished by saying, ". . . and President Lincoln came and made a speech when the battle was over. I can't remember the words, but it was a fine speech."

On the afternoon of July twenty-sixth, Clayton was perched on the spring seat of a six-mule-team Studebaker wagon when it rolled into Springfield. The town was in an uproar; a telegraph message had just been received saying that General John Hunt Morgan and several of his Raiders had been taken prisoner in Indiana and were being transported to the Federal prison at Columbus, Ohio, just forty miles away. Clayton sat by the camp fire that night and listened to the teamsters theorize as to the fate of the famous general. Most of them thought that the Union Army would hang him.

When Clayton finally rolled into his blankets, sleep wouldn't come. He lay there wondering if Cotton too was only forty miles away. He prayed not.

News of Morgan's capture reached General Paine on the same day Paine's wife arrived in Gallatin. Immediately the general put the wheels in motion to host a party in honor of both events. He dispatched handwritten notes to all of the prominent families in Sumner County, "inviting" them to the Fairview Plantation Mansion, just west of Gallatin, for a "Grand Gala."

His officers' wives spent the next week decorating the mansion, and the Fairview slaves were kept busy butchering cattle, sheep, and hogs and baking bread and pastries with which to feed the hundreds of invited guests.

On August second, when the orchestra played its grand march welcoming the guests to Fairview, it was to a nearly empty house. The Southerners had not been intimidated by Paine's command performance and, in fact, had not even bothered to decline his invitation.

It was an embarrassed and irate general who paced his office on Monday, August 3, 1863. "Most of the planters around here are destitute!" he shouted at Butler. "They haven't got a pot to piss in, yet they are still an arrogant bunch that act as though we, not they, are the scum of the earth." Paine shook his fist angrily. "These aristocratic bitches in and around Gallatin are wearing dresses made from their linen tablecloths, but they parade around with their noses in the air as if they were royalty. Their impudence toward our officers' wives is an insult! My wife is no harlot, and I'll not have her treated as one. I won't allow her to be subjected to such rude indifference as these Southern whores showed by shunning our party. How dare they be so arrogant!"

"Blue bloods, General. Blue bloods," said Butler. "They think they're better'n anybody."

"The hell they are!" Paine snarled. "People will do anything when they are destitute. Before this war is over, these grand ladies will be crawling on their bellies begging to kiss my wife's feet"—the general smiled vindictively—"and they will be glad to socialize with officers of the United States Army. My men are not monks, Butler, they are soldiers. They need feminine attention."

"General," said Butler, "no disrespect intended, but if there's any foot-kissin' done around here, Mrs. Paine better wear an old dress she don't mind gettin' the knees dirty on. An' as for your officers . . ." Butler shook his head. "I been livin' in the South all my life an' I ain't never had me no grand belle's companionship."

Paine sneered at the dirty, unkempt man. "My men are not white trash, Butler. There is a difference, sir."

Butler's mouth drew into a tight line. "Southern women might swing their fists at your soldiers, General," he said angrily, "but they won't swing their asses at them . . . not even if those women were starvin', naked, an' barefoot. No, sir, you're whistlin' up a hollow tree if'n you think you can scare or starve these folks into acceptin' you. They ain't goin' to open their homes to your wives or their legs to your soldiers. Course," he smirked, "some of your men have been catchin' them uppity ladies alone an' helpin' themselves . . ."

"Rape and pillage are the God-given rights of the victor," Paine said. "It is not for you to comment on."

"Well, I'll comment on this, General," Butler said. "These folks ain't never surrendered. An' you keep tryin' to treat 'em like they're whipped. Well, they ain't."

"They are beaten!" Paine said through his teeth. "And the quicker they accept that fact, the better. They will succumb, Butler, one way or another." Then he smiled again. "And when they do . . . who knows? Perhaps even you will finally know what it's like to have a real lady instead of a nigger wench."

Before sunrise on August fourth, Cotton walked his jaded horse into Willie's yard. For several minutes he sat slouched, head hanging, in the saddle. Then, gritting his teeth to stifle the pain, he slowly withdrew his sword and cut the thongs he had used to tie his feet to the stirrups.

Dropping the saber, he slid to the ground and crawled up the steps and onto the porch. He reached out, scratched at the weathered door, then fainted.

An hour later Willie was snatched from a deep sleep by Lem's yell. Jumping from the bed, she sprinted toward the front door. Her heart stopped. Lem had kicked the door open and was dragging a man inside. A bright red smear followed the body across the threshold. "It's Cotton!" Lem said. "Get Lena. He's still alive."

It took the three of them—Willie, Lem, and Lena—to raise Cotton onto Willie's bed. And before they had succeeded, they were covered with blood.

Cotton's eyes fluttered open. Willie dropped to her knees beside him and took his hand in hers. "Hello, soldier-boy," she whispered. Then, ever so gently, she bent and kissed his lips.

"Well, Missy," Lena said, picking up a dishpan of bloody water, "he ain't shot up near as bad as it seemed like he was. He sho' nuff must be one powerful lucky boy, 'cause his uniform be so full o' bullet holes it look like a strainin' cloth. Yes'm, the good Lord must like that boy."

Willie finished tying the bandage that engulfed Cotton's

upper chest. "He's lost a world of blood, Lena, and the wounds have gone too long without bein' tended." The girl burst out crying. "Oh, Lena, we can't let him die, we just can't."

The old woman drew Willie against her bosom. "It ain't up to us, Missy. It be up to the good Lord now. We done did all we can."

Cotton slept for seventy-two hours before he regained consciousness. His slight change in breathing woke Willie, on her pallet in the corner. She ran into the kitchen, returning shortly with a cup of sassafras tea, then perched herself on the bedside. "How are you feeling?"

"Like a target." Cotton had been shot five times, and as Lena had said, it was only by the grace of God that the bullets had hit no vital organs.

Willie lifted his head and propped the pillows behind it. Holding the cup close to his lips, she spooned a small amount of tea into his mouth.

"It was dumb as hell, Willie," he said weakly when she had finished. "General Morgan didn't want to cross the Ohio—hell, it was rainin' like pourin' piss out of a boot— but Colonel Duke kept insistin', kept insistin'." He closed his eyes. "We didn't know the country over there, and we were ambushed. But the worst part was that when we got back to the river, it was ragin' from the rain and we couldn't cross. We was penned up, with nowhere to go."

"Please, Cotton," she said, wiping his brow, "please don't talk."

Cotton turned his face so that she wouldn't see his glistening eyes. "They shot us all to pieces, Willie . . ."

Willie laid her cheek against his unshaven face. A moment later, he was asleep.

At ten o'clock on August ninth, Willie's fifteen-year-old neighbor, Lafayette Hughes, pounded on Willie's back door.

"Miss Willie," he said, panting after having crossed the fields at a dead run, "General Paine's soldiers are searching all the barns in the neighborhood, confiscatin' livestock. They're at Pa's right now. They done took our new work-horse, the one Pa went to Kentucky an' bought just last week. If you got any stock, ma'am, you better hide it quick."

"Lem!" Willie cried. "Lem, come out here." The old man appeared in the doorway. "The Yankees are searching everybody's farm again. We can't let them find Cotton's horse!"

Lem wrung his hands in desperation. "They ain't no place to hide a horse, Missy—not where them thieves won't find it."

Lafayette Hughes said, "You could do what ol' Mizz Permilia Lankford did."

"What did she do?" Willie asked.

The boy fidgeted. "Well, ma'am, when Paine's men came to take Mr. Sidney Lankford's prize racehorse, Mizz Permilia took her butcher knife to the barn and cut its throat . . . then told them they was welcome to it."

"Oh, God," breathed the girl. "Mr. Sidney's racehorse was the Lankfords' pride and joy."

"Yes, ma'am", the boy agreed. "But Mizz Permilia said she'd sooner see it dead than let the Yankees take it."

"Well, we're not going to do that," Willie said quickly. "Lem, take some sorghum molasses and sulphur to the barn and rub a mixture of it all over Cotton's horse; then cover the animal with an old blanket. Hurry! The Yankees will be here any minute."

Cotton staggered through the back doorway, draped in Willie's bed sheet. He held a cocked Colt revolver in each hand. "Where's my pants, Willie?" he rasped.

"Get back in bed, Cotton," she commanded. "I'll take care of this." Cotton didn't move. "Please, Cotton. You're in no shape to be up."

"She's right, Massa Cotton," Lena agreed. "You gonna open them wounds, and they's a heap harder to close the second time."

Before Cotton could make a reply, the sounds of cavalry could be heard plainly in the front yard.

With a pleading look at Cotton, Willie darted around the house and ran to the front porch, where a soldier stood rapping on the door. "What do you want here?" she flung at him.

The man turned and tipped his hat to her. "Have you got any horses or mules, miss? We have orders from General Paine to impress any stock fit for military use."

"Since the last time you were here, Captain," she said, "I've bought one old workhorse. But he's so badly galled that he's useless. We can't even plow with him. But if it will stop you people from constantly harassing us, please take him along."

The officer's face reddened. "This is my first time in this area, miss. So I don't know what you are talking about. However, it is my duty to see your animal." The officer and two of his men started toward the barn.

Willie wondered if Lem had had time to cover the horse. Holding her breath, she fell in beside the men.

Inside the barn, Lem was casually forking hay into the horse's manger. He stopped and leaned on the pitchfork handle as the soldiers entered.

"Lem," Willie said, "these men have come for our horse."

Lem nodded at the men. "He sho' nuff is a stinkin', putrefied animal. I's be glad to see him go."

The officer walked to the horse and raised the blanket. Grabbing his nose, he stepped backward.

"This horse is rotten!" he cried. Then, taking a deep breath and turning to Willie, he said, "Lady, I wouldn't touch that bag of bones with a ten-foot pole."

After the soldiers had gone, Willie walked to Cotton's horse and lifted a corner of the blanket. The molasses and sulphur gave the appearance of open, running sores, but it was the stench that nearly turned her stomach. "My Lord, Lem!" she gagged. "That smells like you-know-what."

The old man grinned widely, his toothless gums showing deep purple. "Lena done handed me the slop jar on my way out'n the door. I had to dump it someplace . . ."

The next evening Cotton joined the family at the supper table. "You should still be in bed," Willie scolded.

"I'm almost as good as new," he lied, gingerly picking up a fork and reaching slowly to spear a potato. A moment later he said, "As a matter of fact, now that Morgan is either dead or captured and the command is gone, I've been thinking about joining your cousin, Ellis Harper, and his band of guerrillas."

Willie's fork clattered to her dish. She stared wide-eyed at

Cotton. "You don't mean that?" she whispered.

Cotton frowned at her. "Some reason I shouldn't? Ellis is doin' a good job of keepin' the Yankee sympathizers wonderin' where he's goin' to hit next."

"He's a cold-blooded killer, Cotton," she said.

Cotton shrugged. "Hell, Willie, people get killed in war. That's the way the game's played."

Willie shook her head fiercely. "Not the way Ellis does it. He makes them suffer first. Cotton, please promise me you will return to a regular army unit . . . please." Tears welled up in her eyes. "I love you, Cotton, but I couldn't respect you if you turned out to be like Ellis, and Berryman, and those others who use war as an excuse to rob, and steal, and kill innocent civilians."

"Well, what about the goddamned Yankees?" Cotton asked. "Just before I rode to Indiana with Morgan, we heard that Paine's soldiers had killed six Confederate sympathizers and driven their families off their plantations."

"Two wrongs don't make a right, Cotton."

Cotton took a deep breath. "Here we are, not even married yet, an' you're already tellin' me what to do."

Willie flinched, then said angrily, "Do you want to take the razor strop to me and teach me to mind you, like a good and dutiful wife should?"

"I'd kill any man who ever harmed one dimple in your pretty little a—"

"Cotton!" she cried, clapping her hand over his mouth, her face a fiery red as she glanced sideways at Lem and Lena.

"Well, I would," he said around her hand. "An' that's a promise."

Because Willie insisted, Cotton spent the next two weeks recuperating. Being waited on was a new experience for him. And while he savored it, two things kept hammering at him, spoiling his pleasure. His presence at Willie's farm was an ever-increasing danger to her and her Negroes; and . . . as his body grew stronger, his desire for Willie became unbearable.

He sat on the edge of the bed on the night of the twenty-sixth and watched her comb out her long brown

tresses in the candlelight. It was all he could do to fight
down the urge to rip away her nightgown and take her right
then and there. What made it even worse was his surety that
while it would go against everything she believed, she would
not deny him. He closed his eyes and sighed. I can wait, he
told himself. But he wasn't at all sure. And he didn't want to
find out at her expense. He stood up. "Willie," he said, "I'm
leavin' tomorrow. I'll ride by Summerset an' see the old
folks. Then I'll rejoin a command somewhere . . . a real
command."

Willie's hand holding the comb froze in midair. Then she
slowly lowered it to her lap. For a long time she sat there like
a lovely statue, watching him in the small mirror on her
dresser.

Finally, she laid the comb aside and stood up. Her eyes
were huge in her small face as she crossed the floor to him.
"Make me your wife, Cotton." It was an intense, whispered
plea that stuck him like a blow. "Make me your wife, now,
tonight."

A lump formed in Cotton's throat, nearly choking him.
"Willie," he grated, drinking in the clean, fresh smell of her,
"I would like nothin' more on this earth than to do that. But
you would hate yourself afterward."

"I promise I won't," she cried softly, putting her arms
around him. "I . . . I have this feeling . . . I can't explain
it . . . like I'll never see you again. Oh, Cotton"—she
buried her face against his shoulder—"make a baby inside
of me before you go. Please, Cotton."

"No!" Cotton said, pushing her to arm's length. "I ain't
goin' to disgrace the finest woman I've ever known. I don't
know why the good Lord decided to shine his light on me,
Willie. But I'm sure beholden to him, and for once in my
life, I'm goin' to do somethin' right. I'll get situated with a
cavalry unit an' then I'll come an' fetch you to the chaplain.
We'll get married proper, Willie."

Willie tipped her head up and touched her lips to his. "All
right," she whispered sadly.

"I can't even offer you a last name, Willie—not a real one
leastways," he said. "An' until now, I never thought a last
name was important. I'm sorry."

Tears welled up in her eyes and overflowed. "Then I will

be Mrs. Cotton A. Bastard," she whispered, "and be proud of the name. I love you, Cotton. I love you so very, very dearly."

She clung to him with a desperation born of a deep, inexplicable sadness in the pit of her being, a melancholy so profound that it could well have been diagnosed as an agony of the soul. For she knew that she was touching him for the last time in her life.

CHAPTER 26

It was more like bedlam than a homecoming when Cotton rode up to Summerset. All the slaves rushed to the front yard, and Rufus, who was now fully healed, shouted at them to take Mr. Cotton's horse to the barn, and get Mr. Cotton some hot food and drink, and prepare Mr. Cotton a bedchamber in the house, until Cotton, embarrassed, called a halt to it.

Then the old gentleman and lady were down the porch steps and hugging him as though he were, indeed, their own son.

That night they talked of the war. Mr. Summers warned Cotton that should Paine's soldiers catch him, he would never reach Union headquarters alive.

"They'll kill a man an' just walk off an' leave him lying beside the road, Cotton," Mr. Summers said. "They've become so infernal brassy that they even murder people in front of witnesses."

The old man slammed his fist on the kitchen table. "Not only that," he continued, "but somebody is stirrin' up the slaves, tellin' them they don't have to work, an' encouragin' them to steal everything that the Yankees ain't already stole, an' incitin' them to lie an' cheat." The old man shook his head. "White folks is comin' to hate the darkies, Cotton . . . just plumb hate 'em."

"Who in hell would want to do all that agitatin'?" Cotton asked.

"It's that Mandy wench, the one who ran off from Cragfont a long time ago," Rufus said. "You know— Mandy, who run off with Mista Butler. Well, she came by here a while back an' tried to get all of us to leave here an' go to Gallatin. We threw her off the property. But Fanny slipped over here an' told me that Butler an' Mandy came by Cragfont, too, an' stirred up all kinds of trouble. Fanny said that after Mandy left, Patrick told the Cragfont people that General Paine has promised him Cragfont someday."

Cotton laughed. "The Winchesters own Cragfont. Paine can't take it away from them. Ol' General Winchester was given that property by the United States for servin' in the Continental Army durin' the Revolution. Butler, Patrick, Paine and the whole goddamned Yankee army couldn't get away with a trick like that. Naw, Rufus, Patrick's just a lyin' son-of-a-bitch."

"A year ago I would have agreed with you, Cotton," said Mr. Summers. "But a lot of things have changed since you've been gone. General Paine has folks around here scared to death. And now he's hit us property owners with a tax that most of us ain't got the money to pay." Mr. Summers took a deep breath and released it. "I hate to even think it, much less say it, but if we don't come up with Paine's assessment money, he might own all of our plantations."

"I wish Clayton were here," Mrs. Summers said. "He understands assessments, an' taxes, an' finance . . ."

"Has there been any word of him?" Cotton asked hesitantly. He knew that there hadn't been, because it would have been the first news they would have told him . . . unless they had heard that Clayton was dead.

The old man shook his head. "It's been over eight months—"

"Mr. Clayton's dead," Rufus said. "Ol' Chatty told me she dreamed that Mr. Clayton was goin' to meet his Maker. She dreamed that Mr. Clayton's heavenly father would take him out of a dirty, filthy hell to a beautiful heaven, where an angel would see to his every need."

"Voodoo!" spat Mr. Summers. "Dern it, Rufus, you're an educated man. You know better than to believe in that mumbo-jumbo." Rufus dropped his head.

Cotton didn't comment, but he had seen too many unexplained phenomena not to have a healthy respect for the slaves' age-old religious beliefs. "Did ol' Chatty actually say Clayton was dead, Rufus?" he asked.

"Well, not in so many words. But what else could the dream have meant? She talked of his Maker . . . an' angels, an' a beautiful heaven."

Cotton shook his head. "But dreams can be interpreted in lots of ways."

"Now don't tell me you believe in that African stuff too?" demanded Mr. Summers.

Cotton grinned at the old man. "No, sir, I don't believe in it one bit. But don't tell ol' Chatty that, 'cause she might get irritated and put a spell on me." Mr. Summers frowned at him, then gave an unwilling laugh. Cotton uncrossed the fingers on both his hands.

Clayton Harris had walked nearly thirty miles since leaving Nashville three days earlier. And he was heart-stricken by the changes that had taken place in Sumner County.

Abandoned farmhouses were nearly lost in unkempt yards, where vines growing wild sent ugly tendrils climbing in and out of the ghostly buildings. The places resembled broken, hollow-eyed skulls; nowhere was there a planted field, or even a garden plot. Nor was there any livestock— not a single cow, hog, chicken, or horse. The only fences left were those built of stone; the split rails had long since gone to fuel Union camp fires.

It appeared that every black person in the county was on the road, heading for Gallatin. And very few whites were anywhere to be seen.

A woman and her children were poking through the smoldering remains of a burned-out farmhouse. Clayton cut across the yard and offered his assistance.

"Nobody can help, mister," the woman said wearily.

"We're homeless, with no place to go. My man is in Virginia with Robert Lee, an' there's no tellin' when he'll be comin' back."

"Haven't you got any relatives who would take you in?" Clayton asked. The woman told him she did, but they lived sixty miles away. He gazed at the blackened chimney and the rubble that surrounded it; a family's life lay in ashes. "Why did they burn your home?"

"Some Confederate deserters hid in my smokehouse. The Yankees said I allowed them to do it." In spite of her determination not to, the woman began to weep. "How could I have stopped them?"

"You couldn't, ma'am," Clayton said, turning away.

"I shouldn't complain," she called as he walked back toward the road. He turned to stare at her. "I shouldn't complain," she repeated. "Last week Paine's men arrested a boy up at Richland, named Lafayette Hughes. They said he burned a bridge, but five people swore he wasn't anywhere near that bridge. Paine's men shot him to death. He didn't even get to stand trial. Lafayette Hughes was barely fifteen years old, mister."

Clayton's thin jaws tightened into hard knots; the nature of the war had certainly changed while he was in prison. The woman was going on: "I'll tell you somethin' else you need to know, mister. The Yankees are patrollin' the roads, arrestin' white men. If I was you, I'd cross the fields to where I was goin'."

Clayton nodded. "I'm obliged, ma'am."

It was three o'clock in the morning of September first when Clayton knocked on Summerset's front door. A few minutes later he heard the old man's voice demanding an identification. "It's me, Mr. Summers. Clayton." He rested his forehead wearily against the doorjamb.

The old man snatched open the door so quickly that Clayton nearly fell headlong into the great hall. "Lord! Lord!" Mr. Summers cried, lending him a shoulder to lean on. "Is it really you?" Helping Clayton inside and guiding him to the settee in the hall, Mr. Summers said, "We thought you were dead. All these months, we thought you were dead." Then he ran to the staircase. "Mrs. Summers! Come down here. Hurry!"

A light appeared at the top of the landing, and Clayton saw the old woman in her nightgown and cap, a candle held high in one hand as she peered over the rail. "Who is it?" she asked.

"Well, come on down here an' find out!" cried Mr. Summers.

She looked at the skeleton-thin man who had pushed himself up from the settee, and her breath caught. "Clayton?" she whispered. "Oh, Clayton!" Then she was down the stairs and into his outstretched arms.

Rufus rushed into the hallway brandishing a double-barreled shotgun. Upon seeing Clayton, he stopped, then slowly leaned the gun against the wall. "Master Clay?" he queried, his eyes roving over the pasty-skinned, sunken-cheeked shadow standing before him. "Is that really you, sir?" Clayton nodded. "Lord A'mighty!" Rufus caught Clayton's hand and shook it firmly, refusing to let go.

"Rufus," Mr. Summers commanded, "turn that boy loose an' go wake up Trillie an' tell her to get a fire a-roarin'. Clayton's near starved to death."

Rufus ran down the hall and out the back door. In a heartbeat he was back. Like an old hen fussing over her chicks, he helped Clayton into the dining room and seated him at the table. "Lord, you shore are a sight for sore eyes, Mr. Clay," he said. "We-all thought you was dead."

"Dern it, Rufus," shouted Mr. Summers, "we done told him that."

"It's all right, sir," Clayton said. "There were times when I thought I was dead too."

"Well, we'll have plenty of time to hear about that after you have rested," Mrs. Summers said. "Right now you eat a bite an' then get some sleep." Casting a defiant eye at Mr. Summers and Rufus, she said, "The rest of you leave him alone. Can't you see he's exhausted?"

"You sure you don't need nothin' else to eat or drink, Mista Clay?" Rufus asked for the second time since he had brought Clayton breakfast in bed. "We got to put some meat back on you, sir. You ain't nothin' but skin an' bones."

"I've been home for three days," Clayton said, "and all I've done is sleep, eat, and drink. I'm fine, Rufus, fine."

"Well, you shore don't look fine, Mr. Clay. That prison

near done you in."

"Well, I shore do feel fine, Mr. Rufus," returned Clayton, mimicking the young slave. He lay back against the pillows and sighed contentedly; while in prison, he had dreamed about sleeping in his own bed, and the reality was even better than his dreams.

"Oh, no, sir!" Rufus cried, drawing the covers down. "You can't go back to sleep. I nearly forgot to tell you that Miss Lettie an' Miss Susie an' Fanny is here. They walked over from Cragfont."

Something close to terror washed over Clayton. Lettie, beautiful Lettie. She wasn't a person anymore; she had become a goddess of his imagination, a deity that he had spent many prison-bound months piecing together.

When Clayton walked into the parlor, Lettie rose slowly from the sofa. He was shocked speechless. Before him stood a deathly thin, haggard woman whom he had never seen before. Even her eyes, her flashing, defiant eyes, had a dead glaze that chilled his soul. He had seen that glaze on prisoners who had lost the will to live.

Susie hurried across the room and flung herself into his arms, almost staggering him. She was tall for a twelve-year-old, and already showing signs of becoming a young woman. "Oh, Clayton," she said, kissing his bearded cheek, "I knew those Yankees couldn't kill you."

Lettie came to him and offered her hand. It was cold and clammy. "I'm sorry for what happened to you, Mr. Harris," she said. "I feel that part of it was my fault. If I hadn't insisted that you row us ashore . . ."

Clayton held her hand gently, trying to hide his horror at her appearance. "It was nobody's fault, Lettie," he said, drawing her into his arms and kissing her cheek.

She came into his embrace as a stranger might: emotionless, and without warmth. Nor did she so much as blink when he kissed her, neither drawing away nor responding. Self-consciously, he released her.

Fanny, who had been standing by the sofa, offered him her hand. "Welcome home, Mr. Clayton." If Clayton had been shocked by Lettie's haggardness, he was even more unprepared for Fanny's beauty. She was slim and shapely, and incredibly lovely.

"Thanks, Fanny," he said, taking her hand and squeezing

it. Then, as Lettie sat down primly on the edge of the sofa, he stepped around Fanny and crossed the room, seating himself beside her.

"Have you been sick?" he asked.

As though he hadn't spoken, Lettie said, "Was prison terrible, Mr. Harris? You've . . . lost so much weight, you hardly look like yourself anymore."

Clayton was startled by the comment. It had not dawned on him that his appearance had changed that much. "Prison wasn't bad, Lettie," he said. "The Yankees just didn't have enough food to go around."

"I didn't think it could be as bad as we had heard," Lettie said indifferently. "We've been hearing nothing but horror stories. I'm sick of them."

"They are just that, Lettie. Stories."

"I'm glad." She refused to look at him. Then, rising and glancing around the room as though she were disoriented, she said, "We really must be leaving. I had no idea that seeing you again would be so . . . painful."

Clayton rose. "I was hoping that it would be a pleasure, Lettie. I was hoping that things had changed."

She raised her eyes to his, and there was a glimmer in them that had been missing the moment before. "I really must go." She brushed past him and ran for the door. Clayton caught her there. "May I call on you, Lettie?"

Indecision mixed with fear played across her pinched features. Then she shook her head. "Nothing has changed, Clayton . . . nothing."

He peered anxiously into her face. "Haven't I paid for that one childish mistake made so long ago, Lettie?"

Again she refused to meet his eyes. "Yes, Clayton," she whispered. "But I haven't."

The following Saturday, September fifth, was an unseasonably cold, dreary day. Old Mrs. Winchester had summoned Clayton to Cragfont, and when he arrived, he felt even more chilled, for the stately old house had an air of neglect that was oppressive. Only the smoke rising from the chimney held any suggestion of cheerfulness, and even that was shattered a moment later when Fanny answered his knock; the girl's face was swollen from crying.

Clayton hurried past her and into the parlor, where Mrs.

Winchester, Malvinia, Lettie, and Susie were seated on the large divan. Old Chatty, Sylla, Delphy, and Fleming were standing by the hearth. With the exception of the widow and Lettie, all were in tears.

"Come in, Clayton." The old woman stood and offered her hand, which he dutifully touched to his lips. She had aged greatly. "Thank you for coming," she continued. "We have just received word that my son, George, and my grandson, Napoleon, were taken prisoners at Chicka-mauga."

Clayton tried to keep his face impassive. "I'm sorry, ma'am."

"Tell me," she said, "are the Yankee prison camps as terrible as we hear they are?"

Clayton cut his eyes to the tearstained face of Malvinia, who was fearfully awaiting his answer. "No, ma'am, they're not. Your men will experience certain discomforts, but they will make out just fine."

Hearing the audible sighs of relief around the room, he forced back the bile that rose in his throat as he pictured Johnson's Island and the wretchedness that awaited the Winchester men there.

Mrs. Winchester eyed her family reprovingly. "You prob-ably think we are just weak females, Clayton, the way we are crying and carrying on."

"No, ma'am," he murmured. "I don't think that at all."

Lettie rose to her feet. "Well, you shouldn't. You men had no regard for us at all. You went off to play soldier and left us alone to fend for ourselves. You have ruined our lives." She gazed at him through vacant eyes. "No," she said, "I'm not being honest. You forced us to ruin our own lives."

Pity for Lettie welled up in Clayton, but surprisingly, that was the only emotion he experienced. That was not true, either; knowledge of that very lack of feeling pierced him with a twinge of guilt. "Ma'am," he said to Mrs. Winches-ter, "I've got to go by Wynnewood, and it's a long trek. With your permission . . ."

Mrs. Winchester walked with him to the door. "I'm not pryin', Clayton," she said, "but have you got unpleasant news for the Wynnes?"

"Hall Wynne died in prison, Mrs. Winchester."

"Thank you for coming, Clayton," she said, opening the

door and following him onto the top step. Once outside, she said softly, "Thank you for lying to my family."

He nodded sadly at her. "I knew you weren't fooled, Mrs. Winchester. I'm truly sorry, ma'am."

The old woman gazed across the vast sweep of Cragfont fields, but she wasn't seeing them. She was remembering her late husband, General James Winchester, who had been first captured during the American Revolution, and then a second time during the War of 1812. "They will be back, Clayton," she said strongly. "My men always come home."

Admiration caused the corners of Clayton's mouth to lift ever so slightly. Her statement had the ring of conviction to it.

It was nearly dark when Clayton returned to Summerset. Walking into the office, he found the Summerses and Rufus hard at work at Mr. Summers' desk. Spread out before them were the contents of the safe.

"What's going on?" Clayton inquired.

"Paine's men were here," Mr. Summers said. "They demanded the two-thousand-dollar assessment the general has levied on Summerset. I've got three days to raise the money, or the Federal Government will put a lien on the plantation."

"The son-of-a-bitch," Clayton said.

Mrs. Summers raised her eyes. "Cussing isn't the answer, Clayton." She wondered what had become of the well-mannered, happy boy who had ridden off to war not so many months ago.

Clayton said nothing. Instead, he walked to the table and counted Mr. Summers' cash. Four hundred dollars. "Is this all the money that's left?"

Mr. Summers nodded. "That's all the hard money we've got. Cotton gave us a wad of Jeff Davis, but it ain't good for nuthin' 'cept outhouse paper." The old man's shoulders slumped. "We had good yields in sixty-one and sixty-two, as you know. But the Federals confiscated them . . . and with our work stock gone, we couldn't even plant the fields this year. You saw them, lying fallow."

Clayton frowned. "The army has confiscated hundreds of horses, maybe even thousands. Does Paine have holding pens in Gallatin? Can't we buy back some work stock?"

Mr. Summers shook his head. "Some folks have even tried to steal back their stock. They were shot for their trouble. No, son, Paine ain't about to let us make a crop. He figures on breakin' us, then taking our homes when we can't pay his assessments and taxes. It's a conspiracy, an' he's usin' the Federal Government to help him pull it off."

Clayton's frown deepened. "It doesn't make sense. You signed the Oath of Allegiance to the United States way back when the war started. That should have some influence. But Paine's treating you as though you were a Rebel."

The old man laughed bitterly. "Signing the Oath didn't even carry enough weight to keep 'em from arrestin' me an' Bailey Peyton an' A.R. Wynne back before the Battle of Gallatin and stickin' us in jail at Nashville. We had to post a thousand-dollar bond just to get to come home . . . an' we ain't seen a nickel of it since." The old man slumped in his chair. "Paine intends to own the best plantations in Sumner County—it's plain as the nose on your face. An' Summerset an' Cragfont are heading his list."

"That's what bothers me," Clayton said. "Why is he singling out you and the Winchesters?"

"Cragfont is the most productive Confederate-owned plantation in the county, and Summerset runs it a close second but is owned by a Union man. If he can take both of us, then he'll be home free as far as the rest of the plantations are concerned, no matter who owns them."

Clayton pursed his lips. "Kill the generals, and the troops will surrender." Then he asked, "What does Paine do with all the horses and mules he confiscates?"

"I ain't got the least notion," Mr. Summers replied.

"If he does like ol' Colonel Boone did," Rufus said, "he sells them in Nashville. They were suppose' to go to the Union Army, but they didn't. Colonel Boone sold them for cash and pocketed the money."

Clayton drew up a chair and rested his elbows on the desk. "Tell me how the operation worked, Rufus."

"There really weren't much to it. Colonel Boone would send me to the quartermaster to get vouchers for horses . . ." Rufus went on to detail the process, ending with, "Colonel Boone sold the horses in Nashville to a civilian person he called a 'broker.'"

"Can you remember what the vouchers looked like?"

Rufus grinned. "I memorized the ones Colonel Boone used, word for word, along with every other government paper I got my hands on, 'cause I was never sure what information General Morgan might need."

"Do you think Paine's using the same vouchers?"

Rufus shrugged. Mr. Summers spoke up. "The army never changes nothin'. Sure they're the same."

Clayton leaned back in his chair. A scheme was forming in his mind, and he liked the sensation after the long months of stagnation. "We would need a printing press," he said.

"What are you gettin' at, son?" asked Mr. Summers.

"Colonel Thom Boyers' old press!" Clayton cried, jumping to his feet. "The colonel told me, just before the Battle of Gallatin, that after the war he intended to go back into the newspaper business. He said that he had hidden his press in his barn so the Federals wouldn't get it. Maybe it's still there."

Rufus shook his head. "Mister Clay, if you're thinkin' that we might print up a batch of vouchers an' go to Gallatin an' claim some horses . . . we'd never get away with it."

Clayton shook his head. "I didn't plan on going to Gallatin. I thought that we would go directly to Nashville and sell every horse Paine has in his stock pens."

"My God!" cried Mr. Summers. "That's bitin' off a big chunk, ain't it, son?"

Clayton nodded. "Yes, sir, it's crazy. But that's the very reason it might work."

Rufus frowned. "Gener'l Boone always sent his man to Nashville on the last day of the month, Mr. Clay. That's just the day after tomorrow."

"Then we've got a long night ahead of us, Rufus, because we're going to sell horses in Nashville tomorrow."

It took Annie Boyers several frustrating hours to ready the old press for print. And even more time was spent before Rufus approved the vouchers, but finally they were letter-perfect.

"It's a big chance you're taking, Mr. Harris," Annie said. She wiped her forehead with an ink-stained hand before dropping wearily onto the pile of hay that had covered the press. Then she laughed with tired delight. "If you boys pull this off, it'll be the grandest swindle in the history of Tennessee. May the good Lord be with you."

"Some folks would argue that last part, Miss Annie," Clayton said. "I believe we've played the devil's advocate this night."

Annie Boyers smiled. "There's a touch of larceny even in the Lord, Mr. Harris. Yes, sir. I believe even he will enjoy this one."

"Let's get the press covered up, Rufus." Clayton reached for a pitchfork. "It's almost daylight."

Annie Boyers waved the two aside. "The kids and I will take care of it. You-all get on down to Nashville and do your dirtiest." Again she laughed. "I'd almost be willin' to be called away this very minute, just so me an' the Lord could watch this together."

In less than two hours, Clayton—dressed in one of Mr. Summers' old frock coats, a string tie, breeches and a planter's hat, and carrying a carpetbag—joined Rufus in the johnboat where Bledsoe's Creek emptied into the Cumberland.

"It's a good thing I'm skinny," he told the slave as Rufus guided the boat into the river's swift current. "I would never have gotten into these clothes a year ago. Mr. Summers' legs are about as big around as a poker iron."

"They look real good on you, Mista Horsetrader." Rufus dipped the oars deep. Then, with an uncertain shake of his head, he said, "I just hope this works. They shoot horse thieves around here."

Clayton stood across the street from the "broker's" office until he saw a man step outside and lock the door. Quickly he crossed the cobbles and hailed him. "General Paine sent me," he said. "He's got another herd of horses he needs to dispose of."

The broker impatiently pulled his watch from his vest pocket and studied the porcelain face. "Come back in the morning. I've got an appointment in fifteen minutes."

"The general says the transaction has to be made today."

"Damn it!" the broker said. "Paine gets harder to deal with every month."

Trying to sound indifferent, Clayton said, "I'll tell the general that you don't have time to do business with him. We've got another buyer anyway, and the general has to move the stock tonight; he's expecting a Confederate raid tomorrow . . ."

"He's always got a new buyer. Don't try that hogwash on me. But if he's expecting a raid, well, that's different. Come in. Let's see how many horses he's got." Offering his hand, he said, "My name's Robinson."

Inside the office, Clayton held his breath as Robinson studied the vouchers. Dropping the papers on his desk, the man barked, "Is he mad? He's asking twice what these horses are worth."

Clayton shrugged. "They're a better grade of stock than the last bunch."

Robinson scowled uncertainly. Pressing his advantage, Clayton said, "Mister, if you don't want the horses, say so. I'm tired of waiting for you to make up your mind." Reaching across the desk, he caught Robinson's watch chain and pulled the timepiece from the man's vest pocket. "I've got an appointment in fifteen minutes," he said, "but I intend to keep mine."

When Clayton stepped into the street, Rufus joined him at the corner. He could read nothing in Clayton's stony features.

As they walked down the incline to the wharf, Rufus had to bite his tongue to keep from blurting out the question. Silently he pushed the boat into the channel, and silently they started upstream toward Cairo.

At last the young man could restrain himself no longer. "Did you do it? Did he fall for it? For goodness' sake, Mr. Clay, tell me somethin'."

Clayton tapped the carpetbag and grinned. "Ten thousand, Rufus . . . ten thousand in fine U.S. currency."

The Cumberland River rang with laughter.

"Paine is madder'n the devil, Clayton," Mr. Summers said. "He tried every way imaginable to keep from writing me a receipt for that two thousand dollars. He suspects where that money came from, son. And he's got men beatin' the bushes all over the county, lookin' for an emaciated young man in a frock coat. The only reason he hasn't searched here is because it's too obvious. If he catches you, Clayton, he'll hang you."

"I knew the chance I was taking, sir. I've been giving a lot of thought to what I'm going to do next. I took the Oath of Allegiance, as you know. But the Oath only said that I couldn't fight for the Confederacy, not that I couldn't help feed it. I've sent Rufus out to Robert Mier's place to set up a meeting with him."

"What business you got with that Confederate army recruiter?"

"I want him to authorize me to go to Oklahoma. I want to buy beef for the Confederacy."

"Oklahoma!" Mr. Summers cried. "Ain't nothin' but Indians in Oklahoma."

"That's the point, sir. I've been told that the Indians have cattle by the thousands." Clayton did not mention his vow to inform Montclair Drew's people of their son's death. He knew that Mr. Summers would never understand a man riding a thousand miles to keep a promise to an Indian.

Clayton had one stop to make before riding out of the county, and it was not a call he looked forward to. When he dropped down from the saddle at Cragfont, he unbuttoned his coat and withdrew the revolver that was thrust into the waistband of his trousers.

Susie sped down the walkway. "You've got a new horse!" she cried. "Take me for a ride, Clayton. Take me for a ride."

Mrs. Winchester walked out onto the front steps, then strode briskly toward Clayton. "Paine's men were here yesterday asking about you. They're almost sure it was you who robbed that broker. 'Course, I assured them it wasn't."

The old lady laughed and showed him a copy of *The Louisville Daily Journal*. The headline read: One of The Boldest and Most Successfully Executed Swindles Ever Perpetrated in Nashville. "The Yankees left the paper here when they rode out." She eyed the blanket roll tied to his saddle. "You're leavin' again, aren't you." It was a statement, edged with sadness.

"I'm riding out, Mrs. Winchester. But before I go, there's something . . . I've got to do."

The old lady glanced at the pistol. She knew exactly what he had in mind. "You've changed a great deal since . . .

since the war started, Clayton"—she avoided the word
"prison"—"but you haven't changed that much."

"Yes he has, Granny." Susie gazed at the pistol.
"Clayton's changed a lot."

"Hush, Susie." Mrs. Winchester held Clayton's eyes.
"Well," she said finally, "I suppose we'll never know if
you've changed enough to—"

"Why not, Mrs. Winchester?" he interrupted thinly.

"Because Patrick disappeared from here the day we heard
you were home. We haven't seen him since." The old lady
touched his arm. "You're not a killer, Clayton. You never
were, not even when it was justified."

Clayton remained silent. No one but he knew how much
he had changed.

"Ain't you goin' to say good-bye to Lettie, Clayton?"
Susie looked nervously from him to her grandmother,
knowing that something important had just transpired, but
not understanding what it was.

"Yes," he said, "I'm going to say good-bye to Lettie."

She was waiting in the parlor. She too had seen him ride
up, and she too had noticed the bedroll. For the first time in
months, there was expression in her eyes, and color in her
cheeks. Something close to an overwhelming panic had
gripped her when it became evident that Clayton was
leaving.

Yet when he stood in the doorway looking solemnly at
her, her old feelings of total worthlessness arose in her
throat and nearly suffocated her, erasing the color from her
cheeks and replacing it with that same icy pallor that she
had worn for nearly a year.

Clayton sighed. For an instant when she turned toward
him, he would have sworn there was a hint of pleasure in her
face. "I'm leaving, Lettie," he said. "I just stopped off to tell
you good-bye."

Lettie's stomach twisted and she nodded, afraid to trust
her voice. Clayton's eyes bored into her, startling her. Still
she could not find the strength to speak.

"Someday, Lettie," he said, "we've got to stop blaming
ourselves for Bailey Peyton's death. We didn't kill him; I
know that, and you know that. We've whipped ourselves
enough. It's time we put it behind us and began living
again."

Lettie turned her back to him and leaned her forehead against the window facing. Her body trembled with the long-pent-up need to cry. She wound her hand in the heavy window drapes and worked the fabric into a tight ball.

Clayton wished that she would turn away from the window. The least she could do, he thought, is to face me. Anger welled up within him. Nothing I say gets through to her, he said to himself, nothing. All these months of waiting and hoping have been for nothing. Those endless weeks upon weeks of suffering have been for nothing, all for nothing. He studied Lettie's back. "Such a waste," he whispered. "Our lives have been such a waste." Turning, he walked silently out the door.

"I loved Bailey Peyton, Clayton," she said into the window, her voice almost too low to be heard. "Yet, in a way, I loved you too. But it was his love for me, Clayton . . . his love . . . that gave me the strength to be weak with you."

Tears filled Lettie's eyes and broke over her lashes, and she blotted them with the heavy window drape. "That strength is gone now," she whispered brokenly. "It died with Bailey Peyton." The tears were coming faster. "You say I had nothing to do with Bailey's death, but you're wrong, Clayton. I stopped Bailey Peyton's heartbeat long before that Yankee bullet did. But I can live with that. Yes," she said into the silence, "I can live with that. But . . . " Lettie wound her fist deeper into the drape. "Old Chatty begged me to tell you the truth months ago; she said you loved me . . . that you would understand. She said you would marry me knowing . . . that I . . . carried Bailey Peyton's child. Would you have married me, Clayton? Would you marry me now, knowing that I killed that unborn child? Oh, God, forgive me—please forgive me."

Lettie turned from the window, a child herself, needing love, needing reassurance, but most of all, needing to be understood. She had bared her soul to Clayton Harris, and she felt as drained and vulnerable as was any soldier dying on a battlefield.

But it wasn't Clayton who stood across the room—it was Fanny, horror and pity etched into her features. "Miss Lettie," the girl breathed, "didn't you know that Mr. Clayton left five minutes ago?" And she wasn't quick enough to catch her mistress when she fell, taking the heavy window drapes with her as she sank to the floor.

General Paine was furious for having been made a national laughingstock.

On October 1, 1863, he issued a proclamation prohibiting the Sumner County merchants from selling, trading, or bartering with any citizen who refused to take the Oath of Allegiance to the United States.

Then he initiated a Board of Trade and made it mandatory for all businesses to apply for a permit. As a result, he controlled every item of merchandise that entered or exited Sumner County, and he alone decided when, where, how, and to whom the goods would be sold.

Next, he put his "free Negro" plan into action. Butler and Mandy had been extremely successful in enticing the blacks to leave their masters; Gallatin fairly teemed with contrabands.

On October twentieth, Paine posted a notice at the courthouse: Any plantation in need of field hands was to apply to him directly for the necessary workers.

Paine was well aware that the planters would be enraged at being forced to pay wages for the services of the very slaves they owned. To set an example, he quickly formed a secret alliance with the overseer of Fairview, one of the largest plantations in the county, and made certain that word was broadcast throughout the countryside: Fairview had hired a hundred and sixty Negroes, paying the male workers eight dollars per month and the females five dollars. He also made certain that Fairview at least appeared to be prosperous.

Although the ruse worked to a degree, it did not meet with the success Paine had envisioned, and he found himself with scores of Negroes milling aimlessly about Gallatin. Further infuriating the white populace, he formed the 14th United States Colored Infantry, with the promise that any Negro who enlisted could rest assured that his family would be "well cared for."

Enlistment was overwhelming, and General Paine was obliged to create a tent city to house the families of the new recruits. Gallatin's population doubled overnight.

BOOK III
Freedom Won't Wait

CHAPTER 27

Clayton Harris sat his horse and looked across the sweeping hills of the Oklahoma Territory. It was unlike any country he had ever seen. But what held his attention was the lack of cattle that were supposed to be feeding on the lush grasses; the land was empty as far as the eye could see.

He pulled his coat more securely about his neck to ward off the late-November cold and rode on toward Fort Gibson; situated just outside of Tahlequah, the capital of the Cherokee Nation.

Clayton reported to the Confederate officer in charge, Captain Hawkins, who confirmed what Clayton had feared since arriving in Oklahoma: Like the rest of the South, the people of the Territory were starving.

Hawkins shook his head sympathetically. "Mr. Harris, I'm afraid you've been misinformed about the livestock. What Stand Waite—the colonel who commands the Cherokee Brigade—ain't confiscated, the Kansas jayhawkers have rustled. Hell, there's hardly enough beef for my own garrison. Yes, sir. You've had a long ride for nothin'. However, you're more than welcome to bunk here at the fort an' rest up. I'd sure like to hear what's goin' on back East."

Clayton tried to keep his disappointment from showing —and succeeded. "I'll accept your hospitality for a day or two, Captain, and thanks. But first I've a message to deliver to some people named Drew. Can you direct me to a place called Park Hill?"

"Park Hill." Hawkins grinned. "Any man at Fort Gibson can direct you to the chief's mansion, and will gladly show you the way. Why, they'd even trade their war-horses for a chance to visit with the princess."

Clayton looked at the man.

Hawkins' grin faltered. "Angela Drew, the princess. She's Chief John Ross' niece. Angela is the highest-quality bead-work, Harris." Clayton didn't respond. "That means she's a real looker, Captain Harris."

"How can I find Park Hill, sir?"

After Clayton was gone, Hawkins scratched his head. The pale, skinny Tennessean reminded him of a Yankee; no sense of humor at all.

Park Hill was a stately house by anyone's standards. Its Georgian architecture featured massive columns and porti-coes. A Negro manservant answered Clayton's knock.

"I came to pay my respects to Mr. Ross and the Drews," Clayton said, glancing through the partially open door at the elaborately furnished great hall.

The servant eyed Clayton suspiciously. "Everybody knows that the chief an' Mistress Ross is in Philadelphia, Pennsylvania, under Yankee guard, because old Mr. Lincoln done branded them Confederates an' made them political prisoners." He appraised Clayton from head to toe, taking in his trail-worn appearance. "Where you been that you don't know that?"

Clayton's hand shot out and caught the servant by his shirt front. "I've come a long way, mister, and I'm tired of being quest—"

"Bravo!" came a husky, feminine voice from behind him. "And now that you've put Charles in his place, answer his question."

Clayton turned. Leading a small, hard-ridden pinto horse toward him was a female version of Montclair Drew; the same wide mouth, the same high, chiseled cheekbones, and the same blue-black hair, only hers was a mane that fell all the way to the gentle flare of her slender hips. But it was her eyes that captured Clayton; he was looking into the identical pale-blue gaze that had set Montclair Drew apart from the rest of the universe.

"Excuse me for staring, ma'am," Clayton said, struggling to retain his composure. "I . . . had heard that you were lovely, but . . ."

Irritation flickered across her features. "Obviously you've been to the fort. Did they send you out here to try your luck?"

"No, ma'am," he said. "And if they had, I wouldn't have come. My luck ran out a long time ago."

The girl studied him closely. He has been in jail, she decided. "Who are you, and what do you want, mister?"

Clayton removed his hat. "I'm Clayton Harris, ma'am, from Tennessee."

"I know where you're from," she said. "I knew that by the horse you're riding. I haven't seen a Tennessee plantation horse in the Territory since the war began. What I want to know is why are you here asking for my uncle. As Charles said, everybody, including Jefferson Davis, or should I say especially Jefferson Davis, knows that the chief and Aunt Mary are political prisoners of war, in Philadelphia."

Color seeped into Clayton's face. "I'm probably the only person who didn't know that, ma'am. I'm sorry to hear about Mr. Ross and his wife."

"One doesn't hear much news in jail, does one?" queried Angela Drew.

Clayton's unblinking eyes held hers. "No, ma'am, one doesn't."

"Mister," the girl said with deliberation, "I would suggest that you climb on that walking horse of yours and let him walk on."

Clayton held her gaze. "I'll do that, ma'am. But first I've got to see your mother and father."

Angela Drew's brow furrowed. "My mother is not receiving callers, and my father is away at war. You're right, mister. Your luck has run out."

"Clayton Harris, ma'am."

Angela Drew's half-smile resembled the Mona Lisa's. "If you'll excuse me, Mr. Harris, I've got things to do."

"I intend to speak with your mother," Clayton said softly, "with or without your permission."

Angela Drew's eyes flashed. "Mr. Harris, if you came here looking for trouble, you'll get your fill."

Clayton turned and knocked deliberately on the door.

Angela Drew hurried up the steps and placed herself between Clayton and the entrance. He eyed her angry face, again overwhelmed by her remarkable resemblance to her brother. "Miss Drew," he said, "what I have to say to your mother won't take but a moment."

"Then say it to me. I'll see that she gets the message."

Clayton studied the defiant face. How had he managed to alienate her so? He and her brother had become friends instantly. He sighed; Angela Drew's opinion of him was of little consequence. "I'm sorry, Miss Drew," he said, "but I've ridden a thousand miles to deliver a message . . . to your mother."

Angela's mouth tightened and small lines of tension formed at the corners of her lips. "All right! I'll take you to her. Then you ride out of here. Do I make myself clear?"

Ushering Clayton into a study, she ordered him to wait there. Charles appeared and busied himself with straightening a row of books in the massive mahogany secretary. Clayton wasn't fooled by the man's presence. Then it dawned on him that he wasn't supposed to be fooled; Angela Drew intended that he be aware of the surveillance. Careful people, these Indians, he mused.

A moment later a tall, slender woman entered the room and stood regally just inside the door. There was no mistaking her identity; even though she was in her late thirties, Mrs. Drew was a handsome woman, and Clayton realized that he was seeing Angela in twenty or so years.

Clayton approached her and bowed over her hand. "Mrs. Drew," he said, straightening, "could I speak with you privately, ma'am?"

Mrs. Drew nodded to Charles, dismissing him. When he was gone, she asked, "What is your message, sir?"

Angela entered the room and rushed to stand beside her mother. "Whatever you have to say," she said, "you'll say it to both of us."

Annoyance furrowed Clayton's brows. "No," he said. "My message is private, Miss Drew."

Angela's face flamed and she balled her right hand into a tight fist.

"Don't even think about hitting me," Clayton said. Angela recoiled, astounded. "I saw it in your eyes," he told her.

"Leave the room, Angela," instructed her mother. "I'll speak to the gentleman alone."

"But, Mama . . ."

"Wait in the hall. If I need you, I'll call . . . but I don't think that will be necessary."

Reluctantly, the girl backed to the door. "I'll be right outside, Mama," she said coldly to Clayton.

"Now, Mr. Harris," Mrs. Drew said when the door had closed, "tell me how my son died."

Clayton stared at her. "How did you know, ma'am?"

"Very simply, sir. Angela said that you have been in prison. I would guess, judging by the look of you, that it was a Union prison." Clayton nodded. She continued, "Word reached me that Montclair had been captured. It stands to reason—"

"He died defending a young lad's honor, ma'am," Clayton said. "Montclair was a fine man."

She took a deep, shuddering breath. "He would do that." She raised her eyes to Clayton. "Was it your honor, Mr. Harris?"

Clayton hesitated, then shook his head. "It was a sixteen-year-old boy, ma'am. But, yes, to be truthful, I suppose you could say that Montclair died defending my honor. If I hadn't been a coward that day, perhaps he would still be alive."

Mrs. Drew pursed her lips. "If my son had considered you a coward, Mr. Harris, he would never have asked a favor of you."

Clayton smiled at the lady's tact. "Your son was too much a gentleman to think that, ma'am."

Mrs. Drew frowned. "That's chivalrous poppycock, sir. We Drews act according to the situation. My daughter is a refined lady, sir, but that would not have stopped her from blacking your eye a few minutes ago. Montclair was the same way . . . and obviously he considered you a friend. Can I assume that the feeling was mutual?" Clayton nodded. "Then I shall consider you a friend also," the lady said.

"Thank you, ma'am."

"How did my son die, Mr. Harris?"

"The guards shot him, ma'am," Clayton lied. "He didn't suffer."

The woman sighed, and tears sparkled in her eyes.

Clayton looked away from her grief, pretending to study a painting above the mantel. It was an oil on canvas of a handsome young man who shared many of the characteristics of Montclair Drew. Clayton read the brass plate attached to the bottom of the frame: "John Ross— Cooweescoowee (Large White Bird)—1812."

"Did Montclair ask you not to tell Angela that . . . that he was gone, Mr. Harris?"

"Yes, ma'am," he said, thinking that the Angela Drew he had just met appeared perfectly capable of withstanding the news of her brother's death. "Montclair made it plain that I was to tell only you or Mr. Drew. He wanted one of you to inform Miss Drew."

"I would rather she hear it from her father," Mrs. Drew said quickly. "She will need someone stronger than I to lean on."

Clayton fidgeted. Why are they so apprehensive about telling Angela?

Mrs. Drew blinked several times as though she were just awakening. "I am sorry, Mr. Harris," she said. "Please forgive my poor manners." Clapping her hands, she called for Charles, instructing him to prepare Clayton a hot toddy.

At the door, Charles was forced to step aside as Angela stormed into the room. Immediately her eyes locked with Clayton's. Mrs. Drew took Clayton's arm. "Of course you will stay for supper, sir." Then she added, "I would consider it an affront if you declined."

Fire leaped from Angela's pale eyes, ordering him to refuse. Holding her gaze, Clayton said, "Thank you, Mrs. Drew. I'd be delighted."

The food consisted of boiled vegetables and fried cornbread, served on china plates. It tasted wonderful to Clayton, who had eaten nothing but trail fare for days. The Drews' manners were impeccable. In fact, nothing about Park Hill—or for that matter, what little he had seen of Oklahoma—reminded him of Indians, or at least not the kind of Indians he had heard and read about.

Angela watched his face from across the highly polished table. Then she flashed him a cold smile. "The Cherokee stopped being savages over a hundred years ago, Mr. Harris." Clayton was startled by his transparency. She laughed and continued: "Not that it made any difference to the white man that we had a courthouse, a supreme court, a newspaper, and upper and lower schools. No, those things meant nothing. We were dirty, illiterate savages, and Andrew Jackson had friends who coveted our lands. They forced Uncle John Ross to relocate here, in Oklahoma. Well, Mr. Harris, as you can see, Uncle John has carved out an empire for the Cherokee Nation."

"Angela," Mrs. Drew said, "that will be quite enough."

Angela looked at her mother. "If you will excuse me," she snapped, pushing herself away from the table, "I think I am going to vomit."

Mrs. Drew laid her napkin on the table and told Angela to remain seated. Turning to Clayton, she said, "I apologize for my daughter's behavior, Mr. Harris. There is no excuse for poor manners."

Sullenly, Angela slipped her chair back into place. Then, tossing her head, she asked, "Is it not poor manners to keep secrets, Mama?"

Crimson crept into Mrs. Drew's cheeks. "Mr. Harris has been sent here by the Confederacy to purchase cattle . . ."

"Then he has come on a fool's errand," the girl said. "Oklahoma has been stripped clean, or at least the Cherokee Nation has been. So he has no reason to linger." She turned and smiled acidly at Clayton.

Ignoring her, Clayton said, "It's the same back home, Mrs. Drew. What the Yankees haven't confiscated, the Confederates have. It's a perpetual famine for both factions, the army and the civilians. The army starves the people to feed the army, while the people, in turn, have no seeds or breeding stock that would ultimately produce more food for the army."

"It seems to me," Angela said, "that a young man such as you would be more useful to the cause wearing the uniform of a soldier instead of riding around the countryside searching for cattle where none are available. It's men like you who will lose this war for us, Mr. Harris."

Clayton's ice-cold stare froze the girl. "And just what kind of man am I, Miss Drew?"

Blushing, she glanced away. She had intended for her remark to embarrass Clayton, but it was she who felt humiliated. It left her shaken.

"There are cattle to be had, Mr. Harris," said Mrs. Drew. Clayton's disbelief showed in his eyes. "It's true," Mrs. Drew said. "My brother, Chief John Ross, has a ranch west of here. There are a few cattle there, but it's hostile country, and it would be dangerous for a white man to venture into that area."

"It would be suicide." Angela was unable to keep the challenge from her voice.

Clayton scowled at the girl; she had stretched his patience to the breaking point. "How far is it to the ranch?" he asked.

Angela laughed. "At least one hundred miles . . . but you couldn't get there and back alive."

"Stop it, Angela," her mother said. Then, turning to Clayton, "Not even the Cherokee venture into hostile territory any more than is necessary, Mr. Harris. The Kiowa who live there are an extremely unpredictable people."

Clayton watched Angela from the corner of his eye. The girl had leaned back in her chair and was appraising him contemptuously.

Mrs. Drew's brows puckered in thought. "Perhaps, if one had a Cherokee guide and Cherokee drovers, and traveled by night—"

"Can you get me such people?" Clayton asked.

"I've heard enough of this foolishness," Angela said. "Mother, I have no idea why you are humoring this man, but you know as well as I that no Cherokee is going to guide a stranger into hostile territory. No Cherokee would even discuss it with him. The smart thing for Mr. Harris to do is to go back to Tennessee and tell whoever sent him that no cattle could be found." She gave Clayton a hateful glare. "He wouldn't even by lying, but I'm sure that's of no consequence to him."

Clayton frowned. "I'm sorry that I have offended you, Miss Drew. I assure you that it was unintentional. But I was sent here to do a job, and if it's at all possible, I intend to do it."

Angela flung her napkin onto the table and leaned toward him. "That's very noble of you, Mr. Harris, but your heroics could very easily wind you up on the wrong end of a war lance."

Turning to Mrs. Drew, Clayton said, "About those herdsmen, where do I find them?"

"You don't," the lady said. "As Angela pointed out, they wouldn't even talk to you."

"Then how?"

"Mother!" Angela cried. "Surely you're not serious about helping this man?"

"I'll attend to it, Mr. Harris," said Mrs. Drew, ignoring Angela's outburst. "For now, I suggest that you spend the night here at Park Hill—it's a long ride back to the fort— and we will talk further tomorrow. Charles will see you to your room." Clayton welcomed the invitation; the very thought of a real bed reminded him how truly tired he was.

With lighted candle, Charles led Clayton down the upstairs hall. Opening a door, he said, "Your chamber, sir."

Following Clayton into the room, Charles lit a candle on the nightstand beside a heavy, canopied bed. "I hope you find the room comfortable." Without awaiting Clayton's answer, he stepped into the hall and closed the door behind him.

Clayton was awakened by a gentle shake of his shoulder. "Mr. Harris," came a whisper, "are you awake?"

Clayton sat up. The feeble glow cast by the dying embers in the fireplace silhouetted Mrs. Drew standing beside the bed. Before Clayton could speak, she said, "I am aware that my being here is . . . unseemly, but I could not talk to you downstairs. Angela might have overheard."

"Mrs. Drew," Clayton began, but the woman cut him short. "Please tell me about Montclair, Mr. Harris. Tell me everything you can remember." She caught Clayton's hand and held it tight. "Did he talk about his home? His family? Was he well? Did they bury him decently?"

Clayton felt more than saw her shoulders slump, her tears, an anguished mother's need to hear about her only son. He told her then about Montclair, about his imprisonment, omitting only the truth about his death.

Two hours later Mrs. Drew slipped from Clayton's room

and made her way down the hall to her own chambers. Had she looked beyond, to the staircase at the end of the darkened aisle, she would have seen Angela frozen to the newel post, the book the girl had retrieved from the library clutched so tightly against her bosom that her fingers left indentations in the hard leather.

It took Mrs. Drew the better part of the following day to find anyone willing to ride into hostile territory on the cattle-buying mission. And when she did, she was forced to settle on her twin nephews, Harry and Larry Ross, who were little more than children.

At daybreak on December 4, 1863, Clayton lifted himself into the saddle and followed Harry and Larry west across the frozen, windswept hills. They had not ridden a mile when the boys drew up and twisted in their saddles, watching their backtrail. "What's the problem?" Clayton could see nothing behind them.

"Rider coming," Harry said, squinting. "Can't tell who it is yet."

"You know who it is," Larry said. "I told you she would come."

"She?" Clayton asked. "You mean Miss Drew?"

"It's Angela, all right," offered Harry. "Nobody sits a horse like her."

It was true. Even though Angela was riding sidesaddle, it was obvious that she rode the horse and not the saddle. Her green riding skirt, showing beneath her red-wool blanket coat, shone like new currency against the sides of her black-and-white pinto.

A few minutes later she reined her prancing mount alongside Clayton. "I'm going with you," she announced. She tightened the throat string of her flat-crowned black hat so that the rim shadowed her eyes from the morning sun.

Clayton looked at her levelly. "If the hostile Kiowas are as dangerous as you paint them, I don't want the responsibility of your welfare on my mind, Miss Drew. Turn around and ride back to Park Hill."

Angela flinched as though she had been struck. Clayton smiled; she might have brought first blood, but he cut with a saber, not a kitchen knife.

Her horse reared and spun away, and it took her a

moment to rein it in beside him again. "I assure you, Mr. Harris, that I can take care of myself. And to tell you the truth, I am here because my mother thinks you need a nursemaid. Furthermore, the folks who run the ranch wouldn't turn over a cow chip to you . . . much less a herd. I'm going with you, and that's final." With that, she spurred her horse ahead, across the frost-killed meadow grass.

The two boys swung their eyes to Clayton and waited.

When he didn't speak, Larry asked, "Well, Mr. Harris, what are you going to do about that?"

Clayton continued to stare after the girl; she had a hard head and a sharp tongue, not a combination he liked. He urged his horse into a running walk that forced the boys to break their ponies into a bone-rattling trot, then into a canter, just to keep abreast. "Nothing," he shouted as they came up beside him. "I'm not going to do a damned thing."

The young Indians exchanged sour looks.

On November 28, 1863, the telegraph wire in Gallatin was humming; just the day before, General John Hunt Morgan had escaped from prison. The possibility that Morgan might return to Sumner County prompted Paine to make a hasty and premature decision to establish the position of "superintendent of vacant plantations, farms and estates." He quickly appointed his close associate, Ruben T. Warner, to the office. "Vacant" property meant homes and acreage belonging to any persons who refused to take the Oath of Allegiance. Their holdings would be appropriated for Federal use.

Going one step further, Paine declared vacant those properties belonging to men who were fighting for the Confederacy—regardless of "whoever may pretend to occupy them," as he put it. Thus without further notice, Federal soldiers immediately began evicting women and children from their homes.

Ellis Harper went on a rampage. He wrecked a train at Buck Lodge, burned a trestle at Goodlettsville, and robbed and killed several Union sympathizers.

Paine put five companies in the field with orders to shoot the renegades on sight.

While Clayton Harris rode with Angela Drew across Indian territory, Paine's 106th Ohio Cavalry stumbled upon Harper's gang at its headquarters on Dry Fork Creek, a few miles northeast of Gallatin. The camp was in an isolated hollow that adjoined the northernmost boundary of Willie Harper's farm, an area she had not visited since the war began.

When the Union patrol appeared, the guerrillas scattered, leaving behind over a hundred horses and enough miscellaneous stores to provision a small army.

Willie Harper's childhood friend, William Berryman, was killed outright, but the others escaped.

A local Union sympathizer named Swallows, who, along with Butler and Mandy, was acting as a guide for the Federals, walked arrogantly over to Berryman's body and ground his spur in the dead lad's face.

"Here now," cried the Union captain in charge, "we'll have none of that; we don't fight dead men."

Swallows grinned at Butler, who had dismounted and joined him. "These Yankees ain't got no guts. Do they, Butler?"

Butler eyed the Union captain contemptuously. "That's why General Paine hired men like you an' me to make believers out of these damned Rebels," he said to Swallows. "The general says his new recruits are too . . . squeamish."

"Ain't it the truth," agreed Swallows, grinding his spur even deeper into Berryman's sightless eyes.

After tying the dead man to a captured horse, the Federals rode across Willie's field and dismounted at her front gate.

She met them in the yard. "Evening," she said to the Union officer. Her eyes were riveted to the body draped across the horse.

"Can you identify that Rebel?" the captain asked.

Willie walked closer to the horse and stooped so she could see the dead man's face. She almost retched at the sight. "Yes," she said, biting back the bile. "He's William Berryman."

"Have you known him long?"

Willie nodded. "All my life, Captain."

"You know all the guerrillas, don't you?"

"No," Willie replied. "I know only two or three . . . the ones who grew up around here."

Butler looked down at the girl. "And I reckon you didn't know they were camped on your property?"

Willie swung her eyes to the captain, startled. "Captain, I had no idea they were on my property. Where was the camp?"

"In a hollow across that ridge." He pointed back the way they had come.

"That's not my property, Captain," Willie said, relief evident in her voice. "My property ends a long way this side of that ridge."

"She's lyin'," Butler said. "These bitches know every outlaw in the county. They feed an' protect 'em, an' lay with 'em. How else do you think Harper and his men could disappear so quick? The people around here hide 'em."

"That's not true," Willie said. "I don't agree at all with what Ellis Harper is doing. I told him never to set foot on my property . . ."

Butler laughed and spat a stream that hit the ground at her foot and splattered over her shoe.

"Mr. Butler," the Union officer said, "I am getting tired of your interference in army matters. In the future, sir, if I want your opinion, I'll ask for it." Turning to Willie, he said, "I'm sorry, miss, but it would be best if I took you to General Paine for questioning. Get your things together."

As Willie turned toward the house, her eyes locked with Butler's. The man's gaze dropped insolently to the slight swell of her breasts, then moved to where the wintry breeze had forced her gray woolen skirt tight against her thighs.

Quickly Willie smoothed the garment. Her reaction brought a grin to Butler's lips.

With every step she took toward the porch, Willie could feel Butler's eyes burning into her body. No one had ever looked at her that way, and it scared her. Inside the house, she shrugged into her father's overcoat, then turned to the two old Negroes. "Don't fret about me," she told them, forcing a smile. "I'll be home before dark."

Over a thousand miles away, Clayton Harris sat by a camp fire watching the flames cast delicate, flickering highlights upon Angela Drew's cheekbones. He had, over her protests, demanded that they rest the horses when night fell. Without further argument, she had quickly set a pot to boiling, and now they each sipped from mugs of hot chickory.

"Tell me what to expect when we reach the ranch," he said.

"The worst," she answered, not looking up from the flames. She had been staring into them for several minutes.

"What exactly does that mean?"

"Unless a miracle occurs, Mr. Harris, there's no way we'll slip onto the ranch without being seen by the Kiowa. And it means that it will take an even greater miracle to get us out again." She raised her eyes to him. "Do you believe in miracles, Mr. Harris?"

Clayton smiled at her. "As many as it takes."

Angela turned back to the fire. "You're a fool, Mr. Harris."

"I know that better than you, Miss Drew."

Angela studied the flames, not seeing them. Who is he? she wondered. He was more than a cattle buyer for the Confederacy, of that the girl was certain. What had passed between him and her mother? The thought made her shudder. She looked across at him. "Why are you here?"

Clayton shrugged. "I'm here to buy cattle."

Angela dumped the remains of her chickory on the fire and stood up. "You're a liar as well as a fool, Mr. Harris."

Walking to her horse, she lifted herself into the saddle and hooked her leg over the curved horn. "Mount up, boys," she told her cousins. "We've still got a long way to go if we're to make the ranch before daylight."

In Tennessee, Cotton had also been riding hard. But he had reached his destination. He quickly led his horse inside the Summerset barn and shut the door. He wasn't taking any chances of being seen, since the only people who had horses were either guerrillas or Unionists, and Unionists shot guerrillas on sight.

Walking to the front of the barn, he pressed his eye to a crack between the boards and surveyed the house. Wind whipped through the crack. Blinking rapidly, he cursed the low-hanging snow clouds that had darkened the sky, making vision nearly impossible. Flattening his ear against the opening, he listened, but the only sound that ruffled the stillness was the constant dull ring of a chopping ax; someone, probably Rufus, was splitting kindling.

Cotton sprinted across the yard and entered the house,

stopping just inside the door and listening intently for any sound out of the ordinary.

From the parlor came the muffled voice of Mr. Summers, and a moment later Mrs. Summers' response. Cotton removed his hand from his pistol butt and strode purposefully into the room.

"Well, I'll be!" cried the old man, rising from his chair to shake Cotton's hand. "Christmas has come early!" Then they were all talking at once, and Cotton laughed in sheer happiness.

The Summerses told Cotton about Clayton's return, and of his subsequent hasty leave-taking. They also informed him that two weeks ago Lettie Billingsly had been arrested by Paine and questioned at length.

"It was rumored," Mr. Summers said, "that Lettie's father was mixed up with a former Sumner Countian, Horace L. Hunley, in building something called a 'submarine.'"

"But Paine let her go," Mrs. Summers said, "with a warnin' that she better not try and correspond with her father, because he's being hunted by the Federal Government."

"Now, let me tell you-all some news," said Cotton proudly. "I've talked to the chaplain of our division, an' he said he'd be plumb tickled to marry me and Willie Harper. I'm goin' to tell her tomorrow."

Mrs. Summers was stunned. "Married? You?" Collecting her wits, she rushed to kiss Cotton's cheek while the old man bellowed for Rufus to fetch the only remaining bottle of whiskey.

"This calls for a celebration," hooted the old man. When Rufus returned, Mr. Summers splashed sour mash into three glasses. "Cotton's gettin' married, Rufus," he said, holding his glass high.

"Married?" Rufus looked at Cotton. "Why, I didn't know anyone would have him."

Cotton's eyes narrowed dangerously, bringing a howl of mirth from Rufus.

"To your health and happiness, son," Mr. Summers said, casting Rufus a hard glare. "May both be long-lastin'."

With cheers, the three touched their glasses together, and the two men drank deeply; Mrs. Summers sipped tentatively, then set her glass aside. "When do we get to meet the lucky girl, Cotton?" she inquired.

"If she agrees, we'll be here for supper tomorrow night . . . that is, if the roads are clear of Yankee troops."

Mrs. Summers hugged Cotton to her thin bosom. "I know we will all love her very much."

Cotton nodded happily. "She's the sweetest girl I ever met, Missus Summers, an' the nicest. You'll like her the minute you lay eyes on her."

"Rufus," said Mrs. Summers, beaming, "get all the house servants in here. We've got work to do; we're to have a brand-new bride here tomorrow night. The house has to be cleaned, food cooked . . ."

"Tonight, old Miss? You want all of 'em in here tonight?"

"Tonight!"

Shaking his head, Rufus followed the old lady out of the room, and Cotton could hear them moving down the hall, she making grand plans and he mumbling his answers.

Mr. Summers sipped his whiskey, his faded eyes aglow. "This is wonderful news, Cotton," he said. "Mrs. Summers has needed somethin' such as this to take her mind off the things that's been goin' on around here."

"Like what?" Cotton asked.

"Paine has lured most of the slaves into town with promises of money and freedom. Ours stayed loyal longer than most, but last week a bunch of 'em just up an' left in the night. Can't say as I blame them, tho', what with the Federal Government feedin' an' housin' them for free."

"Well, I sure as hell can blame 'em," Cotton said. "You ain't never mistreated a one of 'em, an' they know it. They've had it good here."

"That's true, son, but it has nothing to do with their leavin'. I know that, so I don't hold it again 'em. We taught our darkies to have principles, dignity, so how can we fault 'em for choosing to starve on freedom rather than to be well fed on slavery?"

"Well, that's true an' dandy, Mr. Summers," Cotton said, "but up on the front line we been hearin' rumors that Paine's confiscatin' the farms of Confederate soldiers and givin' 'em to the slaves . . . an' that the slaves are acceptin' 'em. There ain't no principle or dignity in a dirty trick like that."

"So far, he's mostly done that with the deserted farms."

"Paine is goin' to overplay his hand one of these days, Mr. Summers."

"I've been sayin' that for months, Cotton. Yet he goes right on, gettin' worse all the time." The old man refilled Cotton's glass. "Son, we can talk about Paine any time. Tell me about your girl. Is she built for bearin' children? Can she plow a mule? Is she strong of will and body?"

Cotton laughed. "You'll just have to judge her for yourself, sir. But I'll tell you right now, you won't be disappointed."

CHAPTER 28

In Gallatin, Willie Harper said for the fourth time, "No, General Paine, I did not know that Ellis Harper was camped in that hollow. And that hollow is not on my property."

"Where is his permanent camp, Miss Harper?" That too for the fourth time.

"I've told you, General, that I have no idea where he hides. I don't even know if he has a permanent camp."

"But he is your cousin. You don't deny that?"

"I haven't tried to hide that fact, sir."

"Have you ever seen anyone hung by their thumbs, Miss Harper? You can hear them scream from over a mile away. I hung a man by his thumbs last week because he would not cooperate with me."

"I've told you the truth, General," whispered the girl, tucking her thumbs into the palms of her hands and clamping her fingers over them.

Paine turned to Butler, who sat across the room. "Is she telling the truth?"

"You've said yerself, General, that Rebel women are

twice as mean as the men. I think she's lyin' through her teeth."

Paine studied Willie thoughtfully. "I disagree, Butler. I think she's told us everything she knows."

Butler scowled and swung his eyes accusingly to Willie. "Whatever you say, General."

Paine rose from his chair and leaned across his desk. "If you hear from your cousin, you'd better let me know. Do you understand that, Miss Harper?"

You can go to blazes, General, she thought. "Yes, sir," she said.

"Very well. Butler will see you home."

Willie jumped to her feet. "I would rather go alone, sir."

Paine frowned. "Butler and his . . . wife will escort you, Miss Harper. You forget, ma'am, that the horse you rode here on is government property. They will return it when you are finished with it. That will be all, Miss Harper."

Willie opened her mouth to protest further, but Paine said pointedly, "That will be all, Miss Harper."

With Butler and Mandy flanking her, Willie trotted her horse up the pike toward Richland, fourteen miles away. The night had grown bitter and the sky was spitting snow. But the cold was not what made her shiver and draw herself deeper into her father's coat; it was the way that Butler watched her out of the corner of his eye, the way he kept turning in the saddle and peering over his shoulder as though gauging the distance they had come from Gallatin.

When they had ridden about four miles, Butler nudged his horse close and asked Willie if she had a beau.

She informed him that she was engaged to be married.

"So you're goin' to tie the knot, eh?" He canvassed her with that same upsetting look.

Willie's mouth went dry, and she ran the tip of her tongue across her lips. "Yes," she said, feeling the need to keep talking. "We will be wed as soon as the war is over . . . which, with the way things are going for the South, shouldn't be too many more months now."

"Who's the lucky man?" Butler smiled ingratiatingly at her.

Willie tried to smile back. "He's from Summerset Plantation. His name is Cotton Ferris."

"Cotton!" Butler reached out and caught Willie by the arm. "You're betrothed to that freckle-faced son-of-a-bitch?"

Startled by the hatred in the man's voice, Willie tried to pull away, but Mandy moved in on her other side and pinioned the girl's mount between their horses. Mandy peered around Willie to Butler. "Ain't he the one who got yo' fired when yo' were the overseer at ol' man Summers' place? Ain't he the one what went an' stuck his face in our business when I caught yo' pleasurin' my mammy?"

"The very same," Butler said. He tightened his grip on Willie's arm.

They're both crazy, Willie thought, trying hard not to panic. Then, clutching her overcoat even more tightly about her shivering body, she blurted, "My father will be home by the time we get there."

Butler scoffed at that. "They ain't been a man around your place for months. Don't go tryin' to lie to us."

Willie swallowed hard. She was scared, more scared than ever before in her life. Her mind raced for an avenue out of her predicament, but her normally quick intelligence held no answers this time.

Butler said, "I reckon you're goin' to try an' tell us you're a virgin, too?"

Willie's stomach turned over. "Of course I am," she whispered, praying that the knowledge might spark a glimmer of chivalry in him, "and it's very ungentlemanly of you to ask, sir."

Mandy laughed loudly and nudged her horse hard against Willie's, forcing the girl even closer to Butler.

"Cotton owes me a debt," Butler said, leaning toward her. "I think I'll collect it—now."

Willie dug her heels into her horse's flanks and tried to spin the animal around, but Butler dragged her from the saddle and flung her to the ground between the churning horses.

Willie was up in an instant, but seeing that remounting was impossible, she darted under her horse's belly and scrambled out the other side. The startled animal jumped sideways and lashed out with its hind hooves, catching Mandy's horse in its chest, driving the animal to its haunches and unseating Mandy.

In a flash, Willie was past the floundering horse and rider and running back down the road, toward a farmhouse they had passed a mile back.

Ignoring Mandy, Butler pivoted his mount, spurred it into a gallop and overtook Willie before she had gone a hundred yards. He rode past her, then brought his horse to a sliding stop and stepped down from the saddle, facing her.

Without breaking her stride, Willie threw off her heavy gloves and hurled herself at him, her nails raking for his eyes. She missed, drawing blood only from his cheeks. She kicked at his groin, but her overcoat constricted the effort. then, with a cry of rage, she caught his hand between her teeth and bit down hard.

Cursing loudly, Butler drew back his other fist and smashed it against her forehead, knocking her prone in the powdery snow. She willed herself to rise, but lights kept flashing behind her eyes, and her limbs seemed to be made of lead.

She was barely conscious when Butler popped the buttons from her overcoat. But when he gripped the neck of her dress and ripped it all the way to her waist, she was shocked totally awake by the blast of frigid air that engulfed her naked breasts.

Mandy came tearing through the snow, Willie's horse in tow beside hers. Flinging herself from the saddle, she squatted beside Willie. To the girl's horror, the woman cupped Willie's breasts in her icy hands and kneaded them savagely, pointing out to Butler how very small they were. Then, catching Willie's hair, she drew the girl's head back until Willie could do nothing but look up into Mandy's face.

Willie felt Butler groping at her waist. Another ripping sound, another blast of icy air, and she knew he had torn her dress full length.

"If'n yo' a-goin' to pleasure her, Butler, den get on wif it," commanded Mandy. "I's freezin' to death."

"Please," Willie whispered, "please don't do this." Tears rolled down her cheeks and dropped to the snow.

Butler grinned at her. "I told General Paine I'd have me a real white lady someday." He unbuttoned his trousers and forced Willie's thighs apart. "I'm just as good a man as any of his officers."

Willie's scream when he entered her shattered the night. But the low-hanging, snow-laden clouds absorbed the sound and muffled it as though it had never been uttered.

Mandy laughed delightedly as Butler drove himself into the girl again and again. Then she reached down and caught Willie's face between her hands. She thumbed the girl's tightly clenched eyelids open. "Watch what be a-happenin' to yo', girl," she said. "Yo' bein' pleasured by a real man."

Willie's body convulsed and quivered as Butler slammed even more cruelly into her. In spite of Mandy's thumbs, she closed her eyes and sobbed like a child.

Mandy drew her hand back and slapped Willie hard across the face, splitting the girl's frozen lips. "Yo' jist a baby . . . a crybaby. Yo' white girls is always so high an' mighty, always actin' like yo' too good to spread yo' legs. Well, yo' ain't! Yo' ain't too good for nothin!" Mandy's eyes were wild as she struck Willie again and again.

Then Butler groaned and slumped heavily onto Willie's naked body, his unshaven face pressed hard into her small breasts, his breath quick and hot against her cold flesh.

"First white woman I've had in years," he said. "'Bout forgot how good a white woman was."

Mandy jumped to her feet and shoved her hand into her coat pocket. "Yo' liked pleasurin' her, did yo'?" she shouted.

Butler pushed himself to his knees and buttoned his trousers. "Yeah, I liked pleasurin' her," he said, looking down at the small girl lying forlornly in the snow on her father's overcoat. He was intrigued by the way the snow-flakes mingled with the bloody splotches that stained her thighs, turning the pure-white crystals a deep pink before they melted. Butler laughed. "When 'cold purity' and 'hot lust' mix," he said, "lust wins out every time." He was pleased with the profundity of his conclusion.

Mandy's eyes flared with hatred, not for Butler, but for the girl he had just violated. Dropping to one knee, she sucked in her lips, then spat a stream of saliva into Willie's face.

Willie turned her head away; silent sobs racked her whole being.

Mandy drew a five-shot revolver from her coat pocket, pressed the muzzle lightly against Willie's temple, and without so much as blinking an eye, shot her twice through the head.

"Are you crazy?" shouted Butler as Willie's body quivered in its last throes of death and a puddle of red slush formed under her head. "Look what you gone an' done." Then his eyes bulged, for Mandy had raised the pistol and was pointing it at his chest.

"Now, Mandy, honey," he said, backing slowly away from where Mandy knelt beside Willie's body. "Ain't no white woman as good at pleasurin' as you are. How many times have I done told you that?" The pistol barrel wavered. Carefully, Butler offered his hand to help Mandy up.

Mandy stared at his hand through the falling snow, watching the flakes mingle with the bloody marks left by Willie's teeth. "I's always wanted to kill me a white person," she said, "an' now I has . . . an' I like it. Like it fine." Easing the hammer down on the pistol, she reached up and took Butler's hand.

With a heave, Butler snatched Mandy off balance and wrenched the gun from her. She screamed as he caught the weapon by its barrel and slammed the brass-strapped butt down on her head, knocking her to her knees.

Again and again he hit her, until finally, unable to hit her without kneeling in the snow, he stuck the pistol in his coat pocket and stomped off to his horse. "I should leave you here to freeze to death," he shouted over his shoulder.

Mandy pushed herself to her knees and buried her head in her hands.

"Goddamn you!" Butler cried, mounting his horse and riding over to her. "I should leave you here."

It was an idle threat and he knew it, for if Mandy were found anywhere near Willie's body, he would immediately be tied to the girl's rape and murder. Swinging down from the saddle, he boosted Mandy onto her horse. Then, catching up the reins of Willie's horse, he quickly remounted. "Can you ride?" he asked, seeing that Mandy was holding tightly to the saddle horn for balance. Mandy nodded that she could.

As he turned the three horses toward Gallatin, he looked

over his shoulder at Willie. All he could see was a small, dark mound that was quickly being covered by the heavily falling snow.

Daylight of December 5, 1863, found Clayton, Angela, and the twins bellied down on a windy hilltop surveying a scattered array of teepees and brush arbors that was no more than a half-mile from the Ross ranch house. They had arrived an hour too late to slip into the house under cover of darkness.

"They come in for the winter," the girl said, indicating the Kiowa camp with a nod of her head. "They'll be eating Uncle John's beef instead of hunting buffalo. You can thank the white man for that . . . for taking away our heritage, our pride."

Clayton continued studying the camp. In the cold pre-dawn light, the village looked peaceful. People were beginning to stir about, fires were being lit, and horses milled restlessly, waiting to be herded to new pasture. "How many do you think are down there?"

"Fifty, maybe sixty."

"I count thirteen lodges," he said skeptically.

The girl shrugged. "So?"

Harry said, "There'll be five, six men to a lodge . . . maybe more, Mr. Harris."

"Are all of them hostile?" Clayton asked.

"You bet they are," Larry said. "If they catch you, they'll roast you over a slow fire."

"Well," Clayton said, looking at Angela, "what do we do now?"

The girl appraised him as though he were a fool. "Why, we sleep, of course. When it's dark, we'll slip into the ranch. If the gods are with us, we might make it."

"And if they're not?"

"Then those pistols and that rifle of yours better be more than trinkets, Mr. Harris."

With their blankets wrapped tightly around them, Angela and the two boys lay down beside their horses and were instantly asleep. Clayton lay there wide-eyed.

Cotton donned his captured Federal greatcoat.

"Now, don't tarry, Cotton," Mrs. Summers said. "You

fetch that girl on over here so I can meet her."

"This is a good day to be married on, Cotton," Mr. Summers commented as they walked through the heavy snow to the barn. "It's a whole new world. Yes, sir, that's the way to start a marriage . . . pure an' clean."

Cotton grinned at the old man. "Tell Rufus to keep that upstairs bedroom warm as a biscuit. Tell him I'll kick his ass if he lets the fire go out."

The old man shook his head and scowled. "Maybe that gal will able to clean up your mouth. Me an' the Missus sure ain't had no luck with it."

Cotton grinned even wider. "If anybody can make me straighten up, she can, Mr. Summers."

When Cotton led his saddled horse into the barn lot, the old man caught his hand and shook it firmly. "Me an' the Missus feel like she's one of the family already, son. Go on now, an' fetch her home."

Home. The word held a special meaning for Cotton. But it wasn't Summerset that he was thinking about; Willie had a home of her own, and he was sure that she would want to stay there—and it was only right. Together they would build her farm into a home for both of them. "We'll be here for supper," promised the boy as Mr. Summers gave him a hand up.

"There probably won't be any Yankees prowlin' around after this snowfall," Mr. Summers called as Cotton trotted his horse down the lane, "but you keep a sharp eye out anyhow, you hear?"

Cotton raised his hand in acknowledgment, then kicked his mount into a canter.

In Oklahoma, full daylight bloomed cold and clear under a sun without warmth. Careful not to awaken Angela or the boys, Clayton Harris slipped his rifle from its saddle scabbard, crawled to the rim of the hill and surveyed the Kiowa camp, then the ranch buildings.

The house was a two-building log structure, the separate parts attached by a dog-trot. A small area surrounding the house was enclosed by a five-foot-high palisade of logs that seemed more suited to a fort than to a working ranch.

Clayton was satisfied with the layout; it could be easily defended.

He wasn't aware that Angela had joined him until she said, "The old place used to be a trading post when Uncle John first came here . . . over the Trail of Tears." The last words were not said bitterly, and Clayton was surprised. "If you're any kind of shot with that rifle," she continued, "we'll be able to make a stand . . . provided we get inside the house in one piece."

"You think there's a chance we won't?"

The girl smiled jeeringly at him. "You afraid?"

"Maybe." She looked even more like Montclair when she smiled. Again he wondered why he should not tell her the truth about her brother. "You should be," he heard her say. He tried to remember what Montclair had said about Angela, but he could recall almost nothing. She was not at all the little sister Clayton had expected, and she was certainly not the Angel whom Montclair had painted—far from it. She wasn't even likable.

"I asked you a question, Mr. Harris," came the girl's sharp voice. "Where do you want your valuables sent?"

Clayton studied the Kiowa camp; a half-dozen children were moving the horse herd. "I don't have any valuables," he said.

Angela's gaze mocked him. "Good. I'd hate to think I had to ride all the way to Tennessee to deliver a pocketknife or something."

Or a message, he thought, but "Would you really do that?" he asked.

"What? Deliver your valuables to your home?" He nodded. "Of course," she said, insulted. "Let's get something straight, Mr. Harris. We Cherokee may be Indians, savages to some folks, but we are far more civilized than most white people I've met. We are also highly educated, honest, and trustworthy." She was growing angry, her pale eyes becoming a thunderhead gray.

Clayton looked hard at her. "I wasn't implying that you would keep my belongings, Miss Drew, but I find it difficult to believe that you would ride all the way to Tennessee—"

"I have been to the Smoky Mountains several times, Mr. Harris. Uncle John still owns property there."

Clayton let that pass, for he knew nothing of John Ross or of any Indian holdings in Tennessee; he was surprised to learn that Indians still owned property in the Smokies. In fact, he was surprised by all he had seen thus far of Indians. "These Kiowa," he said, "are they part of the Cherokee Nation?"

The girl threw him a hateful grimace. "You don't listen very well, do you? I just finished telling you that the Cherokee are a civilized people." Shaking her head at his stupidity, she crawled over to where her cousins lay sleeping and rolled into her blankets.

Clayton turned his attention to the windswept hollow, then to the hills beyond. Where were the cattle Mrs. Drew had mentioned? The landscape showed none. Drawing his blanket up over his ears, he resumed his vigilance. It was going to be a long, cold day.

Cotton whistled as he trotted his horse through the hock-deep snow that covered the fields like a neatly turned blanket. The sun had penetrated the overcast, and the world sparkled pure and virginal. He grinned. It reminded him of Willie.

He picked up the Richland road three miles north of Gallatin. Faintly visible on the surface of the snow were the tracks of three riders who had passed sometime during the night. Still whistling, he spurred his horse into a canter and headed toward Richland.

He would have missed the small, snow-covered mound beside the road had not his horse shied violently, blowing hot puffs of vapor from its nostrils in an attempt to dispel the odor of death. Drawing his pistol, Cotton scrutinized the landscape, searching for anything out of the ordinary.

He frowned. Everything appeared normal. Again he reined his horse toward Richland. Again the animal reared and spun sideways. Cotton cocked his pistol and let his eyes move slowly about him. He was to the point of believing that his horse had gone mad when he saw the point of an overcoat collar protruding through the snow.

With a quick look around to be sure that it wasn't a trap, Cotton dismounted and used the toe of his boot to rake the powdery snow from what he was sure was a dead body. Although he was neither fascinated nor appalled by death —he had witnessed too much of it—it was not insensitivity that prompted him to consider climbing back onto his horse and riding on to Willie's. After all, this was his wedding day, and he didn't relish the thought of being caught up in something that didn't concern him.

Cursing himself for a fool, he knelt and finished raking aside the snow. He was perplexed. It was the body of a young girl. With mounting curiosity, he reached out and brushed the snow from her frozen face. "I wonder who she is," he murmured, studying her blood-spattered features. He pushed himself to his feet and dusted the snow from his hands. He would send word to the authorities in Gallatin; it was the best he could do.

Putting his foot into the stirrup, he grasped the saddle pommel and started up. Then he hesitated; something about that body bothered him. He ran his eyes over the thin, exposed torso.

For a moment he didn't move; then, sagging weakly against the saddle, he slid down the horse's side, unaware that the saddle rings were cutting into his cheek. His wide eyes were glued to the girl's naked belly. Barely visible was a small, protruding navel.

Clayton left the rim of the hilltop and crawled halfway to the horses before climbing to his feet and walking upright the rest of the way. He wondered why Angela had not chosen a more sheltered spot in which to spend the day. It seemed foolish to freeze atop an unprotected hill when they could just as easily have camped in one of the many draws or ravines they had crossed.

His eyes wandered to the sleeping girl. She had asked him if he was afraid. Yes, he was afraid; it was a fear born of not knowing or understanding the enemy. But he had not explained that to Angela. She thought he was a coward, and so did the twins, who had hardly spoken a word to him since leaving Park Hill.

Clayton rolled into his blankets. He told himself that it didn't matter what they thought, but he knew it did.

Cotton drew Willie to his breast and rocked her gently, gasping with great racking tears that streamed down his face and dropped onto her frozen cheeks. For an instant it appeared as if they both wept.

Raising his eyes to the heavens, Cotton's lips drew into a grimace that exposed his space-gapped teeth. "I've asked you a thousand times to damn somebody for some stupid thing they did," he shouted, "but I want you to listen real close this time." Then, dropping his head back, he wailed, "I damn you, God! I . . . damn . . . you! You, who damns every fine thing you ever created!"

Then he laid his cheek against Willie's and collapsed into his grief, a man who was, at that moment, more dead than the body of the girl he cradled in his arms.

CHAPTER 29

Cotton buried Willie at her farm. It took him and Lem all day—using double-bit axes, picks, and shovels—to open the frozen ground. They laid her next to her mother. Cotton thought she would have liked that.

After the grave was filled, Cotton, Lem, and Lena stood in the raw December wind, not knowing what to do next.

"She were our baby," Lena said brokenly. "We raised her from a day-ol' chile."

Lem put an arm around Lena. He wiped his eyes with the tattered scarf that hung loosely around his throat. "Why did they haf to take her to Gallatin? She done tolt them the truth about Ellis Harper. She done tolt them the truth."

Cotton remained silent. He had no answer to Lem's question. But he intended to find one.

"What we gonna do now, Massa Cotton?" asked the old man. "We ain't got nobody left . . . nowhere to go."

"How the hell should I know?" Cotton snapped. Then he softened. "I'm sorry, Lem. I ought not to take it out on you an' Lena. I just can't think straight right now."

"It's all right, Massa Cotton. I understan' how you're feelin'."

No, Lem, you don't, Cotton thought bitterly. Nobody knows how I feel. She gave my life a new meaning. How can one person do that for another? He shook his head. "I love you," he whispered to the mound of raw earth. And it dawned on him that he had answered his own question.

He turned to the old couple. "I think Willie would have wanted the two of you to go on livin' here . . . This is your home." When Lem and Lena nodded and walked toward the house, Cotton climbed into the saddle and pondered what to do next. If he returned to the front lines, he would have no chance to pick up a lead toward Willie's murderer. He thought of Ellis Harper. Ellis had informers who might uncover a clue. Yet Willie had pleaded with him not to join Harper's band. "He's a cold-blooded killer," she had said. And while Cotton did not approve of murder any more than Willie had, he could not forget that whoever had murdered her was also a cold-blooded killer.

Cotton looked again at the mound of freshly turned earth—a dirty, ugly scar, out of place in the landscape of glistening-white beauty. Removing his tattered campaign hat, he bowed his head. "I know you would trade your place in heaven if it would keep me from joining Ellis Harper, Willie, but I don't reckon as I've got no choice."

Turning his horse north, away from Lem and Lena, away from Summerset, and away from Willie, he rode across the fields toward the deep, secret hollows tucked between the rugged hills. Somewhere in one of those valleys was Ellis Harper.

General Paine paced his office. "Killing that girl was insane, Butler."

"She tried to make a break for it," Butler lied. "Me an' Mandy figured she was goin' to warn Ellis Harper to stay out of the county."

"You didn't have to shoot her!" Paine shouted. Walking to the window, he gazed unseeingly through the frosted pane. "I've blamed the murder on the nigger contrabands," he said. "And in a way, I guess that's the truth . . . if your whore was indeed the one who killed the girl. I've sent out a detachment of the Eighth Tennessee Cavalry to search for the culprits." Paine swung back to Butler. "Those East Tennessee cavalrymen have already killed one black man who they say 'insulted' a white girl within their hearing. And they begged me, Butler—begged me!—to allow them to kill every Negro in Gallatin."

Butler waved that aside. "I don't see what the big deal is," he said. "Who cares if those East Tennessee hillbillies kill the niggers?"

"You fool!" Paine yelled. "I've worked hard to get this county right where I want it. But even a subdued citizenry can be pushed only so far. If the people of Sumner County thought I was involved in any way with this girl's murder, they would revolt. It's one thing to hang or shoot a man, because people can be deceived into accepting it as a part of the war. But murdering a woman—hell, she wasn't even that, she was just a kid—is like waving a firebrand over an open powder keg." Paine dropped into his chair. "We're going to have to walk on eggs until this blows over, Butler."

Butler said, "I still think you're makin' too much of nothin', General. The people in this county swallow what you feed them, and you've made them like it. You've stolen their stock, their slaves, an' their homes, and you've raped their women. An' they ain't done a thing 'cept complain about it. An' they ain't goin' to do nothin' 'bout that girl bein' killed, neither."

He's a fool, thought Paine, a dangerous fool. "Butler," he said, leaning across the desk top, "listen to me, and listen good. If anything like this happens again, you had better dig a hole and crawl in it, because I'll hang you on the courthouse square, and I'll let you hang there until you rot! I'll not allow the likes of you to destroy what I have worked so hard to build in this county." Paine leaned back in his chair. "Get out of my office before I do the intelligent thing and hang you now."

Angela shook Clayton awake. He rolled out of his blankets and sat up. The night was clear and cold; the moon looked like a sliver of ice floating in a jet pool of frigid water.

Pushing himself stiffly to his feet, he walked to the rim of the hill and peered into the darkness below. The Indian camp was visible only because the breeze had picked up and was fanning the smoldering cook fires into life. The ranch house was lost in the shadows.

Angela joined him. "When we go in," she said, "we ride

straight to the house and take our horses inside with us. If we're seen, the Kiowa will come to investigate. If that happens, let me do the talking." She turned to face him. "Are you prepared to die, Mr. Harris? If they rush the house, I will kill you myself before I'll let them take you alive."

Clayton stared at her. For all your fine schooling and lovely exterior, he thought, you are definitely not fragile on the inside. "Shoot me between the eyes," he said jokingly.

Angela's gaze was level. "If you think I enjoy having to discuss such a thing, you are mistaken. But as long as you are under my care, I'll do my best to protect you, even if it means killing you."

"I'm obliged," Clayton said, "but I didn't know I was under your care. And I don't think I need your protection." Trying hard to suppress his anger, he went on. "I won't be belittled by you, nor will I allow you to make me feel guilty for being a tenderfoot, as you call we Easterners. I'll do whatever has to be done to get this job accomplished. Do we understand one another, Miss Drew?"

"Perfectly!" she snapped.

Larry told his brother in Cherokee that it was about time Mr. Harris started acting like a man.

Harry replied, as they mounted their horses, "Yes, and she deserved it. Sometimes she forgets that she's just a woman."

Angela thought about the brothers' comments. Perhaps she had been a bit high-handed, but she didn't care; it had not been her choice to come on this foray. Even so, that wasn't the real reason for her animosity toward Clayton Harris, and she knew it. What bothered her was the unsettling feeling that he had brought bad tidings to her family.

"Mr. Harris," she said, tying her rolled blanket behind her saddle, "I'm going to ask you once more before we go down there"—she smoothed out the knot, appraising Clayton across her horse's back—"what you and my mother discussed. Whatever it was, I feel threatened by it."

There it was, the very thing Clayton had dreaded: the direct statement. Lifting himself to the saddle, he wondered whether he should continue to lie. He deplored deception, and she had a right to know the truth. Turning his horse toward the waiting boys, he said, "You'll have to ask your mother, Miss Drew."

Angela's face whitened as she slipped her foot into the stirrup, crooked her knee over the pommel extension, and seated herself firmly in the saddle. "Mr. Harris?" she said, riding up beside him. When he turned toward her, she rattled off a long line of Cherokee that nearly smoked in the frigid air.

Clayton rode close to the boys. "What did she say to me?"

The twins looked at one another with embarrassment. Then Angela laughed and spat another string of Cherokee at him.

"She said," offered Harry, "that if you wanted to know what she said, go ask her mother . . . but she didn't hardly say it that nice."

Clayton followed Angela and the boys off the hill, winding down a gully that kept them in the deepest shadows. She's careful, he thought, watching her bob and sway to the movement of her horse as the animal delicately picked its footing down the steep ravine.

Clayton's plantation horse, accustomed to the gently rolling fields of Middle Tennessee, was out of its element in the rough and broken terrain and kept sliding on its haunches as it maneuvered the treacherous incline. Finally the big horse lost its footing, creating a small rock slide as it thrashed and skidded some ten feet before regaining its balance. Miraculously, Clayton stayed in the saddle and managed to keep the terrified animal from bolting headlong into the darkness.

Angela and the boys had frozen in the shadows the moment the commotion began. Cocking their heads toward the Indian village, they scarcely breathed as they listened for the telltale sounds of a camp coming awake.

A dog barked excitedly, then another, and another. But after several minutes they tapered off to an occasional yip. Then everything was quiet.

Clayton released his pent-up breath. Angela asked if his horse was hurt. "Not that I can tell," he replied.

It took them fifteen more nerve-racking minutes before they had worked their way to flat ground. Reining in her horse, Angela told Clayton that the next few minutes would be the most dangerous—when they crossed the open ground.

Clayton glanced at the moon. There's too much light, he thought. "Do we make a run for it?" he asked.

Angela shook her head. "We walk our horses, slow and easy. If anything goes wrong between here and the house, you're on your own." She led off at a slow pace, the boys falling in behind her, Clayton bringing up the rear.

As they crossed the moon-swept plain, their shadows loomed like elongated ghosts leading the way. The girl looked over her shoulder toward the Kiowa camp. A dog had begun barking again. At the stockade, Angela dropped from her horse and swung the gate open. Quickly she motioned Clayton and the boys through, then swung the gate closed again.

Showing her first sign of nervousness, Angela ran to the house and pounded on the door.

A light showed thinly through the threshold crack. "What yo' want at this time 'o night?" came a voice muffled by three full inches of wood.

"It's Angela Drew," the girl said. "Kill that light and let me in." Instantly the light went out, and Clayton could hear the bar being lifted from its iron bracket. Angela pushed the door open and led her horse inside, its hooves loud on the puncheon floorboards.

Clayton and the boys followed. The instant the last horse cleared the threshold, the door was closed and the crossbar fell into place. A moment later the room flickered into light as the wick of a coal-oil lamp was turned high.

Clayton glanced at the interior. The room was twenty feet square, he judged, built of thick, sturdy logs laid with such skill that there was little need for chinking. There were no windows, but shooting loops were placed strategically about the walls. Despite the rumpled bed, the table and chairs, the scattered domestic items, the room had the appearance of a blockhouse rather than a home. The twins caught the headstalls of the horses and took a firm grip. If a battle erupted, the boys would do their best to keep the animals from going berserk and kicking everyone in the room to death.

"What are you doin' here?" demanded the wiry Negro woman who had opened the door. She studied Clayton suspiciously. "Miss Drew," she said, "you know they'll kill that white man if they catch him here."

"We're going to be here for only a few minutes," Angela assured her. "How many cattle are feeding in the arroyos, Maybelle?"

Before the woman could answer, a tall, broad-shouldered Negro man emerged from the adjoining room and leaned an old-style flintlock Plains rifle against the log wall. "A little activity goin' on down at the village," he said. "Maybe y'all got in here without bein' seen . . . but I doubt it."

Angela swung toward him. "How many cattle can you round up, Tom?"

"Not many, Angela," he said, eyeing Clayton. "Three, four hundred."

Angela looked at Clayton. "You think the Confederacy needs that many?"

Clayton nodded. "A thousand times that many if I can get them."

Tom motioned Angela out onto the dog-trot. The girl followed him through the door. Clayton heard the low murmur of his voice, then the higher tones of Angela's. They were arguing.

"What's going on out there?" Clayton asked, taking a step toward the door.

"Don't go out there," Maybelle warned, moving to block the exit.

Clayton caught her by her arm and pushed her aside. When he stepped into the dog-trot, Angela and Tom fell silent. The Negro turned his back and crossed his arms, making no attempt to hide his anger.

"What's the matter, Angela?" Clayton demanded.

"Ask my mother!" the girl said curtly.

"I'm asking you."

"Well, don't! It's none of your business."

Tom spun around and pointed his finger at Clayton. "The Confederacy has done robbed us of about all the cattle in these hills. Chief John Ross hid this bunch to feed—"

"Tom!" Angela cried, cutting the man off.

Ignoring Angela, Clayton asked Tom, "To feed who?"

The man glared at Angela. "John Ross saved these cows to feed the Cherokee women an' children," he said. "These three or four hundred cows is all that stands between them an' starvation."

Clayton looked hard at Angela. "Your mother knew that, didn't she?"

"Everyone knows it," murmured the girl.

Clayton's voice cut like a knife. "Then why did she send us out here?"

Angela raised her eyes defiantly. "Because she obviously owes you a service. We pay our debts, Mr. Harris."

"Even to the point of starving your children?" Not waiting for an answer, he turned to Tom. "The Confederacy doesn't need cattle that—"

"Hush!" whispered Angela, listening intently.

Inside, Maybelle blew out the lantern, throwing the room and the dog-trot into darkness.

Moonlight illuminated the countryside until it was nearly as bright as day, and Clayton could make out several Indians sitting on their ponies just beyond the low stockade. They were watching the house.

Quietly, Angela, Tom, and Clayton slipped into the house and barred the dog-trot door. Clayton removed a plug from a loophole and thrust his rifle barrel through the slot. He took a fine bead on the lead Indian's head. Then the man was gone. He had flipped his leg over his pony's back and dropped lightly to the ground.

"What do you think you are doing?" Angela whispered as Clayton cocked the weapon.

"I'm going to kill that man the minute he steps into the open."

Angela's eyes opened wide as she studied Clayton's calm profile. Quickly she pushed her face against the loop and shouted something in Cherokee. The Indian ducked down behind the gate, and the others galloped their ponies away from the palisade.

After a drawn-out silence, the Indian called out to the girl and they talked back and forth for a full minute. Then the Indian laughed and vaulted onto his pony. He called something to the others, who were sitting their horses a hundred yards away, and they all laughed. Then, screeching wildly, the band galloped off toward the village. Harry, who was holding Clayton's horse, was lifted off his feet as the

Tennessee animal reared and bucked at the yowling of the savages. Even Clayton's skin crawled. The Rebel yell was mere hooting compared to what he had just heard.

"First impressions can be very frightening," Angela said, reading his mind. "They are really not a bad sort, if you happen to be a hostile yourself."

"I'll take your word for it," Clayton said. "What did you say to make them leave?"

The girl's teeth flashed in the darkness. "You'll have to ask my mother." But it was said with amusement, and a very real touch of embarrassment.

Clayton scowled; this was no time for childish games. Facing Tom, he demanded, "What did she say to them?"

Tom crossed his arms. "I don't speak Injun."

Clayton was sure that he lied. He spun back to Angela. "I need to know what you said to those Kiowa, Angela. Our lives might depend on it."

The girl hesitated. Then she said, "I told them that just as soon as I discovered where you kept the money for the cows, I intended to . . . intended to . . ." The girl hesitated, and Clayton could sense her blush in the darkness. "I told them I intended to kill you myself."

One of the boys sniggered and told Clayton that wasn't what she had said at all. "She told them she was your whore woman, and that when she had you naked and defenseless—"

"That's enough!" Clayton shouted.

"Yes, Mr. Harris," Angela admitted. "I said it. I told them that while you were . . . busy, I would cut your throat. They approved of that, Mr. Harris. They understood it. So they left."

Tom lit the lantern and turned up the wick. "You're goin' to have to get out of here," he said. "Them Kiowa are goin' to be back, come daylight."

Angela put her hand on Tom's arm. "I'm sorry about this, Tom. We'll leave two hours before sunup. Now, how many cattle can you spare?"

Clayton dropped the hammer of his rifle to half-cock. "We're not taking any cattle, Angela."

"I'd keep them all if it was up to me," Tom said, ignoring Clayton. "But I might be able to round up fifty, sixty head for you, maybe more." The Negro frowned and looked at

Clayton. "Why didn't the Confederacy send you down to Texas? There's thousands of cattle just roamin' wild down there."

Clayton thought about that. And he too wondered why he had not thought of Texas. Extending his hand to the Negro but looking at Angela, he said, "Thanks for offering the cattle, Tom, but we're not taking them, and that's the end of it."

Ignoring Clayton's hand, the Negro said, "Me an' the twins will bring 'em to Fort Gibson soon's we get 'em out of the coulees. Might be a spell, tho'."

"Good enough," Angela said, returning Clayton's hard look.

The moment the moon set, Clayton and Angela led their horses out the back door of the ranch house. The crossbar fell into place. It sounded final.

Clayton looked toward the village. A teepee glowed like a translucent candle shade, but even as he watched, the light went out, turning the pale tents into eerie silhouettes that reminded him of conical tombstones. He gritted his teeth, wishing he wouldn't have such thoughts. Then a hair-raising war cry erupted in the village.

Angela leaped onto her horse and pivoted the animal toward the hills. "That Tennessee horse of yours better know how to do something other than walk fast," she cried, and she was off and running.

Angela and Clayton whipped their mounts unmercifully, hoping to get one more mile out of them before the jaded animals collapsed.

As Clayton's horse began to falter, Angela pointed to a mesa looming up out of the plains half a mile to the right. He nodded and swung his staggering mount toward the flat-topped hill.

Upon reaching the base of the mesa, they sprang to the ground and forced the blown animals up the steep incline, beating them savagely with the bridle reins. Upon reaching the top, Angela snatched up her mount's front hock, threw her weight against the animal's shoulder, and dropped the horse onto its side. It lay there, too exhausted to rise.

Clayton tried the same maneuver, but his horse weighed a

good three hundred pounds more than Angela's and it took their combined efforts to finally lay his horse over. Then Clayton had to sit on the animal's head while Angela hog-tied its feet—front and back—before it would stay down.

Angela crawled to the edge of the mesa and peered in the direction they had come. Nothing moved. Clayton bellied up beside her. "We might have lost them," she said, scanning the terrain for as far as she could see in the predawn light.

"Do you really think so?"

"No."

A moment later she said, "Well . . . maybe. Indians aren't the wonders of the woods you white fools have painted them to be."

"According to all the books I've read, Indians can track a barefoot man across solid rock," Clayton said.

"Well, we can't," the girl returned. "But we would never let a white man know that."

Clayton was surprised by her honesty, but he didn't say so. "How long are we going to lie up here?" he asked. The sun broke the horizon, bathing the landscape in a cold, metallic gold.

"All day, unless they find us," she said.

"And if they do?"

"Then we'll make a stand. I'd rather shoot down a hill than up, wouldn't you?" She rolled onto her side and raised her eyebrows questioningly.

"How many pitched battles have you been engaged in?" he asked.

"I've never been in any battles, but I've read all of my brother Montclair's books on war and strategy. He's with the Cherokee Brigade, a colonel."

Clayton's eyes widened. Neither he nor Montie had ever mentioned rank, and it came as a shock to find that his friend had held such a high position. Clayton decided that he shouldn't be surprised; Montclair Drew had been intelligent, well schooled, and fearless. Furthermore, he had been a natural-born leader of men.

"What's the matter?" Angela asked, watching Clayton's face. There was an edge to her voice that warned him to tread lightly with his reply.

Feigning indifference, he said, "I was unaware that I was accompanying the sister of a man who outranked me. I will have to be more careful of how I treat you, won't I?"

Angela's scrutiny lasted for a long moment before she turned and made a quick appraisal of the country below. Satisfied, she crabbed backward to her horse and retrieved her blanket, then Clayton's.

Crawling back to him, she said, "The wind whipping across these buttes cuts right through a person." Molding her body against his, she tugged the two covers over them. "Don't get the wrong impression," she warned, her cheek against his, "but we could freeze to death up here. That's one reason I chose this mesa top."

Clayton savored the warmth of her body. "That's about as clear as mud," he said, his lips against her ear. "If there's a chance that we might freeze—"

"See what I mean?" she broke in. "White men won't freeze themselves to death under any circumstances. Indians know that."

"I'm sorry we're not as tough as you Cherokee," he returned sarcastically.

"It's all right." Her lashes tickled his cheek when she blinked. "You can't help it."

"What's your real name?" he asked after a while.

"Angela Drew," she answered, surprised.

"No. What's your Cherokee name?"

The girl laughed; the sound was clear and pure in the morning stillness. "I'm only one-eighth Cherokee, Mr. Harris, but yes, I have a Cherokee name. You would never be able to pronounce it, but it means 'Woman of the Earth.'"

"That's inappropriate," he said. "There's nothing about you that's down-to-earth."

He felt her stiffen. "Not that you'll ever get the chance, Mr. Harris, but if you really knew me, you would say that I am very down-to-earth."

I doubt that, he thought. He said nothing.

A moment later she said, "Get some sleep, Mr. Harris. I'll keep watch."

He told her to wake him if she saw anything, anything at all. She agreed that she would.

When the Kiowa appeared, neither Angela nor Clayton

were aware of it. They were curled tightly together, with
Angela's head pillowed against the curve of Clayton's
shoulder, each of them sound asleep.

Ironically, it was the Kiowa themselves who wasted their
opportunity to slip up on the pair undetected.

After having painstakingly wormed their way on foot up
the rugged mesa and meeting no resistance, the leader
decided that their quarry had not stopped at the top, but
had ridden on to take a stand elsewhere.

Shivering in the bitter cold, the Indian stepped boldly
over the rim of the mesa, then turned and called to his
companions below that the hilltop was empty.

Clayton's horse, scenting the rancid bear grease the
Kiowa wore, struggled violently to break free of its tethers.
Slipping one hoof free, it lurched to its knees, causing the
Indian to take an involuntary step backward.

The movement saved his life, for Clayton flung Angela
from him and erupted out of their blankets thumbing his
Colt revolver at anything that moved.

Hair pipes flew from the Kiowa's breastplate as one of
Clayton's wild shots tore through the makeshift armor and
knocked the startled man over the mesa's rim.

Angela brought her small-caliber hunting rifle to her
shoulder and scanned the hillside for more of the attackers.
Below her, the Indian whom Clayton had shot jumped to
his feet and quickly dashed into a ravine. Angela threw a
shot after him, then grimaced, knowing it had been a wasted
effort.

Clayton sprinted to his horse, which was still thrashing
wildly in an attempt to gain its feet.

Angela's mount, although supposedly well trained, had
bounded upright when the shots erupted and was charging
wildly down the far side of the mesa. In a matter of seconds
it was lost from sight and clear of danger.

Clayton caught his horse's bridle reins and snatched the
animal's head back to the earth. He retied its hooves, then
crawled back to Angela. "See anything?"

"They're down there," she said, watching the hillside.

"Your horse took off."

"I trained him to run with confidence at the first sign of
danger," she said. What she didn't say was that she was

supposed to be on his back.

"Well, you trained him real good," Clayton said dryly.

"Better than you shoot. That Kiowa got up and ran away."

"I hit him solid. He won't go far."

"You didn't hit him at all. He was wearing a bone breast shield. A .36-caliber ball at fifty feet won't penetrate it."

"It penetrated," Clayton said. "But next time I'll use my rifle. I'm a better shot with the rifle anyway."

"You may have to prove that."

"You know something, Miss Drew?" Clayton said, frowning at her. "There's derned little about you that's lovable. You are absolutely nothing like . . ." Too late, Clayton clamped his mouth shut.

"Nothing like who?"

"A woman I used to know," he lied.

"Well, if it's your true love, in Tennessee, don't even think of comparing us."

Clayton turned his attention to the hillside. "Why don't they do something?" he asked.

"They won't make the first move, because they have nothing but bows and arrows."

"You mean to tell me that we rode our horses into the ground getting away from bows and arrows!"

"An arrow can kill you just as dead as a bullet can," returned Angela. Then, pushing herself to her knees, she yelled loudly down the slope, her breath looking like pistol shots in the freezing wind.

"What did you tell them?" Clayton asked.

"I told them that you had a big-bore Hawkins rifle."

Clayton tightened his grip on his Springfield carbine. "What difference does the make of my gun have to do with anything?"

"They know a Hawkins rifle will shoot through their shields. They are afraid of them."

An arrow clattered off of a rock near Angela. She dropped flat and wiggled back to Clayton. "Shoot something," she told him. "They don't believe me."

"What should I shoot at? There's nothing in sight."

Angela peered over the rim. At the foot of the mesa, over five hundred yards below, a half-dozen ponies were tied to a bush.

"Are you as good with that rifle as you say you are?"

"I said I was a better shot with a rifle than with a handgun."

"Well, I sure hope you are, because I want you to shoot one of those horses down there."

Clayton looked down the incline. He saw nothing. "What horses?"

"Those at the bottom of the mesa."

Clayton let his gaze travel along the base of the hill. "For Christ's sake, Miss Drew," he said a moment later, "they're so far away I can barely see them."

Ignoring him, Angela cried out again in Cherokee. Clayton eyed her suspiciously. "I told them you were going to kill their horses," she said. "They laughed."

"I didn't hear any laughter."

"You don't hear it, Mr. Harris, you feel it."

Clayton's eyes narrowed. Was she baiting him? "You've really put the fat in the fire this time," he said, gauging the distance to the horses. "There's no way I can hit one of those horses from here."

"Then give me the rifle," she returned easily.

Clayton stared at her. "Do you think you can hit one from here?"

"No," she said, "but it will beat trying to talk them to death."

Clayton shouldered the rifle, wedging the barrel securely between two stones. Aware that a bullet had a tendency to rise when shot downhill, he dropped the front sight to the horses' hooves. Then he hesitated. At that range, a bullet would lose velocity and fall. He raised the barrel so that it was a foot above the horses, then lowered it again to their feet. In spite of the cold, his hands sweated, chilling immediately and turning numb. To hell with it, he thought, swinging the barrel up and aiming directly at a horse in the middle of the herd. He squeezed the trigger.

With a shrill shriek of pain, an animal on the far side of the herd reared and fell backward, scattering the remaining horses to the four winds.

Angela's mouth fell open. "I don't believe it." She stared at the fallen mount. "I just don't believe it. You actually killed that horse."

Clayton tore open a paper cartridge with his teeth and

ramrodded it down the barrel of his rifle. Quickly he thumbed a priming cap over the nipple. Drawing the weapon to full-cock, he scanned the hillside for the enemy charge he fully expected. When none came, he brought the rifle to half-cock, then peered at the distant animal kicking in its death throes; he felt no elation.

Silence settled like a cloak over the mesa. It was nerve-racking. Clayton became more anxious by the minute, until all he could hear was the hammering of his heart as it pounded against his rib cage. His eyes darted to every nook and cranny in sight, but nothing moved. "Why don't they come?" he whispered to himself.

Angela turned and flashed him a beautiful smile. "They're gone, Mr. Harris. Killing that horse did the trick."

Jumping to her feet, she walked over to Clayton's horse and cut its lashings.

CHAPTER 30

Clayton, with Angela riding double, pushed his horse hard throughout the day. As sunset kissed the bleak landscape into a chilled blush, the girl informed him that they could slow down.

"The Kiowa won't come any closer to Tahlequah than this," she said, relaxing wearily against his back.

"Why not?"

"Because someone might mistake them for 'tame' Indians. And that would be the ultimate disgrace."

"Are you bitter?" he asked. "Sometimes I get the impression that you are."

The girl was silent. Then, when he had decided that she didn't intend to answer, she said, "Perhaps I am bitter, Mr. Harris. When I attended school in the East, I was a naive little girl; it took me a long time to wake up to the facts of life."

Her arms tightened about him, and she continued: "I was at the top of my class, which I assume created a certain amount of jealousy among the other girls. Children in the Cherokee Nation consider it an honor to go to school; they study hard. In other words, Mr. Harris, I was there because

I wanted to be there, while many of the white girls were there because they had no choice."

"What did you do about their jealousy?"

"I did what any Cherokee girl would have done; I thanked them for the compliment of believing me intelligent, but explained that only the least able Cherokee students were sent East to private schools because the superintendent of education in the Nation did not want those students hindering the intelligent ones."

"What happened?"

"They felt sorry for me, of course."

They would, he thought. Then he asked, "What about . . . your social life? I suspect that you didn't want for gentleman callers."

She stiffened and did not answer.

They rode for several miles in silence, until they came upon a small brook that tossed and turned its way down a rock-strewn, wooded gulch. Clayton swung to the ground, then handed Angela down. Both of them dropped to their stomachs and drank deeply, the icy water putting their teeth on edge.

Angela rolled onto her side and dropped her head back, her face raised to the setting sun. A ghost of a smile etched tiny dimples into her rose-colored cheeks.

Clayton gazed at her, captivated by the fine texture of her skin, the gentle arch of her neck, the highlights that reflected from her hair, the pale pink of her slightly parted lips. "You are beautiful," he murmured, surprised by the sound of his own voice.

Angela's long lashes barely parted. "Don't go spoiling your image, Mr. Harris." Closing her eyes again, she drank in what little warmth the sun yet offered.

Clayton got up and unsaddled the flagged horse. Using winter-killed bunch grass, he rubbed the animal down.

Angela tilted her head to the side and appraised him. "Aren't you curious about how other people see you? How I see you?" she asked.

Clayton squatted to wipe down the horse's forelegs. "You've made that fairly plain ever since we met."

"Well, maybe I've changed my mind."

"I doubt it."

Angela's face flamed. "There are several reasons why I react toward you as I do, Mr. Harris. But I'm sure you wouldn't be interested in them."

"Probably not."

Angela's color deepened. "You asked me a question a while ago," she said. "Yes, I had many male admirers, especially in my second year at school." She tossed her head and glared at him. "You said that I am beautiful. Well, you are right, Mr. Harris, but for all the wrong reasons." Clayton stole a glance at her and was shocked by the bitterness that overlaid her near-perfect features. "My brother, Montclair, once said," she continued, "that if my outside ever became as beautiful as my inside, I would be the loveliest girl in the world. Well, it nearly did, Mr. Harris, during my second year at finishing school."

Clayton considered the girl anew. She was not boasting, she was merely making a statement. Angela went on; "The . . . gentlemen . . . were very flattering. And I will admit, they fairly turned my head with their praise. And I believed every word of it . . . because Montclair had said it would be that way." Clayton did not hear anger in her voice. He heard only pain, deep-seated pain. "But they didn't give a flip that I was beautiful inside. No," she corrected, "that's not true. They saw inside of me. But it wasn't my decency they saw, nor my goodness, nor my honesty. All they saw was the Indian blood that runs through my veins."

She raised her head defiantly. "You've heard, I'm sure, that the only good Indian is a dead Indian? Well, that's only true of Indian men, Mr. Harris. The only good Indian girl is one who will . . . who will . . ."

"That's enough, Angela," Clayton said softly.

Angela's lower lip trembled. "Oh, yes," she whispered, "they thought I was beautiful, Lord knows they told me so often enough while they tried . . . their tricks. But not once was I pretty enough to be taken home to meet their mothers, not once." Again her lip trembled, and it was only with effort that she brought her emotions under control.

"Why don't you go ahead and cry?" Clayton asked. "Maybe that would help."

Angela laughed bitterly. "Cry? Haven't you heard that Indians never cry?"

Clayton put his finger beneath her chin and tipped her head back so that he could look into the liquid pools of her pale eyes. He had seen that same look, that same need, in Lettie Billingsly's eyes, and all the hurt and pain of loving Lettie welled up within him, and all the bitterness of knowing that it had meant nothing nearly suffocated him.

Angela saw the change come over him, but still, she was not prepared when he asked harshly, "What makes you think you were worth taking home to meet their mothers?"

Silently, the pools overflowed.

On the fifteenth of December, 1863, Angela's cousins delivered fifty head of beef to Fort Gibson.

The cattle were not the tough, stringy, longhorn breed of the West that Clayton had expected; they were selected breeding stock, principally Hereford—whitefaces, as most people called them. It was obvious, even to Clayton, that John Ross had been looking to the future when he had hidden the herd in the badlands.

The twins dismounted and swaggered over to Clayton. "Well," Larry said, "I see that Angela got you back safe and sound."

"What about you?" Clayton asked. "You boys have any trouble?"

"No," Harry said. "But if the ground hadn't been frozen too hard to make dust, we would have been in a peck of trouble." He went on to say that he and Larry had been forced to hold the herd in a gully for a day and a half because a band of Kansas jayhawkers had camped overnight on the main trail. "We were afraid they'd caught you and Angela for sure," the boy said. "But I slipped up on 'em at night and had a look-see. Hard bunch they were, too!"

Clayton took the boys to the post commander. Captain Hawkins wrote out a receipt for the cattle, and Clayton signed it.

"Those cattle are a sight for sore eyes," the captain said. "They're not going East, Harris; they're staying right here to feed my garrison. We didn't know there were any cows left in the Territory. Are there any more where those came from?"

The twins looked at Clayton, waiting for him to reveal the

whereabouts of the remainder of the herd.

"Not a damned one, Captain," Clayton said.

That evening Clayton stood in the parlor at Park Hill and chastised Mrs. Drew. "Those cattle are breeding stock, ma'am. You knew that. And you knew that Mr. Ross undoubtedly intended to use them to build a future herd for the Cherokee when the war is over."

The slender woman sat on the horsehair divan and gazed silently out the window. "Mr. Harris," she said without turning, "I am the mistress of Park Hill until my brother returns. It was my decision to sell you the cattle, and under the circumstances, I'm sure that John would have approved that decision. I will admit, sir, that I was relieved when Angela told me you refused the cattle. The fifty head we delivered was our way of thanking you for that . . . and . . . for other things."

Clayton grimaced, offended by her original doubt of his integrity. "Mrs. Drew," he said, "I've fulfilled my promise to Montclair, but I've still got the Confederacy to consider. Tom, at the ranch, said that Texas has thousands of cattle . . ."

"Mr. Harris," the woman said, "I must insist that you remain here, as our guest of course, until Mr. Drew returns. He is due a Christmas furlough in two weeks. Surely you can put off going to Texas for two weeks?"

"Ma'am," Clayton said, ignoring her request, "I think that Angela needs to be told the truth about Montclair now. She knows something is wrong, and she resents being left in the dark."

Mrs. Drew sighed and turned to face him. "I know that Angela is blaming you for this secrecy. And I am aware that she is very open in her hostility toward you."

"I can handle that," he said, "but, although she hasn't come right out and accused me of it, she thinks you and I are having an . . ." Clayton blushed.

Mrs. Drew stared at him. "An affair?"

Clayton nodded.

She gave a low laugh. "I am flattered that my daughter believes me still desirable enough to attract a young, handsome man. At the same time, however, I feel like taking her across my knee and paddling her soundly for having such little faith in me."

"I really believe that you should tell her the truth," Clayton said.

"I would like nothing better, Mr. Harris. But I assure you, sir, it would be wiser if her father broke the news. Angela and Montclair were twins, Mr. Harris . . ." Clayton wondered what difference that made. Mrs. Drew continued: "When Angela and Montclair were growing up, they were inseparable. They thought alike. They talked alike, and enjoyed the same games. When Montclair was ten, he broke his arm and Angela suffered so much pain, we had to splint her arm also. And once Montclair got lost in a snowstorm and was forced to hole up for a week without food. Angela lost twelve pounds, Mr. Harris." Mrs. Drew gazed at him steadily. "Need I tell you how much weight Montclair had lost?"

"Incredible," Clayton said. "But, Mrs. Drew, the very fact that Angela is so much like her brother—as you have pointed out—is surely proof that you are shortchanging her strength and courage by treating her as though she were a weakling."

"My daughter is an exceptionally strong woman, Mr. Harris," Mrs. Drew said sharply. "Except where Montclair is concerned." She hesitated. "I will tell you one thing more. And I believe that after hearing it, you will agree that I am correct in wishing to wait until Mr. Drew returns before Angela learns the truth."

Taking a deep breath, she said, "You lied to me about how my son died. Your reason for lying is not important. But I am sure that he was not shot to death. No, don't say a word, let me finish. On the night of December twenty-ninth— almost a year ago—Angela woke up screaming." Clayton's blood ran cold, and he found himself leaning toward the woman, waiting. "I rushed to her room," she said. "Angela was lying on her bed, weeping hysterically, calling Montclair's name and clutching her abdomen."

Clayton stared at her. "Go on," he said, disbelieving what he was hearing but determined to hear it all.

"I don't want to know how Montclair died," she said, dropping her face into her hands. "Angela . . . was passing blood . . . from her . . ."

Clayton's skin crawled. And had he not been certain that

there was no way in which Mrs. Drew could have known the truth about Montclair's death, he would have scoffed at the story. "Mrs. Drew," he said as the lady rose, "I spoke out of turn. You are perfectly justified in your fear for Angela's well-being. And yes, I will stay . . . at least until Christmas."

When Mrs. Drew left the room, Angela entered and quietly closed the door. Leaning her back against it, she watched Clayton coldly. "What did you say to my mother to upset her so?" When Clayton didn't answer, she said, "I think you had better leave Park Hill, Mr. Harris."

Clayton studied her for a long instant, remembering how Montclair had screamed in his last moments. Mrs. Drew had said that Angela had screamed too. "I'm sorry, Miss Drew," he said, "but I'm staying until your father returns."

Angela eyed him defiantly. "You don't hear very well, do you, Mr. Harris?"

Clayton sighed. Even though he understood her better now, he still did not like her. Angela stamped her foot. "You will pack your bedroll, Mr. Harris, and get off this property. Now!"

"I can't do that," he said.

With a cry, Angela struck him an openhanded blow that was quickly followed by another, then another. He made no move to protect himself.

"You coward," she whispered, hitting him with all her strength and watching the blood trickle from his split lips. "You're not man enough for my mother."

Clayton slowly wiped his mouth with the back of his hand. "Are you through?"

"Not by a long shot!" She balled her right hand into a tight fist.

Clayton caught her wrists and pinioned her against the door. "Don't push your luck, Miss Drew," he said. "Don't you know that slapping someone's face hurts?"

Angela smiled acidly at him. "I didn't feel a thing." Then, twisting in his grasp, she jeered, "You won't fight for the Confederacy, nor will you even fight to protect yourself! You stand there like a wooden white man . . . and let an Indian girl beat you to a pulp. Our roles are reversed, Mr. Harris."

Clayton gritted his teeth, his face clouding with anger.

"Oh, so you're getting mad, are you?" she cried. "Well, I'm trembling in my boots, Mr. Harris."

Flinging her aside, Clayton strode through the door, slamming it behind him.

Angela snatched open the door and shouted after him, "You better not be here when my father comes home."

Stalking to the creek behind the barn, Clayton cupped his hands and splashed the icy water over his face, wincing at the cuts and scratches Angela had inflicted.

Never had he been so angry at a girl before, not even Lettie . . . Lettie, who was fast becoming aught but a haunting memory from long ago, so very long ago.

Clayton pictured Lettie the last time he had seen her, standing at the window in Cragfont's parlor. Something in his heart had died when she refused to look at him; and that loss—was it hope?—had left him empty. He had carried that emptiness with him as he crossed the hundreds of miles between Tennessee and Oklahoma. It was with him still, but it had dimmed to a dull, aching sadness, and he knew that eventually that too would fade. Yes, he had changed.

Claudette LaBranche's words seemed to echo in the murmuring brook. "Do not let the South change you." Clayton's face took on lines of bitterness. Claudette was wrong: Places didn't change people. People changed people.

CHAPTER 31

Christmas Day, 1863, was a lonely time at Summerset. Cotton had not returned after Willie Harper's death, and Mr. and Mrs. Summers huddled alone before the fire in the parlor, hardly aware that it was Christ's birthday.

"Folks who knew her say that Willie Harper was a fine girl," sighed the old lady.

Mr. Summers nodded absently. They had already discussed Willie's death numerous times.

Tears rolled down Mrs. Summers' cheeks. The old man's heart went out to her. She had looked forward to the marriage, desperately so.

"General Paine killed her," the old lady cried. "If he hadn't arrested her and made her go to Gallatin, she would still be alive."

"We don't know that," the old man said. But he believed it too.

Getting to his feet, he walked slump-shouldered to his study. The room was cold, but he didn't notice. For the first time in his life, he felt like an old man—a disillusioned, tired old man.

With a sigh of resignation, he lit a lamp and took quill in

hand. He had never intended to call in old favors earned during the Mexican War, but someone had to put a stop to General Paine's madness.

He was aware that other Loyalists, such as Bailey Peyton, Sr., and A. R. Wynne, had petitioned Governor Johnson, complaining bitterly of Paine's atrocities, but he intended to go one step further.

Putting pen to paper, he wrote, "My dear friend Ulysses . . ."

Cotton sat by the potbellied stove in the shack Ellis Harper called headquarters and wished that Christmas would go away. Memories haunted him; memories of Willie—of Christmas a year ago—of popcorn and the trousers she had made for him, of singing and Bible reading. . . .

Ellis Harper, his shaggy brown hair hanging unkempt to his shoulders, straddled a slat-backed chair and painstakingly drew a cleaning rag through the barrel of his Remington revolver and inspected it for powder stains. Not satisfied, he dropped the string down the bore and drew the cloth through again.

Cotton absently wondered how a man who kept his weapons so spotless could live in the pigsty he called a cabin. Strewn everywhere were empty bottles, half-eaten food, and filthy blankets, saddles and harness. A person could hardly find a place to sit down.

"Whoever killed Cousin Willie covered their tracks good, Cotton," Harper said. "But we'll catch the murderin' sons-of-bitches. Just be patient. Somebody will slip up, they always do."

Cotton pushed himself to his feet. "I wish to hell I could get my hands on Paine's throat. He knows more'n he's tellin'."

"Well, he sure ain't gonna come out here an' tell you nothin', an' you can't ride into Gallatin an' face him down. Why, he'd just say what he's been a-sayin', that she was killed by some niggers."

Cotton snapped his fingers. "That's it. If Willie was killed by niggers, like Paine keeps sayin' she was, then the contrabands at the camp in Gallatin would know it."

Ellis Harper looked up from his pistol. "What good's that

goin' to do? You can't get in there to talk to them."

I can't, thought Cotton, but I know someone who can. Walking quickly to the door, he said, "I'll be back in a couple of days, Ellis."

Harper got up and followed Cotton to the open doorway. He watched in silence as Cotton mounted his horse and headed southeast through the heavily timbered woods.

Where was he going? Harper wondered. Gallatin lay southwest.

"I know it's a terrible thing to ask, Fanny," Cotton said, "but I ain't got no other way to turn." He sat on the edge of Fanny's bed and tried to read her face in the darkness.

The girl sat up, hugging a quilt tightly about her. She was still trembling, not so much from the cold as from awaking to find a man in her cabin. And then Cotton's demand had frightened her even more.

She shook her head. "I can't, Cotton. I just can't."

"Hell, all I'm askin' is for you to go down there and poke around a little. You don't even have to ask questions if you don't want to."

Fanny shuddered. The last time she had played spy in Gallatin had ended in tragedy; she still became nauseous when she thought about the three days and nights she spent captive in the Union officers' hotel room.

But as horrible as that had been, it was not the only reason she was reluctant to consider a venture into the tent city that Paine had established for the families of his black soldiers. There was death and sickness there. People were beginning to call the campground the "pestilence house of Gallatin."

She swallowed hard. "I jist can't do it, Cotton. I'm sorry."

Cotton walked to the door and put his hand on the latch.

"Cotton?" He turned toward her "Why is it so important fo' you to find out who killed Miss Harper?" Cotton opened the door. "You must have a reason," she insisted.

Cotton walked outside and closed the door behind him. He had just seated himself in the saddle when Fanny darted from the cabin.

"How will I get word to you?" she asked.

"I'll show up here one night," he said. "I don't know when, but I'll be here."

Fanny nodded and turned to go inside.

"Fanny," Cotton said as she stepped over the threshold. She turned toward him.

"I loved her."

Christmas at Park Hill was filled with disappointment for the Drews. Mrs. Drew and Angela watched the driveway constantly, but Colonel Drew did not appear. Anxiety was plain on Mrs. Drew's face, but Clayton saw something else on Angela's: relief. And he wondered who she was relieved for: her mother? Colonel Drew? or himself?

Clayton stayed away from the house—and Angela—as much as possible, spending most of his time at Fort Gibson, planning at length with Captain Hawkins for his intended trip to Texas in search of cattle. Hawkins, a Texan himself, made Austin, Taylor, the Mustang River, and the rolling prairies come alive for Clayton. So much so that Clayton's original dream to see Texas, the dream that had prompted him to leave college, again became the compelling desire it once was.

"If you can buy cattle at San Antonio," Hawkins said, "an' drive them to the coast, you might find a ship willin' to take 'em around the Florida Keys and up to Charleston or Norfolk. That's about the only chance you got, Harris."

It was enough.

On New Year's Day, Clayton told Mrs. Drew that he could wait no longer for the colonel.

"Clayton," said Mrs. Drew as he lifted himself into the saddle, "you are always welcome at Park Hill. I hope that you will do us the honor of stopping here when you return from Texas."

Angela made no effort to hide her elation at his leave-taking. She stood on the porch and watched him ride west, silently praying that Park Hill had seen the last of him.

In Nashville, Tennessee, on the twentieth day of January, 1864, Ulysses S. Grant, spurred by a letter he had received from an old acquaintance, was investigating a high-ranking Federal officer. He was infuriated by his discoveries; the West Point graduate, Brigadier General Eleazer A. Paine, was entirely unfit to command a post.

Grant strode into the office of his adjutant, General Thomas. "How long have you known what Paine has been doing?" He slammed Paine's file down on Thomas' desk top.

Thomas calmly lit a cheroot and handed it to the general. "I've known for a good while, U.S., but before you go making an issue of Paine's actions, remember that he's a close associate of Governor Johnson."

Grant puffed angrily at the cigar, emitting clouds of blue smoke. "I don't care who he's close to; the man's a black mark against every officer in the United States Army."

"I agree," Thomas returned, taking a long draw on his own cigar, then blowing a deep puff toward the ceiling.

Grant sat on the edge of Thomas' desk. "I believe that we should relieve the general of his . . . kingdom and reassign him to the command of a brigade on the bloodiest front line we can find."

General Thomas shook his head and looked at Grant. "Now, U.S.," he said, "you don't think I'd allow an officer of his caliber to command at the front, do you? Why, some of our own men would shoot him in the back."

Grant nodded. "Exactly."

Thomas continued as though Grant hadn't spoken: "The thing to do is to have the general's conduct inquired into and his position fixed according to desserts."

Grant ran his fingers angrily through his beard. "Then, by God, court-martial him."

Oddly enough, even though the commanding general of the United States Army ordered Paine removed from command, politics still played an important role in military decisions, and the only obvious change in Paine's power structure was a slight reduction in the number of Union troops under his command at Gallatin.

Fanny had been in Freedman's Town almost three weeks and as yet had neither heard nor seen anything that might enlighten Cotton; and in truth, she did not expect to.

Carrying an oaken water bucket, she picked her way carefully around the garbage and exposed cess that was everywhere one stepped and squatted beside a ragged field tent that she shared with a contraband woman named Sadie and her five children. Fanny set the heavy bucket beside the open cook fire, then thrust her cold hands toward the flames.

Her face was smudged with soot and grime, and her coat and skirts were stained with mud, grease, and worse. When her hands had thawed enough that they began to ache, she painfully adjusted the bandanna that hid her ash-blond curls.

Through the thin canvas of the tent, she could hear the wheezing cough of Freedom, Sadie's youngest child, and the mother's crooning voice as she tried to soothe the baby. Fanny picked up a tin mess kit from beside the fire, poured water into it, then dropped in a handful of well-used sassafras roots. Carefully she placed the container over the flames.

The baby was dying with a disease she had never heard of before—the army called it diphtheria—and although the sassafras might not help one whit, at least she felt a little less helpless to be doing something.

Fanny looked around at the threadbare army tents that General Paine had so graciously bestowed on the black people who had come in from the surrounding plantations. Adequate housing, he called it. Adequate housing? Fanny smiled bitterly. The tent city was a filthy pigsty made up of better-than-nothing shelters, less-than-nothing food, and absolutely nonexistent medical care or supplies. Firewood was rationed, blankets were limited to two per family, and there was even a water allowance: one bucket per day for each tent.

Nor had the able-bodied black men who had joined the Union Army been stationed at Gallatin as they had been promised. Instead, they had been marched to Chattanooga, their families left to fend for themselves at Freedman's Town.

As a result, prostitution flourished, as did sickness and social disease; rape and physical abuse were common, as was child molestation. Old people succumbed to exposure; infants died of malnutrition; misery abounded in all aspects of life. Many slaves went back to their masters. But the ones who stayed were free—General Paine said they were.

Fanny lifted the mess tin, wishing her hands wouldn't

shake so, and poured the contents into the Mason jar that served as a drinking glass. The liquid was pink-tinted and weak.

Drawing the tent flaps aside, she was assailed by the stench of sickness that rushed from the small enclosure.

At the rear of the tent, nineteen-year-old Sadie sat on a mildewed army blanket, the baby pressed to her exposed breast. Sitting on the damp ground were her four older children, ranging from two years old to six.

The woman rocked the baby and hummed softly.

"Sadie," Fanny said, clutching the tent pole for support, "we've got to try to force a little tea down her." The woman turned her body away in a protective gesture and her eyes cut threateningly at Fanny.

"Please," Fanny insisted, extending the Mason jar. Then she froze; the baby was pressed tightly against Sadie's nipple, but she was not suckling.

Fanny handed the tea to the oldest child and walked out of the tent. She inhaled deeply, but the very air itself was tainted with the odor of mankind at its lowest ebb.

She struck out toward the Federal guard shack that for health reasons had been moved one hundred yards beyond the perimeter of the camp. By the time she neared the shack, she could hardly place one foot in front of the other. Staggering to a howitzer that was pointed toward the camp, she slumped heavily against the cannon's barrel.

A guard stepped out of the board-and-batten building twenty yards beyond the howitzer. "Get away from that gun, woman," he ordered.

Fanny tried to push herself erect, but she could not find the strength.

The guard eyed her critically. "You sick or somethin'?"

"Yes," she said, gripping the barrel tighter, "I think so . . . but it's not me, Massa, that I come about." She hesitated; her thoughts were becoming incoherent. "I live at tent one-fifty-nine. A chile just died there. She had . . . diphtheria."

The soldier backed up a step and drew his revolver. "Just stay where you are," he warned. "Don't come no closer— not one step—or I'll shoot you."

"Please, Massa," Fanny cried, drawing herself slowly along the cannon to its carriage. "The mama's sick, the children are sick. We need help . . . please help us."

The soldier took another step backward. "I'll shoot!"

Fanny clung to the gun-carriage wheel and stared at him. Then her leaden eyes lifted beyond him to three people who had ridden up to the shack and were dismounting.

"Patrick," she whimpered, and lurched toward Patrick, Butler, and Mandy.

"I told you not to take another step," the soldier shouted, raising and cocking his pistol.

Cotton knocked on Cragfont's front door. Susie swung it wide.

"Well, I'll swan," she cried. "Come in, Cotton, come in. Granny! Mama! It's Cotton!"

Cotton strode self-consciously into the parlor. As many times as he had accompanied Clayton to Cragfont, he had never before set foot in the parlor.

Bowing awkwardly to Mrs. Winchester, then to Malvinia, and finally to Lettie, he said, "I just happened to be nearby an' thought I'd pay you-all a visit."

"Well, we're proud that you did, Cotton," the old lady said. "Won't you sit down?"

"No'm," Cotton returned. "I'll only be here a minute." He glanced at the doorway, expecting Fanny to enter.

"If you're looking for Fanny, she's not back from Gallatin yet," Mrs. Winchester said. "An' quite frankly, I'm worried about her. She should have returned a week ago."

Concern marred Cotton's face. It had been a long shot, sending Fanny to Gallatin alone, but he'd had no choice; if he had sent Rufus, the Federals might well have recognized him. "Mrs. Winchester," he said, striding toward the door, "quick as it gets dark out, me an' Rufus are headin' for Gallatin. We'll bring her home, ma'am."

Lettie caught him at the threshold and took his hand in both of hers. It was the first time she had ever touched him. "I am sorry for what happened, Cotton, truly I am. Fanny told me about Miss Harper."

Cotton was taken aback by Lettie's sincerity. "Thanks, Miss Lettie." Then his eyes narrowed at her. "Paine arrested you, didn't he? Something about your father?"

Lettie nodded. "He questioned me about a boat that sinks under water . . . a thing he called a submarine. He said a Mr. Hunley, who used to live near here, and my father were building one. Paine's crazy, Cotton, crazy as a bed-bug."

Cotton's hands tightened on hers. "When they released you, who escorted you home?"

Lettie blushed and attempted to remove her hands.

"Tell me what happened, Lettie. It's important."

"The general's son, Captain Phelps Paine, brought me home in the general's closed carriage."

"Did he rape you, Lettie?"

She shook her head. "No. I will not go so far as to say that he was a perfect gentleman, but he did not rape me."

Cotton sighed. "Thank God."

It was near dusk when he galloped his horse up the drive to Summerset. And less than thirty minutes later, with Rufus riding double, he stretched the animal into a hard run toward Gallatin.

Fanny fell to her knees and reached out toward Patrick imploringly.

"Patrick," she rasped, "please help me . . ."

Patrick studied Fanny in the gathering darkness, but it was a long minute before he recognized her.

"You know that wench?" Butler asked Patrick.

"She's that Fanny girl from Cragfont," Patrick said. He turned away and walked into the guardhouse.

"If she comes any closer," the guard said, "I'll be forced to shoot her. She's got that diphtheria disease that's killing niggers all over the camp."

Butler took a step backward, but Mandy walked over to Fanny and squatted beside the girl, who had sunk to the ground and lay there breathing shallowly.

"Is it sho' nuff you?" Mandy prodded Fanny with her riding crop.

"Mandy," Fanny whispered, "please help me."

Mandy grinned. "I wouldn't touch yo' wid a ten-foot po'. I never did like yo', Fanny. I jist want yo' to know that a'fore yo' die."

Fanny looked up at Mandy, trying to focus her eyes. "Please, Mandy . . ."

"Go to hell, where yo' b'long," Mandy said. "An' if'n I weren't already sho' you was goin' to die, I'd jist shoot yore head off like I done that sho'-nuff white girl."

Mandy's words raced through Fanny like a white-hot flame, hotter even than the fever that burned in her brain. She reached out and caught Mandy's long skirt. "Murderer . . . murderer," she whispered.

The black girl sprang to her feet and kicked Fanny's hand free. Running her hand into her coat pocket, she drew her revolver and pointed it at Fanny's head.

"Murderer," Fanny said again. Her eyes rolled back into her head and her cheek dropped against the frozen ground.

"Git over here, Mandy," Butler ordered. "You tryin' to ketch the plague too? Put that pistol up an' git away from her, for Christ's sake."

Mandy's fingers toyed with the revolver, undecided.

"Git over here," Butler repeated. "Now!"

"She's done daid anyway," Mandy said, shoving the gun back into her pocket.

The guard motioned to a group of onlookers who had been drawn from their tents by the commotion. "Some of you niggers pick this woman up and take her to tent one-fifty-nine." No one moved. He raised his pistol and aimed it at the crowd. "I order you to move this woman away from here."

Several elderly men came forward. They were terrified of touching the diseased girl, but they were more afraid of disobeying a direct order from a white man.

At nine o'clock that night Cotton tethered his horse a half-mile east of Gallatin and sent Rufus the remainder of the way to the compound on foot.

At every tent that Rufus approached, he encountered the same answer: They didn't know anyone named Fanny, but maybe someone in the next tent could help him.

Rufus jumped to the top of a ragged camelbacked trunk beside one of the tents and looked over the tops of the hundreds of shelters that made up Freedman's Town. She could be in any one of them, he thought frantically. Or she could be in Gallatin, or she could be . . . he refused to say, even to himself, that she could be dead.

Jumping down, he walked to the next tent. He would check every last one of them if it took all night.

It nearly did. It was three o'clock in the morning when he flung aside the canvas doors of tent one-fifty-nine and woke the sleeping occupants.

"I'm lookin' for a Cragfont woman named Fanny," he said to the young woman who had raised herself to peer at him in the dim light penetrating the interior through the open flaps. "A pretty mulatto girl, maybe seventeen, eighteen years old? Kind of blond-haired?"

The woman didn't answer. Rufus backed from the tent and dropped the flaps into place. Taking a deep breath to rid himself of the stench of sickness, he started toward the next tent.

Behind him, a little boy darted out of the flaps. "Dey done come an' taken her an' my baby sister 'way," he said.

Rufus dropped to one knee and gripped the boy by his shoulders. "Who come an' took her away?"

"De boogermen," the boy said. "Dey come and got my lil' sister, and dey got de Cragfont woman, an' dey put 'em in a wagon 'long wif de other daid folks."

"Dead?" Rufus' stomach convulsed. "She can't be dead!"

The whites of the boy's eyes shone in the cold moonlight. "My lil' sister was sho' nuff daid, but de Cragfont woman weren't. Dey taken her anyhow."

"When? How long ago?"

The boy shrugged. "Jist a few minutes, I reckon. Maybe an hour."

"Where did they take your sister and Fanny? Can you tell me that?"

The boy nodded. "Dey take 'em to a place dey call a graveyard, but it ain't. It jist a big ditch been shoveled out'n a field . . ."

"You think you can find it in the dark?"

The boy nodded again.

Rufus followed the child to an overgrown field that bordered on Station Camp Creek, two miles southwest of Gallatin. Parting the bushes, he peered at a wagon parked beside a long, open trench. A soldier, sitting well away from the ditch, was directing two Negro men who were shoveling dirt out onto the bank.

Even as Rufus watched, the men thrust their spades into the turned earth and walked to the wagon.

When they dragged a small body from the conveyance and dropped it into the open grave, Rufus turned to the boy and ordered him to go home. Then, stepping through the bushes, he squared his shoulders and walked toward the wagon.

The soldier jumped to his feet and pointed his rifle at Rufus.

"What are you doin' out here?" he demanded.

"I done come to see de buryin'," Rufus said. "Yo's done got my kinfolk in dat wagon."

"Those people got diphtheria. The whole camp's got it. You too, probably. Don't come no closer."

"Naw, sir." Rufus moved to the wagon. "I ain't got no diphtheria." He jumped up on the hub of the rear wheel and peered into the wagon bed.

Six bodies were covered with a canvas sheet. Ignoring the protests of the guard, Rufus tore back the cover. Fanny, her breath rattling in her chest, lay shuddering and twitching between the corpses of two aged women.

"She's not dead," he said through his teeth. "The boy was right, she's not dead."

"Now you look here," the guard said. "I don't like this job no more'n you, but the only way to stop an epidemic before it gets out of hand is to get rid of the infected bodies as quick as possible."

"But she ain't dead!"

"She will be before morning." The guard dropped his rifle butt to the ground and leaned on the barrel. "I'm sorry, mister, but that's the way it is."

Rufus looked across the wagon to the open trench. His stomach churned, and nausea rose in his throat. "How many live folks have you buried?" he called to the grave diggers.

The men told him they hadn't buried any who were still breathing. But he knew they were lying.

Rufus wasn't aware that he had moved; he would never remember clambering to the wagon seat and whipping the mules into startled flight. Nor would he ever know that the cap failed to detonate in the guard's rifle. All he knew was that he had to get Fanny away from there. He drove the team of mules down Main Street as though the devil himself were riding the tailgate.

Cotton was already mounted when the wagon rumbled into view.

"They'll be right behind me!" Rufus yelled, snatching back on the reins, sawing the bridle bits while at the same time slamming his foot against the brake pole and throwing his weight against it.

Even before the mules stopped prancing, Rufus was over the seat and into the wagon bed.

Lifting Fanny into his arms, he hefted her to his shoulder and climbed down over the rear wheel.

"She's got diphtheria or somethin'," he said, lifting the unconscious girl across the pommel of Cotton's saddle. Then, catching Cotton's hand, he swung up onto the horse's rump. Cotton sank his spurs deep and the animal sprang into motion.

Four miles east of Gallatin, Cotton turned his horse off the Hartsville Pike onto a lane that disappeared into a stand of black oak trees.

"Mr. Cotton," Rufus said, "you know as well as me that this is the way to Oakland. Dr. Mentlo don't work on no slaves."

"He'll work on Fanny," Cotton said, thinly.

Cotton rapped hard on Oakland's front door. When no light appeared, he drew his revolver and pounded harder.

"All right," yelled Mentlo. "I heard you the first time."

The old doctor did not come to the door. But a moment later, Rufus, standing beside the horse, caught the movement as the parlor drapes were cautiously drawn aside. "Dr. Mentlo," he called, "it's me, Rufus, from Summerset."

"What is it, Rufus?" came Mentlo's voice. "Don't you know it's not even daylight?"

Cotton put his hand on the porch railing and leaped to the ground. "Open up, Doc," he said, pushing his face close to the window. "We got a sick woman out here . . . diphtheria."

"Is that you, Cotton?" Mentlo used the tail of his nightshirt to wipe frost from the windowpane.

"Hell, yes, it's me! An' you know damned well I wouldn't bother you if it wasn't necessary."

"Hold your horses," Mentlo said. "Just hold your horses." The drape fell into place and a moment later the front door opened.

"Who you talkin' about, Cotton?" Mentlo asked, stepping onto the porch. "Who's got diphtheria?"

"Fanny, from over at Cragfont."

The doctor hesitated, then said, "Get her out to my office an' lay her near the fireplace. Stack a couple of logs on the grate while you're about it." He turned and started into the house. "Rufus, take that horse to the barn an' hide it. Not the stock barn, the tobacco barn."

Cotton had just laid Fanny on the floor before the hearth when Mentlo appeared with a coal-oil lamp. Setting the lamp on a nearby table, he knelt beside Fanny and thumbed back her eyelids.

"Expose her chest for me, Cotton," he said, rising and rummaging in a heavy trunk that sat near the door.

Cotton caught the neckline of Fanny's blouse and ripped it open to the waist.

"For Christ's sake," the doctor said, "you could have unbuttoned the thing."

Mentlo placed a conical instrument between Fanny's breasts, then moved it over her upper body, listening carefully.

Rufus opened the door and stepped inside.

"Who said she had diphtheria?" Mentlo demanded.

"The Yankees down at Freedman's Town," Rufus said. "They was fixin' to bury her."

"*Bury* her?" Mentlo looked over his spectacles at Rufus. "Don't them damned Yankee physicians know anything?" He sighed. "They probably didn't even examine her."

"What is it, Doc?" Cotton asked.

"This girl hasn't got diphtheria. She's got gallopin' pneumonia." The doctor pushed his spectacles to the top of his head. "I'm not sure we can save her." He stripped off Fanny's clothes while Rufus and Cotton moved a cot close to the fire. The three of them lifted the sick girl onto it.

Mentlo walked to a cabinet. Taking out a bottle, he poured straight shots of whiskey into three glasses and passed one to each of the two men. The third he downed before starting to work on Fanny.

"How bad is she, Doc?" Cotton asked.

"Pretty bad, I'm afraid. Her lungs are full of phlegm . . . she's drowning herself."

Cotton walked to the window. Dawn was breaking, but all he could see was the fear on Fanny's face when he had insisted that she go to Freedman's Town.

Mentlo heated a pan of water and bathed Fanny's face and body. Then he rubbed camphorated oil onto her neck and bosom and covered her with a heavy blanket. Taking an hourglass from the cabinet, he set it on the mantel and told Rufus to give Fanny a quarter-turn every sixty minutes.

"Make her cough," he instructed, "and when she coughs, be sure she spits it up. That's important, Rufus." Mentlo wiped his hands on a towel. "That girl was the best nurse I had when we cleaned up after you boys whipped Johnson's Cavalry in sixty-two. All them Winchester women, even Lettie, pitched in, but Fanny was the best."

"She was doin' me a favor when she caught this pneumonia stuff, Doc," Cotton said without turning from the window. "Don't let her die."

"Damn you, Cotton," Mentlo shouted. "I'm not God, I'm just a physician."

Cotton spun toward him. "You're the closest thing we got to God," he said.

Mentlo took a deep breath and exhaled through his teeth. "You put too much burden on me, Cotton."

Clayton Harris gazed across the swollen waters of the Red River. Texas was on the other side. Texas, at last!

Forcing his mount into the current, he dropped out of the saddle and caught his horse's tail, kicking his feet to help the animal along.

When the two of them pulled themselves onto Texas soil, Clayton scooped up a handful of dirt and let it trickle through his fingers. He had the sensation of coming home. He had no idea of when or how, but the conviction was too strong to be ignored: He would become his own man in Texas.

Rufus quarter-turned Fanny every hour. He worked with infinite patience, for—unknown to anyone but himself—

he was in love with her, and had been ever since the day he had held her, bruised and battered, in his arms at the Johnny B. Hotel.

And the knowledge that she idolized his master made no difference. None at all.

Fanny's rattling, shallow wheeze erupted into another fit of deep-chested coughing. Rufus held her head over the slop jar and commanded her to spit. This time she found the strength to do so. Easing her head back onto the pillow, he blotted the perspiration from her face. "I'm freezing," she whimpered as new beads formed on her brow.

Rufus built up the fire until the mantel fairly smoked, which brought a tirade from Dr. Mentlo when he came in.

And so the hours wore on, with little change until the third day, the seventh of February, when Fanny opened her eyes and gazed up at the whitewashed ceiling. She thought she was dead. But then a pain burst in her chest and she bent double in a spasm of coughing. And she knew it was only wishful thinking.

Rufus held her head over the bucket. "Spit the poison out, Fanny," he urged. "Cough it up an' spit it out. Dr. Mentlo says it's the only way you're goin' to get well."

"It hurts so bad, Rufus," she murmured, but she spat. Then she drifted again into a coma-like sleep.

When Cotton arrived that evening, he caught Rufus' hand and shook it thoroughly. Mentlo had told them that now Fanny had a fighting chance.

For the first time in seventy-two hours, Rufus slept. Cotton sat beside Fanny's bed, and each time she moaned or turned, he was there waiting to make her spit. It was noon the next day before she gained full consciousness again.

Kneeling beside the bed, Cotton took her hand in his. "You damn near died, Fanny."

"Never tell a patient that, Cotton," cried Mentlo as he placed his hearing horn on Fanny's chest. "You'll scare the girl to death." Mentlo listened, then smiled at Fanny. "Sounds much better."

"Fanny?" said Cotton. The girl turned her face to him. "Did you find out anything?" She looked blank. "About . . . Willie's murder."

Fanny closed her eyes. She had made tea for a sick child.

She could not remember whose child. She was aware that something else had occurred, something important. But the harder she tried to remember, the more fleeting it became.

She shook her head weakly. "I'm sorry, Cotton. Nobody knew a thing."

"No," he said, smoothing her damp hair off her forehead, "it's me who's sorry. I nearly caused you to die . . . for nothin'."

On February twelfth, Cotton borrowed Dr. Mentlo's buggy and drove Fanny to Cragfont. He fussed over her as though she were an invalid, carrying her into the big house and placing her in a bed that had been prepared for her in the sewing room. If Fanny had not been so weak, she would have reveled at finally attaining her very own room in the mansion. Her pale cheeks did show a bit of color, however, when Delphy brought supper to her on a tray and with Cotton and the Winchester women watching, spoon-fed her.

And on that same day, in a Dallas saloon, Clayton Harris heard about the Confederate victory in September, 1863, at a place called Chickamauga, near Chattanooga, Tennessee.

He was about to drink to the victory when the bartender said: "Don't celebrate too quick, Master. 'Cause in November, General Bragg lost nearly nine thousand men at the Battle of Lookout Mountain." Clayton didn't hear the rest. Had Cotton been there?

The evening of March twenty-first was balmy for Texas. Clayton Harris was camped beside the Mustang River, forty miles north of Austin. He drank his coffee and gazed at the rolling hills and lush prairies stretched out below. It was a magnificent sight, one that caused his heart to swell. Turning, he walked over to the three stones he had placed on top of one another to mark his claim. Then he frowned, for intermingling with his thoughts for a ranch came a vision of Angela Drew. Why did he think of her, he wondered.

He camped at the Mustang River until his provisions ran out. Saddling his horse, he headed for Austin, sixty miles away. It was the second day of April.

When he reached Austin the following afternoon, he learned that on November 27, 1863, General John Hunt Morgan had been killed at Greenville, Tennessee. For the second time in his life, Clayton got drunk; Morgan had been a friend.

On May 5, 1864, Cotton, wearing a captured Federal uniform, raced his mount up the tracks two miles south of the tunnel he had helped demolish three years before; a Federal construction train was backing slowly toward Gallatin, checking and repairing track and trestle damage.

Cotton reined his horse in alongside the slow-moving locomotive. "We've got track torn up north of the tunnel," he yelled, attempting a Northern accent.

The engineer leaned from his window. "We just came through there. The track's fine."

"The telegrapher at Franklin, Kentucky, says it ain't. He's holdin' the southbound 'til it's fixed."

Shaking his head, the engineer brought the train to a halt, then threw the throttle into forward. "There wasn't any problem with that section of track two hours ago," he shouted at Cotton as the big wheels of the locomotive spun several times on the polished rails before catching. Then, with a hiss of steam and the clanking of cars, the train lurched forward and gathered speed toward the tunnel. Cotton did not follow; he had no desire to witness the carnage.

A mile up the track, a southbound train carrying three hundred men of the 10th Indiana Cavalry, many of whom were riding atop the cars, barreled toward Gallatin.

The collision was earthshaking. And when the smoke and steam cleared, over ninety persons had been killed outright or were mortally injured. The men riding the roofs escaped with minor injuries, for at the last moment they threw their weapons aside and jumped free.

The Louisville Daily Journal wrote: "The fiendish-hearted scoundrels, the cold, calculating assassins, should be hunted down with the greatest of energy, and when caught, drawn and quartered, and their foul carcasses hung up to dry and bleach in the glaring sun of day—a warning to all villains engaged in such fiendish atrocities."

Cotton tried to pass the editorial off as nothing more than a Union paper's rantings, but he could not. He knew that Willie would have agreed with every word written there.

Cotton threw the newspaper aside. "Damn it, Ellis," he said. "This ain't my kind of game."

"It ain't no game, Cotton."

"Yeah," Cotton said, "it is a game, Ellis, and it's gettin' out of hand. After we wrecked that train last week, Paine arrested Dr. Franklin's daughter, sayin' she was harboring enemies of the Federal Government. Hell, Ellis, the enemy was her father, who had quit the army to aid his ailing wife."

"So?"

"It's a pattern, Ellis. Every time we kill a Federal soldier, Paine arrests a Confederate soldier's wife or daughter, just like he did Willie. It's almost like we're somehow playin' into his hands."

"They didn't kill Franklin's daughter."

"Naw," Cotton said, looking hard at Harper, "but they might as well have."

Harper shrugged. "We'll catch one of Paine's men an' cut his cod off. That'll show Paine he can't go 'round deflowerin' Southern women."

Cotton shook his head. Trying to reason with Harper was like talking to an anvil. "An' then he'll rape or kill two more of our women," he said under his breath.

CHAPTER 32

General Paine lifted his tumbler of whiskey to his lips and sipped it slowly, savoring the taste as though it were victory.

"Captain Nyath," he said, pouring the officer his second full glass of liquor, "take a detachment and ride out to Cragfont. One way or another, old lady Winchester has acquired three horses. Confiscate them."

Nyath killed the glass of whiskey and wiped his mouth with the back of his hand. He threw the general a sloppy salute and walked crookedly toward the door. Paine took another sip of whiskey. He would rather have sent Butler to do the job, but Butler couldn't confiscate horses in the name of the Federal Government.

At Cragfont, Nyath and several troopers of the 13th Tennessee Cavalry forced their way into the house. Brushing Fanny aside as she tried to block the door, the captain strode into the parlor.

Mrs. Winchester laid aside her knitting and rose angrily. "I suppose you have an explanation for invading my house without permission?"

Nyath leered at Lettie, who sat frozen beside her Grandmother, but his words were directed to the old lady.

"General Paine gave us permission to go anywhere we damn well please. The general demands that you bring forth all your horses and saddles and—"

"Get out of my house," Mrs. Winchester interrupted, walking toward the man. "And don't ever set foot here again."

The captain laughed and strode over to Lettie. Catching her arm, he forcibly lifted her from the divan and pulled her against him.

"All right!" cried the old lady. "I'll have the horses brought around."

For a moment she was terrified that he would make good his silent threat against Lettie. But he pushed the girl aside and turned to Susie, who had been watching in wide-eyed silence. "Get into the kitchen and tell your cook to fix us some supper," he ordered.

Susie edged past him, then raced down the hall toward the kitchen.

"Chatty! Chatty!" she cried, running into the room. "There's a whole passel of Yankees in the house, an' they're demandin' something to eat."

"Lawd, Lawd," Chatty exclaimed, wringing her hands, "I jist knowed som'pin' bad gwine to happen; I jist knowed it. Las' night I done drempt o' rats de size of o'possums in de smokehouse."

"But the smokehouse is empty, Chatty," Susie said.

"I knows, I knows," the old woman said. " 'Dream o' rats in an empty larder means de rest o' de year gwine t' be harder. I jist knowed som'pin' bad gwine t' happen."

"Well, you better find them Yankees somethin' to eat," said Susie.

Ignoring Nyath, Mrs. Winchester crossed to Lettie and took her in her arms. "Did he hurt you, child?" Lettie shook her head. "Thank the Lord," the old woman breathed. "You've been hurt enough." Then she laid her head against Lettie's cheek and wept.

Lettie's eyes filled with tears; it was the first time she had ever seen her grandmother cry. It dawned on her then how very much the old lady had aged in the past few months.

"Please don't cry, Granny," Lettie said. "Please don't cry."

* * *

Mrs. Winchester did not complain to General Paine. Instead, she wrote a letter to Governor Johnson, in Nashville, charging that Captain Nyath had "entered the house drunk, had stolen three horses, one saddle, a pair of scissors, a shotgun, and thirteen dollars in cash."

She also stated that if steps were not taken to rectify the situation immediately, she would go to Washington and address President Lincoln in person.

Johnson ordered an investigation.

General Paine rose to Nyath's defense, swearing that the "captain was not drunk, had taken only one horse and saddle, and had demanded supper which was at first refused but later provided." Paine countercharged with the standard excuse that the family had harbored guerrillas. It didn't work. Governor Johnson ordered Captain Nyath's arrest.

Although Nyath's court-martial was nothing more than a military farce, the fact that one of Paine's officers had been forced to defend his actions was the first chink in Paine's armor.

Cotton investigated every rumor of murder or rape in and around Sumner County. But the weeks dragged by and he was no closer to solving Willie's death than he had been on the day he discovered her body. Still, he felt that he could not leave a stone unturned or a lead unchecked. On July 4, 1864, he rode to Villine's Inn at Cross Plains, Tennessee, some twenty miles north of Gallatin; a man and his son had been brutally murdered just outside of town, each shot twice in the head. But William Villine, who knew everyone in Robertson County, was unable to shed any light on the killings.

On the plains surrounding San Antonio, Clayton found cattle by the thousands. He devised a plan to drive three thousand head to Corpus Christi and then ship them by steamer across the Gulf and up the coast to Charleston, South Carolina. It seemed simple enough until he tried to put the plan into action.

Not one man was willing to make the month-long cattle drive to the coast. "Mister," said one whom Clayton approached, "the Apache will kill the cattle and burn the drovers over a slow fire."

For days Clayton rode to the outlying ranches, but the answer was always the same: "No thanks."

Finally he found a handful of vaqueros who had ridden in from Franklin and who agreed to hire on. But before the cattle could be rounded up, word came that the Union Navy had blockaded the Texas coast and was occupying Galveston and all ports south.

Packing his bedroll, Clayton turned his horse north and headed back the way he had come, toward the Mustang River, then on to Fort Gibson to report his failure to Captain Hawkins.

On August 10, 1864, Cotton rode to Goodlettsville, eighteen miles west of Gallatin. Three of the Elam sisters had been arrested by Paine for attempting to wreck a train. Word had it that the girls had been molested. Cotton questioned the oldest sister, who was sixteen, but once again he ran up against a stone wall; although the girls had been held at Trousedale Place and questioned at length, they had neither heard nor seen anything that might lead him to Willie's murderer. Cotton was despondent.

Clayton Harris spent the month of August on the Mustang, familiarizing himself with the country for miles around. He became acquainted with some folks named Williamson who lived in a community that was little more than a wide spot in the road some ten miles from his claim. He learned that the land he coveted could be homesteaded. Homesteaded; again Angela Drew stole into his thoughts and he wondered why he associated her with land, permanence, a home. Then he laughed; she had told him that her Cherokee name meant "Woman of the Earth." That had to be the reason. Still, he had the nagging sensation that that wasn't it at all.

Clayton left "Three Stones," as he called his claim, and rode toward Oklahoma and Fort Gibson. He was eager to resign his commission and head back to Austin to file his claim properly.

On September 2, 1864, he was forced to stop at the small town of Waco, on the Brazos River, to have his horse re-shod. While at the blacksmith shop, he learned some disturbing news that made him even more anxious to get to Fort Gibson. As the farrier hammered out the horseshoes, he told Clayton, without the least hint of shame, that he was a Confederate deserter.

"Yes, sir," the smith said, "I was with General Lee for over two years. We fought lots of battles, but in May, when we went against that butcher Grant at what Lee called "the Wilderness"—an' it sure as hell was—we found ourselves fightin' a different war than we'd been used to. Grant wouldn't quit! He just kept sendin' men at us. We killed seventeen thousand of his soldiers; seventeen thousand in one battle! A week later, Grant come at us again, at a place called Spottsylvania. We sent eighteen thousand more Yankees to hell. Still Grant nagged at us—nippin' here, bitin' there—till finally, on the second day of June, he formed up his troops and hit us at a place called Cold Harbor. Hell, that battle lasted four or five days. We must have slaughtered another eighteen to twenty thousand men."

The farrier stopped and looked at Clayton. "I'd had all the killin' I could stomach, mister. I packed up an' come home."

After a long pause, Clayton asked, "How many men did Lee lose?"

The blacksmith drove a nail into the horse's hoof. "Last count I had was somewhere near thirty-five thousand. But that's thirty-five thousand men who can't be replaced. We're losing this war, mister. Yes, sir, in spite of the battles we're winnin', we're losin' this war."

The farrier's words struck Clayton like a sledgehammer. Deep in his brain Angela Drew's words shouted at him: "It's men like you who will lose this war for us, Harris." Men like me? he thought, or men who refuse to fight? He wondered if he were using the Oath of Allegiance as an excuse. No! He was not, nor would he allow Angela Drew to shame his integrity. Still, her accusation left him shaken. The more he thought about it, the more he realized that he was honor-bound to see the war through to its end.

"Well, mister," the farrier said, "guess that does it. You owe me four dollars."

"All I've got is Jeff Davis," Clayton said, counting out

four Confederate one-dollar bills. "I hope it's still worth something."

The farrier eyed the money distastefully, but he took it.

On November 15, 1864, John H. Taylor, of Hendersonville, twelve miles west of Gallatin, was attacked and his son was murdered, shot through the temple.

"Cotton," said Harper as Cotton saddled his horse, "you been runnin' that critter ragged for months an' you ain't turned up nothin'. An' if you ride to Hendersonville, it'll just be another wild-goose chase. Face up to the facts; Cousin Willie's killin' was somethin' that just happened. That's the way war is."

Cotton lifted himself into his saddle, then sat there unmoving. The truth was that he too had finally decided that Willie's murder would go unsolved. Sighing, he swung down and walked back into the cabin.

At Hendersonville, Mr. Taylor wrote in his diary: "There was not a uniform in the bunch. I'm probably wrong, but I'd have sworn the one who killed Paul was a black woman."

On November seventeenth, Harper ordered his men to mount up; he had heard that a Union work crew was at South Tunnel.

At the tunnel, Harper's band captured five black Union soldiers and two white railroad laborers. Harper forced the captives to cut the telegraph wire and to rip up several sections of track.

Still not satisfied, he took a double-edged ax from the laborers' toolbox and walked to the mouth of the tunnel, where the prisoners were sitting with their heads between their knees.

"What are we gon' to do with these men?" Cotton asked indicating the prisoners. "Turn 'em loose?"

"No," said Harper, "I'm goin' to split their crow-complected heads. We're gon' to teach these black bastards that they can't go around actin' like soldiers."

Cotton caught Harper's arm. "You wait just a goddamned minute, Ellis! Those men *are* soldiers."

Harper slapped Cotton's hand aside. "Since when did you turn nigger-lover?"

"I ain't no nigger-lover an' you know it. But let me set you straight about somethin'. Some of the finest folks I know are niggers."

With an icy glare, Harper told Cotton to mind his own business. Then he walked over to the first prisoner.

The hideous murder of the Negro soldiers was reported by *The Nashville Daily Union:* "The guerrillas who are operating in that quarter are not recognized as soldiers; they are robbers and murderers and should be treated as General Sherman says . . . as 'wild beasts.' They show no mercy and none should be shown to them."

General Paine smiled with satisfaction. Governor Johnson would think long and hard before he court-martialed another Union officer. Taking quill in hand, he fired off a dispatch to the governor: "Anyone giving information or any other assistance to guerrillas should be dealt with severely until they fear us as much as they pretend to fear the guerrillas."

Cotton was sick with shame. He was almost glad that Willie was dead for he couldn't have stood for her to know that "wild beasts" applied to him too.

On November twenty-third, Harper captured another work party at the tunnel. This time he marched the prisoners seven miles into the hills. When he called a halt, Cotton rode up to him and demanded, "What are you plannin' on doin' with them, Ellis?"

"What do you reckon?"

Cotton looked deep into Harper's eyes. "I'll tell you what you ain't goin' to do . . . " He eased aside his worn Confederate jumper and rested his hand on the grips of his revolver. "You ain't goin' to butcher 'em."

For a tense minute Harper appraised Cotton. Then he threw back his head and laughed. "You're a real shit-ass, you know that?"

"I reckon."

"If I didn't think so much of you, Cotton, I'd kill you." Harper nodded to the men holding the prisoners. "Turn them loose."

Cotton grinned. He understood what had just passed. And he also knew that if he ever braced Harper again, he would shoot the man dead without so much as a word.

* * *

Clayton rode straight on to Fort Gibson and reported to Captain Hawkins. After relating his intelligence concerning the Federal blockade at Galveston, he got down to business. "Captain, short of bearing arms in a pitched battle, I want to offer my services where I'm needed."

Hawkins studied Clayton for a long minute, then walked over to the table that served as a desk.

Indicating that Clayton join him, he placed his finger on a map of the Oklahoma Indian Territory and traced a line from Fort Gibson, on the Northeast, all the way to Fort Sill, on the Southwest.

"Harris, I need someone to ride to Fort Sill and fetch the payroll for our men here. They haven't been paid in six months and they're gettin' surly as hell. I'd send a detail, but there's a bunch of jayhawkers raisin' cain north of here at Marysville an' we're goin' to have to investigate."

Clayton studied the map. "Sill looks to be about two hundred fifty, maybe three hundred miles from here."

The captain nodded. "And I'm not goin' to lie about it, Harris. The last two couriers I sent were robbed on the return trip. One was killed."

"Indians?"

"Jayhawkers. Deserters. Riffraff. The scum of the earth has come to the Territory to avoid servin' in the war."

Clayton thought that Angela Drew would agree with the Captain wholeheartedly. "I'll need four revolving pistols and another carbine," he said. "When do I leave?"

"The quicker, the better. I'll have the guns waiting for you tomorrow morning."

Clayton walked to the door. "Captain," he said, turning, "has Colonel Drew returned?"

Hawkins shook his head.

Clayton dreaded paying his respects at Park Hill, but he knew that protocol demanded he do so. Taking a deep breath, he knocked on the door.

Angela answered. For a moment Clayton was certain that she would slam the door in his face. "Well," she said as they stared at one another, "the bad penny always returns."

Clayton smiled. "And you are even more beautiful than I remembered."

Although Angela's eyes slitted dangerously, he was not

sorry he had said it; a year had given her a certain hue of maturity that not only emphasized, but strengthened, her beauty.

"Actually," he continued, enjoying her fury, "you are partially responsible for my being here. I have returned to active military duty again, this time in the capacity of special courier for Captain Hawkins. I'm to ride to Fort Sill for the payroll." Angela heard nothing but his first sentence. Angrily she said, "If you will tell me what I said or did to bring you back here, Mr. Harris, I'll see to it that I never make that mistake again."

Clayton blushed. "I was hoping you would approve of my new position."

Before Angela could answer, Mrs. Drew appeared. A moment later Clayton found himself being ushered into the dining room, where dinner was being served.

Angela sipped water from a crystal goblet and appraised him with hostile eyes. He's gained weight, she decided. She was also aware of the summer tan that still shaded his face. Grudgingly she admitted that he was a handsome man— handsome enough that her mother had once visited his bedchamber.

"They'll kill and rob you," she said, setting her glass on the table. "And I will rejoice."

Clayton grinned. "You said that same thing last time I was here, hostiles it was. Who will kill me this time?"

"Jayhawkers . . . road agents . . . Indians." The girl smiled. "It isn't important who kills you, just as long as someone does."

Mrs. Drew rose from the table. "Angela," she said with measured control, "if you cannot be civil to Mr. Harris, then please say nothing at all."

Angela's face paled, and for a second she stared pityingly at her mother. In the next instant anger slashed across her features and she jumped to her feet, confronting her mother.

"Perhaps if you would enlighten me, Mother," she said, "as to why you visited his room last year—"

Mrs. Drew's open palm exploded against the girl's cheek.

Clayton froze, and a deep silence filled the room as the two women stared at one another.

Angela raised her chin stubbornly, but her lips trembled as she spoke. "I won't apologize, Mother. I am not in the wrong. It is the two of you who should apologize." With an air of dignity rare in one so young, she walked toward the door. But halfway there, her aplomb toppled, and pressing her hand to her mouth, she rushed from the room.

Clayton glanced at Mrs. Drew. "Tell her, Mrs. Drew, tell her now."

The woman shook her head. "I can't. I just can't take the chance that the moment she knows that Montclair is dead, she might just curl up and die also."

In spite of Mrs. Drew's offer of his old bedchamber, Clayton rode to Fort Gibson and pitched his bedroll in the garrison stable's hayloft. After rolling into his blankets, he lay there contemplating. No wonder Angela hated him. The sight of her mother coming out of his bedroom that night must have been quite an emotional shock for her. Again he wished that Mrs. Drew dared tell Angela the truth. It was obvious that the girl was dying inside already.

When Captain Hawkins was certain that Clayton was bedded down for the night, he rode to Park Hill despite the lateness of the hour. Charles escorted him into the parlor, where Angela and Mrs. Drew waited.

"Ladies," he said, removing his hat, "I'll come right to the point. I'm sure that Captain Harris—"

"Captain!" Angela exclaimed. "Mr. Harris is a Confederate captain?"

"Yes, ma'am," Hawkins said, surprised. "Didn't you know that he was an officer in Morgan's Cavalry before he was captured?" Angela remained silent. Hawkins continued, "I'm sure that Captain Harris told you of his orders to go to Sill."

The women nodded. "Well," he said, "while I'm certain that Harris will do his best, he's working at a disadvantage. He doesn't know the country between here and Fort Sill. He doesn't know the people, and he's taken the Oath of Allegiance, so he can't even put up any resistance if he's approached by a Federal patrol."

"If he's such a poor risk," Angela interrupted, "why don't you send your own men, Captain?"

Hawkins looked apologetic. "I can't spare one man, Miss Drew, much less a detail."

"Why are you here, Captain?" Mrs. Drew asked.

Hawkins' face reddened. "I am aware, ma'am," he said, "that Miss Drew accompanied Colonel Drew to Fort Sill many times. She knows the trails, and the people between here and there . . . "

"No," Angela said, eyeing the captain coldly. Rising, she started toward the door.

"Hear me out, Miss Drew." When she turned and faced him, the captain said, "I have war correspondence that must be delivered to Fort Sill. I can't entrust it to Captain Harris, because if he were to be stopped and searched . . . but a woman . . . " Clearing his throat, he said, "I believe that if you were to go along, your presence would act as a diversion. Any marauders or Federal troops would not be suspicious of a man and a woman traveling together. The correspondence is crucial, Miss Drew."

"Captain," Mrs. Drew said, "I cannot allow my daughter to accompany Captain Harris unattended to Fort Sill. Why, it would take them three or four weeks to get there and back!"

Angela bristled. "You sent me off with him after cattle."

"The boys were with you."

Not on the way back, Angela thought.

"No, Captain," Mrs. Drew said, "it's out of the question."

She doesn't want me to be alone with him, Angela thought angrily. Aloud she said, "Captain, I will be ready to leave anytime Captain Harris is."

It was still dark, with just a hint of silver edging the soot-black skyline when Clayton led his horse out of the barn at Fort Gibson.

He was surprised to find Angela mounted and waiting.

"What are you doing here?" he asked.

She walked her horse toward him. "How did you know it was me? It's too dark to see."

"The white on your pinto stands out like a sore thumb. Now answer me. What are you doing here?"

"I'm to guide you to Fort Sill." Clayton did not miss the sarcasm in her voice.

"I can find Fort Sill." He lifted himself into his saddle and walked his horse toward the fort's main gate.

"The last two army riders were waylaid," she called after him. "A man and a woman riding together might fool any would-be attackers."

"Go on back to Park Hill, Miss Drew."

Angela nudged her horse up beside his. "I'm going with you, Mr. Harris, and that's that."

"No," Clayton said, "that's not that."

Angrily reigning his horse in before the headquarters building and dismounting, he strode into Captain Hawkins' office.

Rejoining Angela a few minutes later and avoiding her eyes, he handed her a .44 Remington revolver, saying curtly, "The captain says you may need this."

Angela repressed a smile as she accepted the heavy weapon and hefted it several times to get the feel of it. It took both hands for her to cock the pistol. After a few practice tries she nodded her head to indicate that she was satisfied and tucked the big weapon into the inner pocket of her woolen cloak.

Captain Hawkins watched the pair turn their horses and ride west, toward Sill. He wondered if he had done the right thing by forcing Clayton to take her along. Yes, he decided, Angela would get those papers to Fort Sill, and that was uppermost in importance. His eyes followed them until they were swallowed up in the morning mist.

At noon Clayton and Angela crossed the Arkansas River in a skiff manned by a Cherokee; the Indian's two sons swam the horses over and had them waiting on the bank when the boat arrived.

Clayton offered to pay the man, but he refused the money, saying that he was honored to do Angela Drew a service.

The girl threw Clayton a grin that said: "See how easy it is, with me along?"

It was the same when they stopped for the night at a house in the Creek Indian town of Muskogee. Angela was ushered into a bedchamber and made comfortable, while Clayton was shown to the stables, where he bedded down in the cold hayloft.

* * *

It took them five days of hard travel to reach the Canadian River, seventy-five miles east of Fort Sill.

"Well," Clayton commented, eyeing the broad sweep of water, "we could sure use one of your friend's boats along about now."

"You afraid to get your feet wet, Captain Harris?"

"My horse is an excellent swimmer, Miss Drew," he said. "I was wondering about yours."

Angela removed her wide-brimmed hat and tightened her hair where it was drawn into a bun at the nape of her neck. "He'll get me to the other side." She walked her horse to the water's edge. "You just worry about yourself."

Clayton smiled. "You planning on swimming him over, sidesaddle?"

"Something wrong with that?"

He looked at her from under the brim of his hat and considered explaining that the offset point of balance would overturn her small horse, but decided against it.

"I suppose not," he said, riding his mount into the shallows.

As his horse plunged into the deep water and began to swim, Clayton slipped over its rump and caught its tail, allowing the animal to tow him behind it.

Angela leaped her pony into the current and headed it toward the distant bank. The pinto was an excellent swimmer and the rider an exceptional horsewoman.

Clayton, looking back, was annoyed. Angela was getting her boots wet, but very little else about her was even near the water.

It was a long, cold swim, but finally Clayton's horse clattered up the steep bank and stood blowing as though it were winded. Clayton leaned weakly against the saddle and tried to catch his breath.

Angela's horse sprinted out of the water and was halfway up the sharp incline when a ledge crumbled beneath its hooves, causing the tired animal to lose its footing and fall backward toward the river.

Angela kicked free of the single stirrup and tried to throw herself from the saddle, but her long riding habbit caught on the curved horn, and both she and the horse plunged headlong into the icy water.

Clayton ran to the edge of the bluff in time to see the girl vanish into the current.

The Pinto surfaced and began swimming toward the shore. Then Angela bobbed up, spitting water and coughing. The horse scrambled up the bank and stood with its head hanging between its knees. Angela floundered, then sank again. Her cloak and long skirts had become so saturated and heavy that she was forced to fight simply to keep her head above water.

Clayton skidded down the bank to the river's edge, but before he could dive into the current, Angela raised a threatening finger at him.

"Don't even think about helping me!" She sank again. Surfacing, she spat out a mouthful of water. "I'll make it fine without you."

Clayton watched her inch her way toward the shore. As she drew near, however, he splashed in and slipped an arm around her waist. Catching her beneath the knees with his other arm, he lifted her out of the water and carried her to the bank. Surprisingly, she did not protest. . . .

It wasn't until Angela attempted to negotiate the steep incline that he realized how totally exhausted she was. With grudging admiration, he watched her struggle to place one foot before the other. By the time she reached the crest of the embankment, she was crawling. And the moment she was over the top and onto level ground, she collapsed.

Leaving her where she lay, Clayton gathered an armload of driftwood and then climbed up beside her. In five minutes he had a sizable fire blazing.

He squatted, his hands thrust toward the flames, and watched Angela rise, drag the saddle from her horse and untie the sopping bedroll, which she spread out near the fire.

"You'd better get out of those wet clothes, Miss Drew," he advised.

Angela stretched her hands out over the flames and began massaging the circulation back into them.

"You listening?" he asked.

"I heard."

Clayton added a handful of sticks to the fire, then walked to his bedroll and withdrew a heavy woolen blanket.

Returning to the fire, he held the blanket near the flames to warm it. "You can wrap up in this."

"I don't need it." She was standing so close to the fire that her clothes were steaming.

Clayton frowned at her. "Unless you are intending to do some kind of twirling act, your backside will be an icicle before you finish drying your front."

Angela stared into the flames, her face drawn and pinched with cold. "If you think I'm going to undress in front of you, you're mistaken."

Clayton walked off toward the thicket and began gathering more firewood. When he returned, Angela had wrapped herself in his blanket and was seated on the ground near the flames. Her wet clothes lay nearby.

Clayton went again into the thicket and cut several long saplings that he fashioned into a drying rack for her garments. Angela's face flamed as he spread her petticoats over the frame, which amused Clayton. Somehow, he had not expected her to be so modest.

They fried beans and bacon in a tin skillet and washed them down with steaming cups of black chickory. Angela cupped her hands around her hot tin mug to absorb its warmth. Clayton watched her with a twinge of sympathy mixed with admiration. Even though her teeth chattered and her chilled skin appeared translucent, she had not complained.

"It'll snow before morning," she said, glancing at the low-hanging sky.

"It's too warm to snow. Rain maybe."

Angela didn't argue the point. Tiredly, she fingered the blanket she had hung beside the fire; it was still dripping.

"We need to build up the fire if we intend to dry these heavy woolens," she commented.

Clayton added a few sticks. "If we build it any hotter, it'll scorch the fabric."

"I'd rather scorch the wool than wake up in the morning unable to get out of my blanket because it's frozen solid around me."

Clayton pitched the remainder of the wood on the fire and returned to the thicket in search of enough fuel to last through the night. He had gathered a full arm's load and was nearly back to the camp when the snow began—a powdery, light dusting at first, then heavy, wet flakes that quickly transformed the landscape into a lovely, silent wonder. But Clayton wasn't fooled by its splendor; he and Angela were in for a cold, miserable night.

Angela had managed to get back into her damp clothes, and had even coaxed her wet boots over semi-dry socks. Still, her attire was scarcely dry enough to offer any comfort.

The intelligent thing for her to do was to don the extra set of pants and shirt that he carried in his saddlebags. Clayton said so, explaining that the garments would be hidden beneath her cloak. Angela looked at him as though he were demented, and told him curtly that under no circumstances would she ever succumb to such humiliation. A man's clothing, indeed!

The snowstorm's increasing tempo alarmed Clayton, prompting him to move the horses closer to the camp. The mounts dipped their heads and humped their backs, not knowing which way to turn their rumps because the blizzard seemed to be coming horizontally from all directions at once.

Clayton drove their picket pins into the frozen ground and hurried back to the fire. "I've never seen it get so cold so quick," he said, chafing his hands above the flames.

Angela did not respond. Her teeth, chattering again, were stark white against the pale purple of her near-frozen lips.

"We need to saddle up and find shelter," he said.

Angela shook her head and hugged the blanket even more tightly about her throat. "We could get lost in a storm like this," she said thickly, barely able to move her lips. "We'd die for sure."

Clayton squinted into the blinding snow. In Tennessee, he thought, a person might be forced to ride five miles to find shelter, but he would find it. On the Oklahoma plains, however, unless a person knew which way to go, he could ride forever and find nothing. The realization left him shaken.

"What do you suggest?" he asked.

"When we get ready to turn in, we'll move the fire a few feet away and use the ground where it was to bed down on. It will be warm and dry. We'll make it."

Clayton appraised her anew, impressed by her suggestion.

"Why are you looking at me like that?" she asked. "You want your blanket back?"

"No."

"As soon as my clothes dry, I'll give it back to you," she assured him.

He nodded. Would her clothes ever dry on a body that was radiating as little heat as was hers?

When night arrived, it wasn't darkness at all; it was more a dimming of daylight.

Clayton moved the fire, using sticks as tongs as he carried the flaming brands to a location some eight feet distant. Angela immediately rolled into her own damp blanket and stretched out on the heated ground where the fire had been. After piling more wood on the flames, Clayton wrapped up in his blanket and lay down beside her.

In minutes they were covered with snow. Later, when Clayton chanced a peek from under the blanket flap, Angela was nothing but a mound that resembled a grave with no headstone.

He awoke again during the night, cold and miserable. When he raised the blanket flap, bitter-cold air burned his face and a mound of wet snow sifted onto his neck and worked its way under the collar of his coat.

Angela was sitting beside the fire, her blanket drawn over her head and spread open before the flames. Clayton moved to the other side of the fire and imitated her, surprised at the heat the makeshift tent captured.

"Captain Hawkins said that you served in the Confederate Army," she said abruptly. "Did you see much action before you were captured?"

Clayton sensed contempt in the question.

"Does it make any difference?"

Angela shrugged. "I just wondered what people like you, who take the Oath, tell themselves to make their cowardly deeds acceptable so they can live with themselves."

"I live with myself quite easily."

Angela threw him a hateful glare. "So I've noticed."

Clayton watched her across the flames. "What do ladies like you tell themselves when they accuse a man of having an affair? Do they tell themselves that it's their right to pry into other folks' business?" He didn't wait for her answer. "I've never lain with your mother . . . nor would I. Among other reasons, she's too much a lady . . . a fact that you, of all people, should know."

Angela flung her blanket aside and bounded to her feet. Thrust out before her was the heavy Remington pistol. Slowly, she drew back the hammer.

Clayton looked deep into her face. Despite the fact that men had shot at him in combat, he had never seen the menace that lay in Angela's eyes; it was the look of one who could kill in cold blood—and rejoice.

Taking a deep breath, he let it slide between his teeth. "You've had a bone to pick with me ever since I came to Park Hill," he said, "and I'm sick of you and your childishness. You either pull that trigger . . . or learn to act like a decent human being."

Angela's mouth drew into a grim line. Her hand trembled, causing the pistol bore to waver and jump so that at one time or another it was pointed at nearly every portion of Clayton's head.

"You can't even figure out where you intend to shoot me," he said sarcastically.

Rage caused tears to spill down her cheeks, but she released the hammer and lowered the gun. "I promised myself that I would help you get safely to Fort Sill, Mr. Harris. But don't prod me . . . because if you do, I'll shoot your face off."

Clayton glared at her, his anger building to match hers. "The powder's wet in that pistol and you know it. So stop threatening me, Miss Drew. I don't like it."

Angela raised the gun and recocked the hammer. Again that killing look was in her eyes. Clayton supposed that he was seeing one of the most primitive sides of human nature; he had never before witnessed an expression so deadly in another person's face. Then he laughed, and that was a mistake; the bullet tore through the blanket where it was draped over the crown of his hat, carrying particles of blanket and hat with it. Clayton was stunned speechless, and a terrible ringing filled his ears.

For a suspended minute they stared at each other across the fire. Neither breathed as heavy snowflakes settled on their hair, in their unblinking lashes, and on their lips.

Then Clayton was across the flames and wrenching the pistol from her. She fought like a panther, biting, kicking, scratching at his eyes, until in desperation, he hurled her to the snow.

"You fool!" he shouted. "You nearly shot me!"

Angela rolled onto her back and glared up at him. "I shot exactly where I aimed."

Clayton was in such a rage that he was trembling. "Don't you know those pistols are notorious for shooting an inch or two off-center?"

Angela snapped at him, "My pistol is a steel-strapped Remington, Mr. Harris, not an open-topped Colt."

"It doesn't make any difference. That was a stupid trick, Angela. Just more of your blasted childishness."

She pushed herself to a sitting position. "Go to hell."

Clayton's eyes narrowed. "I'm beginning to understand why your mother insisted that—"

"Insisted what?" She bounded to her feet and caught him by his coat lapels. "Tell me, damn you, tell me!"

Clayton pushed her away roughly. "This has gone far enough . . . too far! You should have been told a long time ago."

Angela's eyes never left his face as she slowly seated herself beside the fire and waited. Clayton dropped down beside her and stared into the flames.

She drew her blanket tightly about her, not to ward off the cold, but because of a sudden chill that went deeper than her bones. Biting her lower lip, she told herself that she needed to accept the truth; it was time.

"You asked me a question a while ago about the war," he began. "The answer is yes. I was an officer with Morgan's Cavalry."

Angela's hands twisted the coarse wool of her blanket into a tight knot. She remained silent.

"I was captured and sent to a Union prison at Johnson's Island, Ohio." He looked off into the white nothingness. "Your brother was sent there too, Miss Drew. He died in my arms."

The girl nodded, staring at him. Clayton turned and looked at her; her face was expressionless, her eyes veiled. Her fingers carefully stroked out the knots where she had balled up the blanket. Slowly she drew the cover over her head so that her face was shielded from view.

Without thinking, Clayton reached for her and drew her to him. She did not resist. And her vulnerability, heightened by the simple act of laying her head trustingly against his chest, humbled him more thoroughly than any chastisement he had ever received.

They sat like that for a long while, not moving. Finally Angela removed the blanket from her head and wiped her eyes with its corner. "I knew that Montclair had died," she said in a low voice. "I knew it the day it happened . . . New Year's Day." She stopped and raised her eyes to Clayton's. "All these months. I've refused to admit it, even to myself." She took a deep, shuddering breath and released it. "I knew the day you arrived why you had come. And I was afraid, so afraid. I didn't want Montclair to be dead. I . . . I loved him so much.

"I wanted you to go away and not come back . . . you who would kill him . . . for me. I hated you because of it. But then as the days passed and nothing was said about Montclair, I began to think I was wrong. Deep down, though, I still feared you because you—and my mother—had a secret."

Angela stared at the fire, now no more than glowing embers flaming to life momentarily with each gust of wind-driven snow. "We are a very close family, Mr. Harris, and a very protective family. Obviously that is not only a strength, but a weakness as well . . . " Her voice trailed off, then continued. "If my mother and I had confided in one another, as we should have, perhaps many unpleasant occurrences could have been avoided . . . " Her shoulders slumped. "But we can't undo what's been done, can we?"

Clayton looked away. "No, I guess not."

But all of a sudden Angela Drew was no longer merely Montclair Drew's sister; she had taken on an identity that was every bit her own.

CHAPTER 33

The icy winter weather, the same penetrating cold that Clayton and Angela were experiencing, seemed to stimulate the war effort in the South. The Confederacy was once again teasing its people with renewed hope of victory. On December 2, 1864, Confederate General John Bell Hood, with thirty-eight thousand battle-weary men, was entrenched before Nashville, where Union Major General George Henry Thomas awaited him with fifty-five thousand regulars.

If Hood could take Nashville and then press on to the Ohio River, Jefferson Davis was certain that Lincoln would sue for an end to the hostilities.

The pending battle, no matter who won or lost, represented the beginning of the end of the War between the States. Everyone knew it, including General Eleazer A. Paine.

Paine sat in his office and pondered, aware that the time had come for him to make his move to acquire Cragfont. If he waited until after the Battle of Nashville—and the Union lost—he would forfeit the opportunity forever. Yet if he moved immediately and requisitioned the plantation in the name of the Federal Government, appointing the slave, Patrick, as the new owner and overseer, it would be difficult for the Winchesters to wrest it back, even if Nashville fell.

Paine scowled. "Orderly!" The soldier hurried in. "Have that slave, Patrick, report to me immediately."

On December 7, 1864, General Paine, Patrick, and a detachment of cavalry cantered up the driveway to Cragfont.

Paine appraised the winter-killed fields, the slave houses and barns, and finally the mansion. His lips quirked into a pleased half-smile. In a few minutes it would all be his.

Paine and his troops dismounted. Half of the soldiers were deployed around the house; the remainder were ordered to secure the field slaves in the largest of the servant quarters.

Paine, Patrick, and a handful of men entered the house without knocking.

Patrick sprinted down the hall, through the dining room, and descended the steps into the kitchen. Old Chatty, Sylla, and Aunt Delphy looked up from their chores.

"What yo' doin' here?" Delphy demanded. "Yo' knows yo' ain't welcome in dis house!"

"Shut up, woman," Patrick said. "General Paine says for you-all to get out to the slave quarters . . . now!"

"Well, ol' Gen'l Paine can—" Delphy's mouth clamped shut and her eyes widened as two Union soldiers stepped down the stairs behind Patrick.

"Lawd! Lawd!" Old Chatty wrung her hands. "I jist knowed Gen'l Paine was a-comin'. I drempt las' night 'bout a big ol' hicker-nut tree. But dat big, fine tree was plumb holler; weren't nothin' inside it . . . no wood, no heart. It was plumb empty!"

"Shut yo' mouth!" Patrick pushed the old woman toward the outside door. "Get on up to the quarters where you belong, or I'll take a razor strop to you."

Chatty raised her ancient eyes to Patrick. "Yo' tell Gener'l Paine I drempt dat a big wind done come out'n da no'th and blowed dat hicker-nut tree down . . . "

Slamming the door behind Chatty and the others, Patrick raced to the parlor, where Paine's remaining soldiers had ushered the Winchester women. Upon seeing Fanny, he stopped abruptly and his mouth dropped open. "I thought you had done died," he said disbelievingly.

Fanny looked questioningly at him, not recalling her plea for help that day at Freedman's Town. "You never was right bright, Patrick," she said, wondering what he was talking about.

Paine wasted no time in getting down to business.

His plan was simple. He had made out the necessary papers, confiscating the plantation under the same Abandoned Property Act that he, and he alone, had decreed. He would turn the plantation over to Patrick, who, when the war ended, would merely sign it back to Paine. It was a foolproof plan.

"You no longer own this property," he informed Mrs. Winchester. "Cragfont has been placed on the abandoned-farm list. As of this day, the Federal Government has deeded this property to the free Negro, Patrick." In the silence that followed, Paine turned to Patrick and shook his hand. "You, sir, are the new owner of the house, outbuildings, and acreage."

Swinging back to Mrs. Winchester, Paine smiled thinly. "I have taken the liberty, madam, to have you investigated thoroughly and have learned that you have relatives in Memphis. As an act of kindness, I've also taken the liberty to purchase steamboat tickets for you and your family, from Nashville to Memphis." Paine's smile turned hard. "A carriage is waiting at the end of your driveway at the Hartsville Pike to escort you-all to Nashville."

"General," Mrs. Winchester said, "I am eighty-seven years old. The year I was born, the government of a brand-new nation—the Federal Government of America—awarded my husband, General James Winchester, this property for his service in a war that freed us from tyrants like you. My husband and I fought Indians, the elements, and everything else the good Lord saw fit to throw at us, to keep this place. I have lived in this house for more than sixty-six years, sir. But now you have the gall to walk in here and try to make me believe that that same government is going to take it away from me."

Paine was taken aback. He had not been aware that Cragfont was a Federal grant.

Mrs. Winchester was going on: "I own this plantation, sir, not my son, George, who is at this moment in a Federal prison. You cannot use that abandoned-farm nonsense on me. I am the head of the household here." She laughed in Paine's face. "We're not leaving, General. Take your soldiers and get off my property."

Paine's mouth drew into an angry line; the old woman had put his back to the wall. Should he allow her to flout his authority, every owner in the county would plead the same case.

Turning to the soldiers, he said, "Let them take what they can carry, then escort them to the Hartsville Pike. Should they balk, shoot them."

The widow's face drained and a gray pallor swept over the normal blush of her cheeks. Stepping toward Paine, she raised her hand to slap his face, but the blow was never delivered. Clutching her chest, the slight eighty-seven-year-old lady collapsed.

With a cry of despair, Malvinia dropped to the floor and put her ear to her mother-in-law's breast.

"She's dead," she whispered, raising her eyes to Paine in bewilderment. "She's dead!"

Paine exhaled angrily through his teeth. How untimely, he thought, how utterly untimely. Then a smile crept onto his face.

"I assume, madam," he said to Malvinia, "that Major George Winchester will inherit this plantation. Is that correct?"

Malvinia stared up at him, too stunned to understand the question.

"Then, madam," he continued as though she had agreed, "there is absolutely no question about it; any property owned by a Confederate soldier—which describes Cragfont now—is automatically the property of the Federal Government."

Paine turned to his subordinates. "Bury the old woman, then escort these people off Mr. Patrick's property."

"Yes, sir." The junior officer saluted. And for the hundredth time since being assigned to Paine's command, he wished he had never enlisted in the army.

Susie Winchester, too, knelt beside her grandmother. She looked up at Paine.

"I want you to know somethin', General Paine." Tears streamed down her cheeks. "If I live to be as old as my grandmother, you will have someone hatin' you for the next seventy-five years, 'cause until the day I die I'm goin' to pray for the devil to burn you in . . . where he lives. I hate you! I hate you!"

Paine stared at the child. "She needs to feel the sting of a razor strop," he said.

"No, General!" Lettie slipped her arm protectively around Susie. "You, sir, need to feel a hangman's noose."

With the family watching in horrified silence, the Cragfont slaves hurriedly buried the widow next to her husband in the family cemetery, north of the house. She was not even granted the dignity of a headstone.

Federal guards lounged nearby, their presence a reminder that had it not been for General Paine, Mrs. Winchester might still be alive.

The entire Cragfont slave population followed the Winchesters off the hill toward the Hartsville Pike, but the soldiers who escorted the family stopped the Negroes a quarter of a mile from the house and ordered them to turn back.

Patrick, riding an army horse and wearing one of George Winchester's finest suits, sat straight in the saddle, looking every bit the new owner. He cursed the blacks loudly as they wept and called out farewells to the departing women.

Fanny broke from the group of slaves and ran to the Winchester women and children, who stood in the road looking back at Cragfont, crying openly.

"Take me with you, Miss Malvinia," Fanny implored, catching Malvinia Winchester's hand tightly.

The woman drew Fanny into an embrace. "I'm sorry, Fanny. I wish I could, but General Paine made certain that he purchased passage to Memphis for only the immediate family. He has no intention of losing such valuable stock as the Cragfont slaves—not one of them."

"I am a Winchester!" Fanny cried. "My place is with you. I am family!"

Malvinia stared at her, not knowing how to respond. The officer in charge touched Malvinia's arm. "You've got to be moving on, ma'am. The general's carriage is waiting for you at the highway."

"Why didn't he send it to the house?" Lettie demanded. Then she glared at the guard. "It's because if he's investigated, he can say that we abandoned Cragfont. Isn't that true?"

The officer looked away.

Malvinia kissed Fanny's cheek. "I'm so sorry, Fanny."

"Good-bye, ma'am," Fanny whispered.

Malvinia turned and led twelve-year-old Susie and three-year-old Babe away from Cragfont, away from the land the Federal Government had sworn would be the Winchesters' forever.

Susie slipped her hand from Malvinia's and ran to Fanny.

"I love you, Fanny," she cried, flinging her arms around the young woman. "I want you to go with us; you belong with us. Oh, Fanny, I'll just die without you."

Fanny hugged Susie tight, knowing in her heart that it would be the last time, and thinking that she too would die.

Blinking back tears, she said, "You're grown up now, Miss Susie. You help your mama—Lord knows, she's goin' to need all the help she can get just to keep the family together. Look after little Babe. Oh, God! I love you all . . . I love you."

Fanny turned to Lettie, who was but a shadow of the arrogant girl who had wielded such power at Cragfont, the person whom she had tried so hard to emulate. And Fanny choked back a sob of pity for the Lettie who had been, the Lettie she had admired, the Lettie she had hated.

They appraised one another for a long moment; two young women who had shared so much of one another's innermost dreams, secrets, pleasures . . . and pain.

Fanny suddenly longed to embrace Lettie, an act she had never even considered before . . . but she couldn't summon the courage to make such a gesture toward her mistress.

"Move on, miss," said a soldier standing near Lettie. "The general is becoming impatient."

Lettie nodded and turned down the drive.

"Miss Lettie," called Fanny, "would you like to leave Mr. Clayton a message . . . if'n he comes a-askin', ma'am?"

Lettie hesitated, her mind flashing back to the last day she had seen Clayton Harris, the day she had opened her soul to him in the Cragfont parlor. No, she thought bitterly, not to him, to a room that was empty—as empty as I am.

Lettie shook her head, then walked on.

The news of Mrs. Winchester's death and the loss of
Cragfont swept Sumner County like wildfire, enraging the
citizens, both Confederate and Union, to near revolt.

Letters of protest were fired off to Governor Johnson, but
with Nashville preparing for the battle that could turn the
tide of the war, the voice of Sumner County wasn't heard.

On December 10, 1864, Ellis Harper, Cotton, and a
half-dozen guerrillas dismounted at Cragfont.

Fanny met them at the door, along with old Chatty and
Fleming. Cotton was surprised to see Fanny among the
other house servants. "I figured you went to Memphis with
the Winchesters."

"All of us would have gone, Cotton," Fanny said.
"We begged Miss Malvinia to take us, but there wasn't
enough money for passage."

"We's a-goin' to leave too, Massa Cotton," Chatty said.
"We'ns can't stay here no' mo'. It's jist plumb awful without
old Miss, an' Susie, an' ever'body . . . an' dat Patrick nigger
is worse'n any white massa yo' ever heard 'bout. Why, he
comes in here an' bosses us 'round an' makes us a-wait on
him hand an' foot."

"Where will you go?" Cotton asked.

"I don't know," Fanny said. "Much as we hate the
thought, we've talked about joinin' the folks at Freedman's
Town . . . we really don't have much choice. Oh, Cotton"—
Fanny's eyes filled with tears—"our whole world is fallin'
down all around us. What are we s'posed to do?"

Cotton looked away from her imploring face. He had
no answer. Finally he said, "Go to Summerset, Fanny.
Tell Mr. Summers that I sent you. Tell him all of you need a
home."

The girl wiped her eyes and nodded. Then looking
beyond Cotton to Ellis Harper and his men, still sitting
their horses, she said, "If'n you are here fo the reason I
think you are, please don't do it. He's not worth it,
Cotton."

Cotton's lips drew into a grim line. "Get what you can
carry an' go on over to Summerset." Turning, he walked
back to his horse.

Fleming stepped out onto the stoop. "Marse Cotton," he hailed in a low voice, "we Cragfont folks don' hold wif what done happened here. We wants yo' to know that, suh. An' if'n I was yo', I'd be fo' goin' to the barn an' grainin' my horse . . . if'n yo' understan' my meanin', suh."

In the background, Cotton could hear old Chatty wailing: "I jist knowed sum'pin' bad was gwine to happen, I jist knowed it. Last night I drempt . . . "

Nodding at Fleming, Cotton swung into the saddle and joined Harper's band as they walked their horses slowly toward the barn.

Ellis Harper reared back and kicked open the barn door.

Patrick, who was brushing one of Paine's thoroughbred horses, laid the brush aside and stepped into the aisle that divided the stalls.

"Y'all want somethin'?"

Ellis Harper walked into the barn. "I hear you're the new owner of Cragfont."

"General Paine done give it to me."

"You don't say?" Harper said. Patrick nodded uncertainly. "An' I guess you didn't have nothin' to do with killin' ol' lady Winchester so Paine would give you her property, did you?" accused Harper.

"No, sir!" Patrick said, taking long steps backward until brought up short against a stall door. "Gener'l Paine, he did that. He jist made me the owner of this farm. I didn't have nuthin' to do with killin' ole Miss Winchester."

"It'll be a cold day in hell before you, or any nigger, own Cragfont." Harper drew his sword and stepped deliberately toward Patrick.

"You ain't gwine to cut me again?" Patrick's knees turned to water, and he slid down the door to cower in the barn cess.

"Naw," Harper said, "I ain't goin' to cut you." With a savage overhand swing, he cleaved the saber blade nearly halfway through Patrick's neck just above the collarbone.

Blood spattered the stall door a bright crimson. Patrick's body pitched fulll length and lay there in the muck, jerking and twitching as his heart continued to pump. The slave's mouth opened and closed, emitting a strangled gurgle, and his eyes bulged nearly out of their sockets.

Harper calmly laid the sword blade against the Negro's neck, judging the distance. Then with a powerful double-handed swing, he chopped entirely through Patrick's spine. Another blow and the head rolled free.

Kneeling beside the body, he stretched out the dead man's arms, then laid Patrick's head face-up, in the open palms.

Harper smiled with satisfaction. "It'll be a long time comin' before another nigger takes a plantation away from its rightful owner."

"I thought we were just goin' to run him off, Ellis," Cotton said, his mouth dry and bitter.

Harper shrugged.

Cotton walked outside and swung into the saddle.

"Where are you goin'?" demanded Harper.

"I'm goin' to do what I should have done a long time ago, Ellis. I'm goin' to stop shaming Willie's memory; I'm goin' to Nashville, Ellis. I'm goin' to join General Bate's command . . . if he'll have me."

"You're crazy. Old William B. Bate will probably put you on the front line, just hopin' some Yankee bullet will find you."

Cotton grinned sadly. "A bullet's goin' to fnd us sooner or later anyhow, Ellis."

Harper laughed. "Ain't it the truth. But soldierin' ain't my way of fightin' this war, Cotton."

As it turned out, Ellis Harper was right. On December fifteenth, General William B. Bate's command was engaged in the worst of the front-line fighting at Nashville. The general, although crippled from a knee wound acquired at the Battle of Shilo, was leading the vanguard. That night as Bate's battle-worn Sumner County Confederates huddled around their camp fires, the general, hobbling on crutches, appeared in the flickering light; he was as haggard and worn as they. "You boys did just fine today," he said. "I'm mighty proud of you."

A young soldier looked up from the bloody rag that Cotton was tying around his forearm. "General? Is Hood goin' to send replacements to the front tomorrow? I ain't sure, sir, that I got the guts to go again."

Bate leaned heavily on his crutches. "Son, there are no replacements. I'm sorry."

Tears formed in the youth's eyes, but he quickly knuckled them away.

Bate laid a fatherly hand on the young soldier's shoulder and indicated Cotton with a thrust of his chin. "Son, if you get really scared tomorrow, you just step behind this ol' ex-cavalryman here and regather your courage. You'll be safe, 'cause Cotton's got so skinny since the last time I saw him, he can stand behind his rifle barrel and not show an inch of hide on either side . . . an' I ain't seen the minié ball yet that will shoot through a steel barrel."

The boy sniffled, then laughed. "Thanks, General."

Cotton followed Bate out of the firelight. "We're whipped, ain't we, General?"

Bate adjusted the crutches under his armpits. "Yes, Cotton, we're beaten." He gazed across the thousands of camp fires that glittered in the cold darkness. "By any chance, did you notice the Union soldiers who manned the trenches we tried to take? Did you get a good look at them?"

Cotton shifted uncomfortably. "Yes, sir. I saw 'em eye to eye."

"What did you see?"

"They were black, sir."

"Is that all?"

Cotton frowned, thinking back to the battle. "I believe, sir, they were the Thirteenth an' Fourteenth Colored Divisions. We damn near annihilated the Thirteenth, sir."

Bate sighed. "Yes, Cotton, we did. But I must admit, I was proud of them, the courage those darkies showed under fire."

Cotton frowned at the general, wondering if the man had developed battle fatigue.

"They were our boys, Cotton," Bate said softly. "They were Sumner County slaves, and they fought like seasoned troops."

Cotton's stomach churned. The dead bodies of the Colored Divisions had piled one upon another across the battlefield, their faces gray, their eyes wide and filmed over in death. Yes, they had fought valiantly . . . and if they were indeed Sumner County slaves, they had wreaked havoc on their former masters.

"Well," Cotton said, "it just goes to show that there ain't no pullin' the wool over the damn Yankees' eyes; old

General Thomas knew that even a Southern slave could outshoot the Northern regular army men, so he filled the trenches with 'em . . . an' it worked. They shot us to hell and back today."

Bate nodded. "Who would have thought four years ago that we would wind up being whipped by our own darkies? It's incredible, Cotton, incredible."

Cotton said nothing. He too, like the young soldier a few minutes before, wondered if he had the nerve to face the onslaught again in the morning.

When the dawn of the sixteenth broke, Union General Thomas observed through his field glasses that the Confederates had formed a new line of battle and had thrown up a strong breastworks.

Thomas turned to Colonel McMillan. "Hood doesn't know when to quit, Mac. His troops are worn out, and I'd wager that after yesterday's battle, he doesn't have twenty-five thousand men in those trenches. We've brought up ten thousand fresh reserves." He raised his field glasses and again studied the Confederate front. "This will be a bloody day, but when it's over, the Southern action of this God-awful war will be ended."

Thomas sighed then, and the sound was forlorn and wistful. "It's a shame that so many good men will have to die. Why in God's name doesn't Hood surrender? He knows he's whipped."

McMillan raised his telescope and studied the hills behind Hood's line; Confederate cannon glinted in the sunlight. "Hood wouldn't surrender, General," he said, "if he was the only Confederate alive to wield a sword. Southerners are like that . . . crazy, just plain crazy."

Thomas nodded his agreement. Slipping his binoculars into their carrying case, he spurred his horse into a gallop and rode off to give last-minute instructions to the officers who would lead the first charge.

CHAPTER 34

That same morning, December 16, 1864, Clayton Harris stepped out of the Fort Sill paymaster's office and let his gaze drift across the parade grounds to the sutler's store. The snow that had fallen with such venom was gone except for the shaded places, and the morning sun was fast burning that away.

Angela Drew, carrying an armful of supplies, came out of the sutler's and crossed the frozen ground to the plank walkway where Clayton waited. Together, they strolled toward the livery stable.

"We haven't fooled anyone," Angela murmured. "Everyone at Sill knows why we are here."

"Are you sure?"

"Yes. Look across the street."

Clayton saw a group of men lounging in the morning sun where it heated the plank walk next to the fort's main entrance gate. "They been standing there long?"

Angela didn't turn her head. "Ever since you went into the paymaster's office."

"You know any of them?"

Her mouth tightened. "I don't associate with jayhawkers

and riffraff, Mr. Harris. Of course I don't know them."

Inside the livery stable, Clayton stood in the shadow and watched the men by the gate. There were seven of them, squatting with their backs against the wall; four of them were smoking pipes or cigars. They looked peaceable enough.

Clayton turned to the hostler and nodded toward the gate. "Who are those men?"

The hostler drove his pitchford into a stack of manure and walked to the door. "Buffalo hunters . . . that's what they claim." He returned to his pitchford.

"Are they buffalo hunters?"

"Nope."

Clayton again sized up the men. "What makes you think they're not hunters?"

The hostler spat a stream of amber into a mound of hay beside the door. "Tobacco juice kills worms in horses," he said, indicating the brown spot that was seeping into the hay stems. "I spit in the hay ever' chance I get."

"What about those men? They look like hunters to me."

"Well"—the hostler wiped spittle out of his beard—"they's several things that ain't right about 'em. They're too clean to be buffler hunters, an' they ain't carryin' heavy 'nough rifles, an' they ain't got no wagons, and . . . and they just plain don't smell right. You can smell a hide hunter a mile away. Them fellers stink, but it ain't the right stink." The hostler grinned, his toothless mouth resembling a gopher hole. "Hell, son, they aim to take that there payroll away from you."

Angela stifled a laugh.

The hostler resumed forking manure into the pile. "Ain't nuthin' goes on at this post," he said, "what folks don't know about quicker'n you can fall off a log."

"It's no wonder that all the army couriers are robbed," Clayton said.

"Well"—the hostler leaned on the pitchfork handle—"what I ain't figured out is why they even bother. Confederate scrip ain't worth nuthin' nohow."

Clayton and Angela were ten miles from Fort Sill when Angela turned off the trail and urged her horse up a steep incline.

Clayton leaned on his saddle pommel and watched her as she studied their backtrail. She had done that several times during the day. "See anything?" he called.

"Not yet. But they'll be along. That's why we're quitting this trail."

Clayton stared at her; the trail they were using was rough and dangerous, but the badlands were even worse.

Angela smiled as he joined her on the knoll. "I know seven trails from Fort Sill to Gibson, Mr. Harris. We rode in on this one, and we rode out on it. It's time we made a switch."

All of a sudden Clayton was glad that Angela was there. They dropped over the hill and angled east by north at a slow gallop.

Near noon, Angela reined in at a dwelling that resembled a beehive. It was made of a framework of heavy poles sheathed in grass thatching and tied down with slender wooden rods.

Sitting before the lodge was an ancient woman wrapped tightly in a nondescript blanket that enveloped all but her glittering black eyes. Angela nodded at the woman. Speaking in a dialect that even Clayton could tell was not Cherokee, the girl gestured up and down the path that ran past the wickiup.

The old woman pointed toward Fort Sill. But what caught and held Clayton's attention was the sight revealed when she adjusted the blanket to speak: Where the woman's nose should have been, two grotesque holes caused her face to resemble the visage of a living skeleton.

After several minutes of conversation, Angela passed the old woman a twist of chewing tobacco as leave-taking.

They had barely ridden out of sight of the hut when Clayton edged his mount close to Angela. "What did you talk about?"

"Things."

"What things?" Then, "Are we going to have to go through all that secret stuff again, like we did when we went after the cattle?"

Angela sighed. "I asked her if any white men had been past her place lately. She said there hadn't, which means that the jayhawkers might not know of this trail. Are you satisfied?"

Clayton rode on in silence, but he wasn't satisfied. Angela and the old woman had talked about much more than that, and he felt he had a right to know what had been said.

"What tribe was she?" he asked presently.

"Wichita."

"What happened to her face?"

For a long while Angela didn't answer. "Something bit her nose off," she said finally.

Clayton gazed hard at Angela. "Something bit her nose off, and she doesn't know what it was?"

"Of course she knows."

"Well?"

"I declare!" Angela cried, "sometimes you're not very bright."

Clayton settled back in his saddle. "In what direction am I not very bright? Is it because I don't have the least notion of what chewed her nose off? Or is it because it's some kind of delicate Indian subject that I shouldn't be inquiring about?"

"Both!"

Clayton yanked his horse to a halt. "What happened to her nose, Angela?"

The girl twisted in the saddle, her blue eyes flashing fire. "Her husband did it. He bit her nose off . . . because she consorted with a white man." Angela looked away, but Clayton could see the color creep up the back of her neck just below her hairbun.

"Is that a normal custom?" he asked. "Do all the tribes do that?"

"Some of them."

"The Cherokee too?"

"Occasionally."

What kind of savages could do such a thing? he wondered.

Nashville was nearly obliterated by the smoke from hundreds of cannon and thousands of small arms, and fires that raged out of control as homes burned on the hills surrounding the Union bastion, Fort Negley.

Cotton crouched in a trench so filled with dead and wounded that running blood had turned the frozen ground to a rust-colored mush. Laying his rifle barrel over the edge of the defile, he took aim and fired at the wave of blue-coats advancing steadily toward him. He saw a man stumble, but during the time it took him to fall, another had taken his place.

Cotton dropped the butt of his rifle into the mud and ripped open a paper cartridge with his teeth. Glancing over the edge of the trench at the solid wall of Union soldiers advancing toward him with fixed bayonets, he hurriedly poured the powder down the barrel, stuffed the paper and ball into the muzzle, and rammed them to the breech.

Taking aim, he downed another Federal soldier, only to see two more step into his place.

Time after time he repeated the process—as Confederates were doing up and down the line for as far as he could see—until the Union Army could not advance without climbing over, or stepping on, their own dead and wounded.

Even though the Confederates fought valiantly, giving no quarter nor asking any, grape and canister fired from the Federal cannon emplacements on the hills south of Nashville were taking their toll. Unlike the Union Army, the Rebels had no troops with which to fill in the gap when a man in gray went down.

At three o'clock, Colonel McMillan formed his Union regiments—the 114th Illinois, the 93rd Indiana, the 10th Minnesota, the 72nd Ohio, and the 95th Ohio—into two lines, and with drums beating and colors flying, they marched toward the Confederate trenches. Wave after wave of Union soldiers fell before Confederate fire, but finally the Confederates had no choice but to fall back. The relentless Federal cannonade that followed the Confederates' retreat was heard plainly in Gallatin, nearly fifty miles distant.

The Union commander, General George Henry Thomas, sat his horse on a hill overlooking the battlefield and watched Hood's splendid and courageous army shot into oblivion. The magnificent Confederate Army of Tennessee —the army that had fought with honor all the way from the first Battle of Bull Run to Shiloh, Murfreesboro, Chickamauga, Lookout Mountain, Missionary Ridge, Atlanta, Franklin, and finally Nashville—was destroyed.

Shattered and demoralized, the remnant of men in gray

who could still walk flung aside their weapons and blanket-rolls and fled in total confusion down the Franklin Pike and through the Brentwood Pass.

As General Thomas had predicted, fighting in the southwestern theater was over.

That night as the retreating army dropped in its tracks for a few minutes' rest before pushing on to the Tennessee River and safety, Cotton and a handful of Sumner County soldiers searched out General Bate.

"General, sir," Cotton said, his hat in his hands, "some of the boys ain't been home for months. We was wonderin', sir, if you would mind . . . "

Bate looked at the weary men standing before him. Their faces were powder-burned beyond recognition, their eyelashes singed away, their hands blistered from loading hot barrels. Their eyes were awful to look into; bloodshot, and swollen to mere slits.

"Gentlemen," Bate said in his soft drawl, "when you get to Sumner County, tell my family that I am well, and please pay my respects to the families of my friends who . . . won't be goin' home."

As Cotton started to leave, Bate said, "I don't see that young fellow who was with you last night."

Cotton sighed, then shook his head. "There were no tears today, General. He was a man. He died like one."

Cotton threw Bate a tired salute, but Bate reached out and caught his hand and shook it firmly. "Good luck, Cotton."

Cotton nodded and turned away.

"Cotton," came Bate's strained voice. "How old was that boy?"

Cotton faced his commander, seeing a man old before his time, weakened by the generous sharing of his strength with others, a man whose great heart had been picked away a piece at a time with each prayer he had said over a fallen soldier.

"He was twelve years old, sir."

That night beside the flickering light of a camp fire, General Bate wrote his official report. He was nearing the end of it:

*"About this time, the brigade on the extreme left of our
infantry line of battle was driven back down the hill
into the field in my rear, and the balls on the enemy
were fired into the back of my men. The lines on the
west of Granny White Pike at this juncture were the
three sides of a square, the enemy shooting across the
two parallel lines. My men were falling fast. I saw and
fully appreciated the emergency, and passed in person
along the trenches in the angle built by Ector's Brigade,
where I had placed troops known to be unsurpassed for
gallantry and endurance, and encouraged them to
maintain their places. The men saw the brigade on the
left of our line of battle give way and the enemy take its
place on the hills in my rear, yet they stood firm and
received the fire from all directions with coolness and
courage."*

Bate stared into the fire. Of his entire brigade, only
sixty-five men had escaped death or capture. Sighing, he
finished his report:

*"The command was nearly annihilated, as the offi-
cial reports of casualties show. Whether the yielding of
gallant and well-tried troops to such pressure is repre-
hensible or not, is for a brave and generous country to
decide."*

While Cotton walked through the darkness toward Gallatin, Clayton Harris looked across the camp fire and
secretly assessed Angela Drew's face, trying to picture her
with two open holes in the place where her fine, aquiline
nose should have been.

Even though he had seen the aftermath of Wichita
infidelity, he could not imagine that an Indian, any Indian,
could mutilate a woman's face, make her grotesque for life,
because she had slept with a white man.

Angela poured two cups of chickory and passed one to
him. "I can't make up my mind if Montclair liked you or
hated you," she said.

Clayton frowned. "What makes you say that?"

Angela smiled without malice. "Montclair would have
asked only someone whom he trusted explicitly—or wished
to see dead—to ride blindly into Indian territory. Was he

aware of how green you actually are?"

Clayton sipped his drink; the scalding liquid burned all the way to his stomach. "I doubt that it ever entered his mind."

"Don't fool yourself. He knew better than to send a tenderfoot out here."

"There wasn't anyone else he could send, Angela. Montclair and I were friends as only two people who share . . . " he hesitated, then said gently, attempting to soften the word, "death . . . can be."

"I shared his death too," the girl said with quick anger. Then she did something completely out of character: She touched his hand. "I guess that's one of the reasons I resent you, Mr. Harris. Because you were with him and I wasn't. You saw him die, and I felt it. You held his hand, and I held nothing but a memory."

How fortunate that you didn't see him the way he actually looked at the end, Clayton thought.

"You heard his last words," she continued, "while all I heard was the sound of emptiness in my heart."

"He called you Angel," Clayton murmured.

Angela sighed. "Montclair was the only person who ever called me that. I hated it."

"Why?"

"It made me feel as though I had to live up to his expectations. He always thought that I was God's gift of goodness." She took a quick sip of chickory, then said in tones of sarcasm edged with pain, "Wouldn't he be disappointed?"

An awkward silence stretched out between them.

"Montclair understood human betrayal and weaknesses better than most," Clayton said, thinking of the men who had stood by and watched the Indian die. Rising, he walked off into the night.

Angela watched him go, wishing to call him back . . . but she couldn't.

Turning to the fire, she stared into the flames. Softly her lips formed the words: "But did he forgive them?"

When Clayton and Angela approached the Canadian River, four riders walked their mounts slowly out of the cottonwoods that banked the crossing.

Clayton stopped his horse and drew his coat aside, resting

his hand on the butt of his revolver.

Angela, having wrapped herself in her blanket to help ward off the cold, tugged the heavy wool more tightly about her and drew her horse up.

"Let me do the talking," he warned. She said nothing.

The four men rode to within ten feet of the pair, then fanned out, facing them.

"Did they pay you in gold or scrip?" the leader asked.

"Scrip," Clayton said.

The man grimaced. "Why in the world don't they ever make it worth our while?" Swinging his eyes to Angela, he studied her thoroughly. "I've seen you before. You're that Indian-princess niece of John Ross, ain't you?"

Angela remained silent.

The man smiled. "A woman as pretty as you should be worth quite a ransom."

It was the last sound he ever made. Angela fired through the blanket, the ball striking the man above his left eye. The impact slammed him over the rump of his horse, which caused the animal to run backward over the body and stagger to its haunches.

The three other men, their horses rearing and bucking, attempted to bring their guns into action.

Drawing his revolver, Clayton steadied his cavalry mount and took careful aim at the man nearest him. Then he shot the man out of the saddle.

The remaining two men fired wildly at Clayton and Angela before spurring their horses into a dead run back the way they had come. Clayton emptied his revolver at them, then drew a second one from his coat pocket and took a fine bead before deciding they were out of range.

From the corner of his eye he saw Angela dismount from her horse and drop to her hands and knees. The sounds of painful retching shattered the silence that had enveloped the countryside after the earthshaking roar of the pistols.

Clayton swung down beside her.

Angela raised a tear-stained face to him. "I killed a man, Clayton . . . oh, God . . . I killed a man." She retched again.

"Well, what did you expect? You shot him right between the eyes. Darn it, Angela, I told you to let me do the talking."

"They were through with talking!" she shouted. Then her stomach convulsed and she vomited again.

"There was no need to kill the man, Angela. I could have talked him out of it."

Angela wiped her mouth with the back of her hand. "You just don't understand, do you? The man had made up his mind. As you have said before, I saw it in his eyes. And I assure you, he had no intention of taking me home to Mama."

"For Christ's sake, Angela. The man wasn't even reaching for his gun. You have some kind of stupid idea that all white men are out to . . . that your body is the only thing that interests them."

Angela slowly pushed herself to her feet, her gaze filled with mock curiosity. "Is that right? Please go on . . . I'm sure there's more."

"Damn right there is!" he shouted, wishing he had kept his mouth shut but determined to set her straight. "I don't want your body, lady. And just for the record, from what I've seen of it, it isn't that terrific."

Angela's deathly white face drained to an even paler hue. "You son-of-a-bitch," she breathed. Then she struck him. But the blow carried no force, which surprised Clayton; he knew how hard she could hit.

Before he had time to react, Angela's eyelids fluttered and she collapsed.

Springing forward, he caught her well enough to break her fall and ease her the rest of the way to the ground.

Angered by her delicate faint two minutes after she had shot a man dead, he slapped her face none too gently and commanded her to wake up.

A small stream of blood oozed from one corner of her mouth and trickled down her lip.

At first he thought she had bitten her tongue, but a second later a gout of blood gushed out and spread rapidly over her chin. For a moment he knelt there too stunned to move. Cautiously he unbuttoned her jumper and ran his hand inside the garment, along her shoulder and over her upper chest. When he removed his hand, it was covered with blood.

Don't panic, he told himself. Think. Just keep thinking! Settling back on his haunches, he shut his eyes. If she were a stranger, what would I do? I would try to find the wound and stop the bleeding.

Quickly he stripped her blouse down over her shoulders, revealing her upper chest and the swell of her bosom. He could find no puncture, and again fear crept over him. Frantically he stripped her to the waist.

Still he could not find the source of her bleeding. Fear took a wholehearted grip on him now.

Angela's eyes fluttered open. Moaning, she attempted to sit up, but the sight of her naked, bloody breasts sent her into unconsciousness again.

Clayton hurriedly covered her with her blanket, then bolted to the river and dipped his hat full of water. Taking a deep breath to still his shaking hands, he raced back, and using his kerchief, began bathing her upper body, a task made tediously maddening by the continuous flow of blood from the wound he could not locate. He worked slowly, examining every inch of her skin until finally, when he raised her left arm to cleanse her side, he found the entry hole. The bullet appeared to have hit a rib, but then where had it gone?

Having found the wound, Clayton's near panic abated and he moved with greater surety. Quickly he wrung out the kerchief and folded it into a compress that he bound firmly over the puncture with a strip ripped from her blanket. Covering her again, heedless of the raw December wind that whipped his hair off his forehead and froze the warm blood that covered his hands, he stood for a long while gazing down at her bloodless face.

"Aw, Angela," he whispered, "why did you have to get yourself shot? Why?"

His fingers became so numb that he could no longer feel them. He walked to the river and thrust his hands beneath the icy water. Scooping up a handful of sand, he scoured away the congealed blood and then dried his hands on his overcoat.

While doing so he allowed his gaze to travel the length and breadth of the river. Not fifty yards away, a canoe was beached on a gravel bar near the bank. Judging by the number of tracks on the muddy shore, three of the jayhawkers had paddled the boat across, while the fourth had swum the horses over.

Returning to Angela, Clayton gathered her into his arms and carried her to the canoe. When he went back for the horses, he saw that the outlaw he had shot was sitting up with his shirt open, examining the hole in his chest.

"I'm shot clear through," the man said as Clayton neared.

The bullet had taken him in the chest, above his lungs, and exited out his back.

Clayton cut strips from the outlaw's shirt and folded them into compresses.

"What about your woman?" the man asked. "She goin' to make it?"

"I don't know."

"It weren't me who shot her, mister. Hell, my horse was cuttin' up so much, I never did get off a shot."

Clayton tied the bandage into place, then pushed himself erect. Without further words, he walked to the horses and tied Angela's bridle reins to his horse's tail. As he led the animals toward the river, the wounded man called to him: "Wait a minute, mister. I've got to tell you something."

Clayton stopped and waited. The outlaw grinned nervously. "When you get across the river, you're goin' to find an Injun hut. I just wanted you to know I didn't have no part in what went on over there, no part a'tall."

Clayton shrugged. "Why tell me?"

"Mister, you ain't goin' to like what you see. I don't want you a-comin' back across the river to kill me for somethin' I didn't do."

The jayhawker's warning in no way prepared Clayton for what met him at the cabin. Yet the man had made one correct prophecy: Clayton Harris was outraged. He had the answer to the question he had asked himself: What kind of savage could mutilate a woman? The kind of savage called a human being. It was plain that the jayhawkers had amused themselves with the Indian woman for hours, or perhaps even for a day or two, before she had mercifully died.

Clayton cut her naked body down from the overhead beam where she hung by her wrists and wrapped her in a blanket.

Outside, he searched in the brush lean-to for a shovel or pickax with which to dig a grave but found nothing, not even a grubbing hoe.

Going back into the building, he rummaged through the shambles of the interior until he located enough rope and string to bind the blanket tightly about the body. She was heavy in death, and Clayton was breathing hard by the time he reached a bend in the river, five hundred yards from where Angela lay unconscious in the canoe.

He picked a deep spot in the water below an overhang and slipped the bundle off his shoulder. It dropped into the river with hardly a splash, bobbed along with the current, then slowly disappeared beneath the crystalline waters of the Canadian.

When it was out of sight, he walked to the lean-to, where a travois lay propped against the wall.

After several frustrating attempts, he finally figured out how to harness the makeshift carryall to Angela's horse.

It was night when Angela regained consciousness. For a confused moment she lay silent and motionless, wondering why she felt so weak and exhausted. Turning her head to the side, she let her eyes adjust to the camp fire a few feet distant, and to the man sitting beside it.

"How do you feel?" Clayton stood up and walked over to her.

"What happened to me?" she whispered. Then she sucked in her breath as a deep, burning pain traveled in waves through her upper torso.

"You were shot."

"Shot?" Her voice was barely audible. "I don't remember being shot."

"Take my word for it."

"How bad am I shot?"

Clayton knelt beside her and laid his palm against her forehead. "You were shot in the side, Angela." Her skin was like a live ember. "The bullet's still in there somewhere, but the bleeding has about stopped, if that means anything."

Angela looked up at him. "I killed a man, didn't I?"

"You shot a mad dog, Angela, not a man." He looked away into the night. "I owe you an apology. You were right to shoot first and ask questions later." He sighed and met her eyes. "I'm a fool, Angela. You tried to tell me all along. Well, you're right. Out here, the timid die fast."

Angela ignored his apology. Taking her lower lip between

her teeth, she bit hard to stifle a moan that had formed deep in her chest and was threatening to work its way into a full-fledged scream of agony.

Clayton hastened to his saddlebags and was back a moment later with a small ball of opium. Forcing her clenched teeth apart, he pinched off a generous plug and poked it deep into her throat. She gagged and tried to spit it out, but he kept fingering it into her mouth until she swallowed it.

Angela's fast and erratic breathing began to slow, and the pupils of her eyes dilated as the drug took effect.

"Feel better?" he asked.

"I hurt all over, Clayton." It was not a complaint, and he knew that. "But I hurt the most where the bandage crosses my . . . chest. Can you loosen it any?

"We've got to keep that compress tight, Angela. You're still bleeding."

Tears welled up in the girl's eyes. "Please loosen the dressing . . . please."

Clayton carefully worked the knot apart, then rerouted the bandage so that it crossed above her breast and looped over her shoulder. But when he again pulled the strip tight, Angela screamed and arched her back. Quickly he loosened the cloth.

"What happened?" He caught her shoulders and threw his weight on her to stop her movements. "What is it, Angela?"

"The . . . pressure on my titty. I can't stand it. I can't stand it!"

Clayton tore the bandage open, freeing Angela's breasts.

"It feels like someone is running a red-hot poker into my body and twisting it around and around," she wept. "It's got to stop!"

Clayton's hand shook as he removed the compress and reexamined the wound. It looked awful. Several inches of flesh around the small puncture had turned a blue-black color, and a red line a quarter-inch wide traveled around Angela's rib cage to culminate in another ugly bruise that nearly engulfed her left breast.

Clayton traced the route of the ball with his fingertips, gently prodding and pushing the skin as he went. When he reached the swell of Angela's breast, the girl cried out at him not to touch her, that the pain was unbrearable.

But he had already found what he was seeking; deep in the fleshy underside of her breast there was a hard lump that most certainly had to be the bullet.

Sinking back on his heels, he sleeved a light film of sweat from his forehead. "I found the bullet, Angela," he said, looking down into her pain-ridden eyes. "It's lodged in your . . . " Clayton stopped and looked away.

"My titty? The bullet's in my titty?"

He nodded. "It's deep, Angela, too deep. I've got to get you to a doctor."

"I won't live long enough to see a doctor, Clayton." Her voice was faint.

"Well, what am I supposed to do?" he shouted. "Cut you open with my pocketknife?"

Angela closed her eyes and trembled. "Yes." Her voice was shallow. "Cut the bullet out of me, Clayton . . . "

"No!" He jumped to his feet. "I've got to get you to a doctor."

Angela opened her eyes. There was no mistaking her pain. "Clayton, I'm going to die."

She turned her face aside. a tear broke from her under her dark eyelashes and trickled down her cheek.

"I'm getting you to a doctor!" He ran to Angela's horse and strapped the travois into place.

Pulling the pinto behind him, he hurried back to Angela and lifted her onto the frame.

She looked up at him. Her face had taken on a soft expression. "Did Montclair scream when he died, Clayton?"

"No," he lied, running a thong across her midsection and tying it securely to the sides of the travois. "Montclair died easy. He never made a sound."

Angela bit her lip. "I may not be so brave."

Clayton peered into her face. "You sound stronger, Angela. Just hold on until I can get you back to Fort Sill."

The girl smiled wistfully. "God gives one a repose . . . "

Clayton's heart stopped: the same words Montclair had used just before he died!

Hardly realizing that he had made the decision, Clayton sprang into action. Digging the opium ball from his coat pocket, he forced an even larger piece of it than before down

Angela's throat, then quickly untied the bond that held her to the travois. Gathering her in his arms, he carried her to the fire and laid her on his blanket.

His hands shook as he opened her coat and exposed her breasts. He had no idea of what operating procedures were, or even how to begin an incision. All he knew was that the bullet was embedded in her breast and that it had to come out through a hole made by him.

Withdrawing his clasp knife, he fumbled with the blades, cursing himself for his clumsiness as he attempted to get the smallest blade opened. His breathing was labored, and sweat rivuleted down his face.

Angela lay there looking up at him through glazed eyes; the large dose of opium was taking effect. Clayton judged that she would drift into oblivion soon, but he was afraid to wait for that possibility.

He ran his thumb along the knife blade and thanked the Lord that it was razor-sharp. Then, his teeth clenched so tightly that they ached, he steadied Angela's breast with his free hand.

Placing the point of the blade against her skin, he closed his eyes and drove the steel through her flesh and muscle until it scraped against the soft lead of the ball.

Angela screamed and thrashed wildly. Blood surged over his hand, causing him to nearly lose his grip on the knife.

Clayton flung his legs over Angela and held her down while he probed with the blade to find the bullet again. "Let her pass out!" he cried aloud, not aware that he had uttered a sound.

One more metal scraped against metal. He snatched the knife free and flung it to the ground.

Catching Angela's breast with both hands, he dug his thumbs into the tender flesh beneath the bullet and worked them slowly toward the projectile.

Angela screamed, then screamed again, and the muscle constriction of her chest as she took the deep breaths and released them probably did more to dislodge the fragment than the pressure of Clayton's thumbs could ever have managed. A moment later the half-flattened ball oozed from the incision amid a glop of bloody tissue.

Slowly Angela's screams subsided. She had slumped into semiconsciousness.

Clayton released a long, shuddering breath, then knuckled the sweat out of his eyes, leaving a bloody streak across his face. He was exhausted, more so than ever before in his life, and he wondered why he felt no elation. But he didn't; he felt numb and tired and scared, not even certain of what he had accomplished.

Pushing himself to his feet, he walked over and added more sticks to the fire, then searched out his canteen and washed the blood from his hands. He wished he had a bottle of whiskey.

Returning to Angela, he saturated a cloth and cleansed the worst of the blood from her body to better see the wound. Making a compress of the blood-soaked rag, he again bound the punctures tightly.

With a tenderness that was alien to him, he wiped away the sweat that sheathed Angela's pallid brow. Then he did an even more bewildering thing: He bent and gently kissed her lips. For a brief instant her eyelids fluttered open and she gazed wonderingly up at him. Then slowly her eyes closed again and her breathing became regular.

When Angela awakened, it was nearing daylight. Even though the fire had died to embers, she could see across to Clayton, draped in his blanket and propped against a rock outcrop. It eased her, just knowing that he was close.

"Clayton?" It was too faint to be called a whisper.

"Yes."

"I . . . just wanted to hear your voice."

Scrambling to his feet, he walked over to where she lay.

Angela's smile was weak and her voice was feeble. "I feel a lot better."

Clayton groaned, knowing that she was lying.

CHAPTER 35

After traveling five miles on the earth-jarring travois, Clayton was forced to ply Angela with another heavy dose of opium.

She looked up at him, her face deathly pale. When she spoke, her voice was a dry whisper. "Oh, Clayton, I'm so sick." Clayton ground his teeth; she was burning up with fever. "Would you . . . kiss me again?" she asked.

Bending, he touched her lips; they were parched, but she was unaware of it, for she had slipped into unconsciousness again.

Not knowing what else to do, Clayton dribbled a few drops of water from his canteen onto a kerchief and blotted her face and neck, and then her lips. He opened her blanket to allow the frigid air to cool her skin, and he inspected the bandages for new bleeding. There didn't seem to be any.

Raking a hand in frustration across the stubble on his jaw, he swung into the saddle and urged the horse into a fast walk. He knew that by setting a rapid pace he was taking a chance on worsening her wound. But weighing that possibil-

ity against the surety of her fever and the risk of blood
poisoning, he felt that he had little choice.

Clayton would have missed the wickiup, for it was well off
the trail in a stand of blackjack and post oak, had someone
inside the hut not cast a log onto the fire just then causing a shower of sparks to burst from the smoke hole, illuminating the twilight with a million tiny shooting stars.
Clayton turned onto the faint trail and cantered up to the
hut.

An old woman, wrapped in a blanket, stepped into the
doorway and stared at him through cold, obsidian eyes.
Almost simultaneously, an ancient Indian man carrying a
Brown Bess musket materialized from a blackjack thicket
not twenty feet from Clayton. He walked to the travois and
peered down at Angela.

Clayton twisted in the saddle to face him. "She's burning
up with fever," he said. "She's been pistol-shot."

The Indian stared blankly at him. Clayton tried again;
"She's been wounded." He pointed to his rib cage. The old
man's impassive face didn't waver. Clayton threw his leg
over the saddle and began to dismount. The Indian cocked
the musket and brought it to his shoulder. Clayton lifted
himself back into the saddle and sat there, wondering what
to do next. The Indian lowered the gun, then peered again at
Angela.

The old woman in the doorway called to the man, her
words sounding to Clayton more like gibberish than any
given language. The man answered in the same dialect, then
indicated Angela with a dip of his musket barrel.

The woman jabbed a gnarled finger at Clayton, and her
voice rose an octave as she spoke again. Clayton wondered
if she were instructing the old Indian to shoot him. A
moment later she plodded barefoot across the frozen
ground and peered closely at Angela. Then, pinching her
nose, she backed away from the travois and began a
harangue that rose in tempo until she was shouting at the
old man.

Clayton slipped his pistol from beneath his coat; he had
made up his mind to take Angela away from there as quickly
as possible, and he steeled himself to shoot the man if he
raised his musket barrel so much as an inch.

But the old Indian laid the gun aside and untied the

bonds that secured Angela to the travois. Then, looking up at Clayton, he motioned for him to carry Angela inside.

With the two Indians leading the way, Clayton carefully gathered Angela into his arms and walked into the hovel. The old woman pointed to a rush mattress, and when Clayton laid Angela upon it, she quickly waved him aside, making it plain that he was no longer needed.

The old man caught Clayton's sleeve and led him outside, then attempted to stare him down. Finally nodding, as if satisfied, he opened his fire bag and took out a clay pipe and tobacco. Tamping the pipe full, he called to the woman. A moment later she appeared, carrying a red-hot coal in her open palm. The man lit the pipe, then passed it to Clayton.

Clayton declined the peace offering, which brought more stares from the Indian, but Clayton hardly noticed because he was preoccupied with keeping an eye on the interior of the cabin. Finally Clayton said, "I want to know what's going on in that hut. Either you go in there and find out, or I will."

Although the Indian did not understand English, he did understand Clayton's tone. Snatching up the musket, he pointed it at Clayton, only to find himself looking down the bore of Clayton's cocked revolver. In the silence that followed, as each man decided whether or not to chance a shot, the jingle of saddle harness and the ring of shod hooves could be heard at a distance.

Clayton swung his eyes toward the sounds, then back to the Indian, but the old man was gone. Snatching his rifle from its saddle scabbard, Clayton stepped in front of the door of the hut and steadied the weapon against his shoulder, sighting down the dark trail toward the noise.

A moment later a half-dozen cavalrymen rode into the yard. "You Captain Harris?" demanded a rider, shifting his weight to lean heavily on his saddle pommel.

"I'm Harris," Clayton said, stepping from the wickiup. He dropped the muzzle of the rifle a fraction, but only a fraction.

"You can put the rifle down. I'm Colonel Henry Drew."

Clayton appraised Drew. The man was not what he had expected. His features were finely chiseled like those of his children, but his face was lined and weathered, and had the swarthy complexion of an Indian. Yes, thought Clayton, he looks like an Indian.

Clayton set the gun beside the door. "Angela's been shot."

"Yes, I know," Drew said, stepping down from the saddle. He looked inquiringly at Clayton.

"She's alive," Clayton told him. "Other than that, I don't know. She's an awfully sick lady, Colonel."

Drew ordered his men to dismount, then walked into the hut and knelt beside Angela. He spoke to the Indian woman and she answered him with a shake of her head. Drew spoke again, and she picked up a container from beside the fire pit, and held it up for him to smell. He grimaced, afraid to even guess what was in the poultice.

Rejoining Clayton outside, Drew said, "The old woman says it was you who dug out the bullet?" Clayton nodded. "Good job," said Drew. Then he walked over to his horse and untied his saddle roll.

"My men and I arrived at Park Hill six days after you left." He rolled out the blanket and sat down on it. "We rode out to escort you back from Fort Sill, but you had already left there. You covered your trail well. We lost it, and didn't pick it up again until we got to the river."

Clayton walked over to Drew and squatted beside the blanket. "Did you find a wounded man at the river?"

"Yes, and we found the one you shot in the eye."

Clayton let that pass; Angela could tell her father the truth if she wished to. He told Drew about the four jayhawkers, and about Angela's catching a stray bullet. "It's ironic," Clayton said. "I've ridden into battles where men were trying to kill me—where the minié balls were as thick as a swarm of flies—and I never even got a scratch. But Angela, whom they weren't even trying to shoot . . . somehow that just doesn't seem right, does it?"

Drew shrugged. "Once I saw a man killed by a bullet that ricocheted off the head of the man next to him. We never know what's goin' to happen in battle. If we did, you can bet that none of us would ever fight in one."

Drew fished a cheroot from his coat pocket and passed it to Clayton. Then, clamping another between his teeth, he struck a match on his boot heel and lit them both.

They smoked in silence for several minutes before Clayton said, "Colonel Drew, I told Angela that Montclair is dead."

Drew appraised Clayton through the haze of cigar smoke.

"And how did she take it?"

I wish I could answer that question with any surety, thought Clayton, but he said, "I think she was relieved that it was finally out in the open, sir." Drew's eyes searched Clayton's closely, but the man said nothing.

A tall young Indian, so deeply bronzed that he could easily have passed for a Negro, approached the blanket. He squatted beside the colonel and spoke to him in Cherokee at length, then turned and studied Clayton.

Clayton was certain that the young man's eyes were filled with something akin to hatred, but suddenly the look was gone as though a window shade had been drawn.

"Captain Harris," Colonel Drew said, "this is Sergeant Johnny Runningdeer." Clayton offered his hand, but Runningdeer rose abruptly and entered the hut.

"Runningdeer seems to think that Angela shot that man in the eye," Drew said. "Did she?"

"Yes."

Drew nodded.

"You approve, sir?" Clayton asked, taken aback.

"Don't you?"

Clayton sighed. "The war has twisted things around, Colonel Drew, until I'm not sure what I approve of."

"Tell me about my son," Drew said. "I want to know the truth."

Clayton told the story, omitting nothing. And when it was over, he was again rewarded with a long, drawn-out silence. Finally Drew said, "I'll detail two men to escort you to Fort Gibson in the morning. Have them hurry a wagon back for Angela."

Clayton walked to the hut with Drew, but he hesitated at the door. Johnny Runningdeer was seated beside the unconscious girl, holding her hand. For a moment, before he was aware that Clayton was watching, the Indian's face was soft and vulnerable.

He's in love with her. The thought shocked Clayton. Without being aware of it, he returned Runningdeer's hostile gaze—and gloried in the act. Enemies are made just that easily.

Clayton bedded down a distance from Drew's men. But he could not sleep. He kept thinking of Angela, and of

Runningdeer sitting beside her. When he did manage to drift off, it was a fitful slumber that left him more exhausted than had he stayed awake.

At the camp fire the next morning, Clayton questioned Drew about Runningdeer.

"He's a full-blood," Drew said. "He's what is known as a black Ute." The colonel sipped his chickory, appraising Clayton across the rim of his cup. "He's not a reservation Indian, Harris. He's a terror on the battlefield . . . a real warrior. And he has asked for Angela's hand when the war is over."

"Is that agreeable with you, sir? Would you consent?"

Drew shrugged. "It's Angela's decision."

"But you're her father. Surely Angela would listen—"

"Captain Harris," Drew interrupted, "the women of the Cherokee Nation have the right to choose their own husbands. And if you disapprove of Runningdeer because of his color—which is the feeling I get from you—let me remind you that Angela is not a white woman."

Clayton's lips tightened. What the colonel said about Angela was true. She was not a white woman. Still, he could not imagine a girl as fair and as lovely, and as educated and refined as Angela marrying a man as dark as a Negro. Especially a man who was a warrior, and who doubtless still believed in the old customs that proclaimed women were good for only two things: to satisfy a man's carnal needs, and to labor her life away at back-breaking menial chores.

No, he thought, wondering why he even cared, such a union would indeed be an insult to Angela Drew; she deserved better, much better. "And how does Angela feel about Runningdeer's proposal?" he asked.

Drew shrugged. "She respects Johnny, but she's afraid of him. They come from two different worlds, and she knows that. Still, Johnny is a determined young man. He will press his suit. I would rather she marry a Cherokee. But as I said, the choice is hers."

Clayton excused himself and walked over to his horse. He was troubled by Colonel Drew's words, for while Drew disapproved of a match between his daughter and a Ute, he obviously did not favor a union between her and a white man. Clayton glanced at the wickiup. He would have liked to have said good-bye to Angela, but Drew had told him that the girl's fever had risen and the old woman was keeping her heavily sedated. Angrily he threw his saddle over the animal's back and drew the cinch tight.

Johnny Runningdeer leaned against the building and watched Clayton saddle up. A smile hovered at the corners of his thin lips. "Don't laugh too soon, mister," Clayton murmured beneath his breath. "I'll be back to get her."

He was surprised by the promise.

In Nashville, Ulysses S. Grant stalked past Andrew Johnson's protesting aide and slammed open the governor's office door.

Johnson looked up from the papers strewn across his desk, then glanced quickly at his aide, who cried, "I tried to stop him, sir!"

Johnson glared at Grant. "In the future, General, never enter my office without being announced."

Grant's face mottled, but his words were slow and even. "I don't believe that the Commanding General of the Army of the United States of America needs your permission for an audience, Governor. Nor do I intend to waste my time explaining my presence to some idiot who calls himself your aide."

Johnson studied Grant more closely. The general had gained considerable influence in Washington by taking the defeated Union Army and whipping it into a victorious fighting unit that was winning battles, the result of which assured Lincoln a second term in the White House. "What do you want, Grant?"

"I didn't come here to *ask* you anything," Grant said. "I came here to *tell* you that the President has demanded a replacement for General Paine immediately." Grant took a cigar from his coat pocket and struck a match to it. Blowing smoke toward the ceiling, he said, "If you or your politicians interfere with my orders this time, Governor, I am personally going to kick the seat of your britches until your ass falls out."

Johnson sprang to his feet. "I won't be talked to as if I were one of your soldiers, Grant. I am the Military Governor of Tennessee and the Vice-President of the United States!"

Grant's pale eyes bored into Johnson. "You are nothing

but a goddamned title as far as I'm concerned, Johnson."
Seating himself on the edge of the governor's desk, he went
on: "You can continue to play politics with your lackeys and
bully your civilians, but stop meddling with my army.
Because in spite of incompetent fools like you and Paine, I
intend to win this war."

Johnson sat down again, trying hard to get a grip on the
rage that threatened to send him clawing for Grant's throat.

"Actually, Governor," Grant continued, "I am doing you
a service by coming to you. Paine's actions are the talk of
Washington—there's been a lot of letter-writing from Sumner County. I assure you, sir, the general's not very popular."

Grant took a long, slow draw on his cigar. "You might
give that some close consideration, Governor. Yes, I believe
if I were you, I'd think about that. If I court-martialed Paine
this instant, it might be interesting to see who he would
implicate as accomplices to his high-handed government
murders and thievery. Do I make myself clear, Governor?"

In Gallatin, Paine erupted out of his chair, causing
Grant's young courier to take a startled step backward.

"You pimply-faced son-of-a-bitch!" Paine shouted, shak-
ing the orders at the young soldier. "You go back and tell
Grant that if he thinks he can order me off to Paducah,
Kentucky, he's crazy!"

Paine flung the papers across the room, scattering them
over the floor. "This is my command—Sumner County,
Tennessee. I have worked hard to bring this secesh town of
Gallatin under Union control."

"Sorry, General," the young courier stammered, "but
there's more, sir."

"What do you mean there's more? I read the orders
thoroughly."

"I have a verbal message, sir, from General Grant."

Verbal messages were by far more dangerous than written
orders. Paine slumped into his chair, expecting disaster.

The courier snapped to attention and stared at the wall
above Paine's head. Clearing his throat, he said, "General
Grant says to inform you, sir, that the big boys have left you
sucking hind tit." The soldier dropped his voice until it was
almost inaudible. "He says that you are a disgrace to your

uniform, sir, and that your military career is finished . . . and . . . and that if it were up to him, he'd put you before a firing squad."

Paine's chin dropped to his chest and he made a tent of his fingers which he studied thoughtfully. "A sad day has come to pass," he said quietly, "when a competent, efficient officer, with a superb military background like mine, can be throttled by a drunken bum who has never succeeded at any venture he has undertaken, no matter how trivial."

Ten days had passed when Clayton thundered pell-mell up the path to the wickiup. "The wagon's five miles back," he called to Colonel Drew, who had stepped out of the hut to greet him. Clayton jumped to the ground and led his horse toward Drew. "How is she?"

"She's tolerable. It was bad for a few days. Thought sure she was goin' to die, but she's a fighter."

"Sir," Clayton said quickly, "I would like to pay my respects to Miss Drew."

"I believe the old woman is changing Angela's dressing."

"Is that you, Clayton?" Angela called weakly from inside the hut. "We'll only be a minute more."

Shortly the old Indian woman waddled to the door and motioned Clayton in.

Angela seemed genuinely glad to see him, taking his hand in hers and squeezing it; the touch said more than words. Clayton knelt beside her. She was so pale and drawn that he could hardly conceal the dismay that welled up inside him. "How are you?" he asked at last.

Angela gave him a crooked smile. "I would rather have not been shot."

"I wish it had been me," he said.

"So do I," she agreed.

They both laughed, but the sound had a nervous ring to it, and the silence that followed was tense. Clayton told her that Mrs. Drew had sent her a camelbacked trunk full of clothing; it was coming with the wagon. The girl nodded and lay back exhausted, her eyes searching his face, her hand still clutching his.

"You've got to rest," he said, forcing a smile. She tightened her grip on his hand. Rising to his feet, Clayton found Johnny Runningdeer standing in the doorway. He wondered how long the man had been there. Releasing Angela's hand, he walked to the door, he shouldered Runningdeer aside and stepped into the pale, wintry sunlight.

Colonel Drew joined him and together they walked to Clayton's horse. As Clayton untied the cinch and dropped the saddle to the ground, the colonel said, "Runningdeer doesn't like you much."

Clayton's eyes narrowed. "I can get along with just about anybody, Colonel Drew. But I'm getting to the point where I don't try real hard."

Nodding, the colonel walked out to meet the wagon that was rumbling up the boulder-strewn trail.

The return trip to Park Hill was uneventful until the last night on the trail. Snow clouds had moved in, and they hung thick and heavy over the countryside. Colonel Drew had ordered a canvas stretched at an angle from the side of the wagon to the ground, and Angela's bed had been moved under the makeshift tent.

The snow came out of the west, a bitter, sideways storm that covered the ground before the men could erect their shelters. With his blanket draped over his head, Clayton trudged through the blizzard to Angela's tent. Runningdeer was under the snow-laden canvas talking earnestly with the girl. Clayton cursed under his breath and retraced his footsteps to his own campsite.

Had he bothered to look over his shoulder, he would have seen Johnny Runningdeer stalk from Angela's tent and disappear into the swirling storm. But he didn't look; instead, he rolled into his blankets and wondered if perhaps Colonel Drew were mistaken about Angela's preferences.

Park Hill was a welcome sight, standing with quiet dignity in the barren winter landscape. Angela was hurried into the house and put to bed, while Clayton and the cavalrymen stalled their horses and forked hay into the manger. An hour later Clayton joined the Drews in the parlor.

Mrs. Drew poured him a glass of brandy. "My husband tells me that you have already spoken to Angela of Montclair's death." She settled into a chair across the table from him and stared into his face.

"It was necessary, Mrs. Drew," Clayton said.

"Yes, I suppose it was," returned the lady. "But I would have preferred that you had waited. You were taking a big chance, Mr. Harris."

Angela did her dying months ago, Clayton thought angrily. But he said nothing. He wondered if parents ever really knew their children well enough to appreciate their strengths, or their weaknesses. Certainly the Drews had not the least idea of how truly strong and determined Angela was. No, he decided, the Drews did not know their daughter at all.

CHAPTER 36

Although it was New Year's night, 1865, and the news was several days old, Cotton's elation over an editorial in *The Monmouth, Illinois, Review* was no less satisfying than if the paper had come off the press that very day.

General Paine, having been transferred to Paducah, Kentucky, was, according to the paper, attempting to run the Western District of Kentucky with the same vicious iron fist that he had wielded in Sumner County. The paper screamed: "Paine is guilty of crimes that should hang him on a gibbet higher than Haman's. He should be arrested and arraigned for trial, and it is this editor's belief that he will be speedily court-martialed, speedily convicted, and speedily shot. He is a disgrace to common humanity, and if Lincoln does not see to it that he is punished, he must share his infamy."

Cotton laid the paper aside. "They finally got the bastard," he said to Mr. Summers.

"I thought you'd like that piece," the old man said. "*The Nashville Daily Union* is callin' for an investigation of Paine that would include the time he spent in Gallatin."

Mrs. Summers was sitting in a rocker by the hearth,

knitting. "Do you think anything will come of it, Jonathan?" she asked.

"I doubt it," the old man said. "Too many politicians got a piece of the pie here in Sumner County. They got Cragfont, an' Walnut Grove, the Blythe place, General Donelson's plantation . . ." His shoulders slumped. "I can go on an' on."

Cotton appraised Mr. Summers, and a gentle sadness filled him; Mr. Summers was a tired, worn, old man. Cotton reached over and gripped his shoulder. "Don't you reckon that when the war's over, the plantations will be given back to the rightful owners?"

Mr. Summers covered Cotton's hand with his own. "I hope that's true, son, but I'd not bet on it."

Rufus stepped into the room. "Your blanket roll is tied an' ready, Mr. Cotton, an' I saddled that horse Mista Harper brought you."

Cotton walked over to Mrs. Summers and bent down to kiss her cheek. "I'm ridin' out tonight to rejoin the irregulars," he said.

"Why don't you stay home?" the old lady pleaded. "The war's all but over . . . an' to tell the truth, Cotton, I haven't got a thimbleful of use for that Ellis Harper."

"I been home for nearly three weeks, ma'am," Cotton reminded her. "An' I reckon I'm just too edgy to stay indoors. Besides, with the Yankees patrollin' as heavy as they are, it's a wonder they ain't already searched here."

"Well, they haven't, and they may not," Mrs. Summers said.

"They've done caught a bunch of the boys who come home with me," Cotton said. "An' they ain't lettin' them take the Oath no more."

Fanny burst into the room. "Cotton, the whole yard is full of soldiers. They've surrounded the house."

Before the words were out of Fanny's mouth, Cotton had a cocked Colt in each hand and was dashing toward the hall. Mr. Summers caught him at the door. "Let me handle this," he commanded, snatching the pistols from Cotton and passing them to Mrs. Summers, who quickly climbed the stairs and ran into her bedchamber with them.

Mr. Summers pushed Cotton into the parlor with orders to stay there. Then he walked to the front door, where a heavy pounding suggested that someone was using the buttplate of a rifle for a knocker.

From the parlor, Cotton heard the door open and Mr. Summers demand an explanation. The Union officer replied that he was searching every house in the vicinity for Rebel soldiers. "Well," the old man said loudly, "they ain't no Rebels here, just me and the Missus, an' my house slaves, and my idiot son. But you are welcome to look if you're not satisfied with my word."

Pushing Mr. Summers aside, the captain strode into the dimly lit parlor, where Rufus was busy at the fireplace and Fanny was tucking a lap robe around Cotton, who was lounging in a wing chair.

Rufus' skin crawled as he looked at the man standing in the doorway. Although it had been three long years, he recognized the officer: Wilson, one of the men he had nearly beaten to death in Gallatin. Turning his back to the man, Rufus inched his hand toward the iron poker leaning against the mantel.

Fanny stood frozen; she too had recognized Wilson. The memory of her pain, humiliation, and degradation stabbed through her. A whimper escaped her bloodless lips. Cotton inched his hand from beneath the robe and laid it warningly against her thigh.

The captain's gaze passed over Rufus to Fanny, and then bore into Cotton, who was lolling his head from side to side as if indeed he were feeble-minded.

Crossing the room, the man studied Cotton from different angles. "You look familiar to me," he said. "I've seen you someplace." Cotton continued to loll. A drop of spittle dangled from his lower lip. "Didn't you ride with Morgan?" the man demanded.

Cotton nodded his head vigorously and gave the captain a gap-toothed grin. "Moron, yes, moron!" he shouted. More spittle dripped off his chin.

Wilson took a step backward. "Perhaps I'm wrong," he said. Then, "He been like that all his life?" he asked Fanny.

The girl shuddered as the man's gaze penetrated her. "I don' know, Massa," she stammered. "He's older dan me."

The captain's eyes narrowed as recognition darted in and out of the fringes of his memory. The girl looked familiar, yet she didn't. Snatching up the candle lamp, he held it close to her face.

The son-of-a-bitch recognizes her, thought Cotton. Throwing caution to the wind, he grabbed for the holstered pistol the captain wore. Fanny moved like lighting. Slapping Cotton's hand aside, she shook her finger in his face. "Yo' a naughty boy, Marse Junior. Yo' keep yo' han's off'n this nice man's baubles. Yo' knows better'n to grab at things what don' belong to yo'."

Rufus had also seen the man's reaction to Fanny, and he had turned from the hearth with the poker gripped tight in his hand. The captain spun at the motion. It was the first real look he had had at Rufus, and confusion mixed with alarm marred his face.

"I know these two darkies," he cried, looking from Fanny to Rufus. "The wench is thinner now than she was then, and the buck is bigger, but—"

"An' you know my boy rode with Morgan," Mr. Summers shouted. "An' if you took a good look at my wife, you'd probably think she was your mother. An' considerin' that nary a one of us has been off this place since the war started, that's a damn good trick, Captain." The old man stared contemptously at the officer. "Why, you're as feeble-minded as my boy."

Rufus turned and punched at the fire logs, causing the flames to jump and cast an eerie light across the room.

Captain Wilson shivered. Something was amiss. He looked quickly about the shadowed parlor; all eyes were on him expectantly. He took a quick step toward the door, and then another.

A sergeant walked into the room. "Nobody in the house except an old woman upstairs, sir. You want us to check the barn?"

The captain's gaze swung to Rufus; then to Fanny; then to Cotton.

Again the sergeant asked, "Shall we inspect the barn, Captain?"

Captain Wilson shook his head. "No, Sergeant, I've seen all I want of this place. There's crazy people here . . . crazy people, all of them."

As the soldiers marched down the hall, Cotton heard

Wilson ask the sergeant if any of the people in the parlor looked familiar to him.

When the sound of the troops had died away, Mr. Summers shook his head in dismay. "He recognized the three of you. He'll be back as soon as he figures it out."

No he won't, Cotton thought grimly, but he said nothing; it would be better if the old man had no notion of what he was about to do. "Rufus," Cotton said, "bring my horse around as quick as you can. Fanny, run upstairs and get my pistols from Mrs. Summers. And Fanny . . ." The girl raised her eyes to him, and Cotton could see the nightmarish memories swimming deep in their gray irises. ". . . You were just goddamned great."

Fanny attempted a smile but ended up choking back a sob. Then she fled up the stairs in search of Cotton's guns.

When Cotton walked out the back door to his waiting horse, Rufus, in an overcoat and slouch hat, and with a double-barreled shotgun laid in the crook of his arm, stood quietly holding the bridle.

"Where do you think you're goin'?" Cotton asked.

"I'm goin' with you."

"No you ain't."

"Yes, Mr. Cotton, I am. It's dark, and you might miss."

Cotton stared hard at Rufus. "I never miss."

Rufus stared back. "Neither do I."

Cotton grinned. "I reckon you're figurin' on ridin' double?"

"Unless you're figurin' on walkin', sir."

The two men, riding double, trotted down the lane in the wake of the Union patrol. Cotton asked, "You know what I hate more'n anything else in the world, Rufus?"

"Yes, sir, Mr. Cotton, I do," Rufus returned easily. "You told me several years ago. It's a nigger who's smarter than you."

Cotton laughed and spurred the horse into a gallop.

Clayton Harris did not know Angela Drew nearly as well as he thought he did. On New Year's evening she left her bed and with the help of a servant, donned a soft, finely woven gown and took her seat at the supper table.

The Drews welcomed her unexpected appearance, but

Clayton worried that she was not yet strong enough to be up and about. However, he kept his thoughts to himself.

Angela was quiet throughout the meal. When Clayton happened to look her way, more times than not, he was jolted to find her watching him with an expression that he had not seen before: interest. He wondered what that signified; he had long since learned that Angela's every gesture was founded on meaning.

When the meal was finished and the two men had withdrawn to the sitting room to smoke, Colonel Drew informed Clayton that he was returning to his unit the next morning.

"Going back is a waste of time," the colonel said, "but I want to be there for the finish. Why don't you go with me? No one would ever be the wiser."

Clayton shook his head. "I gave my word, sir."

"Harris," the colonel said, "if all the men in the Confederate Army who took the pledge, honored it, the Confederacy wouldn't have enough men in its ranks to warrant bugle call."

"I'm aware of that," Clayton said, "but it doesn't change my position, sir."

Drew sighed and climbed to his feet. "To oneself be true, or something like that. Well, I'm goin' to bed."

When the colonel's footsteps had died away, Clayton settled more comfortably into his chair and let his mind drift to thoughts of Texas. After the war he would return to Tennessee to see Cotton and the old folks; then he would head for Three Stones.

He didn't know how long he had been meditating before he became aware of her presence; Angela was seated in the chair next to his. For a long while they sat there in the semidarkness lit only by a single candle, neither wishing to break the silence.

Finally Angela said, "I haven't done much to make you like me, have I?"

Clayton thought about the question, then said, "No, I suppose you haven't. But on the other hand, the only thing I've done since I came here that impressed you was to shoot a man's horse."

Angela smiled. "It's about the only thing you've done since you came here that I couldn't have done better."

"Touché," he returned dryly.

"I speak French too," Angela said. "I've even studied fencing."

Clayton ignored the remark. Presently he said, "You mentioned that shooting the horse was 'about' the only thing I've done that impressed you. Is there something more?"

Angela looked directly into his eyes. "Yes, Clayton, there is. Papa told me about the woman at the river. Burying her was a very kind and considerate thing to do."

"Any man would have done the same."

"The men who left her there, didn't."

Angela's eyes reflected the light of the flickering candle as she gazed at him, and Clayton found the smoldering illusion unsettling, for he was more aware of her than he would ever have admitted.

"Another thing that impresses me about you," she continued, "is that you suffered my abuse concerning my mother and never complained. I admire your loyalty . . . and your stupidity."

Clayton shrugged. "You didn't understand what was going on."

"Will you please stop being nice to me!" she exclaimed. "You infuriate me, Clayton, with your constant forgiveness. The only time you've ever acted like a red-blooded man was when I shot at you." The girl's face flushed and she looked away, remembering how he had caught her up and shaken her, how his body had felt against hers when he had held her close before flinging her to the ground.

Clayton jumped to his feet and thrust his face close to hers. She had a way of making him more angry, more quickly, than anyone he had yet to meet. "And the only time you've acted like a woman, much less like the lady you profess to be, was when you were half delirious from being shot!"

Spinning on his heel, he strode from the room, leaving her slumped deep in her chair, her eyes following his every step.

Angela caught him as he opened his bedchamber door. Grabbing his arm, she spun him about.

"I hate you!" she hissed. "I just want you to know that. And when I was shot and I asked you to kiss me . . . well, that was nothing more than a need to be comforted. I would have asked anybody."

"Really?" Clayton raised his eyebrows sarcastically. "And all this time I thought it was because you loved me."

"I hate you," she said again. "And if I weren't wounded, I'd slap your stupid face."

Clayton reached out and pulled the startled girl against him.

"Let me go," she said, looking angrily into his eyes.

"How do you feel?"

"I hurt."

"Bad?"

"No."

Clayton swept her into his arms and stepped into the bedchamber, then kicked the door closed behind him.

Cotton reined in the horse. In the darkened hollow below, he and Rufus could hear the jingle of saddle harness and the mingled sounds of horses blowing and men talking.

"They're taking a breather," Cotton whispered. "Probably be there ten minutes or more."

"How do you want to handle this?" Rufus asked.

"Leave the horse here. We'll work around to the right of 'em, close to the road. When we pick out the captain, I'll shoot him. You unload your shotgun into the patrol to create confusion, then light out for home. I'll head back for the horse." Cotton laughed silently. "Hell, they'll think a Confederate regiment bushwhacked 'em."

The two men crept into the bushes and made their way toward the soldiers. As they neared the road, Cotton gripped Rufus' hand tightly; it was the first such gesture he had ever made toward the slave. Rufus peered solemnly into Cotton's eyes, then nodded; friendships are bonded just that simply. Cotton dropped to his stomach and wormed his way toward the enemy, not fifty yards distant.

The Union patrol was in the process of remounting when Cotton pushed aside a clump of brittle, winter-killed weeds and thrust his pistol through the opening. The captain was ordering the sergeant to hurry the men; he wanted to be in Gallatin before midnight.

The click of Cotton's revolver locking into full cock was lost in the jingle of harness, the clink of sabers, and the voices of the cavalrymen. Slowly, and with careful aim,

Cotton tightened his finger on the trigger. All at once the world erupted in what sounded like cannon fire, and Cotton watched in awe as the captain and his horse went down in a spray of flesh and blood that sent the half-mounted patrol into such a state of pitching and bucking that Cotton didn't even attempt to pick a target. Instead, he emptied both of his revolvers into the frenzied melee. Not waiting to see the outcome, he broke into a long lope for the hilltop where the horse was tethered. He was panting by the time he reached the crest.

The din of shouting, screaming, and cursing that rose from below, filled the eerie darkness with a crescendo that sounded as though someone had opened the gates of purgatory. Cotton ran to the horse and swung into the saddle.

Rufus burst over the rise and raced over to catch the bridle. "Did I get him?" he cried excitedly. "I couldn't tell from where I was layin'"

"Damn right you did. You all right?"

"Damn right I am!"

Cotton laughed delightedly. "Rufus," he said, "just once, before this war is over an' you're a free man; I'd like for you to act like a slave an' do somethin' I tell you to do. Just once!" Rufus grinned at Cotton. "Well, Marse Cotton," he said, "I'se gwine to do that right now, sur. I'se gwine to. 'Light out fo' Home!'" Both men hooted.

"See you when the war's over," cried Cotton, jumping his horse into a dead run. A moment later, amid a clatter of hoofbeats and a spray of frozen earth, he was lost from sight.

As false dawn pushed the blue-black shadows from the bedchamber, Angela snuggled her cheek closer against Clayton's chest and touched her lips to the hollow of his throat. She was contented and fulfilled, happy to be a woman . . . and awed to her depths by what she had just experienced.

Being careful not to awaken Clayton, she crept from the bed and quickly donned her gown, draping it loosely around her bandages. With a longing look at the still warm indentation her body had left next to Clayton in the feather tick, she stepped from the room and hurried down the hall.

She slipped silently into her bedchamber, then carefully eased the door closed and leaned against the panel, listening for sounds that would indicate early risers. Releasing her pent-up breath, she turned from the door and would have screamed had not a hand clasped itself roughly over her mouth.

Johnny Runningdeer wrestled Angela across the room and flung her onto her bed. Then he crossed his arms and glared down at her.

Angela pushed herself to her elbows. Her wounds ached as though they had reopened, but she ignored them. "If you don't get out of here this instant," she spat in Cherokee, "I'll awaken the household."

Runningdeer sneered. "You have shamed not only your family, but the whole Cherokee Nation. You, who are a princess among the people, have lowered yourself to play the whore for a white man, a man who will one day walk away and leave you to face your disgrace alone."

"I have done nothing disgraceful," Angela said. "And if I had, Clayton Harris would not leave me. He is an honorable man . . . and he loves me."

Runningdeer caught her shoulders and shook her savagely. "White people have no honor when it comes to dealing with us. And they know nothing of love; they use that emotion as they use all emotions, to enslave one another."

Steeling herself, Angela twisted free, stood up, and faced him angrily. "I am Indian!" she cried. "As much Indian as you! I went to him freely, and I intend to go to him every night freely! Do you hear? I am free, even if he casts me aside afterward." Her eyes mocked him. "So you see, Johnny, Indians are without honor also."

Runningdeer's eyes moved down Angela's body to where her gown had gaped open when he shook her. A long expanse of naked abdomen and thigh was revealed. His mouth drew into a thin, ugly line. Pointing to the semen that stained her thighs, he said, "The mark of a man runs down your legs. You will never be free again. Never."

Angela snatched her gown tightly about her. "Get out of here," she whispered fiercely.

Runningdeer's coal-black eyes bore into her. "When he is gone and the Cherokee have turned their back on you, I will come. You will beg to be my wife."

"Get out of here," she said again, pointing at the door. "You've got ten seconds to leave, or so help me, I'll call my father."

"And when you are my wife," he said softly, "I will cut your nose so that no white man will ever look into your face again."

Angela Drew was a woman in love. It was March, 1865. Her wounds were all but healed, and she felt wonderful. Although she shared Clayton's bed almost nightly—and indeed was his mate in every sense of the word—and although he had never spoken of marriage, she was daunted not in the least. She loved him; that was enough.

Angela's idolation of him was the only dark spot on Clayton's horizon. No matter how white Angela Drew appeared to be, Indian blood ran through her veins; and the fact that she was intelligent, courageous, and beautiful meant less than nothing to the majority of white people. They scorned interracial relationships with a repugnance that brinked on malevolence, and that particular prejudice was universal. He knew that even Texas would be no exception.

CHAPTER 37

On April tenth, Cotton walked his horse beneath the sweeping branches of a huge maple tree that was donning its spring coat of new greenery with an elegance that only Mother Nature can achieve. He gazed down at a small mound of weed-infested earth. It was the first time he had visited Willie's grave since he had buried her.

Removing his tattered campaign hat, he chose his words carefully. "Well, it's over, Willie. Grant pinned Lee down at some place in Virginia I ain't never heard of an' whipped him . . . us . . . bad. It was at a place called Appomattox, an' Lee had to surrender his army. An' to tell the truth, I reckon I'm glad. We're wore out, Willie. The South is just plain wore out." Cotton took a deep, lingering breath. "The Yankees done turned Gallatin over to the civil authorities, an' the high sheriff has declared me an' Ellis Harper an' the boys outlaws, an' the newspapers is clamorin' for us to be hung. Now ain't that somethin'?"

Cotton twisted his hat into a tight ball. "I let you down, Willie. I done searched ever'where for the people who . . . hurt you. An' I still ain't got no notion who did it. But I promise you, I'll never stop lookin'. An' when I find 'em, you'll know it, 'cause I'll cover your grave with flowers . . . I swear it to you, Willie."

On May 2, 1865, Cotton leaned his cane-backed chair against the wall of Harper's headquarters and chewed slowly on a quid of tobacco, occasionally spitting a stream of amber toward the cold ashes in the fireplace. A Federal courier, his blue uniform crisp and new, stood at attention just inside the door, his eyes darting from one Rebel guerrilla to another until they finally fixed themselves on Ellis Harper. Nervously the courier said, "Well, Captain Harper, you've heard the terms. What is your answer, sir?"

Harper ignored the question and continued pacing the filthy dirt floor, a scowl furrowing his brow.

Cotton fingered the letter lying on the table and silently read the offer for the third time: "The terms are that you surrender your arms and any public property you may have in your possession, give parole not to take up arms against the United States, and to observe and obey the laws in force where you reside.

"Upon complying with these terms, each man will be permitted to remain at his house without being molested by the military authorities."

The offer was signed: Colonel Gilfillan, Provost Marshal, United States Army, Gallatin, Tennessee.

Harper spun toward the courier. "How do I know it ain't a trap?"

"Colonel Gilfillan is an honorable man, sir."

"Don't hand me that hogwash," Harper said. "He's a damned Yankee."

The courier bristled. "I resent that remark, sir."

Cotton grinned at the boy. "How long have you been in the army, son?"

The courier, older than Cotton but looking five years younger, replied proudly, "Almost a month, sir."

"Do you know why Gilfillan sent you out here," Cotton asked, "instead of one of his seasoned troops?"

The young soldier studied Cotton, then shook his head. "No, sir, I don't. But I consider it an honor to have been selected."

"Son," Cotton said, "your commander figured that when you rode in here, you wouldn't live long enough to deliver that message. That's why he sent a green kid as courier. An' that's why we're untrustin' about agreein' to these terms."

Harper drew his revolver and pointed it at the boy. "I still ain't sure he's leavin' here alive."

The courier backed toward the door. "I came here protected by a flag of truce."

Harper thumbed back the hammer and sighted down the barrel. "Don't do it, Ellis," Cotton said, dropping his chair to the floor.

"Damn you!" Harper swung the pistol around and pointed it toward Cotton. "I told you never to brace me again."

Cotton grinned at Harper, but it was without mirth. "If you kill this fella, Ellis, we'll be outlaws for the rest of our lives. I don't know about you, but I want to go home. I'm tired of runnin' and hidin' an' never trustin' anybody, not even our own people. The war's over, Ellis."

Several of the men voiced the same opinion. Harper reluctantly lowered the pistol. "All right." He scowled at the frightened courier. "Tell the colonel we'll meet him a week from today at the bottom of the ridge near South Tunnel. Tell him we ain't lookin' for trouble, but he better be straight across the board with us. You got that?"

"Yes, sir. I'll tell him." With a grateful glance at Cotton, the boy backed from the building and quickly mounted his horse.

When the hoofbeats were lost from hearing, Cotton released his breath. He had truly doubted that Harper would allow the boy to ride away.

On May 9, 1865, Harper, Cotton, and twenty-three guerrillas rode in single file down the long hillside called the Highland Rim. They were edgy, eyes never still, hands always near their weapons.

As they rode out of the woods toward the waiting Federal column, Cotton's mouth was so dry he could hardly produce enough saliva with which to lick his lips. One misconstrued move by either party would result in a blood bath that would make many of the pitched battles of 1864 seem like child's play.

Colonel Gilfillan sized up the men riding toward him. They were a hard, tough lot, and it was obvious that they were nervous. Turning in the saddle, he threw a threatening scowl at his troops. "While this surrender is in progress, if any of you so much as coughs, I'll court-martial the entire brigade. Is that clear?" Not expecting an answer, he faced forward and prepared to meet the notorious Ellis Harper.

The surrender was simple and to the point, with Harper and his men dismounting and stacking their weapons. They stood there quietly, lost and painfully aware of their vulnerability.

The Confederates were mostly young men, underfed, ill-clothed, tired and sickly; yet, even unarmed, they presented such an aroma of danger and menace that Gilfillan wasted little time with formalities. He shook their hands, presented each with a signed parole, then said, "Gentlemen, you are free to go home."

When the Confederates swung into their saddles, a Union soldier began singing "Dixie." In moments the entire brigade had joined in.

As Cotton passed the long line of Union soldiers, a young recruit called, "Hey, Reb, give us a Rebel yell. We joined up too late to hear one."

Cotton studied the young, eager faces that peered up at him. Then, grinning sadly, he said, "You're a lucky bunch of sons-of-bitches, an' you don't even know it."

News of Lee's surrender did not reach Oklahoma Territory until June 23, 1865, over two months after the rest of the nation had ceased hostilities. And equally staggering for Clayton Harris was the simultaneous news of President Abraham Lincoln's assassination.

Although the born-and-bred Southerners, including Angela, showed indifferent sympathy for Lincoln's tragedy, Clayton could not dispel the nagging fear that the South had lost its only Union ally. He felt certain that the loss would haunt the South for years to come.

On the porch at Park Hill, Clayton stood behind Angela with his arm around her, listening to the mournful tolling of the bells that signified the end of a war-torn era. The chimes also designated the finish of his self-imposed exile from Tennessee—and a time of reckoning. He could no longer avoid the issue of Angela's love for him.

Angela felt Clayton's arms tighten around her waist. Leaning back in his embrace, she laid her head against his chest. "I'm frightened Clayton," she said, not entirely sure of what it was that alarmed her, but feeling the threat deep in her soul.

"Of what?"

"Of everything, I suppose. It's all too final—the end of the war, Lincoln's assassination, everything. Washington City is probably a mare's-nest right now with all the politicians vying for new positions in the Federal hierarchy, and we, the common people, always seem to be the losers when a political power struggle is in the making."

"Women aren't supposed to have such thoughts," Clayton chided.

Angela pushed herself free and turned to face him. "I resent that remark, Clayton Harris. Women are affected by politics just as surely as men are. We suffer—perhaps even more than the soldiers do—because men decide to declare war, not upon one another, which is the way it should be, but upon the entire nation, including women and children. Yet we are not supposed to have a voice in our own well-being."

Clayton drew her again into his embrace. "A nation has died," he said, laying his cheek against her hair. "But perhaps an even greater one will grow in its place after the dust settles. One where not only will the slaves be free, but also the women." He tightened his arms about her again. "An old gentleman once told me: 'Never take anything from the soil that you can't put back.' I've thought a lot about those words, Angela. The golden days of the South came straight from the soil—cotton, tobacco, corn—and the Southerners took and took, depending upon the sweat of the slaves' to fuel the engine that kept the entire mechanism stable. Well, maybe in the last four bloody years the South has put enough back into soil . . . that we might start anew."

Angela gazed up into his eyes. "New life will spring from that soil, Clayton," she said, "and we will build a better country than we have yet to imagine." He nodded and his eyes held a distant glint that she had not seen before. She asked, "Was that old gentleman your spoke of, your father?"

"No, but he might as well be; I love him like a father."

"What of your mother?" It was a question asked with timid hesitation. "You've never spoken of her."

"She died when I was very young."

Angela went cold inside. "I'm sorry, Clayton," she said. "I'm sure she was a fine lady."

"Yes, I suppose she was. But I hardly remember her." Clayton was very much aware of Angela's disappointment. Her words, "but not once was I pretty enough to be taken home to meet their mothers," rose up like bile in his throat, and he experienced an unjustified resentment toward her because of the sickening guilt that suddenly gnawed at his insides.

"Darn it, Angela," he said, angrily, "I would have been proud to—"

Angela heard the displeasure in his voice. The coldness within her surfaced so swiftly that she it left her body rigid to his touch.

"Don't say it!" She twisted from his grasp. "Don't you dare say it! Don't insult me, Clayton. It has less than no meaning now."

Clayton caught her by her shoulders and tried to draw her toward him, but she spun free and turned her back to him. Her voice had a quiet calmness when she spoke. "Why did you make love to me, Clayton? Why did you let me fall in love with you?"

"I could not have stopped either one, Angela. I love you too. I've been lying awake at nights trying to sort out our dilemma . . ."

"What is our dilemma?" she demanded, turning to face him. "You just admitted that you love me, and you cannot doubt my love for you. Isn't that enough?"

Clayton shook his head. "Under normal circumstances, it would be, but ours are not normal circumstances."

"Why are they not?" she cried, stepping toward him, hope filling her words. "We are just two young people who love each other . . ."

Again he shook his head. "No, Angela, we're not. I'm a Northern boy who threw his birthright to the wind when he joined the Confederacy. You are a well educated, too-beautiful Indian girl who is considering doing the very same thing were she to join with a white man."

"Would that be so terrible?"

Clayton walked to the edge of the porch and gazed at the distant hills. "Yes, Angela, it would be." He turned toward her. "The Southerners never really accepted me. You know as well as I that beneath their friendly and outgoing facade, they have an Olympian, stiff-necked hauteur that outsiders, no matter how hard they try, cannot penetrate."

"I don't give a fig about joining their social circles," she cried. "I just want to be with you."

"That's the point I've been trying to make, Angela—you'd always be an outsider. They wouldn't accept you. Why, it's been only a little over twenty-five years since the same folks we're speaking of drove your people down the Trail of Tears." He caught her shoulders and looked into her eyes. "Your brother was one of the finest, most courageous men I've ever met. Montclair gave his life for a Southern boy in prison, but it changed nothing; the men despised him for it. And the women . . . no matter where we went, they would spite you. I couldn't live like that, Angela, and even though you believe you could endure their scorn, it would eventually tear you . . . us . . . apart. In the end, you and I would detest one another."

"I'm stronger than that, Clayton," she said, her voice bitter. "My love for you is not so fragile that it can be shattered by nothing more substantial than a wagging tongue."

"And what of our children?" he demanded. "Could you also endure seeing them abused because of their Indian heritage? Could you?" Not waiting for her to answer, he said, "Well, I couldn't! I'd end up killing someone because of it." He took her hand and brought it to his lips. "Try as I might, Angela, I would eventually blame you for my weakness and cowardice, and you would hate me for it."

Angela fought the rising nausea that threatened to send her running for the yard. "We could go away," she said. "Someplace in the East—New York, or Philadelphia. Someplace where my mixed blood would not be a burden." Clayton refused to meet her eyes and she felt the ice-cold numbness return, freezing her.

Clayton shook his head. "You said yourself that when you were in the North, the men were embarrassed to be seen in public with you, that they were ashamed to introduce you to . . ." Clayton scowled at her. "Damn it, Angela. I love you, you know that."

Angela stared at him. "A while ago," she murmured, "you said that after the dust settles, a great nation will grow up out of the soil. You said that Negroes and women will be

free. Well, the Negroes are free, Clayton. But freedom didn't
wait for the South to make up its finicky mind to liberate
the slaves. No, Clayton, freedom won't wait on any man . . .
and neither will I." Tears filled her eyes. "I'm yours for the
taking, Clayton. All you need do is to reach out to me . . .
but the time is now."

He took a deep breath and slowly let it out. "I can't do
that, Angela. Lord knows I want to, but I can't. As much as I
love you, I can't."

"Yes, Clayton," she whispered, "you love me"—she
shook her head—"but you don't love me enough, not
nearly enough."

Angela went to Clayton that night. And her lovemaking
was a sensitive, intimate giving of herself, the total surrender of a woman certain that she will never again see her soul
mate.

She quivered as he entered her, opening herself to receive
him, holding back nothing, melting over him and around
him until they were one.

She was so tender, so passionate, that had Clayton not
been totally caught up in her ardor, he would have understood the pitiful reality: She was trying in the only way she
knew to absorb enough beautiful memories of him to last
her a lifetime. That was the last night she went to him. And
that was the night she conceived.

For two weeks Angela kept to her room. At first Clayton
was worried that she was ill, but when she adamantly
refused to see him, he became angry and spent his days at
Fort Gibson, where a Union commander, having relieved
Captain Hawkins of his command, was in the process of
garrisoning the fort.

Mrs. Drew approached Clayton on Monday morning of
the third week. She told him nicely, but firmly, that it might
be best if he finished his business and returned to Tennessee.

Over Mrs. Drew's protests, Clayton went immediately to
Angela's room, but the girl refused to answer his knock.
Furious, he threw together his belongings and strode to the
barn. As he saddled his horse and tied his bedroll behind
the cantle, he wondered if he were doing the right thing. Was

Angela correct? Did he not care enough? Hesitating in the middle of tying the last knot, he considered the question. Did he love her enough? Yes, he did—and that was the problem: He loved her too much to destroy her.

When he rode back to the house, Mrs. Drew hurried out onto the porch and stopped him from dismounting. "Angela asked me to extend her wishes to you for a safe journey," she said coldly.

"I would like to talk to her, ma'am," Clayton said.

Mrs. Drew shook her head. "My daughter has already said her good-byes to you, sir. I should think you would be gentleman enough to honor her wish not to prolong this sinful affair."

Clayton flushed under the woman's direct stare. "Regardless of what you may think, Mrs. Drew," he said, "I love your daughter."

"I have no desire to hear your excuses for your behavior, Mr. Harris." She pierced him with an icy gaze. "It is enough that you have taken advantage of the hospitality offered by this household. Now, sir, if you will excuse me, I have an unhappy daughter to attend."

Clayton watched her reenter the house. For a long while he sat there staring at the door, fighting a burning desire to kick it off its hinges and search out Angela.

And Angela, watching him through the slit between the drawn parlor draperies, held her breath, praying that he would do that very thing.

Clayton took one last look at the house. Then, touching his spur to his horse's flank, he turned the animal due east, toward Arkansas, and beyond that, to Tennessee.

Mrs. Drew stood in the doorway of the parlor and watched her daughter peep between the drapes; she too had prayed that Clayton would come back for Angela.

When Angela's shoulders slumped and she bowed her head, Mrs. Drew's eyes filled with tears. Crossing the room, she took the girl in her arms. "Even though it's almost too soon to be certain, Angela," she whispered, "you should have told him the truth."

Angela laid her head against her mother's breast. "I would always have felt that I had trapped him into staying. And suppose he had ridden away knowing my condition. I could not have survived the humiliation." She raised her eyes to her mother. "Memories and hope are the two things that keep a woman sane, Mama, and I have an abundance of both."

Mrs. Drew was startled by the strength and determination she saw in Angela's face. And her heart swelled with love. Her daughter had somehow slipped into womanhood without her having noticed.

"I'm so afraid for you," Mrs. Drew said, holding Angela close. "Our friends will shun you; the young men will treat you like a harlot. Disrespect and insults will follow your every step . . . and they will throw your shame in your father's face."

"I love Clayton, Mother, and I want to bear his child," was Angela's only reply.

CHAPTER 38

Just outside of Memphis, Clayton's horse pulled a tendon. He sold the animal for enough to book passage on a steamer bound for Nashville. Hastily he penned a letter to the Summerses informing them that if all went well, he would arrive in Nashville on July 25, 1865. He inquired whether it would be possible for Mr. Summers to arrange transportation to Summerset.

Cotton hitched his cavalry mount to the phaeton. "I wonder why Clayton didn't have us meet him at Cairo instead of Nashville," he complained to Rufus. "It's sure as hell a lot closer."

"Riverboats don't land at Cairo no more," Rufus explained, handing Cotton the reins and adjusting the horse's bridle and blinders.

"Fetch him home in a hurry, Cotton," Fanny said, passing him a basket of food. "We sure have missed him."

Cotton nodded to the girl, then climbed onto the spring seat of the buggy. He was remembering the party at Cragfont, when Clayton had bedded the girl—and Patrick had murdered old Anderson because of it. Cotton shook his head. She still carries a torch for Clayton, he thought, and all he ever brought her was trouble and heartache. Women are strange as hell.

"As Fanny said," put in Mrs. Summers, "we want to see that boy. So don't tarry along the way, Cotton."

"I'll burn the tires off this s.o.b," Cotton laughed, tipping his hat to the old lady. "You thought I was goin' to say son-of-a-bitch, didn't you, ma'am?"

Then he was off down the driveway, the buggy wheels fairly humming.

Cotton made good time, arriving in Nashville late that night. The city was teeming with Federal and Confederate soldiers, most of whom were applying for transportation home. He bedded down near the wharf and slept fitfully, fearing that one of the desperate travelers might try to steal his horse.

The next day he perched himself on an upturned barrel so that he could see the riverboats as they docked. But Clayton did not arrive.

Again Cotton spent a long, sleepless night. He was in a foul mood when at eight o'clock on the morning of the twenty-sixth, he saw Clayton hanging over the rail of the texas deck on a dangerously overcrowded paddle-wheeler. Clayton waved his hat, shouted a heartfelt hello to Cotton, and fought his way through the mob and down the gangplank.

They shook hands and sized one another up, much as they had done six years earlier. Then Cotton grinned and said, "I knew the bastards couldn't kill you."

Clayton gripped Cotton's hand even tighter. "You look good, Cotton, real good."

Cotton pointed him toward the phaeton. "I ain't had no sleep in two nights, or I'd be plumb beautiful."

"How are the folks at Summerset?" Clayton asked, trying to make himself heard above the noise and confusion of another docking steamboat.

"Mr. and Mizz Summers are doin' fine," Cotton yelled. "Me'n Rufus been workin' our butts off plowin' and seedin' an' tryin' to get a crop in the ground. Ain't many slaves left, only Trillie, Rufus, an' Fanny."

"Fanny? What's she doing there?"

Cotton lifted himself into the carriage and waited while

Clayton climbed aboard. Snapping the reins across the horse's rump, he guided the animal through the milling crowds that filled the waterfront streets. "She's living at Summerset now," he said. "Been there since old Mizz Winchester died an' Paine gave Cragfont to Patrick."

Clayton gripped the dashboard tightly, his fingers bloodless against the black-leather upholstery. "Maybe you'd better start from the beginning, Cotton," he said quietly.

As they worked their way toward the Gallatin Pike, Cotton brought Clayton up to date on the events that had occurred during his absence, omitting nothing except Willie's murder.

Clayton was quiet for a long while after Cotton finished. So much had happened; so much had changed; so much was gone. Sighing, he said, "I liked Mrs. Winchester . . . I'm going to miss her." Cotton nodded but remained silent. Clayton asked, "Have the Winchesters moved back to Cragfont now that the war's over?"

Cotton shook his head. "The Federal Government sold Cragfont to some Yankee carpetbagger named Sweeny. He's livin' up there in the big house just as proud as punch, actin' like a gentleman farmer. The truth is, he don't know his ass from a hole in the ground."

"What about Lettie?" Clayton was careful not to look at Cotton. "You haven't mentioned her."

"Last I heard, she went back to New Orleans." Cotton glanced sideways at Clayton. "It's best that she did, Clay. She never was exactly right after Bailey Peyton was killed."

Clayton thought about Lettie—beautiful, spoiled Lettie, his first love. He remembered those early, carefree days, but now they were gone forever, just as surely as the elegant ball gown of the South was gone forever. All that was left of either was a tattered chemise. Still, Lettie Billingsly was special: She was a lovely, sad memory that he would always regard with tenderness.

As they sped onto Gallatin Pike and headed north, Clayton looked out over the countryside. He was appalled by the blackened buildings, charred fences, and overgrown, wasted acreage.

A lone soldier in a tattered gray uniform, his blanket roll slung over his shoulder, stood forlornly in the shadow of what had once had been his home. The burned-out pile of

black rubble was marked on each end by the skeleton of a
tall brick chimney. The man was weeping unashamedly.

Clayton could feel the heartbreak of the soldier, could
taste the bile that was rising in the man's throat. He quickly
looked away. "The whole world's gone to hell, Cotton," he
said with a long sigh.

"Yeah, Clayton, I reckon it has. But now that the war's
over, maybe things will straighten out."

Clayton's voice fell to a murmur. "We've seen the last
plantation," he said as though Cotton hadn't spoken. "We
who came before eighteen sixty-five have seen the last
plantation. It has gone the way of the mound builders, the
pharaohs, Nero's Rome. Never to be again . . ."

Cotton glanced at Clayton from the corner of his eye. "I
don't reckon I'm followin' you, Clay. The plantations are
still here. Different owners maybe, but they're still here."

Clayton shook his head. "A plantation wasn't just a piece
of land, Cotton. Mrs. Winchester tried to explain it to me
once, but I didn't understand then. The whole South—
governed by its own rules, its beliefs, its wants, its needs, its
fears—was an entity within itself. Now that entity is gone
forever. The South as we saw it was the last plantation the
world will ever behold."

Cotton looked ahead, not certain he had understood a
word of what Clayton said.

When Cotton turned the phaeton onto the Summerset
driveway that evening, he was forced to haul back on the
reins with all his strength while slamming his foot against
the brake pole. The wheels of the phaeton locked with a
high-pitched squeal that instantly quieted the screeching of
the tree frogs and the chirping of the crickets. Fanny was
running down the driveway, waving her arms as though she
were demented.

Clayton leaped out of the carriage amid the cloud of dust
that eddied and swirled around the locked wheels and
hastened to meet her.

"Oh, God, Clayton," Fanny sobbed, throwing herself into
his arms. "Something awful has happened!" Without a
word, he lifted her onto the phaeton's seat.

As soon as Clayton was aboard, Cotton kicked off the
brake and brought the buggy whip down hard across the

horse's back. The animal sprang forward, nearly jerking Clayton onto the floorboard.

"I was goin' for Dr. Mentlo," Fanny cried as the phaeton clattered up the drive, swaying dangerously on the curves while Cotton stood against the dashboard and flailed the horse to even greater speed.

Then they were at the house, and Clayton and Cotton were out of the carriage before it stopped rolling. Nor did they slow down at the door; Cotton threw his shoulder against the heavy panel, splintering it against the inside wall with such force that the plaster ceiling was cracked.

Without breaking stride, they burst into the study. Mrs. Summers was sitting on the floor with Mr. Summers' head cradled in her lap. She was stroking his sparse hair and speaking softly to him. Trillie squatted just beyond, dabbing at Mr. Summers' blood-splattered face with a wet cloth.

Mrs. Summers raised her eyes to Clayton and Cotton. "He tried to wait until you boys got home," she said, her voice barely audible, "but . . . I think he's gone."

Clayton placed his fingertips on the old man's wrist; there was no pulse. Putting his arm around Mrs. Summers, he laid his cheek against her white hair. They wouldn't need Dr. Mentlo.

Trillie eased the old man from Mrs. Summers' lap and laid him gently on the floor. "I'll finish cleanin' ol' Massa up, Mr. Clayton," she said. "You-all 'sist Mizz Summers upstairs. I b'lieve she be needin' some time 'lone."

Cotton waited until Clayton and the old lady had started up the stairs before asking the pertinent question.

Fanny took a deep breath, then shook her head as though dazed. "To tell the truth, Cotton," she said, "I'm not certain what did happen. Me an' Rufus was tidyin' up Mr. Clayton's room when Mizz Summers run to the door an' told Rufus to go fast as he could across the fields to Cairo an' fetch the sheriff, who was over there investigatin' a robbery at Mr. Highers' store. Then Mizz Summers told me to hide under the bed an' not come out no matter what."

Fanny hesitated. Cotton wanted to scream at her to continue. But he didn't. And after a long pause while she worked to control her emotions, she said, "I heard them come into the house. It sounded like a bunch of them, maybe eight or ten. I heard Mr. Summers tell them they were wastin' their time, 'cause the safe was empty." Fanny's voice caught, and she looked long and sorrowfully at Cotton.

He wondered at her expression, at the fact that she was slowly shaking her head, at the new tears that were streaming down her cheeks. "Go on," he said, feeling his stomach twist into knots. He sensed that the misery in Fanny's eyes was not due solely to Mr. Summers' death. No, the agony that was tearing her apart was because of something else, and he felt a sudden stab of foreboding. "Go on, tell me!" he cried, clutching her arms so tightly that she winced.

Fanny broke Cotton's grasp and flung her arms around him, burying her face against his chest. "I heard Mandy tell Mr. Summers that he better have money in his safe, 'cause if he didn't, she would shoot his head off. Oh, Cotton, her words brought it all back."

Cotton tightened his arms around her. "Brought what back, Fanny? What are you talkin' about?"

Fanny pushed herself away and blotted her eyes with her sleeve. "I heard Mandy's voice plain, an' it was just like a dream . . . I once had. I was at Freedman's Town, an' I was layin' on the ground, sick, an' I heard Mandy's voice say, 'I'd jist shoot yore head off like I done that sho-nuff white girl.' Only, Cotton, it wasn't a dream, it was real."

Cotton spun away from Fanny and slammed his fist against the wall. Clayton, who had just entered the room, watched the display in wonder. But before he could voice a question, Cotton shouldered him aside and fled.

Anger turned Clayton's face hard. "This is no time for him to go to pieces," he said to Fanny. "We've a lot to do before the sheriff arrives. We need to clean up Mr. Summers and lay him out . . ." Then he stopped and stared at her. "What's been happening here, Fanny? Is there something I haven't been told?"

She nodded. "I remembered who murdered Cotton's fiancée."

"Fiancée?" Fanny's revelation astonished Clayton.

Trying in vain not to weep, Fanny wailed out Willie's story. As the girl finished, Cotton walked into the room with Rufus' shotgun held tightly in the crook of his arm. His face was pinched and white, and his eyes pierced Clayton like bullets. "You goin' with me?"

Clayton drew his pistol from his coat pocket and slowly turned the cylinder, appraising each nipple to be sure the priming caps were in place. Glancing up, he said, "Need you ask?"

Cotton's mouth drew into a thin, hateful line and his cold gaze challenged Clayton. "When I find 'em, I'm goin' to kill 'em, Clay. No sheriff, no trial, no nothin'."

Clayton dropped the pistol into his pocket. "Where do we start looking?"

"I know where they are," Cotton rasped, remembering the group of riders who had been dismounting before the Johnny Bell Hotel when he and Clayton passed through Gallatin not two hours earlier. "Yes," he said, "I know right where we can find the sons-of-bitches."

The phaeton was running full-out when it met Rufus riding double behind the sheriff on the Hartsville Pike a mile west of Summerset. The law officer wheeled his mount off the road as the carriage sped past.

"Damn fools!" he cried, craning his neck and peering down the darkened lane. "I'd like to know who in hell that was. I'd arrest them for reckless drivin'. Did you recognize 'em, Rufus?"

Rufus shook his head. "No, sir, I didn't know them two men." In one sense of the word, Rufus was not lying.

When Clayton and Cotton stepped through the front door of the Johnny Bell Hotel, the desk clerk's mouth dropped open and he took an involuntary step backward. He had seen many dangerous men, but the two facing him were different; they were killers.

Cotton swung the twin bores of Rufus' four-gauge shotgun toward the man, who later swore that they were two swivel cannon wired together. "Put your hands where I can see 'em, mister," Cotton ordered. "And they better be empty."

The clerk very carefully placed his hands on the counter top.

"Which room is Butler's?" demanded Clayton, cocking his Navy Colt.

"An' has he got his black whore with him?" added Cotton, tilting the shotgun muzzles until they were on line with the clerk's head.

The clerk shut his eyes and nodded vigorously. "I told Butler we didn't allow no niggers in this hotel. I told him she'd be nothing but trouble. He assured me there would be no problem. He swore to me—"

Cotton's grin did not reach his eyes. "The son-of-a-bitch lied."

Clayton's voice snapped like a whip: "Which room is Butler's, mister? I'm not going to ask you a second time."

"Top of the stairs, first door on the right."

"If you're smart," Cotton said, still grinning, "you'll get down under that counter and stay there. If we see you when we come back down—"

"You won't, mister. I swear you won't!"

Side by side, the two men walked slowly and purposefully up the hotel stairs. They did not stop at the top; they walked straight to Butler's door and kicked it off its hinges.

A kerosene lamp burned brightly on the washstand, casting the forms of the sleeping man and woman into vivid relief. Upon hearing the splintering of the wood, Butler bolted to a sitting position. "Now look here!" he cried.

Clayton shot Butler between the eyes. Then, taking one deliberate step at a time toward the bed, he continued to shoot the man until his pistol hammer clicked on an empty chamber. Butler died with a look of shocked disbelief on what was left of his face.

With a shriek, Mandy flung herself toward the oak dresser, where her pistol lay. Just as her fingers closed around the walnut grips, Cotton touched both triggers of the four-gauge shotgun. Mandy's breasts and a large portion of her rib cage erupted out her back and splattered across the cabbage-rose paper that covered the wall. Then, as if in slow motion, her body followed, to smash into the wall with such force that it shook the room.

Clayton pulled the barrel wedge of his revolver and removed the empty cylinder. Fishing a loaded replacement from his coat pocket, he inserted it into the gun. Then he picked up Mandy's five-shot, police-model Colt and spun the cylinder. Two chambers were empty. Dropping the gun onto the bed, he nodded to Cotton and together they stepped into the hall.

Clayton looked at the clock on the wall; he was amazed to

find that the double murder had taken less than a minute. The two men stood in the darkened corridor, waiting. But if any of Butler's men were curious about the shooting, they had sense enough not to investigate.

True to his word, the desk clerk was nowhere to be seen when they came down the stairs and walked casually out the front door. Without looking to the right or to the left, they climbed into the phaeton and turned toward Summerset.

As the lights of Gallatin fell behind, Cotton took a deep, ragged breath. "I've waited eighteen months to pay that debt, Clayton." His voice was barely loud enough to be heard. "I promised Willie . . . . Now I can finally put flowers on her grave." Then he broke down and wept.

Clayton laid his hand on his friend's shoulder and stared off into the night. He had never expected to see Cotton cry.

The sheriff showed up at Summerset, along with scores of friends, neighbors, and former slaves, to help bury Mr. Summers. After the last shovel of earth had been turned and the mourners had left, the lawman led his horse over to where Mrs. Summers, Clayton, Cotton, Fanny, and Rufus were standing beside the grave. "Somebody shot Butler and his woman all to pieces in the J.B. last night," he said. "You boys wouldn't know anything about that, would you?"

"Not a thing, Sheriff," Clayton said, his hand inching toward the pistol hidden beneath his coat.

"Didn't figure you did," the sheriff said, looking deep into Clayton's eyes, "cause I know for a fact that you turned your weapons in when you took the parole."

Nodding politely to Mrs. Summers, the sheriff lifted himself into the saddle. Then, leaning on his saddle pommel, he looked down at the two men. "Boys," he said, "slow that phaeton down next time." Pivoting his horse, he galloped off toward Gallatin.

CHAPTER 39

Although the sun had set over an hour before, the late August air was still hot and sticky. Even the fireflies' iridescent glow seemed to add to the sweltering heat.

"On a night like this," Cotton said, fanning himself with his hat as he joined Clayton by the trunk of a giant gnarled-limbed maple that shaded Summerset's front yard in the daylight hours but had little effect on the nighttime heat, "a man ought to be laid up with a good-lookin' woman . . . in the Gallatin icehouse."

Clayton didn't hear Cotton. His thoughts were in Oklahoma as they had been since his return to Summerset in July. Strange, he thought, how distance makes things so much more clear.

Cotton squatted beside him and spit through the gap between his front teeth. "Somethin's botherin' you, Clay, an' it has been ever since you've been home. Did anything happen . . . I ain't pryin', mind you, but did anything happen while you were out west that you need to talk about?"

Clayton started to deny Cotton's question. But that wasn't fair; he deserved an answer. "I've been a fool,

Cotton," he said. "But worse than that, I've been a coward."

Cotton's first reaction was to contradict his friend's charge, but he bit back his retort and allowed Clayton to talk unimpeded.

"I was afraid of popular opinion, Cotton," Clayton continued, "terrified of not being socially accepted . . . so I wronged a fine and decent woman; very probably the bravest, most courageous woman I've ever known." A long silence, then Clayton said, "Lettie was right, Cotton. There's nothing in Sumner County; not for her . . . or for me. Not even the fact that I fought for the South will change that." He sighed. "Not for years to come, anyway."

Cotton fidgeted uneasily. "You're being a little unfair, Clay, both to Sumner County and yourself. Give things a chance to straighten out."

"Perhaps, I am being unfair," Clayton murmured, thinking that he wasn't being half as unfair as he had been to Angela. "But I don't intend to waste what's left of my youth—or hers—finding out, Cotton." *I haven't got that much time,* he added silently. Angela had made that quite clear when she'd said "no, Clayton, freedom won't wait on any man . . . and neither will I." *It may already be too late,* he thought, and felt his stomache tighten. "I'm riding out in the morning," he said aloud. "I'll stop by General Bates' law office and sign my part of Summerset over to you."

"Mr. Summers left Summerset to you an' me, Clay," Cotton said angrily, "because he wanted to give us a chance to make our dream come true! Now, here you are, threatenin' to run off again."

Clayton grinned at Cotton's tirade. Then he said, "Number one: although I deeply appreciate Mr. Summers's generosity, the dream of having one's own plantation was yours, Cotton. Number two: to quote your own phrase, I'm not running from something, I'm running *to* something! or, I should say, to *someone* . . . if she'll still have me."

Clayton climbed to his feet and gazed toward the house. "All I ask is that you take good care of Mrs. Summers."

Cotton also stood up. "You know I'll do that, Clay." Then he sighed. It was the sad sound of defeat. "You sure you want to do this, Clay?"

Clayton nodded. "For the first time in my life I'm finally

sure of something." Turning, he walked into the house and headed straight for the parlor.

Mrs. Summers, Fanny, and Trillie were sewing on a quilt. Clayton stood in the door and watched them, not sure of how to break the news. Finally he said, simply, "I'm leaving for Texas in the morning, Mrs. Summers."

Surprisingly, all the old lady did was to nod. "I suppose I should be surprised," she said, "but I'm not. You've been restless ever since you came home from the war."

"I'm going to Oklahoma first," he said hesitantly. "There's a girl out there . . ." Mrs. Summers' face brightened. He held up his hand. "She's not white, Mrs. Summers . . . she's part Cherokee. I intend to start a new life with her, in Texas."

The old woman studied him for a long while, then said, "Yes, Clayton, I suppose that would be best." Rising, she walked to the door, then turned and appraised him again. "Trillie," she said, "fix Clayton a glass of tea. I'm going upstairs to get something, but I'll be down in a while."

"Wonder what she be a-wantin' from upstairs," Trillie said, pouring Clayton's tea.

Clayton shook his head; his disclosure had apparently not upset her, so he too wondered what had come over her.

Fanny, her eyes glued to Clayton's face, suddenly cast her needlework aside and raced into the hall and out the back door.

Rufus found her perched dejectedly on old Anderson's anvil in the blacksmith shop. "You goin' to try an' hatch that anvil?" he asked, grinning.

"I might."

"You shouldn' have run out of the house like that. Everyone's wonderin' what's the matter with you."

"You know what's the matter with me."

Rufus nodded, then walked over to her and laid his hand on her shoulder. "You think that if Clayton was goin' to love someone who wasn't white, it should have been you."

The girl nodded curtly.

"But he doesn't love you, Fanny," Rufus said gently. "He has never loved you."

Fanny jumped off the anvil and stalked to the forge, where she angrily pumped the huge bellows several times.

Rufus crossed to her and stayed her hand. "I know how

you feel, Fanny, 'cause I feel the same way about you. I've loved you since the first time I ever saw you, but you've never looked at me. Not once."

"An' I won't, Rufus!" she said bitterly. "I made myself a promise before the war that I would never 'llow another nigger to touch me. I vowed that my children would not be slaves."

Anger surged through Rufus. Taking a step closer, he peered into her face. Quickly she backed away, but not before he saw that she was pale and trembling. She's frightened! The realization caused his anger to abate as quickly as it had come. Then it dawned on him that her words had made no sense either. His eyes narrowed in contemplation. "In the first place," he said, watching her closely, "I'm no nigger, Fanny. I'm a black man. Do you understand that?"

She started to brush past him, but he blocked her passage. "Do you understand that, Fanny?"

She trembled even more violently. "Yes," she said. "Yes, I know that."

Rufus frowned, bewildered by the fear in her voice. He wished it were daylight so he could see her plainly. Something was wrong here, very wrong indeed.

"As for the second part of your statement," he continued, "you know as well as me that when and if you have children, they will not be slaves. We're free, Fanny, free! You know that, so that part of your statement doesn't hold water either."

Fanny backed away from him, her eyes large spheres that glistened in the darkness. "Let me go, Rufus," she whispered. "Please let me go."

Rufus shook his head. "Not until you tell me the truth. What are you afraid of, Fanny? Why, you're scared to death."

When she didn't answer, he caught her by the shoulders and shook her savagely. "Tell me the truth, Fanny! Why are you—?"

Fanny wrenched herself free and ran to a corner of the shop. A moment later Rufus could hear her retching.

Quickly he made his way to her. "Fanny," he said, reaching out to her, "Fanny, I'm sorry . . ."

"Don't touch me." She moved further into the corner,

cowering there like a trapped animal. "Don't touch me again!"

Rufus dropped his hand and took a step backward. For several minutes Fanny crouched in the darkness, crying softly. Then she said, "Yes, I'm afraid, Rufus. I'm . . . I'm afraid of men. Me! Who loved being a woman. Me, who used to thank the Lord nightly for havin' made me pretty. Me, who was so trustin' and lovin'. Me, who had such grand plans for the future. I'm afraid of men . . . I'm afraid of you."

Rufus felt something tighten in his chest, threatening to stop his heart. Finally, he managed to say, "What are you talkin' about, Fanny? You've never been afraid of anything . . ."

"Oh, Rufus," she wept, "I wake up at night scared to death. An' I can tell that I've been cryin', 'cause my pillow is wet. I dream about the Johnny Bell Hotel, Rufus, an' I can feel those Yankee soldiers . . . hurtin' me, an' hurtin' me, an' hurtin' me. It's like it's real, just like it's happenin' all over again . . . an' I can't stand it. It's awful, Rufus, just plain awful."

"That was a long time ago, Fanny."

"I know it, but I can't help the way I feel. And . . . it's getting worse. It's getting so that every time a man touches me, just touches me, I get sick to my stomach. I hide it as best as I can. I even force myself to act normal. But sometimes I can't . . . I vomit."

Rufus' mouth went dry; he had witnessed her nausea firsthand. "But if you feel that way," he said, "why are you hurt that Mr. Clayton's leavin'? That doesn't make any sense, Fanny."

She took a deep, ragged breath, then released it slowly. "'Cause he was gentle and kind to me when we . . . were together. I keep makin' myself remember that, Rufus. I keep tellin' myself that if he loved me, I'd feel the way I used to. But I'm not sure!" She buried her face in her hands. "No, I'm not at all sure, 'cause I even cringe when he comes near . . . and I love him. Oh, Rufus, I'm so afraid. All I want is to be me again, to be normal . . . I want it to be like it used to be."

Seconds stretched into minutes. Rufus said, quietly, "There is no 'used to be,' Fanny. You and me an' every slave that draws breath are like newborn babies who came straight from the womb full grown. We have no past; we live only for today . . . an' pray for tomorrow. There is no used to be." Rufus took a step closer to her. "What I just said is not totally true, Fanny," he murmured. "I love you with all my heart, but that's probably the only thing that hasn't changed."

"I know you do, Rufus." It was barely audible, yet he heard her plainly and could not help but wonder if the sadness in her voice were actually pity. He prayed not. "But I don't love you," she went on. "I . . . I don't even desire you . . . or anyone, really."

Rufus turned and gazed sightlessly into the soft darkness beyond the open door of the shop. After a long interval, he asked, "Do you like me as a person, Fanny?"

"Yes, you know I do, Rufus."

"Do you respect me?"

"I've always respected you."

Rufus turned to her. He wanted to take her in his arms, But he dared not. "Well, it's a start, Fanny. Yes, it's a start."

When Clayton trotted his horse up the Park Hill driveway, Colonel Drew, Johnny Runningdeer, and the young twins, Harry and Larry, were unloading farm tools from a buckboard drawn up in front of the mansion.

Clayton quickly canvassed the area, even scrutinizing the far hills in hopes that Angela might come racing up on her pinto. But she didn't appear. Stepping down from the saddle, he walked toward the colonel.

Colonel Drew laid a crowbar on the buckboard seat and turned to meet Clayton.

Clayton extended his hand. "It's good to see you again, sir . . ."

Drew's fist exploded against Clayton's chin, dropping him flat on his back in the hot Oklahoma dust.

Clayton climbed to his feet and blinked his eyes to still the multicolored lights popping just behind his lids. Before he could clear his vision, Drew's fist burst against his lips, this time with a force that hurled Clayton against the buckboard. He would have fallen again, had his arm not wedged itself firmly in the vee of the wagon's spring seat. Blood dripped from the corner of his mouth onto the weathered floorboard.

Drew stepped toward Clayton, his face full of loathing.

Clayton painfully disengaged himself from the vehicle. "Colonel Drew," he said, "I can understand your anger toward me. I can even abide it . . . up to a point. Well, you've reached that point. Don't try to hit me again, sir."

Drew's face mottled with fury. "No! I won't hit you!" he shouted. Wheeling, he stalked toward the house. Over his shoulder he yelled, "I'm goin' to get my gun, Harris. Don't be here when I come out."

"I'll be here, Colonel," Clayton returned angrily. "I've come to see Angela, and I don't intend to leave Park Hill until I do."

When Colonel Drew entered the house, Clayton pulled his pistol from his waistband and walked up to the steps leading to the porch. He stood there, watching the door, his hand becoming so sweat-slick that he wondered if when the time came, he would be able to hold the weapon firmly enough to get off a shot.

Absently he reached up and ran his hand across his split lips, smearing his chcck a bloody red. The big question was whether he could bring himself to actually shoot Angela's father.

Although it was only seconds, it seemed to Clayton an eternity before the knob turned and the door swung inward. Nervously he rested his thumb on the hammer of the pistol while his finger sought and found the trigger. Sweat beaded his face, causing the blood on his cheek to run in small rivulets to his jawline, giving him a sinister and threatening look. Then his pent-up breath burst from his lips and his hand shook with relief; Angela had stepped onto the porch and quickly closed the door behind her.

She was even more beautiful than he remembered. There was a radiance about her, as though a lantern, its wick turned high, was casting a warm glow just beneath the surface of her porcelain-like complexion. Her hair, falling loosely to her waist, was, in contrast, so black that its highlights shimmered a deep blue, deeper even than her icy eyes.

"You told my father that you wouldn't leave until you saw me," she said. "Well, you've seen me. Now get out of my sight."

Clayton gripped his pistol even tighter, his mouth suddenly gone too dry to speak. Although he had not been so childish as to expect Angela to throw herself lovingly into his arms, he was nevertheless taken aback by her bitter reception.

So he stood there motionless, afraid to utter a sound lest his voice betray his dismay at her animosity.

Johnny Runningdeer, standing beside the buggy, was as shocked by Angela's unexpected appearance as was Clayton. Snatching up Colonel Drew's crowbar from the floorboard of the buggy, he stormed toward the house. The twins fell in behind him, chattering excitedly to one another about how the Ute would kill Mr. Harris and probably take his scalp, a feat they had heard about but never witnessed.

Runningdeer hauled up beside Clayton and took a wide-legged stance. The twins held their breath, and Angela's eyes widened in alarm. Drawing back the crowbar, Runningdeer said, "Angela told you to get off this property. Now I'm telling—"

Without taking his eyes from Angela's face, Clayton backhanded Runningdeer across the forehead with his pistol barrel, dropping the Indian flat on his back as though the ground had been snatched from beneath his feet.

Wide-eyed with wonder, the twins knelt beside the unmoving figure. "Is he dead?" Harry asked Larry in Cherokee.

Larry shook his head. "No. But I believe his head's cracked. He's going to be laid up for a long, long spell."

Larry cut his eyes to Clayton, who had not moved or made a sign that anything out of the ordinary had taken place. "Would you ever have believed that Mr. Harris would just up and cold-cock Johnny like that? No warnin' or nothin'?"

Harry shook his head. "I wouldn't have believed that anybody could hit Johnny like that. He's one mean Indian."

Larry nodded. "Well," he said a moment later, "Mr. Harris always was full of surprises."

Ignoring Runningdeer and the boys, Clayton said, "I've come to marry you, Angela."

Angela, who had been studying Runningdeer's prostrate form with mild curiosity, faced Clayton contemptously. "And take me home to the mother you don't have? Is that your intention, Clayton?"

"No," he said, "to Texas, where we will build a new life together."

Angela's hands crept to her abdomen where new life was already building and growing stronger each day. For an instant her face softened. Then, almost as quickly, it turned again to ice. "You waited too long, Clayton," she said. "I am . . . I'm to marry Johnny Runningdeer. I . . ." She blushed. ". . . I am carrying his child."

Clayton's face took on the bloodless hue of death as he noticed the slight bulge of Angela's belly under her long skirts.

Harry frowned at Larry. "I didn't know Angela was going to have Johnny's baby."

Larry scowled at Harry. "She's not, you idiot. It's Mr. Harris' baby. Everyone knows it."

"Shut up!" Angela told the boys in Cherokee, still watching Clayton intently. She fully expected to see rage and contempt on his face, while secretly she hoped to see remorse and loss instead. What she did see, however, left her even more hostile and cold: Clayton was smiling his slow, crooked grin.

"Lying never was one of your stronger points, Angela," he said.

She took a deep breath and released it angrily. "What makes you think I'm lying, Mr. Harris?"

Clayton shrugged. "Simple enough. If you were truly in love with Runningdeer—and were going to be the mother of his child—you would not be standing up there on that porch. No, you would be down here seeing how bad he's hurt. And knowing you like I do, I can safely say that you would very likely have tried to ram that hard little fist of yours down my throat in the process."

"I still might do that," she snapped.

Clayton shook his head, his smile broadening. "Using your own words, Angela, 'You waited too long.' I know the truth now."

"You are despicable," she hissed, blinking back the tears that suddenly filled her eyes. "I hate you so much . . ."

Clayton spun on his heel and strode quickly toward his horse.

Angela watched him go, and that empty, dead feeling that

had been her constant companion for the past three months engulfed her once more . . . only this time it was worse, much worse.

"I wish you had never come back!" she shouted as he reached his horse. Then to herself she added, I could have survived if you had only stayed away.

Turning, she walked toward the door.

"Where in hell are you going?" Clayton called out, hurrying back up the walkway.

"Inside!"

"No you're not, Angela," he said, halting on the top step of the porch. "At least not until I've said all I came to say."

Angela whirled about and faced him. "Then say it and get it over with! I want you out of here . . . forever."

Clayton extended a brown-paper bundle toward her. "A gift," he said, "from a very fine old lady in Tennessee."

"I don't want it."

"Take it."

"No."

Angrily, Clayton ripped away the paper and flung it to the ground. In his hands was a beautiful white-satin gown, embroidered with tiny pearls and edged with exquisite lace. Indeed, the dress would have brought a gasp of pleasure from any woman, and Angela was no exception.

"Mrs. Summers sent you this as a wedding present," Clayton said. "She told me to tell you that she would be honored if you would accept it. And she hoped that it brings you as much happiness as it did her when she wore it over sixty years ago."

A sob caught in Angela's throat, and the tears that had been threatening to come, flowed freely. Hiding her face in her hands, she leaned against the door for support. It was not the gown that had brought on the torrent, no, far from it. As lovely as the gown was, it was not nearly as beautiful as Mrs. Summers' gesture—Mrs. Summers, whom Clayton had said was like a mother to him!

After a long moment Angela straightened and blotted her eyes with the sleeve of her blouse. To Clayton's astonishment, her face was even more drawn and bitter. "Why did you show me that dress?" she demanded. "Do you enjoy humiliating me? Hurting me? Seeing me cry?"

Clayton's mouth tightened, but before he could speak, she

was going on: "You know I gave up the right to wear a white
wedding gown. And most especially not that lovely dress.
Look at me, Clayton!" She smoothed her skirt over her
abdomen, accentuating her rounded belly. "You mock me,
damn you!" Brokenhearted tears of rage filled her eyes
again, and she quickly knuckled them away.

Clayton bounded up the porch steps in two strides and
caught her firmly by her shoulders. Looking down into her
face, he said, "I love you, Angela. You're the finest, most
decent woman I've ever known, and you have every right to
wear this dress. I love you!"

Her lips drew into a acid-like smile as she gazed up at
him. "You love me, Clayton," she said, "but you don't love
me enough."

His hands tightened on her shoulders. "You accused me
of that once before, and I didn't understand what you were
saying. Well, I understand it now, and in a way you were
right, so I won't insult your intelligence by attempting to
excuse my behavior back then."

"Thank you for nothing," she said, and the jeering note in
her voice caused the muscles of his jaws to cord.

Taking a deep breath, he said, "I don't suppose that you
will believe or understand this, but the very nearness of you
scared me. You gave all, and asked for nothing in return
except my love. I had never experienced such unselfishness
in a woman . . . and it confused and frightened me. To tell
you the truth, Angela, I wasn't at all certain that I was man
enough to live up to the standards that came so easily to
you."

Angela was watching him intently. The jeering smile was
gone, replaced by a facial expression that might well have
been carved from stone.

"So I ran," he continued at last. "But whether you believe
it or not, that was the best thing that could have happened. I
needed time to think; to sort out and understand my
feelings . . . to understand myself." He smiled at her. "I've
come to marry you, Angela. So you might as well go try this
dress on and see if it fits. Because I am going to marry you,
and that's the way it's going to be."

Angela stiffened in his grip, her face clouding with
indignation. Before she could speak, Clayton covered her
mouth with his and kissed her long and hard. In spite of her

determination not to, she responded wantonly, melting against him, her arms snaking tightly around his neck.

When they parted, she leaned back in his embrace and studied his face. A smile hovered at the corners of her lips, and her eyes glistened with joy. "I'll always hate you," she said. "I just want you to know that from the start."

Then she sought and found his lips again, softly this time.

And if at that moment Montclair had been watching, he would have been pleased, because Angela Drew was most definitely as beautiful on the outside as she was within.

The End

FROM THE AUTHOR

The story you have just read is basically true. There are so many actual facts woven into the narrative that were I to list them in chronological order, the book would be half again as long. But it would take only a page or two to list the fictitious portions this author has created. The story was written for two purposes: to entertain; and to bring a touch of insight into the complexity of the crises, both mental and physical, that swept the South and its people prior and during the War between the States.

There were so many facets to that awful struggle that no one book could begin to cover all of them. What I have attempted to show the reader in this novel is the people's viewpoint—the scene as experienced by the people who lived the Civil War day to day.

It has not been my intention to shock the reader or to provoke controversy. To that end I chose to withhold revelation of many of the atrocities that actually took place, especially those committed during General Paine's stay in Sumner County. Furthermore, those who had not witnessed them firsthand would not believe them anyway.

ABOUT THE CHARACTERS

- **Clayton Harris**—based loosely on a real person who did indeed throw his Northern birthright to the wind and fight for the South. He did accept twenty dollars from a stranger while on board a paddle-wheeler on the Ohio River. He did teach in a backwoods school where many of the students were older than he. He was captured by the Federals while rowing two lovely young ladies home. And, ironically, his uncle was the commanding officer who released him from captivity upon his signing of the Oath of Allegiance. He did go to Oklahoma to buy beef for the Confederacy. He did go into hostile country for cattle, very much as I described. He made numerous trips from Fort Gibson to Fort Sill to fetch the army payroll; he never failed in his mission, using seven different routes to elude road agents. He did fall in love with an "Indian princess" who was part Cherokee.

More than that I am not at liberty to disclose. The family has asked to remain anonymous, and I am honor-bound to comply with its wishes. However, I will tell the reader that he did go to Texas, and he did become a power among men. In 1901, when the oil business was founded at Beaumont, he became a millionaire.

- **Cotton Ferris**—based on one entry from twenty-five-year-old Miss Amanda McDowell's diary of 1861–1865:
  "Sept. 14, 1863—Monday: I have not a thing in the world to write and am too tired and lazy to make up anything. My school [Amanda was a schoolteacher; one of her brothers fought for the Confederacy, the other for the Union] was small to what it has been. Only 21. I went up to Mr. Cooper's at twelve. Saw Mr. Parchman and —— there. Mr. Parchman is a civil, gentlemanly sort of a man, the other is a perfect laughing machine. Not very bright anyway, at least I think so, but seems as though he could go through showers and sunshine with perfect unconcern, and laugh all the time."

- **Willie Harper**—fictitious. Based very loosely on Miss Amanda McDowell, who was the daughter of a schoolmaster. She was a farm girl and also a schoolteacher. She never owned a slave. She was in love with a young man who fought for the Confederacy. When he joined the irregulars [I feel certain that at one time he rode with Ellis Harper], she was devastated and heartbroken. She never got over it . . . or him, for she painstakingly cut each entry concerning him out of her diary. Such an action could only serve as a reminder.

- **Jonathan and Helen Summers**—fictitious. Based on farm folks I knew in Kentucky when I was a child.

- **Rufus**—based on a paragraph from Mr. Walter T. Durham's book, *Rebellion Revisited: A History of Sumner County, Tennessee, from 1861 to 1871.* As on page 87:

"Morgan was thoroughly familiar with the situation of Boone's troops as he had received detailed
intelligence from a civilian spy. Jim Childress, the
spy, had visited Gallatin posing as a refugee [run-
away slaves were commonly known as refugees, or
contrabands] from Southern conscript officers and
had been permitted free run of the town. There
were no surprises ahead for the Rebels."

Also, I incorporated into the character of Rufus stories
told to me by General William B. Bate's great-nephew,
William B. Bate, Jr. It was Bate's grandfather's slave who,
when told that he was free to go and do what he pleased,
said, "If I'm free to go where I please, then if it's all right
with you, sir, I'll just stay right here at home." Indeed, when
General Bate was wounded at the Battle of Shiloh, it was his
slave who commandeered a wagon and drove the general to
a doctor in Alabama, an act that kept the Confederate
surgeons from having to amputate Bate's leg. The Bate
family (cousins, etc.) had three killed and five wounded at
that battle.

- **Susie Winchester**—Susan Black Winchester Scales, did
  indeed grow up to be a "fine lady." Although "Susie"
  lived at Cragfont for only twelve years (1852–1864), she
  was one of those rare children who paid attention to
  everything that went on around her. But even more
  wonderful, especially for those of us who came later, she
  left her exceptionally detailed memoirs so that we might
  have a true insight to the South during and after its
  "golden days."

  I tried diligently to portray Susie as I saw her in her
  writing and, hopefully, as she saw herself: inquisitive,
  sensitive, provoking, tender yet strong, and above all, a
  very loving and lovely human being. And if she did,
  indeed, despise General Paine until her dying day, he
  was in big trouble, because she lived to be over one
  hundred years young.

- **Mrs. Winchester**—I have attempted to show the reader
  the "ole Mizz" as I saw her in Mr. Walter T. Durham's
  book, "James Winchester, Tennessee Pioneer", and from
  Susie's point of view in her memoirs entitled, "Long,
  Long Ago, Reminiscences of Cragfont, by Susan Black
  Winchester Scales."

I pray the reader grew to love and respect "ole Mizz" as dearly as this writer did, for she was without a doubt a true American heroine.

- **Lettie Billingsly**—fictitious. Based very loosely on Susie's New Orleans cousin, Lutie Breedlove, who spent many of her summers at Cragfont and attended Mr. Mier's School for Young Ladies in New York City. Susie believed that it was Lutie who taught Fanny to dance.

- **Fanny**—born at Cragfont. According to Susie's memoir, Fanny was light-skinned, had long and wavy hair, and was a beautiful woman, with fine features and complexion. Fanny's husband, Eli (owned by the Barrs), was shipped back to Africa after the John Brown incident. Susie said: "Fanny, being young, adjusted herself to the situation."

- **Patrick**—Cragfont inherited him from kinfolk in Virginia. Patrick could read and write. He fell in love with Fanny on first sight. He did indeed, in a fit of jealousy, steal off to a neighboring plantation where he "bludgeoned to death a Negro manservant named Anderson."
  Susie said that after Patrick was returned to Cragfont, he "thereafter wore a troubled look and spent the Sundays reading his Bible."

- **Old Chatty**—I portrayed old Chatty in much the way Susie described her. Even her dialect and rhyme were laid down word for word as Susie recalled them in her memoir.

- **Sylla**—Sylla was Cragfont's weaver. Susie: "Sylla, we children called her 'Lo', [wonder why?] was a good, motherly, sedate woman." The story of Sylla's husband, Sam, attacking the overseer and being brought to Cragfont to see his wife for one last time, was much the way Susie described it in her memoir.

- **Mandy**—Sylla's daughter by Sam. Susie: "Sam's ugly disposition was passed on to the only child of this couple. Mandy was really vicious. When about seventeen, she ran away after one of her outbursts of temper."

- **Bailey Peyton, Jr.**—adapted from Walter T. Durham's book, "Rebellion Revisited, A History of Sumner County, Tennessee, from 1861–1870." The part that Bailey

Peyton, Jr., played in this story is fictitious. His war record, however, is true. He was the only Sumner County Confederate soldier to be buried a hero.

Bailey Peyton's sword, removed from the battlefield by M.C. Tuttle, a Union soldier, was returned to the Peyton family by Mr. Tuttle fifty years later with a gracious letter that stated: "I sincerely trust that it may never be unsheathed again unless in defense of all the Stars and Stripes."

- **Butler**—fictitious, the author's version of the cruel overseer. I could not find any accountings of overseers of Butler's stripe, although I feel certain they were prevalent. I took the incident of Sam attacking his overseer as enough proof to create Butler, for I am reasonably certain that the slave must have been well provoked to have struck his master.

- **Opie Reed**—from Walter T. Durham and Dr. James W. Thomas: "Sumner County, Tennessee, 1786–1986." "Opie Reed was Sumner's [County] unmatched ambassador of good will to thousands who heard his lectures on the Chautauqua circuit or read his many books or articles."

- **General Eleazer A. Paine**—described in Walter T. Durham's "Rebellion Revisited." The reader has scratched only the outer edges of Paine's cruel, devious acts while stationed at Gallatin. They were too numerous to list and, indeed, would have filled a book of their very own. Paine was finally forced to resign his commission on April 5, 1865. An investigation was held, which prompted an outpouring of information about the general's military actions. Detailed accounts of brutality, murder, and executions were offered, as were proof of widespread swindling through assessments, seizures, and the collection of specially imposed fees. Privileges were controlled and sold. Ironically, the Federal authorities refused to allow any Sumner Countians to testify against General Paine at his court-martial.

Was he found guilty? Yes. His punishment: a verbal reprimand.

- **General John Hunt Morgan**—described in Walter T. Durham's book, "Rebellion Revisited." Morgan was finally killed at Greeneville, Tennessee, on September 4, 1864. Sumner County mourned his death for days.

- **Ellis Harper**—Harper was as I described him, and he never changed. After the war was over, he took it upon himself to forcefully return slaves to their former owners (whether they wanted to go or not). He was also known to be acquainted with Jesse James, having been seen in Gallatin on several occasions with the notorious bandit. Harper died as he had lived. In June, 1908, at the age of seventy-two, he was shot and killed in Lebanon, Tennessee.

- **Angela Drew**—Other than assuming the responsibility for telling the reader that she was very beautiful, and very much in love with "Clayton Harris," I am honor-bound to say no more about her. So be it.

ABOUT THE STORY

Almost every word you have read in this book describes an actual happening. I occasionally inserted my characters into predicaments, times, and places where they were not, but that in no way makes the facts any less real.

Even the most trivial-appearing incidents have been gleaned from diaries, letters, word-of-mouth reports from descendants, and most especially from the many years of research by Walter T. Durham, who so graciously allowed me the use of his hard work.

Burkett Nelson presented me with a printed edition of his great-great Aunt Amanda McDowell's diary, titled, "Fiddles in the Cumberland." Because of Amanda's most thorough and painstaking endeavor, I was able to give accurate descriptions of not only the day-to-day occurrences and sicknesses, but of the weather on nearly any given day or at any time. But, more important, I was able to gaze into the innermost thoughts of a lovely, young, unmarried woman in love with a Confederate soldier who turned to guerrilla warfare. She, like Willie, detested it. Amanda's diary was invaluable. Thank you, Burkett.

Another valuable source of information came from Bernarr Creasap, who authored the book, "Appomattox Commander, The Story of General E. O. C. Ord." It was through Branarr's book that I gained a wealth of knowledge concerning the "behind-closed-doors" sessions of military/political chicanery. Also, I learned that high-ranking, professional soldiers are possessed of a human side not normally set down in history books, as revealed by the time General Ord rode into a campaign wearing his houseslippers. Spit and polish?

Judge Robert Lankford related me the story of his great grandmother cutting her favorite racehorse's throat rather than allowing Federal soldiers to confiscate it. Thank you, Judge.

Ann Garrett of Goodlettsville related the story of General Paine's troops setting out to investigate an attempted train wreck (very probably the one for which he arrested the three Elam sisters). In an effort to gain information, Paine's men cast a baby on a burning haystack. The reader might find it interesting to know that the baby (pulled from the flames by its mother) survived and lived to a ripe old age, but was hideously scarred for life.

The story of Willie having molasses and sulphur smeared on Cotton's horse, then covering the horse with a blanket, came to me from my grandfather. He told me that my great grandmother had been warned that the Confederate guerrilla, Quantrell, was going from farm to farm confiscating horses. When he reached my great grandmother's farm, the results were as I described in this story.

Ms. Margaret Johnson told me the story of her relative who slipped home from the war to see his wife and was surrounded by Federal troops. His quick-thinking spouse told the Union soldiers that only she and her idiot brother were home; the story of Cotton's near capture was taken directly from Margaret's description of the incident.

Ms. Eva Denning was gracious enough to allow me access to letters between her ancestors concerning the wounded and sick soldiers of both armies who were welcomed into her people's home for treatment and convalescence. Those letters were a wonderful help for the passages of this book that follow the Battle of Gallatin.

The above are just a few of the references I have incorporated into this story, and it is the relation of just such true occurrences that I hope will have won the reader's confidence in the veracity of my tale.

ABOUT THE PLANTATIONS AND HOUSES

- **Cragfont,** home of the Winchesters, circa 1798. Cragfont has been beautifully restored and is open to the public. It is owned by the State of Tennessee.

- **Elliott Springs,** home of Colonel George Elliott, circa 1825. Elliott Springs (later called Wall Springs) is in fine repair and is owned by Ms. Victoria Laws.

- **Jameson Plantation,** home of James Jameson, circa 1845. Jameson House has been restored to its former grandeur. It is owned by Nathan and Jean Harsh.

- **Greenfield Plantation,** home of the Chenaults, circa 1840. Greenfield has just recently been restored to its former beauty. It is owned and occupied by descendants of the original family, Richard Harsh and his wife Lisa Harsh.

- **Oakland,** home of Dr. Mentlo, circa 1834. Oakland is in fine repair and is owned by Ms. Lennor Story.

- **The Levy Ring House,** circa 1832. The Ring house has been restored to its original elegance and is owned by John and June Garrett.

- **Wynnewood,** home of A.R. Wynne, circa 1828. Wynnewood is in beautiful repair. It is open to the public and is owned by the State of Tennessee.

- **Rosemont,** home of Josephus Conn Guild, circa 1834. Rosemont is in fine repair; it is still owned and occupied by descendants of the original family.

- **Trousdale House,** home of Fanny Trousdale. Trousdale House is in fine repair and is open to the public. It is owned by the United Daughters of the Confederacy.

- **Tillman Dixon House,** circa 1795. Dixona is in fine repair and is owned by a direct descendant of the original family, William (Boo) Young and his wife Faith.

- **Locust Grove,** circa 1797. Locust Grove is in fine repair and is owned by a direct descendant of the original family, William B. Bate (Jr.) and his wife Mary.

- **Fairview,** home of Isaac Franklin, circa 1832. Fairview has been restored to its original grandeur and is owned by Mrs. Ellen Wemyss.

- **Walnut Grove,** home of Charles Elliott, circa 1795. Walnut Grove is in good repair and is owned by Don Wright.

A PARTING NOTE FROM THE AUTHOR

It might interest the reader that in 1954, this author was given a once-in-a-lifetime opportunity to visit with an elderly couple (over 100 years old at that time) who had worn the fetters of slavery during the Civil War. Their unpainted, weatherboard home with a neat, orderly vegetable garden behind it, gave me the feeling of stepping back in time.

Sadly, I was too young to appreciate that God-given opportunity, for all I was interested in hearing about was the time Jesse James and his gang watered their horses at the old couple's well.

One other thing stands out in my memory, even after all these years: I have never met a more soft-spoken, dignified couple.

—D.K.W.